THE UNSEEN HAND

ILLUMIDAR BOOK I

THE UNSEEN HAND

ILLUMIDAR BOOK I

NARCISSE NAVARRE
MARZIO OMBRA

Illustrated by Agata Fiszer

Ink Sorcery
www.inksorcery.com

&

EBON ET NOIR
www.ebonnoir.com

Copyright © 2019 by Narcisse Navarre and Marzio Ombra

Cover Art, Frontispiece, Maps, Calendar, and
Book Design by Narcisse Navarre

Interior Illustrations by Agata Fiszer

Card Deck Illustrations by Charles Bennett & W. Harry Rodgers

Published in the United States by Ebon et Noir LLC,
Warwick, New York.
December 9, 2019

Library of Congress Control Number: 2019914762

The Unseen Hand / Illumidar Book I
by Narcisse Navarre and Marzio Ombra

ISBN 978-0-9846654-3-3 (Paperback)

Second Edition

Also by Narcisse Navarre:

The Olive Grove

An Endless Hunger

Daevil's Tears

Also by Marzio Ombra:

Escape from Skua'Ghagol

Choral Abyss

Glacier Straits

Ursachia

Yrrdrakos

Odyss   Silth

The Faold   Naiara

Cupricha   The Mists

Dar'bas   Eb'anil

Sendayn   Maara   Denietia

Tendaj   Leiss   Kharvissian Peaks

Elizalde   Yohl'debad

Goizonne   Manoelle   Hrryth   Vusk   Ehr'nin

Berinnon   Chloe   Weddingport   Wheatshore

Carremond   Ferencia   Sun Blessed Plains   Ghol'denaan

Longwood or Downs

Talantean Ocean   Xabrielle   Locen   Zherr   Naol

Oldash   Fircrest   The

Edelrohbri   New Hillock

Lereigne

Sevanatil   The Inland Sea   The Xarxet Main

Castan   Messana

Tasana   Faussipo Highlands   Anandoli

Corval   Calantian City-States   Pirensa

K'Tarr   Debendelo

Terranakis & Xio-Bahnn   Sullosia   Mencello   Stellae

Slaukan

Kwllos   Southern Sea

Sea of Sulos

Laremlis

A'DIELIAN RECORD

A Laremlis year has 420 days.

AELIAH

AEPPIA

AEIAD

WINTER SOLSTICE

SPRING EQUINOX

AUTUMN EQUINOX

SUMMER SOLSTICE

Sikel
END OF WINTER

Lusc
NEW YEAR'S DAY

Demmen

Nommen

Triesse

Surlim

Vehron

Tehr

Gath'im
BELFEST

Hel'im
TEMVIS

Dot's

Oredden

Feurge
DAFFOON ALAIN

Cel'im
BEL'TAHIM

Eddelen

Bel'im
BEL'AZAHL

ADULAZAHL

Each month consists of 26 days except Sikel which has 30 days. The last four days of Sikel mark the new year and are celebratory.

DAYS OF THE WEEK

Each week has eight days. Seven days venerate the ancient guardians. The eight is a market day.

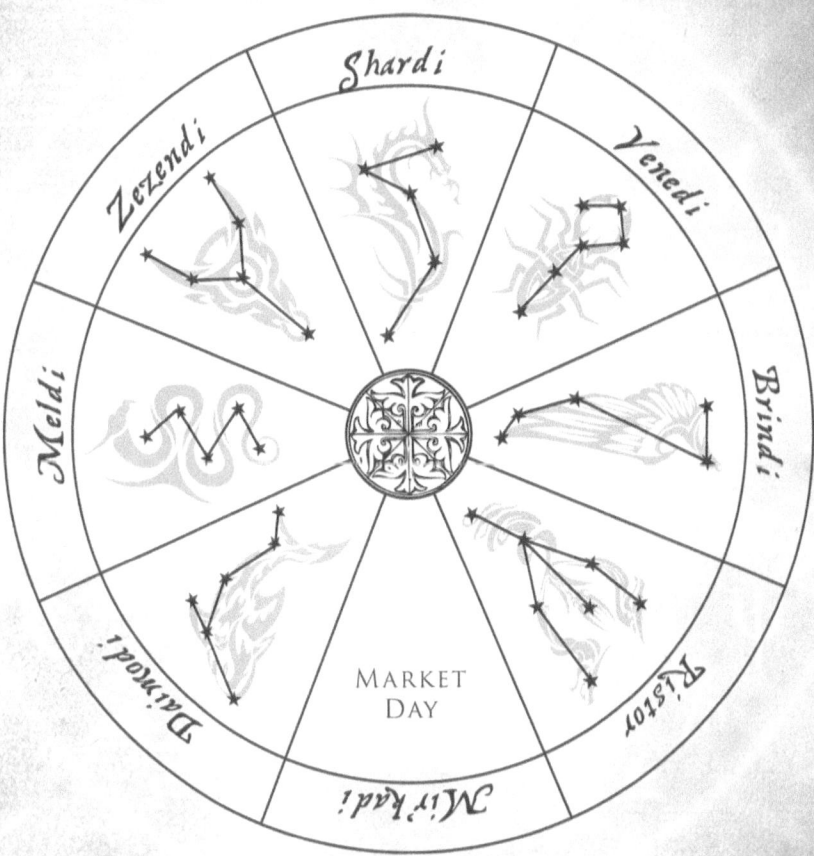

A day in Laremlis consists of 26 hours. Bells tell time in cities and ring every hour. Night is divided into four watches.

SUNDOWN TO NINTH BELL
NINTH BELL TO MIDNIGHT

MIDNIGHT TO THIRD BELL
THIRD BELL TO SUNRISE

Midnight is the 13th Hour.

CONTENTS

LIST OF ILLUSTRATIONS

DEDICATIONS

Narcisse dedicates this book to her brother, Lawrence, whose passion for books rivals hers, and to her husband Rob for supporting her crazy ideas. Her love goes to her grandmother, Gertrudis, without whom neither this book nor any of her dreams would be possible. Rest in peace, Grandma.

—

Marzio dedicates this book to his son, Zack, and his sister Danette for their love and support in all things. He wishes to thank Richard F. Miller, the one teacher who truly inspired him to put his characters on paper— rest in peace. Most of all, he wishes to recognize and thank his best friend and coauthor, Narcisse for believing in him.

ACKNOWLEDGMENTS

A novel is a journey, sometimes an arduous one. Such treks are not accomplished by the writer alone; support is needed. We wish to thank the following people for their feedback and encouragement:

Thank you, Andrei Andrei and Carmen Ungureanu for posing for our posters and postcards.

Thank you, Emily Hare and Agata Fiszer, for making our fantasy come to life with your artwork.

Thank you, Sue Brown, our primary beta reader, for your sincere and honest feedback. Your thumbprints are on these pages.

Thank you to our other beta readers, Marc Irizarry, and Herman Ortega, for your feedback and encouragement.

Thank you to Jakayla Toney for helping us navigate Wattpad. You're a superstar!

Thank you to our Wattpad readers; you gave us valuable feedback and generous support. Special shout-outs to fellow authors Evelyn Hail, Faye Lane, Kelly J. Burke, Rainer Salt, Shannon Tolhurst, Arveliot, Erich Whiteside, Kelsey Kepler, and Lee Dawson. Lastly, a huge thank you to Lily, our first Wattpad super fan who made us smile with her emoji-studded comments.

PART
ONE

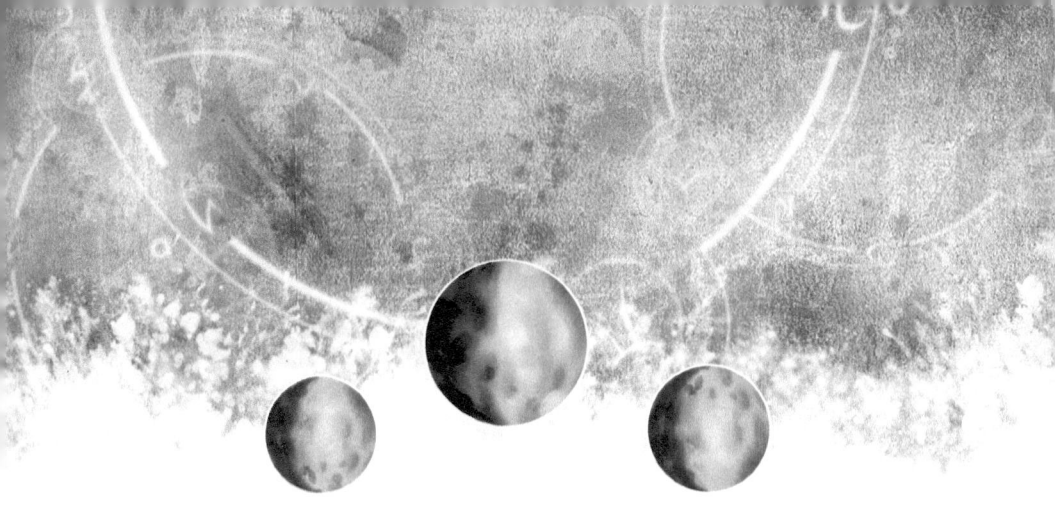

PROLOGUE

Venedi, Seventh of Sund'im, 445 A'A'diel

With nightfall, the grinding of wheels over the well-trodden cobbles and the harsh cries of merchants faded away in the Port City of Reyza. In the sky, the three moons of Laremlis, Aeppia, Aeliah, and Aeiad rose half-faced and bright. Bathed in moonlight, Reyza's architectural jumble acquired a harsh ambiguity—as though nature and all of its pleasantries had been purposely shut out. Edifices clung to the cliff sides like barnacles, stacked one upon the other on ancient masonry that defied the maws of time. Everywhere there was some fragment of whitewashed ruin harking back to the destruction the Three Sisters had wrought.

In two months, the seventeen-year alignment of the moons would pull the tides into the low-lying areas of the city. Even the most accomplished elementalists with their earth-shifting spells would not be able to halt the ocean's devastation. The stone world that Reyzans believed to be so unshakable would inevitably crumble and wash out to sea.

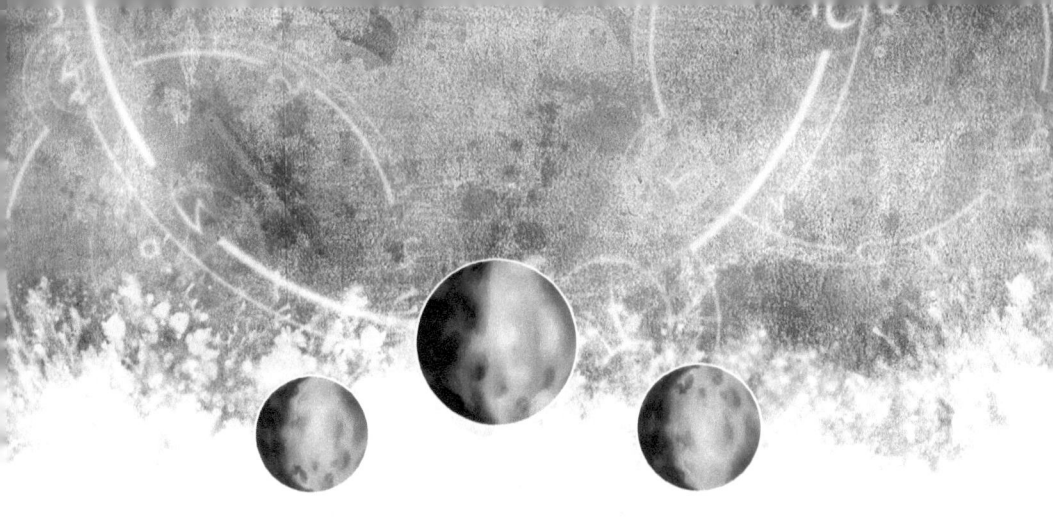

THE STALLION

Venedi, Seventh of Sund'im, 445 A'A'diel

The crowd at The Stallion was thin and long-faced. Ensconced in a shadowy corner, Jarle poured himself a shot of raska and slammed it back. On the night of his most daring heist, the thrill of wrongdoing was absent. His lips felt dry, and his stomach sour. He wished Doshmaan's wives were present to tease him with their wit and wayward hips, but the hour was late, and the women had retired along with the innkeeper.

Marcella, the night hostess, was the only source of brightness among the drunkards and late-night gamblers. The serving girl was tall and lean with dark brown hair and expressive eyes. A curskin like him, she lacked the elongated digits typical of Vendraedi bloodlines.

Jarle watched her as she made her rounds. She waltzed between tables with boundless energy, smiling as she went. She greeted newcomers and ushered them to their seats filling mugs and retrieving dishes along the way. At the stage, she exchanged words with the string player who immediately began playing something more cheerful. Everyone welcomed the livelier mood.

Catching her eye, Jarle raised his cup. The smile that followed warmed him like a ray of sunlight.

With a bounce in her step, Marcella walked to the back and joined him. "Majster Jadien, allow me," she said, refilling his glass.

Jarle slammed back the shot and reclined on the upholstered bench. He took the woman's hand in his and kissed it. "Thank you, Smiley."

The serving girl sat on the edge of the table. "Don't mention it. I can do this all night."

A grin spread across Jarle's lips. "I know you can."

Marcella shook her head. "Flirt. I really should seek employment at a place where I can meet decent men."

"You would be bored to death," mused Jarle.

As Marcella poured him another drink, Jarle spotted a familiar face. Irilio, beloved poet of the court, and his closest friend, entered the tavern and bowed. The swarthy-skinned man wore an embroidered emerald tunic and brown hose. A plumed hat that would have looked ridiculous on anyone with lesser panache adorned his head.

Tickled by fame, Irilio never missed an opportunity to aggrandize his legacy. He greeted all who made his acquaintance with sincere affection and obliged them with a few lines of verse. Everyone loved the poet; those who didn't merely hadn't met him yet.

"Don't look now, but your favorite person has just arrived," said Jarle.

Marcella set down the jar of liquor and tucked loose strands of her hair behind her ear. "How do I look?" she asked, smoothing her skirt.

"Like my favorite Smiley."

The girl turned to face the dining hall, eyes full of anxiety. "My infatuation is silly. Irilio can have any woman he wants. He will never notice a curskin like me."

Jarle drained his cup, then reached up and plucked Marcella's hair sticks. Her dark, wavy mane tumbled long and free down to her waist. He stroked her back, recalling the one time they had made love. "You are beautiful, Smiley, and way too good for Irilio. Besides, he will soon be a married man."

The hostess untied her apron and pulled it over her head. "Jealousy doesn't suit you."

"Jealous? Of that proud peacock?" Jarle scoffed. "Truly, you know me better than that."

The smile faded from Marcella's face as she turned to face him. "Jarle, can I tell you something?"

"Anything."

"The other night, Irilio came here with a cloaked woman seeking a room. When I told him the house was full, he took me aside and offered me a load of sequins to use my quarters. The gods are bastards sometimes."

Jarle crossed his arms. "You agreed?"

Marcella shrugged. "At first, I refused, but he is very charming when he wants to be. Told me that if I did him a favor, he would owe me one. So finally," she sighed, "I gave in."

Jarle sensed more to the story. "And?"

"I snuck upstairs and caught Irilio rutting with his lady friend." A mischievous smirk curled the hostess' ruby lips. "He was with none other than the Rake's wife. That little tidbit is worth more than Irilio's gratitude, don't you think?"

Jarle grabbed Marcella's arm and pulled her down so he could whisper in her ear. "The Rake will kill Irilio if he finds out he's bedding Eloisse. Do you understand?"

Marcella stroked Jarle's face. "So, you knew and didn't tell me? So much for curskins sticking together."

"Gossip is a tasteless trait," Jarle said, pecking her cheek.

"By your definition, you should find me rather unsavory."

"There are exceptions to every rule."

"You are a loyal friend to Irilio. Steer him in the direction of a woman who is not dangerous to his health. Give him a nudge in my direction"—Marcella bit Jarle's ear—"and who knows? I may owe you a favor."

Jarle released her. "Criminal."

Marcella winked at him. "You're one to talk!"

"Get out of here and take this poison with you." Jarle took several coins from his pocket and handed them to her. "You didn't see me."

In the dining hall, Irilio joined the fiddle player and engaged in a duet, which turned into a musical duel. The patrons encouraged the rivalry by banging their metal goblets and stomping their feet in rhythm with the strings.

Marcella tucked the coins into her apron before grabbing the bottle and the glass. "Time to refill cups. Good night, Jarle."

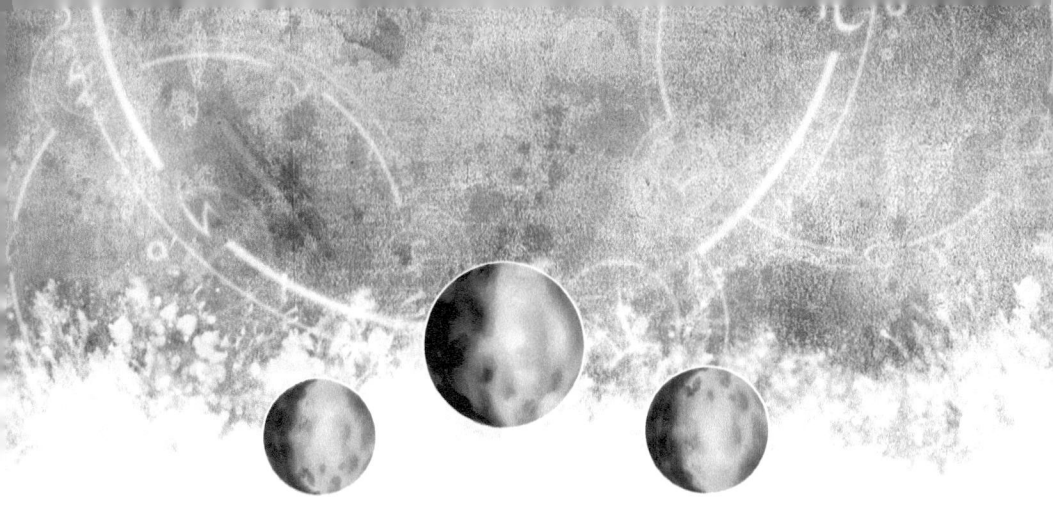

JARLE OF SHADOWS

Venedi, Seventh of Sund'im, 445 A'A'diel

Jarle skirted the counter at the back of the tavern and headed upstairs to his room on the fourth floor. Once inside, he barred the door and opened the travel trunk at the foot of his bed. He rummaged through a jumble of clothes and lifted the false bottom of the chest to reveal the unsavory parts of his life.

Eight daggers lay atop a suit of leather armor fitted with dozens of pockets. Dyed black with crushed graveborer husks, the leather was well oiled and supple. Next to the armor, rested a pair of knee-high boots with padded soles, and a bandolier strung with vials along its length.

Jarle lay his gear on the bed and took inventory of the items: Copper wire, hand-tooled hacksaws, hooks, files, lockpicks, snips, limewood strips, rolled tar paper, a waterproof case of flint and tinder, caltrops, emberstems, and a few hundred sequins worth of gemstones.

Pleased all was in its proper place, he stripped from the waist down and began to dress. He slipped on socks, followed by his breeches. He squatted, stretched, and adjusted his calf and thigh laces until the pants fit comfortably. He tucked his black silk shirt into his waistband, then donned his boots. The cuirass, pauldrons, and arm harnesses required the most fitting. And for a while, he lunged, twisted and crouched until every piece felt right.

Jarle buckled his weapon belt. He slid two throwing dirks into each vambrace and a dagger in each boot. A sense of relief washed over him when he ran his fingers over the corked bottles secured to his bandolier. In all the years stealing for the Mistress of Rats, nothing had brought him closer to the grave than a sip of poisoned wine. By the grace of the gods, he had survived and vowed never to be unprepared again. Over time he learned all he could about dangerous substances, their symptoms, and their cures. The obsession had cost him a fortune.

The midnighter slung the bandolier over one shoulder and secured it to his chest. He tossed his discarded clothes into the chest and locked it. At the open window, he drew his dagger, pointed it at a distant villa, and said a silent prayer to Ven.

The villa's dilapidated coral stucco facade appeared unremarkable—a deception by design. Ca'd'Cel was the home of Tan'os Ensther, a Thrommish fortune-seeker who had risen to Vise and was second in command to Jarle Rigo Iarris, sovereign of Reyza. Robbing the Northman would either end his life or make him rich.

Sheathing the blade, Jarle climbed out the window and dropped down to the roof of an adjacent laundry house. His feet scarcely made a sound as he crossed the building and vaulted over an alley, landing on a crumbling belvedere. He clambered up the brickwork and pulled himself up to the portico of a burnt-out building.

Clouds driven by a chilly autumn breeze rolled overhead. Moving with the shifting shadows, Jarle sidestepped the dark patches of collapsed masonry, then jumped down to the roof of a warehouse. The city blurred as he ran along the rooftops above the web of alleys known as the Tangles. Past Old Gate, he threaded into the heart of the merchant quarter.

Upon reaching the dome of a Venestrae shrine, Jarle paused to survey the estate. Ca'd'Cel occupied a rectangular parcel between two cobbled streets. A moss-covered wall twice as high as a man encircled the secluded garden. On either side of the villa grew two ancient elms whose gnarled branches extended over the street.

On the manor's roof, two guards armored in maille paced back and forth on the parapets while a crossbowman eyed the alley below. Inside the walled courtyard, the glint of steel suggested the presence of at least four men.

Jarle tied his shoulder-length hair at the base of his neck and slipped on a black hood that concealed most of his face. He uncoiled a length of rope he had stashed on the roof some days before and bound it to a marble spire. Working quickly, he pulled a figure-eight descender from his pocket, attached it to the cord, and tossed the line behind the temple. He rappelled down and crossed several courtyards behind a row of shops. The closest building to Ca'd'Cel was a wine house whose walled parcel contained a vine-choked pergola. He scrambled over a stack of barrels to reach the second story, balanced along the railing and climbed up the gutter downpipe to the roof. By the time anyone discovered his tracks, he would be long gone.

Crouched against the shop's chimney, he stared up at the branches towering over his head. The highest limbs of the elm appeared too frail to bear the weight of a child, let alone a man. Many nights he had sat in the same spot considering the risks and the riches. Most times, the promise of wealth conquered fear.

Months before announcing her betrothal to the Jarle of Reyza, Tan'os dangled his daughter like a bit of juicy meat on a hook. Tales of the Thrommish princess' beauty reached far. In hopes of gaining favor, Chaian chieftains sent caravans laden with sheep, and Seh'nahiel lords the rarest jewels. A near-endless procession of starry-eyed merchants and nobles flocked to the Vise's villa never suspecting the maiden's hand had already been promised. Dejected suitors soon found themselves in the dens of courtesans or bawdy taverns, drinking and wagging their tongues.

The stories they told of their experiences in the Ensther household grew more exaggerated with every inebriated retelling. By the time the gossip reached Jarle's ears, every wastrel in Reyza believed Avaren was a watery abomination with fish tails for legs. The sea witch, they claimed, ensorcelled every man who laid eyes on her. And Jarle could care less. The only part of the story that interested him revolved around riches.

The thief emerged from his hiding place and eased himself

over the edge of the roof. His stomach dropped as he let go and landed on the tree. The bough dipped under his weight, sending a shower of yellow leaves spiraling in the breeze, but held firm. One slow handhold after another, Jarle crept toward Avaren's bedroom. He was near the veranda when heavy footsteps signaled the presence of two mercenaries below.

"I wish I were that spineless Jarle Rigo right about now," said one of the guards as he stuffed a smoking pipe.

"Don't invite such misery on yourself, Daber," scoffed the other. "At least you know in which hole to put your cock proper. All the finery in the world wouldn't be worth the buggery."

The men chuckled. The one named Daber struck an emberstem and lit his pipe. "True. I wager the betrothal caused a row between Rigo and that ass-licking Dessian he carries on with."

A rich, woodsy smell filled the air as the other soldier spoke again, "No doubt. That shark-eyed prick is bad news."

Daber puffed before replying, "Oué, he is. The Vise can't stand the sight of him, but he doesn't favor anyone who goes against him, not even his daughter."

"Say what you want, but Ensther pays us better than the miserly lot of this city. As for Mejtress Avaren"—the guard crossed himself—"Cel redeem my soul, I wouldn't risk life as a lizard for one night between her scaly legs!"

After some hushed laughter, the mercenaries resumed their rounds. The maille clinked in time with their steps as they parted, each moving toward opposite corners of the garden.

Jarle seized the opportunity and dropped down to the balcony. Crouching to one side of the glass doors, he studied the entry for tripwires, sigils, or traps. Upon finding none, he used his lockpicks to pick open the lock.

Jarle entered the moonlit room and closed the door behind him.

Avaren's bedchamber displayed the trappings of coddled femininity. Carved beams painted in pastel hues arched to a vaulted, gold-leafed ceiling. From the center of the dome hung an exquisite chandelier whose blown-glass arms held shades in the shapes of lilies. Against the left wall, facing an armoire, stood a bed ample enough for four. Deeper in the gloom, a painted room divider partially concealed a vanity.

As Jarle crept into the room, his eyes fell on the young woman on the bed. Avaren lay on her back with an arm over her head, and the other draped on her belly. Long, lustrous hair the color of starlight framed the beautiful lines of her face. Rosy summits crowned the pearly, firm hills of her breasts, and supple hips flowed out from a slim waist. The smooth pallor of her skin was unbroken, save for a dainty gold chain around her hipbones.

Irilio often proclaimed that love was a dirty trick played on men to ensure the continuation of the species, but as he stared at her, indifference fell from Jarle like a loose garment. Finally, he understood the passion that had inflamed the girl's admirers. He imagined what it would be like to suckle her breasts, lick her neck, and kiss her lovely mouth.

The longer he gazed at Avaren's nakedness, the more intoxicated he became. The air, suddenly suffused with her delightful scent, threatened to strip him of reason. Blood rushed to his loins with the force of the waves that pounded Reyza's jetties. His entire body thrummed with a fierce, almost uncontrollable urge to possess her; to break her open and ride her until his heart gave out.

Bel be damned! He was not risking life and limb to gawk at nubile flesh! He was there for different booty.

Jarle turned away from the sleeping woman and crossed the room. Behind the painted triptych he spied a giant bathtub carved with reliefs of nymphs and tritons. Next to the tub stood a console stocked with folded towels, sponges and toiletries. Vials containing bath oils, perfumes, salts, and sweet-smelling herbs vied for attention. Though faint, he smelled shadowhazel from the moors, chinthistle from Terranakis, cottonbush ground with cinnamon and cloves, rare rainflower from the steppes of A'diel, and a medley of other delights. In the hands of an astute fence, the fragrances could fetch a fortune.

Constructed of malak wood and inlaid with Xio-Bahnnese scenes, the vanity shone like a polished jewel. On the tabletop lay a silver-handled brush and two gold combs. Jarle slipped the treasures into his pocket before testing the drawers. The first held various jars of colored powder, soft circular pads, and small cosmetic brushes. The rest were locked.

Jarle tinkered with the first locked drawer, nudging the tiny tumblers with a pick until it slid open with a satisfying click. A choker studded with rubies and a fire opal necklace with matching earrings rested on a velvet cushion. He pocketed the jewels and began to work on the last drawer.

Beads of sweat broke on his forehead as the tumblers mocked his best set of lockpicks and years of expertise.

"Damnation," Jarle cursed under his breath. Short of smashing the thing and waking the entire household, his only alternative was locating the key. Then, a realization struck him: Avaren slept naked, save for one piece of jewelry which remained well-hidden during her waking hours—a belly chain.

Jarle approached the bed. In the scant light, the fetter glimmered seductively on the luscious swell of the woman's hips. Pressed against her side, he noticed a small heart-shaped key.

From a pocket, the thief withdrew a pair of snips. The blades cut the chain with ease, but before Jarle could swipe the key, Avaren shifted, offering him a full view of her buttocks.

Rooted to her bedside, like a youth catching his first glimpse of cunny, Jarle felt the tingle of magic dance upon his tongue. An eternity passed before his fingers clutched the key.

Gods have mercy! He was losing his mind.

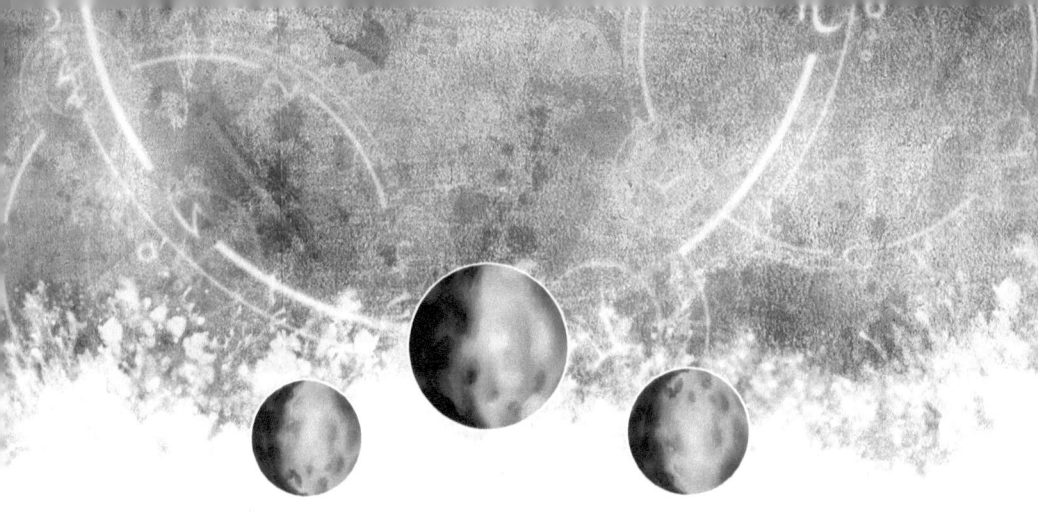

SCENT OF LEMONS

Venedi, Seventh of Sund'im, 445 A'A'diel

A zephyr carried the scent of the Southern Sea over the darkened ramparts of Ca'd'Cel. Captain Varrus Sigolian inhaled the crisp air and surrendered to the urge that had seduced him since sunset. Clad in burnished maille, the head of security of House Ensther approached the low wall that surrounded the southeastern parapet with a casual swagger earned over many military campaigns.

He peered down into the cloistered garden, scanning the shadows beyond the torchlight, and chuckled without mirth. He knew before looking there would be no sign of the intruder.

Four of his men paced along the rows of winter roses and conical topiaries, their armored footsteps keeping time with Varrus' calm heart. As expected, the night was quiet.

Varrus eased his grip on the stone wall and let out a long breath. His future depended on the skills of his mysterious partner.

Jars! What kind of name was that for a rogue? Varrus shook his head. The man's street name conjured images of pottery and spices, not burglary, but what did he know? In a city known as much for its thieves as its merchants, a man's most valuable asset was his reputation and Jars certainly had one.

Varrus had met Jars twice in the Silver Pig, a back-alley tavern in the Tangles where they'd discussed the particulars of the scheme. Jars preferred the darkest corner of the barroom and remained hooded during their brief meetings. The rogue had refused libation and became ill-tempered with idle conversation. When Varrus pressed him for information or made suggestions, Jars threatened to call off the heist. The interactions left Varrus feeling vulnerable, but opportunities to acquire the bounty locked away in Avaren Ensther's bedroom were as rare as finding a virtuous woman in a brothel. Varrus had little choice but to trust the coin he had spent investigating Jars' renown.

The captain rested his foot between two stone merlons. The consequences of discovery caused no worries. Death was a risk he had accepted twenty years prior when he took the vows of a Calantian mercenary. The nervous twinge in Varrus' belly was fueled by the anticipation of living in luxury for the rest of his days.

Years of conflict and mayhem serving at the heels of savage warlords and arrogant nobles failed to tarnish his dream of the simple pleasures of country life. The countless nights spent awake in his tent on the eve of battle, dreaming of a lemon plantation in Lugace Valley were soon to be rewarded. The fantasy of the estate he would buy when he returned home to Mencello summoned a smile. He imagined a verdant valley with neatly planted rows of lemon trees, birds flitting through the groves, and the smell of citrus upon the evening breeze.

Two guardsmen adorned with the blue and silver livery of Thromm approached the pensive captain. The shimmering scales of their armor clinked with their steps.

Varrus maintained his vigil on the cloister as the men neared. He sensed their questions before they asked. "There is nothing to see," said Varrus.

One of the men, a sergeant of some thirty seasons with a bristle of close-cropped gray hair, sidled up to his leader. "The hour grows late," the burly man said, peeking over the ledge. "Do you think it's happened yet?"

All thoughts of lemons banished by the intrusion, Varrus' features twisted into a scowl. His sergeant was a born scrapper, a man with a brutal temperament, quick to throw fists. Cassio had the appearance of a badger given human form. "Care to go inside and see for yourself?"

Cassio aimed his crossbow at the garden below. "My apologies."

"Not necessary, old friend," Varrus said, turning his eyes from the black horizon to face Cassio, "you give voice to what is on my mind as well, but curiosity is pointless. The dice have been cast."

The other guardsman, a young man of twenty summers with shoulder-length brown hair, lifted his eyes to the star-spangled sky. and let out a long sigh.

"Second thoughts, Brath?" asked Varrus.

"None, Uncle—I mean, sir!"

"Out with it." Varrus crossed his arms as he fixed his gaze on his nephew.

"It's just..." Brath's cheeks reddened. "Are you certain Avaren will not be harmed?"

Cassio's laugh was cut short when Varrus dug an elbow into his side. "For the last time, this Jars is a thief, not a murderer. Your sweetheart will sleep through everything and awaken untouched and intact with a few less baubles." Brath flushed hot with the taunt as his uncle continued, "I am worried about you, Brath. Are you going soft? Are you weak-kneed over some split-tailed minx who is beyond your grasp? Will your resolve falter when justiciars start asking questions about the robbery?"

Brath bristled. "Uncle, you need not fear my resolve. It remains as firm as tempered steel."

"For our sake, I hope that is true." Varrus appraised the boy. Although a loyal soldier, his nephew was still wet behind the ears. "In a few hours, there will be chaos. We must all be sure of our tale. The Lord Justiciar's questioning will be relentless; a single missed detail can be our undoing. Never has the Vise of Reyza's home been robbed, let alone under the noses of his trusted guard. If we are to have silk scarves around our throats instead of nooses, our discipline must not falter."

Cassio said, "Varrus, we have been more diligent than tax collectors in lean times. The house guards march their rounds with a precision that would make a clocksmith envious. Aside from the palace, there is no better-guarded villa in Reyza. Even so, no household is impervious. I doubt anyone will discover a gap in our timing or detect any deviation in our duties. Any investigation will determine the Guard of Ca'd'Cel performed with exacting diligence."

Glancing over his shoulder, Varrus sniffed, "It is not outsiders or investigations that cause me concern, Cassio."

Brath's anger flared. "I assure you, Uncle, I will play my part. I shall do both you and our family proud."

"Of course, Nephew," Varrus said, "but only if you do exactly as I have instructed. Say nothing save what we rehearsed, and we will return to Calantia rich men, never more to serve as watchdogs for these Northland pricks."

Cassio grinned. "Oué to that!"

"Now back to your rounds before someone notices. It would not do to make a mistake at this moment." Varrus offered his nephew a reassuring smile and clapped him on the shoulder. "Heed my words, we stick to our plan, and within the week we will be homeward bound with this stinking city behind us."

When his men resumed their rooftop patrol, Varrus returned his gaze to the shadows. He knew better than to count sequins before they were in his pocket, but it was impossible not to daydream. As he inhaled the salty night air, Varrus thought he smelled the scent of lemons.

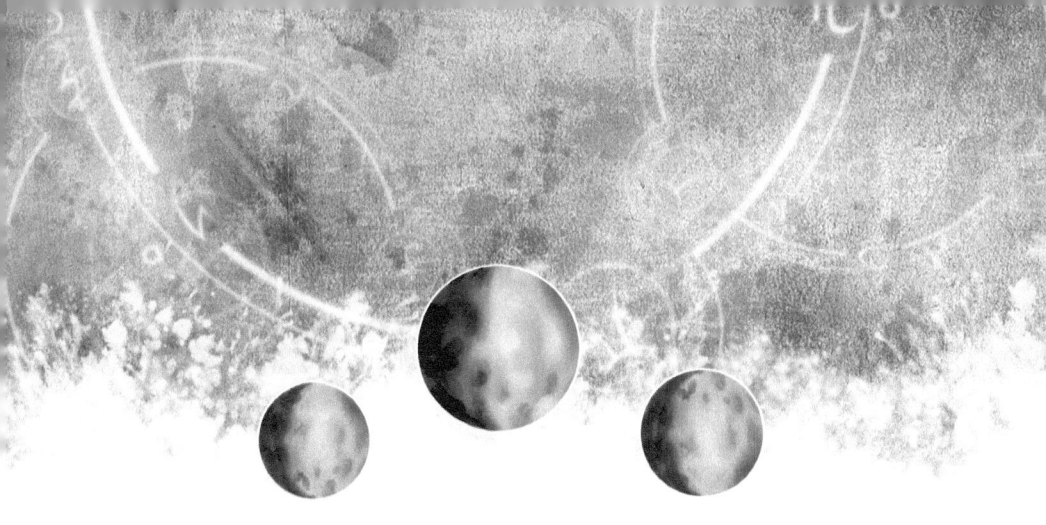

THE MAN IN THE MASK

Venedi, Seventh of Sund'im, 445 A'A'diel

Avaren awoke to a sound akin to the whop a fish makes when slapped down on the chopping block. Startled, she sat up and looked around. Her bedroom was dark; the air redolent with the familiar fragrances of lavender and starched linen. The shadows of the branches that hung over her balcony danced and shifted on the floor.

The house was silent.

Avaren lay back down and pulled the sheet over her head. The sound had been caused by the wind or perhaps the guards out in the hall. Either way, it was much too late or much too early to lie awake. She hadn't slept in days, and her eyes felt like buckets of sand. She curled up and closed her eyes, but sleep proved hopeless. In two days, she would marry a man whose very presence repulsed her. Duty would rule her life, and she would lose what limited independence she enjoyed.

Frustrated, Avaren flung the sheet from her head and turned on her side. She reached under the mattress and ran her fingers over the handle of the dagger she kept hidden. Contact with the cold steel incited angry tears to well up in her eyes. Her father referred to her upcoming marriage to Jarle Rigo as a 'necessary sacrifice.' He plied her with affirmations of safety. Rigo, he said, could be manipulated. She only need suffer the union until a male heir was born. After the child's birth, her father promised her freedom. She would sail to his homeland in Thromm; to the city of Thyra, a backwater she had never seen, and live as she pleased in her step brother's court. She could have a household of her own, choose her lovers at will.

Doubtful.

Avaren pulled the blade free of its soft prison and held it in the moonlight. The weapon was a slim jeweled thing unfit for anything except slicing open letters, but she knew otherwise. Wielded by a trained hand, even a dull kitchen knife could kill. Why her father had taught her to defend herself escaped her, considering her only value appeared to lie between her legs.

Avaren tossed the stiletto on the bed. Thoughts swirled like flotsam. Her father's fleet had rid Reyza of the pirates that plagued her shores. His hard-won political prowess had brought order to the squabbling guild houses, and stabilized the markets. Under his stewardship, coffers overflowed, but she knew he would never be seen as anything other than a meddling outsider. Her marriage to Rigo had the potential to heal the split of power between the Thrommish House of Ensther and the royal line of Iarris, but the cost was her happiness.

Avaren slipped out of bed and walked to the armoire. She opened its mirrored doors and ran her hand over the expensive fabrics. She owned dresses made of tulle and Seh'nahiel silk, bodices embroidered with strings of pearls, petticoats with lace appliqués, capes with gold piping. In the bluish light, colors were indistinct. Deep reds became zaffre; greens indigo; ivories periwinkle. Reaching into the bodice of a rarely worn gown, she withdrew a parcel of folded letters and brought the papers to her nose. Bathed in Aeppia's transformative light, she dared to imagine a different reality.

The scent of wax mingled with traces of almond and vanilla. The parchment had come from her father's study, but the sentiments had not. Paulo was her father's valet and her most ardent admirer. He was handsome and soft-spoken with hair the color of cloves and cinnamon skin typical of Vendraedi stock.

They had rendezvoused thrice in the terraced olive groves that hugged the cliffs. With each subsequent assignation, Paulo had grown bolder and her lady in waiting, Dannia, terser.

Avaren replaced the notes save the last. She unfolded the missive and let her eyes caress the smooth strokes of her admirer's hand.

My pale addonel, our time in the sun grows short. I cannot offer you the riches of a king nor the life of a princess. What I offer is myself, my love, and my eternal adoration. Come to me. Let us fulfill our ardor beneath the sacred temple of the sky and in so doing provoke the gods. I wait for you in our grove. Forever yours, —P.

Paulo's letter had not reached her in time. Dannia had delivered the note after dinner when all chances of escaping her father's scrutiny had expired. Her friend had purportedly acted to safeguard her dignity, but in her kindness, had robbed her of choice.

Avaren folded the note and was in the process of tucking it away when she heard a peculiar clicking coming from the door.

Turning toward the sound, she called out, "Spireo, is that you? Something wrong?"

When the tinkering stopped, it occurred to her that the house was too quiet. The guards stationed outside her door, though mindful, were never entirely silent. On nights when she couldn't sleep, the metallic creaking of their maille was nigh unbearable.

"Spireo?"

After a long pause, a masculine voice answered, "Mejtress, an intruder has breached the garden wall. Please make yourself presentable and open the door, or I shall have to use my keys. Your father wishes you to join him."

Through the thickness of the door, Avaren could not identify the muffled voice.

"Just a moment."

After concealing the note, Avaren slipped into a robe and tied it around her waist. The trespasser was likely a lost soul who had mistaken the villa for a merchant's home, but the distraction could prove useful. While her father and the house retinue were distracted, she could sneak away with Paulo. Rigo Iarris would not have the satisfaction of being the first man between her legs.

When Avaren approached the door, she realized that the latch had already been sprung.

Before she could react, the door swung open and smashed into her side.

Clutching her bruised arm, Avaren staggered back. Fantasies of trysts fled as she stared at the terrifying sight before her. A tall, slender figure stepped over the slumped body of a guard. Crisscrossed over his chest and legs were black bands of spiked leather. He wore two daggers at his waist, and his vambraces held additional blades. An assortment of pouches, pockets, and harnesses held the tools of his awful trade and a black hooded mask hid all but his shark-black eyes.

Cold sweat seeped from Avaren's pores. Even in the gloom, the glistening splatter of what could only be blood shone dark and slick on his armor.

The hooded man rushed into the room grabbed Avaren by the throat. His sclera-less Yerr'draki eyes bore into hers as he shook her with violent glee.

Avaren tried to scream, but only a pitiful sound emerged. Perspiration cooled along her spine as she flailed against his stranglehold. Her palms and knuckles scraped on the spikes of his armguards, leaving bloody imprints. With rage boiling inside her like a gnashing monster, Avaren brought up her knee and connected with his groin. When the man's grip loosened, she stumbled, coughing, toward the balcony. She was almost to the door when the ruffian caught her. He gripped fistfuls of her robe and yanked, tearing the silk along with her hopes. Avaren fell on her stomach. Her fingertips streaked on the glass.

"Help!" she croaked.

In the darkness, they grappled like frenzied hounds. Avaren punched and kicked her assailant, wishing desperately to escape. Choked sobs burst from her lips as powerful hands rained down blows. The man atop her was as strong as a bull with fiendish eyes that shone like hematite orbs. She was fighting a nightmare and losing.

The killer drove his knee down between her shoulder blades and knocked the breath out of her. Avaren bucked and writhed beneath the weight that crushed her, but failed to dislodge him.

Then, out of the corner of her eye, she caught a silvery movement. Turning in the direction of the glint, Avaren spied a metal cord just as it looped around her neck. Instinctively, she reached for her throat and managed to slip her fingers under the garrote.

Above her, the man leaned back while applying downward pressure to her spine. Avaren arched, pulling frantically against the cruel instrument, but it was no use. The tips of her fingers grew numb as the trapped air burned in her lungs. Black pinpoints crowded her vision.

Beyond the glass, she watched the branches of the elms sway. A mellifluous voice filled her ears as the vile wire cut into her fingers. "Your betrothed sends his regards."

Avaren's legs flopped on the floor. Ice raced through her limbs even as hot urine soaked her thighs. Time lost all meaning as the world blurred, and a dull roar filled her ears. She fixed her gaze on the moonlit veranda but saw only the expanse of the sea. Whitecaps danced, enveloped in a fulgor of moonlight that oppressed the heart and withered all impulses. No longer able to feel the weight of her attacker, she surrendered to the siren call and imagined herself drifting like a ribbon of foam upon a lifeless sea.

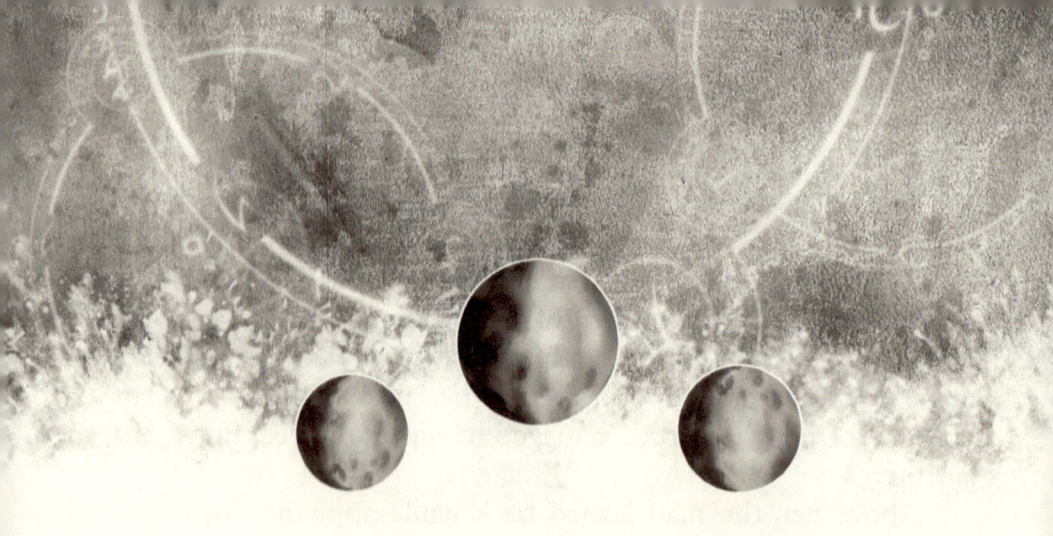

TWO BLADES

Venedi, Seventh of Sund'im, 445 A'A'diel

A tic tremored in Jarle's left eye as he strained to peer through the hinge slit of the room divider. In the gloom, the sounds of struggle and muffled breaths were growing weaker. The midnighter had ample opportunity to end the girl's life with one of his blades, but he was drawing out the deed; relishing her suffering. Jarle clenched his fists and wondered whether the Calantian captain had double-crossed him. Or worse, set him up as the scapegoat for a far more sinister plot.

Common sense demanded cruel indifference, but if he didn't act, the girl would die, and blame for the murder would fall on him. Jarle cursed his luck. Coincidence or not, the attack was ruining his plans and possibly his life. Months of stringent planning and countless hours spent fussing over minute details had all been for naught. That alone merited the intruder's death.

Jarle crawled out from behind the triptych and rounded the bed. He rolled his steps to diminish the possibility of being heard and assessed every shadow.

Outside the wind intensified. And the rustling of the leaves merged with Avaren's wheezing breaths.

The night felt damned.

Jarle crept toward the clashing silhouettes and positioned himself behind the attacker. Reaching out, he grabbed the man's blades and yanked them free of the sheaths. In a burst of speed, he plunged the poniards into the man's kidneys.

Once. Twice. Three times.

Leather, skin, and innards gave way under the stabbing blows. The assassin tensed. He let out an unintelligible gurgle before releasing the garrote. Instinctively he grasped for his daggers but came up empty. The man half-turned, his black eyes wild with bewilderment, before collapsing without so much as a cry.

Jarle unlooped the garrote from the unconscious girl's throat and turned her to face him. He pressed his ear against her lips and listened for breath. Disheveled, made paler by the light of the moons, the woman looked every bit like the specter of death.

"Ven be damned," Jarle cursed. He pulled off his gloves and tossed them. Tenderly, he gathered Avaren in his arms and carried her to the bed. He slid his mask down, took a deep breath, and brought his mouth to hers. The sensation of touching her tear-streaked skin was so sublime that for a moment, the thief forgot his purpose. An inexplicable warmth traveled from her mouth to his as he forcefully blew air into her lungs.

Lightheaded and confounded; feeling as though the floor had suddenly evanesced from under his feet, Jarle pulled back his hood. The tingling that had assaulted the back of his throat when he first encountered Avaren returned.

"Breathe," Jarle coaxed.

After what seemed like an eternity, Avaren inhaled on her own. She coughed and gasped, sucking in air with desperate inhalations. Jarle propped her on a pillow, then covered her shivering body with several thick bath towels.

Assured that the girl was breathing on her own, Jarle kicked the door closed and approached the dead man. He squatted over the body and pulled down the attacker's mask. The gentle profile of the lifeless face sent a chill racing down his spine. There was no mistaking the solid-black eyes and the cross-shaped scar on his cheek. He had killed the notorious assassin known as Mast—a former associate of the Mistress of Rats.

Mast was rumored to have sent more souls to the River of

Dust than kernels in a sack of corn. He had met the assassin once, in the far reaches of Jubbal, when he had delivered him a message from the Mistress of Rats. Mast had welcomed him graciously, with a natural charm that belied his fearsome reputation. Amidst the jingling bells of Ursanii dancers, they shared strong drink and amiable conversation. After their meeting, Mast steered clear of Reyza. Regardless of the assassin's reasons for breaking his exile, he required respect lest his revenant take offense. Jarle took two sequins from his pocket and solemnly placed them in the man's mouth. "May the ferryman guide you."

Jarle stood and turned his gaze from the corpse to the moonlight shining on his boots. He felt like a bird in the coils of a constrictor snake; every instinct screamed at him to flee. Freedom was simple. All he had to do was walk out the balcony door and climb. By sunrise, he could be a wealthy man sailing to a new life.

He took a step toward the exit and paused. On the bed, Avaren struggled to breathe. An angry reddish line marred the girl's throat, and her hands were bloody. The daevil that had been sent to kill her was no ordinary thug. In Reyza, death contracts rarely included a lone killer.

Moreover, whoever had hired Mast could afford an army. It was only a matter of time before Mast's second would finish the assignment. Without help, Avaren would not survive the night.

Ideas of riches, escape, and inevitable culpability fled. All Jarle could think about was protecting the precious, wounded girl.

Jarle picked up his gloves and put them back on. He returned to Avaren's bedside and shook her awake. When her eyes opened, his breath caught. Never in all his life had he beheld such eyes. Orange flecks floated like embers in a tourmaline sea that effloresced with an unearthly light.

Feeling every bit the fool, Jarle smiled.

For a moment, they stared at each other. Then, Avaren's jewel-like gaze turned cold and feral.

Avaren cast the towels aside in search of the discarded dagger. Upon finding it, she swung.

Jarle sidestepped the attack and raised his hands where she could see them. "Breathe, alright. I mean you no harm."

Avaren scrambled off the bed. The blade shook violently in

her grasp as she used her other hand to rub her neck. When she spoke, the words were raspy; barely a hiss. "Why have you done this? Why!?"

Jarle pointed to the dead man. "I am not with that man. I saved your life."

Avaren picked up her torn robe. She peered at the corpse on the floor with equal parts confusion and horror. She shook her head. "I don't understand."

Jarle's chest tightened. The stolen jewels weighed down his pockets like lead. "You are in danger. If I were you, I would run—tonight."

With the dagger still pointed at him, Avaren walked to the bedroom door. Tears sprung to her eyes and rolled down her cheeks. Her ragged sobs filled the room as she fumbled with the door handle. "Don't come any closer."

A gut-punch was preferable to the stark despair in her voice. Her sad, brilliant eyes inspired a profound sensation as though he might die of sorrow should harm befall her. "Let me help you."

Avaren leaned against the wall and opened the door. A sob escaped her as the assassin's massacre was revealed. A dead Zincari guard lay at the threshold, his face frozen in a scream. Blood pooled in an inky puddle beneath his head. His throat had been cut. Beyond him, in the hallway, lay the shape of another corpse.

Avaren drew her gaze away. The sight shredded what remained of her composure. Wracked by sobs, she sank against the wall and shook the dead guard. "Spireo! Gods! What has happened? What has happened? Father?"

Jarle cursed under his breath. Avaren was in shock, unable to listen to reason. The longer he lingered, the more likely the chances that he'd be apprehended. He approached the woman with caution and knelt beside her. She looked up at him like a doe might a hunter. Resignation and doom danced in her eyes.

Jarle reached out and placed his hand on hers, speaking with a calmness he did not feel, "I know that I don't look much different than the man who just tried to kill you, but by all that is holy, I swear I mean you no harm. Please, put the blade down."

Avaren's fingers tightened on the weapon. Her eyes darted to her attacker's body, then back to the thief. Realization dawned in her eyes. "Spireo, he said that an intruder..." Her voice trailed off.

Jarle shook his head. "That was not the guard you heard speaking outside your door. The assassin sent to end your life had already slain him. Mejtress, you are in terrible danger and must leave this place. I can escort you to the palace. You will wed in a few days; Jarle Rigo can protect you."

Avaren shook her head. Her grip loosened on the dagger. "No, he cannot. It is Rigo who wishes me dead."

Jarle pulled the dirk free of Avaren's hand and slid it across the floor. The situation was worse than he could have imagined. "You are certain of this?"

For a moment, Avaren stared into space as though seeking solace in the gloom. "That monster has killed my father, hasn't he?"

Jarle grabbed her upper arm and helped her stand. The sudden closeness sent his spirit soaring. "I suspect he has."

Avaren turned her head and looked up at Jarle. Her eyes blazed, seeming to bore into his very soul. "I do not dare to see what I must. Will you accompany me to my father's chambers?"

Jarle's knees weakened. The girl's voice curled around his heart. "Of course. Anything you desire."

Avaren wiped the tears from her cheek and grazed Jarle's lips with the moisture. "What is your name?"

The thief's throat tingled, and his cheeks warmed as he fought against the question. Revealing his identity would condemn him. "Jarle Jadien," he blurted.

Avaren's eyes scintillated and sparked. She withdrew her fingers. "You will protect me, Jarle."

Inspired by an inexplicable surge of loyalty, Jarle took Avaren's hand in his and kissed the back of her palm. "With my life," he vowed, "I swear it.

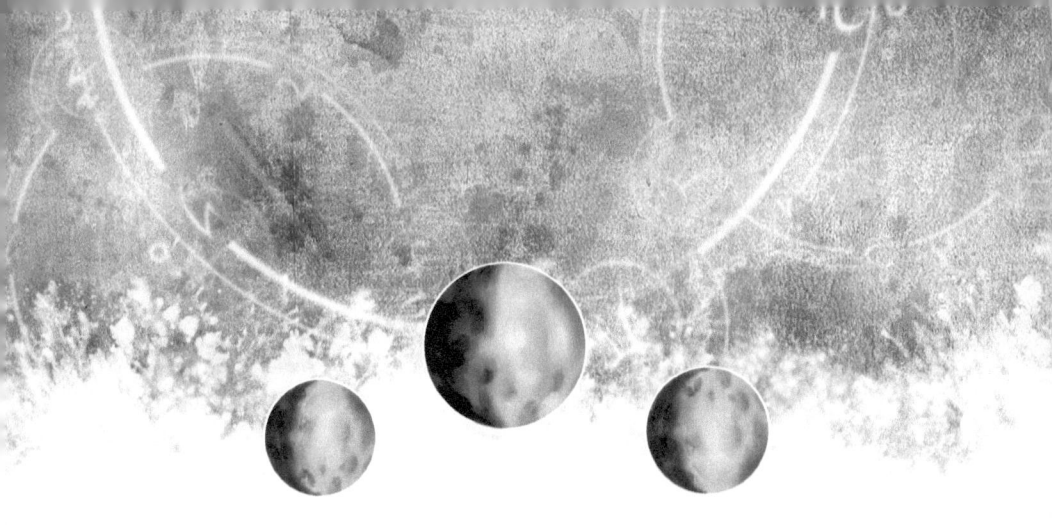

FORKLEAF

Venedi, Seventh of Sund'im, 445 A'A'diel

Jarle pushed open the door to Tan'os' bedroom with his boot. Moonlight filtered through a row of lancet windows, bathing the spacious room in a bluish glow. Tan'os' chamber exhibited none of the luxurious trappings of his daughter's room. Every piece of furniture was functional and austere in its design. Two claw-foot chairs with threadbare cushions faced a giant stone hearth whose dying embers still glowed hot. In the center of the room, on a blackwood four-poster bed with columns as thick as tree trunks, lay dead the Vise of Reyza. Tan'os was sprawled sideways upon plush furs, one hand clasping his bare chest.

In the gloom, the Vise's blood shone black. It glistened on the bed curtains, the pale furs, his arms, and legs. There was no sign of a struggle. Mast had harpooned the Northman's heart with deadly accuracy—a surgical strike that relied on Tan'os' heart to do most of the work.

Jarle had only seen the Vise from a distance, on the rare occasions when he addressed the people from the parapets of Chancellery Square. He seemed larger than life—a pale juggernaut amidst the cinnamon-skinned, slim-fingered peoples of Reyza. In person, the distinction was even more pronounced. Tan'os was the epitome of the Bissatiel bloodline, blond-haired, broad-chested and tall—easily one and a half times Jarle's height. Bulging blue veins, visible beneath his alabaster flesh, ran the length of his arms, culminating at his thick neck. Strands of his blood-smeared hair hung over the side of the bed like a shimmering cascade.

A pang of sadness clenched Jarle's chest as he considered the corpse of Tan'os Ensther. He could not recognize the noble lord or the brave sea captain who had once defended Reyza from the scourge of sea-faring marauders. He saw only the face of a man plagued by a thousand troubles, disfigured by his last harrowing moments spent among the living.

The sharp planes of Tan'os' face were chiseled in a silent howl.

Jarle blocked the door, preventing Avaren from entering the room. "You do not need to see this," Jarle said, his voice low. "Your father is dead. We should go."

"No!" Avaren said, pushing past him. "I must see him."

The girl clambered onto the bed and smoothed back her father's hair. "Papa!" she sobbed, cradling the dead man in her arms. "Oh, Papa."

Jarle winced at the sight of the grief-stricken girl. In the moonlight, her pallor held a radiance, not unlike the marble quarried in the Canyon of Parryos, whose flawless white sheen was coveted the world over. Her long hair fell over her bare shoulders, possessed by a mysterious luminescence. Jarle squeezed his eyes shut, but the strange aura surrounding her remained. He blinked again, rubbed his eyes, and forced himself to look elsewhere. As he did so, his mind cleared.

Suddenly it dawned on him—there was no struggle because the Vise had been poisoned. The corded, cramped muscles along Tan'os' arms and his facial expression were the results of paralysis.

Jarle crossed the room and seized Avaren's wrist, pulling her hand away from Tan'os' face. "Poison," he cautioned, sniffing the air. Mingled with the odor of spilled blood, oiled wood, and Avaren's alluring perfume, Jarle's trained nose picked up a faint, bitter scent. It reminded him of Esh'fah sauce, a fermented condiment favored in Ghossian cuisine. Jarle narrowed his eyes, surprised by Mast's choice of poison.

"Forkleaf," Jarle said. "It paralyzes the body."

The rare herb grew high on the frozen peaks of Blackspur, the Thrommish capital's mountainous hold, where the air was thin. The substance induced excruciating pain, followed by debilitating spasms that caused the heart to beat faster until it burst from exertion. Forkleaf explained the copious amount of blood that had gushed from the wound in the Vise's chest.

"Your father died quickly," he lied.

Avaren looked at her bloodstained fingers, then at Jarle. "We can't leave him here," she said, her voice cracking. "We must give him a proper burial so that his soul may cross the River of Dust."

Jarle covered the dead man's body with one of the furs. He then took two sequins from his pocket and dropped them in the girl's palm. "Here, say a prayer for him and see that he makes it to the halls of his ancestors. Hurry, we don't have much time."

Avaren placed the coins over her father's open eyes, careful to avoid contact with his blood. "Leave me a moment."

Without further words, Jarle crossed the room. He stood beneath the eave of the door, his back to her to allow her some privacy. Behind him, Avaren began to sing in a language foreign to his ears. Though he could not understand the language, her lamentation caused Jarle's heart to swell with grief.

The song transported the rogue back in time, to the dingy confines of his childhood home—a soot-stained hovel by the docks. He was twelve when he'd knelt by his old man's side hoping for a miracle that never came. His father, a second-generation curskin, died in a flea-infested bed, coughing up blood, without even a dirge or a coin to usher him to the next world. No funeral pyre marked the passing of Tulot Jadien—the man who taught Jarle what little honor he had. Kindness had earned his father nothing but maggoty bread, threadbare pockets, and a watery grave.

Moved by the monody and painful memories, Jarle blinked away tears.

Avaren ambled past him as though in a trance and walked down the hall.

Jarle followed her. "What are you doing?"

"There is a secret passage beneath the stairs. We can take the servants' stairwell to get there. I will show you, but first, there is something I must do."

Jarle scanned the empty hall. "Whatever it is, do it fast."

Avaren paused before a doorway and grasped the handle, but didn't turn the latch. Sensing her trepidation, Jarle pulled her aside and opened the door.

The scene that greeted him was as morbid as the last. Upon the bed, half-covered by a sheet was an olive-skinned youth whose complexion had grown ashen in death. Beside him, strewn like a rag doll, lay a pale, naked girl with hair the color of summer wheat. Her eyes were wide and bloodshot. Mottled bruises circled her neck where Mast's hands had wreaked their havoc. The valet's clothes had come off in a hurry and were thrown about while the woman's dress lay folded neatly on a chair. The pale blue silk was embroidered with pearls and dotted with topazes. It was the gown of a queen, not a servant.

Outside the room, Avaren brought a hand to her mouth. "Please tell me he isn't dead."

Jarle shifted to let her pass. "I am sorry."

As she stared at the entangled, naked bodies, Avaren heaved and nearly vomited. Betrayal, grief, and fear twisted her features into a mask of anguish. She reached out and brushed back a strand of the youth's hair, before turning her back to the massacre. Tears spilled down her cheeks, and she shook like a leaf in a breeze. "He lied to me! She lied to me. They all lied to me!"

"Quiet," Jarle hissed.

Avaren turned and smashed her fist into Jarle's face. "Do not speak to me, mongrel!"

Jarle squinted against the pain. He grabbed Avaren and shook her. "What in Ven's name are you doing? Do you want to get us both killed?"

Avaren flailed wildly in his hold, landing several kicks near his groin.

An icy thrill ran along Jarle's spine as he heard footsteps and clinking chain maille coming from the stairwell. If he didn't subdue Avaren's outburst, he would be slaughtered by the Calantians where he stood. He needed to think—fast.

Jarle spun the girl around and pinned her against his chest. He clamped his hand over her mouth and nudged the door closed with his boot. "By Ven's scaly cock, be quiet."

Outside, the guards emerged from the stairwell and rushed into the hall. The staccato sounds of their armored boots quickened as they charged past the valet's room toward Tan'os' bedchamber.

Cold beads of sweat ran down Jarle's neck as Avaren writhed in his grasp, croaking muffled curses into his hand.

Jarle released her shoulders and grabbed Avaren in a chokehold. When she brought her hands up to struggle, Jarle swept her feet, throwing her off balance. Slowly, he eased her down while tightening his hold. He applied gradual pressure to her neck until she slumped unconscious into his arms.

Jarle lay her down, then rolled to his feet and pressed his ear against the door. Down the hall, the guards were assembled in the Vise's room, locked in a heated discussion. Jarle strained to hear but couldn't discern their words. With any luck, they would tarry over Tan'os' body long enough to allow him to slip undetected down the service stairs.

Still feeling the sting of Avaren's blows, he returned to her side and hoisted her in his arms.

"By the fires of Y'rth!" Jarle swore. Never had a woman compelled him to such folly.

SILKY PROMISES

Venedi, Seventh of Sund'im, 445 A'A'diel

Jarle Rigo Iarris' fingertips tapped ominously on his lover's back.

Beneath the sheets, the man groaned. "Sleep, Rigo, for gods' sake, or the morning will find you red-eyed and ill-tempered."

Rigo's long, bony fingers retreated. "How do you do it, Neylen? How can you sleep knowing that at this very moment, Tan'os Ensther and that cunt daughter of his are making their journey to the River of Dust?"

Neylen rolled on his back. "I forbid you to squander another night worrying about that giant fool."

Rigo cocked his head to one side. "Remind me again why your plan is infallible?"

Neylen sighed and folded his arms under his head. "Trust me; there is no need to brood. By morning, the Vise and his daughter will be dead; removed beyond all concern. The man I commissioned is one of the best."

Rigo twirled Neylen's long braid between his fingers. "And if he lives?"

"If who lives?"

"Tan'os!"

Neylen gave his lover a piercing look. "You haven't been listening, have you?"

"This is serious, Neylen. What if Tan'os somehow survives?"

Exasperation tinged Neylen's voice. "Then you shall pretend to be shocked about the attempted assassination and launch a proper investigation. The criminals will be brought to justice, tried, and found guilty. As a wedding gift, you will present your bride their heads on a platter, and afterward, live joyously ever after. You will sire many children, grow fat and lazy, and forget all about me."

Nervous laughter burst from Rigo's lips. "Aren't you a smug one!"

Neylen threw the covers off his body and flashed him a charming smile. "I am confident; there is a difference."

Rigo met the Dessian's black eyes—the signature trait of his Yerr'draki ancestry. The glossy obsidian orbs, like those of a shark, revealed no emotion. "Always so amusing, your kind."

"My kind?" Neylen feigned offense. "I am not so different from you. We desire the same things, do we not?"

Rigo's face softened as he recalled the Feast of Bel'Tahïm; the night he had met Neylen. Sacred pyres illuminated the squares and wreaths of greenwood adorned every home. The scent of ash and revelry traveled upwind from the ocean to the noses of the wealthy, whose lavish masquerades often dictated the course of politics. Spring flowers hung in garlands inside his winter garden, where couples twirled to the music of the bards. The Dessian diplomat arrived in a coach drawn by windbeasts, whose lashing tongues sent palace valets scattering. All eyes turned to Neylen, whose bronzed flesh gleamed with gold dust. The man took two steps at a time, strutting into the banquet hall like a long-forgotten god.

Rigo sucked on Neylen's nipple before nipping it with his teeth. "Yes, I suppose we possess many desires in common. Mutual hatred for that northern prick tops the list."

"Despite what you may believe, I do not share your bed out of gratitude, though I am grateful for your commitment to my nation's plight. But let us not discuss business. Trade is as dry a subject as Dessia's vistas." Neylen grabbed Rigo by the scruff of his neck and brought his face down over the planes of his abdomen. "Use your mouth, Highness, allow me to put your mind at ease."

Rigo grazed Neylen's belly with his lips and allowed the Dessian to guide him. He flicked his tongue over his lover's penis, then established a slow, gulping rhythm. Slowly, like a snake swallowing its prey, he worked the huge shaft down his throat.

Neylen arched his head back and caressed Rigo's shoulders. "Mmm, just like that," he moaned.

Rigo suckled the upthrust cock, taking pride in his newfound abilities. He loved the way Neylen's body quivered with the right twist of his tongue; the way his head rolled and his toes curled. In Neylen, Rigo had found an ally, a mentor, and a confidant. He could not recall a happier moment than the night they plotted the Vise's demise.

Neylen's stomach muscles rippled as his cock disappeared into Rigo's mouth. "This night,'" he said breathlessly, "Tan'os meets his death at the hands of Maél Aodhan, a fiend known as Mast, whose poisoned blades are said to have sent more souls to Ven's Needle than entire wars."

When Rigo rose to respond, Neylen pushed him back down. "I'm not finished," he gasped. "To obscure our involvement...I hired..." Neylen trembled as his glans plunged into the confines of Rigo's throat. "The Hand of Fate! By Thul," he hissed through clenched teeth. "Don't stop!"

A frisson of delight tightened Rigo's belly. Every Reyzan feared the Hand of Fate. People spoke of the frightening, mythical figure of a thousand faces only in whispers. The Fate's enemies died in their sleep, or worse, they disappeared, never to be heard of again.

Rigo's eyes welled up with tears as he surrendered to the furious pace set by his paramour's hands. Excitement mingled with desire as Neylen's thighs trembled, and his groans filled the room. Hot flesh impaled his throat and expanded.

With an explosion of breath, Neylen convulsed and emptied himself in Rigo's mouth. Rigo squeezed his eyes shut and struggled to swallow the thick cream. When he looked up, the Dessian smiled.

"Are you pleased?" Neylen asked.

Rigo wiped tears from his eyes. "Yesss, yes," he purred.

"Come then," Neylen said, patting the bed, "sleep. Tomorrow will challenge us."

Rigo crawled under the sheets and curled against his lover's side. A satisfied grin curved his lips. By sunrise, Tan'os Ensther and his kin would be dead.

SHATTERED DREAMS

Venedi, Seventh of Sund'im, 445 A'A'diel

"We are well and truly fucked by the gods!"

Varrus didn't respond to Cassio's epithet. His attention was consumed by the corpse sprawled upon blood-soaked furs. The cold grip of doom clutched at his bowels as a roaring sound filled his ears. Tan'os Ensther, the Vise of Reyza, lay assassinated in his bed.

Captain Varrus Sigolian, a veteran of countless campaigns, felt his blood turn to ice. Fate was a cruel bitch. In an eyeblink, his daydreams of lemon groves transformed into phantasms of the gallows.

Cassio leaned his bulk against one of the bedposts and rubbed his brow. He glared at Varrus. "The opportunity of a lifetime, you said. No one would be harmed; it would just be a simple robbery. You swore this Jars was only a burglar! What happened?"

Varrus reeled with disbelief, replaying every caution taken in a jumble of memories. He had been diligent, used several reliable sources, spent more than adequate coin, and had been careful to cover his tracks. Only after he convinced himself that Jars was genuine had he agreed to the plan. "I checked him out thoroughly! He is just a burglar!" The protestation rang hollow; the proof of his failure lay upon the bed.

Cassio thrust his finger toward the remains of their employer. "Does that look like a porch climber's handiwork to you? The Vise lies murdered, in his chamber—on our watch! We are dead!"

Acid churned in Varrus' belly. A dozen scenarios played out in his mind. None of the outcomes made him feel any less sick. The heavy-timbered walls of the bedchamber seemed to loom inward, coinciding with the tightness in his chest. Cassio was right. They were doomed men.

"What is the matter with you? Say something." Cassio shoved his palm into Varrus' shoulder, jarring him from his dire thoughts. "What in Ven's name are we going to do now?"

"Do? There is nothing that can be done. The Vise is dead. No one can change that, not even one of the soulbound."

"We can run. It won't be the first time we have had to retreat from unpleasant business. We could disappear into the jungle—or steal a boat."

The idea of flight was tantalizing, but fleeing into the jungles surrounding Reyza without resources was suicidal. They would be dead within days. As for stealing a ship, any vessel they might hope to commandeer would never outrun the Thrommish fleet.

"There is no escape for us this time, old friend." Varrus shook his head. He hadn't survived a lifetime of campaigns dwelling on fortune's fickle nature; it was time for action, not self-pity. Setting his jaw, he leveled his eyes into Cassio's angry stare. "If we are to see Calantia again, we must think and do so quickly."

"Thinking is what got us into this mess!" Cassio spat. "We were fools to believe this plan would work."

Before Varrus could reply, Brath's voice rang out through the dark halls, startling the men. "Uncle! Come quick, Avaren is gone. The thief is dead!"

Varrus and Cassio looked at each other, hope flaring in their eyes.

"If she still lives—"

"We may have a chance!"

The two men rushed to Avaren bedroom. Cassio glared at Varrus as he stepped over the lifeless body of their comrade, Spireo.

Inside the room, they found Brath standing over the body of

a man clad in black leather.

"Did you kill him?" asked Varrus.

Brath shook his head. "No, I discovered him like this."

"Mejtress Avaren? Where is she?" Varrus said, looking around the room.

"She's gone. I think he raped her." The words spilled with breathless abandon from Brath's mouth. "We must find her."

Captain Varrus leaned over the corpse for a better view of the man's face.

"Fuck me with a poker!" Varrus rose up to face Cassio and Brath. "This isn't Jars."

"Well, who in the Seven Hells is he?" Cassio's hands balled into fists. "You said Jars worked alone."

"He does. He did."

"Listen to me," Brath snapped.

The two men broke off glaring at each other to face the youth.

Brath stooped over the corpse, careful to avoid his blood. He pointed to the matched handles of the daggers and the empty sheaths on the belt. "He was done in by his own daggers. Perhaps Avaren killed him, or he had a falling out with the thief you hired. And here," Brath said, pointing to the wire garrote wrapped around the dead man's fingers. "Maybe he tried to strangle her?"

Cassio rubbed the stubble that darkened his broad chin. "If she was being garroted, how could she have stabbed him in the back with his own knives?"

"Forget that, for now," Varrus barked. "Brath, see if there is anything to identify this man. Anything we might use to cover our asses."

Brath complied with his uncle's orders and searched the dead man. The contents of the belt pouches revealed little. He found several vials, small hacksaws, spiked knuckles, wire and a handful of Reyzan sequins. The young Calantian was about to rise when he noticed a hidden sheath in the man's boot. He drew the stiletto and examined it in the moonlight streaming through the balcony door. The blade was stained with blood and a dark, greasy smear. Brath dared a hesitant sniff at the substance.

"Poison!" Brath said, jumped to his feet.

"Be quiet. Another outburst like that will attract the cloister guards. We need to figure this out." Varrus glowered at his nephew's lack of discipline before turning his attention to Cassio. "It occurs to me that if we find the girl before anyone else does, we might get out of this with our necks intact."

Cassio considered the expression on his friend's face, then nodded. "Oué, we might even be heroes if we rescue the Vise's daughter and kill the assassin."

Brath strode toward the door, the envenomed dagger clenched in his fist. "We have to find Avaren. She could be wounded or worse."

The two veterans followed the youth.

"Yes, Brath," said Cassio, "let us rescue your princess and save our own asses as well."

FISHEYE

Venedi, Seventh of Sund'im, 445 A'A'diel

Even the gloom of night could not attenuate the grandeur of Ca'd'Cel. The finest carpenters in Reyza had crafted the balcony that ringed the hall of the villa. Ornately carved columns rose at regular intervals, marking the boundaries of the parqueted floors. A curved staircase with carpeted steps connected the first and second story, and on the walls, a multitude of paintings vied for attention.

Jarle made no sound as he walked toward the servants' stair. He offered silent thanks to the long-forgotten craftsmen who constructed such an unshakable floor.

Though his muscles strained, it was not Avaren's weight that concerned him, but the need to safeguard someone other than himself. He despised the feeling of having his hands tied in a house crawling with mercenaries eager for a kill. Every stride invoked the waking nightmare of getting stabbed in the back.

Jarle was nearly at the servant stairwell when someone called out, "There he is! He's got Avaren!"

Abandoning stealth for speed, the thief ran down the stairs, taking two steps at a time. Behind him, the thuds of boots grew louder. The guards were closing in fast.

Realizing that he could not outrun them with Avaren in his arms, Jarle stopped on the corner landing between floors. He lay the unconscious girl at the foot of the staircase and eased back into the shadows.

The first man to rush down the stairway was younger than him. He held a dagger above his head—an almost comical gesture when combined with his utter lack of agility. In his blind rage, the young Calantian failed to see the woman at the landing. He let out a shout and tried to slow down, but his momentum thrust him forward. The soldier leapt over Avaren and lost his balance.

Jarle emerged from hiding, grabbed the guard, and used the man's impetus to slam him headfirst into the wall. Reeling from the blow, the guard dropped his blade. The weapon clattered noisily down the steps.

Not waiting for the guard to recover, Jarle kicked his leg out from under him and sent him careening down the next flight of stairs. The sound of crunching bone joined an anguished scream.

The youth attempted to pull himself up and collapsed once more. "It's a trap!" he yelled, warning his comrades.

Jarle retreated into the darkness and waited. He recognized the man who followed on the young guard's heels. Captain Varrus Sigolian descended with caution. He crouched next to Avaren and felt for a pulse as he peered into the shadows. Behind him, footsteps signaled another man.

Doubting he could take both men simultaneously, Jarle pulled two daggers free of his wrist sheathes and let them fly.

The movement triggered Varrus' battle-honed reflexes. He dodged out of the path of the first dagger only to be impaled by the next. The blade struck true, sinking hilt-deep into his throat.

Varrus's sword fell from his hand with a deadened clang. Hot blood filled his esophagus, spilling out of his mouth and nostrils. With a shuddering gurgle, the Calantian captain fell backward.

Midway down the stairs, the injured youth cried out, "Uncle! What's happening?"

The thief scarcely had time to draw his daggers as another guard appeared. The soldier was well built and nimble, brandishing a broadsword with a long reach. Shoving past his dying comrade, he leapt over Avaren. Spittle burst from behind clenched teeth as he swung in the shadows.

Jarle ducked the blow. He scrambled along the curving wall seeking an opening in his opponent's guard. The Calantian was not intimidated by darkness or cramped quarters. Worse, the youth was still yelling—a sound that would attract anyone Mast hadn't already killed.

"Kill him! Kill the bastard!" The exhortations resounded in Jarle's ears.

The Calantian pressed the attack. Jarle twisted away from another powerful strike and lost his balance. He crashed into the wall, and before he could recover, the guard kicked him in the hip. Jarle cried out, barely scrambling out of the way of another swing. Sparks flew as metal scraped stone.

Again and again, the sword sought blood. Deadly strokes sliced the air, forcing the thief to dodge for his life.

Sweat dripped from Jarle's brow. Each narrow escape caused his hip to throb. He needed to end the skirmish soon, or he would perish.

The Calantian was a practiced soldier used to sparring with armored men. His was the art of clashing swords, charges and battle cries. With each miss, Jarle sensed the man's frustration growing—an observation he used to his advantage.

Jarle baited the soldier to greater fury with fruitless swings of his poniard.

The Calantian bared his teeth. "You'll need more than that toothpick, you son of a whore."

The man's voice inspired the youth, whose voice had grown weak with exhaustion. "Don't let him get away, Cassio."

The thief evaded a sword strike and lunged in with his dagger. Cassio sidestepped, reversed his thrust, and drove the broadsword's pommel into Jarle's rib cage.

The blow resounded with a loud crack. A strangled grunt burst from Jarle's lips as he staggered back, daggers at the ready. "By the looks of your teeth, you need a toothpick more than I do." The bluff stole the air left in Jarle's lungs.

Cassio thrust his weapon forward with all his power. Jarle deflected the swing, but the force of the parry jostled his entire body. He cried out in pain and missed his footing on a step.

All appeared lost when Avaren abruptly stirred from unconsciousness behind Cassio. She let out a moan and distracted the Calantian long enough for the thief to move past his guard. Jarle lunged upward and buried his blade deep into the soft flesh of the guard's inner thigh and struck bone.

Cassio stumbled and fell backward. He struggled to keep his sword raised as he fumbled for the hilt of the dagger stuck between his legs.

Jarle crawled back up to the landing. Every breath sent stabbing pain coursing through his battered ribs.

"I've dealt you a fatal wound," Jarle panted.

The Calantian's face twisted into a grimace. In a show of bravado, he pulled the dagger out of his injured groin and took a swing. "May the Spider Queen take you, backstabber!"

In the distance, Jarle heard shouts. More guards were approaching. "Know this; I did not betray you. Nor did I kill the Vise. Send my regards to the ferryman."

Gritting his teeth against the pain, Jarle hobbled to where Avaren lay. He sheathed his daggers before propping her up, then slapped her face. "Avaren," Jarle whispered, "wake up."

The stinging slaps caused the girl's eyelids to flutter, but they did not open. Avaren let out a soft, sleepy moan.

Jarle gripped Avaren's jaw to stop her head from lolling back. "How do I find this secret passage?"

"Fisheye," Avaren murmured.

Jarle shook Avaren's shoulders. "Fisheye? What do you mean?"

When the girl said nothing more, Jarle slammed his palm on the floor. "Shit and thunder!"

Avaren had said the passage was under the central stair. And while Varrus had not mentioned any tunnels, Jarle knew what every street urchin in Reyza sooner or later discovered. A network of limestone caverns crisscrossed the city.

Passage or not, he had to think fast. In a few moments, the villa would be swarming with guards, and he was in no condition to fight. Fleeing through the main entrance was suicidal. The servants' quarters were less risky, but there was no telling they would avoid detection. Their only hope was to hide.

Using the wall for support, Jarle scooped the unconscious

woman into his arms. He rose, biting back a scream as the pain in his ribcage flared. Sweat dripped into his eyes and down his back.

Barely alive, one hand pressed against the gushing wound, Cassio watched the thief pass.

Jarle's breaths burst from his nostrils with each labored step down the stairs. Midway down the flight, Jarle paused before the wounded Calantian soldier. The youth lay across the steps immobile, except for the rise and fall of his chest. His right leg was bent at an unnatural angle and appeared broken. Jarle considered setting Avaren down to ascertain that the man wasn't feigning unconsciousness but to do so meant losing precious time.

"If you wish to save your hide, don't get in my way." When the threat failed to rouse the guard, the thief stepped over him. As he did so, a bolt of pain shot through his calf. Jarle cried out and stumbled down a few more steps, before setting Avaren down. In a haze of agony, he turned to see the Calantian soldier holding a stiletto in his grip.

"You won't get far," the guard spat.

Jarle touched the wound. His leather armor prevented the blade from penetrating deep, yet the superficial scratch felt like burning pitch. To his horror, the muscles of his thigh cramped with violent spasms. Fire spread through his veins, and his heart began to pound like a galloping stallion. Jarle fought against the wave of panic that threatened to strip him of reason as his worst fear came true.

He'd been poisoned.

Every thief was wary of the proverbial dagger in the back, but the dread of poison had tormented Jarle for as long as he could remember. His compatriots taunted him for his near-obsessive compulsion to carry all kinds of exotic and mundane antidotes. It was this very paranoia that he hoped would save his life. Jarle's mind flashed to the corpse of Tan'os Ensther; to the curled lips locked in a scream and the corded, twisted muscles.

By all that is holy! Forkleaf.

Jarle's fingers moved with unprecedented alacrity as he pulled ampules and small jars from the pockets sewn into his bandolier. His head swam and his vision blurred. The toxin was spreading through his body like wildfire. The searing sensation swept through his groin until his balls felt like they were being boiled.

In his panic, he could not recall which jar contained the antidote for forkleaf. He willed his cramping fingers to pop open the little cork caps. Two and three at a time, he downed one foul-tasting elixir after another. He drained every vial he carried, gulping down every drop. Several wheezing breaths later, the fire in his loins and legs began to subside. The muscle spasms that wracked his legs eased along with the strained, arrhythmic beating of his heart.

"I am going to kill you," Jarle said, crawling up the stairs toward the Calantian guard.

The youth began to pull himself up, one step at a time; the broken leg trailing behind him. "The killer is here! Hurry!"

A bitter taste tainted Jarle's throat. The sound of the guards rushing through the house thundered in his ears. He had two choices. He could kill the man who had poisoned him and most certainly be captured or attempt to save the girl.

Jarle stopped his pursuit and hobbled back to Avaren. He hoisted her over his shoulder and limped out of the cursed stairwell. Should he manage to survive, he would thank Old Man Warrick for the potions with a fistful of sequins. He emerged beneath the sweep of the grand stairs and looked around. Above him, the guards had discovered Mast's crimes and were scrambling a search party. Somewhere in the courtyard, a bell tolled. Jarle's head pounded with the sound.

Although the fire in his body had subsided, the pain of his wounds continued to smolder. The paintings that lined the villa's walls swirled into a dizzying kaleidoscope. Exotic animals, lofty ladies and all manner of personages peered down from their painted prisons. Their eyes seemed to pinpoint his location while their smiles mocked his predicament.

Jarle swallowed and resisted a wave of nausea. He had not defeated one of the world's most feared assassins only to be apprehended like some amateur. The secret door had to be near.

Fisheye. Fisheye! What fucking fisheye!?

Most of the paintings were too small to mask a secret passage except one. The large canvas that captured the rogue's attention was mounted in a gilt frame inlaid with mother-of-pearl. The subject was a mythical seascape painted in vibrant colors by a master's hand.

In the painting, two rough black rocks thrust out of a frothing sea. Perched with one foot upon each outcrop, a muscular, naked man stood facing the ocean. The painted hero hurled a fishing net into the raging tempest. Even a street rat could recognize the classic myth of Danikos ensnaring the Southern Gale. Jarle's father had recounted the story when he was a boy. It was the tale of a man who achieved the impossible only to be undone by his pride.

The sounds of guards in the stairwell prompted urgency. Jarle lay Avaren down and ran his fingers along the perimeter of the frame. He pulled at the frame's corners, expecting it to slide open, but the painting didn't budge.

Jarle rubbed his brow as he studied the masterpiece. His head pounded, and his heartbeat thundered in his chest—a counterpoint to the guards' approaching footsteps.

The artist had captured the intensity of the famed Southern Gale; the churning water was translucent, highlighted in pastel shades that reflected the distant sunset. Leaping in the salty spray near one of the painted rocks, a small fish seemed to stare at Jarle.

Jarle rolled his eyes before he breathlessly offered a prayer to Ven. He held his breath, pushed his thumb into the fish's eye, and felt a soft click. He exhaled with a huff when the frame quietly opened to reveal a passageway. The tunnel's walls were rough-hewn, and the floor surfaced with slabs of marble. Rusted sconces fitted with moonstone blocks shed a dim, bluish glow.

The thief grabbed Avaren by her arms and dragged her into the opening. He closed the frame and leaned against the wall, nauseous and disoriented. Whether from having imbibed too many antidotes or the poison itself, his malaise was worsening.

Hidden by only a rectangle of painted canvas, Jarle listened to the shouts of soldiers as they searched the downstairs living area. The proximity of the guards would prove fatal if Avaren awoke and made a sound.

Move your ass or get caught like a tosser.

Jarle fought the growing numbness in his extremities. He stooped down and picked up Avaren despite the white-hot throbbing of his ribs.

It took all his willpower to avoid screaming.

He shuffled down the passage, arms straining, unsure where the journey led. The tunnel curved; the walls narrowed. Pockets of slick algae thrived under the pools of blue light. Moisture trickled down the limestone walls. The smell of the sea intensified.

Twice Jarle slipped and scraped Avaren's legs against the rocks. A clammy, cold sweat broke out on his body and soaked his limbs. He had lost track of time and direction when the passage abruptly ended in a circular stairwell.

In a haze, Jarle followed the winding stair and emerged onto a ledge. The floor of the landing was paved with lapis colored tiles that had long lost their luster. Beyond, stretched a cavern that opened to the sea. The sight would have filled him with gladness, except for the floor-to-ceiling iron gate standing in his way.

The ebb and flow of the crashing waves matched the rush of blood at Jarle's temples. The tortuous burn of forkleaf had returned to his leg. Each breath was a hammer blow against his ribs, and his arms shook from the strain. Unable to go farther, Jarle lay the girl down and tested the bars. The gate was locked.

Dropping to his knees, he searched his pockets for his lockpicks and found a pearl necklace instead. Tremors shook his limbs and stiffened his fingers. The world spun; the floor gave way. Jarle collapsed on his side, facing the girl. Avaren's cherry-red robe had come undone, exposing her beautiful breasts, but all he could see were the mottled bruises around her neck.

Slowly, the thief's eyelids grew heavy, and the pain began to fade. "Avaren," he breathed, "Forgive me."

TAKE A DEEP BREATH

Brindi, Eighth of Sund'im, 445 A'A'diel

The sun was high in the sky by the time Avaren awoke. The crash of surf echoed in the cavernous tunnel. Dull pain spread behind her eyes as she squinted, staring past the iron bars that marked the secret entrance to her father's home. The acrid smell of saltwater and bat droppings filled the air.

Avaren gripped the bars and stood. A delicate exploration revealed tender bruises on her neck and arms; scraped knees. She took a step forward, then stopped. Her legs trembled, and her stomach felt sour. Frightful visions of her father's clouded eyes and Paulo's bruised flesh assaulted her. Death had deformed her loved ones' faces into grotesque, bloodless masks that would forever haunt her.

Avaren had lived a sheltered life and was wholly unprepared for the grief that tore her insides. She fell to her knees as sudden tears rolled down her cheeks. "Papa," she cried, "I love you, Papa. Why—oh gods—why has this happened?"

For a long time, her strangled sobs joined the roar of the sea.

When there were no more tears left to shed, Avaren crawled to where her rescuer lay. The man's olive complexion was ashen, and his half-open eyes roamed haphazardly. Avaren shook him. "No, no, no, you can't die."

She gripped his face. "Please, tell me what I can do. What is wrong? Are you hurt?"

Jarle smiled dreamily as he tracked her movements with unfocused eyes.

Avaren followed the man's gaze down to her chest where her robe was parted at the front, and drew it closed. "What are you smiling about, fool?"

Jarle attempted to respond, but his effort resulted in a muffled groan.

Part of her wanted to claw the man's eyes out; to blame him for the cruel world that had destroyed her father and her lover, but she could not. It was time to return the thief's favor.

The thief had helped her when all seemed lost, and she wasn't about to let him die. She removed the man's hood and slapped his cheek to focus his attention. "Blink if you can hear me."

Jarle blinked once.

Relieved, Avaren exhaled. "I am going to try to help you. Blink once for 'yes' and twice for 'no.' Can you move?"

Jarle blinked twice.

The man's lips were dry and bluish. Avaren checked him for signs of bleeding and found none. "Why can't you move? Are you poisoned?"

One blink.

Avaren considered rummaging through Jarle's many pockets, then thought better of it. "Is there something in these pockets that can help?"

Two slow blinks.

Avaren got up and walked to the iron gate. Reaching up, her fingers danced along a narrow ledge until they closed around a key. Her hand trembled as she unlocked the rusty bolt. She had opened the gate that led out to the ocean a thousand times, but this time, would be her last. With her father dead, the place she called home was nothing more than a tomb.

When the gate creaked open, Avaren walked through it to the opening of the cave. Light filtered through the canopy of clouds, bathing the jagged mouth of the cavern in a warm glow. Eight armlengths below, white-crested waves rose and fell against the

cliff face. Red-footed gulls squawked, riding the drafts that swept up from the sea in search of a meal. To the west, partially hidden by the haze of sea spray, stretched the docks. The tall masts of great ships bore the colorful standards of Ghul'denaan, Wheatshore, A'diel and her father's homeland of Thyra. Two vessels from the Calantian city-states; of Stellae and Pirensa were being unloaded on smaller wharfs. The cries of dockworkers carried on the morning breeze.

Avaren looked behind her to the immobile man on the ground, then returned her gaze to the blue expanse of open ocean. If she managed to stay alive, she would ensure Rigo Iarris paid a blood-debt for taking her father's life.

Avaren took off the robe's waist tie and used it to bind her hair in a ponytail. She returned to the poisoned man's side and removed her tattered robe. Ignoring Jarle's wide-eyed stare, Avaren hooked her arms under his armpits and began pulling him toward the mouth of the cave.

Huffing with effort, she positioned Jarle's body until he lay at the very edge of the drop-off. She stood over him and studied the swirling, foaming waves. She knew the ebb and flow of the morning currents well. Timed right, the man would fall three or four armlengths at most, before being dragged out in the undertow.

*
**

Jarle had imagined his death many times. He long presumed Ven's vengeance would come in the shape of a dagger or a jilted lover, perhaps even as a glass of poisoned wine, but never the sea! The idea of having cheated death thrice over only to be murdered by the very socialite he risked life and liberty to protect was beyond absurd.

Through the bright trails of light that clouded his vision, Jarle's eyes grew wide with horror as the waves crested, then crashed against the rocks. He protested with rapid blinks, but the woman above him appeared oblivious to his plight.

Paralyzed, with poison beating in his veins, the thief prayed to his maker.

"Take a deep breath," was the last thing Jarle heard as Avaren pushed him into the churning waves.

The impact of the fall battered Jarle's broken ribs. He howled in pain; lost precious air. For an eye blink, he floated on the seesaw of the waves that smashed against the rocks, then sank, paralyzed and helpless, beneath the churning surface. His heart pounded against his temples. His blood raced. Panic gripped his mind as the light of the sun faded. The pressure in his ears built up until all he could hear was a high-pitched scream.

Damn her to Hel!

Seized by the undertow, Jarle sank fast. He held his breath until his lungs burned like two furnaces, then exhaled in a silent scream. His breath escaped in a stream of bubbles. Black dots began to crowd his vision.

Jarle was certain he was on his way to the River of Dust to join all the souls he'd dispatched to the underworld, when suddenly, Avaren appeared before him. The woman was a monster in every sense of the word. Her eyes burned with azure fire, glowing like two moonstones in the dark. Her hair drifted in the current like wisps of pale smoke. Beneath the surface, her pallor was stark, and her skin as translucent as milk glass. Bluish veins pulsed at her throat, and her teeth were sharp like those of a tigerfish. When she spoke, the melodic sound of her voice cut through the piercing shrill that throbbed in his ears.

"Breathe," she said.

Jarle fought the urge to scream as two sinuous black tails whipped behind Avaren's back. The tentacles were long and muscled, covered with dark green iridescent scales that shifted in the currents that buffeted their bodies.

Despite his fear, a delightful shiver raced along Jarle's skin when Avaren pressed her mouth to his. The thief quaffed the warm, fresh air that filled his lungs, unable to summon the courage to look down.

Were the girl's lovely legs a mass of writhing tentacles?

Jarle's stomach dropped. Never in his life had he felt such desperation. He willed his limbs to move, to thrash, to follow the direction of the bubbles that escaped their locked mouths, but it was no use. Avaren held him in a tight embrace.

Around them, the current shifted as though the ocean obeyed

some unspoken command. They moved through the blue-green morass in a series of thrusts and twirls; a weightless dance that threatened to make him ill. Disoriented and panicked, with no idea of where they were headed, Jarle focused on the only thing he could do—breathe.

THE HIDDEN GROTTO

Brindi, Eighth of Sund'im, 445 A'A'diel

The coastline of the Reyzan peninsula was treacherous. Below the roiling surf, razor-sharp reefs thrust up from the shallows. The coral labyrinth with its unpredictable currents had claimed many ships whose wooden ribs littered the ocean floor. On land, narrow pebble beaches gave rise to imposing limestone cliffs with pleats and tucks where a myriad of birds raised their young. Above the bluffs, half-swallowed by the jungle, stood the colossus of Umad the Snake. Constructed with the donations of pilgrims who worshiped at the Temple of Ven on Minstrel Rock, the stone guardian warned would-be raiders.

When Avaren surfaced with the thief, three leagues northwest of Reyza, only Umad's giant head was visible above the jungle that spilled over the cliffs. Overhead, redbills and gulls squawked, skirting the waves in search of a meal.

Avaren hooked her arms under Jarle's armpits and hoisted his face above the surf. Her savior was limp in her arms and his ashen skin mottled with reddish blotches. Part of her wanted to let go; to watch the thug slip beneath the waves; see his eyes bulge, and his mouth gulp for breath.

Avaren's tears spilled hot and bitter into the sea. The morning sun held no warmth, and the frolicking birds no joy. She cursed the indifference of the clouds, the cliffs, and the breezes that caressed the surf. She cursed Rigo, the man in her arms, and all the souls in Reyza.

On any other day, she might have found her whizzing through the coral maze; chasing schools of glimmering fish or collecting baubles from the shipwrecks. She would return home at high tide and enjoy a meal with her father, who would admonish her for missing her lessons. After his departure to the palace, she'd sneak to the kitchen for a game of Thrarttas with Paulo where they enjoyed sweet wine under the watchful eye of the servants.

On any other day, the ones she held dear would still be alive.

Avaren took one of Jarle's gloved hands and held it above the water. His digits, though slender, were a third shorter than those of typical Vendraedi males—a telltale sign that the ruffian was a curskin. Curskins were the lowest of all people, mongrels born of mixed bloodlines without any of the endowments of their antecessors. Even criminals of pure pedigree held a higher status than curskin do-gooders. Damned at birth, the unblooded curs had had little choice but to turn to a life of crime.

Avaren released Jarle's hand and thrashed her powerful tails against the current that threatened to dash them against the coral. Flanged rows of gills along her back flared as she sucked in her breath. The man's dead weight, coupled with the effort of synchronizing her breathing to his, had sapped her strength. Her arms felt like bowed strings and her fingers cramped where they dug into Jarle's armor.

Keeping his chin above the waves, Avaren towed the rogue into a ring of coral spires where the surf broke with a deafening roar. "We are almost there," she gasped, unsure if the man could hear her. Wrapping one of her áel-like tails around the paralyzed man's waist, she shifted to face him. "We have to go under one last time. If you can hear me, blink."

Jarle opened his salt-reddened eyes and then closed them once more.

Avaren uncoiled her tail from around his body and circled her arms around his waist. "On the count of three, take a deep breath. After I pull you under, I'll pause to give you air. One, two, three."

When Jarle filled his lungs, Avaren pulled him into the depths with uncanny swiftness. She swam through a narrow crevice on the ocean floor and into an underwater tunnel. Her black-finned tails beat against the riptide currents and propelled them through the silty murk. Before them, tiny crabs scurried along the walls, and blind cave áels hissed, fluffing their sand-colored dewlaps. Wedge-headed galefins darted back into their rocky spawning beds, their green, glowing eyes marking the contours of the passage.

Avaren wove through the tight turns until the narrow walls opened into a vast, underwater system with branching tunnels. She placed her mouth over Jarle's and allowed air to flow into his lungs, before shooting upwards toward an opening illuminated by shafts of light.

Jarle gulped for air as they emerged in an underground pool open to the sky. Thick, twisted roots hung down from the edges of a hole where the cave's roof had collapsed. Mosses, bright-hued ferns, and tangled vines choked the circumference of the oculus. The air was warm, redolent with the scent of late-summer blooms, moist verdure, guano, and alkaline earth. Around them echoed the sounds of the jungle; hoots and howls; the singsong of birds; a waterfall gushing in the distance.

Avaren pulled Jarle's paralyzed body to the shore and slithered beside him. Sharp pebbles wedged themselves under the scales of her coiling tails, and the gills on her back opened and closed like those of a landed fish. For the span of several hacking breaths, she belonged to neither land or sea. Her tails thrashed like writhing áels as she crawled forward onto dry land. She cried out as the cartilaginous tissues of her lower extremities shortened, and scales softened into to flesh. The gills fused with the skin on her back, and her monstrous teeth retracted into her jaw.

Exhausted, Avaren flopped onto her back and stretched her legs. She blinked away the nictitating membranes over her eyes and stared at the clouds drifting through the sky. For a long time, she pondered the intolerable length of time that existed between sunrise and sunset and all of the terrible events that could transpire in one day.

Beside her, the thief rolled his eyes, trying to communicate, but Avaren did not stir to help him.

For the first time since she had discovered the cave, she felt like a stranger within its walls. The ancient grotto bore traces of many storms. Striations of salt crystals left behind by high-water lines limned the walls, and in what remained of the ceiling, stalactites had begun to form.

Shadows lengthened. Bats fluttered. Beyond the opening, the sky blazed with a depth of color that bards would struggle in vain to describe in their ballads. The sunset's glorious majesty did little to raise her spirits. Inside, Avaren felt hollow.

As blackness swallowed the contours of the cave, a chilly breeze caused Avaren to shudder. Curling on her side, she brought her knees to her chin and clenched her eyes shut. She had never spent the night in the cave or anywhere but the comfort of her own bed.

Loneliness wrangled with despair. Visions of her father's smile wrestled with the memory of his blood-splattered body. Her nostrils filled with the coppery stink of blood. Her nightmare had just begun.

MORTAL REMAINS

Brindi, Eighth of Sund'im, 445 A'A'diel

Jarle Rigo Iarris paused before the entrance of the royal crypt and turned to face Ther'oldo Ers, the ambassador of Thromm. "A word of warning before we enter," he said, putting on his most sympathetic face. "You have heard the preliminary reports of what happened at Ca'd'Cel, but I am not confident that you are prepared for the sight that lies beyond this door. Tan'os Ensther did not die quickly."

Ther'oldo hailed from Blackspur, the capital city of his northern homeland and was of a Bissatiel line that had for generations bred giant men. Despite his old age, he had an impressive build and towered a full armlength over Rigo's head. He looked down at Reyza's ruler and met his gaze. His impassive blue eyes did not reveal the turmoil that brewed in his heart. "The Vise of Reyza was slain in his home while defending it against thieves. One thug is dead, and the other escaped, presumably after kidnapping Avaren Ensther. Is that correct?"

"Yes, that is—accurate." Rigo shrank from the Northman's stare. "However, the evidence points to a brutal struggle, one that has left the Vise's mortal remains in a frightful state."

Ther'oldo's gaze did not waver. "Like Tan'os, I am a son of

Thromm. We are not weak-hearted people who spill our stomachs at the sight of gore. Open this door, let us proceed."

Rigo nodded to one of the guards in his entourage. The soldier stepped forward, unhooked a key ring from his belt and unlocked the sepulcher. The scent of camphor, incense, and herbal oils filled the hall as he pushed open the door.

Inside the royal tomb, walls of polished stone rose in graceful sweeps to a domed vault. Larger than life statues of Reyza's former rulers circled the perimeter of the chamber. The serene sentinels stood with their heads bowed to the platters they held in their hands. Upon the discs, urns of gold inlaid with precious stones immured the ashes of the deceased. In the center of the room, above a catafalque of clean, understated design hung a brass chandelier whose ever-burning elemental flames illuminated the corpse of Tan'os Ensther. The smoke wafting from several censers diffused the golden light and hovered about the body like a mist.

Rigo withdrew a silk kerchief and held it to his nose to guard against the fumes. "Apologies for the scent. Although I have retained the very best undertakers to embalm the body, they are not accustomed to the funerary practices of the North. Reyzan custom does not allow for the preservation of corpses." Rigo gestured for Ther'oldo to enter. "After you, Ambassador."

Ther'oldo ducked under the door and approached the slab. Tan'os lay on his back, hands at his sides. He was naked save for a modest length of black silk draped over his hips. In death, his skin appeared waxen, nearly translucent. A direct result from the loss of blood caused by the numerous gashes that marred his flesh.

The oils the embalmers had used in their efforts to mask the scent of death, had only partially succeeded. The nauseating stench of dead meat filled the room.

Ther'oldo did not turn to look at Rigo as he addressed him; instead, he forced himself closer to the body, bending down to examine the gaping wounds. The multiple stab wounds denoted an almost rabid frenzy on behalf of Tan'os' murderers. "The Vise appears not to have been slain, so much as butchered," Ther'oldo said. "Are you certain this was a robbery and not an assassination?"

Rigo remained by the tomb's entrance, handkerchief to his nose. "It is still early in the investigation, but the testimony of the surviving guards points to betrayal and theft. It appears that the Zincari Captain made a deal with the thieves and allowed them access to the villa."

Ther'oldo leaned forward and studied the bulging tendons that distorted Tan'os' face. "I would speak with these witnesses myself."

"Of course. However, I am told the inquisitors are still prising information from them. My men are skilled at what they do, but it may take days before we know all the facts. I have assigned Lord Justiciar Poldar Tsardon to lead the investigation personally. I shall ensure you receive a full copy of his report upon your return."

"My return?" Ther'oldo turned to face the regent. "Just where is it you think I am going?"

Rigo waved his kerchief. "Thrommish custom demands every effort be made to bury a great personage in the soil of his homeland before putrefaction takes hold. Anything less would damn a soul to wander the River of Dust without respite. Surely you intend to escort the Vise's body to Thyra for a proper funeral."

Ther'oldo stroked the back of his neck. Rigo was correct. The body's stench was proof that a departure as early as the following morning would be required to ferry the body home in time for a burial. He needed time to think. "Speaking of funerals, where is the body of Dannia Jarnïs?"

Rigo hesitated. "Mejtress Avaren's maid-in-waiting?"

"The very same. Dannia is also of noble blood, the youngest daughter of Olørn Jarnïs, the Trezur of Carr."

"Her remains are in the room adjacent." Before Ther'oldo could interrupt, Rigo pressed the matter of the funeral. "There are two Thrommish vessels currently in port, the *Helicon*, and the *Guldvind*. I understand that you have recalled the rest of the Southern Fleet from their respective ports of call, but it will take weeks before the vessels arrive. Respectfully, Ambassador, I must insist that you sail north even at the peril of leaving Reyza undefended. Tan'os Ensther was a great man who deserves to be buried in the native soil of his land."

Ther'oldo balled his hands into fists. "I am not going anywhere!"

Rigo masked his dismay with the kerchief. "Tan'os Ensther

served my nation with utmost loyalty. I will not allow you to send a hero of Thyra to the afterlife with as much importance as a barrel of pickled fish."

Ther'oldo prayed for the forgiveness of his dead kinsman. "Tan'os Ensther's body will not go north in either of those ships. His daughter is missing, and I will not abandon her plight."

Rigo snapped, "I am making every effort to find the whereabouts of my future bride. Do not use his daughter as an excuse to damn Tan'os' eternal soul. You know very well that if Mejtress Avaren were here, she would demand her father receive a proper interment."

Ther'oldo slammed his fist on the stone slab. "I have sent word of Tan'os' death to Thyra, *Your Highness*. If you think that his son will sit idly and wait for the delivery of his father's corpse, you are sorely mistaken. It is likely that Strommarch Rhiess will dispatch the Northern Fleet; he may even make the journey himself. My countrymen will demand answers for these crimes, and I shall remain here to see that those answers are found."

Rigo raised his eyebrows. "The Strommarch will not be pleased with your decision regarding his father's remains."

"Perhaps, but that is my concern. Tan'os Ensther would expect me to utilize those ships to scour every harbor from here to Carr in search of his daughter, and that is precisely what I intend to do."

Rigo shook his head. "There is no evidence that the perpetrator of this crime left aboard a ship. All vessels have been forbidden to set sail and are currently being searched. With all due respect, Ambassador, your motives for denying Tan'os a funeral ring false."

Ther'oldo turned his back on the mauled corpse of his kinsman and walked over to where Rigo was standing. He was pleased when the smaller, younger man took a step back. Looking down at Rigo, Ther'oldo spoke, his tone solemn. "I took an oath to represent Thromm's interests in Reyza and have no intention of leaving her shores at this critical moment. I intend to hire a private investigator to unearth the truth behind these murders and the whereabouts of the missing princess. In the interest of continued amity between our two nations, I humbly suggest that you appeal to the mages to stave off decay for both bodies—at your expense— until such a time as Thromm is satisfied that Tan'os Ensther and members of his household were the victims of a robbery, and not a more sinister crime."

Frustration underscored Rigo's polite tone. "Out of respect for the memory of Tan'os Ensther and our good relations with Thyra, I will acquiesce to your requests."

Ther'oldo took a step back from the Jarle. "Thank you. I believe this concession to be a constructive step toward normalizing relations between our two nations."

"I am glad we have reached an accord. Let us leave Tan'os in peace now." Rigo sidestepped the old man and left the room. He waved his kerchief to the guard who had opened the tomb—a silent instruction to close the door.

Ther'oldo followed him down the hall. "I am aware of Lord Justiciar Tsardon's politics and wish to have your assurance that he will not interfere with whomever I hire to conduct my private investigation."

Rigo stopped and offered the diplomat a patronizing look. "As these are trying times, I will overlook your insult to Lord Justiciar Tsardon. If it pleases you, I can bestow an agent of your choosing a writ granting them the authority of a Chief Justiciar for the duration of your inquest. Further, I shall have the Lord Justiciar spare some of his soldiers as well."

The door of the royal tomb closed behind them with a quiet finality.

Ther'oldo bowed as low as his old age allowed. "On behalf of Thyra and Blackspur, I thank you for your generosity and concern. I shall endeavor to pass on your heartfelt condolences to the Ensther family."

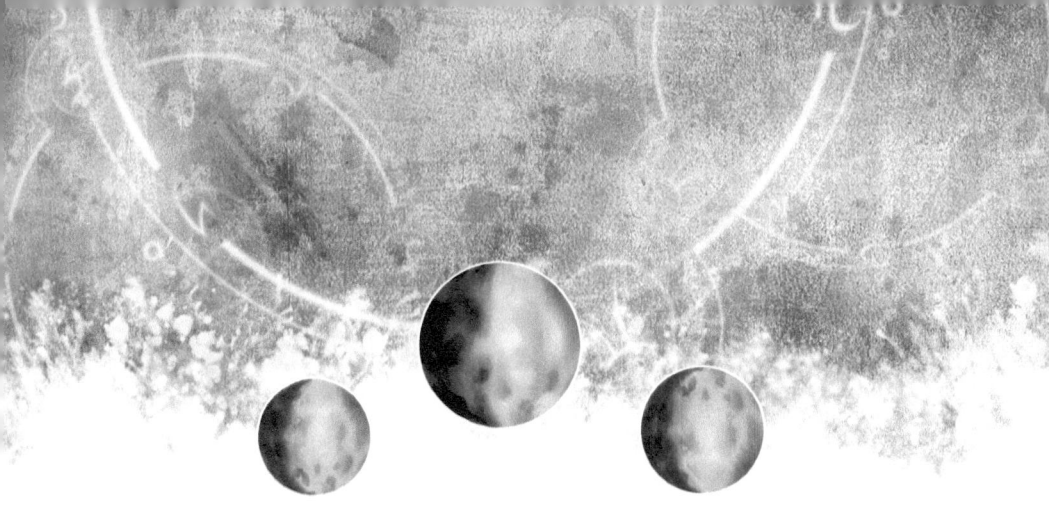

DAEMON IN THE FLESH

Brindi, Eighth of Sund'im, 445 A'A'diel

The iron and glass doors that led to the balcony of the royal bedroom were open, and a cool breeze rustled the curtains. From the dim interior of the bedroom, Neylen watched his lover pace from one side of the balcony to the other. Rigo had discarded his jacket and vest, which lay rumpled on the floor, and his hair was a disheveled nest of curls. Rigo bit his nails as he walked, a habit Neylen found irksome, if not outright revolting.

Neylen left the shadows and stepped out to the balcony. Straightening his shoulders, he prepared for confrontation. Rigo was in a black mood which could only mean that his meeting with the Thrommish ambassador had not gone as planned.

Neylen lowered his eyes and bowed his head. "You sent for me, Your Highness."

Rigo ignored him. He paced back and forth a score more times before pausing to face the bronze-skinned Dessian. "I have news," Rigo hissed. "That frozen old fuck is not going back to Thyra."

Neylen lifted his head and looked into Rigo's eyes. The Jarle was twelve years his junior with large, pale blue eyes and soft sensual lips. When he was angry, a hot blush tinged his youthful complexion which served to weaken his masculinity. There were times when, in a certain light, Rigo appeared every bit an androgynous figure; like the fabled sylphs of his desert land. The thought triggered a smile which goaded Rigo's anger.

Neylen cleared his throat. "That's not entirely unexpected."

Rigo threw up his hands. "How can you stand there looking so calm? Everything you said would happen has not!"

Neylen walked to the railing and looked over the city. Below the palace ramparts, staggered terraces of villas and plazas cascaded down to the glimmering sea. Thin pines rose artfully from the chaos of buildings and gulls floated on the breeze. "The continued presence of Ambassador Ers does not complicate matters. He is alone, and without the Vise, he is nothing more than a toothless hound."

Rigo stepped up to the railing and joined Neylen. He leaned on his elbows and ran his hands through his hair. "A toothless hound that will be sniffing about. He intends to conduct his own investigation and forced my hand into signing a writ bestowing his man the temporary rank of Chief Justiciar."

Neylen's expression was placid as he stared out to the shimmering ocean beyond the harbor. "That is a minor complication. Lord Justiciar Tsardon has followed our instructions regarding the evidence. Whatever the ambassador's man discovers will only serve to solidify our official account. Regardless, we should have the ambassador and whoever he hires closely watched."

Rigo clenched his fists. "There is more. Ers insists that I keep Tan'os' body, and that of Avaren's maid-in-waiting magically preserved to stave off decay until Thromm is satisfied with their findings. That could be weeks or months."

Neylen fixed his gaze on the Collegium's spire opposite the palace. "Risking the damnation of Tan'os' soul is not the most intelligent decision."

Rigo dropped his head into his hands. "Even after death that ill-begotten son of a northern whore continues to squeeze my balls! The Collegium mages are as double-dealing as the thieves of this city. Once they realize that I have little choice in the matter of the preservation of the bodies, they will demand an exorbitant price. And then there is Ers' implied threat of the Northern Fleet and my brother-in-law, Strommarch Rhiess descending on this city. Did I mention my sister despises me?"

Neylen felt his stomach drop. The coup which he had so carefully crafted was unraveling, and if he didn't reign in the threads soon, Rigo would turn on him. "This is a rather unexpected turn of events. Please, allow me to share the brunt of this expense. I insist."

Rigo shook his head. "No. The exchange of coin between our nations will rouse suspicion. Even I cannot escape Council scrutiny when it comes to finances."

Neylen turned to his lover and cupped his cheek. "Once we untangle ourselves from this affair, we will profit. You have my word."

"I hope you are right." Rigo straightened, leaned his hip against the banister and roughly undid his silken cravat. The garment joined the others on the floor. "What of the Calantian, has he spoken?" Before Neylen could reply, Rigo held up his hand. "A word of warning, my ears are fatigued by word of endless misfortune, so do not speak if you bear ill tidings."

Neylen leaned against the balustrade and crossed his arms. "The Calantian guard confessed everything. Mast's killer appears to be a member of the Jewelers' Guild. The interloper goes by the street name of Jars."

Rigo's ears shone the color of ripe tomatoes. "Who is this pathetic fuck and what was he doing in Tan'os' villa?"

Neylen kept his tone cool. "He was born and raised in the Tangles, the bastard son of a curskin potter and a prostitute. His birth name is Jarle Jadien."

Rigo cut Neylen off with an incredulous snarl. "The scum's name is Jarle!? I will see these damned curskins pay for their mockery!"

Neylen ignored the outburst and continued, "It appears that Tan'os' guards hired this thief to steal jewels belonging to your betrothed. The Calantians planned to split the spoils with the interloper."

Rigo raised his eyebrows. "And this Jars was there purely by coincidence?"

Neylen nodded. "It appears so."

Rigo scoffed in disbelief. "Listen to me carefully, Neylen.

Tan'os was respected, if not loved. People are not comfortable with murder, rape, and missing women. They expected a wedding, and they got a bloodbath. If we don't produce a culprit and at least pretend to care about what has happened to the Vise of Reyza, we will have a mob on our hands. As if that weren't enough, Thyra's Northern Fleet is capable of pounding Reyza's bastions into dust. Let's not forget how Tan'os achieved power. The Strommarch's ships remain in Thyra, for now, but they will sail south soon enough."

A lopsided grin crossed Neylen's lips. "Then it is rather convenient that we have someone to blame, isn't it?"

Rigo met Neylen's pitch-black eyes. "You cunning snake."

Sensing Rigo's change of mood, Neylen pulled the youth against him. The Jarle was lithe, seeming almost petite against his body. "We could use this," Neylen whispered in Rigo's ear. "Just what kind of man breaks into another man's home, steals his riches, murders innocents in their sleep, kills the Vise and then absconds with his daughter, your wife-to-be, the future mother of your children?"

"A savage," mused Rigo. "An absolute monster!"

"Precisely." Neylen bit Rigo's ear before running his hand over the curve of his lover's buttocks. "This Jars is the worst kind of monster, a daemon in the flesh who must be found, tortured and executed for all to see. Round up the thief's family and the people who know him and question them. Have the Lord Justiciar issue a tempting reward for his capture."

"Yes," Rigo gasped. "I want a hundred criers in the streets this very evening. Let them shout the thief's name loud and clear. Jarle Jars Jadien is henceforth a wanted man and an enemy of Reyza." Rigo pulled free of Neylen's arms and paced past him. He looked toward the docks where the setting sun tinged the water in molten gold. "What news from the port? What says the harbor master?"

Neylen's livery collar shone in the setting sun. "Tsardon searched all of the ships as you commanded. There was no sign of the girl. I am told that the *Tasirny* and the *Howl of the West* sailed before the harbor was closed."

Rigo tapped his fingers together. "I will send word to Ther'oldo and inform him of these developments. He made his intention clear regarding the Thrommish ships currently in port. I will suggest that the *Helicon* and the *Guldvïnd* give chase. The less Thrommish presence in this city the better."

"That is a splendid idea," Neylen agreed.

Rigo stopped his pacing. "I want that curskin half-breed, and that northern whore found. I will have Tsardon search the Tangles and the beaches. I will turn this city upside down if I have to!"

Despite his cool composure, Neylen's head ached and his lips felt dry. "I will have my personal Durauk Guard aid in the search. If they don't ferret them out, the Hand of Fate surely will."

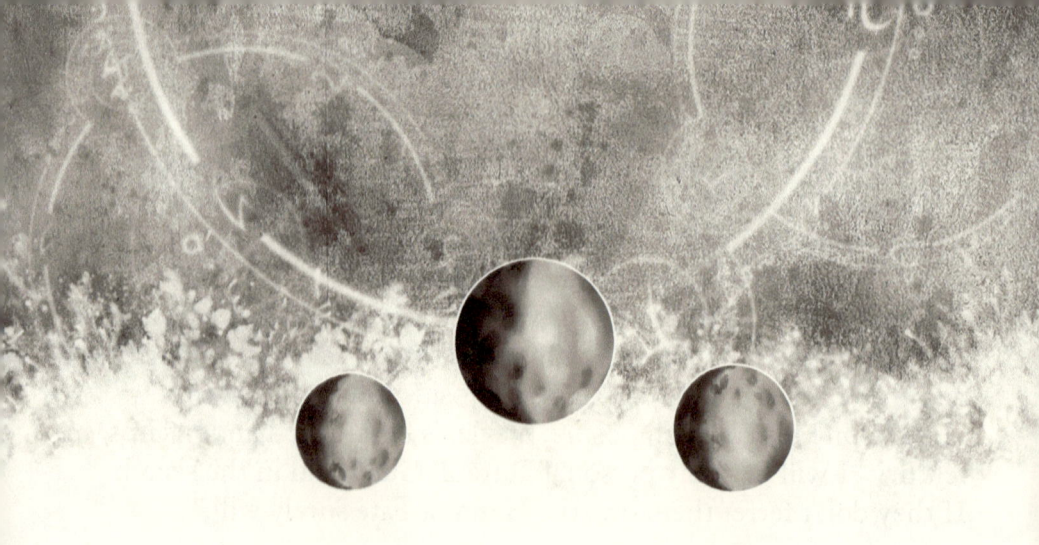

SUNKEN TREASURE

Ristor, Ninth of Sund'im, 445 A'A'diel

Distorted memories of the massacre swirled in Avaren's mind. Ashen faces. Cold flesh. Blood. She struggled to breathe; writhed under the assassin's weight.

"Help!"

Avaren awoke to the echo of her scream and a thousand wings beating in unison. Morning light had not yet stolen into the aperture of the cave when the bats returned to their roosts. The tiny creatures circled the quiet pool before darting into the dark recesses of the cave.

Beside her, sprawled on the shore with his boots still in the water, lay her rescuer. Jarle was unconscious; his fingers curled into a claw-like grip; his breaths shallow. Avaren got up and crawled to the man's side. She brushed the hair away from his face and pressed her palm to his cheek. Jarle was cold to the touch; his lips so pale they appeared bloodless.

Gently, Avaren slapped the man's cheek. Jarle didn't stir nor move a muscle. Looking at him more closely, it occurred to her that the man appeared frozen, his limbs locked in a strange torpor. Avaren thought back to the moment when her eyes had met the thief's in the landing below Ca'd'Cel. She had asked questions to which Jarle had blinked back answers, but she couldn't remember what they were. Avaren swallowed hard. She couldn't remember anything past—"Paulo." Her voice sounded weak and raspy, and her throat was sore from the assassin's handling.

Suddenly, Avaren didn't want to remember. She wanted to forget. The sight of Jarle's anguished pose banished the memories and returned her to the present. The madness that caused her to ignore her rescuer's injuries the previous evening was gone. It didn't make a difference if she knew what was wrong with the man or not. He was hurt, and she needed to help him.

Avaren's hands trembled as she began to undo Jarle's armor. She unlaced his pauldrons and vambraces and tossed them aside in her urgency. His bandolier and hood followed suit. The wet leather straps that held his cuirass were difficult to unthread, but the chest piece gave after a few hard tugs. Cuirass, weapon belt, boots, hose, and gloves landed in a pile.

Piece by piece, she undressed him until all that remained were his breeches and shirt. A search of his pockets yielded a wire similar to the one the assassin had used to strangle her, mirrors, a pouch of spikes, a wax-sealed cylinder, a set of files, several items that seemed to have no purpose whatsoever, and finally, her jewelry. Earrings, necklaces, combs, and brooches twinkled in the morning's early light. The thief had stuffed the entire contents of her vanity into his pockets!

Rising to her feet, Avaren walked away and paced along the shore in a futile effort to remain calm. Her face grew hot, and her heart pounded in her chest. After Rigo and her father's murderer, Jarle was the lowliest creature ever to cross her path.

The curskin thief represented all the ills of Reyza and its loathsome underworld; the greed and lust of its shiny-eyed hawkers; the lopsided, claustrophobic tenements where newborns were discarded in tubs of fish guts by impoverished mothers; dockside streets crowded with urchins, beggars, drunkards, and whores; bawdy taverns; fetid gambling halls; cathouses; and every manner of evil that lived and breathed in the city's rotten underbelly.

Some believed curskins were a plague sent by the gods to punish the seven bloodlines for interbreeding. Her father had openly sided with those that thought they should be rendered sterile—a belief that had always irked her, considering that her mother was a creature from beyond the realm of men.

The jewels dug into Avaren's palms. Her head ached. It was possible that Jarle wasn't working with her father's killer, but it was just as likely he had lied.

Avaren exhaled and straightened her shoulders. Years spent in the company of governesses had taught her how to comport herself in all manner of situations, including the company of men. She had learned the differences between vulgar flirtations and the coquetries favored in court. Most importantly, she had learned to control her temper.

"Fire in the heart fills the head with smoke." Avaren quoted the late Mejtress Trudchen who had burned the mantra into her heart with her paddle. She took several deep breaths until the roaring fire of her rage had banked to embers.

Feeling smug with the knowledge that she would make him pay for his crimes, Avaren returned to Jarle's side. She stuffed the jewels back in his pockets along with all of his tools. What good were jewels or the suitors who had procured them? Idle days of girlish games and lavish fetes had vanished along with her dignity.

Avaren unsheathed one of Jarle's daggers and used it to cut open the front of his shirt. Removal of the garment revealed a blotch of purplish bruises centered on a lump on the right side of his chest.

Slowly, Avaren set the dagger down. She had seen a similar injury before.

Some years ago, a rearing horse had kicked one of her father's footmen and broken his ribs. The man had been in so much pain that for weeks, he cursed the act of breathing. By the look of the swelling, Jarle had at least one broken bone, perhaps more. How the thug had managed to carry her down hundreds of steps to the villa's landing was a mystery. The pain must have been excruciating.

Avaren stood and walked to an opening in the cavern wall. She squeezed between two calcite columns and stepped into a natural tunnel that led deeper into the cave. The rough corridor sloped up, twisting and turning before opening into a vaulted chamber fringed by rows of stalagmites.

Beams of sunlight pierced the far reaches of the cave, illuminating the rushing waters of an underground waterfall. Smooth-lipped plateaus and steps had formed where the cascade's runoff had pooled throughout the centuries. Tiny crabs scurried in the dark.

Avaren climbed down to the vault's sandy floor and walked past the sunlit gallery and into the shadows. She had discovered the place on her tenth birthday six years prior and had since explored it with the zealousness of a curious child. While her father had believed her to be swimming in the shallows, she had whiled away the hours exploring windswept reefs in search of shipwrecked treasure.

For years, the hidden grotto had served as a refuge—a place where she had found respite from the tight-laced routines of Ca'd'Cel; where she could be herself and dream. With her father dead and no home to return to, the cave seemed nothing more than a hole filled with broken, useless trinkets. Worn curtains embroidered with silver thread hung over a sleeping pallet of layered blankets stolen from the villa's linen closets. Coins manacled together by coral and the passage of time were piled high inside broken chests. Barnacle-encrusted platters, mangled chalices, and rusted weapons rested on crates bursting at the seams with dredged baubles. An assortment of wine bottles and sand-filled glasses cluttered the innards of a lopsided cabinet. Moth-eaten shirts and gowns from bygone eras rested on chairs whose cushions had long ago disintegrated.

Avaren brushed aside the cobwebs and began to search for the one item that could save Jarle's life. She found the small trunk beneath a brass ewer. The chest with hammered silver ribs appeared untouched by time and the salt of the sea. Inside, nestled in red velvet, was a portrait of a Seh'nahiel nobleman and a cut-crystal vial. Avaren took the bottle out and shook it until the liquid inside shone a bright, pale gold.

She had found the magically preserved chest not far from the port of Reyza where her father had said the *Ruarch* had sunk. Many of the objects she'd salvaged might have once belonged to the ship's crew, but she had never disclosed her findings to her father. The secret cave and its contents were her only link to a mother she had never known—a woman her father had rarely talked about and likely considered a monster.

Avaren took a gown from the back of a chair and shook it out, sending a cloud of dust into the air. She slipped into the threadbare dress and tucked the small vial between her breasts. With a quick pull of the hair tie, she freed her brine-soaked locks. A quick search revealed a set of ivory combs which she used to wrangle her unruly mass of curls at the top of her head.

The horse-battered footman, she recalled, had been bound around the torso with starched linen strips. Jarle, Avaren concluded, needed warmth, rest and bandages to support his ribs.

Avaren rummaged through piles of tattered garments until she found a long swathe of Seh'nahiel silk. She gave the fabric a few hard tugs and was pleased when it did not tear. She then grabbed one of the woolen blankets from the bed and headed back. Through the years she had scavenged many treasures from the sea but never had it crossed her mind that she might one day trawl a man. Saving a curskin thug who was just as likely to help her as violate her seemed reckless, but the man was street smart and might yet prove useful.

Jarle had come in contact with her tears and had appeared under her thrall, but she couldn't be sure. Only time would tell if her supernatural charms would affect him as powerfully as it had others in her father's circle.

Avaren returned to Jarle's side and dropped the bundle of blankets. The shallow rise and fall of the thief's chest coupled with patches of reddened skin worried her.

Then, the realization struck her. Jarle's claw-like fingers, the tension in his neck, and the stiffness of his body reminded her of her father.

'Forkleaf paralyzes the body. Your father died quickly.'

Visions of her father's wide-open eyes filled her with dread. "Poison!"

Avaren grabbed Jarle by the arms and dragged him away from the shoreline until his feet rested on dry land. She laid the silk perpendicular to Jarle's torso and began to thread the cloth around his chest. The act of lifting the man left her breathless and made her head throb. She wound the fabric half a dozen times and secured it with one of the stolen brooches. Once finished, she reached between her breasts, withdrew the magical vial, and shook it until the golden glow returned.

Curiosity had driven her to taste the contents of the potion once before. The draught had made her feel light-hearted and caused a subtle tingling at the back of her throat. Within a day all blemishes and childhood scars had faded, leaving her skin as smooth as a babe's bottom. Avaren wasn't entirely sure what the potion did, but there was a chance it might help Jarle. She unstoppered the vial and took a drink. The liquid soothed her sore throat and caused the tension to drain from her limbs. The painful bruises on her arms and face began to fade along with her headache.

For a moment, Avaren felt woozy and out of sorts. She stared at the ruby-studded brooch that held Jarle's silk bandage. The delicate dragonfly with silver wings had arrived in a glass box alongside a bouquet of roses—a token of some merchant whose name she hadn't bothered to learn. She had tossed the jewel among the rest never imagining that it might one day serve to bandage the thief who had stolen it.

Thief. Curskin. Criminal. Avaren ran her fingers through Jarle's shoulder-length dark hair and allowed herself to view him as a man. Strong arms chiseled with lean muscle led to a broad back which tapered down to a narrow waist. Between his hip bones began a trail of dark hair that ran up the center of his chest and branched out over his nipples. His face was handsome with prominent eyebrows that curved elegantly over deep-set eyes. An elegant and aristocratic nose led to full sensual lips that were as kissable as—Paulo's. Avaren withdrew her hand.

She placed her thumb over the opening of the crystal vial and tipped it over Jarle's mouth. The golden drops sparkled in the sunlight before disappearing between the thief's parted lips. Avaren watched in awe as color crept back into his cheeks. His face softened, and his fingers relaxed; a subtle tremor shook his legs. Then, as if by a miracle, the man opened his eyes.

A smile brightened Avaren's face but did not linger. The man was looking at her with the adoration a hound might lavish on its master. His eyes were unfocused, and the corners of his mouth curled with the hint of a smile.

"How do you feel?" Avaren asked.

Jarle raised his hand and caressed a strand of Avaren's pale hair. "Alive," he replied.

The sudden closeness to the man made her uncomfortable, and she shrank from his touch. "That's comforting."

Jarle balled his fists and tried to rise, but the pain in his ribs hobbled him. Wincing, he lay back down.

Avaren stoppered the empty vial and draped a blanket over his body. "You need rest; your ribs are broken."

Jarle caught Avaren's wrist when she went to rise. "Thank you."

A spark of anger flared in Avaren's eyes. She wrenched her hand free and stood up. Her eyes darted to the pile of daggers. "Do not ever touch me without my consent again."

Jarle squinted into the sunlight and clutched the blanket to his shivering body. His dark eyes burned into hers, cold and challenging. "I meant no offense."

Avaren wanted to lash out; to scream, to tell the son of a dog that his very presence offended her, but instead she just nodded. Despite her privilege, status, and priceless jewels, she was homeless, orphaned and as powerless as the curskin before her. Without another word, she turned and fled.

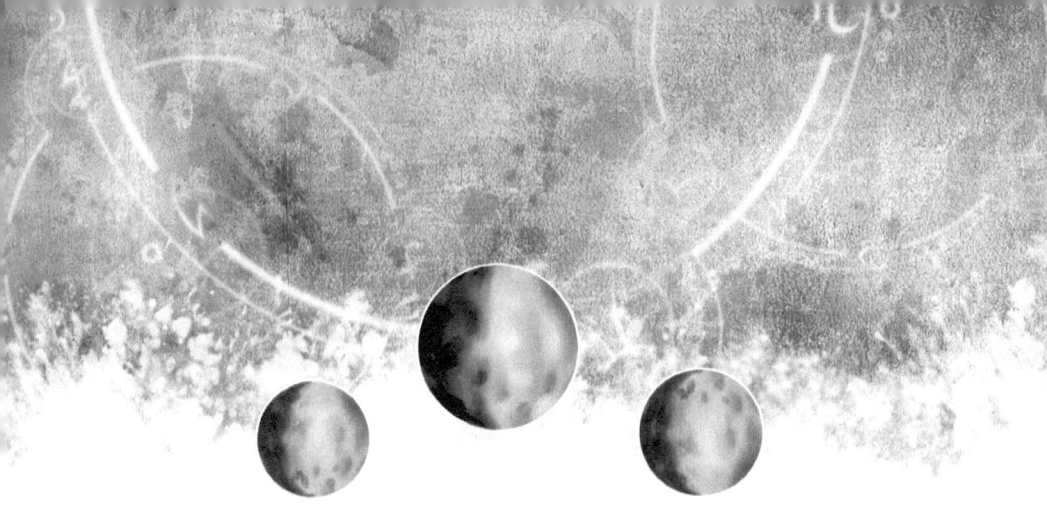

THE DRAGON OF REYZA

Ristor, Ninth of Sund'im, 445 A'A'diel

The setting sun surrendered the city's streets to shadow. Braziers sprang to life, illuminating a row of buildings nestled along the base of the cliffs below the palace. The government offices along Governors' Row were designed in harmony with the palace, but with a modest grandeur to distinguish their lesser stature. A single structure broke the architectural harmony; a brutalist, granite keep that was as incongruous as a brick among porcelainware.

For over three hundred years, the Chancellery fortress had stood unchanged while more fanciful architecture rose up around it. The city's original settlers had built the monolithic building, and as such, it had become an icon of Reyzan resilience.

Behind the keep's wall, wrought-iron braziers illuminated the flagstone courtyard at the base of the tower. The wavering pools of light gave the quadrangle a festive flair as a cool breeze blew in from the ocean.

In the center of the courtyard, Sodke the executioner leaned against his tall iron rod and surveyed his work. Flat on the ground before him, a sobbing wreck of a man was tied spread-eagle upon a wagon wheel.

The condemned prisoner was old. The gray in his beard spoke of seventy winters. Thick loops of hemp rope bound the man's waist to the hub of the wheel. His bony ankles and left wrist were secured to the rim with loops of rawhide that bit deep into his flesh. The man's right arm lay twisted, the pale skin marred by oblong purple blotches where Sodke's rod had smashed flesh and shattered bone.

Sodke nodded to his assistant, a lithe young man called Owl after his large, intense eyes. "Quickly now, the evening is fading. It will be night soon, and I've yet to sup."

"Hurry, hurry," Owl grumbled to himself as he bent over the moaning man. "Always on about food." Owl grabbed the wrist of the broken arm. An agonized howl dispelled the tranquility of the Chancellery courtyard.

Ignoring the scream, Owl threaded the old man's ruined limb between the spokes. He performed the grisly duty with disdain, as though he were weaving a ribbon through a wreath on festival day. A few expertly knotted loops of rawhide secured the arm in its tortuous position.

"And you're always going on about the women." Owl's efficiency earned a nod of approval from Sodke. For all his laziness and complaining, the boy was a deft apprentice. "Let's do the right leg next."

Owl kneeled on the unfortunate man's leg, pinning it under his weight. He pulled a loose end of the knot and secured the ankle. "Ready?"

"Aye, pull hard and hold it steady. Three blows." Sodke held the rod like a lumberjack holding an axe. He raised his arms above his bald head, ready to swing. "Now!"

Owl ignored the gibbered pleas for mercy as he grabbed the man's ankle with both hands and rolled to the side. He pulled hard, bracing his feet against the tread of the wheel until the captive's leg was fully extended. "Strike!" he grunted. "Strike him now, for the love of Ven. This codger is stronger than he looks."

Sodke's rod whistled downward three times in swift succession. The prisoner's shrieks took on a hopeless, warbling note like some macabre bird singing at sunset.

Owl rolled his eyes, mimicking the sobbing man as he twisted the broken leg through the spokes. As Owl finished securing his handiwork, Sodke stepped to the other side of the wheel. "Left arm."

The prisoner writhed and pulled at the bonds of his undamaged arm with animalistic desperation. Foul curses exploded from the old man's mouth.

The unexpected outburst sent Owl tumbling backward onto the flagstones. He landed on his rump with a startled laugh. Sodke scowled—he had no patience for nonsense, not while dinner awaited. A nudge with the rod spurred his assistant to action. "Left arm."

"Aye, aye. I heard you." Owl's smile twisted into a sneer as he rolled to his feet. "Come now, old geezer, settle down. There's no point in making everyone's night rougher."

The prisoner continued to struggle, glaring at Owl with venomous hatred. He spat a bloody gob onto Owl's pants. At the same moment, he pulled his left wrist free of its bindings with a triumphant, "Ha!"

*
**

Deneven D'Neir stood in contemplative silence behind one of the windows of the Chancellery's waiting room. He fixed his eyes on the scene being played out in the torchlit courtyard below. The imported Ferencian glass panes weren't thick enough to mute the screams of the condemned prisoner. Life in Reyza was not for the weak or foolish. Beneath the veneer of prosperity, the port city remained faithful to her violent past. Justice was swift and harsh by necessity.

For a moment, Deneven's focus shifted from the courtyard to his reflection. A weary face looked back; the wild waves of dark hair were more gray than brown, and the years had carved deep lines into his face. Barely in his fifties, Deneven could pass for a man a decade older. The war which had cost him his leg, coupled with the weight of his former office, had taken a toll on his proud features.

In the seventh year of the conflict with Five Isles, Deneven had been bestowed the title of Chief Justiciar. Jarle Draos Iarris had granted him the distinction in recognition of his ardent defense of the city and his success in leading the resistance through endless days of close-quarters fighting in Reyza's streets and back alleys. In those days he had been the rallying defender; the fierce hero; the symbol of the unconquerable soul of Reyza.

Outwardly, Deneven had played the role with stern vigor, but the bloody attrition suffered by his unit horrified him. As the war went on, the stony resolve within him eroded until he grew sick of the stench of blood and the screams of the dying. When forced to mete out his first death sentence, to a deserter, he did so with a heavy conscience. For weeks afterward, the condemned man's final pleas haunted his conscience.

After the war, Deneven was promoted to the office of Lord Justiciar. Recalling the ugly street justice required during wartime, he dedicated himself to reforming the Chancellery. Honor demanded the condemned be recognized as fellow men, regardless of their crimes. It was his first commandment that all sentences be carried out professionally and without undue suffering. Judging by the spectacle taking place in the courtyard, the dignity of the Chancellery was a notion that his successor, the current Lord Justiciar, did not espouse.

The doors to the Lord Justiciar's office swung open. Deneven feigned unawareness. Instead, he watched the executioner's assistant struggle to catch the old man's flailing arm. For a moment, it appeared as though the black-clad boy was trying to grab a dodging snake. If it weren't for the fact that the old man would soon expire, the scene would have been humorous.

Lord Justiciar Poldar Tsardon stepped up to the window alongside Deneven and gazed out as the boy lunged after the prisoner's arm and missed. Then, he shifted his gaze to Deneven's reflection. "It appears that the rascal refuses to cooperate."

Deneven refused to return the man's gaze. He maintained his focus on the doomed contest. The executioner smashed the end of the rod into the prisoner's testicles, crushing them. The man howled in pain, no longer able to avoid Owl's grasp.

Tsardon smiled. "The outcome is always the same; rebellion only results in suffering. Resistance is a waste of effort."

"Is it?" Deneven gritted his teeth as two sharp screams rang out below.

"You disapprove?"

"I find your methods reprehensible, and your amateur implementation inexcusable."

"Ah, yes, it's true that Sodke and Owl are having difficulty. But allow them some leeway. Breaking a man on the wheel is an old technique, rarely used—until now." The Lord Justiciar turned to face Deneven, a reptile smile on his lips. "Practice will lead to perfection."

Deneven remained quiet; the implied threat was only an opening volley. A series of shrieks erupted from the courtyard as scorching brands burned the soft parts of the old man's body.

"Ah, the singing has begun." Tsardon clapped his hands. "Almost worthy of the opera house, wouldn't you say?"

"I am afraid we do not share the same tastes in music, Lord Justiciar."

"Yes, of course. You prefer boozy caroling in popular taverns. You always did fancy yourself a man of the people." Tsardon snorted with disdain. "How does it feel to be one of them now?"

"I like it just fine," Deneven lied.

"It is most heartening to hear that the famed Dragon of Reyza finds his retirement agreeable."

Deneven resisted the urge to punch the sanctimonious self-satisfied smirk off of his successor's face. Instead, he chided himself for allowing Tsardon to goad his wounded pride. "Who is he?" asked Deneven.

Another series of cries penetrated the windows.

"A thief and a traitor. You might know him. Goes by a rather colorful street name—some treacherous rodent-like vermin."

"The Weasel?"

"Yes, that's it. A vile name for a vile man."

Deneven squinted trying to discern the face of the man threaded upon the wheel. The Weasel specialized in street swindles. He talked money out of gullible foreign sailors. Deneven had fought alongside the man during the war; the old man was no traitor. "What exactly is his crime? What could he have done to deserve such an execution?"

"Executed? Who is being executed? Tonight, the useless

sod serves as a warning to all who dwell in the Tangles. In a few moments, my men will roll the wheel along the cobbles of Commerce Road. The prisoner will be released at the docks."

"A warning?"

"Yes, a warning. The Weasel is the last person to have spoken with Jarle Jadien, the killer of Tan'os Ensther and the kidnapper of his daughter. I suspect that he refuses to tell us where to find his friend Jars out of some sense of loyalty. Although witnesses swear to have seen the two of them conspiring the day before the murders, the old man insists that they were only 'chatting about the weather.' The weather!" Tsardon's fists clenched until the knuckles grew white. "I will not be toyed with by curskin mongrels. I will find Mejtress Avaren and her kidnapper even if I have to torture every last thief in Reyza."

Deneven stared at the ruined man on the wheel, his stomach knotted with cold horror. It was madness. The Mistress of Rats would never tolerate Tsardon's unwarranted brutality without responding in kind. "The Thrommish Fleet is on its way south as we speak and you seek to ignite a street war?"

"Your feelings for the underworld of Reyza are well known, Deneven D'Neir. Let me remind you that your compromises with the so-called Jewelers' Guild while you held this office bordered on treason. Unlike you, I don't believe that 'rats' hold any loyalty to Reyza." Tsardon's words were as sharp as arrows. "I am certain that the scum of this city know where Jars is holed up with Mejtress Avaren. That is, of course, if the curskin pig hasn't already killed her. Regardless, dead or alive, I intend to find them both."

"How are you so confident that Jars Jadien is the killer? As I recall, the man is a jewel thief, not a kidnapper or murderer."

"It seems he has switched trades. Jars cut a deal with Varrus Sigolian, the Calantian captain of the guard of Ca'd'Cel. He offered Sigolian a share of the spoils so long as he and his company looked the other way while the villa was burglarized. Jarle informed the Calantian captain of his intention to loot Mejtress Avaren's dowry—which he did, right after he and his partner killed the entire household."

"Who was this partner?"

"Unknown."

Deneven frowned. "Explain."

"There is not much to reveal; I am afraid." Tsardon straightened his goatee with a lackadaisical tug. "The man was dressed in black leather and looked every bit the typical midnighter. He was found in Mejtress Avaren's bedroom, dead from a stab wound in the back. None of my soldiers recognized his face."

Deneven's gut tightened. "I want to see the body for myself. Tonight."

"Impossible. Jarle Rigo was so incensed with rage and grief he ordered the dog's corpse to be chopped to bits and flung into the sea. I had a sketch of the perpetrator's face rendered before we dumped him into the harbor. You will find it in my report."

Deneven's lips tightened into a thin line. Jars was a skilled thief reputed to have ended a few lives but only when pressed by extenuating circumstances. Jars was one of the rare rogues who took artistic pride in clean thefts. He was also notorious for being as elusive as smoke. In any event, he was not known as a particularly violent thief, certainly not as an assassin. Nor was he known to work with any partners.

"Assassination is a trade few practice well; one that requires a motive and usually a patron. Have you compiled a list of suspects that might wish the Vise's demise?" Deneven asked.

"That would include at least half the city," Tsardon scoffed.

The story did not sit well with Deneven. "Has demand for a ransom been presented?"

"No, and I don't expect one. There was enough wealth in the Vise's villa to purchase a kingdom."

"So why kidnap the woman?"

"Asking me to divine the workings of a curskin's mind is like asking me to transform myself into a swine." Before Deneven could interject, Tsardon continued, "If I had to guess, I'd say that Mejtress Avaren's honor is in great peril. She is a handsome woman of status; exactly the kind of prize a curskin would wish to sully. I hope that she is alive and that we find her soon."

"We agree on the latter." Deneven reached into the inside pocket of his greatcoat and withdrew a letter with two large seals. He presented the document to Tsardon. "I assume that you know why I've come."

Tsardon snatched the letter. "Chief Justiciar Darkor Phennas has already conducted a thorough investigation. We have several confessions from the Vise's guards. We know what happened and who is responsible. Jarle Jadien and an unknown partner murdered Tan'os Ensther during a robbery. To waste our efforts on another investigation merely to assuage a frightened diplomat is an insult to this office."

Deneven shook his cane at Tsardon as he spoke, emphasizing every word. "You cannot be serious. A frightened diplomat is exactly the sort that needs reassurance."

"There is nothing more to be gleaned from this tragedy, D'Neir. Your days as a justiciar are over."

Deneven spoke calmly. "That document you hold in your hand is signed by Jarle Rigo Iarris. It grants me the powers of a Chief Justiciar for as long as Ambassador Ther'oldo Ers feels it is necessary to investigate Tan'os Ensther's death and his daughter's disappearance."

When Tsardon opened his mouth to speak, Deneven cut him off. "My commission makes your full cooperation and the resources of the Reyzan Guard available to me. To start, I require copies of the raw transcripts of the interrogations you have conducted."

Tsardon studied the letter. "I shall have copies made and delivered to you."

"Excellent."

The Lord Justiciar looked as if he had taken a mouthful of sour milk. "It seems you have found your way back into the Chancellery. Don't get used to it."

It was Deneven's turn to be smug. "I require the use of the squad assigned to the Vise's quarter. I believe the Fifth Constabulary Company still patrols that district under Lieutenant Garentas."

Tsardon reexamined the decree. "Yes, the Fifth is still assigned to the Vise's district. However, it says here that any resources assigned to you must not diminish the efforts of the official investigation. At the moment, all of my resources are bent to the task of finding Mejtress Ensther and her kidnapper. I will instruct Lieutenant Garentas to assign you two of his men." Tsardon handed the letter back to Deneven. "I am afraid that is all I can spare at the moment."

Red-hot anger flashed across Deneven's grizzled eyes. "Two will suffice. As for the matter of the Calantian prisoners, I prefer to speak with the captain of the Vise's guards myself."

"Then you can go to the River of Dust, with my blessings."

"He is dead?"

The Lord Justiciar nodded. "He was killed by Jars during the abduction."

Deneven's jaw tightened. "I was informed that you took several prisoners from the Vise's villa. Do any still live?"

"Regrettably, they failed to survive the interrogation. Except one—Sigolian's nephew, a stupid boy named Brath. Feel free to speak with him for all the good it will do." Tsardon raised his eyebrows. "Though you will need to wait until tomorrow. We are finalizing some last details for our records."

"You will afford me time with the captive." There was a harsh edge to Deneven's words.

"Of course!" Tsardon snapped. "But be aware that the prisoner is to be torn apart with hot pincers in Archway Square at seven bells tomorrow evening."

The tension between the two men was heightened by a bloodcurdling scream, followed by curses coming from the courtyard.

Tsardon walked to the door and held it open for Deneven. "Now if you'll excuse me, I must grant clemency to The Weasel before Sodke's enthusiasm ruins his purpose."

Deneven limped toward the exit. "Before I go, there is another matter I'd like to address. I wish to examine Tan'os Ensther's body. I assume his corpse is in the morgue?"

"That is impossible. The Vise's body has been taken to the Collegium. The mages are preserving his corpse for the long voyage home. You know how the Thrommish are about their heroes—proper interment in home soil and all that nonsense."

Deneven placed his hand on the door to prevent Tsardon from shutting it. "I see. Surely you documented the state of the Vise's body upon discovery. Do you have a detailed report of his wounds or is that unavailable as well?"

"A copy of the notes and illustrations documenting the wounds suffered by Tan'os Ensther will be included with all reports. I assure you that my investigation is beyond reproach."

"Dead prisoners, missing corpses?" Deneven did not remove his hand from the door. "Sounds like careless work to me. Then again, you were always more of a peacock than a bloodhound."

The Lord Justiciar's face reddened. "You infer I have acted in bad faith, and I will not stand for it! Despite our differences, I took the same oath as you. If you find it impossible to accord me respect, at least show it for the office you once held."

"You are correct, Lord Justiciar." Deneven bowed stiffly. "It is reassuring to hear you have not forgotten the Oath of Justice. Apologies."

"You will find that protocols have been followed at every stage of the investigation and properly documented." Tsardon exhaled sharply and tugged his uniform into place. He smoothed his hair as the color faded from his cheeks. "We have indeed been rivals since our days patrolling the streets, so your antagonism is not unexpected. I acknowledge that you believe what happened to you was unfair. However, I remind you that it was you who chose your fate."

"Next, you will tell me that you had no hand in my forced retirement." Deneven snorted.

"There you are wrong." Tsardon straightened his shoulders. "I proudly take responsibility for my contributions to your ouster. You expected professional loyalty to subvert my sworn loyalty to the Jarle of Reyza. You thought yourself infallible and are too blinded by hubris to see that the path to your ruin was your policy of tolerance for this city's rats. But this is an old debate and no longer relevant now that you have retired. Please remove yourself from my office and find your way out."

Deneven crafted a dozen barbed retorts in his head before deciding to walk the high road. "Good evening, Lord Justiciar."

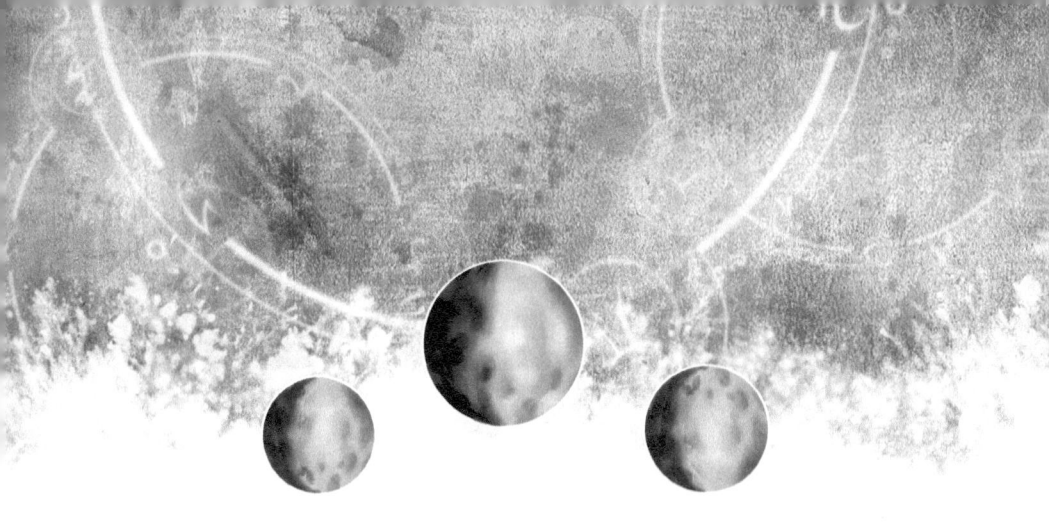

TESTAMENT

Ristor, Ninth of Sund'im, 445 A'A'diel

"Brath Barathac, I understand that you have formally confessed to your guilt in the robbery and subsequent murder of Tan'os Ensther, the Vise of Reyza. And that you continue to defend your innocence in the matter of Mejtress Avaren Ensther's disappearance. According to this transcript, you claim that you tried to rescue her? Would you have me believe that you are both a villain and a hero in this tragedy?"

When the prisoner failed to respond, the prison guard rapped the back of his head with his fist. "Answer him, you murdering piece of dung."

The battered, naked young man nodded weakly without raising his head. In the guttering torchlight of the interrogation cell, Brath's hair shone like spun gold. Bruises and dried blood marked the boy's body; evidence of previous interrogations. Any lingering resistance appeared to have been whipped, burned, and torn from him.

"That will be enough of that, Sergeant Kethen." Deneven was no stranger to the cruelties of Reyza's prison, nor was he unsympathetic to the prisoners' suffering. He turned to the boy. "Accept my apologies for having forgotten my manners. Please allow me to introduce myself. I am Chief Justiciar Deneven D'Neir. I have been retained by the nation of Thromm to enquire into the matter of the Vise's murder and his daughter's kidnapping. Do not expect clemency; your fate is sealed." Deneven tapped the parchment. "I only have questions and attentive ears to offer you. However, you need not fear any further mistreatment."

Brath lifted his head to examine the man seated across the table for the first time. Both of his eyes were blackened and swollen. "If you please, sir, might I have some water? My throat is parched."

"Certainly," Deneven's response was aloof but not unkind. He was mindful that Brath would soon be the paying the harshest of prices for the crimes against his employer. "Sergeant Kethen, please bring the lad a mug of water from the guards' rain barrel, not the prisoners'. Also, a bowl of soup. He wasn't sentenced to be starved to death."

The guard grumbled an acknowledgment at Deneven and approached Brath. With a grimace, Kethen leaned over and yanked the chains attached to Brath's manacles. Brath winced as the iron bands cut into his chafed wrists but refused to cry out.

"He is still quite secure, as you can see." Deneven snapped. "I will be quite safe until you return."

Kethen spat. "Believe me; I am not worried about your sorry hide—*sir*."

"Make me wait for that water any longer than necessary, and you will have cause to worry about your continued employment." Deneven reached for his valise and proceeded to take out a worn leather notebook, quills, and ink. He paused after dipping the tip of the feather pen in the dark liquid. "And Kethen, no extra *flavoring*."

Kethen opened the cell door and stepped into the dungeon hall. He slammed the heavy oak door shut and barred it. "Don't go anywhere."

Deneven waited until Kethen's footsteps faded before returning his attention to the young man.

"I am aware that you have already provided your version of the events, but I would prefer to hear it from your lips rather than trust the dubious objectivity of the scribe's pen. We can wait for

Kethen to return if you wish. However, I expect he will tarry in his errands."

"No, sir, it is all right. I will speak." Brath spoke with shallow breaths.

"Please tell me when you first learned of the plot."

"As I told Inquisitor Franca, I was surprised when Uncle Varrus pulled Cassio and me aside after morning briefing. I think Cassio knew what my uncle was going to say, but I didn't. Uncle Varrus told us that he had found a way for us to retire. He said we would be able to go home to Calantia as rich men and never have to work for Thrommish vermin again."

"Your uncle disliked the Vise?"

"Oh, no, sir. I mean, well, Majster Ensther was a difficult man to work for, but he was fair enough. It's just, well, being from Calantia and all..."

Deneven nodded. A legendary love of the homeland burned in Calantian hearts. The gluttony of its city-states had devoured the once-thriving empire. Waging endless battles over land, trade, and power, Calantia's ravenous Dolcarrs preferred to waste expendable troops before risking their elite cavaliers. The famed Zincari, once the flower of military tradition and honor, had devolved into a mercenary army willing to work for the heaviest purse. It was said that the Dolcarrs spent Zincari lives for victories with no more regrets than a baker burning logs to heat his ovens. Any non-landed Calantian wishing to be a professional soldier had but two options available—fight for a Dolcarr or leave Calantia for employment in foreign lands.

The Zincari who traveled abroad found their martial skills and discipline well valued, but their nationality received little of its former respect. Most employers treated expatriate Calantians little better than war hounds.

"Working for House Ensther was my first contract," Brath continued. "Uncle Varrus brought me in as a favor to my mother. According to Cassio and Uncle Varrus, Majster Ensther was better than most employers. He demanded discipline, but he wasn't cruel or disrespectful." Brath took a deep, shuddering breath. His eyelids fluttered, and for a moment, Deneven thought the boy might collapse.

"Brath?"

The boy jumped in his seat. A sharp gasp escaped his split lips as he settled back into the chair. "Sorry, sir. I didn't mean any disrespect; it's just that I am so tired. They haven't allowed me to sleep."

"I understand. You were about to recount what your uncle told you that morning. Please continue."

"Uncle Varrus told us that we had a rare opportunity and that we needed to be bold and act. My uncle claimed we could hire a professional burglar to slip into the villa, steal Avaren's finery, and escape without detection. Uncle Varrus said that Jarle Rigo wouldn't let her wear gifts given to her by other men; that the jewels would simply go to waste. Cassio suggested that if we created a gap in the patrol timing, the theft would be possible. We would take the roof watch to ensure no one accidentally spotted the thief from that vantage. And that is what we did."

"You both agreed to this plan without question?"

"No, sir. Cassio demanded reassurances. He was worried about the thief either being an amateur or betraying us."

"A sensible concern." Deneven set down his pen and leaned back in his chair. "What was your uncle's response?"

"My uncle told us how he had found the thief and how he had confirmed the man's reputation."

"Brath, I have a bit of a problem with this story. I understand why your uncle would be interested in this larceny, but I wonder why a thief would be willing to even speak with the captain of the Vise's guard. How could he be sure it wasn't a setup—that your uncle wouldn't detain him right then and there, then turn him in for a reward? You see my point, do you not?"

The boy shuffled uncomfortably in his seat. "The robbery was my uncle's idea. He knew there was no way we could do this without an expert's assistance."

"Thus, your uncle set off to hire a thief to burglarize the Vise's household like he would a carpenter to build a cabinet?"

"Not like that, sir. Uncle Varrus told us that he spent his off-duty hours in the Tangles, carefully enquiring after a skilled thief with a professional reputation. He spent quite a bit of time and gold in his search. He said criminals were easy to find in Reyza;

that the trick was finding the *right* sort. But it wasn't impossible if one knew where to look, and he knew exactly the right tavern."

"And that was?"

"The Silver Pig. It's near—"

"I am familiar with the tavern. Easy enough to get in touch with a rogue there." Deneven picked up the quill and noted the name. "Did your uncle say how they met?"

"Uncle Varrus didn't tell us much, but he swore he was careful. He said that he had become an expert in the solicitation of shady business. That's how he found Jars, or rather, how Jars found him. Afterward, he spent more coin confirming that this fellow was who he claimed. The thief had it all planned—he knew a fence and promised to split the proceeds with us."

"What about after the theft? Did your uncle reveal where he was to meet Jars afterward to divide the spoils?"

The boy's brow furrowed. "I heard him tell Cassio he was going to meet the thief at a warehouse near the mudflats, in an alley called Cat's Gut."

"Cat's Cut," Deneven corrected the boy. The alley was a quiet, narrow passage between some of the older, more rundown warehouses in one of the poorest quarters of the city. The lane was so narrow that few people knew of it; fewer still traveled its path—a perfect spot for a clandestine meeting. Deneven made a note to investigate the warehouses nearby. "Back to the morning when your uncle told you about his plan. Is there anything else that was discussed?"

Brath nodded, "As soon as my uncle finished telling us his plan, Cassio demanded no one be harmed."

"Interesting. Cassio demanded, did he?"

"Yes, sir. I insisted too." Brath's cheeks flushed with earnestness. "I didn't want anything bad to happen to Avaren."

"That's twice now."

"What's that, sir?"

Deneven set the pen down gently. His gaze remained locked on Brath. "That is the second time that you have referred to the daughter of Tan'os Ensther as Avaren, not Mejtress Ensther or even Mejtress Avaren."

Brath's gaze dropped. "I meant Mejtress Avaren, sir."

"No, you did not. You referred to her in the familiar, Brath, because you two were close. Am I correct?"

Color rose to the youth's cheeks in a rush. "It, it isn't like that."

"How is it then?"

Brath refused to look at Deneven. "You have to believe me; we didn't do anything wrong, just kissed—a little. It was nothing, I mean it was not nothing, but—" Brath looked up, struggling to find the words.

"How do I know it wasn't you who set this all up?" Deneven's voice was harsh. He leaned forward with his hands on the table. "How do I know you aren't lying to me about this? Maybe you had Tan'os Ensther killed and arranged to elope with his daughter, but the whole plan went awry."

"No, sir! It… it was not like that!" Brath was so upset by the accusation that he began coughing violently. "I… I swear it."

Deneven watched the boy choke until he was convinced Brath's outburst was sincere. "All right, Brath, settle down. I don't think this was your plan. Tell me about Mejtress Avaren."

Tears cut through the grime on Brath's cheeks as he gasped. "She was kind to me, sir, she was kind to everyone. I watched her live in that house; I saw how her father treated her. He treated her like a possession, no different than his coveted casks of Zherrian Ale! I—I felt sorry for her. One night after a dinner party, she seemed especially lonely. I told her a joke, and it made her smile. I don't know how it happened to be honest, but we wound up hiding in the linen closet. We kissed, I swear, just kissing. It was the best thing that has ever happened to me, but it never happened again. She was more interested in Paulo anyway."

"The Vise's valet?"

"Yes. The two of them would find ways to sneak away sometimes. The guards turned a blind eye. We all pretended not to notice." A hard look crossed Brath's eyes. "I would have given anything for Mejtress Avaren to look at me the way she looked at Paulo. And what did the bastard do? He seduced Mejtress Dannia, bedded her late at night while she wore Mejtress Avaren's dresses. Made me angry. Still, we never said anything, because, as I said, Avaren was always kind to us."

"I see." Deneven pursed his lips. After a long pause, he

continued with his interrogation. "Did you see the Vise's body?"

"No, sir. When Uncle Varrus and Cassio went to check on him, I went to ensure Avaren's—Mejtress Avaren's—safety."

"That is where you discovered the second thief?"

"Yes, in Mejtress Avaren's bedroom. He was already dead, stabbed in the back with two daggers."

Deneven pulled the sketch from the papers of the official report and slid it over to show Brath. "Is this the dead thief?"

"No, sir." Brath looked up as Deneven returned the sketch to his papers. "The dead thief had a rounder face and a scar on his cheek."

"Who was the second thief?"

"I do not know, sir, but I have thought about it, and I think Jars betrayed us and brought in a partner." Brath's face grew red as the words tumbled forth in a torrent. "I think his associate tried to rape Avaren! I would have killed him myself, but he was dead when I got there. I was so upset that when I realized one of his daggers was poisoned, I wanted to give Jars a taste of his own medicine."

Deneven looked up sharply. "Poisoned? How do you know?"

Brath blinked, appearing light-headed from his outburst. "It had this oily black sap on the blade that smelled like the fish sauce the Ghossians douse their meals with, but worse."

The pen traced words on the parchment; the implication absorbed Deneven's thoughts. *What sort of poison smelled like Esh'fah sauce?*

"You are certain?" Deneven confirmed.

The boy nodded. "I stabbed Jars with that blade."

"Tell me about your encounter with Jars."

"He ambushed us in the stairwell used by the house staff. The bastard dropped Avaren on the stairs, causing me to trip. I was distracted, and he threw me down the stairs. That's when I broke my leg. I couldn't see, but I heard fighting, heard him kill my Uncle. Cassio almost had him, but Jars stabbed him too."

"Go on." Deneven's gaze intensified.

"Cassio was down; I think he was dying. I heard Jars kick his sword away before he tried to wake Avaren. That's when the thief spoke."

"Did you hear what he said?"

"Yes, sir, but it was all lies."

"Allow me to be the judge of that. What did Jars tell Cassio?"

"He said that he didn't betray us; that he didn't kill the Vise."

"I see." Deneven frowned. It didn't make sense that Jars would lie to a dying man. Why take the time? Perhaps he hadn't known Cassio was dying and was attempting to pin the murders on his dead partner, or was there something else missing? Deneven set the question aside. "Then what happened?"

Brath scowled. "I heard Jars slap Avaren. He demanded that she tell him about a secret passage, but she only uttered nonsense. This made the thief angry. He lifted her and carried her down the stairs, but I played dead. When he stepped over me, I stabbed him with the poisoned dagger."

Deneven paused writing and flipped through the copy of the official transcript. His stomach tightened; there was no mention of poison or a poisoned dagger. He made a note to check the stairwell. "Why do you think Jars slapped Mejtress Avaren?"

"To wake her. She was not conscious." Brath suddenly straightened. A small grunt of pain escaped his lips. "They wouldn't tell me, sir. Please, I must know, is Jars dead? Did I kill him?"

Deneven looked up from his writing. "We haven't found a body, so I suspect he may be alive despite your efforts."

"He kidnapped Avaren, and I let him escape." Brath slumped in his chair; head bowed as his shoulders began to shake.

Deneven heard footsteps outside the cell. Kethen had dragged out his errand as long as he dared. "Did you mention the poisoned dagger to Inquisitor Franca?"

"Yes, sir."

"How about Paulo's relationship with Mejtress Avaren?"

Brath shook his head. "No, sir, only you."

"Good. If you care about Mejtress Avaren and her safety, do not tell anyone what you have said to me tonight."

The boy's voice grew hopeful. "You think she is still alive?"

"Yes, and I intend to find her."

"Then I will take my secrets to the grave, for her sake." Brath's lips tightened with a newfound resolve.

Deneven considered the boy as Kethen unlocked the cell door. Physically, Brath appeared less than twenty seasons of age, but his eyes were those of an old man; one who had come to terms with his mortality.

"Here's your food and water, scum." Kethen slammed the mug and a steaming bowl of soup down on the table in front of Brath.

"That's enough, leave him be."

Brath gave Deneven a weak smile of gratitude before he sipped the water. The expression on his face was akin to that of a thirsty man enjoying the finest Seh'nahiel wine.

Deneven packed his valise then stood while Brath finished the last of his water. Time was wasting, and he was satisfied there was nothing else of value to be gleaned. The investigator struggled to find words for the young man who would be executed publicly in a matter of hours. He placed a hand on the youth's shoulder. "Tonight, as you face your fate, I want you to think of Mejtress Avaren Ensther. You deserve to go to the River of Dust with thoughts of her on your mind."

Kethen couldn't resist joining in. "Yes, scum, that's right, die with the thought of Mejtress Ensther and what you did to her!"

"Yes, sir. Avaren will be in my thoughts as well as in my prayers." Brath lowered his head to hide his wistful smile from the guard. "May addonels guard over her."

THE CATCH

Mir'kadi, Tenth of Sund'im, 445 A'A'diel

Jarle was accustomed to the nighttime noise of the crowded Stallion and found neither sleep nor comfort in the silent cave. By the time dawn blazed across the sky, he had twice counted the roots that dipped into the pool and twice cursed his fate. Stealing from Tan'os Ensther was the worst idea he'd ever hatched.

It was close to mid-morning before the thief summoned the strength to ease himself into a seated position. His ribs ached, and his stomach felt like a bubbling cauldron. He dug his fingers into his thighs and massaged the tendons in his legs. Pins and needles assaulted his flesh as sensation slowly returned.

Jarle wiggled his toes and circled his ankles. If luck favored him, the poison would work itself out of his body, and he would regain full mobility. If not, his days of prowling the streets were over. He would be left hunched and trembling like Old Man Warrick after his wife had accidentally poisoned his stew.

Jarle unlaced his breeches and pushed his pants down over his hips. The leather had stiffened with the briny water and clung uncomfortably to his legs. Every tug caused pain to rip through his chest, but despite his suffering, Jarle smiled. He hadn't seen the girl in almost a day, but the concoction she had given him, had improved his condition considerably. He still felt queasy from having swallowed too much water, and his body ached, but the crippling paralysis had lifted.

Free of the waterlogged pants, Jarle leaned back on his hands and caught his breath. Above his head, clouds rolled, and the foliage that lined the opening of the cave rustled in the breeze. With the sun's arrival, the moonflowers, which had released their heady fragrance during the night, closed their petals. Somewhere in the distance, the roar of a beast joined the sounds of the waking jungle. Howls, chirps, and birdsong filled the silence.

Looking at his breeches, Jarle frowned. The leather was caked with sea salt and coarse to the touch. Carelessly tossed in a pile, the rest of his gear fared no better. His once-supple cuirass, gloves, and sleeves had dried in a crumpled, dirty heap. If he hoped to wear any of his armor again, he needed to find a way to rinse it with fresh water. But to do so, he needed to walk.

As Jarle rolled to his knees, he bit down the urge to scream. He massaged his muscles until his legs felt like hollow logs crawling with wood mites. Once the blood was flowing, he willed himself to stand. He had almost succeeded when he noticed a shadow gliding beneath the water.

Jarle's stomach knotted as the arc of a black-scaled tail broke the surface of the pool. Visions of black tentacles and burning eyes; of desperate gulps of air, and the sea's unwelcoming coldness assaulted his thoughts. The girl, or sea monster, or whatever she was, could not be trusted.

Jarle reached for his dagger, lost his balance, and fell sideways on the pebbly shore. Before him, Avaren crawled out of the pool naked, her pale hair streaming over her shoulders and buttocks. Powerful tails splashed in the shallows sending sparkling droplets scattering in all directions before turning into legs. When she rose, seeming more like a goddess than a flesh and blood woman, Jarle's jaw grew slack.

Rivulets of water trickled over Avaren's face and dripped down over the full, firm globes of her breasts. Jarle gawked, transfixed as droplets beaded at her nipples, before tracking down over her taut belly. In one hand, she held a fishing net filled with oysters, kelp and flopping fish, and in the other a dagger.

"You must be hungry," Avaren said.

Jarle's eyes roamed the breadth of her exposed body. He'd be thrice-damned if he weren't dreaming. Standing before him was a woman so extraordinary that a man might see her likeness but once in his lifetime. The desire he'd felt when he first laid eyes on her returned in a wave of suffocating heat. He yearned to crush her breasts against his chest, spread her marble-smooth thighs, and thrust into her with wild abandon. Instead, he crossed his arms over his privates, suddenly wishing he hadn't removed his pants.

"I am—hungry," Jarle admitted.

Avaren dropped her dagger on the shore and tossed the net at his feet. "Since I have gathered, it is only fair that you cook. I leave the shucking and butchering in your capable hands."

Jarle looked into Avaren's eyes and found no hint of contempt. She appeared bemused, almost playful.

"What's the catch?" Jarle asked.

Avaren gathered her hair, and twisted it, wringing out the water. Failing to catch his innuendo, she went on to describe the contents of the net. "Bluespine oysters known the world over for their buttery taste, two galefins and broadblade kelp."

Jarle fixed his gaze on the triangle of silken hair between her legs and offered her a lopsided grin. The girl attempted to appear aloof, but the color on her cheeks and her shallow breaths revealed nervous excitement. The game she was playing with him had been played and lost by far more experienced women. "When the moons rise, a feast will await you, but only if you answer one question. Where in Ven's name are we?"

Avaren turned and sauntered along the shoreline. Pausing at an opening in the cavern wall, she turned to face him. "We are three leagues north of the city along the coast. I call this place Sigrün's Beard. See you at dusk."

When the girl slipped out of sight, Jarle smiled, overcome with elation. The cave suddenly didn't seem so dismal nor the strange sounds forlorn. He stared at the quivering, suffocating galefins and sympathized. "I know exactly how you feel," Jarle said, before vigorously massaging life back into his legs. He had dinner to prepare, and a goddess to impress.

As bleak and disheartening as the previous day had been, the present one was proving fortuitous. Blood rushed to Jarle's head as he wobbled to his feet. He unwrapped the braies that hugged his hips and tossed it aside, enjoying the freedom of his inflamed loins. He took a few steps along the shore, then waded into the shallows, cherishing every sensation below his waist. Pebbles dug into the spaces between his toes, and goosebumps raced up along his thighs.

Beyond the shallows, the water grew darker with depth, culminating in the shadowy crevice of an underwater tunnel that seemed to have no end. The sight banished his arousal and caused a sickening iciness to settle in Jarle's belly. He took a few steps back and held onto one of the roots before dipping his head beneath the water's surface. He scrubbed the layers of crusted salt, sand and dirt from his hair before washing the rest of his body.

To Jarle's surprise, the pool water wasn't salty. The revelation made him giddy as he cupped handfuls of water to his lips. The layer of rainwater on the surface of the pool tasted sweeter than any inebriant he had ever sampled.

Thirst slaked, Jarle finished his ablution. He emerged from the pool, sat on the blanket, and began to assess what remained of his equipment. The thief whistled when his fingers closed around a jumble of stolen jewelry. He withdrew one of the silver necklaces from the rough leather pocket and dangled it in the light. Flanked by two lavender leadochrite trillions, the ostentatious fire opal glowed as though possessed by an inner light. Only three stable leadochrite mines existed in all of Ibea—two were in Dessia— which accounted for the gems' considerable value. Whoever had procured such a gift was wealthy beyond avarice.

Jarle tucked the necklace back into the pocket and withdrew his emberstems. Water had eaten through the sulfur tips, rendering them useless. He tossed them aside and began to search for his tinderbox. "Ven's sake!" he groused, noticing that nothing was in its proper place. "Where did she put my tinderbox?"

Jarle breathed a sigh of relief when his hand closed around the wax-sealed cylinder that held his fire-making tools. He had grown up near the docks, where fishermen unloaded the day's catch to esurient swarms of black flies, and the thought of eating raw fish turned his stomach. Luckily, there seemed to be enough driftwood, fallen branches, and biwarra-nut husks to make a fire.

Jarle set the tinderbox down and regarded his pants. He loathed the idea of wearing cold, wet pants through dinner, but they needed a wash. Reluctantly, he gathered his armor and waded back into the shallows to scrub each piece. He chuckled, wondering what Avaren would do if he dared to serve dinner naked. His broken ribs soon chastised his levity.

It was early afternoon by the time Jarle finished cleaning his armor. After hanging all but his pants and boots on the roots to dry, he began to get dressed. The wet pants proved as trying to put on as they had been to remove. Each yank of the tight breeches caused a throbbing ache in his chest. Sweat broke out on his brow.

Exhausted, hungry and in pain, Jarle lay down on the blankets and slept. When he awoke, the sky was no longer blue. Clouds tinged with the coral hues of sunset raced over a mauve sky, and the nectarous scent of moonflowers filled the air.

Bracing his bandaged ribs, the thief donned his boots and weapon belt. He wobbled to his feet, then limped along the shoreline picking bits of biwarra-nut coir, small branches, and driftwood for kindling. He made a pile on a sandy spot between two rocky outcrops near the far wall of the cave and gathered stones to create a firepit. The month of Sund'im marked the end of warm summer nights. Triesse would bring wind, rain, and chilly nights making fire a necessity.

Jarle made a hole in the sand and lined it with stones. He filled the pit with the kindling, then cut into the wax that sealed his tinderbox. He withdrew a few strands of oiled yarn, tucked them under the pile of driftwood, and struck the flint against the metal cylinder. Jarle's chest swelled with joy as the tinder took. Bending over the smoking pile, he blew until steady flames began to lick the driftwood.

In his lifetime, Jarle had gutted more fish and shucked more oysters than he cared to remember. While he tended the fire, he cleaned the galefins with the skill of a seasoned fisherman and cut them into tender cubes. Next, Jarle pried open the spiny oysters and scooped out the buttery meat. He used the flat-leafed kelp to wrap the fish and oyster combination into tight satchels in hopes that the kelp's saltiness would transfer to the bland fish. Instead of string, Jarle used young vines to tie each packet closed.

As each packet came in contact with the fire, the kelp popped and hissed, filling the cavern with the delicious scent of grilled fish. Jarle's mouth watered, and his stomach growled with anticipation as he turned each fragrant bundle. He doubted The Stallion's chef could top his ingenuity.

While the fish roasted, Jarle brushed off the blanket and brought it closer to the fire. He tossed the fish guts at the far end of the pool and rinsed out the largest oyster shells to serve as dishes.

Catching his reflection in the water, Jarle winced. Rough stubble covered his face, and his hair was a mess. He no longer stank, but he looked like a bedraggled savage.

Rifling through the pile of spiny oysters, Jarle selected one with wide-set spikes. He ran the shell through his hair, grimacing as it caught in the tangled knots. After a few fruitless yanks, Jarle abandoned the idea. He tossed the shell into the pool and tied back his hair with a leather cord.

Pleased with the compromise, the thief ran his fingers over his chin. Rippling water and a poniard weren't ideal tools for a shave, but he was determined to impress the girl.

Unsheathing his blade, Jarle bent over the surface and pulled the flesh taut over his cheek. Carefully he grazed the edge of the dagger over his stubble. One smooth cheek later, he groaned in agony. The crouched position was nigh unbearable and caused his anger to flare.

"Damn her!" Jarle cursed. He could scarcely believe he was shaving to please a woman who likely hated his guts. Because of Avaren, he was a wanted man; a fugitive with at least two broken ribs that would take months to heal.

Avaren had called him a dog never suspecting that he was willing to live up to the insult. A male dog would give rise to his sexual needs and mount anything; a bitch, another male dog, a human leg, and even a spoiled little darling.

Jarle finished shaving and stood. With the easing of his pain, clarity returned. Blaming Avaren would not change his situation. Even if he could prove his innocence of the deadly plot, he would die in prison or at the hands of the Mistress of Rats. He had foolishly vowed to protect the girl, and knew he needed a plan, but brilliance rarely struck on an empty stomach.

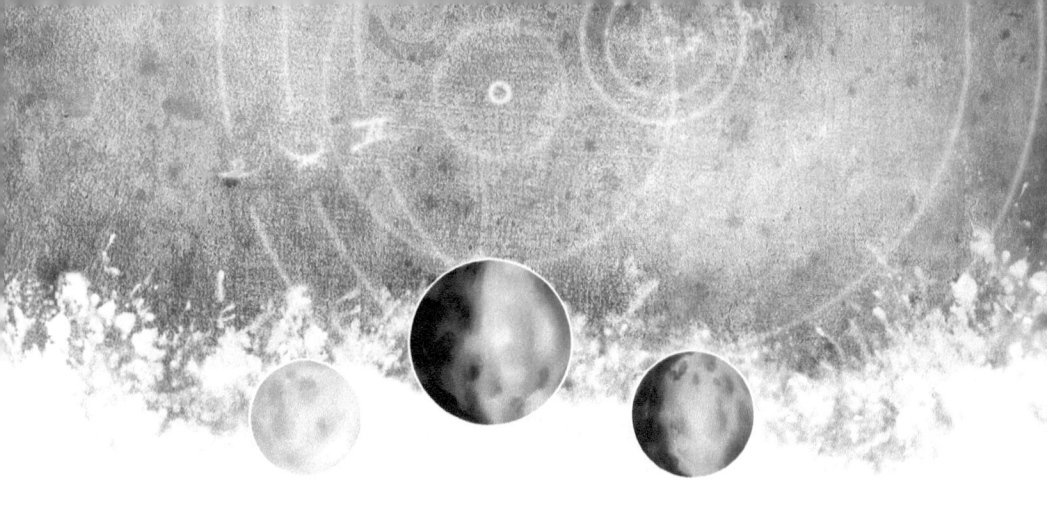

A GAMBLING MAN

Mir'kadi, Tenth of Sund'im, 445 A'A'diel

The sunlight that streamed through the soaring, ogee-arched windows of Tan'os Ensther's bedchamber illuminated a chaotic scene. A pair of sturdy chairs lay smashed near an upturned table beneath the windows, their splintered limbs echoed by the hulking four-poster bed at the opposite side of the room. The Vise's two-handed sword lay on the floor, stained with dried blood.

A large curio with glass doors stood against the wall and appeared to be one of the few pieces of furniture that hadn't been destroyed. Behind the bed hung a timeworn tapestry depicting one of the most epic sea battles in Thrommish history, the Conquest of Pellandar Bay. The violence of the naval onslaught was mirrored by the stench of death and the room's disarray.

Beneath his wrinkled brow, Deneven's eyes shone with intensity. Contemplating the chaos, the newly deputized Chief Justiciar sought to make sense of the grisly events. Something about the scene did not feel right.

Deneven leaned on his cane with a grumble and shifted his weight to his good leg. He had paid copious coin to various craftsmen, but none had yet crafted a wooden leg that didn't cause his stump to ache.

Behind him, one of the two guards assigned to aid his investigation cleared his throat with an exaggerated cough, stirring Deneven from his reverie.

"What is it?" asked Deneven, his tone flat.

"Begging your pardon, sir. Lord Justiciar Tsardon was quite explicit in his orders. You were to be given until noon to inspect the building, and it is almost that time." The young guard's curled mustache quivered as he wrinkled his nose. "The Lord Justiciar wants the villa to be properly cleansed."

"What is your name, Lance Corporal?"

"Ionaden Kesner, sir."

Judging by the angle of the sun's rays upon the floor, Deneven judged it to be mid-morning. "Corporal Kesner, I am quite aware of the time. I have at least another hour."

"Yes, sir, I only meant to—"

Deneven turned to face the doorway where the cavalrymen stood. "I know what you meant." A quick up-and-down flick of his eyes was all Deneven required to assess the soldier. "Your armor is fit for a cavalcade, not a single nick or dent to be found. You've not been in battle. Indeed, I wager a year's pay that you've yet to kill your first man. Bah, don't try to deny it. One look at you and I know all there is about you. Soft hands, plump cheeks. You are the coddled spawn of some grasping courtier, or lesser merchant, seeking a quick path to power through service in the decorated Ca'Dezer Cavalry." The timbre of Deneven's voice grew dark. "You'd best become accustomed to this stink. Own it, inhale it as you would the aroma of your momma's stew on a cold winter day. Some days the air will be filled with the odor of your enemies' shit and gore, others with that of your comrades' blood. One day the stench may be your own." Deneven hobbled to stand nose to nose with the paling youth, "You chose death's trade when you accepted that sword and armor. You are a Reyzan Ca'Dezer; we eat steel and spit daggers. Right now, you look like some dainty Ferencian noble sniffing his bride's cunt. Now cease wrinkling your nose and grow some hair on your balls."

The cavalryman raised his chin and straightened. "Yes, sir."

With a dismissive snort, Deneven eyed the stiffened guard but said nothing further. He turned and walked back into the room, the clunk of his peg leg on the wooden floor startling in the stillness. He stopped at the side of the bed and dipped his head.

Tan'os Ensther might have been a salt-soaked, blunt-nosed bastard, as brutal and cunning in politics as in battle, but he had not been without merits. Despite his foreign birth, Tan'os had used his position to improve the lives of Reyzan citizens. The Thyran warlord had been tough but fair in all his dealings, never giving an advantage to anyone, including his kinfolk, something Deneven had always respected. In many ways, the iron-willed foreigner had treated his adopted city better than its native-born monarch.

"May Nogh's icy ship speed you to Evershine Bay, Tan'os Ensther." The simple Thrommish prayer was the least he could offer the gods on behalf of the Savior of Reyza.

Deneven closed his eyes and inhaled. The coppery stink of blood fused with the reek of voided bowels. According to the official report, the Vise had been killed while defending his home against nighttime prowlers. The illustrations in the report that documented Tan'os' wounds indicated a desperate struggle, further evidenced by the damaged furniture and the bloodied two-handed sword.

Opening his eyes, Deneven studied the wall near the bedside where two sword hooks hung empty, then turned to where the sword lay upon the floor. He looked toward the door with a puzzled expression. "Did anyone move the sword?"

After a long pause, one of the guards dared to look into the room. "Pardon, sir?"

Deneven sighed and pointed to the sword with the tip of the cane. "Did anyone move the sword?"

"No, sir, everything in here is exactly as we found it."

"You have been in this room before?"

"Yes, sir, my squad was the first to arrive when the alarm was sounded."

"What is your name?"

The young man snapped to attention. "Lance Corporal Eskander Johar, Fifth Company, sir."

"Please describe everything you saw here." Deneven stared at the young man intently, both hands perched on the tip of his cane.

"I cannot, sir." The young guard swallowed. "I was in the girl's room."

"How about you, fancy boy? Were you here?"

Corporal Kesner bit back his retort and responded with a curt nod. "Yes, sir."

"And?"

"Exactly what you see, sir." The words were crisp and clipped. "The Vise was dead. He was on the floor, there by the window, hacked near to pieces."

The investigator nodded to himself and turned away from the guard. He walked over to the sword. Streaks of dried blood coated the blade, and continued, uninterrupted on the floor around it. Deneven bent over, leaning his weight on the cane as he examined the droplets. A lack of movement marked the stains, as though the blood had been sprinkled from above. Curiously, none of the stains were smeared as often happened amid furious swordplay.

One of the assailants had been killed in Mejtress Avaren's bedroom by a double strike of daggers from behind. His alleged accomplice, Jarle Jadien, had escaped with Avaren Ensther as a hostage. If all that was true, then whose blood coated Tan'os' blade?

Deneven straightened and clomped over to the Vise's bed. The bedding was soaked in the Vise's blood, as were the drapes. Deneven stared at the bloodstains that covered the mattress and curtains. He had killed enough men in the war to know the signs of arterial spray when he saw it. Such wounds did not allow for long engagements. Even a giant man such as Tan'os would have bled out quickly.

Deneven's heart began to hammer in his chest. He walked across the room to the glass curio that dominated the far wall and peered at the contents inside. The curio's shelves held an assortment of playing cards—eight decks in all. Each deck of cards had been arranged in a fanned spread to feature the artistry of the illustrations. Deneven contemplated a particular set; the artwork on the thin rectangles of wood was well executed, but among the other decks, it seemed shoddy and cheap.

Cheap, thought Deneven, shaking his head. The cards had cost him two months' pay and a year of lessons. Thrarttas was not a game for faint passions. It was a game of intellectual strategy that required extensive knowledge of the ancient myths. The element of chance was the draw, but it was the keen mind of the player that determined the card's fates. Thrarttas was challenging to learn and nigh impossible to master.

Deneven smiled, recalling the day when Tan'os had convinced him to take up Thrarttas. He had beaten Tan'os at Primeta, Deneven's preferred gambling game, five times in a row when the suggestion to play another card game had come. A year and a thousand sequins later, Deneven had handed his custom Thrarttas deck over to Tan'os in his first and last game. The betting of decks was a rare occurrence, tantamount to a duel. Deneven tapped the glass. His defeat had been the Vise's way of evening the score.

Adjacent to his former deck, lay an extravagant set of cards fashioned from thin slats of ivory. He had seen the suite of cards before. The deck belonged to the head mage of the Collegium, Arcanist Olos.

Deneven stared at the stark black and white cards. In over fifty years of playing Thrarttas, Olos was rumored to have never lost a match. The center card in the fanned display depicted a beautiful woman with six arms, Sherzadeen, the Daemon Queen of Spiders. It was a card of webs, seduction, and deceit. Deneven couldn't help but wonder about the match that could have been won with such a card. Tan'os had played a legendary game with a Thrarttas master and triumphed. Extraordinary.

Deneven was about to leave the room when he noticed two rectangular depressions on the narrow carpet near the curio.

Deneven furrowed his brow. "Where are the chests?" he asked.

"Excuse me, sir?" Corporal Kesner asked. "What chests?"

"What chests? The chests that created those marks, you fool." Deneven pointed to the marks on the woven rug. "What has become of them?"

Lance Corporal Johar stepped forward and spoke. "The Vise's coffers were taken to the palace, under the command of Lord Justiciar Tsardon, sir. He was concerned their contents might be stolen."

"So much for leaving the villa undisturbed and intact," Deneven muttered. He took one final glance at the room then stepped out into the hall. "Do either of you know where the daughter's bedroom is?"

"Aye, sir," the guards replied in harmony.

"Well, lead on, then. Time is wasting."

A few moments later, Deneven and his minders stood outside the bedchamber of Avaren Ensther. "This is where the slain guard was found?" Deneven pointed to the blood outside the door.

"Yes, sir," Corporal Johar confirmed.

Deneven stepped over the gore as best he could. When he was inside, he looked around with awe. The opulence of the girl's room made the Vise's bedroom seem like a monk's niche.

Deneven limped over to where a large dark red stain had soaked into the carpet. He was disheartened to find that dozens of bloody footprints had tracked through the evidence. Tsardon was cutting corners on discipline, training—or both.

Fucking politician.

Deneven lingered over the bloodstain, taking note of the spot where Jars' mysterious partner had expired. Slowly, he turned in place, taking note of the layout of the room. His gaze settled on Avaren's vanity whose drawers lay open.

Behind him, Corporal Johar spoke up with confidence. "We detained all of the surviving Calantian guards for questioning. None were in possession of the stolen property, but we remanded them to the palace dungeons for inquiry..." The youth's voice trailed off, realizing that he had spoken without having been addressed.

The breach of protocol was unusual. Deneven stroked his chin thoughtfully; his curiosity piqued. He remained with his back turned to the guards while he motioned for the soldier to approach. "At ease, Corporal Johar. Please, join me." Deneven was pleased when the young guard sidestepped the blood on the carpet. "Tell me what you saw here when you arrived," Deneven demanded, pointing to the puddle of blood on the floor.

"We found a dead man dressed in black leather. He had two daggers stuck in his lower back."

"Did you notice any signs of struggle?"

Eskander pointed to a palm print on the glass balcony door. "Chief Justiciar Phennas believes that there was a struggle between Mejtress Avaren and one of the intruders, as evidenced by the imprint of her palm on the balcony door. As for the dead man, the Chief Justiciar believes he was ambushed from behind."

Deneven walked to the glass doors. The handprint was indeed smaller than a grown man's. Turning back to face the guard, Deneven said, "Describe how the dead man was positioned."

Eskander pointed as he spoke. "He lay face down, both arms at his sides, legs slightly apart. Two daggers were buried in his back."

"According to the interrogation report, there was a wire garrote found in the room?"

"Yes, Chief Justiciar Phennas believes that the now-dead man used it in an attempt to murder the girl, sir," Eskander said.

Deneven put on his gambling face. "What makes Phennas think the man's intent was murder? Perhaps the garrote was used to render her unconscious? Maybe the intruders meant to rape her, then kidnap her. It's possible they didn't use the garrote on Mejtress Avaren at all, but on the guards outside."

"Well, those are possibilities, sir, but I believe that murder was his intention. Mejtress Dannia Jarnïs and the Vise's valet Paulo Cova were both found strangled." Eskander's voice betrayed his enthusiasm. He stepped over the puddle of blood to the bed. "See the way the bedding is disarranged? It looks as though someone was violently dragged off of the bed. Now look here, based on the location of his body, the garrote, and the handprint, attempted murder seems the only likely explanation."

Deneven crossed the room to examine the bed. "I see," said Deneven coolly. "What do you make of these towels on the bed? Do you suppose the perpetrators bathed Mejtress Avaren before attempting to end her life?"

Eskander looked at the bed with consternation. "I don't know, sir. Perhaps Mejtress Avaren was bathing when they broke into her room?"

Deneven walked to the bedroom door and looked around. Not far from the threshold lay a slim, jeweled dagger. "The door does not seem forced." Deneven motioned for Eskander to join him. "But, what do you make of this?" he asked, pointing to the blade.

"Looks like a letter opener, sir," Eskander replied.

"Oh, it's no letter opener. Hand it to me, please?"

Eskander picked up the dagger and handed it to Deneven.

"Do you think the girl used it to defend herself?"

Deneven turned the weapon in his hands. It was just one more clue missing from Tsardon's *detailed* reports. Chief Justiciar Darkor Phennas had been hired after he had retired. Deneven had no way of proving if the investigator's sloppiness was a result of deliberate subterfuge or plain incompetence. "Quite possibly. Tell me, did you see the dead man's face?"

"Yes, sir."

Deneven set the dagger down on the bed and continued to look around. "Describe him, please."

"Tall, muscular, but without the bulk of a warrior. Clean-shaven. Shoulder-length black hair tied back in a tight bun at the nape of his neck. His face was fair-featured but weathered, with soft cheekbones, a straight nose, and solid black Yerr'draki eyes. He had a very distinctive scar on his left cheek shaped like a cross. I don't recall much else, as we were all reassigned to secure the front gate by the Lord Justiciar."

"Thank you, that was very helpful." Deneven managed to keep his voice steady while his thoughts roiled; caught in a raging storm. Just as with Brath, the soldier's description bore no resemblance to the sketch contained in the official report. Indeed, the revelation of Yerr'draki ancestry and the cross-like scar struck Deneven like a thunderbolt. As Lord Justiciar, he'd spent years investigating the trail of carnage left behind by a man with just such a scar—a killer named Mast.

Deneven forced his breathing to remain steady. It had been a stretch to believe that a professional thief would drastically change his modus operandi for such a high-profile job, but even more of a stretch to accept that an assassin who always worked alone had aligned with a partner. Something about the whole affair reeked and it wasn't the gore. Without realizing it, the young soldier had confirmed his growing suspicion—Chief Justiciar Phennas had knowingly tampered with the crime scene. Deneven made a mental note to have a bottle of Debendelo Red delivered to Captain Garentas for lending him such an astute soldier.

"Kesner, you stay here." Deneven turned and walked out the doorway. "Come along, Corporal Johar. Let us see where the fight with the guards occurred."

The old veteran moved with a natural gait that belied his wooden leg. The soft clomp of Deneven's cane was the only clue that he was less than whole. Eskander followed the former Lord Justiciar down the servant's stairwell to the first landing.

"This is where we found the bodies of the captain of the guard, Varrus Sigolian, and his sergeant, Cassio Serda." Eskander pointed out each location. The dried blood that covered the stones appeared black in the flickering torchlight. "Right down there is where the surviving conspirator, Brath Barathac, was found. He claimed to have stabbed the thief who abducted Mejtress Ensther."

"I heard the survivor's testimony. It is not uncommon for a captured conspirator to portray himself as trying to stop the very crime which he encouraged."

Deneven descended the stairs and paused. He poked about with the tip of his cane and was rewarded with a slight tinkling sound. The investigator stroked his scraggly gray beard, then bent down to retrieve a small glittering object. "What do you make of this?" Deneven asked, raising a small glass vial to the torchlight.

Eskander approached to study the tiny object. "It is an apothecary's jar, sir."

Deneven delicately sniffed at the opening of the vessel. "Used to contain oil of tarbark."

"Is it poison, sir?"

"The exact opposite. It's an antidote used to neutralize certain toxic concoctions." Deneven handed the vial to Eskander, becoming slowly aware that the landing was littered with similar vials. He picked up another container and sniffed it. "Curious, this is extract of amphrosis," he said, wrinkling his nose at the bitter scent, "another antidote."

Deneven bent down to scoop up more vials. "This one is essence of indictine, and this blue-stained one is tambor root sap. All of these seem to have held antidotes to assuage the effects of various poisons. Indictine and amphrosis taken together can lead to lunatism." Deneven's heart began to beat faster. Once again Brath's testimony was proving truthful where the official report had fallen short. He was on the trail; the mystery of the case had seized him.

Eskander met Deneven's eyes. "Why so many different

antidotes?"

Deneven slipped the empty vials into one of his belt pouches. "Tell me, what else did you find on the deceased thief?"

"Well, we found two daggers in his back that we suspect were his because they fit his scabbards, plus various tools commonly used by thieves." Eskander closed his eyes, recalling the scene. His eyes flew open with realization. "In the stairwell, right here, we found a small boot dagger. It had blood on its tip and some black oily substance."

Deneven nodded to himself, once again the corporal had inadvertently corroborated Brath's version of the events. Deneven withdrew the jar with a thin coat of blue residue and turned it in his fingers. "It seems that the justiciar who investigated before me was right. Whoever was stabbed here was prepared to avoid being poisoned—too prepared. There is only one moonlighter in this city who would be paranoid enough to carry both tambor root sap and essence of indictine. Jarle Jars Jadien."

"You know of him?"

"Yes. He's one of Reyza's most notorious rogues with a well-known fear of poison. They call him 'Jars' because he is rumored to carry all manner of antidotes on his person. So at least one part of this mystery is solved. Jars Jadien was indeed here on the night of the murders."

"Is it possible this Jars person and his partner had a falling out? Maybe the dead thief wanted to kill Avaren and Jars wanted to kidnap her for ransom?"

"Never jump to conclusions. There are several scenarios for how this could have played out. An argument is one, but something tells me there is more to this than a duo of squabbling thieves." Pain in his stump prompted Deneven to rub what remained of his leg. He leaned toward Eskander and whispered conspiratorially, "Say nothing and follow my lead."

Deneven hollered in a tone that always sent men scrambling, "You there with the weak stomach, this investigation requires more time! Go to the Lord Justiciar's office and inform him that Deneven D'Neir requires exclusive access to the villa until midnight."

"B-but sir," Kesner complained at the top of the stairwell,

"my orders are to keep watch over you."

"Lance Corporal Eskander seems capable of subduing a one-legged geezer if he has cause. Go now at once, or I will have your hide for disobeying my orders. And if you need to, remind Tsardon that if he declines my request, Majster Ther'oldo Ers will file a formal diplomatic complaint with the Council!"

The young guard's mustache twitched, but he put forth no other protest as he stomped down the stairs. When the echo of the slammed front doors faded, Deneven smiled at Eskander. "We have a while before your comrade returns. Let us take advantage of that to speak freely. Please enlighten me with your opinion of what transpired here. What do you believe happened to the girl?"

"No body; no trace of her whereabouts." Eskander shrugged. "I do not know, sir."

Deneven led Eskander out of the stairwell and into the light. "Well, it is clear that she fled, whether against her will or willingly is yet to be determined."

Eskander shook his head. "Willingly? Why would she go willingly and with whom?"

"Walk the streets long enough, and you will see and hear all manner of things. All that we know for certain is that she is not here." Deneven walked with the guard past the grand stair, to the front door. "Now, do you wish to know the truth behind this mystery?"

Eskander nodded solemnly. "I do, sir."

Deneven met Eskander's eyes. "Do you take the Guard's Oath—to effect justice for those offended, to uphold the laws of Reyza and dedicate yourself to protecting the city, regardless of personal cost, even unto death—sincerely?"

"Yes, sir, I spoke those words freely and from my heart."

"Then help me unravel this conundrum and bring to justice the killer of the Vise and his household. Help me find Avaren Ensther."

"Yes, sir!" Eskander's words were genuine but strained with worry.

Deneven placed a hand on the cavalryman's shoulder. "Be at ease; I will ensure that you do not violate your lawful orders."

Eskander exhaled. "Thank you for your confidence, sir. How

may I be of assistance?"

"We know that Jars made it out of the servant stairwell with Mejtress Avaren and that he did not die from being poisoned. We are aware that the cloister guards didn't find anyone besides Brath alive when they searched the villa, and that Jars and Avaren are missing. We need to discover what happened after Jars took the antidotes. Unfortunately, your peers' careless tromping has removed any spoor we might follow."

"So, we are at an impasse?"

"Yes, we need assistance—from an expert." Deneven smiled. "Do you know of a place in Gavalene Hill by the name of the Grinding Wheel?"

"How could I not?" Eskander blurted. "We are always dealing with complaints about that place."

"Excellent. You are to go there and fetch me a man." Deneven ignored the confused look on Eskander's face. "He is a Seh'nahiel ranger, goes by the name of Redmane. In all likelihood, you will find him drunk, or worse, but no matter. You are to bring him here immediately before your comrade returns. When Redmane protests—and he will—tell him these words exactly. 'The Dragon is calling in all of his markers.' He will know what that means."

"But, sir—"

Deneven cut Eskander's protests short. "I understand that your sensibilities are offended. I ask that you trust me and that you bear in mind that for over twenty years, I served as the Lord Justiciar of Reyza. Mejtress Avaren's life may depend on your expediency."

Eskander stood at attention. "Yes, sir."

Deneven opened the front door of the villa. "The man you are to fetch is light-hearted and feckless, but there is no better tracker in the city. Now go, before any more time is lost."

THE GRINDING WHEEL

Mir'kadi, Tenth of Sund'im, 445 A'A'diel

The traders were well into their haggling when Eskander reined his charger onto Ardaran Road. Two and three-story buildings butted up against each other along the thoroughfare like the walls of an angular canyon. The ringing of tinkers' hammers echoed off the white plastered façades, a shrill counterpoint to the clamorous buzz of negotiations. It was midday and Tinker's Notch was crowded with throngs of customers seeking the district's artisanal wares.

Eskander rode down the boulevard, the steady hoofbeats of his stallion heralding his presence. His tunic bore the ochre and sky-blue checkered pattern of the Ca'Dezer Cavalry; the uniform assured his unhindered progress more than the iron-shod hooves of his warhorse. The crowd parted before him like a school of baitfish around a gliding shark.

Various aromas vied for attention. The spicy scent of roasting meats roused hungry bellies while imported Terranakan perfumes enraptured the senses. Paid shills sang out promises of quality and low prices, tailoring their spiels to the passersby like fishermen angling for the big catch.

Eskander spurred his horse into a canter as he turned into a less crowded street. The pale stones of Therander Lane gleamed in the morning sunlight, creating a magnificent path that ascended straight from Tinker's Notch into the heart of Gavalene Hill. Unlike the Tangles, where decades of dirt clung to the buildings, the villas that lined the winding streets of Gavalene reflected the sun's brilliance.

Eskander's destination, the Grinding Wheel, was an inn that straddled the border between the privileged elite of Gavalene and the sweaty plebeians of the craftsmen's ward. Twenty years prior, the building had housed an upper-class hostel known as Gentry's Rest. The previous owner, a disgraced noble, had sold the establishment to a Calantian whoremonger as a farewell insult to his former peers.

As Eskander steered his horse along the side of the inn, a grubby boy emerged from the stables. "May I take your horse, sir?" the boy asked, straightening his hat.

"Stabling won't be necessary," Eskander said, tossing the boy a copper coin. "However, I would appreciate it if you would keep Phraxes here company while I go inside."

The stable hand tucked the coin into his patched jerkin and tipped his hat. "Yes, sir, gladly."

Eskander took off his embossed, steel helm and handed it to the boy. He adjusted his scale armor with a few short tugs and smoothed back his sandy brown locks.

The Grinding Wheel was built in the revival style that had fallen from fashion a hundred years prior. The exaggerated curves of its gabled roof were a stark contrast to the symmetry and square proportions of neighboring homes. It had been years since the weather-stained walls, and mossy alcoves had received any attention. Above the sweeping veranda that ran the length of the inn, the establishment's namesake hung from a chain. It was a worn blacksmith's wheel covered with chipping scarlet paint that advertised the building's ignoble purpose. The Grinding Wheel was one of Reyza's most notorious brothels.

Inhaling deeply, Eskander straightened his shoulders and strode up the steps that led to the tiled porch. He placed a hand upon the brothel's wooden door and paused to look around. Across the street, curious onlookers assessed his intentions. Eskander narrowed his eyes and glared at them with such vehemence that all but small children cringed before returning to their business.

Eskander pushed open the door with chagrin. The Grinding Wheel was the last place he wanted to be seen entering.

The interior of the brothel was as posh as the outer façade was distressed. Eskander stepped into the vast, vaulted foyer. Mahogany walls soared up to a dome inlaid with jade. Brocade curtains shielded the parlor from daylight, imbuing the room with an intimate ambiance. Tendrils of rillweed smoke swirled between the wooden pillars and curled around the fronds of ferns planted in marble urns. Music emanated from a second-floor balconette where an unseen trio of musicians strummed a tranquil melody.

Beyond the glow of the oil lamps, Eskander discerned scantily clad men and women lounging on velvet couches and settees. Tucked away in alcoves, some of the concubines lay with companions, indulging them with wine, food, and shameless caresses. From a shadowy corner, a girl with golden tresses arched, letting the décolletage of her robe slip down to reveal a pair of pert, tawny breasts. Closer to Eskander, a copper-skinned woman with sultry eyes and wide hips dipped her hand between her thighs before beckoning to Eskander with glistening fingertips.

Eskander swallowed hard, then looked away. He was less unsettled by the women's flirtations than the idea that anyone of worth, let alone a Seh'nahiel noble, could be found in such a despicable locale.

The Grinding Wheel was among the last places Eskander would ever expect to find one of the arrogant and aloof citizens from the great City of A'diel. The Seh'nahiel held as much esteem for Reyza as they did for a steaming turd. They were an insular and condescending lot who treated other bloodlines with a detached imperiousness that bordered on contempt. Were it not for their deft politics, powerful magic, and incredible wealth they would not be tolerated in Reyza, let alone welcomed.

Eskander had minimal experience dealing with Seh'nahiel, and that suited him just fine—the nobles of Reyza required enough ass-kissing and hand-holding as it were.

Eskander stepped into the dim brothel's parlor and glowered at the nearest concubine. The brown-skinned woman rose from her divan and approached him with the slow, predatory steps of a huntress. Her hips swayed with promise as she circled him, eyeing him like a piece of meat. "We don't get the pleasure of entertaining many from your order, but the ones who do frequent our establishment never disappoint. The Ca'Dezer certainly know how to ride."

Eskander raised his chin. "I am not interested in your entertainment."

The woman's fingertips traced up along Eskander's arm as she turned to face him. "Are you certain? We can provide many forms of diversion, good sir."

"I am not here for a woman," Eskander replied.

"You wish the pleasure of a boy?" the woman asked.

Heat rushed into Eskander's cheeks. "What!? No, I seek a man!"

Eskander winced when the woman let out an amused giggle. He could have kicked himself for stammering.

The woman's heated glance dropped to Eskander's groin. She licked her lips. "I seek a man as well."

The seductress knew her trade well and was gifted in the dance. Eskander gritted his teeth and ignored the tightening in his breeches. He continued with a more professional tone. "Mejtress, I am here on official business."

"Oh, I see." The woman's demeanor shifted as swiftly as storm clouds. A scowl replaced the inviting shine in her eyes as a patron pulled away from the embrace of a concubine and began to dress with haphazard alacrity. The woman placed her hands on her hips and squared off in front of Eskander. "Well, then you best be quick about it. You are bad for my business."

"*Your* business?"

"Yes, *my* business. Let's knock off the little-boy-lost act, shall we? I am Lyssandra, and the Grinding Wheel is my house. If you are here about noise complaints, I have already paid my fines this month. Your comrades have already plundered a full week's worth of earnings to leave my girls in peace. I am not paying you one filthy sequin more until next month."

Eskander clenched his fists. "I am no grifter here to pry money from your hands, nor am I aware of any complaints or fines. If city guardsmen are extorting you, tell me the names of these criminals and I shall see to it they are properly dealt with. The Ca'Dezer Cavalry serves all of Reyza without prejudice."

Lyssandra let out a whistle of disbelief. "Listen, I don't know who you are or what you've been drinking, but you do know you are in Reyza, yes? The city guard, including your precious cavalry, serves its own interests first. As for ratting out your peers, I do not need any more enemies. I am quite satisfied with the list I've made over the years." Another patron slunk out the front door. "So, unless you have personal needs to be fulfilled—out with it, or out with you. Every moment you stand here is costing me sequins."

Eskander held no illusions about his peers in the city guard. Ever since Lord Justiciar Tsardon had taken office, standards had diminished. The prestige of public service was fading, and accusations of corruption galled his sense of honor. He lowered his voice. "Despite your experiences to the contrary, not all of us take our vows lightly. That said, I accept your decision to avoid reporting this crime. Should you change your mind, I am Lance Corporal Eskander Johar of the Fifth. I promise I shall do everything in my power to provide the justice you deserve."

"Right now, I desire to have you on your way. How may I hasten your departure?"

"As I said before, I seek a man—a Seh'nahiel known by the name of Redmane."

Lyssandra's expression turned to stone at his words. "I do not know of any person by that name, Seh'nahiel or otherwise."

Drawing himself upright, Eskander summoned the full force of his authority. "Whores by profession are practiced liars. I have little doubt that you are an expert in your trade. Therefore, I will ask you a single question and caution you to consider your answer before speaking." Eskander spoke with steely calm, his words crisp and clear in the smoky air. "Should I believe your answer there will be no need for further investigation. However, if your words ring false, I shall summon the entire Fifth Cavalry to surround and search your brothel from top to bottom. They will be thorough, though being horsemen, do not expect them to be gentle or polite. All infractions uncovered, no matter how trivial, will be cataloged, reported, and prosecuted." Eskander's voice grew cold. "Should

I find this Redmane present, I shall personally see to it that you are immediately seized and imprisoned in the dungeons of the Chancellery of Justice until such a time that you may be brought before a tribunal. A woman of your vocation is surely familiar with the tales of the prison's hospitality. The choice is yours."

The color drained from the woman's face, and her eyes darted away. He could sense her struggle with the idea of betraying a patron's trust. Tired of delay, Eskander brusquely stepped forward until his armored form loomed over the scantily clad woman. Lowering his voice to a menacing timbre, Eskander growled, "Where is Redmane?"

When the woman's eyes fluttered, Eskander thought she might faint. He grabbed her arms to stop her from falling and held her. Mistaking his intent, Lyssandra's eyes shot open, and her bladder released its contents. "Please don't arrest me! He's in the gallery! Sweet addonels have mercy; he's in the back!"

Eskander guided the trembling woman to a nearby divan. "Where is this room?"

Lyssandra raised her finger and pointed to the far corner of the parlor. "Behind the tapestry."

Eskander looked at the defeated woman with a twinge of regret. He preferred a lighter touch but wasn't past striking the fear of the gods into unwilling citizens when his duty demanded.

"Thank you for your cooperation. My offer to free you of your troubles still stands." With that, Eskander crossed the parlor, ignoring the harlots who darted past him to console their mistress.

The cavalryman swept the expensive tapestry back with a forceful swipe to reveal a secret door. From beyond the door came muffled laughter. Impatience goaded him to yank the door open and be done with it, but he reconsidered. Regardless of his opinion, Deneven seemed to hold great respect for the Seh'nahiel in question. More importantly, the justiciar believed the foreigner's aid was necessary to rescue the Vise's daughter. Eskander quelled his urge to kick the door down and knocked instead.

When there was no response from inside the chamber, Eskander inhaled deeply. He knocked again, his mailled knuckles denting the wood.

The laughter stopped. A moment later, the latch was unlocked from the other side. With a creak, the door opened. A young woman peeked through the crack, her bright eyes traveling the length of Eskander before settling on his face. "Well, hello there, handsome! I think you have the wrong room."

Before Eskander could reply, a foreign-accented male voice called out from the depths of the room, "Is that the wine?"

The woman smiled at Eskander as she called back over her shoulder. "No, sweetness, only a lost soldier."

"I am not lost. I am Lance Corporal Eskander Johar of the Fifth Ca'Dezer Cavalry. I have come here to speak with Redmane." Eskander stiffened, bracing to push into the room should the girl attempt to close the door.

"I am not accepting any more visitors at the moment, as my arms are overflowing." Feminine giggles accompanied the man's muffled laughter. "However, if you have wine, I am confident we can spare a moment for you."

Eskander gritted his teeth. "Deneven D'Neir dispatched me. He has instructed me to inform you that the Dragon is calling in all his markers."

"If that is what he wishes so be it. Tell Dennie I will call upon him tomorrow to settle accounts. As you can imagine, I am presently and quite pleasantly engaged." The sound of a slap on a firm rump followed by a pleasured squeal punctuated the reply.

"My apologies." Eskander clenched his fists, but his tone remained cordial. "Chief Justiciar, D'Neir, is adamant that you speak with him now."

"Bel's furry balls! The old man's timing is damned inconvenient. Trinn, please let our guest in."

The girl winked at Eskander, then opened the door wide to reveal a sumptuous chamber. Lurid paintings framed in gold adorned the red velvet walls. A tangle of naked, nubile bodies writhed in a nest of luxurious sheepskins and silk-covered pillows. Eskander made out the forms of three women lying upon another body. Only the man's feet were visible, dangling from beneath the mound of soft, moaning flesh. Heedless of Eskander's presence, the women continued to kiss, suckle, and caress their client with enthusiastic devotion.

The man raised a hand between two supple thighs and waved

in Eskander's general direction.

The woman who had opened the door gestured to an elegant chaise. "Have a seat."

Eskander ignored the offer. "Majster, we need to leave now. I insist."

Giggling girls tumbled from the furs, revealing a long-limbed man less than twenty seasons of age lying amongst the pillows. Redmane was unlike any Seh'nahiel Eskander had ever encountered. He didn't appear anything like a pampered noble. The man's athletic body rippled with strength. His features bore the dignified, angular contours of his brethren, but his youthful complexion was browned from countless days spent under the sun. Battle scars marred the smooth skin—some severe enough to have brought the man to the threshold of death.

The Seh'nahiel rolled to his feet with the grace of a jungle cat, then brushed aside long, auburn locks from his face. His emerald eyes glowed with an inner light—proof that Bel'Eldriim blood flowed through his veins.

"As you wish," said Redmane. He stepped past the edge of the sleeping pallet and spread his arms.

The woman named Trinn poured water into a copper bowl, then set it at Redmane's feet while the other women fetched vessels of oils and soft cloths. The Seh'nahiel noble was engulfed in a flurry of activity as the women laved his body with fragrant oils and combed out the knots in his hair.

Shocked by the man's lack of shame, the cavalryman averted his eyes and cleared his throat. The brash youth bore no resemblance to any skilled woodsman he knew.

A warm, roguish smile appeared on Redmane's lips as he looked beyond Eskander. "Hello, darling."

Eskander turned in the direction of the ranger's gaze and froze. A few paces beyond him stood a monstrous dog-like creature with raised furry hackles. The pitch-black brute was twice the size and brawn of the biggest war-dog he had ever seen. The beast's eyes blazed like hot embers, and when it opened its maw in a silent snarl, it revealed a volcanic inferno burning within. He could feel the intense heat of its breath.

Eskander's hand instinctively moved to the sword at his

side. The reaction prompted a warning growl from the hellish creature—a powerful, rumbling sound like that of an earthquake.

"Easy, girl, Eskander here is a friend." At Redmane's words, the ferocious beast's fiery tongue suddenly lolled, and her tail began to wag so hard her rump shook. "Go play now. I will call you when I need you."

The beast let out a distorted bark and bounded away through the open door, seeming more like a faithful hound than a monstrosity borne of nightmares.

"I take it that's the first Khorvassian vulk you've ever encountered."

Eskander forced himself to relax and released the hilt of his sword. He smoothed his hair in a blatant attempt to mask his unease before turning to face Redmane, "I thought vulks were a myth—a legend made up by the barbarians of Cypricha to keep outsiders away from their sacred mountains."

"Vulks aren't a myth; Shenn is as real as real gets. However, you aren't completely wrong. Vulks do tend to discourage folks from wandering the Khorvassian Peaks." Redmane moved to allow the women to strap worn, well-oiled leather armor onto his body. The seal-brown armor was more scarred than the flesh it protected. "Don't let Shenn worry you. She only attacks those who wish me ill."

"I intend no threat, sir, but I *will* see you to Deneven."

"Indeed, I have no doubt of that." Redmane's chuckle was light and carefree. "Trinn, please have my horse brought round. And Lance Corporal Johar's as well."

"Thank you, that won't be necessary. My horse is saddled and ready."

"I see. Then let us make haste." Redmane strapped a Seh'nahiel long sword to his waist. The narrow blade was magnificent. Eskander calculated its cost at two years of his salary, assuming he could ever find one for sale. The weapon appeared as well seasoned as the man and his armor. The tracker then slung a carved bow over his shoulder that made the sword seem plain by comparison. Faint traces of green light pulsed along the wooden grain of the longbow's ribs. Eskander let out a soft gasp. The mystical properties of Draengale Wood were legendary.

Redmane gave the girl named Trinn a lingering, sensual kiss before plying each of the women with a fistful of A'dielian-minted gold coins. After brief farewells had been exchanged, he clapped Eskander on the shoulder. "Let's go see Dennie."

REDMANE

Mir'kadi, Tenth of Sund'im, 445 A'A'diel

"I heard they put you out to pasture, you stubborn old goat."

"They tried, but I found a way out of the corral." Deneven smiled and embraced the robust Seh'nahiel. For the first time since he had undertaken the commission to investigate the Vise's murder, Deneven felt optimism bloom in his chest. Redmane was eccentric, even by Seh'nahiel standards, but there were few better rangers than the Bel'Vandrari, fewer still who owed him a favor.

"Your soldier says you wish to call in your markers." Redmane considered the circular fountain in Ca'd'Cel's cloistered garden. In the center of the marble waterworks stood the Lady of Storms, a demigoddess venerated in Thromm. Sculpted in the form of an angry, wild-haired woman, the statue cast sprays of water from her outstretched hands. "He proclaimed your desire was urgent." Redmane winked at Eskander. "Since this is the Vise's home and he is recently deceased, I presume you require my tracking skills."

The justiciar nodded. "Had you been as astute when I drew that straight, you wouldn't now be in my debt."

Redmane smiled. "That was a memorable wager! Next time will see a different victor."

Deneven raised his graying eyebrows. "You will need a

great deal more practice to forge that boast into truth. Age and experience provide advantages over the enthusiasm of youth. In the meantime, I am more than pleased to continue collecting your markers."

"Some markers are easier to repay than others." Redmane adjusted the bow slung on his shoulder. "If sniffing about is all that's required to settle my account, I will honor your request and consider myself lucky."

"Indeed." Deneven's amusement faded. "Eskander, if you please, I require a moment with my friend."

The cavalryman's eyes flicked to the ranger before he saluted and strode to the front entrance of the villa. Deneven eased himself onto a marble bench that faced the fountain and laid his cane across his lap.

Redmane unslung his bow and leaned it against the bench before sitting next to his friend. He studied diamond-like droplets that arced from the statue's hands while he waited for Deneven to speak.

The justiciar lowered his voice, "What do you know of this matter?"

Redmane relaxed, his grass-green eyes drawn to the scintillating cascade. "Only what everyone else knows. The night before last, a thief broke into the Vise's home, killed him, and kidnapped his daughter. If the wanted placards are to be believed, he is a decent looking curskin. A man named Jarle Jadien goes by the street name of Jars. The reward is substantial."

"But not significant enough for you to take on the hunt yourself?"

Redmane turned his gaze to Deneven. "Since when do I care about money?"

Deneven smiled. "True enough."

"Don't get me wrong; I did think about getting involved. Avaren's a rare beauty. I saw her once—from afar. But even from a distance, she turned my head. Naturally, her predicament called to me."

Deneven's humor evaporated. "Naturally," he scoffed. "Your instinct for heroism has involved you in far graver matters. It may be the death of you yet."

Redmane smirked. "Wise counsel coming from the Dragon of Reyza."

"You haven't answered the question. Why are you not hunting for her?"

"Bad timing, my friend, nothing more and nothing less. I must depart Reyza by dawn tomorrow if I'm to reach the Alderwylde in time for the Festival of Moons." Redmane's fingers brushed stray locks of long auburn hair behind a long-pointed ear. "There is no event more sacred for us Bel'Vandrari."

"Let's not forget the week-long orgies and the wine," Deneven mused.

The Seh'nahiel's laughter was as bright as the sunlight. "You'll not find me complaining."

The creases around Deneven's eyes crinkled as he offered his friend a smile. "There are times I envy you, young man."

Redmane sobered. "You may think me fickle, but my oaths as a ranger of the Fheydian Grove are as unyielding as your loyalty to this city."

Deneven sighed and nodded, "I know, friend. I meant no insult."

"None taken." Redmane's brows furrowed, "What can I do to alleviate your concerns?"

"I have been commissioned by the Thrommish to uncover the sequence of events that led to the death of Tan'os Ensther and to discover the whereabouts of Mejtress Avaren Ensther. I am aware of your political allergies, but surely you recognize the danger Reyza faces. The Thyran fleet is under sail as we speak. I need answers."

Redmane looked over at the cavalryman standing at the villa's entrance. "You don't believe the official version?"

"Suffice it to say that I am keeping an open mind." Deneven's voice grew hushed, "The Chancellery has rushed this investigation and provided me with a lackluster report. I am working mostly from second-hand accounts and instinct; I need something more substantial before I draw any conclusions. All I ask is that you do not speak to anyone regardless of what you discover henceforth."

"I understand, Dennie. You have my confidence and my assurance that before this day is through, you will know what truly happened here."

The Seh'nahiel brought his fingers to his mouth and blew a sharp whistle. Moments later, the ranger's vulk cleared Ca'd'Cel's outer wall as effortlessly as a horse might an ornamental hedge. The muscular beast bounded to her master's side, tongue lolling like a happy pup.

"Hello, Shenn. I see you haven't found better company yet," Deneven mused.

The vulk's eyes blazed with recognition as she sidled up to Deneven. From his vantage at the villa's entrance, Eskander winced when the beast flashed her jagged black fangs and snuffled the old investigator's hand.

Shenn's tail wagged while Redmane scratched her head. "I never claimed she had any sense of refinement. She's direct and eager to please, like the women whose company I enjoy." Redmane's eyes flashed with glee before he grew serious again. "Please, indulge me, I need a few moments alone with Shenn before we enter the villa."

"Of course," Deneven watched the ranger and his companion head out the main gate.

Eskander's eyes widened at the ranger's departure. He approached his superior with quick strides. "He is leaving?"

Deneven remained seated on the marble bench. He grasped his right thigh with both hands and massaged the stiffness from his crippled leg. "Be at ease. Redmane's capricious manner belies his true spirit. I imagine he is circling Ca'd'Cel for signs of entry. That vulk of his has a keen nose, keener than any hound's."

"Frightful creature," bristled Eskander.

"You have no idea."

"What does that mean?"

"Both man and beast are formidable. Only a fool would think Shenn a pet."

Before Eskander could press the conversation further, the Seh'nahiel and his companion reappeared at the gate. "After examining the exterior of the compound, it occurred to me that if I wanted to breach the villa's walls unseen, I'd use the trees. I suspect your thief may have done the same, but there is only one way to find out."

Without breaking stride, Redmane walked to the far side of the garden, where a sprawling elm grew in the corner. As he drew closer to the wall, the ranger's pace quickened to a run. He leapt, grabbed a low branch, and swung upward, scrambling into the gnarled boughs with no more effort than the monkeys in the jungles outside Reyza.

Eskander shook his head. "Were it not for his pointy ears, I would take him for a wildman rather than a Seh'nahiel."

The comment elicited a soft chuckle from Deneven, "He would consider that a compliment."

Redmane twisted through the lush foliage with ease. He stepped on a long jutting limb, placing one foot after the other he traveled farther from the trunk. Shenn jumped and scampered below her master, her excited barks echoing off the stone walls. The Seh'nahiel stopped and called out, "Ho! Deneven!"

The justiciar rose from the bench with a stifled groan. Silently, he cursed his missing leg. His stump seemed to ache only when bad news loomed—which was often. The grizzled veteran leaned heavily on his cane as he limped around the fountain with Eskander by his side. When they reached the tree, they peered up into the branches.

Redmane hung down by his knees. "There are several bent twigs, and the bark is scuffed. Someone slid along this branch very recently," he explained. "I will meet you inside the house, come upstairs to where this balcony is." The tracker gestured to his eager hound. "Shenn, go with Dennie."

The ranger was already in Avaren's bedroom by the time Deneven and the soldier entered. The vulk trailed in after them, broad snout to the floor. Redmane crouched over the dry bloodstain while the beast sniffed. "Who died here?" he asked.

"That is where one of the two assassins—I mean thieves—died," Eskander offered.

The investigator glowered at the cavalryman.

"Assassins?" Redmane rose, watching Shenn circle the gore.

Deneven crossed the room and closed the balcony door. He leaned on his cane as he addressed Redmane, "The official report states that two men broke into the villa to burglarize the estate. The bloodstain belongs to Jars' accomplice."

The Seh'nahiel stroked his chin. "There's at least one tree climber; I will stake my reputation on that. Shenn can follow this man's blood trail if you like."

"The dead can wait for now," Deneven said. "There is a missing young woman who may still be alive. I need to know where she went."

"Understood." Redmane gave a whistle that drew the vulk to rapt attention. He looked around and approached the bed, gesturing for Shenn to follow. The tracker held out a pillow for the beast to sniff, then spoke with firm, clear words, "New target. Track!"

After latching onto the scent, the hound began moving throughout the room in what appeared to be a random circuit. At the door, Shenn paused and lowered her nose to the ground, snuffling in all directions.

"Come on, girl, the freshest scent." Redmane patted the vulk's black scruff.

The animal gave a soft rumble as though confirming the command then locked on a trail. She led the men out of the bedroom and down the hall, back to Tan'os Ensther's room. Shenn sniffed around the threshold, entered, and went straight to the blood-splattered bed. Despite her muscular bulk and monstrous claws, her tread was no louder than a cat's.

"Hold up, girl." Redmane approached his companion. The vulk sat on her haunches and stared up at her master with a frightful, canny intelligence.

Deneven stood inside the doorway and shook his head. The vulk hadn't sniffed near the window where Tan'os' body had purportedly lain, nor had she gone to the man's bloody sword. "Makes no sense," he murmured.

"What do you mean?" asked Eskander.

The justiciar turned to the cavalryman. "Why would Avaren go to her father's bed if Tan'os was already dead by the window?"

"The room was dark. Perhaps she ran to the bed, expecting to find him there," Eskander posited. "Or she could have heard sounds of a struggle and rushed in to find her father leaning on the bed for support. Could she have fled the room or been subdued before Tan'os' ultimate demise?"

"Shenn insists the woman came directly to the bed after leaving her room. She didn't go by the windows, or anywhere else in this chamber." Redmane shrugged. "Shall we continue to trace the lady's steps?"

As though in a daze, Deneven nodded, "Yes, let us see what other mysteries await."

Redmane patted the vulk's shoulder. "Shenn, continue."

The men followed the vulk back out of the bedroom and into the hall. Shenn's nose brought them to the doomed valet's room, where she paused inside the doorway and sniffed around in circles.

"What is it?" Deneven asked.

Redmane folded his arms, braced his back on the door frame, and watched the vulk trot back and forth. "She lost the scent."

"She what?" Eskander blurted.

"Something must have changed," Redmane explained, without taking his eyes off the hound. "Just give her a moment."

"What changed?" Eskander asked his voice tense.

Redmane rolled his eyes. "Perhaps the girl sprouted wings and flew away."

Eskander was about to retort when Shenn barked and trotted past him, back out into the hall. Redmane and Eskander followed the vulk into the servants' stairwell, pausing briefly on the blood-stained landing before continuing down to the first floor.

Lost in thought, the veteran investigator hobbled down the stairs behind them. The vulk paused before a large painting beneath the grand stair and pawed the ground.

"The trail ends here," Redmane said, gesturing to the mythically themed canvas. "I have a silver trade bar that says there's a secret passage here."

"Fool's bet." Deneven declined without humor as he stepped past his friend to examine the ornate frame. "Look for a concealed catch or lever in the woodwork."

The three men took turns, pushing and pulling the carved features along the frame. Frustrated, Deneven scowled and stood back, his knuckles white on the knob of his cane. Redmane joined his friend and watched the soldier continue to poke and prod the heroic figure of Danikos.

Eskander threw up his hands. "Are we to be stymied by a

painting?"

"Ven's black heart, this is nonsense! A woman's life is at risk." Deneven gestured to the soldier. "Cut it."

Eskander hesitated. "Are you certain, Majster D'Neir? This painting must be priceless."

"I have a signed decree from Jarle Rigo Iarris stating that I may proceed as I see fit with this investigation. If the Chancellery of Justice has a problem with property damage, they can hold me accountable. Now cut it!"

The guard drew a dagger and sliced through the canvas along the bottom of the frame, then cut upwards along the edges. Redmane rolled the painting upward as Eskander separated the top side. The removal of the canvas revealed a door with a brass button near the lower corner. Shenn pawed the knob until the door flew open, then bounded into the narrow passage, disappearing from view. Redmane shoved the rolled-up painting into the cavalryman's arms and followed the vulk.

Eskander moved to enter after the ranger, but Deneven stayed him. "I need you up here. Corporal Kesner will return shortly. When he arrives, prevent him from entering the villa grounds until we are finished. He must not see Redmane leave."

"Understood, sir. I will distract him."

"Thank you, Corporal Johar." Deneven watched the young officer depart, grateful that he could trust at least one of his two assistants.

Redmane's voice wafted up from the passage. "Hey, Dennie, you'll want to see this!"

Deneven cursed his aching leg as he struggled down the uneven tunnel. With every painful step, he felt his anxieties over the conflicting evidence grow. The echoing sounds of Shenn's barking could only mean that the vulk had found something. He called out to the ranger, "Did you find Avaren?"

"Alas no, but I do know where she went," came the reply.

Deneven's heart skipped. He was aware of the secret passages that twisted beneath the villas of Reyza. During the war, combatants had used the tunnels for shelter and the element of surprise. But none of the passages he'd ever used proved as spacious or well lit as the cavern beneath the Vise's estate.

Redmane crouched before an open iron gate and lifted a pile of red silk as Deneven approached. "A woman's dressing gown, crimson. Not a lot of blood mostly smears."

"The wearer was wounded?" Deneven asked.

Redmane unfurled the torn robe with outstretched hands. In the bluish light, the gown looked like a bloody phantom. "I don't think so. None of the stains are saturated or centralized. My gut tells me this is someone else's blood." The ranger handed the garment to Deneven, then picked up a black leather hood. "Also, there's this—thief's mask, dyed black, expert stitching. Another trade bar says it belongs to the tree climber."

Deneven took the mask and wondered about the face and the man it had obscured. "Anything else?"

Redmane directed Deneven's attention to the gate. "The key is still in the lock. See those fresh scrapes in the corrosion? Someone opened this door recently." The Seh'nahiel stepped around the bars pointed out a trail on the ground. "According to the story told by the dust and grit, a barefoot person dragged someone through here. Your thief was either incapacitated or dead, as he posed no resistance." The ranger jumped down to the remains of a wooden platform anchored above the churning water. "I believe the girl dragged the man to this spot."

Deneven's peg leg echoed on the tiled floor as he stepped closer to the edge. "Then what?"

The ranger pointed to the crashing waves. "She pushed him in the drink."

"She drowned him?"

Redmane shrugged. "Seems so."

Deneven stared at the foaming surf. Had Avaren somehow overcome the thief and avenged her father? "Where did she go after that?"

"This is going to make your head hurt." Redmane tossed a broken piece of masonry into the sea. "She followed him in."

"What?" Deneven blinked in disbelief. "Why?"

Redmane gave Deneven an apologetic smile. "I can only tell you what happened, not why. All I can say with certainty is that Avaren's trail ends here." Redmane turned his eyes to the sun-dappled harbor. "I am sorry, my friend."

"Could they have hired a boat?"

The ranger pointed to greenish patches of algae. "The seaweed on the side of the cliff is undisturbed and anywhere else where one might moor a boat shows years of disuse. Steadying a boat against the ledge without scraping the sides is impossible in this churn."

"A boat could have been anchored beyond the breakers." Deneven mused, "It isn't too far of a swim."

"That delicate wisp of a girl?" Redmane gave his friend a sympathetic shake of his head. "I doubt the strongest swimmer I know could handle that chop. Then there is the undertow to consider. The current here is considerable. Trying to swim in that water is suicide."

"You're suggesting that Avaren killed herself?"

"I've seen stranger things in my life." Redmane shrugged. "A sound swimmer would be challenged to keep their head above those waves. What chances exist for a disabled man or a grief-stricken noblewoman after a night of horrors? Is it possible? Yes, but I wouldn't wager on it unless she dabbles in magic."

"Agreed. Short of sorcery, jumping into the sea doesn't make any sense. Neither does suicide." Deneven refused to accept that Avaren Ensther was dead. He had met the beautiful young woman a few times. Charming and polite, Avaren comported herself with the utmost charm. In their brief interactions, he had sensed an inner strength and a keen mind. After a lifetime spent assessing people, Deneven was sure the girl was not the type to kill herself, but only the gods knew what had happened to her the night her father died.

Sensing his dismay, Redmane placed a hand on Deneven's shoulder. "I am sorry, Dennie. I wish I could have led you to a better resolution. I suggest checking the harbor by the docks. Their bodies may wash up in due time."

Deneven nodded. "No apology necessary, my friend."

"What now?" the tracker asked.

"Avaren Ensther's trail has grown as cold as her father's corpse." Deneven handed the mask to Redmane. "I still need to discover what happened in the villa. Let's start with the owner of this mask."

Redmane nodded. He held the black leather garment out for

Shenn to sniff. "New target, Track!"

The vulk barked and bolted back up the passage. Redmane and Deneven followed in silence.

*
**

"You are telling me that Jadien's trail is nearly identical to that of Mejtress Ensther?"

Redmane peered through the glass panes of the balcony door at the long elm branch. "Shenn's nose doesn't lie. He climbed down the tree, entered through this door, then followed in the girl's footsteps—or remained by her side—until she pushed him into the ocean. Now we know for certain that Jadien is our tree climber."

Deneven paced. The burning pain in his stump inflamed his frustration. He chewed his bottom lip as he put the pieces together. "Let's investigate his accomplice."

Redmane led the vulk to the pool of dried blood. "New target. Track!"

As the vulk began to follow the scent trail, the ranger grabbed the vanity's stool and set it down before Deneven. "Wait here."

"I don't need pity," Deneven snapped, immediately regretting the outburst.

With a wink, Redmane jogged out of the room. "I'll holler when I need you, old goat," he called out from the hall.

Deneven stewed, formulating several witty retorts which went unsaid when the ranger chased after his beast. The justiciar gritted his teeth and pushed his pain and anger deep down. He couldn't recall the last time he'd walked so much without pause. With a resigned sigh, he set his walking stick on the floor and unstrapped the wooden appendage. Relief washed through him as soon as the polished cup detached from the nub of flesh. He dropped the leg next to the cane and proceeded to rub the pain away.

The young woman's room was a dismal tableau of a life cut short by tragedy. Past the half-closed triptych, Deneven's gaze fell on the bathtub with the fanciful carvings of fish and other sea life. He recalled all that he had learned, unable to dismiss an absurd idea, an old wives' tale spread by idle gossips with wagging tongues. Still, Deneven found comfort in the thought that maybe Avaren was the daughter of a naera.

"Horseshit," Deneven swore. He shook his head like a drunk trying to clear his vision. "A stupid fantasy prompted by pain."

Disappointed with himself for indulging the daydream, Deneven stooped and retrieved his wooden leg. He strapped it back into place with punishing tightness. He was a man of reason and wasn't about to start believing in children's tales.

With his limb secured, the justiciar picked up his cane and hobbled out to the railing that circled the second floor of the villa. He looked down in time to see Redmane and Shenn trailing across the living room.

Deneven called out, "What have you found?"

Redmane stopped and looked up. "The dead thief's trail leads to scene after scene of murder. Judging by the bloodbath both upstairs and downstairs, I doubt anyone lives to tell."

Deneven nodded. "Unfortunately, you are correct. According to the report, he killed the maids, the cook, the house guards, and even a young stable hand. Enlighten me, where did he go in the Vise's room?"

The ranger crossed his arms. "Your mystery man went straight to the bed, then came back out. He didn't walk around or linger. Whatever happened was immediate and final; the bloodstains on the curtains and mattress tell the tale. Give me a little more time, and I will tell you how he infiltrated."

"Before you go, what can you tell me of the blood splattered on the floor of the Vise's room and the disarray?"

Redmane patted Shenn's rump. "Hints at a brawl. Do you want me to take a closer look?"

"Not necessary. Please, continue following the perpetrator's scent."

Deneven leaned on the railing and rubbed his temples. The story unveiled by the evidence bore little semblance to Tsardon's report. The inconsistencies were many: The lack of blood where Tan'os corpse had supposedly lain. That Avaren had gone to Tan'os' bed where all signs pointed to an arterial wound. The fact that the sketch of the dead thief looked nothing like witness accounts. The list went on.

With full access to the home, the duo would have had ample opportunity to steal the goods and escape, yet the villa's strongboxes remained untouched.

"Highly unlikely," Deneven said aloud.

He felt confident that Tsardon had falsified the inquest report and that subsequent efforts to conceal the truth resulted in a sloppy and rushed coverup. The thought chilled him to the bone.

The sound of Shenn's bark snapped Deneven from his reverie. He watched the Seh'nahiel ranger climb the stairs with apprehension. "Have you concluded your circuit?"

Redmane nodded. "Shenn traced the man's scent to a hay pile in the stables. The man could have snuck in a delivery cart and waited until nightfall. Perhaps his first victim was the youngster."

"Wonderful, just wonderful."

"By the look on your face, you are not happy, Dennie."

"Not in the slightest." Deneven pursed his lips and straightened.

Noting Deneven's change of mood, Redmane clapped his friend's shoulder. "I regret that I must now take my leave. The journey ahead requires preparation. Care to join me for a drink before I depart?"

Deneven clasped hands with his friend. "No, thank you. I think I will remain here a while longer. May you enjoy the holiday with your kin."

"May Bel smile upon you and yours." The Seh'nahiel gave his friend a sympathetic smile. "Come the alignment, seek high ground. Stay dry, old goat."

After Redmane's departure, Deneven stared at the living room below and wondered what other plots had gone wrong on the night of the murders. As he turned the evidence over in his mind, he kept coming back to the unlikely partnership. Much to his chagrin, there was only one person in all of Reyza who could elucidate the machinations of thieves and assassins—the Mistress of Rats.

SEH'NAHIEL WINE

Mir'kadi, Tenth of Sund'im, 445 A'A'diel

What remained of the afternoon light had dwindled by the time Jarle removed the dumplings from the flames. The food smelled good, but the charred red kelp was crispy and burnt. Jarle shrugged. If the girl was half as hungry as he was, she would be content with anything resembling a meal.

"Dinner is served!" Jarle called out. "But don't dress up on my behalf. What you wore earlier is perfect."

As night fell, darkness enveloped the fringes of the cave. The bats fled in shrieking clouds, leaving behind the stillness of the jungle and the crackling of the fire. Beyond the circumference of the firelight, the moons shed their pearly luster over the pool.

After what seemed like an eternity, Jarle heard the sound of bare feet. "Hope you're hungry," he said in the direction of the sound.

"Smells delicious," came the reply.

Avaren stepped into view wearing a sheer, wine-hued gown that clung to her curves. Strands of luminous pearls wove through her braided, snow-colored hair and glistened in the firelight. Her eyes shone with a color beyond anything that existed in the natural world, sparkling like dual fire opals in an aqua sea.

Jarle wiped his palms on his breeches and extended a hand, beckoning the woman to sit.

A smile danced on Avaren's lips as she revealed two goblets and a barnacle-encrusted bottle from behind her back. "Here's my contribution to the feast," she said, handing Jarle the bottle.

"Much obliged," Jarle said, unable to tear his eyes away from her.

Avaren sat next to the fire and set the goblets down. "Please, open it."

The soft-spoken demand broke Jarle's reverie. Suddenly, it dawned on him that he was holding a bottle of wine. "How did you—where did you find this?"

"At the bottom of the reef, near a wreck south of Firehill." Avaren smoothed the fabric of her dress. "There is more where that came from."

Jarle's eyes grew wide as he studied the vintage. "Mejtress, do you know what this is?"

Avaren knitted her brows. "Wine?"

"No, not just any wine. Look here." Jarle pointed to a hand-blown mark depicting an eye surrounded by flames. "Sunblood."

Avaren shrugged. "What does it mean?"

Jarle gazed at the bottle with incredulity, hunger temporarily forgotten. "I have only seen two other bottles like this. They sold at auction some five years ago. A merchant by the name Dhalsim purchased them—eccentric man, I am told. He paid a king's ransom. I am no wine expert, but the Sunbloods are not known vintners—at least not traditionally, but"—Jarle pointed to the symbol—"there it is. Someone in that cursed family brewed this."

Avaren crossed her arms. "I imagine someone did brew it, Majster Jadien."

"I know you don't think that highly of me." Jarle eased himself down on the blanket. "Just call me Jarle."

Jarle rolled the neck of the bottle in the heat of the flames until the resin seal grew soft. He produced a small hook from one of his pockets and pushed it down along the inside rim of the opening. When he felt the hook clear the resin topper, he turned it and pulled.

The bottle opened with a pop, suffusing the air with a

provocative bouquet. The scent of summer flowers joined that of opiate smoke, dark cherries, and aged leather. Around them, the shadows shifted, seeming to dance in a sinister rhythm. From the darkness came the sound of tinkling bells and a woman's joyful laughter.

"Did you hear that?" Avaren asked, looking around.

Jarle put the lip of the bottle to his nose and inhaled deeply. The heady scent of the wine and the girl's beauty ensorcelled his senses. "The Sunbloods are known for their sorcery. That's a good tingle. Gods know what daemon breathed life into this wine."

"You are sensitive?" Avaren asked, narrowing her eyes.

Jarle poured the ruby wine into the goblets. "Does that surprise you?"

"I didn't think that cur—"

"Go on, finish your thought," Jarle urged.

Avaren took a deep breath, then spoke, her tone flat. "I didn't think that a curskin could possess such a rare talent. Very few can naturally detect magic; even most blooded mages, cannot."

Jarle offered Avaren a cup. "Had I been born into privilege, I might have been a suitable candidate for the Collegium."

Avaren swished the offered goblet; changed the subject. "To revenge," she toasted, raising her glass.

Jarle was about to drink, then paused. "Never drink to such folly lest you seek to invite death into your life."

Avaren's eyes flared hot. "Death has already entered my life," she snapped.

Jarle's eyes narrowed to slivers. "Let us drink to a turn of fortune for you and yours."

The chalices clinked with a heavy, hollow sound. Avaren and Jarle drank in silence; their thoughts held captive by the vintage's mysterious allure. Every sip banished the chill in the air until their bodies grew warm and their faces flushed. Worries slinked away, replaced by comforting thoughts as they plucked joyous memories from their decanters.

When they drained the first cup, Jarle poured a second round. "Best wine I've ever had," Jarle said, raising the goblet to his lips.

A contented expression brightened Avaren's face. "Blackvin has a similar taste, but it lacks the intensity."

"It's beguiling," Jarle said, "a perfect complement to my cooking." The thief placed two kelp sachets on an oyster shell. He cut the vine that held the packets closed and motioned to the meal with flair. "This evening, I impress you with a fire-grilled galefin and bluespine oyster dumpling wrapped in broadleaf kelp. The contrast of the crispy kelp and the buttery stuffing is delightful. Enjoy."

Avaren chuckled, accepting the dish. "Thank you, Majster Cuisinier."

Jarle placed a hand over his heart and took a slight bow. "Thank you for gathering, esteemed huntress. My stomach is overjoyed."

Avaren unwrapped the dumpling and took a bite. Her eyes opened slightly as the succulent strips of oyster mingled with the tender chunks of steamed fish. The kelp lent the dish texture as well as a subtle spicy flavor. "Not bad," she mused.

Pleased with the girl's reaction, Jarle wolfed down one of the sachets. He chewed fast, moaning with pleasure, then washed down the last bite with a swig of wine. The meal was simple but flavorful. "It's not every day that a man like me gets the opportunity to dine in such a romantic setting with one of the most desirable women in Reyza. Add to that a priceless bottle of Seh'nahiel wine and I dare say this is one of the best evenings of my life."

As soon as Jarle uttered the words, he regretted doing so.

Avaren's face twisted into a scowl and her eyes sparked like hot coals. "I am so pleased that the murder of my family has provided you with one of the best days of your pathetic existence."

Upset that his attempt at humor had been so ill-received, Jarle finished his glass and poured himself another. The girl's words were filled with poison for which he had no antidote. He finished what remained of the second fish dumpling, and drained the goblet in one gulp.

Avaren flinched when Jarle flung the goblet into the pool. "Perhaps I misunderstood what you meant," she quickly said.

Jarle lay on his back and watched the embers swirl into the darkness as the silence between them deepened into a chasm. He felt certain that Avaren would find fault with his person no matter what he said or did.

After a long while, Avaren spoke again, "I shouldn't assume

the worst. Please, accept my apology."

Jarle didn't look at her. "For what it's worth, I am sorry for what happened. I know what it's like to lose a father."

Tears welled-up in Avaren's eyes. "How old were you when you lost yours?"

"I was twelve," Jarle said.

Avaren finished her meal and set the shell plate to one side. She lay down on the blanket beside the thief and propped her head on an elbow. "Tell me about your family."

Jarle crossed his arms under his head and stared up at the jumble of vines that encircled the opening. "My father's name was Tulot. He was a potter; owned a small shop by the docks where he scrounged living making jars, amphorae and the like. He made the mistake of falling in love with one of the serving girls of a well-to-do merchant family. Every time she came for a case of oil jugs, the sun shone a little brighter, or so he once told me. The serving girl's name was Yara. She was Vendraedi with cinnamon skin like mine and hair so dark it shone indigo in the light. Over the course of several months, my father wooed her, until finally, Yara returned his affection. One passionate night became two and three, and so on until Yara became pregnant—with me. When she began to show, she lost her position as a servant and was cast out on the street. My father desired above all else to make my mother his wife, but Yara refused, claiming that she wasn't going to waste her youth and beauty raising a potter's curskin brat."

"She didn't marry him?" asked Avaren.

Jarle shook his head. "No, she didn't. She broke my father's heart through and through. A few days after I was born, my mother abandoned us, leaving my father the task of raising me. Gods know, I nearly died. My father didn't know the first thing about taking care of a baby. Fortunately, some of the neighbors took pity on him and helped my father feed and rear me. My father spent what time he could with me, teaching me how to fish and cook, make pottery, mend my clothes, keep clean. He taught me to love and honor my mother despite the hatred she bore us. My father was a good man. What little honor I have, I owe to him."

"How did he die?" Avaren asked softly.

"When I was ten, the year when you were born, the Three

Sisters aligned and brought with them the floods. My father's workshop washed away, and we were ruined. He started over for my sake, but two years later, he contracted the red fever and passed away. We had no money for a proper funeral, so he was laid to rest at sea. I went to my mother hoping she'd take me in, but she didn't want anything to do with me. From there on in, I was on my own."

"You were so young; how did you survive?" Avaren asked.

"I stole. I fought; slept in a different place every night. I fell in with a bunch of other urchins like me until eventually we were rounded up by a woman who gave us work. It was dangerous work, but she fed us, put a roof over our heads, and taught us how to survive."

"My mother also left me. Her name was Egeria. I never knew her," Avaren admitted.

Jarle turned on his side to face Avaren. "She is one of the legendary naeras like the rumor-mongers say, isn't she?"

Avaren hesitated. "Would that frighten you?"

It was Jarle's turn to pause. "Perhaps."

Avaren searched Jarle's eyes. "You don't strike me as the superstitious kind."

"But alas, I am superstitious, like my father and his father before him." Jarle reached out and caressed a strand of Avaren's pale hair. "What of your mother? Tell me about her."

Avaren met Jarle's eyes. "Haven't you heard? She is a witch who commands the waves, eats sailors' souls, and rains down lightning upon the ships that dare cross her straits."

"Sounds lovely. Is your mother the reason your father forsook the sea?"

A look of sadness crossed Avaren's eyes. "You are too close to the truth for comfort. I am what remains of my father's greatest fear. He didn't speak of my mother much, but I know he was taken to a place beyond the world of mortals and held captive. Once, when he was deep in his cups, he told me that the entire crew of his ship drowned at the hands of creatures like me. Somehow, he managed to survive and escaped with me, a child who was half Bissatiel, half naera. After that, he vowed never to sail again. Fearing that someone might discover my lineage and accuse him of soulbindery, he kept me hidden. Needless to say, my childhood wasn't easy on either of us."

Jarle grazed his knuckles against the smooth skin of Avaren's arm. "I have so many questions; I don't even know where to begin. Did you have tails when you were a baby?"

Avaren nodded. "Until I was eight, I didn't have very good control over my transformations. My body shifted without warning. Sometimes the change lasted a few hours, sometimes days. My father was my sole caretaker in those early years. I had no nursemaids and no playmates and spent most of my childhood behind closed doors splashing in a bathtub. My father never said it, but I knew he begrudged the part of me that was like my mother. When I finally learned to control my abilities, our relationship began to improve. My father purchased Ca'd'Cel for its access to the sea. Suddenly, a whole new world was revealed to me. I feel at home in the ocean, but sadly I can never live there."

"Why not?" Jarle asked.

Avaren shrugged. "I am not like my mother. I have limited control over the change. When I am on land too long, I begin to suffocate and must return to the sea. And after a day or so of being in the water, breathing becomes as difficult as inhaling sand. I wish I knew the cause, but I don't."

Jarle met her eyes. "I think you are remarkable."

Avaren shook her head. "Remarkably cursed, I think."

Jarle leaned back, resting on his elbow. He studied the curve of Avaren's waist where the silk hugged her hips. His stomach dropped, then clenched. A warm fog fell over his mind as he gazed at her. "If beauty is a curse, then I am inclined to agree."

"You are just like the others," Avaren accused.

Jarle shook his head. "I am nothing like the others. They brought you gifts. I stole them."

"True." Avaren smiled.

"Avaren, I know that I offend you, that I stand accused in your mind as the same kind of villain who killed your father, but I am not like him. I gave you my word, and I intend to keep it. I will protect you."

Avaren tucked a lock of her hair behind her ear. "But will you help me?"

"Yes, of course. I can escort you north, to safety. We should be able to reach Thromm in three months along the South Road, faster if we hire a ship."

"No," Avaren said. "There is nothing for me in Thyra except my estranged half-brother who, like my father, will find a way to marry me off."

Deep lines creased Jarle's forehead. "You did not wish to marry, did you?"

Avaren knitted her brows. "Why would I desire to marry the man responsible for my father's death?"

"You honestly believe it was Rigo Iarris who ordered the assassination?"

"Of course, it was Rigo!"

"How do you know?"

Avaren swallowed hard. "The man sent to kill me whispered it in my ear. Rigo wanted me to know that it was he who was sending my soul to the afterlife."

Jarle looked out over the misty water recalling the way Mast had toyed with Avaren. The Mistress of Rats had banished the assassin from Reyza under penalty of death. Mast was a vile man, but faithful to his oaths. Whoever hired him must have offered a vault-full of sequins to convince him to risk a confrontation with the guild mistress. Rigo ordering the murder made more sense than he wished to admit.

"What reason would Rigo have to kill you? Why not simply break off the engagement?" Jarle asked.

Avaren shook her head. "My father was not a kind man. He loved me, yes, but that did not stop him from using me to assert his power. He used people for his own ends, Rigo included. Two months ago, a heated argument took place between Rigo and my father with regards to our betrothal. In a rage, Rigo attacked my father with a dinner knife of all things." Avaren swallowed hard. "My father slammed his elbow into Rigo's face, broke his nose, then drove the knife through the offending hand, pinning Rigo's palm to the table. Rigo's resolve buckled, and he agreed to the marriage, but I'll never forget the hatred that burned in his eyes. My father stepped too far."

Jarle rubbed his eyes. The story that Avaren was spinning went far beyond the public's understanding of Reyzan politics.

Tan'os, it seemed, had far more control over the throne than anyone thought possible. "People have been hanged for less. Were there witnesses?"

"Yes, a few courtiers were present. Rigo ordered the palace guards to arrest my father, but they ignored the order. I think it was the first time Rigo realized he was a regent in name only. After the incident, Rigo began asserting himself. He charged the four guards who disobeyed his orders with treason and had them executed. He then contravened my father's wish to exile a Dessian diplomat and personally removed several long-standing members of the Council."

"I take it the Council was not pleased with Rigo's newfound assertiveness?"

"You don't follow court politics very closely, do you?" Avaren scoffed.

"Rumors and gossip don't particularly interest me unless there's coin to be made."

"Until the matter of our arranged marriage, Rigo was content to indulge his diversions and drain the city's coffers while my father ruled in his stead. Many in the Council, including the Collegium mages, tolerate him for the sake of his title, but don't owe him any loyalty."

"How did your father convince the Council to choose you as the next Jarleina? Surely there were other eligible noblewomen."

Avaren's voice grew quiet. "My father had his means of garnering allegiance."

"Ah, blackmail, deceit, and bribery—the real currency of our esteemed city. Alas, we are both its victims. Know this; the man sent to kill you was one of the most feared men in Ibea. His name was Maél Aodhan, but his street name was Mast. Lord Justiciar D'Neir spent years pursuing him in vain. It's safe to assume that whatever happened between your father and Rigo, was serious indeed. Your betrothed wanted you very dead and spared no expense to achieve it."

"You knew him?"

Jarle hesitated to answer. The less Avaren knew about the Mistress of Rats, the better. "Barely. Years ago, I was hired to deliver the man a letter. I never saw him again until I sank my daggers in his back. I shudder to think whom Rigo could have hired as Mast's second."

"His second? What do you mean?"

"When taking out a contract for someone's life, it is customary to hire not one, but two assassins in case the first assassination attempt fails. If we hadn't fled when we did, Mast's second would have inevitably ended your life."

Avaren looked down, unable to look Jarle in the eye. "If it hadn't been for you, that animal would have killed me."

Jarle reached out and raised Avaren's chin. "If it weren't for you, my head would be on a pike for all to see in Chancellery Square."

Avaren moved closer to Jarle and rested her head on his shoulder. "Do you mind if I stay here tonight?"

Jarle's heart skipped as Avaren's tear-streaked cheek met his skin. In a rush, her emotions filtered through him as though they were his own. He felt her rage and her grief; the edge of her desperation and something more—attraction? The tingling at the back of his throat warned him magic was afoot, but not wishing to shatter their temporary truce, he gently stroked her hair. "Sleep, Avaren. I will watch over you."

BAT SURPRISE

Daimodi, Eleventh of Sund'im, 445 A'A'diel

The summer gardens along Via Elgabarr blurred into a sea of color as the Vise's carriage wound its way to the palace. Inside the carriage, Paulo flashed Avaren a mischievous smile before closing the velvet curtains. He tossed his plumed hat on the upholstered seat and dropped to his knees. The valet slipped his hands under her skirts, grabbed the back of her thighs, and pulled her buttocks forward. "Did you do as I asked?" he said, coaxing her legs apart.

Heat rose to Avaren's cheeks as she ran her fingers through Paulo's hair. The inside of the carriage felt like a brick oven. "You should have seen the look on Dannia's face when I told her I only needed garters."

Paulo bunched Avaren's skirts at her waist to reveal her nakedness. He planted a kiss on her inner thigh and inhaled her musk. "You're so beautiful," he whispered. "I'm going to devour you."

Avaren's heart raced. She draped one leg over his shoulder and teased the bulge in his breeches with a stockinged foot. "I want you to, but only if I can please you in turn."

With a groan, the youth buried his face between her legs and began to lap her honeyed core. Avaren closed her eyes and tossed her head back. Each bump heightened her fear of discovery while every lick brought her closer to a climax. "Paulo," she gasped, "I'm so close. So close..."

Avaren's dreamy susurrations roused the thief from his slumber. Jarle opened his eyes to find the girl curled against his side with a bare thigh draped over his groin, and an arm across his chest.

Jarle closed his eyes then opened them again, half expecting the beauty at his side to vanish in a wisp of mist. Beneath the weight of her leg, his erection felt like an iron ingot in his pants. *Merciful gods.* Avaren was so close he could smell the smoke and brine clinging to her hair. The scent summoned images of her rising naked and dripping from the pool. He imagined what it would feel like to lay claim to all her pale, glistening flesh; to swallow her moans; to hear his name shouted from her beautiful lips.

The impudence was short-lived. Jarle ran a hand through his hair and peered over Avaren's shoulder. Ashes were all that remained of the cooking fire. A dented goblet lay on the sand; its insides stained with the mysterious ruby vintage they had copiously imbibed. Jarle was grateful for the alcohol and the Seh'nahiel witchery trapped in the bottle. They had both deserved pleasant dreams and a good night's rest.

Through the opening, clouds spread like ghostly fingers across a charcoal sky. The morning was damp, and chilly gusts howled through the cavern's hollows like lovelorn specters. Brilliant flashes of lightning preceded angry rumbling, and soon, fat drops of rain began pelting the pool.

Careful not to wake the sleeping girl, Jarle angled free of her embrace and drew the blanket over her. He stood and walked into the pouring rain, gratified by the sobriety brought on by the cold. The raindrops felt like flechettes against his skin as he relieved himself against the wall. With his bladder drained, desire returned with a fury. Looking down between his legs, Jarle shook his head. He was as rigid as a flagpole.

He glanced over his shoulder to ascertain Avaren was still sleeping and slipped into the shadows. He was wanted for the murder of the Vise and the kidnapping of the man's daughter—grave offenses that would cost him his neck—but all he could think about was rutting. The woman made his blood boil and clouded his ability to think.

The thief shoved his pants down with an urgency he hadn't felt since first discovering his cock and handled himself with desperate, hurried strokes. He climaxed with shuddering gasps, his moans drowned by rolling thunder.

The release left him feeling weak and forced him to brace himself against the wall. Each gulp of air felt like a stab to the ribs, but the pain failed to lessen his arousal. He was disappointed to discover that his needs were far from quenched.

*
**

With a lazy stretch and a satisfied yawn, Avaren awoke to the stench of burning hair and roasting meat. Her dreamy smile vanished at the sight of the rainy gusts pelting the pool.

Not far from her, the thief sat by the firepit roasting four unrecognizable black husks on a spit. "Good morning," Jarle greeted.

Avaren grimaced at the charred carcasses and drew the blanket over her shoulders. "What's good about it?" she groused.

Jarle pointed to the fire. "Breakfast is almost ready."

Avaren wrinkled her nose, disgusted by the smell. "What are you cooking?"

"This is"—Jarle looked at the blackened creatures and creased his forehead—"bat surprise?"

Avaren raised her eyebrows. "How in the world did you manage to catch four bats?"

Jarle grinned. "I have good aim."

"What did you do, stone them to death?" Avaren crawled forward for a closer look. The small animals on the coals had been gutted and skewered with green twigs.

"I killed them with my daggers."

Avaren's gaze swept over Jarle's muscled chest before returning to the fire. "Eat one of those, and I'll share some of my raska."

Jarle chuckled. "I'm beginning to suspect that our elegant accommodations come with a cellar."

"A few waterlogged bottles do not a cellar make," Avaren

mused.

"True." Jarle turned the stick in his hand. Bat surprise didn't look appetizing, but the slightest possibility of raska was. He bit into the scorched wing and chewed until his jaw ached. Swallowing, the thief smiled. "It's crispy, tastes just like chicken."

"Liar." Avaren winced.

"You did say, raska, right?" Jarle offered her the skewer. "You sure you don't want some?"

"Gross." Avaren turned her nose up. "It occurs to me bat meat might make a decent fishing lure."

Jarle set the skewer down. "Good thing you owe me a drink, I need one more than ever."

They both started when a bolt of lightning streaked through the blackened sky.

"We should shelter from the storm on the other side of the cave," said Avaren. "The weather's getting worse."

Jarle stood up and began gathering his armor from the dangling roots. The wind had picked up and was blowing a fine mizzle in their direction. "Does this area flood?"

Avaren pointed to the lines of pinkish sediment along the cavern wall. "I've seen the water rise about an armlength here, depends on the tides and the time of year."

Jarle made a sack using the net Avaren had used to catch their meal and piled his armor into it. He slung it over his shoulder and stomped out the fire. "Lead the way."

Avaren gathered her skirts and circled the cavern, careful to avoid the sharp rocks. She slipped between two calcite columns and tapped a ledge above her head as a warning before ducking into the passage.

Jarle followed Avaren into the darkness. The narrow corridor sloped upwards, meandering through the center of a much larger cave system. To the left and right, they passed smaller grottos and plateaus that branched off into the shadows. The only illumination came from areas where the cavern ceiling had collapsed, exposing the cave to the elements. The rocky walls were slate-colored with striations of calcite, dolomite, and quartz. "How long have you been coming here?"

"I found this place a few years ago."

"I am surprised your father allowed you wander so far from the city," Jarle commented.

Thunder rumbled. Lightning lit up the jagged contours of the cave.

Avaren spoke, raising her voice above the howling wind. "After our move to Ca'd'Cel, we rarely spoke of my underwater escapades. For years I came and went as I pleased. But after my sixteenth birthday, everything changed. Once the talk of marriage began, my comings and goings came under scrutiny by chaperones, tutors, and guards. It was unbearable. More than once, I wished I had been born poor and mutt-faced."

At the top of a small ledge, Avaren flattened her back against the stone and slid through a crevice.

Trailing behind her, Jarle stared at her swaying hips. The delicate silk of her dress clung to her curves like a sheet of vellum. Beneath the folds of the fabric, her sculpted buttocks quivered with every step. Jarle adjusted his pants but found no relief. Avaren muddled his senses and made him throb with an ache that threatened his sanity. He couldn't help but feel pity for the poor sods who had wooed her in vain.

"If you still wish it," Jarle offered, "two swift kicks to your face will do the job."

"You are a terrible man," Avaren quipped.

"Maybe so, but I'm incredibly attractive, and I make delicious dumplings—two very endearing qualities," Jarle replied.

"Watch your head."

The warning came too late. The thief smacked his head on a low-hanging outcrop and cursed, "Ahhh f—!" Pursing his lips to stop himself from unleashing a string of curses, he let go of the sack and rubbed his forehead. If he had been watching where he was going, instead of staring at the girl's rear, he wouldn't have broken his skull.

Avaren turned to face him and picked up the bundle. "Are you alright?"

"I deserved that for not paying attention," Jarle said.

"I would have thought a man in your profession would be more graceful," she teased.

Jarle bent down to take the net from her hands and froze as

searing pain shot through his ribs. "As graceful as a three-legged pony," he said, bracing his chest.

Avaren looked into Jarle's eyes. "This is all my fault. I knew you were in pain and asked you to exert yourself."

"I don't regret cooking. We both needed a meal." Jarle leaned on the wall and took a long, deep breath. Avaren's sudden closeness was making everything worse. Did she have any idea what she did to men? "Broken ribs don't mend overnight."

Avaren brought her hand to Jarle's chest and slid her palm over his chest. "You need to rest."

Jarle grabbed the net from her hand and winked. "Thank you for patching me up. Pink is not my color, but the silk wraps help with the pain."

Without further words, they continued on their way through a series of claustrophobic passages before emerging into a natural amphitheater ringed by mineral columns. The hanging stalactites resembled the sharp, toothed maw of a shark. In the gauzy light, Jarle discerned the outlines of half-rotted coffers brimming with treasure.

The thief's eyes shone as he spied the gleam of coins and silverware, strings of pearls, scattered weapons, and carved statuettes. Barnacle-encrusted bottles, tattered gowns, keepsakes, and candelabras were piled high between the stalagmites; swathes of colorful silk hung over a nest of dried kelp. Against one wall, a cascade gushed into a natural basin, creating a shallow pool.

Dazzled by the wealth strewn before him, Jarle let the sack drop, then crouched to pick up a handful of pearl necklaces. His mind raced as he attempted to place a sequin value to the scattered objects. He imagined the bewildered faces of the fences when presented with such opulence. "Where did these riches come from?"

"Shipwrecks." Avaren parted the silk curtains and plopped down on her makeshift bed. "I like pretty, shiny things."

Jarle wiped his face as though to awaken from a lucid dream. He thought back to his youth; to days spent hoisting up fishing nets under an unrelenting sun. "When I was younger, I used to sail out with the dawn fishing crews. Occasionally, we'd trawl a rusted bauble or two in the catch. The men would fight over the scraps like rabid beasts, only to spit thrice and commiserate about their awful luck. 'Wish it Were a Pretty Naera,' they would sing clubbing the fish to death." Jarle's dark eyes sparkled as they met Avaren's. "The irony! Think of the poor souls battling sun and sea for a meager wage never suspecting the precious hoard beneath their oars. Naeras aren't just real, they're crafty too! Are you sure you aren't a figment of my imagination? I feel as though I've died and gone to heaven."

Avaren reclined back and began to sing. Her voice cut through the roar of the storm and the gushing cascade.

> "Amidst white-capped waves, his vessel nears,
> Assuréd horrors of the deep.
> Delightful music to his ears, the siren with a voice so clear.
> Could it be she who tore the ship asunder?
> Naera's daughter, oh, naera's daughter will pull you under."

Switching melodies, she intoned the popular fishing song:

> "Wish it were a pretty naera,
> With shiny, scaly fins,
> Wish it were a pretty naera
> With smooth and pearly skin
> Oh, you pretty, pretty naera
> Don't' drag me out to sea
> Cause I'm a salty sailor
> And my sweetheart waits for me."

Cutting the ditty short, Avaren nodded. "I've heard the tales, read the stories, and know the songs."

From Myrsi's fruity intonations to Gracelynn's modulated vibratos, Jarle had been spoiled by the variety of beautiful voices that graced The Stallion's stage. He thought he had heard the pinnacle of a decent voice box until he listened to the naera sing. She had sung twice, and twice he had been captivated. The woman's voice was unearthly; silvery and smooth, with a dulcet quality that left him breathless. Jarle tossed the necklaces back into the pile. "Your voice is sublime. I've never heard its equal."

"Thank you." Avaren's eyes shifted from bright blue to a midnight shade. She rummaged under the blankets and withdrew a corked ceramic jar. "Care for a drink?"

The thief's lips curled into a grin. Careful not to injure his ribs, Jarle bent down and picked up two dented chalices from the gleaming pile. He rinsed the cups in the waterfall, then joined Avaren on the bed. He handed her a goblet and sat down. "What's a highborn girl like you doing with a jar of raska? This slag will singe the toe hairs off a Logarian bogbeast."

"I've heard that and more," Avaren said, uncorking the jar. "I understand raska turns decent women into nightwalkers."

The pungent scent of honey, burnt cedar and plums seduced Jarle's nose. He extended his cup. "Truly? Tell me more."

Avaren poured a drop of the dark brown liquid into each of the goblets. "I'm certain you are very familiar with such women."

Jarle clinked Avaren's cup and slammed back the shot. As the liquor blazed a fiery trail down to his belly, he was—for a moment—enveloped by the warmth of The Stallion and Marcella's smile. Despite the company of a legendary naera and a cave full of wonders, he missed home.

Avaren's hacking cough snapped Jarle from his reverie. The tears in the girl's eyes revealed her gaffe. She had no experience drinking hard liquor. Jarle took the bottle and poured himself another drink. After pounding it back, he refilled her goblet. "Seems you have quite a way to go before you become one of those women."

Mimicking Jarle, Avaren clinked goblets and drank the liquid in one gulp. "Unholy mother of—." Avaren gritted her teeth and squeezed her eyes shut. Her cheeks blazed beet red. "My stomach's on fire."

"This raska business was your idea," the thief reminded her.

"I admit; I truly wanted to see you gag on that disgusting meal." Avaren wiped her mouth.

Jarle grinned. Each drink eased the pain of his broken ribs. "I hadn't quite noticed that you enjoy torturing me."

Avaren lay back and rested the cup on her stomach. "The Fates are cruel," she said, circling the rim of the glass. "I wished for a different life for so long. I wanted to be free like the serving girls to love, and come and go as I pleased. I lay awake so many nights praying that I wouldn't have to marry Rigo, never once imagining how the gods would end up fulfilling my wish."

Jarle's eyes followed the line of the girl's shapely shoulder down to her slender fingers. "How little you know about the people you envy. The servants you speak of barely have anything to eat. Many live in squalor fearing their masters' whims. Twenty-seven years have taught me that no one is free. Everyone answers to someone."

"I never thought of it that way."

"And why would you?" Jarle shrugged. He poured himself another shot, then set the raska down. "You have led a privileged, sheltered life—a good life. Don't spend too much time courting guilt. It's a useless emotion; a warning sign at best, and a shackle at worst. Your wishes for freedom did not cause the tragedy that befell your house." Jarle chugged back the shot. "Look around you," he said, waving his hand, "there is enough wealth in this room to afford you the future of your choosing."

"Are riches all you care about?"

The thief set down his cup and corked the jar. "I could have remained hidden; allowed the assassin to have his way with you. My pockets were already full."

Avaren frowned. "I didn't mean—"

"Forget it," Jarle said, rolling to his feet.

Avaren sat up and tossed her cup aside. "Jarle," she said, seizing his wrist, "I would like it if you stayed here. There is room for us both on this side of the cave. The soft bedding will help you recover; you'll be warm and dry."

Jarle twisted his arm free of her hold. "What do you want from me?"

"It's all yours," Avaren said. "My jewels; everything here—take it! But please, help me."

"Ven's sake," Jarle snarled, "I already vowed that I would protect you and see you to safety. What more can you desire?"

"Revenge!" she blurted. "I want you to kill Jarle Rigo Iarris!"

Jarle ran his hands through his hair. "Why? So you can continue in your father's footsteps and earn yourself an early grave? Rigo hired Mast. Do you have any idea what that means? You should be dead three times over. Fate is not cruel, lady, she has smiled upon you. By the gods' graces, you are still alive. Take this wealth and make a new life. Let the past be the past."

"Do you think I can do that?" Avaren's eyes blazed. "Everyone I ever cared about is dead. Do you hear me? Dead!!!"

Jarle reined in his temper. "Listen, I know you are angry and grief stricken, but you are not thinking straight. Going back to Reyza and attempting to kill Rigo is madness. I refuse to add regicide to my long list of sins."

Clenching her fists, Avaren stood and faced the thief. "I am going back to Reyza with or without your help."

"All you rich folk are the same, always thinking the world owes you something. Well, guess what, sweetheart, it doesn't." Jarle closed the distance between them until his nose almost touched hers. "I saved your life. You saved mine. The scales are even. I am willing to escort you to your family in Thromm. But from there, you are on your own. If you want vengeance, get it yourself!"

A CURSKIN, A THIEF, AND A LIAR

Daimodi, Eleventh of Sund'im, 445 A'A'diel

Avaren had a vague understanding of the power her supernatural bloodline possessed. Her father had told her tales of her mother, Egeria—a daevilish creature, whose tears could crush a man's will and whose voice commanded the seas. Unlike the naera who had enslaved her father in an elemental world of eternal storms, Avaren had never willingly subverted a man's will.

Summoning all her courage, Avaren wrapped her arms around the thief's shoulders and kissed him. She gasped when the man grabbed her by the hips and pulled her roughly against him. Jarle's arousal pressed hot and urgent into her stomach, and his dark eyes burned with hunger. Moments later, he released her and winced.

The realization that her savior was in pain sent color rushing to Avaren's cheeks. Flustered, she stepped away. "Apologies," she blurted. "I don't know what came over me. I should be helping you get better, not worse."

Exasperated, Jarle adjusted his breeches. His breaths came hard and heavy, and for a moment, he didn't speak. "You have nothing to apologize for," he said, his voice hoarse.

Avaren sat down on the blankets and looked up into the earthy pools of his eyes. "Today I was to wed Rigo. After my coronation as Jarleina, a grand banquet would have taken place in the palace's winter garden. I would have danced and dined beneath garlands of flowers and globes of ever-burning flames. In a different world, I'd like to think that things could have been different. Perhaps Rigo and I could have worked past our differences. My father would still be alive." Avaren stared down at her hands. "Have you ever been in love, Jarle?"

The thief sat down next to her. "Every time I'm in the arms of a beautiful woman."

"You jest." Avaren gripped her knees and watched her knuckles grow white. The man was sitting close to her. All she needed to do was turn, wrap her arms around him, and let her nature run its course. But the brusqueness of his desire had frightened her. Jarle was not like Brath or Paulo or any of the gullible courtiers she had charmed. He was crass, experienced, and intimidating.

Jarle lay back on the blanket and tucked an arm under his head. "I thought I was in love once when I was younger with this girl named Marcella." Jarle smiled. "We grew up together on the streets, helped each other out; covered each other's back." Jarle's smile faded. "But it never went anywhere."

"Why not?" Avaren asked.

"We parted ways. Marcella fell in love with my best friend."

Avaren sighed. "I thought I was in love also."

"Your father's liveryman?"

Avaren's stomach clenched with the thought of Paulo. "Yes, we kept our relationship a secret. No one except my handmaiden knew about us."

"Was she the woman in his bed?" Jarle asked.

Avaren nodded. "Her name was Dannia. I thought she was my friend. When I saw her in Paulo's bed; saw my dress draped on his chair, I felt sick." A lump formed in Avaren's throat. "At that moment, I felt more jealousy and rage than grief from seeing them dead. How is that possible? What kind of person am I?"

Jarle turned to his side and reclined on his elbow. "In one night, you lost your father, your lover, and your friend. Do not judge yourself so harshly."

Avaren wiped away tears. "Paulo and I—we—were close. I thought I was special; that I meant something."

Jarle reached out and squeezed Avaren's shoulder. "You were going to become the wife of a king. How do you think that made your lover feel? He was your father's valet with neither the wealth nor the power to possess you. You were far beyond his reach from the moment he laid eyes on you. If Paulo did have feelings for you, he must have been raging inside. His actions were no different than those of a rabid dog biting the hand that feeds it."

Avaren put her hand to her breast and felt the invisible pull of grief—that cord that forever tied the dead to the living. "You are right. Paulo and I had no future. We both knew it."

Jarle took Avaren's hand in his and stroked the top of her wrist with his thumb. "You have been marked by a tragedy, nipped by frost in the bloom of life, but the horror you have experienced doesn't need to define you."

Jarle's gentle caress sent a flutter rippling down Avaren's belly. The sensation caused her to lose herself in the thousands of raindrops echoing in the cavernous gloom, the gushing of the underground stream, and the tender pressure of their clasped hands. The man's gaze made her feel warm and out of sorts.

Avaren pulled free of Jarle's grasp. "That was very poetic."

Jarle rolled onto his back. "Roughness is all you expect from a man like me. It's a shame I will never be anything more to you than a curskin, a thief, and a liar."

The man was exasperating. "You may be all those things, but you're all I've got."

"Then the situation is grimmer than you thought," Jarle scoffed.

Anger flashed in Avaren's eyes. With a quick motion, she rolled over the rogue and straddled his hips. She dangled her breasts over his face to distract him while her fingers wrapped around the handle of his blade. "You are no better than the filth the fishermen scrape off their feet when they step out of the dockside latrines. But you have your uses."

Jarle strained his buttocks together, forcing his hips up between the girl's spread thighs. He seized her face between his palms. "What might that be?" he growled.

Avaren pulled the dagger free of its sheath and pressed the tip against the thief's belly. "Teach me how to fight—help me avenge my father's death."

Jarle ran his thumbs along the smooth flesh of Avaren's cheeks, then pulled her down into a passionate kiss.

The silky pressure of the thief's tongue dancing with hers threatened to strip her of reason. Desire and fear mingled until one was indistinguishable from the other. For the first time in her life, she felt as though she were drowning. Losing her nerve, Avaren tightened her grip on the weapon and dragged it lower until the flat of the blade pressed against his stomach.

Jarle's breath stifled in his chest. "I will teach you," he gasped.

Avaren ran the tip of the blade over the tight leather of Jarle's breeches, threatening his inflamed loins. "I am my father's daughter. You will find me an astute student."

"Of that, I have no doubt." Jarle kicked up his hips, grabbed Avaren's arm, and tackled her onto the furs. Before the girl could react, he straddled her hips and pinned her wrists above her head. "The first thing you need to learn is never to let a blade get that close. By Ven, do you have any idea what you do to me?"

Avaren winced as Jarle's fingers choked her wrists. She dropped the knife. "Let go of me."

Jarle eased his grip but did not release her. He marveled at her beautiful features as he wedged himself between her thighs. His thumbs grazed her open palms. "Is that what you want?"

Avaren's inexperience loomed over her; her stomach dropped. Rebellion against her father's edicts had fuelled her tryst with Paulo, but over months the flirtation turned into a tumultuous affair that had tested her efforts to remain chaste. Only fear of her father's wrath had prevented surrender to baser desires. Tempered by a lifetime of hardship on the streets, the thief was nothing like her father's valet. Jarle was dangerous and unpredictable— qualities she found thrilling. "I have never slept with a man," she admitted.

Jarle released her wrists and grew serious. "You trust me enough to speak from your heart. Thus, I will speak from mine. I have never slept with a man either."

In spite of her nervousness, or because of it, Avaren burst into laughter. "You are an idiot!"

Jarle gritted his teeth as he rolled to his feet. He winked at her.

"A moment ago, I was a terrible man no better than the filth of dockside latrines. Idiot sounds like a compliment."

Avaren's laughter faded, but levity remained. "Thank you. I needed that."

Jarle picked up his dagger and sheathed it. "You have a beautiful smile," he said, extending his hand. "Ready for your first lesson?"

"Lesson?" Avaren accepted Jarle's hand and stood. She was surprised he could walk, let alone concentrate. "Are you certain you are well-enough to spar?"

Jarle picked up a pair of sandals from among the pile of clothes and tossed them at Avaren's feet. "You'll need shoes."

Avaren slipped her feet into the old leather sandals and laced the straps up her calves. "Very well."

Jarle circled the naera, appraising her strengths. "You are well proportioned and in decent shape. Swimming has conditioned your arms. Judging by the muscles of your left forearm, you've practiced with a sword too cumbersome for your strength—a Thrommish flat blade if I were to guess. If you are serious about learning to fight my way, you have to forget everything you've learned about combat."

Avaren crossed her arms. "Why's that?"

Jarle paused behind Avaren and leaned in close, his voice a whisper against her ear, "Because shadows can't be slain."

When Avaren turned around, the man had disappeared. Her eyes darted to the swaying silks and the reflections on the ceiling before scouring the heaps of treasure. Avaren sensed no unusual noises or movement. "You've made your point," she called out.

Jarle emerged from behind a column and stepped behind the girl without a sound. "Unlike the sword, the poniard is lightweight, quick to draw, and easy to conceal." Jarle unsheathed his blade and presented it to Avaren. "It favors the element of surprise, especially when wielded by an unseen hand."

Avaren grasped the dagger and turned to face Jarle. "I am not unversed in its use."

Jarle raised his eyebrows and beckoned for the girl to attack him. "Show me what you know."

Hot blood rushed through Avaren's temples as her fingers

tightened around the handle. She circled the man, seeking the best angle from which to strike, then lunged for his neck.

Jarle sidestepped the attack, grabbed the girl's wrist, and disarmed her. In one swift movement, he locked her in a chokehold and pressed the tip of the dagger against her kidney. "You have some skill, but little patience," he said, releasing her. "When using a short blade, calculating your attack is essential. Wait for an opening. Misdirection is your ally."

Avaren narrowed her eyes. "Perhaps I will stab you while you sleep?"

A grin danced on Jarle's face as he handed her the blade. "Again."

Avaren attacked as soon as her fingers closed on the handle of the blade. She feigned left, ducked and jabbed forward. When Jarle avoided the thrust, Avaren kicked, aiming for his thigh.

Jarle weaved out of the way. "Well done."

Avaren couldn't believe her eyes. The man was fast. Without a word, she lunged forward and slashed wildly at his midsection.

Jarle used the girl's momentum to send her scrambling into the decrepit coffers. Before Avaren could recover, he stepped behind her and pressed his dagger to her throat. "The dagger is a weapon requiring an intimate connection with your victim." Jarle used the weight of his body to keep the girl unbalanced. "Is that what you desire, Avaren, to be a killer? Was it not enough to have death breathing down your neck? Are you so eager to cross the River of Dust?"

Avaren swung her arm up and elbowed Jarle in the ribs. The man's sharp cry filled her with immense satisfaction. "It is because of my recent experience with death that I wish to learn to fight."

Winded, the thief stumbled back. His face grew pale, contorted by pain. He gripped the girl's shoulder to brace his fall, then dropped to his knees, struggling for breath.

"Gods!" Avaren cried. "Apologies."

Jarle appeased her with a raised hand. "I deserved that," he coughed.

Avaren felt wretched for worsening the man's injury. "No, you didn't. You were trying to help me—you've been trying to help me all along. Forgive me."

With Avaren's help, Jarle hobbled to the furs and lay down. He looked into Avaren's eyes and gave her a weak smile. "Ribs willing, we can resume your training tomorrow. I will teach you how to defend yourself, but I will not make you a killer. You deserve better."

Avaren's breath fluttered in her throat as she bent over the wounded man. "So do you."

Jarle caressed the girl's pale hair. "Can we start over?"

Avaren placed a hand over Jarle's chest, watching him. The man's cinnamon skin reminded her of dark molasses and his eyes of stormy seas. Never in a thousand years would she have considered the curskin commoner as anything but an animal to be feared or tamed, but the attraction she felt for him defied her prejudices. She craved to taste his sensual lips again and feel his hands upon her skin. "Kiss me," she whispered.

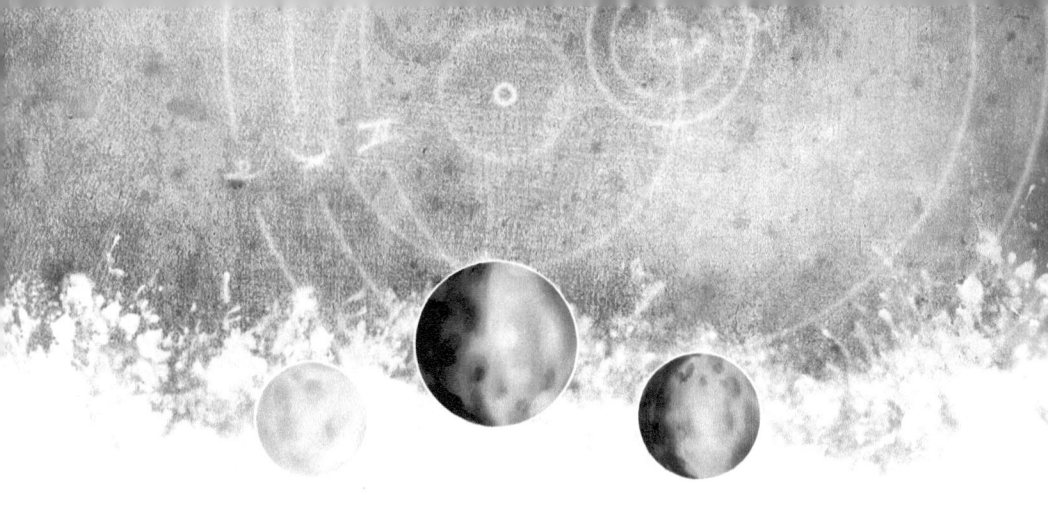

THE NAERA'S EMBRACE

Daimodi, Eleventh of Sund'im, 445 A'A'diel

When Jarle met the soft warmth of Avaren's tongue, a heady thrill quickened his pulse. The breathless, dizzying rush he felt when they had first kissed returned along with the knowledge that he had succumbed to an irresistible attraction.

As the storm raged, the sensual dance of their lips communicated what words could not. Time slipped away as did the morning's downpour. Thunderclouds rolled off into the distance, protesting with roaring grumbles as shafts of brilliant sunlight pierced the openings in the cave.

When the kiss ended, they were both panting and unfocused. Gazing at Avaren, Jarle felt like a supplicant granted the favor of a goddess. The naera's eyes were sphinxlike—suffused with the color of the southern shallows, and her lips swollen from his kisses. Beneath the translucent crimson silk of her dress, the outline of her naked body enticed his touch.

Jarle traced the contour of the girl's ribcage and cupped a firm breast. He teased her stiff nipple with his thumb, praying she wouldn't stop him.

Avaren draped a thigh over his hip and swept her fingers over an old scar on his chest. "How did this happen?"

Jarle swallowed hard. The woman lay so close he could smell her arousal. Her musk, combined with the smoky perfume of her hair, created an intoxicating bouquet that ensorcelled his senses. His breeches caged him in a sweltering prison. "That was"—Jarle searched for words—"a near miss."

"And this one?" Avaren guided her finger lower, to a mark above his hipbone.

In that intimate closeness, Jarle knew Avaren was as aware of him as he was of her. His mouth curled in a mischievous smirk as he smoothed his palm under the fabric of her dress. "Another close call."

A coquettish smile danced on Avaren's face as she tugged the laces at the front of his pants. "How close?" she asked against his lips.

Before Jarle could respond, the girl shoved her hand into his pants and stroked his manhood with a firm caress. The touch sent a rippling thrill through his body and caused his hips to recoil, but as her hand insisted, he thrust into it with barely-controlled lust.

"By all that is holy, do not goad me," Jarle warned, running his fingers through her mane of pale curls. He kissed her cheeks, her chin, the long elegant line of her jaw. "What is it you desire?"

Avaren pulled her hand free and knelt over him. She unhooked the brooch that held the dress together and tossed it into the darkness. The silky fabric slid off her shoulders, revealing her breasts. "I want you," she whispered.

Jarle's hands wandered along her bare arms, before turning inwards to lavish the seductive softness of her flesh. He clasped the underside of the full globes and feasted on her nipples. "Avaren, if we do this, there is no going back."

Avaren reached down and fumbled with the straps of her sandals, all semblance of grace and delicacy lost in her eagerness. "I want to. What about your injuries?"

Jarle laced his arm around her waist and rolled over, taking her with him. The motion sent a stab of pain searing through his ribs. "Consider yourself lucky," he gasped.

"You are certain?" Avaren kicked off her shoes.

Jarle inhaled. The woman was all around him, clouding his judgment and driving him mad. The touch of her skin, the sight of her breasts, her round, naked hips beckoning beneath the silk; made him nauseous with almost adolescent desire. Swooping down, he kissed his way down to her chest. He sucked her taut nipples, groping and massaging her body, before nuzzling down to her groin.

"Never been better," Jarle lied.

With far more gentleness than he felt, Jarle eased the dress down over Avaren's legs. He covered her hips with kisses, following the line of her smooth, glistening thighs. Avaren was as wet and aroused as he'd hoped. The silken skeins of her lust clung to her petal-soft skin—her body's primitive plea for a hard cock to fill her. "Delicious," Jarle said, stroking her velvety folds. "Open your legs; let me please you."

* **

The man's touch was so slight, so alluring that for a moment, Avaren wasn't sure if her strangled cries were of protest or encouragement. All else faded except the tempestuous ache building inside her. "Oh, gods"—Avaren grasped the woolen blanket and arched her hips—"that feels so good."

Jarle stroked her with deliberate slowness. His fingers swam in her slippery heat while avoiding the swollen pearl at her center.

Gazing at him, Avaren realized she no longer cared about her reputation or society's judgments. If pleasure could grant her a moment's reprieve from the grief and rage that consumed her, she welcomed it with her entire being. "Kiss me," she begged.

Jarle hooked an arm under Avaren's back and wedged his hips between her legs. He claimed her mouth with decadent carnality, tasting her in bouts of fervency and savoring licks.

Canting her head, Avaren ran her fingers through Jarle's dark curls and tugged. The slow, deep thrusts of his tongue so perfectly mimicked what she wished would happen between them that she grew unbearably wanton. Arching upward, she crushed her aching breasts against his chest and pulled him closer with feverish need.

Jarle traced the curve of her buttocks, moving with her until his erection pressed thick and threatening against her cunt. His mouth traveled to her jaw, then her ear. "Easy," he purred, caressing her as though calming a skittish mare. "Let me take care of you."

Burning hotter than a raging furnace, Avaren nodded. Her body didn't know the difference between a prince and a criminal. "Please," she begged.

Jarle's lips slid along her throat, sucking and nipping. "Please, what?" he asked, his breath gusting over the pebbled tip of her breast. As he waited for an answer, he tortured her nipple with feathery licks.

The greediness of his warm mouth was a delightful torment. "Touch me. Lick me. Make me not want to care."

Satisfaction burned in the rogue's gaze as he scuttled down to her loins. "Where do you wish to be licked?" he teased.

"You know more than I!" Avaren protested.

"I will soon know what you enjoy better than anyone," Jarle promised in a husky tone. "But for now, I'm still learning. Show me what you desire."

Avaren grasped a handful of his hair and lifted her hips in a flagrant offering. "I want your tongue inside me."

Jarle bared his teeth with a look of such feral pleasure; only a fool would mistake it for a smile. He squeezed her tensed buttocks with an approving groan.

Avaren sensed the humid warmth of his exhale before he made contact with her sweltering cleft. The sound that escaped her was so raw and needy that an embarrassed flush colored her face. But when his mouth covered her vulva, and his cheeks hollowed in a drawing pull, she stopped caring about what desperate sounds she made.

Jarle lashed her clitoris with ruthless skill while his fingers worked in rhythm with her writhing hips. Tilting his head, he licked into the clenching, spasming channel, until he was fucking her fiercely with his tongue.

Enflamed by a climax beyond her wildest imaginings, Avaren's thighs tensed, and her hips bucked with demanding passion. Quivering and gasping, she tried to pull free of Jarle's embrace, but he overpowered her. The man between her legs was surely a daevil from the deepest parts of Hel with an appetite to match.

Jarle plumbed her clenching depths and continued to pleasure her until her toes curled, and her thready moans filled the cavern.

He swallowed her juices, nibbled, and sucked, leaving her weak and trembling. "Please, no more," she pleaded. "Mercy."

Jarle lifted his head with reluctance and wiped his mouth on her inner thigh. He bestowed seductive kisses on her skin and eased her back to sanity with reverent caresses. When she had regained her bearings, he sat back on his haunches and pried apart the rest of the laces. Between his legs, his manhood jutted—proud and thick.

Avaren sucked in a sharp breath as her gaze fell on his magnificent cock. She had expected his body to be uniformly fit, but in this matter, she was at a disadvantage. Her eyes traced the sinuous veins that coursed the rigid length. The man was ragingly aroused, and she wondered if her body could accommodate him.

Cel help her.

"Please, say something," Jarle said gruffly.

Avaren swallowed hard as imagined reprimands filled her mind. Voices from governesses, tutors, and court braggarts joined her father's thundering rebuke of the curskin scourge. Bedding Jarle would debase her, and make her something worse than a whore. She would be unmarriable; shunned by all respectable members of society. She didn't care.

Rebelling against the phantom chorus, Avaren dipped two fingers into her cunt in a lurid invitation. Jarle was a curskin with a dangerous past, a thief, and a killer. Far from frightening her, the observation excited her. "Long have I wished to free myself from the shackles of my virtue."

Jarle's expression darkened into a mask of lust. He pushed his breeches down and crawled over her. "Avaren, you have stolen my sanity. I want you more than I have ever wanted anything. Tell me you want this as much as I do."

"I do." Avaren smoothed her palms over his narrow hips. "I want you inside me."

Jarle hooked the back of Avaren's knee with the crook of his elbow and flattened her leg against her chest. He slipped his hand between their bodies and grasped his cock. Once flush with her entrance, he thrust into her with a hard, decisive stroke.

Thoughts fled. Together, they let out a long, strangled gasp, then grew still.

"You are divine," Jarle confessed.

Avaren gritted her teeth as she endured the splitting sensation in her loins. "You're big," she whimpered.

Jarle released her knee and smoothed back her hair. He kissed her lips and cheeks; as he pushed into her with agonizing slowness. "The pain will pass," he assured.

As though caught in a dream, Avaren watched Jarle's mouth cover one of her nipples. With each slow stroke of his hips, the sting of penetration melted into a dull, quiet ache. She closed her eyes and ran her hands down his back, sensing she had, at last, stumbled into the mystery of her own body. Jarle's skin smelled of sun, salt, and sweat. He was hard and male—everything she didn't know she was missing and urgently craved.

"More," she breathed, her tone ripe with desire. "I need more..."

The man's nostrils flared, and his lips pulled back to reveal his teeth. He gripped the supple globes of her ass and spread her open with his knees. His hips reared then slammed forward, impaling her with bruising strength. "You're so fucking tight," he gritted out. "So damn beautiful."

Eyes locked on his, Avaren moved restlessly beneath him, relishing each punishing thrust of his cock. She moaned and arched, sank her teeth into his shoulder; left a mark.

Jarle placed his hands on the bed and supported his weight as he pumped into her with a frantic rhythm.

Avaren took advantage of the sudden freedom to wrap her legs around him and pull him deeper. Her breath escaped her with a loud cry as he slid inside her to the root. The inexorable fullness made her fear the end of her life was near. Tears welled up in her eyes and spilled over her cheeks as she clung to him, defenseless against the domineering rhythm of his body.

Together they crashed and churned until Jarle could no longer hold back release. He skewered into her with a dozen vicious thrusts, before pulling out with a feral growl.

"A-va-ren!"

Jarle braced himself, gripped his cock, and stroked until his cream spurted on her belly. His back bowed, and his neck arched as a pained ecstasy warred with vulnerability.

Awed by the ferocity of his orgasm, Avaren embraced the trembling thief. When their mouths met, the kiss was soft and indulgent, lacking the fury of moments before. Perspiration and semen sealed their torsos together as they held each other in the dark.

Avaren nibbled Jarle's jaw. "There was a moment when I thought I might die," she confessed.

Jarle cupped her face in his hands and stroked her hair. "I don't have words to express how you've made me feel."

"Is that good?" Avaren asked.

"It's better than wonderful."

Avaren wiped her tears on his skin to further solidify her enchantment. "Thank you for pulling out when you did."

"Believe me when I tell you it wasn't easy." Jarle rolled off of her and lay at her side. The motion ripped an anguished groan from his lips. "I'm a curskin, and you are of noble blood. A child would only complicate our situation." Jarle offered her a smile. "Are you in a lot of pain?"

Avaren bit her lower lip. Her loins yet glowed from the exquisite penetration. "You fared worse than I."

"Curse these ribs."

Avaren propped herself on her elbow and stared at the sticky mess between them. To her surprise, the thief's erection had not waned. His organ was still engorged; smeared with her vestal blood. She opened her mouth to speak, then fell silent, cheeks blazing with embarrassment.

Jarle followed Avaren's gaze, then frowned. He squeezed her thigh with a reassuring caress, then slowly stumbled to his feet. He cast off his boots and took his pants off before staggering to the pile of treasure. He picked up a tattered shirt and walked to the gushing cascade.

Avaren laughed when Jarle flung his head into the frigid water and let out a high-pitched howl. "You are harebrained; you know that?"

Jarle laved his body with the rag, then rinsed it and wrung it out. He swaggered back to the sleeping pallet and flexed his arms. "Certainly, you meant charming."

Avaren's lips curved into a girlish grin. The evenness of the thief's sun-kissed skin betrayed how often he went about without a shirt, while the thickness of his biceps and the roping of his abdominal muscles revealed endless hours of conditioning. Unlike the coddled courtiers and the gluttonous merchants who had wooed her, Jarle exuded power and strength. He was hard like sculpted warm marble, and she wanted him. She yearned to touch him and breathe his scent into her lungs. "Charming is a bit of a stretch," she lied.

Jarle lay down beside her and dabbed her clean with the wet cloth. He took his time, admiring her nakedness. "By the gods, you are perfect."

Avaren caught his wrist. "And aching for you."

Jarle tossed the rag aside and pulled her into his arms. "You are not alone. Let me fill you," he purred, temptation incarnate. "I want to make you come."

"Not yet." Avaren crawled over him like a stalking lioness. She sucked the hard disc of his nipple and smiled. "I should spare you further torments, but I'm afraid I'm heartless."

"Torment me at your peril." Jarle hissed and grabbed her hips with possessive force. "Broken ribs or not, I will pin you down and fuck you as you deserve."

Avaren angled free of his grasp and nibbled her way down his stomach. Pausing shy of his sex, she licked her lips. "You are mine to do with as I wish."

Jarle caught a fistful of Avaren's hair and gazed into her eyes. "Avaren," he breathed, "I am in danger of losing all that has up to this point distinguished me. I've never felt as I do now."

Avaren stilled, eyes blazing. Her breath panted across his skin. "Men always say such things at such times, do they not?"

"Burning Hel! Yes," Jarle said, holding her face in his hands. "Sometimes, we even mean it."

Avaren engulfed the thick crest of his cock, moaning when a salty bead flowed over her tongue. The time had come to demonstrate she wasn't entirely unversed in the art of pleasure.

THE TANGLES

Meldi, Twelfth of Sund'im, 445 A'A'diel

At the northernmost edge of Reyza, the ancient Jungle Gate loomed above the Southern Road like a giant woman squatting to relieve herself. Beneath the splayed pillars, hundreds of people milled about in choreographed chaos. It was the B'hadia, Departure Day, the tumultuous spectacle that kicked-off a perilous two-month journey to distant Dessia.

Brawny stevedores sang a bawdy tune to keep their rhythm as they tossed heavy crates from man to man. The workers stacked the reinforced boxes upon stout, iron-wheeled trade drays that lined the road like miniature fortresses.

Threading through the lines, cursing teamsters guided huge, woolly-coated thrasks. Bred for the arid journey, the mighty beasts chewed their cud as their masters harnessed them to the sturdy, oaken yokes of the caravan wagons.

Among the turmoil, armed men loafed in idle clusters, rubbing the hangover from wine-weary eyes. The guards, glorified sellswords, and would-be-adventurers paid little heed to the preparations. Their commission began when the last crate was secured. Months would pass without the taste of wine or a full night of restful sleep. Until the horn to decamp sounded, the guardsmen savored their last moments of lassitude.

In the shadow of the towering gateway, seasoned traders held sideways conversations while their eyes tracked the movements of their cargo. Talk and gossip helped distract them from darker thoughts of what lay ahead.

Within the hour, the line of wagons would begin a journey of desperate sprints from outpost to outpost through the wastelands of Chaia and Ellaia. On the eastern edge of the savage tribe lands, the trek would transform into a grueling race against the elements and bands of nomadic bandits. Despite precautions, one in nine wagons never arrived at its destination. The wooden skeletons of failure littered The South Road and inspired chilling campfire tales that often began with, 'They headed out late.'

Tired of the veterans' teasing, a nervous young noble with a pale, sweat-slicked face, stood apart from the throng. The novice trader pursed his lips and rested an unsteady hand on the ancient pillar. He appeared on the verge of spilling his breakfast onto the cobbles.

On the far side of the plaza, a street urchin watched the ashen-faced merchant with the compassion of a lion eyeing a gazelle. Glori sucked her teeth with her tongue, seeking to draw out a bit of stray bacon while she waited for an opportunity to rob the man.

The young trader painted the stones with his bile, then wiped the vomit from his mouth with a square of silk. His eyes darted about in embarrassment as the scene drew amused chuckles.

Glori smiled as she snuck behind a rain barrel. She felt neither contempt nor glee over the youth's discomfort. The man's anxiety was justified. Had she been born male, she could have been the one feigning confidence in the shadow of the gate.

Shy of twelve seasons, Glori was as savvy about the B'hadia as any of the graybeards. In another time, before the Fates had shat upon her family, she had lived a life of privilege. Her father, Huago, had been a successful trader and braved the road to Cartuj twice a year to trade olive oil for silk. Every departure, Huago hugged his three daughters before uttering his habitual words. 'After this B'hadia, we will have enough sequins to live the rest of our days in luxury.'

Memories of her father's broken promises fueled Glori's anger.

Luck had abandoned her the day Huago perished, becoming a heap of vulture-picked bones on the dusty plains of Chaia. The death of the family patriarch and the loss of their goods to a raiding party had left Glori's family deep in debt. The creditors had claimed their due with the same mercy the barbarian horsemen had shown her father. Within days, bankers confiscated their modest villa and cast her and her kin out into the street. They salvaged little except the clothes on their backs and a few personal belongings before being shoved out into the cold.

By the week's end, the flesh peddlers who procured fresh meat for the brothels of Gavalene propositioned them with dishonest work. Pride, and morality, they argued, couldn't fill their growling bellies or keep them warm on winter nights. Some nobles, they soon learned, enjoyed debasing the remnants of their former competitors' houses and paid ample sequins for the pleasure. Displaced children always fetched decent coin.

Her eldest sister sold Glori to a despicable establishment where she toiled day and night in the kitchens dreaming of escape. When Glori finally broke free, she ran until her lungs gave out and vowed never to speak to her sisters again.

Few souls endured the streets of Reyza alone, and soon, the homeless girl joined a ragtag bunch of orphaned children. They scraped by with careful thefts and ever-alert senses, but within the year, they found themselves cornered, facing another unsavory proposition.

"Ha!" The memory faded as Glori pushed the stubborn bit of bacon free with the tip of her tongue. She swallowed the piece of meat and grinned, focusing on her mark.

The noble failed to regain his composure. With a sudden lurching gush, he vomited once more unto the cobbles. To calm his nerves, the trader closed his eyes and rested his forehead against his wagon. To Glori's delight, the man began to recite the Dessian alphabet.

The urchin plastered a wide-eyed look of innocence on her grubby face and snuck behind the murmuring young man. The substantial pouch tied to the man's belt promised a bounty of sequins.

Ignoring the acrid stink of vomit, Glori glanced at the lazy guardsmen and the cluster of gossiping traders. Satisfied the men were distracted, she whipped her dagger out from its hidden sheath and severed the loops holding the purse with a well-practiced jerk.

"Mine!" Glori cried as the heavy bag dropped and filled her hand.

The sudden release of weight from his belt roused the noble from his trance. "Stop! Thief!"

"Bye!" Glori's heart pounded with excitement as she dashed off, running as fast as her muddy feet would take her.

Save for some laughter and a few verbal barbs; the workers ignored the nobleman's cry. The hungover caravan guards gripped their weapons and scanned the crowd lest the purse-snatching prove a distraction for a more daring robbery, but otherwise remained grounded.

Squinting against the sun, the girl cut through the sea of people like a minnow among rushes. Ducking the occasional hand that reached out to slow her, Glori sprinted beneath the swaying belly of a thrask. The wooly beast lurched onto its hind legs thwarting the red-faced merchant from mimicking the spritely maneuver. Losing his balance, the man skidded on a steaming pile of droppings.

"Idiot!" Glori goaded.

Cheers and quick wagers rose up as the chase drew attention. Each missed grab and successful dodge elicited excited shouts as the pursuit made its way along the street.

With a gleeful, mocking laugh, Glori bolted into a dingy alley barely wide enough for three people to walk abreast. The plaster walls of timeworn tenements loomed high above the narrow canyon, ensuring sunlight never shone on its filthy cobbles. Halfway down the winding corridor, she slowed and glanced back.

"Balls!" Glori cursed when the gasping noble appeared. She had underestimated the man's endurance.

The urchin clenched her teeth and loosed a shrill, taunting whistle before skipping around a corner into an even tighter passageway. She stood at the end of the alley, smirking as she tossed the purse from hand to hand.

"I'm going to crack your skull, little brat!" The merchant cried, charging headlong into the alleyway. As his hands stretched to seize the pouch, a burly figure emerged from a hidden entryway and slammed the enraged man onto the cobbles.

The young trader lay on his back, stunned. Anger gave way to fear. He scrambled backward like a crab seeking to get away, but rough hands yanked him to his feet.

"Here now, where are you going in such a hurry?" a gruff voice demanded. "You nearly knocked Golias here off his feet."

The outrage on the noble's face provoked peals of derisive laughter from Glori.

"I-I b-beg your pardon?" The nobleman squinted, trying to clear his vision as two thugs, pushed him against the wall. "I was chasing a thief, a boy. He stole my money. Surely you saw him? I will compensate you."

"You see a boy anywhere, Ianto?" Golias flashed a sharp smile at his companion. "This dim-witted buffoon wants us to rat out this poor little girl."

"Let's see what reward he has to offer." Ianto grabbed the terrified merchant with his beefy hands and turned him back and forth. "Nothing of value, except this handsome jacket and his leather boots. Reeks of thrask shit too!"

"You are fortunate, my friend. Today, the toll for leaving the Tangles just so happens to be your coat and boots."

"W-what?" The noble shook his head. "My coin purse contains all I own in the world. Be merciful for the love of Ven."

"You heard him, thimble-dick. Strip!" Knives appeared as false smiles disappeared.

"P-please, don't kill me." Fear of his impending death banished all thoughts of lost wealth. The merchant's fingers trembled as he unfastened the buttons of his coat. He handed the garment to one of the muggers. Shivers shuddered through his lean body as he bent down to remove his boots.

"Thimble-dick? That's giving him too much credit," laughed Golias. "Hurry lest I decide to use you like the woman you are!"

The heaviness of the pilfered pouch distracted Glori from the scene unfolding before her. She couldn't imagine why anyone in their right mind would carry all his trade funds on his person. The bag contained enough sequins to keep her cozy and well-fed for years. She daydreamed of spending the money, debating what to buy first. The thought of giving two-thirds of her prize to sluggards like Ianto and Golias rankled her mood. Granted opportunity, she would hide half of the coins and divide the rest.

The noble tossed his footwear in his attackers' faces before bolting barefoot on the muck that covered the alley.

When Golias gave chase, Glori snuck behind the men and slipped out of view.

"Fucking oaf," Ianto said, picking up the boots.

Golias stopped midway down the passage and laughed, watching the man flee. "That was easy. Now, let's catch the little rat before she swipes our cut."

*
**

Glori wandered through the maze-like twists of the Tangles, smug with self-satisfaction. The thought of bamboozling Golias and Ianto thrilled her. The last time she had tried to cheat them, she had found herself broke and limping for a month. Golias had a temper, but it burned out faster than a lit fart. Ianto was the one who scared her. Many whores wore permanent marks of the enforcer's disfavor.

Quickening her step, Glori threw a nervous glance backward and ran into a man walking in the opposite direction.

"Pardon me, majster," Glori muttered to the grizzled old man. She moved to walk around him but found her way blocked by his cane.

"It is not my habit to pardon thieves." The man's hand shot forward and yanked the stolen purse from the girl's hands. "Not even one as young as you."

Surprise gave way to anger. Glori drew her dagger. "Give that back."

The walking stick snapped sideways, the silver handle striking the urchin's knuckles with a crack. Glori yelped as her weapon clattered on the stones. She stared at the man who dared attack a thief in the Tangles and flicked him a rude gesture. "You'll be sorry you did that."

"Not at all, little spider."

Glori went to step back when the cane swirled, reversed, and hooked her feet out from under her. She tumbled to the ground, staring at the cripple with disbelief. The geezer was insane. Suddenly, Golias and Ianto seemed worthy of their share of the loot. She let loose a shrill whistle.

The old man dangled the purse with idle disdain. He leaned on the cane, grinning down at the urchin. "My gratitude. You have been most helpful."

Glori spat. She could outrun a limping old fool, but there was no way she could abandon the fat haul of sequins. "You are daft."

The walking stick remained motionless as the girl stood. "I've heard worse in my time."

Unsettled by the man's calm demeanor, Glori whistled again. The enforcers were nowhere to be seen. Frustrated, she eyed the dagger lying on the stones.

As though sensing her thoughts, the man flicked the stick with a sharp, precise snap and sent the blade skittering beyond temptation.

Moments later, a gruff shout announced the arrival of Golias. "Hey! What's this nonsense?"

Glori flashed her opponent a smug smile. "You are going to get it now, you stupid gimp."

Ianto stepped up behind the urchin and cuffed her sharply. "What are you doing with this geezer?"

"He stole my—our—money!" Glori snarled, rubbing the back of her head.

"Is that so?" asked Golias.

The thugs drew their knives, then hesitated as recognition flickered across their faces.

"Great Sherzi's tits!" cursed Ianto. "Do you not know who this is?"

"The dimwitted cripple who took my sequins?" Glori eyed her partners as though they were as crazy as the old coot. Something was amiss. The geezer appeared as unruffled as a theatergoer, while the ruffians scanned their surroundings for signs of ambush. Confused, Glori pointed to the stranger. "Who is this mad prick?"

Ianto's voice grew colder than a child's tomb in winter. "The Dragon of Reyza; the great war hero himself."

"This old man?" Glori wrinkled her nose. She found it

impossible to connect the one-legged greybeard with the title of Lord Justiciar. The old-timer appeared more apt at cajoling bartenders for free ale than commanding the Reyzan City Guard.

"Indeed," said the man leaning on his cane. "I am Deneven D'Neir."

"That's the Lord Justiciar?" Glori stepped back so quickly she nearly fell. Her stomach clenched in knots as she searched for a way out of the unexpected mess.

"Not anymore." Golias stood taller, eyes narrowing with hatred. "Now, he is just an old man with a walking stick who bakes for a living."

"I am going to enjoy taking our money back," snarled Ianto.

"I have no more need for this, or you," Deneven said, tossing the purse. The bag bounced off of Glori's chest, scattering the coins on the pavers. Glori dropped to her knees and began pocketing the sequins as fast as her fingers could handle.

"Giving back the money isn't going to save you, old man." Golias gripped his blade tighter, dropping into a fighter's crouch. Ianto flanked him in a similar stance.

"Perhaps not, but this will." Deneven reached into his coat pocket and withdrew a gemmed ring that glinted in the gloomy canyon. He tossed it to Ianto, who caught the sparkling bauble with his free hand.

Golias glanced at his friend. "What is it?"

Ianto's face twisted into a scowl as he sheathed his dagger. He handed the ring to his partner. "It's one of hers. He gets a pass."

Glori gawked at the shiny jewel in Golias' hand. "Whore-shit. That is not her ring."

"Indeed, it is," Deneven said with calm confidence. "I am here to talk to your mistress."

Golias turned the band in his fingers, his cheeks flushing with anger. Turning to Ianto, he snapped, "How many of our brethren has this shit-eating eunuch thrown into the dungeons? I'll be ass-fucked by all three of Jubbal's magic bulls before I give him free passage, let alone escort him to see her. You know what he did to my Pop." Golias tossed the ring at Ianto.

Ianto snatched the jewel with one hand and slapped the back of his friend's head with the other. "Fool; this is her token. You know what she will do if we defy her."

Golias tightened his grip until his knuckles shone white. "So, we have no choice but to take this piece of shit to see her?"

Deneven tapped his cane. "As you have confirmed, that is her ring, and her audience is my demand."

"Yes, we are compelled to comply with our mistress' dictates. We will take you to see her." Ianto placed a restraining hand on the shoulder of his friend. Golias shrugged it off and straightened, stuffing his dagger into its sheath.

Ianto sneered at his partner. "However, she also has rules about escorting such visits, correct, Golias?"

Golias furrowed his brow. "What rules?"

"The rules regarding visitors." Ianto sighed with frustration when Golias failed to grasp the subtlety. "Remember? Secrecy?"

The flash of understanding lit up Golias' eyes. He grinned at Ianto. "I do believe you are right."

Ianto smacked his open palm with his fist. "Favor or not, no outsider is allowed to see the way to her lair."

Golias flashed his rotten teeth. "What a shame we don't have a blindfold or a hood with us. But don't worry, we have a solution." Without warning, the two thugs sprang at Deneven.

"Beat him blind!" shouted Glori.

The Dragon of Reyza was not an exaggerated title bestowed in irony. Enemies, not friends, had granted the former Lord Justiciar the well-earned epithet. Expecting the attack, Deneven spun on his wooden leg and evaded Ianto's grasp. In the same motion, he thrust the tip of his cane into the bulge between Golias' legs.

Golias collapsed with a howl that caused Glori to drop the coins from her hands. All thoughts of money evaporated as the grizzled veteran began to move with the alacrity of a man half his age. The cane swung around in a flashing arc and smashed Ianto's nose, causing an explosion of gore.

Clutching his ruined face, Ianto joined his groaning friend on the ground. Glori stumbled back when the old man turned and looked at her. The reptilian intensity of Deneven's eyes chilled the urchin's blood. They were the eyes of a killer.

"P-please, s-sir, mercy! I will t-take you to her!"

Golias plodded to his feet with a snarl and grabbed Deneven

with both arms. Deneven regarded the thug as though he were an insect. The brass handle of the cane glittered as the justiciar reversed his grip before slamming the metal knob into the left ear of his attacker. Golias slumped to the stones motionless.

Once again, the dead-eyed gaze settled on Glori. The girl's mouth moved, but no words escaped. Fearful that her silence might be mistaken for defiance, the urchin frantically nodded. She would do anything to avoid the Dragon's fury.

To Glori's horror, Ianto kicked Deneven's peg leg out from under him and sent the Dragon sprawling. Time slowed to a crawl as the violent ape began to rain his bloodied fists down on the old man like a frenzied drummer. Still half-dazed, Golias rolled to his knees, ripped the wooden leg from Deneven, and raised it like a club.

Glori dove at the thug's legs and tripped him, sending the wooden leg flying. "Stop it!" she barked. "Stop before you kill him, or the Mistress will hurt us bad."

"Stay out of this, rat!" Golias shoved the urchin and rose to his feet. Murderous rage burned in his eyes as he kicked the unconscious man.

Fearing the worst, Glori threw a handful of coins at Ianto to get his attention. "Ianto!"

"What?" growled the enforcer.

"She will murder us all if we disobey her!" warned Glori.

The fire in Ianto's eyes quelled with the girl's words. He cursed in frustration before rising to prevent Golias from doing more damage. When the ruffian didn't stop, Ianto slapped him. "Enough!"

Slowly, Golias reined in his anger.

"He is out cold," Ianto said, looking down at the one-legged man. "We have done enough; any more and we risk her wrath."

Golias shook his head as though trying to dislodge something from his ear. He picked up the wooden leg and scowled. "Fine. The bitch can have him."

Ianto wiped the blood from his shattered nose before he helped Golias sling the unconscious man over his shoulder.

Golias glared at Glori. "Pick up every fucking coin and meet us at her safe house. Try to fuck us, and we will hurt you worse than we hurt the Dragon."

"You don't scare me," Glori lied, shoving the last handfuls of coins into her pockets.

Ianto spat, then followed Golias into the bowels of the Tangles.

DESSIAN MERCY

Meldi, Twelfth of Sund'im, 445 A'A'diel

The cliff face beneath the palace of Reyza concealed a subterranean network of storerooms, kitchens, and servants' quarters. The lowest levels held the dungeons and a tangle of natural seaside passages that stank of rot and mold. In the earliest days of Reyza, when a fortified tower had stood on the site of the palace, the passages doubled as prisons for the fledgling nation's most hated enemies. Dubbed 'salons' by a long-forgotten jailor, the dismal chambers had remained unchanged for hundreds of years.

Unlike the cells in the upper dungeon, the salons were crude. Each consisted of a barred door and a single window carved into the cliff face to allow a narrow beam of sunlight to filter through. The outer walls were scored with cracks wide enough for seawater to flow with the rise and fall of the tide.

At the center of each cell stood a stout wooden pole with a set of manacles bolted at its apex. The chains were long enough to allow the unfortunate captives to stand upon a wooden rung during low tide with their wrists extended above their heads. When the sea crept in, discomfort turned into a fight for survival. The prisoner was forced to cling to the algae-slick post and keep their head high to avoid drowning until the tides ebbed. Crabs, rats, and other vermin took advantage of the perch. Through the years, many a forlorn soul had chosen a watery death over the fate of a thousand bites.

In the darkness, the wail of a sobbing woman echoed from one of the salons.

"Please," the woman cried, struggling against her bonds. She was soaked to the bone, her clothes ripped to shreds.

"Tell me what you know of this, Jarle, or by the Gods, I will rip out your tongue!" Rigo yelled.

"That would be counterproductive, Sire," Neylen said from the shadows. "Why don't you offer our guest some incentive, perhaps a cold glass of water?"

The woman's feet slipped on the rung. She regained her balance, then looked up from under a bedraggled nest of curls. Her eyes looked from one man to the other, yet failed to focus. "I am so thirsty," she croaked, "please have mercy."

Rigo snapped his fingers to the jailer. The man stepped forward, keys jingling, and took up a pitcher. He poured water into a wooden cup and held it to the woman's trembling lips.

The woman drank heartily, draining the cup in one long gulp. Rigo watched with disgust.

"Give her another," commanded Neylen, "and let us hope it brightens her disposition, else I sense less charitable acts in our future."

The jailer did as he was told. Again, the woman drank, nearly choking as she swallowed.

Rigo looked Neylen squarely in the eye. "You must be referring to your future. The ambassadors from A'diel have arrived, and they have their petticoats in a bunch. I don't suppose you want to explain to them why the price of marble is lower in Reyza than it is in A'diel."

"I defer to your mastery of diplomacy, Sire. It is a matter more suited to one with your skills." Neylen bowed. "Please allow me the menial task of debriefing our guest."

Rigo's voice echoed as he stepped out of the cell. "We will discuss the matter later."

Neylen motioned for the jailer to release the woman from

her bonds. While the brute unfettered the shackles, the Dessian stepped around to face his prisoner. He allowed a genuine smile to light his face. "My apologies, Mejtress Yara. Allow us to begin again on a more proper note." Neylen bowed with a practiced flourish. "I am Lord Neylen J'zab Akkalon of Cartuj."

The woman shivered, rubbing the welts along her arms where the manacles had dug into her flesh. She stumbled backward and slipped on the slick stones. With a thud, she struck the wall. Fresh tears welled up in her eyes as she rubbed the back of her head. "Please," she said, "I don't know anything else. I swear it."

Neylen stepped forward and helped the woman to her feet. He spoke in a soothing tone. "Then you have nothing to fear. Please, do not be afraid. My temper is far cooler than that of our beloved ruler. Indulge me with a moment's conversation before your release."

Yara grew wary. She had experienced naught but misery since she had arrived at the palace. "Conversation?" she asked.

"Only if it pleases you."

The woman nodded, sensing a glimmer of hope. "I want to help, of course. I have never broken the law. I mind my own business, I do."

"I am pleased to hear it," Neylen beamed. His genial tone grew effusive, "Loyalty is well rewarded."

"Thank you for your kindness. Am I free to go now?"

"Certainly! I am sure you wish to be out of those filthy clothes. I shall arrange to have you provided with new attire. Something fine, perhaps, a suitable reward for your cooperation. What is your opinion of Dessian silk?"

Yara ran a hand through her matted hair, pushing it back so she could study her interrogator more closely. "Dessian silk is among the finest in the world, but I live a modest life. Sunlight would be gift enough."

"Nonsense, sunlight is only the beginning of my gratitude for your forthrightness. You shall have both in abundance."

The woman dropped to her knees and wrapped her trembling hands around Neylen's ankles before kissing his muck-encrusted moccasins. "All holy Cel bless you and yours, sir. I have two birds, lovely animals from Naraj. I long to see them."

"Naraj! Have you been there?"

The woman sobbed. The stress of her incarceration, though brief, had made her question whether she would die in the palace dungeons. "No, sir, but I have heard tales of the Black City."

"Oh, it is exquisite! We call it Naraj ne'Doqua e Dessia. It means Naraj, the Jewel of Dessia. There is no city more fabulous in the world. Her obsidian towers put those of A'diel to shame." Neylen paused, looking around the chamber with disgust. "But, this is no place to talk of such magnificence. Come, let us seek sunnier vistas."

Neylen helped the woman stand. He led her out of the cell through a low stone arch and into a hall lit by oil lamps. The woman walked before the Dessian, not knowing where she was being guided. Behind her, Neylen followed. They passed vaulted stone cells. Most were empty, and the occupied ones, silent.

At the end of the hall, Neylen extended his hand, urging the woman to climb a mossy stairway. "Rigo is holding court," Neylen explained. "We cannot have you pass through the halls looking like a pauper. It would cause a scandal. I'm afraid we'll have to exit through the upper dungeons to the back garden."

They climbed several flights before arriving at a landing where Neylen knocked on a barred door with a peculiar rhythm. When it swung open, a gush of fetid air rushed into the stairwell, bearing with it groans and agonized screams.

"My apologies, we are quite full at the moment. I ask that you steel your nerves."

A shiver ran down the woman's back at the sight of the sprawling dungeon. Low stone arches joined thick pillars, creating an arcade that cut through the heart of the dark prison. Smaller passages, each harboring a theater of pain, branched off from the main corridor. The first chamber they passed housed several suspended man-shaped cages, heavy with their sorrowful burdens.

Neylen ushered Yara past the prisoners' outstretched arms, deaf to their pleas for mercy. The dank stench of sweat and feces mingled with smoke and charred meat. "Come, let us not linger here. These sorry wretches do not understand the value of cooperation like you do, dear. Fresh air awaits just ahead, do you see it?" Neylen pointed to the far end of the main corridor, where a jailer stood by a bright doorway. Through the archway, the sun shone bright—a promise of Cel on the far side of Hel.

Yara nodded, squeezing her palms to her ears to block out the screams. She cursed the names Tulot and Jarle a thousand times in her mind. "Yes," she said, "can we go now, please?"

The sound of torment appeared to set Neylen at ease. A beatific smile appeared on his lips as though he were listening to a concerto. He placed a hand on the woman's shoulder and guided her past a series of bloody scenes along their path.

The variety of torments went far beyond expediency; they were the artistic creations of sadistic genius. On a stone bench, a man was slowly pulled apart by hooked chains and pulleys. Not far from the wretch, two women shrieked while their bodies were sewn together.

They paused at the entrance of a vaulted chamber where a man wearing an elaborate gag sat at a table. One of his arms was outstretched and bare, pinned down by bored-looking thugs. A muscular ruffian with hawkish eyes stood across from the prisoner, his intense gaze focused on the man's flesh.

Neylen leaned over to whisper into Yara's ear. "Observe. This technique requires great skill. I have heard this is how the Sullosians fashion gloves for their nobles."

The torturer seized a thin knife and began to slice around the man's exposed forearm. A ribbon of dark red blood spilled onto the grooved tabletop. The man groaned horribly through the leather strap that covered his mouth. Heedless of his victim's cries, the torturer dropped the knife and took up a pair of rusted pincers. As though performing on a stage, the sadist clipped the forceps onto the severed edge of the man's flesh, then yanked, hissing with exertion. The man's skin rolled off his hand with a wet rip followed by muffled screams.

"There!" Neylen clapped his hands as the torturer held up the flayed, dripping skin that quivered like a jellyfish. "Perfection. I warrant that it is fit for the hand of a Sullosian Thurikha."

Yara put a hand to her mouth, holding back the urge to retch. The door was near. She could see the greenery thriving in the golden sunshine. A few more steps and she would be free.

The Dessian blocked her path. "Before we part, there is

something that I would have you clarify."

Yara looked past the man's shoulder to the brilliant sunlight and wrung her hands. Neylen's smug expression worried her. He was savoring her wretchedness with the gusto of a gourmand enjoying an excellent meal. "Yes?"

"You told the jailer that you had not seen your son Jarle in over ten years and didn't know of his whereabouts. Is that correct?"

"Yes, I have not seen my boy since he was very young. I abandoned him to the streets," she admitted. "I don't know where he is, sir, I swear. Last I heard he was in Reyza. Why am I being held? Has my son committed a crime?"

Neylen put his arm around her shoulder and shook his head with feigned shock. "You mean to tell me that no one has told you why you're here?"

Yara trembled like a reed in the wind. "No, sir," she croaked.

"Your son stands accused of murdering esteemed Tan'os Ensther, the Vise, and Savior of Reyza. He is also wanted for theft, rape, and the kidnapping of the Vise's young daughter."

Yara began to sob and dropped to her knees. "Why punish me? He is a stranger to me! I have done nothing wrong."

Neylen looked down at the sobbing woman without pity. "Mejtress Yara, I don't believe you have entirely told me the truth."

"I have told you everything! I have nothing more to say."

"Then kindly explain why an estranged son you haven't seen in a decade provides you with a substantial monthly stipend."

"What?" Yara looked up. Confusion danced in her eyes before a thread of recognition blossomed on her face. "Majster, I—"

"You lied." The Dessian bent down and grabbed the woman's arm, hoisting her to her feet.

Yara took one last look through the open door, realizing that she would never set foot in the palace gardens. She would die in a stagnant hole with no one to mourn her. She shook her head and tried to pry herself free from the Dessian's vise-like grip. "I didn't know the money came from him! Please, you have to believe me."

"In light of this revelation, I think it best we continue our conversation until I am satisfied you have told me everything." Neylen's black eyes shone in the light of the braziers as he led the woman away from the sunlight.

THE MISTRESS OF RATS

Meldi, Twelfth of Sund'im, 445 A'A'diel

Deneven opened his eyes to darkness. A searing line of fire throbbed on the side of his forehead. Every heartbeat thundered against his temples. He would be feeling Ianto's fists for days to come.

A tight roll of cloth cut between his clenched jaw to secure a wad of silk stuffed in his mouth. He was blindfolded and tied to a chair with what felt like leather straps.

The captive justiciar used the only senses that remained unfettered, intent on determining his situation without betraying his return to consciousness. The smell of glowing coals and an undertone of tantalizing spices teased his nose but revealed little of his whereabouts. As the silence deepened, Deneven's stomach dropped. The lack of discomfort in his leg meant his wooden leg was missing.

"You are still a terrible actor." A feminine voice as cold as the breeze from an ice-bound mountain gorge broke the silence.

Despite the long years that had passed since their last conversation, Deneven recognized the voice. He was in the presence of the Mistress of Rats; the woman he'd known during the war as Fhaen.

The woman removed the blindfold from Deneven's eyes. As blurriness gave way to sight, Deneven blinked, barely able to believe his eyes. He was sitting in the candlelit kitchen of a small apartment that he had not set foot in for over twenty-two years. Time had passed, but the cramped room was the same as he remembered it. Memories of a time when things were much simpler flooded his consciousness. The rekindled emotions were far more painful than his bruises.

Across from his chair, flames sputtered inside a ramshackle coal stove. A familiar tea kettle hissed among the glowing embers, a curl of steam wisping from its dented spout. In the far corner, a tallow candle guttered, filling the room with shifting light. The apartment that had once witnessed laughter and the urgent passion of lovers was—in those flickering shadows—nothing more than a museum of broken dreams.

"I see that you haven't forgotten, but don't flatter yourself by thinking that keeping this place had anything to do with nostalgia. Considering the rising prices of villas in this city, it was purely a business decision." Fhaen remained out of view. "Besides, a rat can't have too many hidey holes."

Deneven didn't buy the lie for a moment. He turned his head to catch a glimpse of his hostess. The dancing shadows served their purpose, creating a theatrical milieu that was at once warm and intimidating. The irony of the situation was not lost on him. Fhaen was using his own techniques against him—illuminate the prisoner, obscure the interrogator.

"I would apologize for Golias and Ianto's rough handling, but we both know how much you enjoy that sort of thing." Fhaen placed her hands on the back of his chair. "My instructions were clear should you ever come looking for me, but pride can often supersede reason. Some years back, you jailed poor Golias' father for commercial fraud. He was guilty, but you know how it is between sons and fathers."

Fhaen was near enough that Deneven could smell her fragrance, a heady blend of lush jungle flowers and aromatic herbs. Jacaya! The perfume inspired memories of endless nights spent entangled between the woman's legs. Fhaen still played dirty.

Some things never changed.

Deneven gritted his teeth as his loins stirred. Tied as he was, there was nothing he could do to hide the awkward tension in his pants.

As if sensing his discomfort, Fhaen reached out from behind him and caressed the gash on his scalp. Her touch sent a spasm of hot agony coursing through him, but Deneven refused to give her the pleasure of a groan. The fingers moved away from his wound, and the cord of twisted silk loosened and fell free from between his swollen lips.

Deneven spat out the wad and inhaled. He managed a cavalier tone despite the lightning bolts of pain that blazed behind his eyes. "Your men are weaker than I remember."

"Is this why after nearly twelve seasons of silence, you finally return my ring? To make poor jokes?"

"I am confident that you are aware of my reasons."

"I would hear it from your lips," Fhaen whispered in his ear.

The warmth of Fhaen's exhalation against his skin stirred Deneven's feelings into a bonfire. He inhaled her scent, recalling the long, terrifying night that had prompted two doomed comrades to seek solace in each other's arms.

Five Isles' warships were bombarding the city, and fire was raining down on them. They were wounded and bloody, retreating through the inferno of the Tangles when a building collapsed, blocking their path. Pinned between burning timbers and an advancing army, they had taken shelter in an abandoned tavern. The fateful night had sparked a romance that had burned brightly for two years. Ironically, the love and peace they had found during the war had vanished during peacetime.

Deneven repressed the memories. "I need your help, Fhaen."

Fhaen emerged from the darkness. Midnight-blue Seh'nahiel silk swirled as she stood before Deneven. Time had not diminished her beauty, only matured it like a fine wine. In the dozen years since they had last spoken, Fhaen had changed little save for a few more wrinkles on her honey-colored skin. Her long hair still framed her elegant features, flowing like a gray waterfall over her shoulders.

"Let us forget the last two decades or so and everything that has ever happened between us for one moment. Set aside how many of my people you have jailed and executed. Even with all your accounts settled, kindly explain, why the fuck I would help you?"

"Our past."

Even though he anticipated it, the slap shook Deneven, filling his head with a white flash of pain. His ears rang, and his senses reeled. He closed his eyes against the pain and clenched his bound fists. "That is enough, Fhaen. Hear me out or send me on my way, but untie me. I am not interested in the bedroom games we used to play."

The whispering seductress was gone, replaced by a tigress. "It appears that there is still some fire in the Dragon's belly." Fhaen stood with her hands on the flare of her hips. She bent to examine Deneven's face, prodding his darkening bruises. "Nothing life-threatening, your wounds will heal." The woman finished her examination, arching an eyebrow. "Injury aside, you appear healthy enough. I don't detect any senility in your eyes."

"I don't know if that is a blessing or a curse," Deneven said.

Fhaen leaned closer until her nose almost touched Deneven's. "How dare you come here after all this time and ask me to help you? Our past is nothing to me but a bitter memory. You sacrificed everything we shared for personal glory."

"Even had I foreseen the consequences of my decision to become Lord Justiciar, I would have still pursued that office."

"Exactly. People are expendable, including lovers. So long as your pride gets satisfaction."

Their eyes burned into each other for what seemed like an eternity before Fhaen stepped into the shadows. She returned with a chair, which she set down in front of Deneven. The woman placed her foot between Deneven's legs and withdrew a stiletto from a sheath in her leather boot. She twirled the blade in her hand as she considered her prisoner. "You look like shit."

Deneven eyed the glinting blade. "You are as lovely as ever."

Fhaen settled into the chair with a huff. "I am too old for dancing. Let us cut to the heart of your purpose."

"You are aware of my current employment?"

Fhaen leaned back in her chair, toying with the point of the stiletto with the tip of a finger. "You have been hired by the

Blackspur Ambassador to investigate the Vise's death and find his daughter. I imagine that you have come here to discover why I had the Vise killed and where I have stashed the girl. Is that about right?"

"Almost." Deneven tested his bonds to relieve the tingling in his wrists. "I may be paid from Thrommish coffers, but I still work for Reyza's best interest. What most people don't know is that the Northern Fleet is sailing south as we speak. The result of my independent inquiry has the power to preserve the peace or provoke war. Fhaen, I need answers."

Fhaen slipped the dagger into her boot. "I suspected the Thrommish might sail, but hoped they would not."

Deneven licked his bloodied lips. "Tan'os' methods were harsh, but he was good for Reyza. Under his rule, we enjoyed peace. Trade was never better for everyone, including your so-called Jewelers' Guild."

Fhaen stood up without a word. She turned her back on Deneven to tend the coals under the kettle. "War is not good for my business."

"What do you know of Tan'os' death?"

Fhaen grabbed a poker. She prodded the fire, sending a rush of embers swirling up into the chimney. "I did not sanction the death of Tan'os Ensther. And even if I had, what would you do? Arrest me?"

"Do you prefer to have this discussion in the dungeon?"

"Same old Deneven," Fhaen scoffed. "You speak as though you stand a chance of laying your hands on me again."

Deneven narrowed his eyes. He, too, could play dirty. "As I recall, you rather enjoyed the last time I laid my hands on you."

Fhaen's grip on the fire poker tightened. "Leave our past out of this if you wish to continue this conversation."

Deneven exhaled slowly before changing the subject. "The Thrommish do not believe the official story."

The prodding stopped. Fhaen put the poker down and rose. She walked across the room to a cabinet and withdrew a delicate teacup and a small, octagonal tin. She popped the lid off the tin with a deft twist and threw a pinch of dried herbs into the porcelain cup. "Of course not, what the Chancellery is peddling is absurd."

Deneven watched her fuss with the tea. If she was the same woman from his nostalgic memories, Fhaen was in the midst of internal debate.

Returning to the fireside, Fhaen lifted the boiling kettle from the embers and poured steaming water into the cup. A sour odor with an unsettling thickness filled the room. Fhaen returned to Deneven's side with the teacup in hand. "Drink this; it will help with the pain."

Deneven looked at the brew with consternation. Unstrained, dark leaves swam in the brownish liquid. The aroma stung his eyes.

"Drink." The order was tinged with annoyance as she held the cup to his lips.

Deneven drained the tonic in a long swallow. He imagined that licking a barroom floor at closing time would begin to approximate the brew's awful taste. The foul fluid warmed its way down to his belly, where the heat blossomed much like lamp oil poured on a fire. The brief bloom of heat burned away the pain, leaving a comforting glow in its passing.

Fhaen crossed her arms. "You shouldn't trust me."

"Who says I do?"

Fhaen dropped back into the chair. She crossed her legs and laced her fingers around her knee. "Ask your questions."

"Why do you think the official report is absurd?"

"It doesn't make sense for a single man to be able to sneak into the villa, slay the entire household including a Thrommish war hero, then kidnap the girl past a battalion of Zincari mercenaries."

"Care to tell me how one of your rats wound up as the prime suspect in the Vise's death?" Deneven leaned forward, wincing as his head wound flared, "No burglary or assassination occurs in this city without your knowledge, if not your blessing."

"I cannot tell you why Jars was in the villa that night. What I can say is that Jars is one of the best second-story men I have known. A jewel thief, yes, but not a killer."

"You expect me to believe that one of your best midnighters broke into the Vise's villa without your knowledge?"

Fhaen uncrossed her legs and leaned forward. "I know exactly how I sound, Chief Justiciar D'Neir! Surprise, surprise. The Mistress of Rats is denying any knowledge of the presence of one of her thieves in the Vise's home and the subsequent disappearance of his daughter." Her voice softened as she peered into Deneven's eyes. "You know me, the real me. Age has taken its toll, but the fire within me burns as true as ever. Tell me, am I lying to you?"

Time and tide might have changed her methods and appearance, but within the woman's eyes, the fierce street-fighting girl he'd once loved looked back. Fhaen was right; he knew her well enough to recognize the truth in her eyes. "I am not as talented as you when it comes to calling your bluffs."

"You know I had nothing to do with the Vise's death, or you wouldn't have risked coming here alone." Fhaen's eyes narrowed. "So how about you quit playing Lord Justiciar and ask me what you really want to know?"

Relaxed by the tonic, Deneven exhaled as the burning pain diminished. Like Fhaen, he had grown weary with the verbal sparring. "What type of poison would be described as an oily black sap that smells worse than Esh'fah sauce?"

"Is this a riddle?"

"Humor me."

Fhaen studied the ceiling while she thought. "Sounds like thresherweed oil. Or perhaps forkleaf."

"Which one would work best on a blade?"

"Forkleaf, no doubt there."

"Where might I acquire forkleaf in Reyza?"

"Forkleaf is as rare as a grimmalkin's mercy and complicated to obtain."

"Why is that?"

"Forkleaf only grows on the highest slopes of Blackspur. That alone makes it hazardous to harvest. Then there is the matter of reducing the plants to a usable oil—a very exacting and treacherous process." Fhaen's eyelids closed to slits. "Ah, so that's how the Vise died."

"That is my suspicion," admitted Deneven.

"Then, I can tell you for certain that Jars did not do it."

"For certain?"

"You need to understand something. Forkleaf is one of the most reviled toxins in the underworld. The vindictive substance is known to turn on its handler in a single careless instant. It paralyzes the body and causes excruciating pain. I wouldn't wish such a death even on you." Fhaen swiped a long gray lock from her eyes. "Only the most sadistic or insane assassins dare to handle this poison. Jars would never use it. He's terrified of being poisoned."

Deneven's cheeks felt warm. "How about a pleasant-faced Yerr'draki with a cross-shaped scar on his left cheek?"

Fhaen straightened in her chair, then whispered under her breath, "Maél?"

"What did you say?" Deneven stared at Fhaen.

"Maél," Fhaen repeated. "Maél Aodhan. You knew him as Mast."

Deneven's jaw grew tight. Anger welled inside him like magma within a volcano. "I know full well who Mast is and that he once worked for you. I also know that you exiled him from Reyza. Banished or not, an assassin of Mast's reputation is not hired in a back alley or rum shack like some common cutthroat. You are the Mistress of Rats; the Queen of Shadows. No assassin of his talent could be hired without your knowledge!"

"You are wrong." Fhaen shook her head. "The Vise's death was as much a surprise to me as it was to you. I can assure you that the guilds did not tender Mast's contract."

"That is a wagonload of—"

Fhaen cut Deneven off. "I will say this one final time; I did not authorize nor was I aware of the plot to assassinate Tan'os Ensther. Mast has not been one of mine for over eight years. I banished him from the city, and forbid his return under penalty of death. He is an outsider—a freelancer."

"Why should I believe you?"

Fhaen's eyes flashed. "Do you recall the Antillios family?"

"Of course." Eight years prior, the entire family of one of the richest men in Reyza had been slaughtered. The assassin had forced Lord Antillios to witness the rape of his wife and the butchery of his children before slitting the man's throat. Even for Reyza, where violent death was not uncommon, the murders had been shocking. Deneven had personally led the investigation. "That was Mast's work?"

"The contract was to kill Edgard Antillios only." Fhaen's face grew stony in the candlelight. "I won't pretend I was unaware of

Mast's penchant for violence, but the bloodbath he left behind was depraved. Banishing him was far more than just good business. Murder is a tool, not an amusement." Worry gave Fhaen's eyes the shine of wet glass, "Where is Mast now?"

Deneven knew better than to push for more details. Fhaen's military experience and fierce commitment to her code had enabled the consolidation of various street gangs into a single underworld organization. She reigned over her empire with more professional restraint than the so-called respectable merchant lords who sat around the Council's table. The Mistress of Rats was not one to risk losing control of her hard-won position over the chaotic deeds of a lone wolf. "He's dead," Deneven replied.

"Good. How did he die?"

"I suspect that Jars, your *peaceful* thief, stabbed him in the back. What reason would they have to work together?"

Fhaen pressed her lips together. After a long silence, she answered with a terse, clipped tone. "I do not know."

"Do you know who Mast worked for after you sent him away?"

Fhaen shifted, smoothed her dress. "The last time I had any contact with Mast was to settle accounts. He was in Ehl'ahim. I assumed he went there to be closer to his new clients."

"And who might those clients be?"

Fhaen raised her eyebrow. "You know as well as I do."

"Dessians," Deneven said quietly.

"Yes, Dessians." Fhaen cocked her head. "Do you truly think Ambassador Akkalon's only interest is buggering our beloved ruler? Everyone knows that at the last Council meeting, Tan'os humiliated Neylen, quashing all hopes for a trade treaty with his country. That is who you should be interrogating instead of me."

Deneven's mouth was dry, and his head felt fuzzy. "Supposition is not evidence."

"You will never change, will you?" Fhaen shook her head in disbelief. "How much evidence do you need? Who benefits most from the death of Tan'os and possesses the wealth to make it happen? The guilders of Reyza? Even if they could bring themselves to part with the coin required to hire someone like Mast, they aren't fools. You said it yourself; their coffers overflowed under Thrommish administration. The Seh'nahiel? Everyone knows they share their bed with Thromm. The Calantians are too busy scrabbling over their hereditary plots of dirt. Five Isles? Ha! They shit their pants at the sight of Thrommish pennons. That leaves only one nation on the map with the most to gain."

"Those are my suspicions, but I need proof. I need to know who hired Mast."

"I can't help you there."

"You have eyes and ears everywhere."

"Not anymore." Fhaen's voice grew terse. "My spies have been expiring like flowers in a drought. I suspect there is a mole among my rats and until I ferret them out, I am quite deaf."

"I see. What about Avaren Ensther?"

Fhaen released an exasperated sigh. "I know nothing of the girl or her whereabouts. If someone were holding her for ransom, you would have heard demands by now. She is either in hiding or dead. I would wager upon the latter. Contracts for challenging assassinations are typically issued to multiple assassins to ensure complete success."

"Is there anything else you can tell me about Jars that might help me locate him?"

Fhaen leaned back into her chair. "Tsardon's men have been quite thorough rounding up all of Jars' known acquaintances. Few remain on the streets who know him, fewer still who would willingly acknowledge it. Tsardon even had his mother arrested—a woman who abandoned Jars when he was a boy."

Deneven's brow furrowed. Fhaen's revelation roused the ache in his temples. Proving a Dessian connection would be all the more difficult if Tsardon continued rounding up every possible witness. He had little doubt that confessions would be forthcoming, all swearing to the official version of the events. Deneven felt the odds shifting against him. "Is Jars the type to save a woman from being raped or killed?"

"Jars isn't the type to lose himself in pretty eyes and parted thighs, but he does possess a sense of honor."

Deneven's heart skipped a beat. Could Avaren be in hiding with an accidental protector? Perhaps there was hope for finding the girl alive after all. "If Jars is on the run, do you know where he might go to ground?"

Fhaen gave Deneven an incredulous smirk. "It amazes me how quickly you forget that we are thieves. People like us trust no one, especially with dogs on our trail. We are not in the habit of discussing our safe houses. If we did, they wouldn't be very safe, now would they?"

"I suppose not."

"If Jars is hiding and he has the girl," Fhaen watched Deneven intently as she spoke, "he will not reveal himself until he decides the time is right."

Deneven's eyelids felt heavy. The tonic had done more than eliminate his pain; it had relaxed him more thoroughly than drinking a bottle of potent wine. His gaze wandered to the teacup. "What was in that tea?"

Fhaen settled into the chair across from Deneven. She peered into his eyes and found whatever it was she sought. A satisfied smile curved her lips, "I didn't poison you. But now it is your turn to answer my questions."

"No," Deneven slurred.

"Yes." Her smile disappeared. "Jars Jadien defied me. He broke into the Vise's home without my permission. He may or may not have been working with Mast. Regardless of his reasons, I cannot tolerate insubordination. You of all people know the rot that grows from treason. He must answer to me."

Deneven shook his head, "I can't help you."

"You will," Fhaen reached out to brush Deneven's cheek with a fingertip. "What do you know about that night in the villa. What did you discover?"

The drug's influence was insidious. Deneven wanted to tell her what he knew, and he did. As he blurted all that he had discovered, Fhaen grew more and more impatient. "Yes, yes, you already mentioned that Jars stabbed Mast from behind. You've also told me twice now how the ranger's dog tracked them to the water's edge. Where did Jars go after that?"

A series of knocks sounded at the door to the back stairs of the apartment. Fhaen sighed in frustration. She pulled the gag up and tightened it around Deneven's mouth. "Don't go anywhere."

Deneven blinked as Fhaen opened the door and stepped through. Before the door shut, he caught sight of a leather-clad man with a mask that concealed his nose and mouth. The conversation was quiet enough that Deneven could hear the intonations but not the words. From the sound of it, the news the man was imparting was not making Fhaen happy. Deneven breathed in and out through his nostrils rapidly in an attempt to rouse himself from the drug's effects.

He was distracted when the front door of the apartment opened, and a plump young girl with flaming red hair walked past him as if though were a piece of furniture. Deneven's eyes widened. The pre-adolescent girl was the spitting image of Fhaen, her hair almost as red as an apple.

Deneven watched the girl open a cabinet and take out a loaf of bread. She sliced a piece with a serrated knife before returning it to its place. Next, she took down a large jar and fetched a spoon from a pot of utensils. The girl hummed to herself the way contented children do when they've not a care in the world. She scooped out a wobbling spoonful of jam and spread it on the bread.

When the girl looked at him, Deneven froze as if thunderstruck. The girl's eyes pierced his with an intense clarity that was eerily familiar yet defied recognition. He watched her raise a single finger to her lips as she shushed him.

The tonic's effects strengthened, causing the world to tilt beneath his feet. Deneven struggled to retain focus. The girl took a mouthful and munched happily. The sudden opening of the back door and the reappearance of Fhaen caused both of them to start.

"Yvina!" Fhaen's lips tightened with anger.

"Yes, Momma?"

Momma? The word smashed through Deneven's drug-induced cloud like an avalanche. *When did Fhaen have a daughter?*

Fhaen's eyes flicked to the gag around Deneven's mouth as she grabbed the girl by the wrist and dragged her into the bedroom, slamming the door behind them.

Deneven's heart pounded as he strained to listen. His vision was growing cloudy, and with each blink, his eyelids threatened to remain shut.

Behind the closed door, Fhaen's words were muffled yet audible. "How many times do I need to tell you to stay away from that scoundrel?"

"Glori is not a scoundrel!" The girl protested. "She is nice; she's my friend."

"You listen to me, Yvina," Fhaen snapped. "I pay a daevil's fortune to send you to the academy to learn how to be a proper young lady. I will not have you become another one of my rats. Stay away from Glori. And no more skipping history lessons! Do I make myself clear?"

"Yes, Momma."

"I've had more than enough aggravation this day!" Fhaen's voice strained with frustration, "Stay in this room and practice your letters."

A moment later, the bedroom door snapped open, and Fhaen returned. She sat down and removed the gag. Her eyes glittered as she peered into Deneven's eyes. "Oh, for the love of Ven! Of course, you are going to pass out on me now!"

Deneven fought against the growing compulsion to sleep. It took all of his willpower to bring the question to life, "When did you have a dau—"

The walloping slap to the side of Deneven's head ended the conversation and sent him into blackness.

WHISPERERS

Mir'kadi, Eighteenth of Sund'im, 445 A'A'diel

Rime thickened along the *Swoughünd's* hull until the ship began to list sideways. The cries of her captain pierced the morning fog, sending sailors scampering into the frozen harbor. Men and women rushed to the docks with pickaxes and clubs, ready to free the trapped vessel from the ice.

Ice floes the size of barges washed down from upriver into the channel and buckled upon one another, blocking access to the sea. From somewhere in the mist, Gøran heard the sound of cracking wood. Eight carracks loaded with lumber, precious furs, and ore had fallen prey to the ice.

"Ring the bell, or we'll lose the fleet!" Gøran yelled.

A ruddy-cheeked urchin bolted up the snowdrifts, falling several times before reaching the lookouts' hill. "Ring the bell!" he cried. "Ring the bell!"

Over the roar of splintering wood, groaning ice, and the cries of men, a bell began to peal. It rang twice, paused, then rang twice again. The pattern repeated, piercing the white haze that enveloped the Thrommish port of Thyra. A quarter-hour passed before the first villagers arrived. Bearing clubs, shovels, and pickaxes, they joined the sailors.

"Fight the ice!" he yelled to the motley crew. "Fight!" Armed with a massive hammer, the sea captain joined the fray. He hadn't anticipated a deep freeze for another month and planned to sail to the southern port of Carr at week's end. The weather had different ideas.

More and more people poured onto the docks until the sound of breaking ice became a roar. Somewhere, a giant sheet of ice groaned and shattered, sending half-frozen men fell into the frigid waters. Gøran cursed his luck, beating the hull of his frozen ship with renewed vigor.

The sun rose to the cries and songs of tired men. The first ship to escape the icy prison was the *Erika*. When her hull bobbed up and righted, the force snapped her mizzenmast in two. Suspended by ropes, the mast swung before smashing into the quarterdeck. The nightmarish sound of splintering wood ground Gøran's ears.

"Ymithra's hoary snatch!" Gøran bellowed. "Fetch timbers!"

The cold seeped under Gøran's fur cloak, invading every pocket of warmth, while his cooling sweat soaked his garments. Beneath his heavy mittens, the skin on his hands reddened and chapped. Thyran winters, an old adage told, froze flesh and soul alike.

Gøran toiled alongside his men until late afternoon when the sun dislodged the bulk of the ice. Bleary-eyed and trembling, he sought refuge in his cabin. Upon opening the door, he thanked Cel for the invigorating heat that greeted him, then smiled as the pile of furs on his bed stirred.

"You do not fear being crushed by the frost gods, do you?" Gøran closed the cabin door behind him and shirked his cloak.

A woman twenty years Gøran's junior, with green eyes and olive skin, surfaced bare-breasted from beneath the covers. "Gods do not write men's destinies."

"But women certainly do," said Gøran, his mood growing lighter.

The woman licked her lips suggestively. "Come, find your warmth between my thighs," she invited.

The myriad of wrinkles on Gøran's face crinkled as he smiled, feasting on the goosebumps that raced across Vira's body. The petite Calantian woman had inspired more joy in the last five years than all of his wives combined. The Bissatiel man tossed his mittens and kicked off his boots. In two steps, he crossed his cabin to the foot of the bed and threw the covers over his head. The squeals of the woman filled the room as he closed his cold-chapped hands around her ankles. Gøran pulled her down and was about to pry her legs apart when a heavy knock at his door interrupted their horseplay.

"What?" Gøran growled.

The muffled voice of his first mate came through the door. "Urgent news, Captain. A Whisperer has ridden north from Lyrin."

Gøran eased himself from the pelts and adjusted his breeches before throwing open the door. "A Whisperer, you say?"

The first mate eyed the woman in the captain's bed appreciatively. "Yes, he demands to see you immediately."

Gøran straightened and slicked back his snow-white hair. "Vira, go," he said to the woman.

Vira slipped her feet into her fur boots and wrapped herself in a pelt. She walked past the two men and smiled. "I'll be in the galley, warming my belly with your wine."

"The nerve on that one," mused the first mate.

Gøran's eyes grew grim. "It seems we cannot appease the gods this day. Escort the riders to the chart room."

Gøran closed his cabin door and entered the adjacent chart room. He had heard of the mysterious sect of Seh'nahiel messengers who rode like the wind but had never met a Whisperer in person. Rumor said that they rode fearlessly to their destinations, passing unseen even through the midst of battles. Neither inclement weather nor adverse terrain deterred the elemental spellcasters. Gøran's palms began to sweat as he sat behind his cluttered desk and waited.

The captain stood when a strong wind slammed the door open. Ledgers and maps flew from their shelves. Oil lamps extinguished. Three riders cloaked in crimson, bearing the sigils of A'diel, stepped into the room. Their feet made no sound upon the weathered planks. The wind died down but continued to buffet the riders. Their long hair and cloaks whipped about; caught in an unseen storm.

Two of the riders stood on either side of the door, hands over

the pommel of their blades as a third man moved forward. "You are Captain Gøran Rarikian, Commander of the Northern Fleet of Thyra?"

Gøran straightened to his enormous height. "I am."

The man pushed his hood back to reveal a gaunt, yet hauntingly beautiful face. "I am Anadern Stormsinger, Twelfth Herald of the City of A'diel." Driven by a sudden gust of wind, the door to the chart room slammed shut. "I have ridden north from Lyrin to deliver a message from Ther'oldo Ers, the Blackspur Ambassador in Reyza. Do you accept?"

"Aye." Gøran nodded.

The Whisperer's slim body convulsed as though struck by lightning. The uncanny wind howled and whirled in a supernatural tempest and an inner light shone from the depths of Anadern's sea-green eyes. Through his lips came a distant, disembodied voice. "Captain Rarikian, listen carefully. On the seventh of Sund'im, Tan'os Ensther was murdered along with most of his household staff. His daughter, Avaren Ensther, recently betrothed to Jarle Rigo Iarris, is missing. Jarle Rigo has issued a public decree accusing a local thief by the name of Jarle Jadien of the deed, but I have reason to suspect this information. I will do everything in my power to learn more about this heinous crime and recover Tan'os' daughter. Such news should not be delivered from the lips of a stranger. I leave it to you to inform Strommarch Rhiess Ensther of his father's demise and his step-sister's disappearance. Know that Blackspur has been informed of these events. The Størmman has divested full authority to the Strommarch of Thyra to proceed as he deems necessary. May Cel grant you fair weather."

As the Whisperer uttered the last word, he slumped forward and dropped to his knees. His two protectors rushed to his aid and helped him to his feet. When the wind ebbed to a soothing breeze, Anadern spoke again, "We are sworn to secrecy under penalty of death. Our lips and hearts are sealed. Our protocol requires that I remind you that threatening the life of an A'dielian Herald constitutes an act of war. With your permission, we will take our leave."

A storm brewed behind Gøran's gray eyes as he nodded his consent. "Your reputation precedes you. I don't expect you would take no for an answer."

Though visibly exhausted, a smile blossomed on Anadern's face. "A mere formality, Captain," he said, managing a shallow bow. "May fortune smile upon you."

THE GREAT HALL OF THYRA

Mir'kadi, Eighteenth of Sund'im, 445 A'A'diel

The Great Hall of Thyra was silent save for the crackling of logs in the hearth and the howl of the wind beyond the timbered walls. Two wooly greathounds basked in the heat of the fire, muzzles resting upon their forelegs. The dogs' eyes glittered as they regarded the somber giant who stood before the roaring flames wringing the cold from his fingers.

Gøran drew in a long breath and turned his gaze upward. The fireplace formed the base of a colossal sculpture of the Celestial Tree. The carved flames, draped by basalt roots, represented the forges of the underworld. The tree's gnarled branches stretched upward, supporting hundreds of jade leaves that appeared to rustle in the wavering firelight. An arched niche in the center of the massive trunk housed a statue of Issatiel—the Anvaari whose mythical blood ran in the veins of every Bissatiel. Twice as tall as Gøran and carved from a single block of white marble, the majestic figure thrust his sword toward the heavens. Surrounded by addonels, the divine icon presided over the hall like a vengeful, ruby-eyed god.

Gøran's lips moved in silent prayer; a supplication to the progenitor of the Bissatiel bloodline on behalf of Tan'os Ensther's soul.

"Admiring our artwork, Captain?" came a voice from the shadows.

Gøran turned in the direction of the feminine voice. He pressed his hand to his heart and bowed. "I wish that my purpose were so trivial, Marchess Eva."

A woman with hair the color of rusted iron stepped into the pool of light. She wore a white wolf pelt draped on her shoulders and an ivory gown embroidered with thousands of tiny pearls. Her sinuous body glimmered as she approached Gøran with the elegance befitting a queen. "We do not see you in our hall nearly as much as we'd like these days."

Gøran swept back his hair and straightened his shoulders. "My duty lies with the fleet, my lady."

Eva's dress snaked over the flagstones as she circled him. Her fingertips trailed along his hip. "All these years and the air still grows heavy between us," she whispered. "Why is that, Captain?"

Gøran lowered his gaze and drank in the sight of her beauty. Five years had passed since he'd last seen her, but time had not tempered her allure. Eva was as slim as the moment she had boarded his ship nearly two decades prior. Defiant of the cold that assaulted Thyra's shores, her caramel skin glowed with the promise of southern warmth.

Gøran tore his eyes away lest desire preempt the mournful nature of his visit. He responded to her question with a platitude. "I am forever your humble servant, Marchess."

The warmth of Eva's voice was drowned out by the shrill whistling howls of the arctic wind. "The freeze comes early this season. When do you sail to Carr?"

Gøran gazed into the shadows where ancient tapestries depicting naval battles adorned the cold stone walls. "We sail as soon as the weather permits, though the destination depends on your husband's will."

Eva faced the hearth and held out her delicate, long fingers to the fire. "You have come for Rhiess, I presume?"

Gøran nodded. "Yes, Marchess, I bear urgent news."

At the far end of the cavernous room, a door creaked on its hinges. Rhiess Ensther's voice boomed across the hall, "Gøran, take care with my wife. You know very well of her ability to bewitch us, mere mortals."

Gøran smiled curtly, suddenly wishing he were elsewhere. Rhiess' jest doubled as a warning for past transgressions.

Eva turned to face her husband. The heat of the fire caused a soft blush to blossom on her cheeks. "I think you might be right about my charms, dear husband, for I have convinced Captain Rarikian to dine with us this evening."

Rhiess' heavy riding boots echoed in the empty hall. The shaggy dogs barked and leapt to their master's side. Their tails wagged with such vigor their haunches wobbled. Rhiess paused to rub the scruff of the hounds' necks before extending his arm to the captain in greeting. "Friend, it's been too long."

Gøran relaxed when Rhiess clapped him on the shoulder. "Indeed, Strommarch. I shall be mindful not to allow duty to deprive me of your gracious hospitality."

"Good." Rhiess eyed his wife. "The *Erika* needs repairs, and this blizzard won't break for another day. The men can endure your absence for one night. Dinner it is."

Gøran felt his stomach drop. Eva had cornered him. "You honor me, Strommarch. Thank you."

Eva looked from one man to the other and smiled. "I will leave you to your affairs and see that a grand feast is prepared."

Gøran gave Eva a slight bow. Rhiess kissed her cheek. For a moment, they both watched the redhead as she strolled in the direction of the kitchens.

Geniality faded as soon as Eva closed the door behind her.

Rhiess spoke in a tone that affirmed his authority. "What news? Why have the Whisperers come?"

Gøran met Rhiess' steady gaze. The Strommarch of Thyra was broad-shouldered and tall with icy blue eyes that could bore into a man's marrow. He was every bit Tan'os' son in physical appearance, if not in temperament. Rhiess had a generous heart, and it pained Gøran to cause him grief. "I received grave news from Reyza, my lord."

Rhiess narrowed his eyes. "Has something happened to my father?"

"Tan'os Ensther is dead, my lord. Murdered." Gøran's throat

knotted. "My condolences."

The news drained the color from Rhiess' face and dulled the luster in his eyes. The Strommarch gripped Gøran's upper arm and bent forward as though the wind had been suddenly knocked out of his lungs. After a moment, he inhaled. "Who dispatched the Whisperers? Are you certain we are not being deceived?"

"I am sorry to be the bearer of such news, my lord. The message was sent by Ambassador Ther'oldo Ers."

Rhiess released Gøran's arm and turned toward the fire. He placed a hand on the stone mantle and stared into the flames. As though spurred by Tan'os' vengeful ghost, a burning log cracked and flared, sending sparks swirling into the chimney. One of the hounds responded with a hollow whimper.

Gøran's guilt prevented him from placing a comforting hand on Rhiess' shoulder. His betrayal had tarnished their friendship and made him a stranger in the Great Hall. It didn't matter that Rhiess had forgiven the flagrant affair he'd had with his wife; or that he had raised Eva's firstborn—a bastard—as his own. Rhiess' clemency had only made Gøran feel worse. Were it not for his son; he would have fled Thyra years ago.

"Tell me everything," Rhiess demanded, his voice strained.

Whether from the heat of the fire, guilt, or grief, Gøran felt lightheaded. His coat felt tight, and sweat soaked his woolen trousers. "The message was brief, my lord." Gøran stared up at the avenging figure of Issatiel. The statue's ruby eyes seemed to flicker with divine judgment. "On the seventh of Sund'im Tan'os and the members of his household were slain. Thank Cel, your half-sister, Mejtress Avaren was not among the dead. She is, however, missing. Jarle Rigo Iarris has made it publicly known that your father died in a robbery perpetrated by a local thief by the name of Jarle Jadien."

Rhiess took a step back from the fire and rubbed his face with both hands. A modicum of disbelief crept into his face. "My father's killer is named Jarle?"

Gøran met Rhiess' eyes. "The irony of the fact was not lost. Ambassador Ers claims to have his doubts about the robbery, but he didn't elaborate. He did say that he was investigating the crime and would do his best to find Mejtress Avaren, who, according to the missive, was scheduled to wed Jarle Iarris."

"Aye, I knew of the upcoming wedding. Anything else?" asked Rhiess.

"Ers sent word to the capital. The Størmman of Blackspur has granted you full authority to deal with this situation as you see fit."

"Ers is a good man. He's always been an ally." Rhiess clenched his fists as he tried to hold back tears. "We shall discuss matters this evening after I've had a chance to gather my thoughts."

Gøran cleared his throat quietly, "I am sorry for your loss, my lord. Many will remember Tan'os Ensther as a hero, but I will remember him as more than that. He was like a brother to me."

Rhiess clasped Gøran's hand. "Thank you, Captain."

Without another word, Gøran turned on his heels and vacated the hall. He stepped through the immense doors into the blizzard and left Rhiess Ensther to his grief.

COMMAND OF THE FLEET

Mir'kadi, Eighteenth of Sund'im, 445 A'A'diel

The Strommarch of Thyra sat at the edge of his bed as the Marchess paced. Eva glided through the pools of moonlight that spilled through the blue and yellow honeycomb panes of their bedchamber with ephemeral grace. Her skirts trailed over the flagstones, silent as a shadow. Dyed black with ice beetle wings, the woolen dress she wore hugged her curves as elegantly as the finest silk.

His people believed that the bosom could grieve for eternity beneath diamonds, yet rejoice at the touch of wool. The rich and the poor in Thromm mourned equally—a custom Rhiess admired. Yet despite his woolen attire, his heart remained heavy.

Rhiess mourned his father from a sense of duty rather than loss. Tan'os had shown him little favor as a boy, preferring to dote on his half-sister in later years. He had always lived in his father's shadow, working tirelessly for the interests of a city which recognized only one name: Tan'os Ensther.

Rhiess was not bitter. Whatever shortcomings Tan'os possessed as a parent, he had compensated with a talent for leading men and his passion for commerce. His father had used his position as Vise of Reyza to negotiate favorable trade agreements and treaties that had enabled Thyra to thrive.

As a result of Tan'os' acumen, the Port of Thyra had grown from a forgotten harbor to a burgeoning cultural center. The resultant renaissance had inspired artists, sages, and mathematicians to migrate north and settle in Rhiess' court. Assuming relations with Reyza remained stable, Thyra might one day rise above its backwater reputation and join the ranks of Terranakis and A'diel as a hub of commerce and learning.

Rhiess lifted his eyes and gazed at his wife. The arranged marriage to Eva Iarris had been one of his father's political machinations, but also Tan'os' greatest gift. His love for the petite Vendraedi shone even in the darkest nights.

Rhiess buttoned his cassock. "Tonight, we dine as paupers, poorer for the loss of my father."

Eva stopped pacing. "The only gratitude I owe Tan'os is that he brought us together. Tonight, I mourn only for your loss."

Rhiess smiled a mirthless smile. "By all means, speak your mind, wife."

Eva crossed her arms. "Have I ever done anything other?"

"Never," replied Rhiess. "Your honesty is one of your most endearing qualities. What did you and Gøran speak about today?"

Eva fixed her gaze on her husband. "Don't tell me Gøran still bothers you after all these years?"

Rhiess stood, smoothing the dark sleeves of his vestment. "He would bother me, dear wife, if I thought you still had feelings for him."

Eva motioned to the circular mirror that faced their bed. "Gaze upon yourself in the looking glass and be reassured, husband."

Rhiess stood and faced the mirror. "If it is my good looks and my youth that keep you loyal, I fear I must worry, for both those qualities will fade."

Eva walked behind her husband and wrapped her arms around his waist. "Look at us," she said, peeking around his arm to gaze into the age-spotted glass, "we are not of this world. It has no bearing on us because we are happy. It's true," she said, pressing her cheek against his back, "you were not the first between my legs, but you and my children are the joy of my life."

Rhiess stared into the mirror. His hair was long, nearly as

long as his wife's, and his eyes were of a gray color that changed with the seasons. He and Eva made a handsome pair. He stroked his wife's arm, content in the knowledge that whatever happened between Reyza and Thromm would not diminish the affection between them. "You are wise, my love."

Eva stroked Rhiess' shoulders. "I know that your half-sister is somewhat of a stranger, but I fear for her. Women's lives are fragile in the hands of men. Death can sometimes be a blessing."

"Aye," agreed Rhiess. "Avaren is but a child, not much older than you were when you came here. Regardless of whom my father favored, I do not wish harm upon my sister. Although, after our last encounter, I doubt she will judge me favorably."

"You were angry with your father and lost your temper. The girl must know by now that you are sorry for hurting her feelings. Either way, we cannot alter the past. All we can do is steer the future."

"You are serious about going to Reyza?" asked Rhiess.

"I must." Eva released her husband and walked to the fire. She grabbed an iron poker and stoked the flames. "In my heart, I know Rigo is behind all this. My brother is an arrogant fool who is not beyond trading the welfare of his people to satisfy his foolish pride. If Reyza breaks the treaty with Blackspur, I fear for the whole of Ibea."

Rhiess crossed his arms. "We both know you do not care about the fate of an entire continent, Eva. What are you not saying? Where is that honesty I treasure?"

Embers swirled into the smokestack with each of Eva's thrusts. The flames licked higher, casting their orange light upon the friezes that lined the room. Eternally caught in the throes of a raging, marble ocean, the carved ships flickered in the meager light.

"I don't discuss my childhood for a reason," Eva said, setting the iron back in its stand.

"I believe the time has come for such a conversation," said Rhiess.

"We will be late for dinner."

"Gøran can wait."

Eva relented. "Pour me some ale. With your permission, I will divulge my grievances against your father; Ven save his soul."

Rhiess walked to a console and took up a pitcher of ale. He poured two goblets and handed one to Eva. His wife's truths tended to rip flesh from bone.

Eva took a seat on one of the two chairs that faced the fire. Rhiess joined her.

The firelight danced upon her features as she spoke. "For years, my nightmares have caused you concern. And for years, I have evaded your inquiries. I have withheld the horrors of my past to protect what love remains in your heart for your father."

"Whatever wrongs my father has done me, I have forgiven." Rhiess drank deeply. "He didn't deserve to be murdered."

Eva turned to her husband. "The Fates, like the winds, do not care about what people deserve."

"Speak plainly, wife."

"Yes, of course. Rhiess Ensther despises long-winded intercourse unless he is in bed." Eva set the goblet down. "My mother, Leila Osueldo, was of Calantian stock, the daughter of Iago Osueldo, a man renowned for his temper. At the age of fourteen, she married my father, Jarle Draos Iarris, a man she had never met. She married him because it was her duty, but eventually grew to love him, or so she once told me. My early childhood was peaceful; happy even. Children are so often oblivious to the turmoil of the world." Eva sighed. "My parents sheltered my sister and me from the trouble in their marriage. We knew nothing of the gossip at court; my father's string of mistresses, or the heated arguments that raged behind closed doors. But as I grew up, the cracks in the veneer of my familial portrait, became harder and harder to conceal."

Eva crossed her legs and relaxed into the chair. "I remember the first time I met your father. Neesa and I were spinning tops in the ballroom when we were startled by one of the hunting hounds. We screamed and ran. We bolted into the corridor, straight into your father's boots."

Rhiess nursed his drink. "When I was young, my father seemed larger than life."

Eva nodded. "We were awestruck. My sister and I had never seen a Bissatiel man before. We fell back wondering if we had just met one of the legendary Sigrün. Your father bent down and held his hand out. 'Godagg lasses,' he said. It was one of the only times I saw Tan'os Ensther smile."

"Tan'os Ensther was never one for humor," agreed Rhiess.

"I didn't see him much after that. Whatever dealings Tan'os had with my father went on in the war room or in the royal study; places my sister and I were not allowed to enter. Tan'os rarely joined our family for dinner or private affairs. Your father always remained an outsider; my parents never trusted him."

"I never assumed that my father was well-liked. Reyza needed his ships to win a war. Everyone knows that it was convenience, not love, that forged the bond between our nations," Rhiess said.

Eva took up the goblet and sipped the Zherrian ale. She stared into the flames, allowing the silence to deepen before continuing. "On the eve of my tenth birthday, I snuck out of my room. As was my habit on cold nights, I crept to Mama's bedchamber. As I approached, I realized that my mother was not alone. Father was in her chambers; yelling. The argument concerned Lady Reanne Badradeis, one of my mother's handmaidens. Reanne was my mother's third cousin. She had come from a smallholding near Mencello to live at court. Five years my senior, she was buxom and beautiful—gifted with a bright disposition. Reanne had caught my father's fancy, and my mother was enraged. I think Mama would have tolerated the whole affair if it had proved fugacious like the others, but it was not so. Reanne was different."

Rhiess shifted in his seat. "I am sorry to say, but this is not that uncommon. Rulers often favor mistresses over wives."

"There is more to it than mere infidelity," Eva snapped. "My mother was young, and after two daughters, all of Reyza expected news of a son. The birth of my sister, Neesa, left my mother barren—a condition that was kept a secret from both court and Council. Mother's inability to bear children vexed my father and fueled his indiscretions. He wanted to punish her for shaming him."

Rhiess raised his eyebrows. As far as anyone knew, Rigo Iarris was the legitimate son of the late Jarleina. Suspecting the worst, he asked, "What did you overhear that night?"

Eva drained her cup in one swallow. "Reanne had conceived a

child—a boy according to the midwives. Naturally, my father was overjoyed. At long last, Reyza would have a male heir. Instead of banishing his mistress as my mother had begged, he pressured my mother to accept Reanne's child as her own."

Eva's knuckles whitened around her cup, but her voice remained cool. "You may think this was a reasonable request, but you didn't know my mother. The argument boiled over. Things were thrown and smashed. I couldn't see what was happening, but I heard every word. That night, Jarle Draos Iarris beat his wife and threatened to kill her if she didn't do his bidding. He warned that if she so much as touched a hair on Reanne's head, he would brand her with hot irons. Through enraged sobs, my mother pleaded for my future, claiming I was the rightful heir of the throne. My father was unmoved." Eva stroked her forehead. "Rhiess, when I heard my father curse the day my sister and I were born, my world shattered. Until that moment, I had believed he loved us."

Rhiess' heart ached for the sadness and anger that burned in his wife's bosom. He wanted to pull Eva into his arms and embrace her, but he refrained. "Did you tell anyone about what you overheard?"

Eva shook her head. "No. I was too young to understand what I had witnessed. All I knew was that my mother had changed. She withdrew from everyone, including me." Eva closed her eyes and took a deep breath. When she opened them again, they were glossed over with despair. "My mother's beautiful hair grew brittle and fell out in clumps when I combed it. She lost weight. Dark circles appeared under her eyes."

Rhiess placed a hand on Eva's knee. "I am sorry, Eva."

Eva offered Rhiess a small smile. "It didn't take long for my mother to disobey Father's wishes. Reanne grew bold with the brat in her belly and didn't miss an opportunity to salt my mother's wounds. One evening while we were embroidering, Reanne began to mock my mother's inability to bear children. Mother remained silent during the ordeal; didn't even miss a stitch. When Reanne finished deriding her, Mother asked her to fetch wine. With feigned clumsiness, the upstart spilled it on my mother's lacework. Mother snatched the silver ewer from the pregnant woman's hands and proceeded to beat her within a breadth of her life. If it weren't for the guards, Reanne would have died that night. Blood and wine covered everything."

"I assume the child survived?" Rhiess asked.

Eva nodded. "Reanne lost an eye and part of her jaw, but as the gods would have it, she lived. The following day, without my mother's permission, Father announced to the court that the Jarleina was with child. He proclaimed that his wife was in fragile health, beseeched blessings for his unborn son, and dispatched Mother to the Retreat of Silos." Eva stared into the flames. "My hopes drowned in the cheers that rose in all corners of the city that day."

The hair at the back of Rhiess' neck bristled with the confession. "What part did my father play in all of this?"

Disgust tinged Eva's voice. "A contingent of mercenaries under Tan'os Ensther's command escorted my mother to the cloister. To this day, when I close my eyes, I can still hear my mother screaming for justice from inside her windowless carriage. I never saw her alive again. Six months later, she returned to the palace in a casket."

Rhiess rubbed his forehead. "You believe my father had something to do with your mother's death?"

Eva hurled her goblet into the fire, sending shards of broken glass scattering. "Tan'os was desperate for a foothold in Reyzan politics! He would have done anything to gain Jarle Draos' favor!" Trembling with anger and grief, Eva rose from her chair and knelt by her husband's side. She set his cup aside and grasped his hands in hers. "I have no proof that my mother was murdered, but I will never forget the coldness in Tan'os Ensther's eyes when I began asking questions. Not long after, Tan'os convinced my father to arrange the marriage between us. Our wedding didn't just solidify trade across the Crossroads; it also distanced me from Reyza."

Rhiess wiped the tears from Eva's eyes. "What happened to Reanne?"

"She jumped to her death from one of the palace windows three days after Rigo's birth."

A quiet rage began to burn inside Rhiess' chest. "My poor wife, you should not have let this secret fester for so long. Why didn't you tell me sooner?"

"Because I didn't want you to hate your father as I hated mine. Besides, what good would this knowledge have done?"

Rhiess lifted Eva's chin. "Who else knows that Rigo is a bastard?"

"After my brother's birth, accidents befell many who were loyal to my mother. Some of her handmaidens did not return from Silos. With Tan'os' demise, I suspect all knowledge of Rigo's illegitimacy is gone."

At long last, Rhiess understood his wife's desire to return to her homeland. Gently, he brushed back a strand of her hair. Eva was braver than most men and possessed a keen mind. At that moment, he knew that if he stood in the way of her ambitions, he'd be no different than all the men who had already robbed her of choice. Rhiess spoke softly, afraid of the words he uttered next, "What is your desire, dear wife?"

Eva gazed into her husband's eyes. "Give me command of your ships! Let me go to Reyza and claim the throne that is rightfully mine."

PART
TWO

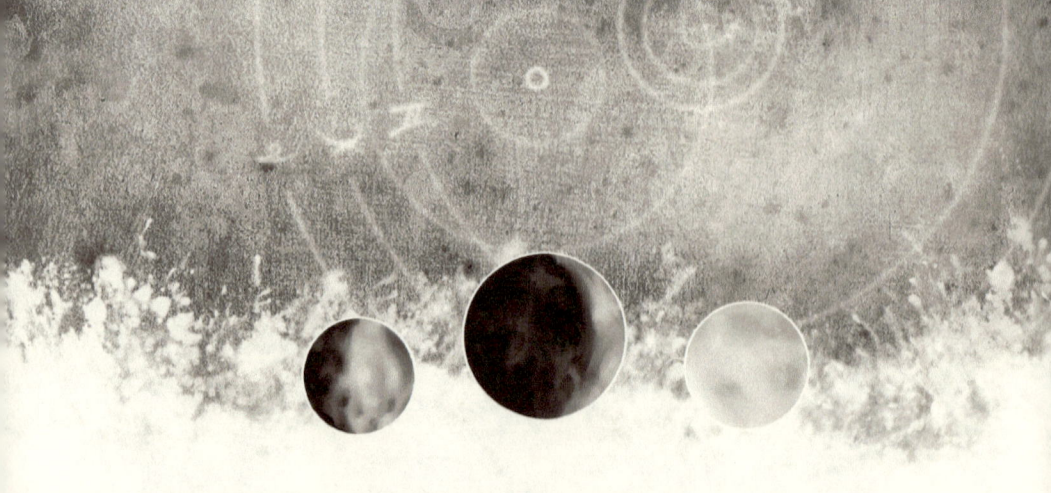

THE JOURNEY SOUTH

Daimodi, First of Triesse, 445 A'A'diel

Flames licked dangerously high inside the wood-burning stove in Gøran's cabin, yet the chill pressed on. The cold stiffened the fingers and twisted the faces of the sailors into static grimaces. Since their departure eight days prior, a steady rain had pelted the fleet, covering every surface in a treacherous layer of ice. The *Swoughünd's* crew labored over the creaking planks, fighting the encroaching rime with axes and clubs.

Gøran gazed at his men through the clouded panes of his cabin window. "Poor souls," he said, his breath misting. "They look neither up nor down, but straight ahead, their eyes fixed on some distant destination. Even the anchor-faced ones move as though death has claimed them."

Eva sat at his stateroom table, huddled under a woolen shawl. Her slender fingers pulled at the cloth, drawing it tight around her shoulders. "I sympathize. Cold weather is not my ally."

Turning away from the window, Gøran appraised his guest. "Winter on the Valga Sea is harsh. There is no comfort to be gained this day, only suffering. Shall I warm some ale?"

"I prefer ghavha," said Eva.

Gøran walked to the potbelly stove and rummaged through

the cupboard until he found a tin of ghavha leaves. He flexed his fingers and grimaced. His swollen, aching joints were a constant reminder of forty years spent at sea. He crushed a handful of the tea into a strainer and set a kettle on the hot plate. "I don't know how you southerners stomach ghavha. Vira drinks it morning, noon, and night; claims she can't live without it. Every time I drink it, I feel like crawling out of my skin."

"I've been living in Thyra for over fifteen years, and I have yet to figure out how you northerners stand tzuica. The smell of that plum slag is enough to sour my appetite."

"Tzuica is not the greatest of culinary achievements, but it's potent, and puts the heat back into men's bones."

Eva brushed back a strand of her hair. "I think Thromm's only gastronomic achievement is salting."

Gøran grabbed a mug and wiped it clean with a cloth. "Oh, I don't know. We are also experts at smoking just about everything: Goat, bear, boar, seal, fish, mushrooms, sage, tarbark, the list is endless. And don't forget baking. We make excellent bread."

"Your expertise ends at kneading the dough." Eva's face betrayed the hint of a smile. "You haven't tasted good bread until you've eaten a sweet bun from The Crusty Loaf. There is none better, I assure you."

"Sweet buns, she says!" Gøran chuckled softly. He placed the strainer inside one of the mugs and waited for the water to boil. "Bissatiel lads need hardtack as rough and as dark as the winter to make them strong, not pastries made with that teeth-rotting powder you enjoy so much."

Eva raised an eyebrow. "I concede, Thrommish flatbread is as daunting as the climate."

When the tea kettle wheezed, Gøran filled the mug to the brim and brought it to the table. "Daunting, indeed. This storm is stubborn, but she'll break."

Eva curled her long fingers around the steaming cup. Despite the cold, her eyes radiated warmth. "They all break, don't they, Gøran?"

"Are we still talking about the weather?" Gøran fetched a mug for himself and took a seat next to his guest. Reaching down, he grabbed a ceramic decanter at his feet and uncorked it. "I always did have a soft spot for that mote in your eye," Gøran said, pouring himself a shot.

Eva wrinkled her nose at the pungent scent of fermented liquor. "My husband likens it to a bird in flight. Raolph has it too."

The crows' feet at the edge of the captain's eyes deepened with his smile. "He's quite a handful, that boy. I caught him skulking about Vira's cabin a few weeks ago. I took the opportunity to teach him how to tie some knots. The boy says he wants to be like me someday and sail to distant lands."

"All boys dream of such adventures," Eva mused.

Gøran hooked his boot on the leg of one of the wooden side chairs and pulled it so he could rest his feet. He crossed his legs on the cushion and slammed back the shot. "When he is older, perhaps you'll allow him to sail with me."

Eva brought the cup of ghavha to her lips and sipped slowly. "Raolph is destined to inherit Thyra. The less he knows about you, the better."

"Yes, of course." Gøran gulped down the liquor in a single swallow and sucked his breath through clenched teeth. He slammed the mug down, then quickly refilled it. "He should honor the man who raised him, not a worthless fortune-seeker like me."

"This journey will feel twice as long if we go on sparring like this." Eva reached out and steadied the decanter as a wave rocked the ship. The cries of men joined the creaking of planks and the snapping of the sails. "You're not obligated to suffer my company, Captain Rarikian. I understand that your mistress' Calantian blood runs hot."

Gøran studied Eva's face. The richness of her green eyes reminded him of opalescent lagoons where warm shallows lapped at golden sands. He drained his drink and offered her a smile. "You should know, you share your mother's fire."

Eva's eyes grew flinty and unreadable. "Speaking of the dead bodes ill fortune."

"Apologies." Gøran took the tzuica from Eva's hand and corked it. "Eva, I do not wish to revisit the past. We have suffered enough. I want us to reconcile and find a way to move forward." Gøran thrust a finger at the frost rimmed window. "Look out there; all Hel has broken loose. You have a husband who loves you, a beautiful family, a city that worships you. Give the word, and we'll turn back. This is no place for the mother of my only child."

Eva's right eye twitched. "How dare you presume to tell me, the Marchess of Thyra, where my place is?"

Gøran threw up his hands. "Ven's sake, woman, you are impossible."

Eva swiped her arm across the table. The decanter and the mugs shattered on the floor, sending ceramic pieces scattering. "The impressionable young woman you once seduced with a bottle of that cheap swill is dead!"

"So I gather," said Gøran, slamming down his fist. "My fleet is yours to command, Marchess."

"Of course, it is. Do not patronize me."

"Don't play that card with me!" Gøran pushed the chair with his foot so hard it fell on its side. Standing up, he glared at the woman, eyes like daggers. "You are not going to Reyza to avenge Tan'os' death. We both know you hated the man; despised his very name. I pray to the gods you consider the implications of waging war."

"I find it ironic that you now wish to play the role of my conscience. I suggest you concern yourself with this storm, not my intentions," snapped Eva.

"Unlike the ice that threatens my ship, the coldness between us is a lost cause. At least on deck, I can be useful." Gøran walked across the cabin and threw the door open. Gusts of sleet robbed the room of its meager warmth. "When you decide to include me in your plans, you know where I'll be." Without bothering to shut the door, Gøran disappeared into the storm.

*
**

Vira wound her forearm around a length of rope and said a prayer to fair-weather deities as a barrel of pickled whitefish broke free and rolled toward her like a charging bull. Narrowly missing her, the cask skipped past her and smashed into a coil of rope. The stench of briny fish, coupled with the seesaw motion of the ship, caused her to spill the contents of her stomach.

Soaked to the bone, Vira clawed for her life as another crashing wave dragged her past the quarterdeck's stairwell. She was about to be washed out to sea when warm fingers locked around her forearm.

Vira's eyes widened. Above her, obscured by the pelting sleet, stood the windswept figure of the Thyran Marchess. Eva wore a woolen shawl draped over a knitted dress. The mourning garment offered little protection against the cold. "Thank you, Marchess," Vira croaked. "Please, get back inside before you freeze to death."

Eva helped Vira to her feet. "What in the Seventeen Labyrinths are you doing out here?"

A surge of warmth blossomed from Eva's grip and raced up Vira's arm. Blood returned to her numb fingers, and her trembling subsided. Surprised by the sudden comfort, the Calantian pulled her hand free. "Marchess, how did you—"

Eva took off her shawl and draped it over Vira's shoulders. "Answer my question."

Vira brushed strands of frozen hair from her face and scanned the rimed deck. Everywhere she looked, hulking mariners fought for their lives; their shouts unintelligible in raging winds. High on the rigging, gray silhouettes grappled to contain the *Swoughünd's* black shrouds. The vessel that had weathered a hundred winter storms creaked and groaned as though she were about to snap in half.

"Vira!"

Eva's voice pierced the cold haze of her consciousness. With sluggish pupils, Vira focused on the Marchess. Her teeth chattered as she spoke. "We're taking on water. The planks below decks have sprung. Durra, the carpenter, sent me to warn Gøran!"

Eva turned toward the bow in time to see a white-capped wave spill over the ship. "We need shelter. We'll be swept away if we stay here."

Vira squinted against the wind. Beneath her feet, the hull complained, and the floor lurched. Waves struck the deck like the fists of an elemental god, sweeping cargo and men into the churning abyss.

From somewhere in the chaos came the sound of splitting wood. Startled, both women looked up in the direction of the sound. Above them, a black sail snapped free, flapping like a vengeful specter.

Vira gripped Eva's arm, panic beating at her temples. "We are going to die!"

"Do not say such things, lest the daemons of the deep take heed!" Eva wrapped an arm around Vira's shoulders and helped her to the nearest ladder.

Shivering, Vira descended into the darkness. Above her, Eva shouted something, but her words were lost in the roar of the storm. "I can't hear you!" Vira cried.

Moments later, the *Swoughünd* listed, and a wall of icy water rained down on her. The Calantian woman lost her grip and crashed on the flooded deck below. Black briny water roiled around her numb limbs stealing the last vestiges of warmth. She tried to rise, but her legs became tangled in her wet skirts. With each roll of the ship, glacial torrents poured down from above. "Help!" Vira choked, cursing the sea and all things in it.

*
**

As the ship keeled to the port side, Eva grabbed hold of the wooden stair rail. Spluttering, she pushed her hair from her eyes and scanned the compartment below. "Vira!" she called out, "Where are you?"

The *Swoughünd* righted with an ear-grinding sound sending a deluge of water streaming below decks. Eva climbed down and waded in the knee-deep deluge in search of Gøran's mistress. Relief rushed through her when she spied the woman clinging to the base of a stanchion. "Hold on!" she shouted as the ship rolled once more. "I'm coming!"

Another surge of seawater drowned Vira's pleas. The downpour knocked Eva down and sent her tumbling into a post. Wrapping her hands around the beam, she pulled herself upright only to be shaken anew as the *Swoughünd* shivered from bow to stern.

In the seesawing darkness, Vira gained her bearings and burst out laughing.

Eva shook her head. "You find this amusing?"

"Did you hear that?" Vira shouted.

"What? The ship falling apart?"

The Calantian lumbered to Eva's side. "Gøran's done it; he's turned the bow aweather to meet the storm head-on! Better to charge the waves than to be rolled by them!"

"If you say so." Eva grabbed her skirts and plodded through the ankle-deep water toward the next set of stairs.

Vira gripped her arm and pulled her in the opposite direction. "Your cabin is the other way, Marchess."

"No!" Eva yanked free. "You said the ship was taking on water. Take me to the breach. Now!"

"Follow me," Vira said, trudging into the dark.

The pair descended and followed the meager glow of the moonstones until the sound of sloshing footsteps stopped them. A young sailor emerged from the shadows and scrabbled past them. Behind him, a second man followed. Ice crystals covered his beard and brows. Eyes wide with fear, the giant man closed his fist around Eva's wrist and yanked, dragging her down the gangway. "Death is down there!" he warned, fingers digging into her flesh. "Durra and his mate are dead! All is lost!"

Eva slammed the heel of her palm into the crazed man's face. "Let go of me!"

The sailor did not relinquish his hold. "Death! Death!" he lamented, oblivious to the blood spurting from his nose.

Vira unhooked a metal sconce and swung, smashing the back of the mans' knee. The impact brought the delirious man to his senses. "Daemons take you both!" he cursed, limping away from them.

Vira tossed the makeshift club aside. "If the carpenter is dead—"

Eva cut her off, "We are needed more than ever. Go!"

Vira slogged on with Eva close behind. Together, the women wound their way through the *Swoughünd's* labyrinthine passages, descending ever deeper into the ship's lower decks. The flagship of the northern fleet was a juggernaut with eight decks, each a fathom and a half tall to accommodate the Bissatiel crew.

The stentorian din of the storm took on a diabolical tone in the bowels of the ship. Beneath the waterline, the bedlam of the crashing waves took on a deeper, more fearsome resonance as though they were trapped inside a funerary drum. The women plodded through the corridors, sloshing through floating debris before emerging into a cavernous hold packed with grain sacks.

The only light came from two moonstone lamps that swung and spun as the ship swayed. The bodies of several dead sailors bobbed in the bone-chilling water. Within the shifting shadows, four men shored a section of leaking planks with a massive timber brace while two others tried to hammer planks over the breach. With each roll of the ship, salty water sprayed into the hold, bathing the weary sailors. Submerged thigh-deep in water, the men were half-frozen to death.

"Samish," grunted the liveliest man, "We can't hold this much longer! We need another brace."

Vira climbed over a stack of sacks and shouted, "No! You need more oakum!"

The sailors spared her a desultory glance before ignoring her.

Scrambling down, Vira rejoined Eva. "These men are cooks and stewards from the galley and don't know what they're doing. Braces and nailed slats alone won't seal the leaks."

Eva studied Vira's eyes. "You sure?"

Vira rubbed her upper arms and nodded. "Oué. My father is a merchantman. I know a thing or two."

Moved by the conviction in the Calantian's eyes, Eva imbued her voice with authority until her words filled the disordered chamber and drowned out the chaos. "I command you to follow Vira's orders as though they were my own! Fail to do so, and I promise that should the icy depths not claim you, my executioner's axe will!"

Vira nodded and turned to face the sailors. "Amanuel, Ugtag, grab mallets and oakum; start filling the gaps. You, Samish, help Torvald with the brace. Be ready to secure it on my command. You two—get on the bilge pump and don't stop until I tell you to. The water is rising too fast."

Confused glances passed among the mariners before their eyes settled on Eva.

"You heard her—MOVE!" Eva's command cracked through their consciousness like a whip. The sailors leapt to their assigned tasks as though stung by Ven's daemons.

Vira waded through the chest-deep water and began ferrying

bundles of tarred fiber to the men. The ship quaked as it skirted another swell, causing Torvald to lose his grip. The middle-aged man rose but didn't return to his post. He stared blankly at the gushing hole, bluish lips agape.

Eva braved the waters and reached the man. She placed her hand against his icy cheek and summoned from her core, the healing gift that could whisk away fatigue and revive even the most helpless of souls. A surge of lifegiving warmth traveled from her fingertips to the exhausted man's frozen skin.

Torvald eyed Eva with wide-eyed wonder, then shook off his lethargy. He put his back against the brace and pushed. "We can do this!" he urged. "We can save the ship! Keep working!"

Eva's heart thundered in her chest. Unsanctioned magic was as forbidden as soulbindery and punishable by death, but the risk seemed worth it. The Ingvizitorij couldn't very well judge her if she were dead.

Before the Marchess could further ponder the consequences of using her gift, another sailor fainted. Eva slogged to his aid, but upon touching him, she recoiled. The mariner's dying heartbeat echoed within her own body—a distant, slow pounding that plunged her senses into freefall. A chilling shiver raced through her spine as the mariner's filmy eyes met hers, and his lips broke in a black-toothed smile. "He's gone," she said to Vira.

Eva pushed the corpse aside and wrapped her hands around the bare arm of the man named Samish. Determined not to lose another soul to the cold, she channeled her lifeforce into him. When color suffused his cheeks, Eva shook him. "Push, or I will have your bones scattered to the Seven Winds."

Eva's threat, coupled with the fear of foundering, focused Samish's attention. "Aye, lady. I will hold fast until Ven takes me."

Vira scaled the pile of sacks and replaced the dead sailor. She swung the wooden mallet with both hands, pounding the tarred rope into the leaking gaps. "Stop the pump. Secure the first brace, then get the next support ready. On my mark, push against the hull with all your might!"

While the sailors complied, Eva renewed everyone's strength with her warming touch. Flushed with newfound vigor, the grateful mariners returned to their tasks, never suspecting the cost that healing exacted on their savior.

Each remedial exchange sapped Eva's energy and her ability to stave the cold. Shaking uncontrollably, the Thyran ruler dragged herself through the algid water to a heap of sodden grain. She tried to climb, but her hands proved useless. Her fingers resembled lumps of frozen meat. "Vira," she called out, unable to feel her legs. "Has the water stopped rising?"

Vira abandoned her task and crawled to Eva's side. "Oué. The shoring is holding, but if this storm continues, there's no telling."

A fog of exhaustion descended over Eva's mind. Her body felt heavy and limp. "You have d-done good work. G-go," she gritted. "Don't d-die down here."

Vira beckoned to the youngest sailor. "Amanuel, carry the Marchess to her cabin—now! Torvald, keep the pumps going and watch for new leaks. Samish, get help, so this crew can warm their bones. And for all that is holy, inform the captain."

Vira's voice echoed, faint and distant. Eva smiled as the handsome stranger lifted her into his brawny arms. "*Swoughünd* is Thrommish for Black Swan," she said in a lazy slur. "Did you know that?"

Amanuel nodded. "By Nogh, stay with us, my lady."

Vira cleared the flotsam clogging the flooded passage to make way for the laden sailor. More than once the man tripped, and tumbled as the ship tackled the storm.

"Tell my children that I love them," Eva mumbled.

Vira held Eva's frozen hand in hers. "You will tell them yourself, Marchess. Takes more than a little gale to drown this blackbird."

Eva's eyes fluttered open as a bolt of lightning forked above her head, and rain pelted her face. In the moonlight, black clouds roiled and flashed, and the wind howled like the spirits of the damned. For the first time in her life, she considered that she might die. "Is that the sun I see rising?"

"Shh," soothed Vira. "Conserve your strength."

Eva channeled the last of her reserves to combat the shivering spasms that wracked her body. Only time would tell if the battered ship would reach Reyza. As exhaustion overwhelmed her, she thought of Rhiess and her children, laughing, in the fields of summer wheat.

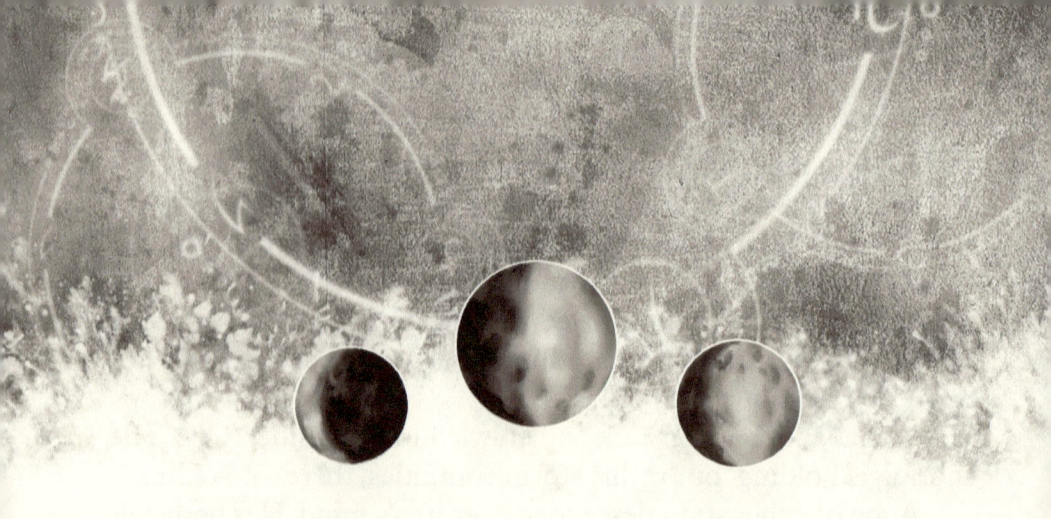

ÁELS

Shardi, Fourth of Triesse, 445 A'A'diel

A flash of distant lightning glinted off the thief's sharp blades as he thrust forward. Jarle rolled, leapt to his feet, then feinted to parry the blows of an invisible enemy. His face remained serene throughout the frenzied dance of precise footwork and quick lunges. Only his eyes betrayed the intense focus required for each combination of critical strikes. A month had passed since Avaren had brought him to the grotto, and a week since he had felt healthy enough to engage in his training regimen. With each practice session, strength returned to his limbs.

Overhead the wind quickened, and the clouds turned to a leaden gray. Thunder chased the violent flashes of lightning, booming through the cavernous depths. Moments later, heavy drops began to pelt the pool.

Submerged a hand's breadth below the surface, Avaren rolled over and gave Jarle a brief glimpse of her buttocks before circling the perimeter with lazy undulations. The girl's long, white hair trailed behind her as she wove amidst the dangling roots.

Jarle stabbed forward twice more with both daggers, then returned the blades to their sheaths. He smirked, slicking back his rain-soaked hair. "Welcome back, beautiful."

Avaren surfaced, her opalescent eyes gleaming. "Come for a swim," she invited, her voice sweet.

Jarle's gaze traveled down the length of her tail, where the scales became smaller and smaller until they glimmered like jewels on a delicate set of armor. The fronds of her caudal fins unfurled like feathers, the various shades of purple and blue highlighted with tempting glitters of silver. The sight tightened his breeches and sent white-hot longing pulsing through his veins. The overlapped scales lent her hips a lush outline and filled his mind with images with previous watery romps. "Last time we tried that, I almost drowned."

"You would have gone to Ven a happy man." Lying back, the naera grazed her nipples. Beneath the water, her dual tails twisted and writhed like coiling pythons. "Join me."

Jarle unbuckled his weapon belt and kicked off his boots. He had promised Avaren that her body would cease to ache, but he had lied. The bullish cravings of his cock, coupled with her lusty whims, had kept them delightfully sore. Some days they didn't bother to leave the blankets, eschewing food for lazy pleasures. Others, they fornicated like fiends, thrashing in the shallows. "What of the storm?"

"Let it come!" Avaren circled a mass of dangling roots. "I'm already wet."

Jarle shoved his pants off and dove in after her. He swam to the center of the pool, wrapped his arm around one of her tails, and pulled the splashing squealing girl against him. "Wet, are you?"

Avaren wound her fingers in his hair and crushed her mouth to his. Entangled, they sank into the cool depths and exchanged each other's breaths through ardent kisses. Jarle caressed her, letting his hands roam greedily over the curves of her supine body. He squeezed her breasts and teased her beaded nipples, ran his fingers over the slick scales rejoicing in the softness at her apex. The naera's sex, he had discovered, was a wondrous organ camouflaged by fan-like flanges, which merged with a man like sucking lips. The initial discovery had been so shocking, he had swallowed a mouthful of water and almost hacked out a lung. Far from dissuading him, the experience left him yearning for more. The woman in his arms thrilled him in ways he failed to describe. He was mad for her, enamored beyond reason—addicted. Obsessed.

Reaching down, he guided his cock into her velvet-soft channel and exhaled into her kiss. A gush of bubbles floated upwards as her gills flared. Locked in the suffocating embrace, they found their rhythm. She clawed his back. And he kissed her, breathing the precious air her lungs extracted from the sea. His tongue plunged and retreated along with his hips, both seeking to drive her wild. He wanted her as crazed and desperate as he felt.

Jarle rolled with her, probing with the iron-hard length of his penis, absorbing every nuance of her fevered response. He discovered a spot that made her shiver and exploited it, stroking over it again and again. He held his breath when she climaxed, enjoying the delicate ripple of her muscles around his thrusting cock. Then, he slowed, grinding in and out, so he could watch pleasure take her. He loved the way her silky body accepted his possession, how her tendrils tightened, the opalescent glow in her eyes during release. Entranced by her beauty, Jarle ignored the change in temperature or depth. They foundered into the abyss until his lungs ached, and the surface rippled distant and wan.

Avaren uncoiled her tails and propelled them to the shallows where they were met by fat drops of rain. "You alright?"

Jarle nodded and gulped for air, feeling light-headed. "You take my breath away."

In the clearing, the wind howled, and lightning forked through angry clouds. Leaves blew in through the opening, and thunder boomed through the hollow recesses of their sanctuary.

Avaren brushed her lips against his ear and soothed him with a caress. "You're shivering. Let's go inside."

Jarle swam to shore without protest. As much as he enjoyed their watery escapades, they often came at a price. Chills wracked his body, and his eyes stung from the salt. "The storm is worsening," he said, picking up his gear.

The naera glided to the pebbly beach and pulled herself out of the water. Her gills flared, and her tails thrashed until the iridescent scales softened into pearly skin. In an eyeblink, cartilage turned to bone, fins into flesh. She heaved, gritted her sharp teeth, and clawed the sand in a state of pain or ecstasy, Jarle could not tell. Moments later, she stood with the dignity of a noble-blooded princess and whisked his chill away with her sultry gaze. "I'm not finished with you."

"I suspect not," Jarle said, offering his arm, "though you might be the end of me."

Hand in hand, the lovers retreated to their sanctuary and collapsed on the silk-veiled bed. Swollen with autumn rain, the waterfall gushed into the worn basin filling the shadows with a fearsome roar. The lichens, ferns, and mosses trembled in the languid breeze, and the dredged treasure gleamed with each flash of lightning. The scent of silt, moisture, and brine mingled with the musk of arousal.

Jarle claimed her with frenzied passion, his hands finding purchase on her slippery flesh. He sucked the taut points of her breasts, tangled his fingers into her wet tresses, lost himself in the feel of her liquid heat. Each push into her pliant body asserted a shocking revelation: He needed her with an urgency as violent as the world that had bred him. Avaren would dictate the path his life would traverse because he couldn't proceed without her.

Gasps became soft noises that built in volume until the naera cried out, head back and mouth open—eyes glazed in a way that pushed him toward release. He pinned her to the kelp bed, driven by the thought that if he plumbed deeply enough, he would find his center in the molten embrace of her womb. "Avaren," he gritted, pulling out at his most vulnerable moment. "I love you."

The storm surge rushed through the underwater caverns, and the howling wind drowned their moans as they quenched each other's hunger twice more. Time slipped away, and the darkness deepened until only the glow of the cooking fire danced on the rain-slicked walls.

Desire sated, the lovers curled under a threadbare blanket and listened to the rainfall.

"Are we skipping dinner again?" Avaren asked, planting a tender kiss on Jarle's jaw.

"Not a chance." Jarle caressed the length of her back, rubbing the cold from her limbs. "How does áel surprise sound?"

"Again? I feel bad for the poor things, all cozy in their holes."

Jarle nibbled the ridge of Avaren's collarbone. "How will you learn to fight if you regret killing sea snakes?"

Avaren shrugged. "I don't think that's a fair comparison."

"You're right." Jarle grew pensive and pulled her close. "Áels are nothing like people. They won't betray us or hurt us or plot against us. They are content in their rock caves, never wanting for more. They hunt when they hunger and sleep when they tire. They live by the grace of the currents in a moonlit paradise."

Avaren bit her bottom lip and reached between Jarle's legs. "They do have some similarities to men."

Jarle rolled on top of her, wedging his hips between her thighs. "Can't possibly imagine what you mean."

Avaren wrapped her arms around the man's neck and stole a kiss. "I think we are a little bit like the áels, no?"

"When you first brought me here, I was convinced I had landed in Hel." Jarle pulled back to look at his lover. "Since then, this place has grown on me."

A crack of thunder reverberated through the stone columns with a low-pitched resonance. Avaren cuddled into Jarle's arms. "Life is strange," she said. "I never would have imagined that I would meet someone like you, let alone—"

"Let alone what?" Jarle asked, stroking her back.

Avaren's luminous eyes met his. "Fall in love," she whispered.

Jarle raised her chin with his hand until their noses touched. "Before meeting you, I held romance in contempt. In my mind, love was like raska. It confused the senses, replaced reason with delirium, and when the drunkenness ended, all that remained was a soul-wrenching ache far worse than any delights. I could control my thirst for liquor, why not some meddlesome ardor? I foreswore the emotion and vowed never to allow myself to fall for it again. It was an oath that provided my friends with endless amusement." Jarle peered into Avaren's eyes, his voice grew serious. "Avi, I was comfortable in my credo until the night that I set foot in your bedroom. When I saw you, something changed. I cannot explain it. I don't want to explain it." The words began to tumble from his lips, becoming ever more impassioned. "You've altered the course of my life, given me something to live for. Many nights I've watched you sleep wondering, hoping that someday you might feel for me what I have felt for you since the moment we met."

Jarle kissed her cheeks, her lips, her eyelids, his face alight with joy. "I know that what we share may not last. You are a princess and am an unblooded cur, but by the gods, right now I am the happiest man alive!"

Heat rushed to Avaren's face. "Really?"

Jarle swooned as though he'd downed a goblet of Seh'nahiel wine in a single swallow. A giddy smirk spread across his face as he embraced her. "Yes. You've made me eat my vows. If I'd known love was this wonderful, I would have succumbed to it years ago."

Avaren playfully punched his ribs. "I take it a dangerous man like you has had many lovers?"

"At least five times the number of your suitors," he confessed, "but I can't remember their faces or their names."

"What is it you do recall?" Avaren said, straddling him.

Jarle gripped the girl's ass and pulled her down. He sucked one of her nipples. "What does it matter?"

"I'm intrigued," said Avaren, trapping his cock between her thighs. "Tell me."

Jarle groaned as her legs squeezed. "I have led a rather unremarkable existence. Truly, I swear it. If you are curious, there are a great many things I can bore you with."

A lopsided smile crossed Avaren's face as she rubbed her slick cunny on his shaft. "A liar like you," she teased, "is so beneath me."

Jarle dragged his hands over the swell of her hips. "Happily beneath you, my lady." He reached up and pushed Avaren's wet hair behind her shoulders. "Release me, and I promise to make you the best áel you have ever tasted."

Avaren rolled off of him. "I'm famished. But rest assured, we shall continue this interrogation later."

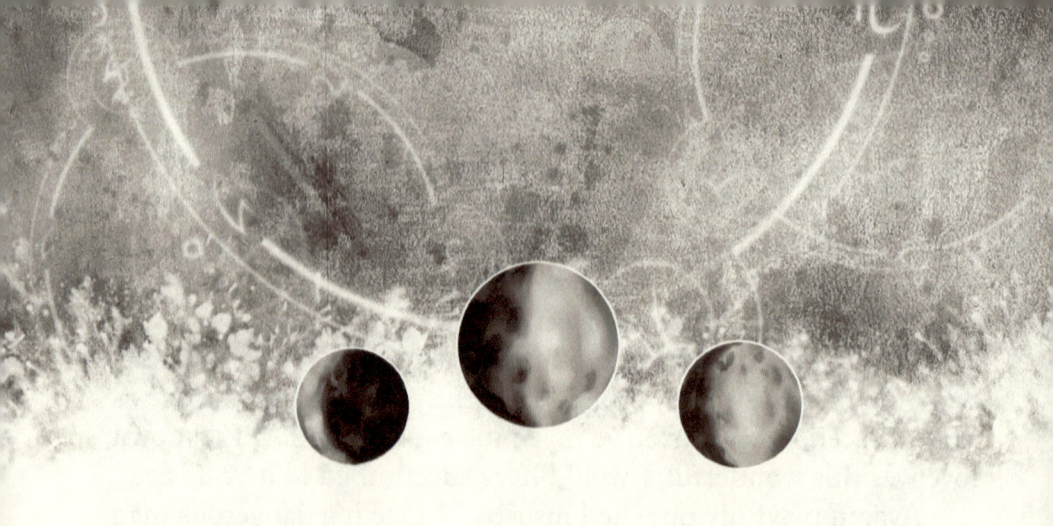

AFTER THE STORM

Mir'kadi, Eighth of Triesse, 445 A'A'diel

A week passed before the storm-scattered Thrommish fleet reunited. The *Swoughünd* cruised along white-capped waves; her black sails luffed to catch the southerly wind. Outside the rondel glass windows of Gøran's cabin, clouds drifted through a crisp blue sky. The sound of ropes grating against pulleys and the creaking of wood roused Eva from her repose.

Propped on a heap of pillows, the Thyran Marchess stared at her bandaged hand. All that remained of her right ring finger and pinkie was a relentless, throbbing ache. She found it ironic that the hands that had prevented so much death had fallen prey to something as mundane as frostbite. Eva sighed. Had she managed to remain conscious, she could have healed the damage and avoided the amputations. There was no sense in dwelling on what could have been. She had once sacrificed her heart to Gøran in the *Swoughünd's* wooden belly; two fingers were a lesser loss.

At the foot of her bed, Vira slumbered in an overstuffed armchair, seeming more like a sleeping child than the captain's mistress. The Calantian's eyelids fluttered as she dreamt. In the days that followed the violent storm, Vira had taken excellent care of her. And Eva was grateful. Thanks to the woman's quick wit, the vessel had weathered the gale.

Vira started awake when the ship lurched into a trough. Her eyes flew open, and her hands gripped the arms of the chair as though expecting to find herself elsewhere. The storm had left a lasting impression on everyone aboard.

"Bad dream?" Eva asked.

Vira ran a hand through her dark curls and nodded. She looked out the window and squinted. "I was dreaming of those cold waters again, but I see I have no reason to worry. The sun is bright in the sky." Vira reached out and held Eva's uninjured hand. "How are you this morning, Marchess?"

Pleased to feel the weight of a gentle hand, Eva smiled. "I am content to be alive. Ven willing, I will see my children again. How about you, dear Vira? When will you take my advice, and get some proper rest?"

Vira leaned forward in her chair and shook her head. "I owe you my life, Marchess. It is an honor to care for you."

"Will you tell me one of your stories today?"

Vira lit up. "Did I tell you about my sister, the one who lives in the foothills of Anandoli?"

"Another one? How many siblings do you have?" Eva teased.

"There are six of us altogether. Mariella is the youngest and the most headstrong. She is five years my junior."

Eva arched her brow. "So she's a child?"

Vira blushed. "I am not as young as you think. Mariella is nineteen seasons old and as wild as the mountain goats that prance in the Farangeppo. She left Stellae with a traveling caravan headed north to Anandoli."

Eva recalled that the coastal city-state hosted a heavy Thrommish presence. "Anandoli is a large city with a scenic harbor, is it not?"

Vira nodded. "Oué, Marchess. The weather is fair, and towering pines that grow like green needles line the streets. The people are poor, but their smiles are as bright as the sunshine that graces that part of the world. There is a festival called Festa Vesia that reveres the mythical founder of Anandoli. Vesia holds sway over the tides and protects the lives of unborn children. The festivities last a full week, and at its zenith, a maid embodies the role of the goddess.

For two years now, the people have chosen Mariella to act the part. Everyone in Anandoli loves her. My little sister is a legend."

Eva patted Vira's hand. "I see you've left the best story for last. Dare I ask what goes on during this feast?"

Vira winked. "Lots of drinking and carousing."

"Sounds like I need to spend some time in sunny Anandoli."

Vira reclined in her chair. "There is an old saying in Calantian. *Esos óu véinn do Calántia sómpreis tournéiren.*"

"Those who belong to Calantia," Eva translated, "always return?"

Vira beamed. "Oué! Well done, Marchess! Did you ever visit your mother's lands?"

Eva nodded. "When I was a child, we spent some time in the Osueldo territory. The countryside was unlike anything I had ever seen. I recall vast stretches of tilled fields and orchards with outcrops of brush forest and sparkling rivers. My sister and I used to play chase in the olive groves surrounding my mother's ancestral fortress. Mosses and ivy choked every breadth of mortared stone. Silly us, we believed the place enchanted and spent one entire summer looking for little people. From the top of the battlements, we could see the spires of Mencello and the sea."

The Calantian sighed. "So, you see, the saying is true. Calantia calls to you."

"One day, I will take my children and visit," Eva mused.

"Did you find the little people?" Vira asked. "Where I grew up, we called them the munkacelli. Legend tells they are small hooded creatures that live in the bowels of the aqueduct. They enter houses through the keyholes and steal food and riches."

"In Reyza, we have similar folktales of spirits lurking in the deep. And don't get me started on Thyran superstition. The yarns northerners spin are far less sunny than Calantian ones."

Vira was about to speak when the door to the stateroom opened. Gøran stepped through, bearing a gleaming tray of food.

Eva forced a gracious smile as the man placed the breakfast platter on her lap.

Gøran tousled Vira's curls. "Get some rest, sweet flame, but before you do, stop in the galley. The cook insists on feasting you like royalty. Be assured; our brave Marchess is in fine hands."

Vira gathered her blanket around her shoulders and stood. "I will return later to help you bathe. Enjoy your meal, my lady."

Eva gave the woman a curt nod. "Thank you, Vira."

With Vira's departure, Gøran removed his plumed hat with a flourish and hung his greatcoat on a peg. The captain had bathed and oiled his beard before donning the formal colors of Thromm. A black coat embroidered in silver complemented his slim-fitting, dark blue breeches. Beneath the jacket, he wore a starched white shirt and a cravat of yellow silk. Gøran's knee-high leather boots shone with a mirror polish. The man was nearing sixty but looked more distinguished than many Vendraedi half his age. Time tended to be kind to the Bissatiel bloodline.

Eva appraised him appreciatively. "You look like someone I met a long time ago."

"In another lifetime, my lady." Gøran lifted the kettle and poured Eva a cupful of steaming ghavha. Silver gleamed in the morning sunlight.

Eva eyed the silver service. "What's the occasion, Captain?"

"Do I need special dispensation to dote on my beloved ruler?" Gøran put the teapot down.

Eva smiled. "We were in this very room when you looked at me in all seriousness and said, 'What a fine gown you're wearing, perchance I may talk you out of it.' Of course, you didn't. You couldn't talk your way under a woman's skirt if your life depended on it."

Gøran chuckled. "Fortunately, I am a man of action, not words."

Eva reached for the cup with her injured hand and paused. The levity of the moment fled when her eyes settled on her missing fingers. "Thank you for breakfast," she said, her tone flat.

"No need to thank me. I am here, in fact, to extend gratitude on behalf of my crew and myself. The mariners you saved told me of your heroism." Gøran eyed the linen bandages wrapped around Eva's right hand. "I am sorry that your selflessness carried such a heavy price."

Eva raised the teacup with her left hand and brought it to her lips. "My heroism? Vira saved the day, not I. You chose wisely; your Calantian firebrand understands the workings of boats. If she wields a man half as well as a mallet, I suspect you are a happy man."

The man chuckled. "Aye, Vira, played her part and is receiving her due accolades. But everyone knows that were it not for you; we would be drifting corpses in a frozen sea."

Eva sipped, savoring the spices added to the ghavha leaves. After a long silence, she set the cup down and leaned her head back. "If your men had any sense in their hollow skulls, they will not speak about what transpired in the hold."

The man sat in the armchair and clasped his hands. "I told the crew you were injured attempting to seal the breach. That is all they know. The men's morale and their loyalty have increased on account of your sacrifice. As for Vira and the sailors who witnessed your gifts, do not worry. They have sworn oaths to carry your secret to their graves."

Eva unfolded the napkin. "Good. Some secrets hold keys to doors that should remain closed."

The man leaned forward. "Eva, please talk to me."

Eva rubbed her forehead. "When the water was rising, all I could think of was how I felt when my mother died. She left me much too soon. Her death haunts me to this day. I wasn't ready to leave my boys--to have them toss and turn at night, waking up soaked in sweat, wondering about my last anguished moments aboard this ship." Eva considered her bandaged hand. "I lost two fingers, but I am alive and will be able to see my sons again, to wrap my arms around them, and to watch them grow into men. I made a fine choice."

Gøran nodded. "We have conquered impossible odds and suffered the insufferable for the sake of love. I wish I could trade places with you now and take away your pain away."

Eva patted Gøran's arm. "Nothing can be done."

Gøran rested his palm on Eva's hand. "Eva, I know that our past is complicated and that we don't always agree, but my loyalty to you has never wavered. Why did you leave the security of Thyra? Why embark on this journey to Reyza?"

Eva closed her eyes. "Too often, circumstances force women to experience the world as spectators. The will of men has dominated so much of my life. I go to Reyza to take back what is mine."

"What's on your mind, Eva? I can't navigate blind. Twelve ships can lay waste to the port and destroy treaties and trade easements that have taken decades to forge. We know very little about what has happened. Tan'os' murder is unprecedented, yes, but we should be cautious about how we proceed."

"Tan'os made insidious enemies. His death was a matter of time."

"Why do you say so?"

"The future comes to me in dreams and portents. I can read the waves beneath your rudder, leaves swirling in the river, clouds drifting in the sky. Sometimes I think I'm going mad, and then, when I can't stand the throbbing in my head, my visions begin to make sense." Eva stared out the window, debating whether to confide in Gøran. Her nightmares around the time of Tan'os' death were fraught with disjointed images. She often found herself trapped below the surface, pounding her fists against an iron sea. Then there was Rigo's incessant cackling followed by blood--so much blood. "On the day Tan'os died, eleven days before the Whisperers arrived, I awoke screaming from a nightmare. I felt sick as though my whole world was bottom side up. I heard my brother's laughter in my head, felt Tan'os' pain, heard his dying gasps."

Gøran stood and began to pace. "We have no evidence that Rigo sanctioned an assassination. Supposing he did, we must still rise above personal gain. The security and economy of Thyra and the whole continent depends on our actions. How long do you think we could occupy Reyza before we had a revolt on our hands or daggers in our backs? Is it your intention to blockade the city, to cause innocent people to starve? Think, Eva. I will not unleash the might of Thromm because you had a bad dream."

"There are many things you do not know."

"Then perhaps it's time to enlighten me."

"Rigo is a bastard. Tan'os was one of the few souls who knew the truth."

"Most rulers are bastards, present company excluded."

"Don't be dense. What I mean is that my brother is not the legitimate heir." Eva's voice grew steely. "My father desired a male heir despite my mother's inability to provide one. When one of his mistresses became pregnant with a boy, he forced my mother to pretend it was hers. When she refused, my father had my mother killed. I believe it was Tan'os who carried out his orders." Eva paused. Her lips tightened, and her jaw clenched. "As I grew older and more outspoken, my father sought to silence me. Once again, the Vise provided an agreeable solution. He convinced my father to marry me to his son. I was shipped off on this very ship, sent to Thyra to be forgotten. You asked me to tell you, and there you have it." The fire returned to Eva's eyes. "The throne of Reyza does not belong to Rigo; it never has. I go there to deliver a long-deferred justice."

Gøran crossed his arms and mulled over the confession. "Your brother will do everything in his power to suppress such a truth."

Eva gazed out the sunlit window. "I do not know what we will find when we arrive. I only know that I am destined to do this."

Gøran leaned at the foot of the bed. "I do not favor hunches. But, I have seen too much to deny the wisdom of the gut. We will reach Reyza in two weeks. The Southern Fleet, under the command of Captain Athanasios, will be expecting us. In such situations, their orders are to remain neutral and avoid involvement until commanded otherwise. When the fleets unite, we will number eighteen. That's enough military might to scare the piss out of that pompous boy."

"Please pour me another ghavha."

Gøran refilled Eva's teacup and set the teapot down.

"Thank you." Eva took the cup with her right hand, holding the bowl between index finger and thumb. She took a long sip. "In the last few years, my communications with my brother have consisted of brief letters, likely written by his advisors. We have not seen each other in fifteen years. I cannot tell you what kind of man he has become."

Gøran's brows knitted together. "We must be cautious, or we'll have the mages to contend with. Many of our former allies no longer hold power. Deneven D'Neir stepped down as Lord Justiciar over a year ago, and Arcanist Olos is so old his magic tricks stink of mothballs. I hear the old kook spends his days being spoon-fed while nestled in the bosoms of his serving wenches."

Eva grabbed a crusty, buttered roll from the breakfast tray, and took a bite. The look of anguish in Gøran's eyes was unbearable. "Do not pity me," Eva scolded. "Stop lamenting and have one of your clever men craft me something suitable for my hand. I understand you pirates are wily at that sort of thing."

The word pirate brought a smile to Gøran's face. "It's been years since you referred to me with such endearment. Bosun's Mate Svelik carves wood in his spare time and prides himself on his artistic ability. I am sure he would be honored to ease your pain." Gøran lifted the silver cloche to reveal a plate of eggs, crispy potatoes, and browned sausages. He cut into one of the juicy links and presented the morsel to Eva's lips. "Now, if you would allow it, my lady, this humble brigand, would like to help you with your breakfast."

The scent of fried eggs and pork fat caused Eva's stomach to growl. She was slim, but not from lack of appetite. With Gøran's help, she ate heartily, finishing the meal by mopping up the yolks with a piece of bread. When she had swallowed the last bite, she gave the captain a wink. "Your cook has outdone himself this morning."

"I will extend your compliments," Gøran pronounced, stacking the empty dishes on the tray.

"Even the worst of weather can't get between me and a meal," Eva said, wiping her lips with a napkin.

"Some things never change." Gøran donned his overcoat. "That hole in the hull continues to weep like a festering wound. I will instruct Svelik to visit you this afternoon when he's done overseeing the ship's repairs. In the meantime, I will fetch the surgeon."

Eva cringed at the mention of the healer. "No need. I am faring much better."

Gøran grabbed the platter. "You have surprised our healer with your speedy recovery. He tells me your wounds are almost healed. Favorable news, don't you think?"

Eva straightened. "Henceforth, my rehabilitation and general health are not open for discussion. Your surgeon does well to keep his miraculous conjectures to himself. I have not yet forgiven him for sawing off two of my fingers."

Gøran took his tricorn off the peg. "You know very well that

I gave the order. In my position, you would have done the same."

Eva wanted to scream, but there was no point in venting her outrage. Boiling over would only encourage visits from the butcher Gøran called a doctor. "You were Tan'os' first mate on the *Ruarch* before granted command of the Northern Fleet, were you not?"

"I see you are changing the subject," Gøran said, adjusting his collar. "I served on that cursed ship, and would rather not discuss it."

Eva pressed on. "Surely, you can dispel the strange rumors circulating about Tan'os' daughter and her mysterious birth. Perhaps later this evening, you will indulge me with your tale."

Gøran put on his hat. "Us pirate folk are a superstitious lot. Some stories are best forgotten or told with our feet planted on hard-packed soil. The *Ruarch* and ninety-seven souls met their watery destiny long ago. I reckon you won't find many who are willing to sate your curiosity, my lady."

"I don't need many. I need you."

"I will tell you after we dock, and I've had a chance to imbibe enough liquor to regret it."

"That's easily arranged."

A blustery wind pushed into the room as Gøran opened the cabin door. "As you said earlier, some doors are better kept closed."

Eva nodded. "And some keys, forgotten."

"Rest well, Marchess," Gøran said, closing the door behind him.

Eva focused on the sunlight filtering through the window and drew the blankets up to her nose. Suddenly, she wished she were basking under the Calantian sun.

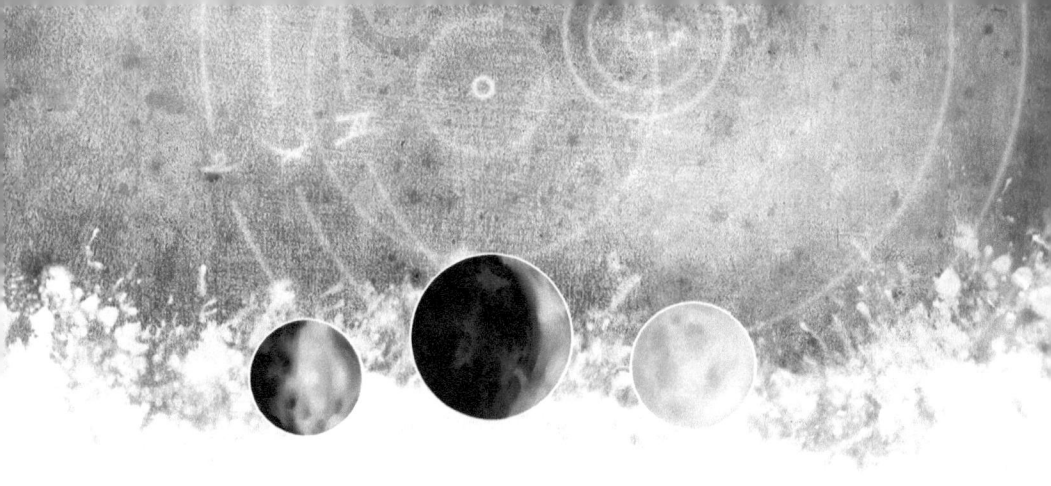

BREAKFAST IN PARADISE

Meldi, Eighteenth of Triesse, 445 A'A'diel

The morning's chill roused Jarle from strange dreams. He yawned, pulled his boots on, and stood. He picked up one of his blades and crossed the cavern to a shallow pool of writhing áels. The creatures were soon becoming his least favorite food.

Jarle plunged the dagger into the water and skewered one of the sea snakes. He waited for the áel to stop thrashing, then cut the glossy skin around its gills. He held the fish's head in one hand and yanked its sleek coat with the other. The scaly sheath peeled away, exposing pink ribbed flesh. He lobbed off the head and tossed it back into the pool along with the scales. The surviving áels fought for the morsels, biting and hissing in a writhing mass.

The sight reminded Jarle of Avaren's aquatic form. In the sea, the noblewoman became an ophidian creature of legend. And though he had often witnessed her transformation, her duality proved challenging to reconcile. As a naera, Avaren breathed and moved through the currents as effortlessly as a sinuous reedfish. Below the waves, she exhibited an unquantifiable joy—an exuberance as bright as the sun. His lover walked on two legs, but her soul belonged to the ocean.

Jarle deboned the animal, scraped out the guts, and discarded the entrails. He grabbed a metal salver and placed it on the coals to heat while he seasoned the meat with sea salt, wild garlic, and chives.

Upon hitting the hot pan, the headless áel wriggled as though still alive. Revolted, Jarle held the meat down with his blade and daydreamed of Reyza's wharf side taverns, heaping platters of slow-roasted meats, and tankards of fizzy ale. Beyond the steady noise of the pouring rain and the splash of feeding áels, he could almost hear the laughter of the buxom wenches and the boastful banter of gamblers casting dice. His mouth watered at the thought of a crusty slice of bread slathered with melted butter. He longed for the bustling streets, the crowded, colorful markets, and the scent of perfume and pastries. He missed city life.

The pop and sizzle of the cooking fire stirred Avaren from her slumber. Stretching her arms, the girl favored the thief with a drowsy smile. "Is it still raining?"

Jarle smiled, silently scolding himself for the maudlin indulgence. The view of Avaren's soft curves as she rose from the blankets banished all thoughts of Reyza. The woman made his heart soar. "Yes. This weather is stubborn."

Avaren sauntered to the cascade and began to wash. "In a few weeks, the seas will dredge the glaciers from the south, and trade in Reyza will slow to a crawl. Winter currents are treacherous. We will need to leave soon."

Jarle savored the sight of her shapely backside as she bent over to wring the water from her hair. "Must all good things end?"

The naera finished her ablutions and buffed dry with a swathe of silk. "Storms won't stop blowing for our sakes. Besides, I don't think you can stomach áels much longer. Civilization calls to you."

Jarle flicked his hair aside with the tip of his blade. "I confess, there are moments when I miss the rooftops and alleys, the back corner of the Silver Pig, and its spicy stout, but I can't say that I wish to return to the life I had. To quote my best mate, Irilio, 'The senses, desires, luxuries, melodies, and all that makes life delightful enrich and deepen the mortal genius, but the soul can scrape heaven only in exile of such indulgences.'"

The girl rummaged through the dredged treasure and selected a massive livery collar set with aquamarine cabochons. She donned the chain and approached the fire. "Your friend sounds clever."

Jarle's heart nearly stopped at the sight of her. In the firelight, the gems glowed like stars upon her skin. "Irilio's wisdom ends with a beautiful face. We share the weakness in common."

Avaren flaunted her breasts, running her fingers over the golden links. "I suppose my latest fashion would stupefy him."

Jarle chuckled. "Aye. He'd look at you and say something banal like, 'Even the Three Sisters are invidious of your radiance.'"

"And what would you say?" Avaren picked up a metal mirror and began to comb her hair with a spiny shell. In a month, her tresses had grown down to her thighs.

Jarle rinsed his hands and approached his lover from behind. He wrapped his arms around her waist. "You are a vision, a goddess made flesh."

Avaren smiled at their reflection in the polished dish. "Whoever thought thieves could be so glib?"

Jarle kissed the top of her head. "Whoever dreamed naeras were real?"

"Do you think other legendary creatures exist?" Avaren asked.

Jarle stroked his lover's arms. "The Sigrün are said to live in the frozen wastelands of Cypricha, and woodland spirits in Belvaaste. When I was a child, my father told me tales of the serpent of Jubbal. Many swear the dragon's tears feed the Blue Spring to this day."

Avaren discarded the mirror and turned to face him. "Legends claim that naeras leave their watery realms during lunar alignments when the veil between the dreaming and the waking thins. I wager satyrs and serpents venture forth as well to carouse with randy maidens."

"Aye. The Ingvizitorij would claim you are daemon-spawned and hunt you. The mages and scholars would dissect you. Frisky satyrs like me, well, we'd simply devour you." Jarle grabbed Avaren and slung her over his shoulder. "If you are a dream," he said, twirling in place, "may I never awaken."

Avaren let out a happy squeal as Jarle bit into her hip. She slapped his naked rump, seeking to escape. "Put me down, you furry beast," she cried.

Jarle munched on her thigh. "This is the least you deserve for almost drowning me yesterday, nymph."

"No guts, no glory," she replied, wiggling in his grasp.

Jarle spanked her and tossed her on the bed. He fetched plates and goblets from the pile, rinsed them in the cascade, then returned to the fire. "Breakfast's almost ready."

Avaren draped a blanket over her shoulders and rolled out of bed. "Want to give that Seh'nahiel wine another try? I think we have a few bottles left."

Jarle carved the áel and served the fillets. "I don't normally imbibe this early," he said with a shrug, "but I see no reason to adhere to tradition."

Avaren rifled through a heap of tarnished baubles and pulled a crusty bottle from under a mangled shield. She brought the wine to the firepit and tucked the seal into the coals.

As the wax sizzled, the hairs at the back of Jarle's neck bristled, and a familiar tingle tickled his throat. "I swear this vintage is haunted."

The naera sat by the fire and gazed at the thief through snowy lashes. She smiled and tossed her silver hair, which shone like gleaming sun rays in the dark. "Yet we remain constant to its mystic charms."

When Jarle cut the topper with his blade, a heady scent seduced their senses. Lightning flashed, and thunder roared. A warm gust of wind brushed their skin and filled the rupestrian hideout with the attar of roses. Along the walls, the mineral deposits sparkled as though illuminated by lamplight.

The thief poured the precious liquid into a pair of dented cups. He handed one to his lover with a sheepish grin and lost himself in the jeweled beauty of her eyes. Whatever elemental trickster had dwelled in the old bottle had fled, but not before pulling his heartstrings. "To the old—wisdom and treasure," he toasted.

Avaren raised her goblet. "To the young—all health and pleasure."

They sipped heartily and in high spirits before digging into the meal with their hands. The spicy flavor of the garlic and chives complemented the earthy bouquet of the wine. Upon finishing their meager repast, they stretched their legs and basked in the warmth of the fire.

Avaren ran her fingers through Jarle's hair before tracing an old scar on the back of his neck. "What happened here?"

Amused by her exploration, Jarle refilled their goblets. "A shard of glass."

Avaren kissed the faded line. "A window?"

The thief laughed. "No, try a widow."

"Was she widowed before or after she tried to cut your throat," Avaren asked.

Jarle shrugged. "She became one afterward."

The girl pinched his ribs. "You are a frightening man, Jarle Jadien."

"Aye." Jarle drained his cup, his mood growing darker. "You can do much better."

"Why say so?" Avaren said, refilling his glass.

"I haven't been entirely honest with you," Jarle confessed. "There are some details about the night of the murder, which I haven't divulged."

Avaren's eyes narrowed. "Like what?"

Jarle pulled the blanket tight around his shoulders. "Months ago, I heard a rumor that a man was looking for a partner to clean out a stash. After a few inquiries, I met with Varrus, the captain of your father's guard."

Avaren set the bottle down. "Captain Sigolian betrayed our house?"

The thief nodded. "Men born under calamitous stars have no choice but to serve. Our coin purses, and our debts steer our destinies. Change requires risk, which is almost always driven by desperation."

"I don't understand," Avaren said. "My father paid his retinue well."

Jarle gazed at the crackling flames. "Tan'os' wages could not fulfill Varrus' dream of returning to Calantia. Our meetings were few and tense, but when I asked him why he was willing to undertake the gambol, he mentioned his great-grandfather's lemon orchards. The earnings of a sellsword kept food in his belly, not much else."

"What if Varrus had hired another burglar?" Avaren's voice faded to a whisper. "I'd be dead."

"More than likely." Jarle sighed.

Avaren stared down at her goblet. "Why did you do it?"

"This won't make any sense to you, but the truth is that I wanted to put an end to my life of crime. With enough coin, I could disappear, start over. Misery drove me to your door as surely as it did every man who conspired against your family."

"You steal for a living. Surely you were not as strapped as Varrus. Why not retire or invest in a business?" Avaren asked.

Jarle took a sip of wine. "My life is complicated."

"I'm not going anywhere," said Avaren.

"After my father's death, I had to sift through trash or steal if I wanted to eat. The Tangles were rife with urchin gangs bound together by a common purpose. Survival meant everything. In between beatings and scuffles, petty thefts, and muggings, the Mistress of Rats noticed me. Her people took me in, clothed me, fed me, taught me how to fight. For a decade, I was a bottom-feeder, getting by on the jobs no one else wanted. I dreamt of being recruited into her inner circle, of wealth and prestige, never realizing the cost of such success."

"Ah, you are indebted to her."

"Aye. Once the harpy sinks her claws into you, you are bound forever to the guild."

"How does it all work?" Asked Avaren.

Jarle scoffed. "The racket is shockingly simple. Behind the reputable merchants and businesses that specialize in art, silver, and jewels is the Mistress of Rats. Jewels and precious objects are sold, tracked through the city, and eventually stolen. Artisans melt the metals, cut and reset the gems, and fences move the merchandise. The process goes on and on," motioned Jarle. "People like me do the stealing, risking our hides for a small cut of the haul. The jewels, the paintings, and sculptures are all accounted for—there is no cheating the Mistress, not if you want to live. After each caper, we have to pay for our safe houses, our armor, our weapons, and our contacts. What's left is never enough to break free." Jarle drank the goblet dry. "Once you work for the Mistress, the only way to quit is to die. She doesn't let any of her rats retire until they pay their debts. I took Varrus up on his offer because I didn't want to live that way anymore. I didn't want to find myself as old as the

Weasel still working the streets." Jarle looked at Avaren. "I may be sick of eating áels morning, noon, and night, but the truth is that I'd continue to do so if it meant I could live the rest of my days in peace by your side." Jarle ran a hand through Avaren's hair. "After all that has happened, I feel as though making love to you is the closest I will ever get to paradise."

Avaren stood and held out her hand. "Come to bed. Let us enjoy our heaven while we can."

Jarle joined Avaren on the blankets and drew her close. He caressed the lovely line of her jaw. "Avi, you are my beautiful dream," he said, gazing into her eyes. "There isn't a night that goes by that I don't thank the gods for guiding my footsteps into your bedchamber."

Avaren straddled his hips and wrapped her arms around him. Her eyes swirled and sparked with a feral glow. "I'm glad you stole my dowry and my heart."

Jarle's breath caught when Avaren slid down along his body. The girl smelled of wood smoke and sea salt, and she felt delightfully warm. "I love you, and I want you to be happy."

"There is only one way to ensure my happiness," Avaren whispered against his lips. "You know what I want."

Sparks of anticipation tightened the thief's stomach as he thrust into her clenching heat. "Aye. You shall have all you desire and more."

Clinging to each other, they moved like raging autumn seas. Their caresses grew heated as their mouths devoured rather than communed. Their fiery passions burned away the cold, and their moans joined the howling wind.

Jarle dug his fingers into Avaren's flesh and plunged into her with the raw force of his need. He delighted in the sound of her moans, her musk, and the pliant yielding of her body.

Beneath him, Avaren clung to his neck. Her breasts brushed against his chest, and her fingers wound into his hair. She bit his neck and moved her trembling lips to his. "Jarle," she coaxed, "tell me what I long to hear."

The back of the rogue's throat tingled, and his breath hitched. He lifted Avaren's buttocks with ecstatic fury and surged into her, feeling as though he might shatter if he resisted. "Rigo must die," he gritted, reeling at the edge of control.

Avaren tangled her fingers in the thief's hair and kissed him with a fervor that threatened to draw his soul out through his mouth. Unable to think, Jarle flexed his loins and surrendered to the urge that had seduced him from the moment he first saw her. He leaned forward, grasped her waist, and reveled at having her body entirely at his command. When his frame shuddered with the thunderous tremor of release, he rammed into her with sadistic thrusts. Almost crying with the excruciating sensation, he climaxed inside her in a slippery outrush. "Avaren," he breathed, unwilling to withdraw, "I love you more than I value my life."

T⊙ MANY TANKARDS

Mir'kadi, Twenty-Fourth of Triesse, 445 A'A'diel

Late autumn in Reyza consisted of sharp, stinging winds, and chilly days of hazy light. Wild gusts from the currents of a cooling sea, rattled the dockside hovels and howled through the Tangles with eerie delight. Fall was a time when fishermen cast out early and begged the gods for sunny days.

In the darkness before dawn, a dense fog roiled along the cliffside of Firehill. The swirling mists reduced the lighthouse's blazing beacon to little more than a feeble beam that probed the darkness beyond the Reyzan peninsula.

Kaban Ulstor stood at the edge of the public dock and yawned loudly. The sleepy fisherman scratched the morning scruff on his jaw with one hand while the other directed his stream of urine down into the harbor. He shuddered as he stuffed his cock back into his bedraggled pantaloons, as much from relief as from the chilly breeze blowing in from the sea. Rain was coming; he could smell it. Kaban rubbed his eyes and nodded silent salutations to the misty shapes of his comrades as they prepared to head out for the day's fishing.

Clasping his hands, Kaban prayed, "Hear my humble plea, mighty Ahitsura, give your humble supplicant generous and gentle seas this day." Dozens of throats quietly echoed the prayer as the fisherman and his comrades pushed their dories into the blackened water.

Kaban leaned down and set his shoulder to the squared stern of his boat and shoved hard. His bare feet sank deep into the cold sand as the boat scraped into the gentle swells. "Fuck me thrice," he swore as he waded into the cold water before sliding into his dory.

"Cold enough to shrink Bel's hairy balls," came a cheerful voice from the darkness.

"Then yer lucky to not have any, Sola!" Kaban called back as he took up his oars and rowed.

"He's got you there!" shouted another voice.

"Maybe, but I've got enough cock to satisfy your skinny wife and that tavern wench you carry on with!" Sola laughed.

"The one he swears is not his sweetheart," came another reply.

Several different voices continued the banter as the fishermen of Reyza rowed out to sea. The playful hazing was a morning ritual as old as the city itself.

Kaban was about to hurl another insult in Sola's direction when hazy shapes as large as warehouses slowly drifted into view. A thrill of fear shot through the fisherman as he lifted his oars and squinted into the gloom.

The first ruby rays of dawn pierced the fog illuminating the reefed sails and fluttering pennons of gigantic warships. Anchored bow to stern, the vessels blocked the harbor in an unbroken line. Under cover of night, the Northmen had sailed into the port unseen, without the aid of lamps or harbor pilots. The colossal dreadnoughts from the north dwarfed Reyza's merchantmen and fishing vessels like swans among common ducks.

"Thromm!" Kaban shouted aloud as his stomach dropped.

The fishermen's excited shouts filled the darkness.

"Looks like fish and women will be in high demand today!" Sola yelled in a half-hearted attempt to sound cavalier.

"Giants eat for ten!" shouted a fellow.

"Hide your wives!" advised another.

Although the Thrommish had not issued demands or threats, there wasn't a single soul in Reyza who believed the Vise's murder would go unanswered. As Kaban stared at the intimidating black juggernaut before him, the last thing on his mind was fish.

The immense flagship of the Northern fleet floated in the stillness, her spars towering above the mist. The three-hulled angular monstrosity cast an opaque belt of shadow on the darkling glassy shimmer of the sea, obscuring hopes and foreboding doom. Fearing for the safety of his family, Kaban spat and began to row toward shore.

*
**

With the arrival of the Northern Fleet, a hushed tension descended upon Reyza. It was palpable in the suspicious glances of merchants and the whispers of women as they bustled between errands. Droves of Thrommish sailors—fearsome, pale-haired giants who stood half an arm's length above the average Reyzan—poured into harborside taverns like starved and lusty dogs. Whatever perils they had faced during the long voyage south had left them with a voracious appetite for women, drink, and solid ground beneath their feet.

The fleet's quartermasters engaged every available carpenter, sailmaker, and rigger the port had to offer. Local shipwrights accustomed to repairing dories and caravels labored alongside their Thrommish peers in the formidable task of restoring the storm-damaged vessels.

Two companies were deployed from the Chancellery to keep the peace. The Fifth Company comprised of Ca'Dezer Cavalrymen and outfitted with gleaming scabbards, and indigo cloaks funneled through Nahiel's Arch and positioned themselves at the foot of Gavalene Hill, while the Sixth City Guard Company marched to the docks.

Meager light pierced the cloud cover, sending shadows racing between the crowded slums that rose like a toothy grin along the cliffs. In the alley behind the ramshackle Portly Otter Taverna, a chubby, ruddy-cheeked girl, struggled to hold her pants up while balancing a slimmer girl on her shoulders.

Glori motioned to the girl beneath her. "Hold still, Yvy."

"I'm trying," the girl complained, shivering in the cold. "Why do I always have to be on the bottom?"

"You know why." Glori craned her neck to peer through the grimy window. "Because you're stronger than me."

"I know," Yvina shook her shoulders. "I just like hearing you say it."

Glori wiped the grunge from a windowpane. "Oh, damn!"

"What?" Yvina shifted. "What is it!?"

"Captain Brianni has brought the entire Sixth inside to arrest the Thrommish churls!"

"Is he crazy?" Yvina wondered aloud.

Impetuous Captain Brianni, known for excessive drinking and brawling, led the Sixth City Guard Company. Unlike the Ca'Dezer, who counted among their ranks well-trained nobles, mercenaries, and adventurers, the Sixth was cobbled together from a motley crew of peasants and ne'er-do-wells who had been suckling their mother's teats when Reyza had last gone to war. The Sixth was better suited for rolling drunkards and shaking down whores than challenging hardened sea rovers.

From inside the Portly Otter came the muted sounds of shouting and furniture breaking. "Tell me what's going on, Glori!" Yvina whined, tugging her friend's pant leg.

"Stop moving, and I will tell you. I can barely see inside!" Glori's fingertips grew white as she pulled herself higher along the wooden wall to peek through the clean spot on grimy windowpanes.

Squinting, she stared as half-dressed prostitutes used tankards, jugs, and wooden platters to defend themselves from the writhing mass of brawling men. Steel glinted in the amber light of lanterns as weapons appeared. Angry shouts and anguished cries followed as daggers and swords cut through limbs and impaled tender flesh. The terrified screams of people trying to escape the fray joined the cacophony of chaos.

"One of Brianni's goons smashed the big blond Northman we were trailing with a bench. Shit and sequins, all Hel is unbound," Glori said breathlessly. "The Sixth is outmatched three to one. Today is gonna be one profitable day for the undertaker!" The urchin flinched as a wooden flagon narrowly missed the window.

Yvina scowled as Glori shifted on her shoulders. "Which big blond one? They all look the same."

"Oh, Yvy, I wish you could see this! It's a riot in there!" Glori giggled with excitement. "Big blondie just threw Corporal Cabbage into the liquor shelves! I swear he broke every bottle."

"Good, he is a mean jerk," Yvy said. "What else do you see?"

"Oooh! Someone just trashed the portrait of Mejtress Dorno."

Yvy released a low whistle, "Majster Dorno won't like that at all. He paid a fortune to paint her ugly mug."

"No! No, he won't," agreed Glori. "I wouldn't much like it either if in a bell's time everything I owned got trashed by a bunch of drunken foreigners. Lift me a little, will you?"

Yvina braced her legs beneath her friend and stretched. "What's happening now?"

"Brianni is causing a shitstorm, as usual, his guards have pulled their swords. The giants don't seem to care; they're throwing fists and chasing ladies."

"Fists against swords?"

"Yeah and—" Glori sucked in her breath sharply. "Your momma is not going to like this."

"What do you see? What?"

"I think the Mistress' favorite watering hole is about to go up in flames!" As soon as Glori said the words, the scent of burning tallow filled the air. Yvy lowered down from her tiptoes. "How bad is the fire?"

Glori eased herself off the chubby girl's shoulders. "Two lanterns just hit the curtains. Come, let's get back and tell the Mistress before this shit gets worse. Stopping all-out war may just come down to us little people!"

Yvina hiked up her pants and followed Glori around the corner. The girls darted beneath a low alcove, then rushed down a set of slippery stone steps. At the bottom, they made a left into a vaulted passage beneath the prying eyes of the alley.

"My schoolmate Sallima lives next to the Otter. Shouldn't we help put out the fire?" asked Yvina.

Glori thought about it for a moment then quickened her pace along the passage. "It's daylight, and there are a hundred people in the Otter. Besides, isn't Sallima always complaining about that flea-infested hole she calls home? Come on, what we've seen today has to be worth some coin."

"Don't you mean everything you've seen?"

"Well, sure, but you've made it all possible. You know me," Glori said with a wink. "I never leave a friend out in the cold."

"I've been in the cold all day while you go sneaking around," groused Yvina. "And you still owe me for delivering that letter the other day. I still have the bruises on my backside from that sod's boot."

Glori frowned. "I promised to pay you, didn't I?"

The clouds delivered on their threat, and a cold, steady rain began to pelt the cobbles. The friends broke into a run as the chilly downpour soaked them to the bone. Yvina's pants slid down and tripped her. She fell onto her hands and knees in a puddle. She released a string of curses worthy of a sailor, hitched her pants up, and started after Glori once more. "This is really bad, isn't it?"

"Well, I can tell you this much; those giants didn't come down here for a sunny holiday."

"You think Jars did what they say he did?" asked Yvina, falling into a breathless pace beside her companion.

Glori cringed at the mention of the name. "Shut up, fool. There's a large enough reward on his head that anyone who even whispers his name can be rounded up and tortured. You know what they did to old Weasel!" Glori traced the sign of Ven in mid air. "By Adur's cock! They broke every bone in his arms and legs, then blinded him. I'll be damned if I wind up like that."

Yvina nodded. "Momma says we'll be taking care of the Weasel for the rest of his life. I'm sorry, Glori. I won't mention him again. You'll see, I'll get better at this."

"Sure you will," Glori said before ducking under the alcove of an abandoned house wreathed in vines. "Now listen to me. Your momma is gonna be plenty mad about you spending the day with me."

"I don't care. I am my own woman." Yvina stood in the cold rain, her arms crossed in front of her chest in defiance.

"Sure you are, Yvy! But I would hate for you to get whipped again on account of me."

"I can take it."

"I know you can, but I have a better idea."

"I'm listening." Yvina remained planted as the rain plastered her fiery hair to her face.

"If you let me do the talking, I am certain that our news will overwhelm any upset the Mistress might have." Glori motioned to her obstinate friend. "Would you please get out of the rain?"

Yvy relented and joined the urchin in her erstwhile shelter. She swept soggy locks from her eyes. "Momma won't be happy about me skipping lessons, and she'll be furious about the Otter."

"That's true, but I think when we tell her about the other stuff we found out, she'll be so tickled that she'll forget all about you running out on that silly tutor of yours." Glori grinned. "Didn't I tell you the excitement around town would give up valuable information?"

Yvina wrung out her hair. "Yeah, yeah. Drunk men are loose with their coin, cocks, and tongues."

"That's right." Glori nodded, "Think about it, Yvy. When I tell the Mistress that Eva Iarris is here in the flesh, she is sure to forgive our caper. I can't wait to see the look on your momma's face when I tell her that the Marchess of Thyra is gallivanting around town disguised as a sailor with a wooden hand!"

"I think you are overly optimistic as my tutor always says. My mother forgives nothing. I'm still going to catch a whipping." Yvina's mouth curled into a sly smile. "Think she'll reward you?"

"I think she will."

"Well when she does, you owe me half. I know my numbers, and by my calculations, your debts are mounting."

Glori shook her head with a resigned smile. "Like mother, like daughter. Trouble, as the bards say, almost always wears a skirt. Well, except maybe you, Yvy. Better a skirt than those pants that are too big for you."

Yvy punched Glori's shoulder. "Don't change the subject. You give me half, deal?"

Glori rubbed her arm. "Deal."

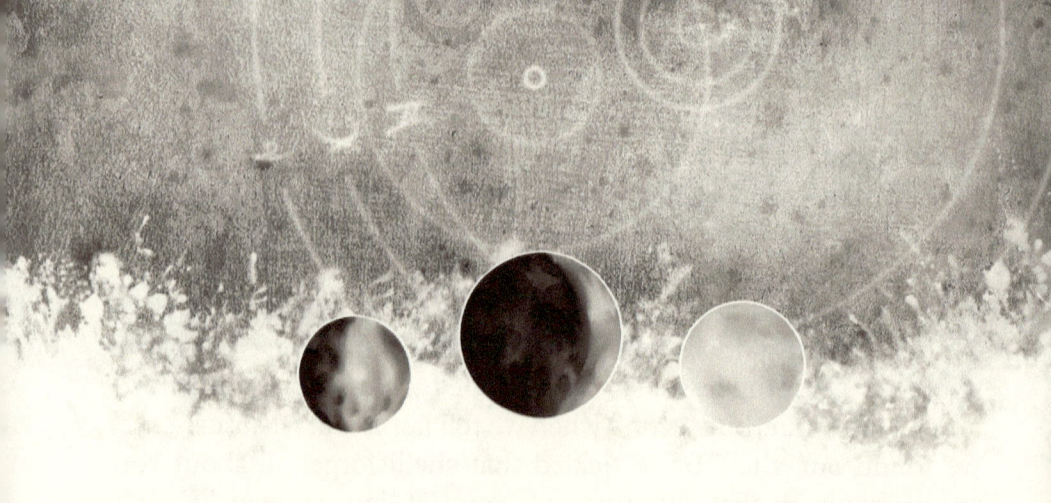

THE RUARCH'S DESTINY

Mir'kadi, Twenty-Fourth of Triesse, 445 A'A'diel

Eva paced back and forth like a caged tigress. The small, sumptuous quarters above the Swallow's Nest afforded a welcome change from the rocking drafty cabin aboard the ship, but her sour mood precluded all enjoyment.

She paused at the window, hoping to see something other than the inferno that raged unabated. Madness! Within hours of debarkation, sailors stormed the port like savages. Men, women, and children armed with buckets and bags of sand formed snaking lines through the streets. Trembling hands passed bucket after bucket in hopes of saving the flaming slums.

With each clang of the fire bell, Eva's headache worsened. She watched the mayhem for as long as she could bear it before closing the curtains. Her journey to Reyza was nothing if not ill-fated. Tears welled up in her eyes as she loosened her cravat with her left hand.

"Why?" she asked. "Why did I return?"

Frustrated, Eva surrendered to the plush, welcoming bed. She lay in the gloom, head throbbing with the peals of the bell. The air that wafted through the cracked window reeked of cinders and misery. As the faraway shouts faded, Eva cursed the mages in their lofty towers for failing to quench the flames. Knowledge was useless without practical application.

Shadows traversed the crossbeams. Eva ran a hand over the smooth lamb's wool sheets and wondered how many strangers had lain upon the soft, well-used mattress. Her mind drifted to the first time she had set foot on the deck of the *Swoughünd*. The sun beat down on the harbor, and her clothes clung to her body in the sticky heat. Shirtless sailors swabbed the ship's black decks, tying ropes, and loading cargo. She had never seen so much indecent, sweaty, male flesh. Unlike the dark-skinned Reyzans, the Thrommish were blue-eyed with hair as white as clouds. Like a conquering giant, Gøran appeared and silenced the whistles and catcalls with his booming voice. Eva smiled. Years, distance, and love for her husband had done little to douse her yearning for the father of her firstborn.

At the sound of footsteps outside in the hall, Eva sat up. A knock followed. "Who goes?" she asked.

"It's me," came Gøran's voice.

Eva unlatched the door and opened it. The disheveled man who entered did not resemble the man who had accompanied her hours earlier to Bherengello's, a respectable inn renowned for epicurean delights. The captain wore a sailor's garb. Gone were his polished boots and the pressed overcoat with gleaming buttons. An unbuttoned white shirt revealed the planes of his muscular chest, and his graying hair was tousled. The man stank of cheap liquor and held a lavender paperboard box in one hand.

"You look how I feel," said Eva, closing the door behind him.

A smug smile spread on the man's face. "Then, you must feel great."

"Your men arrive like a pack of hungry wolves in search of meat, and you join them?" Eva motioned at his garb. "You're a disgrace!"

Gøran moved past her to the liquor cabinet and produced two glasses. "They're your countrymen also, don't forget."

"What do you think you are doing?" Eva asked, snatching the cups away from him.

"Pouring us a drink."

"I believe you've had enough."

"Not enough to forget your sweet buns." Gøran handed Eva the box.

"Careful," Eva warned as she untied the twine and opened the lid. The trio of sticky pastries from the Crusty Loaf made her smile. "Mmm, I remember these from when I was little."

A lopsided grin appeared on Gøran's face as he appraised her. She wore slim trousers, a white linen shirt, and an unraveled cravat. The top three buttons of her blouse were open, revealing an enticing swath of skin. "Did anyone ever tell you that you make a damn fine man?"

Eva sought a retort but found laughter instead. "Not fair! You can make me laugh when I most want to be angry with you."

Gøran plucked the glasses from her hands and set them down on the table. He withdrew a round, black ceramic bottle from the cabinet and smiled. "Drink with me."

"My head hurts," Eva demurred.

"Raska cures headaches," the man said, filling the cups halfway.

Eva crossed her arms. "Only to create worse ones the following morning."

"One drink! Indulge me."

"Only one," said Eva.

"And then what?"

The implication warmed her cheeks and caused her to stutter like a bumbling ingénue, "W-what?"

"You heard me," the captain said with a wink.

Eva accepted the drink. "Must we always wind up here?"

"Here?" Gøran drained the liquor in one gulp and slammed the cup down. "You can't be referring to finding ourselves halfway around the globe in a bedroom drinking raska. And yet here we are, two sailors watching the world burn."

Eva shook her head. It was unbecoming of her station to be alone with a man. If word of their rendezvous spread, there would be a scandal. She set the box of pastries down on the nightstand. "Who knows about my whereabouts?"

"The crew won't betray your wishes for secrecy. No one suspects the honorable Marchess of Thyra is holed up with a deplorable sea dog in a shoddy part of town. Such conspiracies don't cross the minds of simple men." Gøran's gaze lingered on the curve of her breasts. "Sneaking about was your idea."

Her intention to land undetected to regain her bearings and recover from her sea legs had only resulted in a terrible headache. The glass trembled in her hand as she brought it to her lips. It smelled pungent and noxious. She drank, squirming as the alcohol torched its way down to her belly. "This is a drink for commoners and whores. Fitting," Eva said with a grimace.

Gøran grinned. "Which are you?"

Eva's heart thundered as loud as the fire bell. She sucked in her breath as the man fixed her with his smoldering gaze. "You forget yourself!"

"No, I remember what you choose to forget," Gøran said with quiet urgency. The giant man wrapped his muscular arms around Eva and lifted her into an embrace. His mouth sought hers for a passionate kiss.

The sensation of Gøran's lips coupled with the warmth of his body unleashed a rush of repressed emotions and with them the memories of long ago. When the captain crushed her against him, she felt as though she might faint from the ache in her heart. The kiss was temptation and damnation, an indulgence that would set fire to her world. Turning her head, Eva ended gasped, "I can't."

"Do you deny that you feel something for me still? I have spent countless nights dreaming of this moment. When you married Rhiess, a part of me died. You can't imagine what it's been like to see my son raised by another man. You can't tell me we are in this room to spin the tale of a doomed voyage of all things!"

Eva held back her tears, refusing to meet the man's gaze lest her resolve falter. "Please, stop."

Gøran lowered her but did not release her. With a gentleness at odds with his size, the sea captain lifted her chin until their eyes met. "Eva, I know I am twenty years your senior—a rough man who is neither well-educated nor well-versed in courtly manners. As you have pointed out many times, I am a brute. I have little to offer another man's wife, least of all a queen, but I have waited fifteen years for a chance to tell you how I feel. By the gods, woman, I love you!"

The proclamation struck her like a physical blow. Eva's breath fled, and her stomach dropped. "What can we do?" she asked, looking away.

"Take this cursed throne and stay here to rule over it. I will deploy half the fleet to Thyra and remain here with the rest to protect your interests. We can be together. Think about it."

"You are mad."

"Since I laid eyes on you."

Eva closed her eyes, mind racing. Staying in Reyza presented many possibilities. She could send for her children and carve a new life for herself. Her chest ached at the thought of abandoning Rhiess, the man who had shielded her from disgrace.

Eva breathed and regained her senses. "What of your woman, Vira?"

Gøran pecked Eva's cheek. "She is not important, Eva."

Pain pounded her temples. "How easily men lie!"

Gøran gripped her waist and pulled her roughly against him.

"Is hating me the only thing that makes your icy heart beat?"

"You seduced me when I was only a child. I fell in love with you!" Eva's tone turned steely, "I swallowed my feelings and gracefully accepted my husband's forgiveness while your bastard grew in my belly. How do you think that made me feel? Now you proclaim your emotions? Here? At this moment? Allow me to remind you that it was you who distanced yourself, not just from me but also from Rhiess and our son. You became a stranger to the very people you claim to love to assuage your pride and avoid discomfort. I have perfected the art of hating you."

The wintry bite in Eva's words doused the warmth in Gøran's eyes. He released her and stepped back. "I understand what this is now. I'm nothing but another piece of your righteous revenge falling into place."

Eva straightened her shoulders, her face a mask of quiet rage. "That's the beauty of being a man! When things don't go your way, you can walk away unhindered. You sail to sunnier shores and sow your seed in fresh bellies while we women are abandoned and left to suffer. Do you have any idea what it's like to lie with a man whose father likely killed my mother? Do you? Of course, you do not, because revered Captain Rarikian is a hero. Pretty maids flock to his cabins, and men fumble over themselves to be able to say, 'I served with him!' You cannot understand the burden I carry because you don't know what it's like not to be free. You don't have a fucking inkling what it's like not to have personal choice."

Gøran bowed and headed for the door.

Eva scoffed. "Where do you think you are going? I have not dismissed you."

Gøran's hand froze on the latch. He turned to face her and straightened. He stood solemnly, arms at his side, staring over Eva's head. "How may I be of service, Marchess?"

Whatever palliative effect the raska had provided had been undone by her rage. The pain in her skull throbbed with a vengeance. Eva closed her eyes and rubbed her temples. A long while passed before she spoke. "I still care for you, Gøran. Ven have mercy on me, I do."

Gøran remained silent, his eyes on her.

"What you desire is an impossibility. I am the wife of Rhiess Ensther, and I love him. I will not betray him again, especially not with you."

"I see," Gøran said bluntly. "I will not bother you again."

Eva let out an exasperated sigh, "Why must it be all or nothing with you?"

"If I cannot have you, there is nothing. To believe otherwise invites a pain I'd rather not endure."

"You stupid man, stop acting like a child because I will not open my legs for you."

Gøran exploded, "You think this is about sex?"

"Isn't it?" Eva's lips tightened.

The statement struck Gøran like a slap. He blinked. "In the beginning, it was," he said, closing his eyes, "but what I said before is true. I love you; I don't want you to despise me."

Eva turned and gazed out the window. The fire bell ceased to ring. "I don't hate you, but we cannot unwrite our history."

"What do you want, Eva?"

Eva met Gøran's gray eyes. "Be my friend—my ally."

"Friends," Gøran scoffed. "We have a son together!"

"Yes, we do," Eva said. "Raolph is a wonderful young man. We have both made sacrifices to allow him the life he deserves. Do not piss on the idea of friendship. There is more to a relationship than fucking." Her tone softened, "I want you in my life, at my side, but with the absence of intimacy. It is all I can offer you."

Gøran stood in silence, his brow furrowed as an internal debate raged within him. Before Eva could speak, he interjected, "How do we do this?"

"With small steps and clear minds." Eva offered.

"I apologize for my behavior. You deserve better."

"Forgiven." Eva nodded toward the raska, "Pour us another. My headache returns."

Gøran refilled their glasses. "You won't tell Vira about this?"

Eva shook her head. "No. Though as a friend, I advise you to consider your relationship with her. Vira deserves better too."

"You are right." Goran raised his cup, "To new beginnings?"

Eva toasted and drank.

"Now what?" Gøran poured another round.

"Tell me what you know of the *Ruarch* and Tan'os' daughter as this is the primary reason we find ourselves here. Sit down."

Gøran plopped down on an overstuffed chair and eyed her with steely eyes.

Eva grabbed the box of sweet buns from the table and sat on the bed. "You are staring, Captain."

"Apologies." Gøran broke off his gaze and looked out the window. Outside, the clouds had broken, and the three moons were shining. In the distance, beyond the rain-slick tiled roofs, the sleek shape of the *Swoughünd* floated on mirror-smooth water.

Eva crossed one leg under the other. "Go on, speak."

The grizzled captain rubbed his face with both hands and sighed. "At the turn of the century, Thyra was nothing but a forgotten city on the fringes of a marsh ruled by Strommarch Ultaf who died without a male heir."

Eva's stomach grumbled as she plucked a frosted pastry. True to its name, the bun stuck to her fingers. "A common woe."

Gøran nodded. "Ultaf elevated Tan'os, his dead brother's son, rather than one of his bastards, rumored to be many. The Strommarch took his nephew under his wing at the age of six and tasked my mother, his most cherished cousin, with the boy's rearing. I was ten at the time."

Eva took a bite of the sugared dough and stifled a satisfied moan. The argument had left her hungry. "I didn't know you and

Tan'os were so close. Your lineage explains why my husband didn't outright kill you when he learned about our affair."

Gøran narrowed his eyes. "Times like this, I wish he had."

"Please, continue."

"In our youth Tan'os and I were inseparable. One day—I'll never forget it—three Seh'nahiel barques sailed upriver. Tan'os was thirteen at the time, and I had just completed my rites of manhood. That morning the keep was in an uproar. Ultaf ordered a grand feast prepared in honor of our guests. Eagerly, we climbed the watchtowers to view the spectacle. It was like nothing we had ever seen. Unlike the oiled oakwood planks of our ships, the Seh'nahiel vessels' hulls were smooth as glass. Their sleek sides bore colors we had never seen—Canary, bloodwood, and ash, inlaid to form fantastic patterns. At the tips of their spars, long red flags streamed like fire drakes. Unlike our rustic scrollwork, their golden prows boasted carved maidens with arms outstretched."

Gøran's eyes misted with the recollection. "My eyes grew wide when the first passengers disembarked. The men and women were slender with long, pointed ears pierced with precious jewels that glinted in the light. I thought them frail until I saw the savagery in their glowing eyes. The craftsmanship of their armor and weapons made ours appear basic and crude. Their feet made no sound as they walked. I recall wondering if the Anvaari gods of old had been summoned to our shores."

Eva licked the frosting from her fingers. "Seh'nahiel have that effect, don't they?"

"Aye, they do." Gøran paused, then continued, "Before that fateful day, Thyra and A'diel shared a tenuous peace. The delegation deliberated for three days with the Thyran Circle. On the fourth day, our cities signed a trade treaty. As a token of goodwill, their leader, Yaereene Zylbella, who still lives I might add, bestowed the *Ruarch* to Ultaf."

"Sounds like love at first sight," Eva teased.

Unprovoked, Gøran continued, "You couldn't possibly imagine. Ultaf called the barque a primped whore, but Tan'os and I saw her virtues. The *Ruarch* was the finest ship we had ever seen—a wolf among our clumsy sheep."

Eva considered whether to indulge in another of the sugary

treats. She heard the words coming out of Gøran's mouth, but could only listen to her inner turmoil. She thought she had slain the defiant young girl content to be taught new tricks by a salty old dog, yet Gøran's earnest advances tempted her. Confusion tied her stomach into knots. She had children to consider, and the honor of a kingdom. Most importantly, she loved Rhiess.

Sensing her distraction, the captain cleared his throat. "Eva?"

Eva's forehead creased with distress. "Yes?"

Gøran rose and took her hands in his. "I know what you are thinking," he said, kneeling before her, "but you and my son are the only souls in Laremlis for whom I would give my life without hesitation. I will not fail you."

The fire drained from Eva's body. She set the box aside, leaned forward, and clasped the man's broad shoulders. "Yielding to temptation would have been a terrible mistake."

"I cannot apologize enough for my impulsiveness."

Eva nodded and reclined on the bed. "Please, continue."

"Is this how you would spend the evening?"

Eva nodded. "Indeed."

"All the rumors are true," Gøran said, sitting by the fire. "Ultaf gave the *Ruarch* to Tan'os three years later to commemorate his coming of age. Together, we sailed out in the spring of 409 and didn't set foot in Thyra's halls for four years. We returned when Ultaf summoned Tan'os to wed Lady Fienna of Wrens."

Eva relaxed into the pillows; her headache diminished. "Considering how rarely Fienna comes down from Wrens' Vane, I presume their marital bliss short-lived."

Gøran took another swig. "Not at all. Lady Fienna dug her talons into Tan'os so deep I feared he would give up the ocean forever. For months after their wedding, they left their bed only to appease the necessities of life. Rhiess was born a year later."

"She's a sweet old woman who embraced me as her daughter the moment she met me. She dotes on her grandchildren as much as she does, Rhiess." The smile prompted by the happy memory faded. "My husband never speaks of his parents' marriage. What happened?"

Gøran sighed. "Eventually Ensther tired of his landlocked life and abandoned his family for the sea. After a few years, Fienna and Tan'os reconciled their differences through letters, but the passion never rekindled."

Eva grew pensive. "Fienna found companionship with her steward—a much younger man. He was a good stepfather."

Gøran nodded. "Mikveil is a decent man."

"How did Tan'os become involved with the war with Five Isles?"

"Tan'os was a gifted captain. He learned fast; assimilated knowledge and ideas from foreigners who crossed our paths. Unlike old Ultaf, he wanted to see Thyra thrive like some of our more cosmopolitan neighbors. He admired the opulence of Goizonne and A'diel, envied the wealth of Reyza and the cargo from Terranakis. Convinced Thromm should dominate the waters from the Valga to the Southern Sea; he directed our efforts toward enriching Thyra. Sailors flocked to his command seeking fortune, and soon, the *Ruarch* numbered one among hundreds of vessels. With new trade routes plotted, treaties and commissions followed."

Gøran took a swig of raska before continuing, "Everything went well until privateers from Five Isles began to plunder our cargo. The larger our fleet became, the more losses we suffered. Tan'os hated to lose. It didn't matter whether he lost one man or a hundred pounds of Wendingport cheese. He would rage just the same. Jarle Draos didn't waste any time seeking him as an ally—a wise decision if you ask me. Tan'os armed his ships and entered into a bloody conflict that spanned a decade. Without Thromm's help, Reyza would have burned to the ground."

"Yes, I remember the war—the constant state of fear we all lived in." Eva pointed to the fireplace. "Please, toss another log in the fire."

"After we weakened Five Isles, peace returned to the seas. At your father's request, Tan'os remained in Reyza, and the protection of Thyra fell to me. That's when our navy split into the Northern and Southern Fleets." Gøran added wood to the flames and stoked the coals with a poker until the fresh log ignited. "In 428, Ensther sailed north with the *Ruarch* to renew our trade agreements with A'diel. After several weeks, he departed with a hold full of Seh'nahiel silk and a secretive passenger—a highborn, pregnant woman."

"Who was she?" Eva asked.

"I remember the look in his eyes when he described her. The pale-skinned arcanist from House Sunblood brandished the beauty of her ancient bloodline. She had luminous eyes, the color of amber, and hair so black it shone indigo. Tan'os never told me her name, nor could I find it in the A'dielian manifest. Tan'os often wondered if his mysterious passenger brought on his sorry luck. Honestly, I don't doubt it."

"Why? What happened?"

"At first, not much. The voyage fared well for a week before the crossing soured. The first mate became ill and died, followed a day later by the ship's quartermaster. Men reported strange whisperings during the day and nightmares at night. The scuttlebutt grew malicious, and within a score of days, a disciplined crew turned treacherous. 'Throw the soulbinder overboard,' they cried, believing the ship cursed."

"Of course, they blamed the woman," Eva scoffed.

"As time wore on, life aboard became stranger. Some claimed the stars in the sky shifted. Tan'os confessed that for the first time in his life, he lost all sense of direction. For a month, the *Ruarch* wandered aimlessly at sea."

"How is that possible?" asked Eva. "You said it yourself, the route to Reyza is routine."

Gøran shrugged. "How did you heal dying men in my hold? Some mysteries defy explanation."

Eva crossed her legs. "What of the pregnant woman?"

"As the situation worsened, Tan'os feared for his passenger's safety. He confined her to her stateroom and posted guards outside her cabin. Hours later, the wind died, the sails grew slack. The *Ruarch* floated listlessly in a swirling fog for days. Rations ended, and the ocean yielded no catch. Sailors began to chew the leather of their boots and scabbards. Some perished from thirst; others jumped overboard. Inevitably, Tan'os began to suspect the rumors about the woman were true."

"Did he confront her?" Eva asked.

"Aye." Gøran tugged at his beard. "After a few more days in the windless morass, he pressed her to confess her role. The noblewoman pleaded for her child's life; claimed innocence of the *Ruarch's* plight, but Tan'os was unconvinced. The night he threatened her life, a storm came. Thunder, lightning, and rain raged while relentless waves washed some of the crew out to sea. The sea rose around them like claws, ripping the *Ruarch* apart at the seams. The few poor bastards left on deck beheld the worst horror of all. The water beneath them writhed with black tentacles. Above the roar of the storm came the sound of voices. Beautiful creatures unlike any they had ever seen emerged from the storm-tossed waters—women with skin like moonlight, and long, streaming hair the color of snow. Singing their Helish songs, a score of them climbed aboard the foundering ship and ensnared all in their path."

"It sounds like a nightmare," Eva said in quiet horror.

"Through the thick curtain of rain, Tan'os spotted the beacon blaze of Firehill. They were sinking but a league from Reyza's harbor, but in that weather, it may as well have been a thousand. Terrified, Tan'os leapt into the ocean, preferring to drown than die at the hands of the monstrous women. Clinging to a plank, horrified beyond measure, he watched as pale hands and black tails dragged his men to the abyss. Tan'os never forgot the screams and the terror of that night. He swam toward the shoreline, but the suction of the sinking barque pulled him under."

Eva frowned. "What about the Seh'nahiel woman?"

"The storm of 428 devastated Reyza and coincided with the lunar alignment. It took the city over two years to recover from the damage. Many ships sank along Reyza's reefs. Drowned men littered the beach like seaweed. The Sunblood passenger presumably drowned."

Eva raised an eyebrow. "Obviously, Tan'os survived."

"Everyone thought him dead." Gøran leaned forward, "Until a year later."

Eva stared at Goran. "You jest."

"No. Dock hands discovered Ensther wandering along the shore half frozen to death with an infant in his arms. He couldn't recall where he had been, but claimed the child was his."

"So what are you telling me—that my sister in law is a sea monster, an offspring of those infernal women; that the *Ruarch* drifted into some other realm?"

"Aye. Growing up, you must have heard the rhymes. 'When the moons are up on high, the Three Sisters part the sky, mortal and immortal fates are tied.'"

Eva frowned. "Rubbish. The alignment is nigh. Do you see naeras anywhere? Face it; this yarn is an old man's fantasy to justify having raped some undeserving wench whose child he took pity on."

"I knew Tan'os, Nogh guard him. He was not a superstitious man, yet I saw the fear in his eyes when he told me this tale. After the incident, he never set foot on a ship again. He was thirty-five, hardly an old man." Gøran reclined back. "As for his daughter, naera or not, one thing is certain; the girl is Starborn. You can see it in her eyes."

Disbelief spread on Eva's face. She had expected some useful facts but had gotten an old wives' tale instead. The story Gøran imparted made the gossip surrounding Avaren's origins sound tame. "Starborn, daughter of a naera, is quite the claim."

"I'm not the only one who believes such a thing. Ask around."

"People like to spread tales about gentility. If I believed everything I heard, I would attest Rigo has the head of a swine and a cock long enough to reach Dessia."

"Does he not?" Gøran corked the Raska bottle.

"For a moment you had me, you really did," said Eva.

"Only a moment?" Gøran chided. "I have told you all I know. Truth or not, I cannot say."

"Get some sleep," Eva said, pointing to the door. "That's an order. We'll need our wits tomorrow when we visit Ambassador Ers."

The captain stood and bowed. "Pleasant dreams, Marchess."

THE HAND OF FATE

Daimodi, Twenty-Fifth of Triesse, 445 A'A'diel

Candlelit shadows danced within the coral-encrusted alcoves of Neylen's villa. Perched high on Gavalene Hill, Ca'Ithas' decorative masonry boasted red marble banding and chevron-patterned limestone. Casement windows rose tall, culminating in clover-shaped arches that opened onto ornamented balconies. Though compact, the villa's elegance surpassed the neighboring estates like a jewel among river stones.

Reserved for the comfort of visiting regents, Ca'Ithas, had never served as a permanent residence. Thus, the Reyzan Council was outraged when Rigo bestowed the national treasure to a mere ambassador.

Within the walls of Ca'Ithas, Neylen paced, rapt in thought. The hem of his black silk robe whispered in his wake as he circled a ring of columns that supported the dome above his bedchamber. As the Dessian made his rounds, the flames in the sconces elongated, drawing toward him like cobalt shards to a lodestone.

In the sunken center of the room, a trio of cinnamon-skinned youths lay sprawled and spent, their dark hair spilling over brocaded pillows. The concubines' bitten and bruised flesh scripted the testimony of a sadistic orgy that had lasted hours.

Neylen turned his gaze from their sweat-slicked bodies to the domed ceiling, where a glittering mosaic depicted the mythical battle between Bessellyn and the seven-headed drake. The artist had chosen to render the climax of the fight when the famed shield maiden had severed one of the beast's heads. The hydra's gushing blood, conceived in polished red tiles, formed the pattern under which he slept. He had lain awake, many a sleepless night, pondering the fate of the defeated drake.

The myth was among Neylen's favorites, told to him by his mother. In ancient times, when the Seh'nahiel capital of Lyrr'cadea thrived at the peak of its glory, Jassindora Ar'Nohva dispatched her fiercest warrior to destroy the invading tribes of Yerr'draki barbarians. Believing the conflict would end with the death of the enemy's living god, Bessellyn hunted Yarvisirg, the seven-headed dragon. After a long and bloody battle, Bessellyn severed four of Yarvisirg's heads and felled the beast. Triumphant, the shield maiden returned with two of the fearsome trophies as proof of the creature's demise. Ar'Nohva transformed flesh to stone and placed the dragon heads atop the towers of her palace as a warning to all who would challenge Seh'nahiel supremacy.

The hydra was wounded, not destroyed. And in a score of years, the living god resurged, inspiring a new generation of Yerr'draki tribes to seek vengeance. In the second invasion of Lyrr'cadea, Jassindora Ar'Nohva and her champions perished, and the splendorous city was reduced to smoldering ashes. Through rape and slavery, the once-pure Seh'nahiel bloodline became tainted with Yerr'draki blood. The few who escaped the massacre fled their ancestral lands and crossed the ocean to Ibea.

Neylen scanned the shadows, sensing a familiar presence in the cupola. The idea of his deadly associate spying on his earlier diversions sent a frisson of delight racing down his belly. He casually allowed his silken robe to fall open and reveal the effect the thought inspired. "The mosaic seems ill-suited for the home of visiting kings," he said aloud. "I often wonder if the bloody head cutting serves as a warning or an invitation."

When no response came, Neylen approached the window and looked out. The villa's topiary garden defied winter's grasp, refusing to surrender to the elements. The rose bushes in the marble urns still bore masses of yellow blooms. The land in Reyza boasted a vitality rarely seen in his native soil, where the sun withered both throat and root.

With a whispered incantation, the Dessian caused a trickle of heat to surge along the length of his body. In Reyza, even the warmest rooms felt cold and damp.

"How long have you been watching?" Neylen asked, his breath misting on the windowpane.

"Long enough," came the curt reply.

Reaching down, Neylen stroked himself, imagining the sorceress' warm mouth engulfing his cock. He turned in the direction of the voice. "Your timing is impeccable."

Tendrils of ink-black smoke seeped forth from the shadowed alcove. The vapors spiraled around the dome before descending in a sudden rush and coalescing into a feminine form. From the mist emerged a youthful woman clad in supple black leather that clung to her curves like tar. Crisscrossed along her back were two short swords with carved bone handles. When she removed the mask that concealed her features, a long dark braid uncoiled down her spine. The woman regarded Neylen with hazelnut-colored eyes set deep beneath angled brows. The fine laugh lines on her cheeks betrayed thirty seasons, perhaps more. The woman's gaze didn't waver as she tucked her mask into her belt. "Sleep eludes you yet again?"

The sorceress' reputation was legendary. She was known in the streets only as a terrible, indefinable fear, a shadow that could—if provoked—find her way into bedchamber and privy, nursery and kitchen. The Hand of Fate, people called her, anointing themselves upon uttering the cursed name.

Neylen savored his arousal, giving flight to the lurid thought of clasping his hands around the woman's neck while he defiled her. "We are not so different," he replied.

"True, we are both serpents."

Neylen's robe glided over the marble floor as he approached the mysterious entity. While the rest of the world thought her a phantasm, he knew her to be flesh and blood. Beneath the dyed leather armor was the soft body of a woman who, by the nature of her profession, surely enjoyed violence. "Men by their very natures crave danger and diversion. I find it thrilling that both can be found in the arms of a woman."

"Or a man." Before Neylen's eyes, the woman transformed into a frail old man—an eye blink later, into a callow youth. "I suspect you prefer boys."

"I wonder, Vess, what could entice you to reveal your native form?"

"Trust me; you would not enjoy the sight."

Neylen reached out and raised the boy's chin so he could peer at his neck. "This scar upon your chin does not change with your guise. An exceptional blade must have inflicted a wound which proves impervious to your infernal powers."

Vess returned to her original form. "An old gift from Tan'os," she said unamused.

Neylen's hand wrapped around the woman's slender throat. His lips brushed against hers. "Does your new master please you?"

"I have come to collect my due," she replied.

Against the warmth of his inner thigh, Neylen felt the flat of a cold dagger. His mouth curved into a grin when the sword dug into the delicate flesh of his groin. The threat to his manhood should have filled him with terror, but it only heightened his desire. There was no thrill quite like tempting Fate. "It is a pity that your steel did not taste Mast's blood or finish off Avaren Ensther. However, I am a man of my word. I will deliver payment on one condition."

The blade slid higher until Neylen was forced to stand on his toes. "I'm listening," said Vess.

Neylen eased his grip and delivered a caress. His knuckles trailed down the valley of her breasts. "I desire a continued partnership—of course."

Vess withdrew the blade and fondled his testicles with her leather gloves. The hard planes of her face melted into a beatific smile. "The night is young."

What the dagger failed to do, her rough handling accomplished. A shiver ran down the length of Neylen's spine, deflating his arousal. The Dessian shrank away from the woman, suddenly wishing he hadn't initiated such close contact. Releasing her, he tied his robe closed. "Let us discuss terms," he said, motioning toward the strewn pillows.

Vess eyed the sleeping trio with disgust. "In private," she said, sheathing her dagger.

"Let us retire to the library," Neylen said, moving past her. As they walked, the only sound came from the rustling of his footsteps on the polished floor. Vess' eerie silence caused Neylen to doubt whether she was still behind him, but he resisted the urge to look.

Along the hall, oil lamps in the shape of winged drakes sputtered to life as he approached a double set of brass doors. With a leaden clang, the latch lifted, and the massive portal opened, untouched by mortal hand. Stepping aside, Neylen motioned for Vess to enter. "After you."

The moment the woman crossed the threshold, a myriad of candles ignited, bathing the study in a warm glow. Bookshelves crammed with leather-bound tomes lined the walls, rising to a coffered ceiling inlaid with coral, lapis, and debossed carvings. In the center of the room, an assortment of maps, scrolls, and books rested on a wooden table. An iron-mantled fireplace occupied the space between two windows. Close to the hearth, a pair of chaises faced each other separated by a card table.

With a whispered incantation, Neylen caused the pile of logs in the hearth to ignite. The flames leapt into a cheery blaze sending a gust of heat into the room. With a flourish, the Dessian motioned to a sofa. "Please, make yourself comfortable."

Vess studied the wooden cards fanned on the table. "I didn't know you played Thrarttas," she mused.

"I am but a humble initiate. My skills are not yet worthy of even the youngest courtier." Neylen walked to the fire, picked up a kettle from a trivet, and hung it on the crane. The hook swung into the flames with a creak. The scent of mulled spices filled the room. "Do you play?"

Vess pulled the deck apart with a few deft flicks, splitting the stack into eight separate spinning sections before rejoining them. She fanned the cards at a dizzying speed, whipping them from one hand to the other. "I dabble."

Impressed, Neylen raised an eyebrow. "A thousand years will pass before I dabble as well as you."

"The key to the dominion of Thrarttas is the Lovers," Vess

said, pulling a colorful card from the shuffle. Upon the face of the card, beneath a stylized flowering arbor, a man and a woman made love. "Without the Lovers, the Empire is thrust into perpetual war, draining your pockets and your patience while creating a game so unbearable it is not worth playing. Many have forsaken the game for this reason."

Neylen narrowed his eyes. "Continue."

Vess pulled another card with a flourish, flicking it casually between her fingers, before laying it on the table. "Represented by a child trapped inside a ribcage and a crook-shaped constellation of winter stars, Ven, Lord of the Needle, whether through time or misfortune, will trump all. The Lovers are like the innocent in the cage of bones, oblivious to death's woes. You see, it's impossible to play Thrarttas without knowledge of the ancient myths. The best players are, in some ways, mystics. Arcanist Olos, a long-time mentor of mine, retains the rare honor of having lost only once. He believes that our history is cyclical, that our destinies are scripted before birth."

"What are you getting at?" asked Neylen.

Vess placed the stack of cards over the card bearing the guise of the skeleton. From thin air, she drew The One, a hideous card of a snake gobbling an egg. "Reyza is a prosperous nation, but try to strangle her, and you will find history repeating itself. The serpent eats its own tail."

Neylen's stomach dropped. "Is that a threat?"

"Sound advice," said Vess, meeting Neylen's gaze. "Reyzans despise foreign influence. The people tolerated Tan'os because he truly loved this city, but in the end, Fate was less than kind to him. Don't make his mistakes."

Though soft-spoken, the woman before him was dangerous. He knew little about her, but with every meeting, his suspicions that she practiced soulbindery grew. "You are very astute for a woman," Neylen said, knowing his barb would sting.

Vess grinned. "And you are petty for a man."

"The truth hurts," Neylen admitted. "Care for a drink?"

Vess set the cards down and took a seat. "Suit yourself. I do not partake."

"I wouldn't have taken you for an ascetic, especially in this weather."

The woman unbuckled her scabbard. She set the twin blades down next to the sofa and reclined back. "Business and pleasure rarely coalesce."

With his bare hand, Neylen grasped the scalding handle of the kettle and withdrew it from the fire. He took a ceramic cup from the mantel and poured the hot wine. The scent of cloves and cinnamon replaced that of leather and oiled wood. He took a seat across from the sorceress and savored the sweetness and warmth of the spiced brew. "Let us discuss business."

Vess crossed her legs. "Earlier, you mentioned a partnership. What do you propose?"

The Hand of Fate had been Tan'os Ensther's informant. She had been the puppet master in the shadows, pulling strings, nudging opinions, and slitting throats when necessary. She was spymaster, assassin, arcanist, and political schemer in one. "I seek an alliance similar to the one you had with the Vise."

"Before or after he fell from my favor?" chided Vess.

"Before, naturally," Neylen clarified. "I value my throat."

The firelight caused Vess' eyes to glow like those of a cat. "That sort of relationship will cost you."

"Name your price," Neylen countered.

"For my continued advisement, I require eight thousand sequins worth of diamonds delivered on a bimonthly basis."

Neylen set the cup down and rose from the chaise. He paced across the hearth—thinking. The sum was outrageous, but he kept his expression calm. The financial fate of Dessia depended on a revised trade treaty, and he had been charged to accomplish the feat by whatever means possible. Without information, he would achieve nothing, or worse, find himself at the end of a noose. He steepled his fingers and brought them to his lips. "I will agree to this sum for a year, after which I expect a renegotiation."

"That is acceptable. Deliver the first payment as well as what you owe me to Quartermaster Merritt on the *Jiulia*. She sets sail for Goizonne at dawn on the fourth of Nommen."

"You shall have payment well in advance, you have my word," said Neylen.

"Excellent," said Vess. "Now, allow me to prove the wisdom of your acquiescence. Deneven D'Neir has spared no effort to solve the murder and locate Avaren Ensther. He hired a ranger from House Sunblood to aid in his investigation, a rebellious noble who whiles away his days chasing game and women. However, the man is a gifted tracker. He discovered that Avaren and Jarle were together in the caverns beneath Ca'd'Cel the night of the murder. As of this moment, the current whereabouts of Jars and Avaren remain a mystery. In his desperation, D'Neir met in secret with the Mistress of Rats, an effort that resulted in frustration as well as several nasty bruises. Left with no other trails to follow, the former Lord Justiciar believes the pair drowned."

"I have my doubts," said Neylen tersely. "If they had drowned, they would have washed up by now as all corpses do in the rip currents of Firehill. As for Avaren, she could have jumped into the ocean and swam to the docks. Once there, she could have seduced one of the sea captains to carry her away. Two ships sailed before Rigo closed the port on the day of the murder. She could be as far as Calantia by now."

Amusement danced in Vess' eyes. "I haven't earned my riches by chasing every hunch that tickles my mind. Good fortunes are made by manipulating the outcomes of situations as they arise. Don't waste your energy worrying about two people who may or may not be alive."

Neylen frowned. "So the all-seeing Fate knows as much as I do? That doesn't exactly inspire me with confidence. What if they resurface?"

"Assuming they are not dead, the best way to deal with them will depend on the circumstances of their reappearance. Consider this, finding Avaren alive may better serve your aims. The girl can be used to sway public opinion. Rigo can marry her and look like a hero, then execute the thief publicly as a wedding present for his new wife."

"Why wait?" Neylen licked his lips, "You could turn yourself into Avaren long enough to end the investigation. You could marry Rigo and become the next Jarleina."

"There is not enough money in the world to lure me into that trap." Vess clucked her tongue. "Besides, you would make a better queen than me."

Neylen gave Vess a solemn glance and ran a hand through his hair. "I am not exchanging my braids for the vulgar coifs that pass for fashion in Reyza."

Vess laughed. "Let us focus on the present, shall we?"

Neylen pushed the kettle back into the fire. "Alas, you are right. Please, continue."

Vess reclined on the pillows, crooking an arm under her head. "The official investigation paints Jars as a disturbed person, a thief and rapist who breaks into Ca'd'Cel, kills the Vise, and kidnaps his daughter. Your misdirection is well-timed, but Reyzans are, by nature, distrustful. From the alleys to the great halls, tongues are wagging with all manner of rumors."

"And what does the Hand of Fate have to say about all this?"

"Profit can be reaped from chaos."

Neylen crossed his arms. "Fortune from misfortune. I understand your mind all too well. Can Deneven D'Neir's investigation expose us?"

Vess shook her head. "I have read the preliminary report he intends to deliver to Ambassador Ers. He has privately identified Mast as the culprit behind Tan'os' death but has not found proof of our involvement. Deneven is too much the patriot to risk a war over baseless suspicions. He will only report to Ers what he can prove beyond a doubt."

"Speaking of his employer, how fares the Thrommish Ambassador? I'm tempted to poison the meat shanks he favors, and in the absence of malice, pray he chokes upon them."

"My spies in his household tell me that Ther'oldo met with Chief Councilman Pallas and Councilman Regestres yesterday to draft a document in defense of the Treaty of Thyra. They intend to present their arguments during the upcoming Council session."

"The treatise must not be renewed," growled Neylen. "Dessia will be strangled by higher tariffs on marble and the exchange of diamonds! How can we prevent this?"

"I understand your frustrations. However, even first-year apprentices at the Counting House know that the trade of marble and diamonds is among the most lucrative in the world. Once the levies on Dessian goods disappear, your country's wealth would rival A'diel's in a few short years. Many speculate that your nation will use the newfound riches to muster an army and crush the warring clans in Chaia and Ellaia. With their demise, Dessia would gain access to untapped resources and several natural harbors. Tell me, Ambassador, if that comes to pass, which nation could compete in a market governed by Dessian diamonds? Unlike the Seh'nahiel, who practice self-restraint, the Yerr'draki are renowned warmongers." Vess tapped the card deck. "Thrarttas tells us so, as does the exquisite mural above your bed."

Neylen grew impatient with the Fate's smugness. "You have yet to answer my question."

"Blackmail. Hostages. Money. But a soft touch is required. Both Councilman Pedrias and Councilman Gheneveve have already taken a bribe. Others will follow."

"Excellent." Neylen relaxed slightly. "They are powerful men whose voices are respected. What news from the Northern Fleet?"

"Marchess Eva Ensther is in Reyza. She sailed with the fleet in secret."

"Rigo's sister is here!?" Neylen fumed. "You waited until now to share that information? What does she want?"

Vess met Neylen's black gaze. "The Marchess cares not for the untimely death of her father-in-law. She is here because she believes she is Draos' rightful heir. Given the opportunity, she will linger and cause disruption. Your future and the profits of your nation depend on maneuvering Eva Iarris to depart amicably. Supporting the Treaty of Thyra, for now, is the only logical option. Do advise Rigo."

"Damn the gods," Neylen hissed. "The throne goes to the male heir, not the eldest child. What in the name of Thul gives the woman the idea she has any claim?"

Vess grew silent. The shadows from the fire danced in the far corners of the room as she pondered her response. "Eva is an obstinate woman who has always resented her arranged marriage to Tan'os' son. She stands second in line to the crown and has a formidable military advantage."

Neylen shook his head. "Rigo is prideful and will provoke and humiliate his sister." Neylen withdrew the kettle and refilled his cup. "Do you believe her capable of slaying her brother?"

"Eva doesn't want to bloody her hands with regicide or a war of occupation that can result in revolt. A bankrupt republic serves no one, and violence will only discredit her claim. I assure you, Eva does not yet possess any legal means to contest the throne. She is more annoyance than threat." Vess' eyes grew as sharp as daggers. "That said, you must impress upon your lover to tread softly in her handling. The public has little faith in his ability to rule, and Tan'os' murder weighs heavily upon their hearts. If another tragedy should befall the city, I am not confident that you will outlast the storm."

Neylen drained his wine in one gulp. "Have you any good news?"

Vess' tone grew soft, "I do indeed."

"Then, by all means, do not hold your tongue."

"It appears that Eva Ensther is involved in an adulterous relationship with Captain Gøran Rarikian."

Neylen ceased his pacing and sat down. He leaned forward, his black eyes shining with intensity. "Is that a fact?"

Vess nodded. "Eva and Gøran shared a room at the Swallow's Nest where the walls have eyes and ears. She was disguised as a sailor—inventive perhaps for the backwoods of Thyra." Vess grinned. "In Reyza, women are more discreet in such affairs."

The Fate's information was proving to be worth the price. "What else?"

Vess swung her legs around and stood up. "The Mistress of Rats has a new spy in court, a musician by the name of Hemsley. He is the eldest son of the merchant Henroth Nares, who has recently done rather well in the wool business."

"I shall see that his tongue is ripped out," said Neylen.

The assassin slung the blades on her back and buckled the straps. "I have given you a small glimpse of my hand. We will meet again once my payment is delivered."

Neylen bowed. "I look forward to our next meeting. Perhaps you can indulge me in a match of Thrarttas."

Vess smiled. "I'd hate to part you from such a fine deck."

"Are you so sure you'd be the victor?" asked Neylen.

"I never underestimate a man who keeps a copy of *Lyeen's Histories* on his shelf."

"Your powers of observation are a wonder." Neylen escorted

Vess to the door. "Before you go, there is one more matter."

"That is?" Vess asked, taking a few steps into the darkened hall.

"My investigation has revealed that Jarle is friends with a young courtier—a poet by the name of Irilio Errion. I am sure you have heard of him. In any case, I want to bring him in for questioning, but his family's affluence makes this difficult—that, and Rigo is very fond of him. Perhaps you can find a way to deliver this upstart into my hands."

"Consider it done. Sweet dreams, Ambassador," Vess said, fading from view.

Neylen squinted in the gloom, searching for the source of the voice, and found only flickering shadows. His stomach lurched. He doubted he would sleep, let alone dream.

UMADI WILDS

Meldi, Twenty-Sixth of Triesse, 445 A'A'diel

Before dawn, a furious storm gathered and broke, and renewed rains added their quota to the inundation of the cave. The rain-swollen cascade echoed with a fearsome roar, drowning out the sounds of the flitting bats and the sloshing áels. Beyond the colorful silks of their sleeping pallet, salt stains rimmed the grotto's walls. Similar watermarks marked the walls of alleys in the Tangles—grim benchmarks of floodwaters. The highest and faintest of the lines trailed above where they lay. The tides cared naught for the lethe of moon-eyed lovers. In a few days, no low-lying place would be safe from the pull of the Three Sisters.

The fierce chill that caused Jarle to shudder from head to foot could not be cured by raska. "The day grows old," he said, stroking his lover's back.

Avaren buried her face in his shoulder. "May it wither and die."

Jarle curled his fingers around a strand of the girl's pale hair and inhaled her fragrance. Avaren filled his senses, caused his heart to drum a beat that was both wonderful and frightening. At last, Jarle understood the woeful ballads sang by minstrels in honor of parted lovers and the anguish that drove the fishwives to pace the docks in search of familiar sails. "Nothing would please me more than to stay with you."

Avaren turned away from him. "The alignment is coming whether we want it or not. The tide has already flooded many of the passages. We have lived a dream and must now awaken."

The thought of parting filled Jarle with a terrible ache. He pressed against her and kissed her shoulder. "We can still make different choices. You can travel north and reunite with your brother, or stay with me. I can charter passage on a ship, and we can disappear in some distant corner of the world where no one will ever find us."

Avaren shook her head and shrugged free of Jarle's embrace. "My father's death must be avenged. You know as well as I do that Rigo will never stop hunting us."

"So you claim." With the slowness of a condemned man, Jarle rolled out of bed. He donned his linen braies and slipped into his breeches. The salty water had stiffened and cracked the leather, rendering what remained of his armor useless. He pulled up his threadbare socks, followed by his boots. Killing Rigo was madness, but the debate was pointless. Avaren refused to listen to reason. Jarle put on his gauntlets and picked up his blades. Steel glinted as he twirled his daggers in mid-air, caught the black quillons, and slid the weapons into their sheaths.

When Avaren turned to face him, her eyes gleamed in the darkness like two beads of mercury. "You made a promise," she reminded him.

"I always keep my word," Jarle said, grabbing the empty jar of raska.

He walked to the gushing cascade and filled the vessel to the brim with water before corking it. "Do you know where Firehill is?"

Avaren nodded. "Yes."

Jarle slipped the water jug into an old leather satchel, then knelt by the girl's side. "In five days, at dusk, meet me on the dark side of Firehill, where the fishermen hang their nets to dry. If you don't see me by midnight—"

Avaren placed a finger on Jarle's lips and shook her head. A sadness came upon her, and her eyes grew moist. "Do not finish the thought," she said. "Do not doubt. Succeed, and I promise we will start a new life—together."

Time stood still as their lips met, and their hands grasped, desperate to bring their bodies as close as life and breath would allow.

Jarle raked his fingers through Avaren's tousled hair, and kissed her deeply, again and again, smothering her gasps and sobs, adding his own muffled words of endearment as his hands, lips, and body trembled with choked emotion. When at last they parted, breathless and flushed, he cupped her face. "Gods give me strength; I will live if only to gaze upon you again."

"Please, be careful," Avaren whispered.

Jarle was tempted to crawl back into the furs, to make love to her, and convince her to run away with him, but instead, he pulled away. Once on his feet, he turned and fled, weaving silently through the stone columns. At the edge of the pool, he eased down into the waist-high water and waded to a mass of tangled roots.

A cold drizzle buffeted the thief's body as he climbed the woody stalk to the surface and clambered over the lip of the cave. At the top, he glanced down at the glittering pool. Nestled in a thick bramble of twisted vines, the partially collapsed cavern was well hidden. Inadvertently, Avaren had discovered a defensible hideout.

After a quick adjustment of his vambraces, Jarle drew his daggers and began to chop his way through the wet foliage.

The path Jarle had cleared the previous day to forage for wild tubers was already overgrown. Beyond the cave opening, the trees jealously guarded every patch of light. Ferns as tall as a man, armed with needles, presided over the jungle floor while corded vines as thick as his arm speared upward, reaching for the dense canopy a score of manlengths above.

The Umadi Wilds was the primary reason Reyza had only ever been conquered by sea. Unlike the steamy jungles elsewhere in Laremlis, the impregnable wilderness thrived in freezing temperatures, and proved impervious to sharp winds, sea salt, and sandy soil. All who tried to cultivate the green morass failed, leading sages to surmise that the jungle was either a natural wonder or a cursed patch of land.

Jarle knew as much about the wilds as he did about sewing dresses. For street urchins who had grown up in the tight confines of the city, the wilderness beyond Reyza's bastions was a source of mystery, if not outright fear. Rumors told of strange, savage people who lived like beasts amidst the undergrowth, and of soulbinders who exploited the jungle's remoteness to cast their daemonic rituals. By far, the most fantastic accounts were those of the legendary monsters that preyed on foragers and adventurers.

The hair on Jarle's arms prickled as he recalled Al-Safan's account of what had become of his hunting expedition. The fat man's anecdote of richly-plumed cockatrices swooping down from the trees and turning his men to stone had been easy to dismiss while sitting in a cozy tavern enjoying a mug of ale. Neck-deep in foliage, Jarle wasn't so sure that the hunter had concocted the fable to entertain a dull crowd.

The thief glanced up at the dense canopy. Months ago, he had believed that cockatrices, manticores, and man-eating trees were nothing but chimerical figments conjured by sunbaked minds. But after sharing a bed with a naera, a fantasy made flesh, all he could hope for was that addonels and protective spirits also existed.

The thief chopped his way along the jungle floor, looking for his previously traveled path. At a thicket of native biwarra trees, he knelt and dug around with this dagger until he unearthed four yellow yams the size of potatoes. The tasty tubers were easy to roast on an open flame and remained fresh for weeks. Jarle thanked the gods for the yams before stuffing them into his pack. Survival had less to do with careful planning than luck.

Continuing on his way, Jarle forged into previously unexplored territory. He sliced through the stubborn, prickly growth, swatting beetles and bloodthirsty moths. On occasion, he discovered what appeared like a glade or pathway and pursued it a short distance, only to find another tangle of creepers. Above his head, long pendants of foliage laden with colorful festoons of flowers hung from the branches. Exquisite as the orchids and other plants were, Jarle became wary of their vitality. Their perfume sickened him; their colorful glory palled upon his sight. The oppressive greenery was too brilliant, too unfamiliar, too unlike home. He longed for the restraint of Reyza's formal gardens, for roses in mossy urns, clipped topiaries, and climbing vines tempered by whitewashed plaster.

In the afternoon, the rain ceased, and the sun appeared. Fleeting sunbeams pierced the dense growth and illuminated his path, before disappearing once more, abandoning him to darkness. Jarle's only sense of direction came from the sound of the crashing surf. If he followed the cliffs and kept the ocean on his right, he would reach Reyza in a couple of days.

As the day wore on, Jarle sensed he was being watched. As the feeling evolved into a palpable dread, he quickened his pace and began to chop in the direction of the sea. Sweat poured from his pores, and his arms trembled from fatigue, but he kept on, determined to escape the unseen horror.

By evening, Jarle reached the bluffs that overlooked the flinty waters of Basalt Reef. At the top of the promontory, the jungle's lushness was beaten back and scorched by the winds. The air on the point was fresh, unlike the thick, oppressive humidity of the primeval wilds.

Thankful for a moment's rest, the thief slid his pack off his shoulder and withdrew the water jug. He took a long drink and stared over the waters in the direction of home.

Highlighted by the sun, whitecaps beat against the imposing cliffs. The crashing waves dispersed in clouds of spray through which redbills darted in search of prey. In the north, the storm trailed its tattered skirts. Thunderheads flashed in the distance, their rumbling faint.

Jarle corked the jar and returned it to his satchel. In the sky, nestled amidst the clouds, shone the pale gray disks of Aeliah and Aeiad. Alongside the two full moons loomed Aeppia, the Lorn. Jarle spat, damning the Three Sisters and the destruction they would soon cause to the bottomless pit of Thul.

The beacon atop Firehill illuminated the shreds of mist that hugged the cliffs. The familiar sight should have given him hope, but instead, it made him anxious. He had asked Avaren to meet him in five days at the lighthouse, but he had no idea how he was going to fulfill his promise.

Leaving the edge of the cliff, Jarle cut his way back inland, pausing only to regain his bearings and slake his thirst. As darkness closed in around him, the sense of terror returned. Pausing mid-swing, Jarle clenched his weapons and turned, eyeing the shadows in all directions. Crouched on a branch of a tree, he spied a massive cat-like beast with multiple appendages and incandescent eyes. The creature's coat shifted, blending with the hues of the jungle and tricking his senses. The entity's unblinking orbs possessed a hypnotic quality that held him in a trance.

Unable to move, Jarle cursed under his breath. "Fucking Hel, what am I doing?"

The monster fanned its scintillating appendages, causing the air to glimmer, before leaping down from the tree. As his terror subsided,

Jarle rubbed the back of his neck and stared at his daggers as though seeing them for the first time. His hands shook, and around him, the sounds of the jungle grew louder and more defined. He heard the staccato sound of night ravens and the throaty howls of spiral creepers. Beneath the verdure, the scampering of small caprids and the high-pitched stridulation of insects became unbearable. Above him, a crimson and aqua feathered bird flashed among the hanging vines, vanishing as quickly as it had appeared.

Suddenly and inexplicably, Jarle felt a bitter agony greater than he could withstand. The fierce tension of his strained nerves gave way with a cry. "I won't do it!" he screamed at the trees. "This is madness."

In his mortal anguish, Jarle released his weapons and fell like a drunken man to the ground. He rested his brow on a pillow of moss and clutched at the moist loam. Deep sobs heaved his breast as burning tears forced themselves from his eyes—tears which seemed to wring his life-blood from him in their fiery rain, yet tears which saved him in that awful moment from insanity.

The more he resisted the thought of killing Rigo, the more his body trembled. Cold sweat erupted on his limbs, and a splitting pain set fire to the base of his skull. In the back of his throat, he felt the familiar itch of magic.

The thought that Avaren could be so accomplished an actress; that all her loving words and caresses could be false; that all the ardent affection lavished on him were a lie, unfolded like a terrifying nightmare.

"No!" Jarle clutched his knees and closed his eyes. His mind drifted to the first time Avaren's opalescent gaze met his—the effect not unlike that of the monster in the trees. Her beauty was disconcerting, and her eyes the source of all inspiration. He imagined kissing Avaren's jaw and inhaling her scent. He recalled the soft weight of her breasts when he cupped them in his hands, the feel of her thighs against his.

Jarle wiped away his tears and straightened. "She loves me," he said, reassuring himself. "And I love her."

With the vision of his heart's desire, Jarle's pain ebbed, and his breathing returned to normal. He brushed himself off, grabbed his weapons, and stood up. With a deep, brave breath, he stepped toward the thick foliage that barred his way and began to chop once more. Each swing of his daggers and every subsequent step forward brought him closer to his purpose—the arms of his beloved.

Swing after swing, Jarle asserted his affirmations. "I must protect Avaren. Rigo must die." With each repetition, strength, and resolve flowed through his body. He cut tirelessly, ignoring the ache in his arms and the chafing of the leather breeches against his skin. Avaren had given his life purpose and opened his heart to the wonders of love. He would conquer the wilds and the very fires of Y'rth to please her.

Night fell swiftly in the jungle, and with it came a flurry of activity and sound. Everywhere Jarle looked, he saw the abomination's glowing eyes. City life ill-prepared a man for the rigors of the wilderness. The light of three nearly full moons was useless in the pitch-black tangle.

Jarle stumbled and fell in the darkness, cursing himself for not having found a suitable place to camp during daylight hours. He settled in the hollow of a tree and curled into a ball. He took a sip of water to quench his hunger pains and prayed that the abomination that stalked him would spare him.

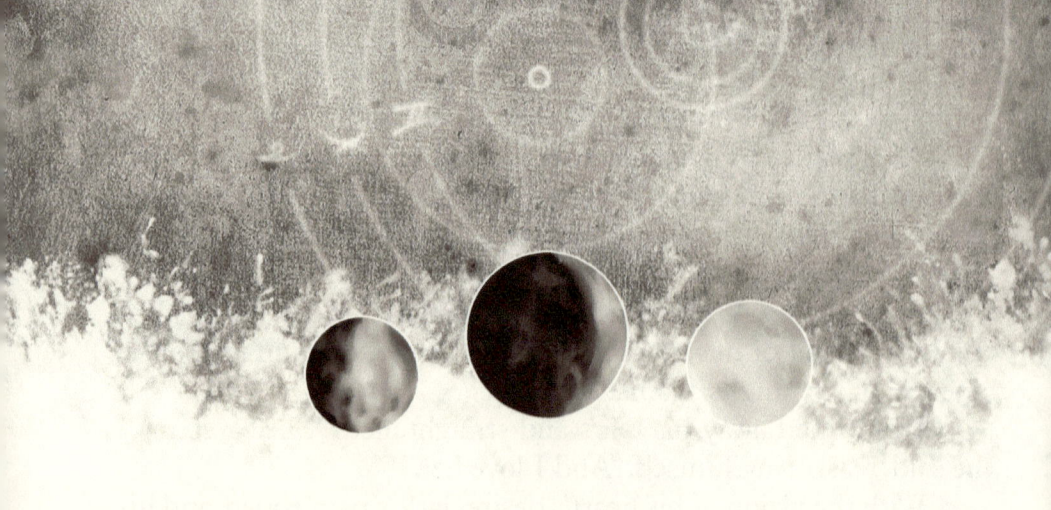

SHERZADEEN'S GRASP

Zezendi, First of Nommen, 445 A'A'diel

In the gloom, Avaren listened to the wind. It echoed through the cavern like whispering supplicants on their way to the Temple of the Venestrae. The sibilant sound stirred memories of the previous summer when she had accompanied her father on the pilgrimage to Minstrel Rock. On the fourth of Hel'im, they had climbed the ten thousand steps leading up to the shrine to commemorate the Midsummer Feast, the day when Reyzans venerated the dead.

Orange and purple streaks colored the sky by the time they reached the monastery's portico. Clad in black-cowled robes, they ate spicy noodles from ceramic bowls and welcomed the rising sun. Even dressed in beggarly garb, her father eclipsed the other worshipers. He stood a head taller and broader than most. His loose snow-white hair blew in the breeze, and his eyes shone as blue as the glaciers from his homeland. On the summit, overlooking the patchwork of red and white rooftops and the placid sea, Tan'os Ensther held her hand and kissed the top of her head. In that solemn moment, he told her he loved her and entrusted her with the safekeeping of a box of secrets that could destroy his enemies should he meet an untimely demise. Tan'os, a schemer who had won a kingdom through daring plots, had predicted his own doom but failed to imagine the eventuality of hers. Luck, in the form of a curskin thief—a lowly son of a potter—had intervened and saved her life. Thus, she still had a promise to fulfill.

Avaren secured a knife to her leather belt and swam to the center of the pool. As she dove, a myriad of tiny scales erupted along her skin, shimmering in the afternoon sunlight. Mid-glide, her svelte legs elongated and transformed into a pair of muscled, black-finned tails. Her first gasping breath caused her gills to open in the spaces between her ribs. Like rows of bloody claw marks, the flanged slits flared and filled her lungs with fluid. Twirling in the chilling currents dredged up from the depths, Avaren opened her glowing eyes. The translucent membranes ensured clear vision underwater even in near-darkness.

In the arms of the sea, unchained from the world above, Avaren breathed free. Every transformation served to remind her of who she was—a naera's daughter, a creature of two worlds—one mortal and one altogether unknown.

Where the layer of rainwater mixed with the brine, the water took on the consistency of oil, becoming blurry and thick. Avaren navigated the indigo blackness with ease, thrusting past the freshwater lens until she entered a deep shaft.

Spectacular mineral formations, sculpted through the course of millennia into the shapes of stony curtains, fringed the flooded cavern. Between the undulating folds, a passage branched off and led to the reefs that skirted the coastline. Beneath the outgoing tunnel, floated a corrupted film of pinkish vapor that stank like rotten eggs. The miasma obscured the sinkhole and prevented deeper exploration.

Avoiding the noxious broth, Avaren plunged into the well-traveled shaft, zigzagging through the narrow opening with the grace of an áel. In the wake of her thrashing tails, a vortex of silt stirred, obscuring the tunnel behind her. Jarle despised her preferred mode of travel with good reason. The underwater passages were dizzying and claustrophobic. Twice, the thief had swallowed so much water that he cursed the day she was born.

In the distance, a bright, sea-green dot grew larger as she sped toward the light. With the grace of a seal, Avaren glided beneath a rocky outcrop, then reared upwards, emerging into open water.

Upon her tongue, she tasted churned shores and seafoam—the essence of winter, glaciers, and storms.

The curling waves swept the coastline before crashing against the distant, lichen-covered cliffs. Avaren surrendered to the lulling motion of the undertow as she navigated the swaying forest of seaweed and red kelp. Colorful starfish and spiny urchins rested on the muted siennas and violets of the reef while tiny fish munched on the corals. Beams of scintillating sunlight illuminated a shoal of silverfins as they escorted her to the surface in a brilliant, shimmering cloud.

In the sky, the silhouettes of the Three Sisters loomed low, pulling the waters, and her very marrow inland. Tendrils of fog clung to the cliffs and veiled the spilling jungle in a haze of gray. The forlorn view constricted her chest. She felt wretched for manipulating Jarle, the one person who cared about her, but she could not ignore her father's last wishes nor her desire for revenge.

With a heavy heart, Avaren turned seaward and dove. She descended into the murky depths and twirled in the blue expanse, edging along the base of Basalt Reef, whose skeletal symmetry had been sculpted through the years by the wreckage of hundreds of ships. She ducked under a barnacle-encrusted mast and darted through an opening into the blackness of a sunken hull. In the gloom, with six broken arms and a missing head, lay the shattered colossus of Sherzadeen, the Spider Queen of Hel whose cult had long ago disbanded.

Fish weaved through the Spider Queen's eye sockets and pecked at a giant anemone that made the statue's grinning face its home. Avaren clenched her jaw and descended for a better view of the creature. Though spindly, the anemone's iridescent tentacles were as long as a man and armed with deadly barbs. In hindsight, she wished she had stashed her father's coffer in the cave rather than the goddess' thick skull.

Avaren cursed, sending a stream of bubbles racing toward the surface, then began to scour the wreck for anything that might help her dislodge the venomous creature. Her knife was worthless against the anemone's reach, as was the pile of coral-sheathed futtocks and crushed amphorae. Deeper still, her search yielded clumped remains of roofing tiles and fragmented slabs of quarried stone—more useless objects.

For a moment, she floated upside down and stared at the broken, grinning head with purplish hair. She felt at ease beneath the waves but was no expert in marine life. She had spent most of her life in stuffy salons surrounded by tutors and diplomats. All she knew about anemones was that their tentacles tasted lovely when breaded and pan-fried in butter. As she pondered the delicacy, her father's often-used adage came to mind.

Expect problems, then eat them for supper.

With a smile on her face, Avaren bolted toward the shallows. It was time to get creative.

*
**

The riptide currents that drove ships to their watery doom stirred the bottom of Basalt Reef. Avaren circled along the towering boulders and canyons, spreading disks and wavering fans. Fluted coral branches trembled in her wake, before returning to their lolling motions. The vibrant strangeness of the reef was unlike any of man's sordid, angular creations. There was no pattern, no order to the sprawling network of tiny amorphous skeletons whose brilliant facade marked thousands of years of death. The chaotic, overgrown garden boggled the senses. The sea sang a deep song—a melody both benign and malicious with the power to delight and destroy.

Below her, timid áels poked their heads from the labyrinthine outcrops while above, glimmering shoals flashed, spiraling like autumn leaves in a whirlwind. Farther on, Avaren sensed the shadows of roving mid-water predators and the eerie keening of leviathans. She followed the ridge of the coral beds and glided inland, where fishermen dared to brave the treacherous currents.

In the shallows, the naera swerved among the kelp streamers seeking anything that might help her oust the anemone from its perch. Half buried in the sand, she spied a trawling net. The mesh was tangled and pinned down by a wooden plank too deep to unearth.

Avaren cut a piece free with her blade and began to fold the net into a bundle. In the current, the sheet proved as unwieldy

as the creature she intended to snare. After chasing the netting for what seemed an interminable eternity, she gained a newfound appreciation for the fishermen who trawled for catch each dawn.

By the time the naera returned to the broken effigy, every one of her muscles throbbed with fatigue. Undeterred, she dove into the darkened hull and unfurled the net while keeping an eye on the creature's movements. The anemone's many arms radiated like a sunburst from a flat center, where a blue-fringed opening expelled bits of refuse. The feelers trembled in the gloom, swaying idly in the currents until she drew too close. Aware of her presence, the writhing tentacles undulated in her direction.

Avaren slung the mesh on one of the colossus' broken arms and searched the shattered hull for debris. The coral had clumped most of the remains of the cargo into hard, stony mounds. Using her knife, she hacked at a pile of pottery and pried off a chunk. Her eyes glowed with mischief as she weighed the lump in her hand.

Let's see how you like this meal.

With a flick of her tails, Avaren hovered into position above the pulsating orifice and released the block of fused shards. The debris sank like iron. Beneath her, the tendrils jerked in unison, too clumsy to stop the object's trajectory. The refuse bounced on the bluish tissue, then disappeared into the gaping hole.

The anemone shuddered and gurgled before a myriad of spindly appendages shot out from its base. One of the tentacles made contact with Avaren's arm and seared an angry line across her skin. Blinding pain drove the naera back, forcing her to weave through the whipping tangled mass. The underwater world tumbled as she dipped and dove. A cloud of dirt rose up around her while she kicked. Sharp rocks scraped her arms, and wounds opened on her hands when she grasped the coral-encrusted wreckage. Through the murkiness, she heard what sounded like a throaty sucking sound, followed by a thud. The old hull creaked, and the beams bowed as the creature began to move.

The anemone slithered off of Sherzadeen's head and advanced in her direction. Fighting a wave of terror, Avaren flattened herself against the ship's side to escape the flailing tentacles. The weal on her arm throbbed with every beat of her heart. She couldn't risk another sting, but neither would she abandon her father's box.

Avaren swam behind the icon's torso and waited for the organism to return to a more tranquil state. After a while, the thread-like tendrils retracted, and the thicker ones returned to their gentle loll. The naera gripped the loose end of the net and took a deep breath. The buoyancy of her expanded lungs caused her to drift upwards. At the top of the hull, she used a beam to propel herself over the amorphous creature.

At a turtle's pace, she unfurled the mesh, stretching it like a giant blanket over the writhing mass. With a silent prayer to Danikos, Avaren kicked hard and swooped down to smother the scattered tentacles. With uncanny speed, the monstrosity unleashed its vile appendices once more. Using the beast's instinct to her advantage, Avaren circled it and dragged the net in her wake. The more the creature fought, the more tangled it became.

Avaren squealed with delight when the giant anemone detached its stalk from the stone and slithered toward her. Ignoring her bleeding palms and her cramping muscles, she towed with all her strength until the unbalanced monstrosity listed and toppled on its side. She gritted her teeth in the silt-stirred murk as she wrenched the wrangled monster toward Sherzadeen's torso.

The sea creature's lashing, in conjunction with her yanks, caused it to roll in her favor. A repulsive sucking sound echoed between the ship's wooden ribs as the anemone sucked on the rubble scattered on the sandy floor before disgorging it. Avaren toiled in the current, strangling the bilge-sucking abomination until it collapsed in a gelatinous heap.

Too weary to rejoice in her victory, Avaren tied the net to the statue and swam to where her father's coffer lay hidden. Sherzadeen's colossal face appeared to smile at her as she chipped away the reddish coral lodged in the hollow skull. Amidst a cloud of bloody-hued silt, Avaren pried the box free and turned it in her hands. Where the inlaid wooden lids touched, a magical seal glowed a faint blue.

"Thank the guardians," Avaren said, relieved to find the coffer undamaged. She tucked the slim parcel under one arm and began the long swim to Reyza. The time to fulfill Tan'os Ensther's last wish had come.

GRIMMALKINS

Shardi, Second of Nommen, 445 A'A'diel

Jarle dreamt of being devoured by hungry beasts and awoke to the sound of a woman's scream. Startled, he reached for his weapons and surveyed his surroundings. Dewdrops glistened at the tips of ferns like diamonds. A layer of fog enveloped the verdure and broke the patches of sunlight into crepuscular beams. Among the expected howls and screeches of animals, Jarle heard the chopping of a blade. The scent of wood smoke and sausage reached his nostrils.

Armed men.

Gathering his gear, Jarle clambered through the bush in the direction of the sound. In his wake, a multitude of blackbirds flew into the canopy. Above the murmur of flapping wings and squawks, came voices.

Through the vines, Jarle spied two men whose aspect spoke of endless days spent at sea ingesting salted fish and watered raska. One of the ruffians, a bald, scarred man with a considerable paunch examined at a maggoty rabbit carcass inside a cage. "This one's empty. Damn vultures picked the meat clean."

The camouflaged trap was simple but effective. Vines reinforced with tar held the cage's wooden ribs together. The prey they sought was sizable.

Unlike his companion, the second man was lean with a full head of oily curls. "Let's check the others," he said, exposing a mouth full of rotten teeth.

Jarle stayed on the marauder's heels as they cleared a path through the foliage. An icy frisson traveled down his spine as another feminine cry pierced the canopy.

Could it be Avaren?

The thief didn't pause to think. The mere thought of the men's grimy hands touching Avaren's pearly splendor consumed all reason. Heart pounding, Jarle snuck behind the pair as they paused for a short rest. The bald one leaned on the trunk of a tree, while the slim one swung his parang and stretched his shoulder.

The hairless man handed his companion a waterskin. "Seems Macario is having fun with his little bitch again. I hope he changes his mind about giving us a turn."

The wiry man drank his fill. "Macario's lost his wits. He says she's a noblewoman, but I don't believe him. The fires of Hel possess her. One of these days, that soulbinding wench will unleash a pox on us."

"Don't tell me you believe that daemonic rubbish!"

"She raises the scruff on my neck. Her eyes are unnatural like she's no woman at all, but something else."

"Then you're blind! The little minx has a fine ass, and a set of tits like"—the stout man paused looking for the right words— "like Mama's holiday dumplings! Why should we allow Macario to enjoy all that plump juicy meat by himself?"

"Cause his cock and his brains are bigger than yours, you dumb sod."

"Guess I'll settle for your sister then."

"Careful, Lauven."

The bald man stroked his gut. "She still looking for an honorable man?"

The slim marauder smiled a black toothy grin. He stoppered the wineskin and slung it over his shoulder. "My sister is only a few years your senior, still capable of bearing strapping lads."

The man named Lauven shook his head and moved on. He swung his blade with broad strokes and began to chop into the thicket once more. "Aye, I should think about settling. As much as I enjoy plowing Rosie, she's not the kind of woman you bring home to Mama."

"Aye. The sooner we ditch this place, the better." The black-toothed man followed his companion into the jungle. "But sailing past the Thrommish blockade is as likely as steering a dinghy 'round the Horn of Ktoth. We're stuck in this ass-tearing morass and won't see the inside of a brothel or eat your Ma's dumplings anytime soon."

The bald man swatted at a swarm of flies. "Some say war's brewing."

"May Zezen swallow every one of the Bissatiel pricks!"

The duo cleaved their way through the underbrush to the location of another trap. Impaled in its hind leg by the cage's spiked door, a grimmalkin struggled to escape. Blood covered the beast's sleek black coat, and its eyes gleamed with baleful intelligence.

Jarle ducked into the undergrowth and gaped. He had seen grimmalkin pelts for sale in the bazaar but had never seen the feline itself until—yesterday. Muscled like a greathound and dark as a shadow, the feliform fiend possessed áel-like appendages which extended from its sides and flailed at the sight of the poachers. The underside of the tentacles flared to expose rows of menacing barbed hooks.

Lauven whistled and circled the wounded beast. "Look here, Corle, we caught ourselves a kitten."

Corle licked his blackened teeth. "That's a heap of black gold right there."

Lauven wiped the sweat from his shiny scalp. "How Macario's little plaything managed to kill four of these I'll never know."

"She stole their souls; that's how! "Corle tossed his parang from one hand to the other. "Here, kitty, kitty, time to part with that sweet hide."

Grimmalkin hide was said to protect from magic and curses—boasts that Jarle refuted with logic. The rare pelts cost a fortune. As a result, unscrupulous merchants dyed bear and thrask fur with ice beetle husks and black walnut to imitate the effect. The pelt's only magic, Jarle assumed, derived from its capacity to impart a semblance of power and wealth to its wearer. But as he peered into the creature's indigo eyes, he reconsidered. The tingling at the back of his throat confirmed the presence of magic. The grimmalkin was no ordinary jungle cat.

"Don't get too close," warned Lauven.

"Nothing's easy these days," said Corle. "Go sharpen a long pole. I'll see if I can wrangle its other leg with the rope."

Jarle tensed as the corpulent man passed him in search of a sapling. He slipped into the underbrush and waited for the poacher to begin fashioning his spear before making his move. Keeping to the soft moss, Jarle crept through the shifting shadows until he could smell the man's stink. He then darted from the foliage and stabbed sideways into the man's throat.

The poacher gurgled. The coppery stench of blood filled the air as blood sprayed from his mouth. Jarle drove the second dagger into the man's eye socket, then controlled his fall. The marauder perished in frightful, almost comical convulsions.

Jarle wiped his blades on the dead man's armor and sheathed them. Without a moment to spare, he circled back toward the man named Corle. Unaware of his partner's death, the black-toothed thug focused on the creature. He shuffled to the left, cast the rope and missed. Jarle snuck out from the shadows and walked behind the man. When Corle turned in the direction of the sound, Jarle kicked him hard in the stomach. The blow sent the man crashing into the cage.

The grimmalkin flattened its ears and shot its appendages through the wooden bars. Four black tentacles wrapped around the poacher and slammed him back against the cage. Frantic, Corle drew his blade but didn't have time to swing. The fiend bit the man's head and crushed his skull between its jaws. When Corle stopped twitching, the grimmalkin flung the broken man toward Jarle and fixed him with its indigo gaze. The appendages flailed, then settled on the ground.

Jarle cringed as bits of brain and blood seeped from the thug's cranium. His mind screamed for him to run, but his legs refused to obey. Was the creature trying to communicate? The thought was absurd. Jarle's heart pounded a staccato rhythm as he walked toward the cage. "Ven's sake! Why do I get the sense you can understand me?"

The beast lowered its head and retracted its claws. Jarle approached until he was standing close to the wounded beast. "You could have had me for dinner last night," he said, "but since you spared me, I will help you." When the creature made no sudden moves, Jarle sprung open the latches and pried the door open. With a yelp, the grimmalkin angled free of the enclosure and limped into the shadows.

After the predator disappeared, Jarle stripped Corle of his armor. With trained efficiency, he undid the buckles and belts and made quick work of the switch. He squatted and stretched; adjusted arm straps and leg guards until the leathers conformed to his body. He strapped the dead man's parang to his waist and transferred his thieving tools.

With a huff, Jarle hoisted Corle's body over his shoulder and dumped the corpse into the underbrush. The morning fog had dispersed by the time Jarle returned to where Lauven lay. He relieved the man of his jewelry and flung his weapons into the umbrage. He then rolled the corpulent man under the shade of an antler-leafed tree and covered him with vines.

Aching from exhaustion, Jarle followed the trampled trails and the scent of roasted meat back to the poachers' camp. The encampment lay nestled in a clearing sheltered on one side by a crescent-shaped ledge. Five oiled calfskin tents ringed a bonfire. Above the flames, a hunk of unidentifiable meat cooked on a spit. Not far off, fleshing beams held cured, outstretched hides. Four cages similar to the two he had seen in the jungle occupied the far reaches of the overhang. One contained a red-furred hog and the other what appeared to be a huddled person. A pelt concealed the top of the cage.

As Jarle circled the camp, he counted five men in various states of dress and a woman who wore an eyepatch to conceal a disfiguring cicatrix.

Their leader, the man, called Macario, was middle-aged and broader than the rest with arms as thick as tree trunks. A dizzying pattern of indecipherable symbols covered his bare chest, and the dual tines of his braided beard reached his belly. The look in his eye marked him a hungry man. Jarle knew the look well. He had once been like Macario, eager for riches, excessive drink, and discord.

The thought of Avaren caged and abused caused a sharp pain in his chest. Come nightfall, Jarle vowed, Macario would regret every last vile seed he'd ever sown.

THE SOULBINDER'S HOWL

Shardi, Second of Nommen, 445 A'A'diel

No shrub larger than a footstool had escaped the machetes of Macario's men. The encampment was bare save for a handful of gnarled trees ringed by tall ferns. Jarle cursed under his breath and shrank into a bower of vines outside the camp's perimeter. Hidden within the cluster of lush, glossy leaves, he settled on his rump, took a swig from the water jar, and resolved to wait for the cover of darkness.

Macario paced the camp, his decorated skin slick with sweat. He paused to stare into the jungle with an expectant scowl. "Rose! Yene! Get over here."

The one-eyed woman and a gangly-limbed man with a crooked nose walked over to their tattooed leader. The woman cocked her head, "What the fuck do you want?"

"Lauven and Corle are dragging their asses," Macario said. "Go find those sluggards and bring them back here."

Rose shook her head. "Send Ferret instead."

"Ferret's got the night watch. Take Yene and go." Macario approached Rose so that she was forced to step back and tilt her chin up to meet his steely glare. "Say one more word about it. Go on, say something."

Rose turned her head and spat. The man named Yene swallowed hard and grabbed his short sword. "Come on, Rosie."

Rose huffed and followed the skinny poacher into the green morass. After their departure, Macario barked orders at the remaining men who quickly set about stretching pelts on empty wooden frames.

With two of the marauders out looking for their dead comrades, only three remained in the camp. Jarle gritted his teeth and resisted the temptation to act before he confirmed the captive was indeed Avaren. He stared at the cage, willing the prisoner to put her face to the bars and end the ambiguity, but his curiosity went unanswered.

The sun shone high in the sky by the time Rose and Yene returned. Macario set aside the hide he was scraping and stood. He wiped his palms on his breeches and narrowed his eyes as Rose advanced.

The female ruffian tossed a blood-stained parang and a portion of Corle's face at Macario's feet. The weapon hit the tattooed man's boot. "That's all that's left of 'em," Rose spat.

Macario glared at his comrade's flesh, then at the woman. "You want to tell me something?"

Rose squirmed under the intensity of Macario's scrutiny. She glanced down at Corle's remains and the bloody weapon and shifted her weight from one foot to the other. "Apologies, just that I was rather fond of ol' Lauven. Daevils know what this accursed jungle has done with him."

Macario turned his attention to the man behind her. "Yene, was it an animal?"

The man nodded. "Best I can tell, Macario. I think they found a live grimmalkin half caught by the trap. We found some fur, blood, and cat tracks leading into the bush. We only found Corle, no sign of Lauven."

"The wilds are dangerous. Corle and Lauven knew that when they joined us," said Macario. He favored Rose and Yene with a wicked smile. "Your shares have just improved."

The woman bent down, collected Corle's jaw, and walked away in silence.

By evening Jarle had memorized the thugs' patterns. Every

hour or so, two men checked the traps and cages and fetched water from a nearby brook. The rest scraped and prepared the hides, drinking and gambling between chores. In the afternoon, several new animals were brought in, skinned, and butchered.

Shadows lengthened, and the sky turned violet. Men settled around the campfire. Jarle angled closer, hoping for a better view. Through the sliver between hides, he spied bare feet and a swath of thigh. The thugs had not offered their prisoner food or water. *Savages!*

A pockmarked, rail-thin man sliced some flesh off of the hanging roast and distributed slabs of it into eager, dirty hands. "Shall I cut a piece for your pretty, boss man?" he asked, as Macario neared the cages.

Hunger and worry turned Jarle's stomach into a seething pile of coals. He watched from the edge of the camp, fingers clenched on the pommels of his blades as Macario taunted the prisoner. A vision of Avaren, disheveled and trembling against the cold, shrinking away from the man's filthy hands formed in his mind.

Jarle swore dire oaths of vengeance to every god and goddess he could think of should his beloved be harmed. He bit down the urge to charge into the clearing. He could kill two, maybe three, but not before Macario crushed her neck. Years of training had taught him that impatience killed more thieves than hangmen.

He needed to wait.

Macario looked back to the campfire with a roguish grin. "Think some meat might sway her ladylike disposition?"

One of the men shouted, "I got some meat for her."

The poachers licked their lips and narrowed their eyes. "Let the little beast out to feed," someone called out.

Jarle let out an involuntary hiss when a petite Seh'nahiel girl sprang from the cage. She was young with long, black hair and eyes the color of swirling gold. Though grimy and covered with unsightly bruises, her features betrayed a noble lineage. Her long, slim legs propelled her past Macario's grasp and into the darkness. Ropes bound her hands, and a dirty rag gagged her mouth, but there was no mistaking the fire smoldering in her eyes.

Laughter and whistles filled the camp as the thugs fanned out around her.

The waif ran behind a drying rack and got a hold of a skinning knife, which she waved before her. The blade flashed in the moonlight as she turned to face one man, then another.

Macario walked toward her, arms open. "Come, put that thing down before you hurt yourself."

The men's lascivious eyes devoured the sight of her naked breasts and buttocks. In the firelight, her primal movements tightened breeches and slackened jaws. Only Rose refrained from joining the fray, choosing instead to crawl into one of the tents.

Macario sidestepped the strike and lunged. He tackled her to the ground, but not before she grazed his arm with a stinging cut. The men cheered as he pinioned her beneath him, squeezing her wrists until the knife slid out of her fingers. The girl writhed and kicked, lashing out with unexpected strength. Her defined muscles spoke of arduous labor, but also served to beautify her physique.

"She's a wild ride, this one," boasted Macario, easing off of her to display her wares.

The dark-haired girl jerked under her captor. She twisted to her belly and bucked her hips to toss him. Macario pushed her face down into the dirt until she was forced to raise her rump to escape the pressure on her neck. He pried her knees apart with his thighs and undid his pants with his free hand. Encouraged by jeers and epithets, he thrust into her.

Jarle slammed his fist into the dirt. He'd already lost a day lingering around the marauders' camp and couldn't risk a further delay. Shame mingled with relief as the girl's muffled cries filled the clearing. He was glad Avaren was safe, but could not abandon the poor girl to such cruelty.

The woman's suffering grated Jarle's nerves and tested his self-control. He crouched at the base of a tree and retrieved the ceramic jar from his pack. He uncorked it and took a drink of water wishing it were raska, but he doubted any amount of liquor could numb him to the callous spectacle.

Jarle breathed a sigh of relief when Macario tired of his sport and dragged the reticent waif to the campfire. After removing her gag, the marauder sliced a hefty piece of roast and tossed the meat on the floor. Men laughed as the girl bent down and tore at it like a wild animal.

Despite the abuse, her will to survive was strong. "More!" she demanded.

"Hear that, boys? She wants more of my meat!" boomed Macario.

"More!" the girl repeated, eyes glowing bright with hatred.

Macario's smile disappeared. He shoved the abused girl to the ground and cruelly pressed a knee into her chest. Careful to keep his fingers clear of her snapping teeth, the burly man shoved a filthy wad of rags into her mouth. He tied a greasy leather cord around her face and secured the gag. Satisfied with her silence, he growled in her ear, "You will get more when I am ready to give you more."

Jarle shook his head. There was no person alive who was invulnerable to suffering, but some had the will of the Seven Winds. The Starborn Seh'nahiel girl, young as she was, had more spirit in her than the entire band of thugs. She possessed eyes that had seen too much, too soon. No matter what Macario did to her, he would never break her. Lucky for her, the bastard hadn't realized it yet.

The black hand of night, full bellies, and a long day of hard work finally exhausted Macario's company. One by one, the men cast aside boots and armor and crawled into their tents. Macario was the last to retire. He walked the perimeter of the camp and inspected the snares before he too disappeared into his tent.

A lone lookout remained on guard; the man named Ferret. Short of stature and as portly as the caged hog, he reminded Jarle of a toad. He paced around the encampment until his comrades fell asleep, then settled by the warmth of the fire. As time passed, he lost interest in the safety of his compatriots and indulged in his wineskin.

Jarle sidestepped the traps set at the edge of the clearing and moved through the shadows. The hiss and pop of the campfire filled his ears as he snuck behind the inebriated lookout. He waited for the toad-like man to lift his wineskin, then struck. With a quick motion, Jarle gripped the man's greasy forehead, yanked his head back, and slammed his dagger into the base of his skull. With a ghastly crunch, Ferret slumped dead.

Jarle scanned the camp as he eased the corpse to the ground.

He pulled his blade free and wiped it clean on the man's chest before using it to relieve the lookout of his coin purse.

Jarle straddled the log previously occupied by the guard. He cut off a chunk of boar and wolfed it down. The flesh was dry but well spiced. After a month of bland fish and yams, the meal tasted like heaven. Jarle gulped from the wineskin and chased it with another piece of meat. Long had he lived by the precept to never forgo a good lay or a good meal. Life in his circles tended to end early and unexpectedly.

When he couldn't eat another bite, Jarle got up and walked to the drying rack. He took two of the cured grimmalkin hides and let his hands slide over the fur. The texture was silky and light, imbued with a peculiar nighttime sheen. The itch of magic tickled his throat.

Shadows danced on the underside of the crag where the girl was caged. The place smelled of sweat, feces, and dried urine. From within the cage, two gleaming amber orbs studied him as he approached. Recalling that Seh'nahiel could see in the dark, he raised his palms in a gesture of goodwill, "I mean you no harm," he said in a hushed voice.

A low groan escaped the captive's mouth as she pushed herself to the far side of the enclosure.

Jarle stood his ground. "I may look like one of them, but I'm not. I'm going to release you. Nod if you can understand me."

After a vigorous nod from the trapped girl, Jarle edged closer. He withdrew his thieving tools and set to work on the crude bolt. In an eyeblink, the latch clicked open, and the door swung.

Hope shone in the girl's eyes. She angled forward, her chafed knees sinking through the spaces between the bars. Jarle moved to assist her but paused when she tensed. He held his hands open once more and backed away. "I can't imagine the horrors you've suffered. I'm sorry for what these motherless curs have done to you. If you allow me, I will cut you loose. But please don't make a sound, you'll get us both killed."

The girl climbed out of her prison and offered him her wrists. Jarle cut the rope, then removed her filthy gag. He picked up one of the pelts and draped it over her bare shoulders. The girl was small and malnourished, not much older than Avaren.

"Let's go," Jarle said quietly.

The disheveled girl rubbed the rawness from her wrists and spat out her gag. "*Leh'siehn,*" she whispered.

Jarle managed a smile, but his heart was full of sadness. "You're welcome. Let's go."

Jarle draped the other grimmalkin pelt over his shoulders and ushered the girl along the back of the crag. They crossed a patch of moonlight, then ducked into the undergrowth. Upon finding a safe place, he turned to her. "Stay here while I go find you some clothes. When I return, we will go."

When the girl didn't reply, Jarle returned to the clearing. He moved past the dead sentry, circled to Rose's tent, and listened. From inside came the sound of soft, rhythmic breathing. Jarle parted the folds of the shelter and crawled inside. Nuzzled in a sheepskin bedroll, the woman shifted but did not awaken. He nabbed her boots, vest, and leather leggings, then headed back to the thicket.

Halfway to his hiding place, Jarle caught sight of the girl running toward Macario's tent. A gleeful smile danced on her face as she swung Ferret's blade over her head. Astonished by her audacity, Jarle stumbled. He dropped the stolen goods and waved her down. "This way!" he hissed. "Gods be damned; get over here!"

Jarle gave up silence for speed. He got to his feet and bolted into the safety of the shadows. "Fucking shit!" he cursed, debating what to do. The girl was either insane or witless.

The instant Jarle resolved to help her, a man's blood-curdling scream woke the camp. The Seh'nahiel girl burst out of Macario's tent. Bathed in the light of the aligned moons, and splattered with blood, she resembled a daemon from the Pits. She held a parang in one hand and a clump of dripping meat in the other. Rooted in place, Jarle gawked as the girl flung the gory gobbet into the flames. The macabre offering caused a swirling column of blue fire to shoot into the sky. The wicked light filled the moonlit clearing with unnatural brilliance.

Macario half crawled, half stumbled out of his tent. "My balls!" he screamed, clutching his bleeding loins. "Fucking cunt; I will kill you!"

Groggy men floundered out of tents and reached for their

weapons. Jarle's heart lurched as they converged on the naked girl.

Whispering winds swept through the jungle toward the clearing. Leaves rustled, and branches snapped. The girl cried out to the heavens in an incomprehensible language. Obeying her cursed commandments, the spear of flame spiraled around her, writhing like a serpent's tongue. The poachers ran and shouted as horrific specters emerged from the blazing whirlwind. Phantasms ripped apart the first man who dared to attack. His entrails scattered in the howling storm. The girl's raven hair flew upwards. She lifted her arms and continued to chant the bizarre words.

The sight raised the scruff on Jarle's neck and drained the color from his cheeks. At the back of his throat, he tasted blood. At last, he understood why the Ingvizitorij hunted soulbinders with merciless obsession.

Daggers in hand, Jarle turned and broke into a desperate run. Against the backdrop of infernal gusts and the shrieks of dying men, he pulled the grimmalkin pelt tight around his shoulders. Even the supposition that the fur could confer the wearer immunity to curses inspired a shred of hope.

Dizzy and disoriented, the thief stumbled through the undergrowth. Panic beat at his temples as he swung at the vines that clutched his legs like leafy constrictors. When his heart nearly gave out, his mind flashed to the gruesome pair of daemonic fiends that had sprung from the fire. Unable to continue, Jarle collapsed to his knees and did something he had not done since his father's death. He prayed.

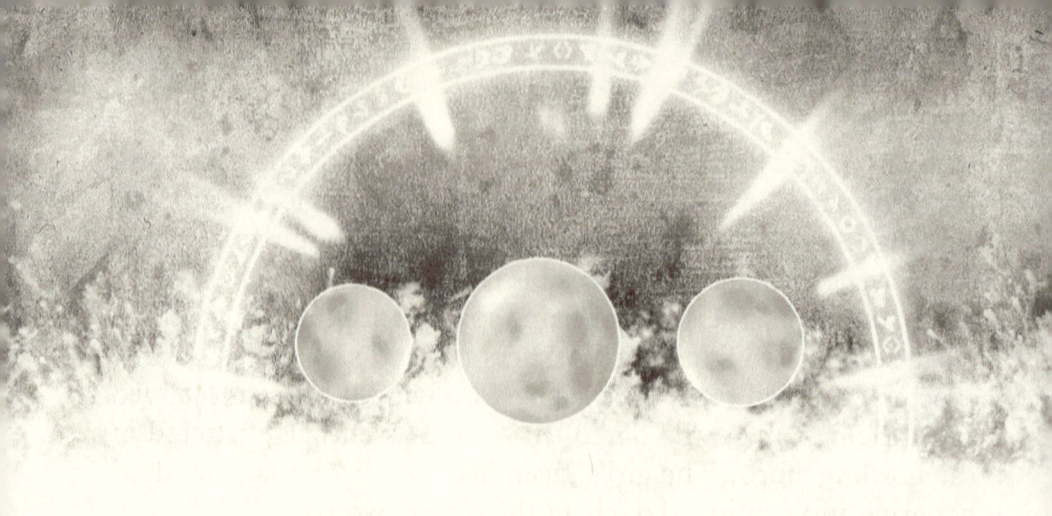

BLACK HEARTS

Shardi, Second of Nommen, 445 A'A'diel

From the palace balcony, Neylen observed the chaos in the streets below. The Three Sisters glowed brightly in the night sky, seducing the tides with their splendor. In a week, the swollen sea had submerged the docks and began to lick the edges of the Tangles. A procession of torches snaked upwards toward Gavalene as citizens fled the flooded areas around Old Gate. A unit of mounted Ca'Dezer, their armor shining in the moonlight, blocked the refugees from climbing farther up the hill. In the other direction, the silhouettes of the Thrommish ships floated on the bay like a murder of crows. The sight unnerved him.

Rigo threw his arms up. "Look at them! They are scampering toward high ground like rats fleeing a burning ship."

Neylen turned his back to the sea and studied his companion. Rigo wore a crimson and black embroidered doublet of Dessian silk—an extravagant luxury reserved for coronations and funerals. Armazine hose the color of crushed bone, and talon-shaped aggrafes completed the ensemble.

"Do you think hosting a pretentious gala during this catastrophe is wise?" Neylen implored.

Rigo scoffed, "Does the grand stirrer of shit lose his nerve in the Twelfth Hour?"

The banquet in Eva's honor had occupied the servants for three days. Along the parapets, every torchiere blazed, illuminating the palace with magnificent brilliance. Blue pennants bearing Thromm's crest—a serpent chasing its tail—hung from every balustrade and window. The royal silver-service had been procured from the vaults and polished to a mirror finish. Scullery maids scrubbed floors while chambermaids dusted curtains and dressed bedrooms with fine linens. Rigo insisted on perfection, and Neylen complied by instructing his guards to punish spiritless service.

Neylen brought his wine glass to his lips and sipped. Arguing with Rigo affronted him. Thus, he resorted to sarcasm. "Let the poor sods drown and starve. We shall rule over a people who despise us and judge us as vainglorious fops interested in fetes and lascivious entertainment! What's more, we will host games—contests of sword mastery like they do in Cartuj so that daily bloodshed can wash away the drudgery of decency."

Rigo cocked an eyebrow and let out a hearty cackle. "Is this your way of telling me my crimson doublet is too much? Understandable. It is ill-considered to give my sister another reason to despise me." Rigo held his hand out to Neylen. "Come, help this vainglorious fop out of his flashy clothes, we have some time before the regale begins."

Neylen ignored the offered hand and draped his arm over Rigo's shoulders. They walked past the glass doors of the balcony and into Rigo's bedchamber where a roaring hearth battled the chill. The crash of surf against the bedrock of the palace—a sound that for a long time robbed Neylen of sleep—had become a welcome melody. Even the dampness which seeped in from every crack was preferable to the scorching heat of his homeland. Though he loathed to admit it, Neylen was beginning to feel at home in Reyza.

Rigo's valet, an older man, named Hennes, sprang into action as they entered the room. He closed the terrace doors and drew the curtains.

Neylen waved his hand at the underling. "Leave us."

After a deep bow, Hennes withdrew and shut the chamber doors behind him.

Rigo seized the goblet from Neylen's hand and set it down on a console. "Give me your mouth, for I fear I will taste only bitterness tonight."

Neylen pulled his lover into his arms. The Jarle had many faults, but absent recriminations, his lips were divine. He gripped Rigo by the nape of his neck, where a silk ribbon held back his mane of blond curls and kissed him with firm, moist pressure. Thus embraced, they stumbled to the edge of the dais, which supported the royal bed.

Neylen's hands glided like shadows along Rigo's body as he disrobed him. He untied laces, unhooked aggrafes, and cabochons until the young man's warmth graced his palms. The crimson doublet landed on the floor in a crumpled heap. With a whispered incantation, Neylen dimmed the globes of elemental flame that illuminated the bedchamber and eased his paramour into the luxuriant bed.

Rigo clenched his thighs around Neylen's hips. He unhooked the eyelets of the Dessian's doublet and began to undress him.

Neylen slipped a hand beneath Rigo's undershirt and caressed his smooth, still-hidden flesh. "You are trembling," he said, halting his advances.

Rigo exhaled. He gazed into his lover's fathomless black eyes and stroked his chest. "I sometimes wonder whether you are made of stone. Has your black heart ever loved, Neylen?"

Neylen withdrew his hand and smoothed the silk shirt over Rigo's belly. In the gloom, Rigo appeared older than his years. Worry lines creased his brow, and his gaze betrayed insecurity. Beneath him, Neylen didn't see the regent of one of the wealthiest nations of Ibea; he saw only a vulnerable young man desperate for affection. Rigo had been ignored by his father, rebuked by his sisters, overshadowed by Tan'os Ensther, and finally seduced by his own manipulative schemes.

Neylen stroked Rigo's cheek. "I came to Reyza seeking political gain and new trade opportunities for my nation. To the east, we have an impassable sea, and to the west, a sprawling desert wasteland filled with warring savages—our situation is what you Reyzans call a rock and a hard place. I was prepared to do anything to sway your disposition. I brought with me black diamonds from the mines of Kes, bolts of our finest silk, and an entourage of my nation's most striking dancers to woo you. I shall never forget how your eyes bored into mine as two of the loveliest women of Naraj wove sensuous patterns in the space between us. Most men would have been awed by their bronzed bodies and the mystery behind their obsidian eyes, but you gazed past them." Neylen caressed Rigo's lips with his thumb. "What could I offer a man so disinterested in female beauty and wealth?" he asked, the planes of his face softening into a smile.

Rigo's eyes sparkled. He massaged the bulge between Neylen's legs before replying, "Enlighten me."

Neylen turned Rigo roughly onto his stomach. He seized the waistband of Rigo's leggings and tugged, exposing his buttocks. Rejoicing in Rigo's excited gasp, Neylen straddled the back of his lover's thighs. He kneaded each pale globe in his hands, parting and squeezing each cheek while pressing Rigo's hips against the bedding. When the Jarle squirmed with desire, the Dessian bent over him, letting his hot breath accentuate his words. "Loyalty," Neylen said.

Rigo moaned, gripping the sheets with his fists.

Neylen wrapped his fingers around Rigo's wrists and slid against him to whisper in his ear. "There isn't a single person I have loved who I didn't eventually betray. I assure you, Your Highness, my loyalty is immensely more valuable than my love."

CIRCUMSTANTIAL EVIDENCE

Shardi, Second of Nommen, 445 A'A'diel

The air in the parlor of the Thrommish Embassy was thick with unease. Ambassador Ther'oldo Ers wiped his brow with a linen handkerchief. The clock on his mantelpiece read a quarter past six, a half-hour past the appointed time—and still, no sign of Deneven! Across the room, Marchess Eva and Captain Rarikian spoke in hushed tones and glanced in his direction. Ther'oldo smoothed his doublet and walked to the window. He needed air.

Outside, night had fallen. In the triple moonlight, the shrubs cast eerie overlapping shadows across the courtyard. The stark scene invited heaviness into Ther'oldo's heart. Despite the luxuries of his office and the excitement of courtly maneuverings, he missed the warmth of his wife's meaty thighs and the roaring hearth built by his great-grandfather's hands. He yearned for his countryside estate near Carr with its wild ravines and rolling hills. He pined for the mists that slithered down the mountains at dawn and cloaked the meadows with dew. Ten seasons had passed since he had last set foot in his home. With Tan'os dead, his responsibilities in Reyza had trebled, diminishing his hopes of returning to Carr. The dream of walking among the swaying pines whose height defied the clouds faded into a distant memory.

"I'm too old for intrigues and politics," Ther'oldo confessed to his reflection.

"Pardon, Ambassador?" Eva asked.

The woman's query snapped the diplomat from his musings. Ther'oldo turned from the window and faced his guests. "I believe Deneven's arrival is imminent," he bluffed.

Eva's gaze lingered on the diplomat's wrinkled brow. "The justiciar is renowned for his punctuality. It is unlike him to keep us waiting."

Ther'oldo nodded. "Perhaps he was delayed at the Old Gate on his way up from the Tangles. The Collegium warns this is a powerful alignment. Sections of the city that escaped flooding in the past are now submerged. Even Reyzan sorcery cannot halt the encroachment of the sea."

"Time cares not for excuses," mused Eva.

Ther'oldo was about to respond when the sound of hoofbeats redirected his attention. The silhouette of two riders passed through the villa's iron gates. "He's here!" Ther'oldo exclaimed, his mood lifting.

Eva crossed the room and joined the old man by the window. Outside, the Deneven sat atop a plodding plow horse that dwarfed his escort's Namurese stallion. The Ca'Dezer rider alighted and took the justiciar's steed by the reins. He steadied the animal long enough for the older man to dismount. Once off the horse, Deneven unbuckled his saddlebags and withdrew a leather document case which he handed to the younger man.

"D'Neir has grown thick around the waist," Eva noted.

"Age favors no one," huffed Ther'oldo.

*
**

The parlor's gilded doors flung open. Clad in a black, thigh-length jerkin devoid of ornamentation, Deneven doffed his plumed hat and knelt on his good knee. Behind him, the swarthy cavalryman removed his helmet and followed suit. His poleyn clanked on the wooden floor. Both men's faces were flushed, their faces red from the cold.

Deneven bowed his head and pressed his hat to his chest.

"Marchess."

"Lord Justiciar, D'Neir," Eva acknowledged with a nod.

"Former, Marchess," Deneven corrected. "Apologies for my delay. The water is rising faster than expected, and many of the streets are impassable." Deneven leaned on his cane as he rose to his feet. Behind him, the cavalryman remained kneeling, his head bowed. Proper etiquette dictated a royal soldier remain prostrate in the presence of Reyzan nobility.

Eva examined the soldier, her eyes lingering on the document case in his hand. "Introduce us."

Deneven noticed the two, permanently clenched wooden fingers in Eva's black glove, but pretended otherwise. The last time he had seen Eva, she had been a child—bony and long-limbed. The woman who stood before him was as far from his recollection as Xio-Bahnn was from the shores of Reyza. Some women didn't need embellishment or great beauty to bend a man's will. Even in her woolen mourning dress, Eva commanded respect. Her eyes shone with an inner light—a sharp intellect that could, if provoked, cut deep. She stood straight-backed and poised, confident of her station. Draos' little girl had grown into a queen.

Deneven gestured toward the soldier with his plumed hat. "This is Lance Corporal Eskander Johar. He is one of two men assigned to me by your brother to aid in my investigation."

"More likely to keep a close eye on you," said Eva. She tilted her head toward the Thrommish sea captain, "I'm sure you remember Captain Gøran Rarikian, Commander of the Northern Fleet."

The giant man stepped forward with a welcoming smile and clasped Deneven's arm. "Fortune and fair weather. Despite the circumstances, I'm glad to see you again."

Deneven clapped Gøran's shoulder. "You as well, old friend."

Gøran eyed the purple bruises marring Deneven's complexion. "I gather the Dragon of Reyza continues to add battle scars to his collection. Let me guess, resistant suspect? Or a risky gambol?"

"A little of both," Deneven said. "I'm a lame dancer."

"A story worthy of a drink!"

Deneven smiled. "Another time. Perhaps after a few rounds of that weak firewater, you insist on calling proper liquor."

"Weak? I will pit your raska against my tzuica, glass for glass! I assure you it won't be me waking up on the floor!"

"My hangover from our last wager yet lingers. Mere mortals shouldn't compete with giants," Deneven quipped.

Ther'oldo crossed the room to greet the investigator. He clasped Deneven's hand and smiled politely at Eva. "Please," he said, pointing to the chaises, "let's sit down. We have much to address before Rigo's dreaded banquet."

With a dismissive wave of her hand, Eva gave the guard leave to rise. Eskander stood and bowed before handing Deneven the leather document case.

Deneven held his hat and cane in one hand and the valise with the other. "Ambassador, with your permission, I would like to attach my men to the retinue guarding the embassy until the alignment is over."

"Thank you, additional security is most welcome." Ther'oldo looked at Eskander and pointed to the double doors leading away from the parlor. "Young man, you will find Brent stationed in the gatehouse outside. He can give you instructions."

Eskander acknowledged the ambassador with a curt nod. He saluted Eva, then turned on his heels and strode away from the warmth of the fireplace. As he moved, his armor gleamed in the candlelight.

Eva walked to the fire and settled into one of the overstuffed chairs. She crossed her legs. "I see the illustrious Ca'Dezer is still quite the beauty pageant."

"Can't argue with you," Deneven said. He waited for the assembled company to sit before joining them. "Thanks to Thromm's vigilance, these noble whelps have never seen war. However, even in peacetime, you can find a few, like young Eskander, who demonstrate promise."

The coals glowed in the iron firebox, providing comfort in the drafty room. Four high-backed settees surrounded a low table upon which rested a tray of dainty sandwiches.

"How thoughtful of you to provide finger sandwiches, Majster Ers," Eva commented without humor.

The diplomat's face paled. "It wasn't my inten—"

"Of course not," Eva snapped, holding out her goblet.

Ther'oldo picked up a pitcher of wine and filled her glass along with everyone else's. The claret vintage shone ruby against the backdrop of the flames. The group took their first sips in silence; the death of Tan'os Ensther and the kidnapping of his daughter merited no cheer.

Deneven broke the awkward silence. "I wish we were meeting under more pleasant circumstances. As I'm sure Majster Ers informed you, the leads to Avaren Ensther's whereabouts are dry."

Eva's eyes narrowed, and her eyes grew as cold as tempered steel. "Do you believe the girl is alive?"

"Although I wish it were otherwise, the facts do not support her survival. And yet"—Deneven hesitated—"there is no evidence of her demise either. My gut tells me she still breathes."

Eva set her wine glass down. "Your gut? Surely you do not expect us to pin our hopes upon your belly."

Deneven straightened in his chair. "I questioned the last surviving conspirator personally before he met the noose. I cashed in every favor owed me in my hunt for information. I searched the harbor and the beaches where—pardon my brusqueness—corpses wash up. I have conferred with the Collegium mages and scoured as far south as the land permits. There is no trace of Mejtress Avaren nor the thief named Jars."

Gøran drained his glass of wine and poured himself another. "Are you certain she is not within the city?"

Deneven met the grizzled captain's gaze. "I cannot state anything for certain."

Ther'oldo shook his head. "If she were in the city, we would have found her," he blurted. "Avaren Ensther is no ordinary woman; she can't blend in with the locals. Rigo's reward is substantial, a worthy prize for anyone with eyes and ears."

Eva wrinkled her nose. "Is she so distinctive? Can she not pass for a Thrommish lass?"

The ambassador leaned forward in his chair. "Marchess, Avaren's beauty is legendary; her eyes shift in color between helfire and sapphire. Her fame drew suitors from as far as Terranakis. How else do you think the Ensthers amassed the fortune that brought about this tragedy? True or not, the people think she is a soulbinder and would sooner spend the night in the dungeons than grant her shelter."

Eva shot Gøran a sideways glance before addressing Deneven, "Do you believe the rumors, Majster D'Neir; that Tan'os' daughter is a sea witch with the ability to mesmerize men and summon the tides to her bidding?"

The question caught Deneven off guard. "I base my beliefs on facts, not rumors, Marchess."

"That was not my question," pressed Eva.

Deneven rubbed his forehead. He chose his words carefully. "Reyzans possess a fondness for tales that glorify or denigrate their rulers, beloved or otherwise. Tan'os Ensther's charms never won him any friends. If I may be blunt, common folk considered Tan'os a usurper—a hard-nosed foreigner who meddled too far in Reyza's affairs. People tolerated him because his methods yielded coin and security. Not surprisingly, this lack of affection, coupled with the girl's unusual appearance, led to ugly rumors." Deneven's expression softened. "I met Mejtress Avaren on a few occasions. I found her to be a well-mannered, intelligent young woman— certainly no water-dwelling sprite or enchantress. She does possess striking features which I attribute to her Starborn birth, nothing more."

Eva picked up one of the finger sandwiches and nibbled. When she finished, she brushed a few crumbs from her lap. "In your report, you state that Avaren and the thief named Jars fled together; that their trail ended at the edge of the cavern leading out to sea. What do you think they were doing there—before they leapt into the churning waters of the bay?"

Deneven loosened his cravat. "I have a few theories. Based on the Calantian mercenary's confession, Mejtress Avaren was unconscious. Jars could have been working with accomplices and arranged for a boat and crew to wait for him. He could have left Reyza on one of the two ships that sailed that night or taken the kidnapped girl to a secret place beyond the city walls." Deneven observed Eva's reaction as he continued, "It is also possible that Mejtress Avaren resented her upcoming marriage to Jarle Rigo. Perhaps she saw an opportunity to save herself from death and an undesired marriage and went willingly. Maybe she seduced the thief, who then killed his partner in a dispute."

"Preposterous!" Ther'oldo banged the table. "The Vise's daughter is a proper young lady. She would never think of eloping with the killer of her father—least of all a filthy, unblooded curskin." The consternation on Eva's face goaded Ther'oldo into silence.

"I am merely suggesting that many potential explanations can correspond to the facts," Deneven said coolly. "All we know for certain is that Avaren and her abductor are missing without a trace. Escape via one of the two ships is the most likely possibility in my estimation."

Once again, Ther'oldo interjected, "The Southern Fleet scoured the ports of call of the Tasirny and the Howl of the West and found no trace of them."

Eva shook her head. "I have witnessed firsthand how men treat proper ladies aboard ships, Ambassador. If my sister-in-law boarded one of those vessels, I doubt very much that Thrommish sailors seeking a noblewoman would find any trace of one."

Gøran took a sip of wine. "Speculating about the girl's whereabouts will not yield results."

"Indeed," agreed Deneven. "I intend to continue the search."

Eva's gaze fell on Deneven as intense as a falcon's. "Not on Thyra's coin."

"I don't understand," Deneven began, "Why would you aban—"

With an exasperated gesture, Eva cut him off, "We appreciate your efforts, Justiciar. The matter of my husband's half-sister is important, yes, but there is a much greater concern you have not addressed. What of Majster Ers' suspicions that Neylen Akkalon conspired against the Vise? Does evidence exist to support this claim? Do you believe in this conspiracy?"

Eva's terseness set Deneven's mind whirling. He leaned forward on his seat and clasped both hands over the handle of his cane as he mulled over the possible reasons Eva had to sail to Reyza. His expression remained placid as he spoke. "Circumstantial evidence exists of a coverup, yes. However, the Dessian emissary is a skilled diplomat and currently holds favor with Jarle Rigo. Raising such an accusation without ironclad proof will create a scandal that will discredit Thromm in the eyes of the Reyzan Court, and ultimately the Council."

"I think the moment has come for us to stop wasting wealth and time on a fruitless investigation. You offer us nothing beyond what we already know," Eva said, her tone clipped.

Ther'oldo poured himself another glass of wine. "Marchess, I hired Majster D'Neir as an independent investigator because I did not trust Lord Justiciar Tsardon's competence, nor his allegiance to truth. Deneven has worked diligently to unearth the facts and divulged his findings in full. What more can we ask of him? The murder reeks of a conspiracy, but without a witness or new information, we have nothing to refute Tsardon's official report. There isn't a single judge in the High Court who would entertain a case based on presumption and circumstance. Isn't that correct, Deneven?"

"I wish I could offer more," said Deneven. "Apologies."

Eva stood, not bothering to conceal her frustration. Her green eyes bore into Deneven's, and her cheeks flushed. "I cannot justify keeping the Northern Fleet in Reyza because some petty thieves, acting on their own accord, killed my father-in-law during a robbery!"

The sound of Eva's footsteps and the howling of the wind filled the silence. Deneven studied Eva as she paced back and forth across the parlor. Her sudden outburst justified his decision to withhold knowledge of Mast and the use of poison. Eva had not braved the diabolical currents of the Crossroads to avenge Tan'os or to find Avaren. She lusted for occupation and war.

A knock on the door interrupted the precarious calm. Ther'oldo cleared his throat. "Enter," he called out.

The doors opened to reveal a mousy servant. The woman looked around nervously at the grim faces and curtseyed. "The royal carriage is here, Ambassador. Shall I fetch the cloaks?"

Ther'oldo's gaze fell on Eva, whose back remained turned to the group. "Please do, we mustn't keep Jarle Rigo waiting."

PRISON OF MEMORY

Shardi, Second of Nommen, 445 A'A'diel

Avaren surfaced from the benighted depths of Reyza's harbor in the hulking shadow of a Thrommish frigate. Above her, a trio of fretted lanterns shed their reddish glow over the aftcastle and the gilded letters that identified the vessel as the *Swoughünd*—juggernaut of the Northern Fleet.

Absent the chop caused by the cape's crosswinds; the ocean was as still as a millpond. Across the sky, a garland of stars framed the full moons, and to the west, low clouds flashed with distant lightning. The air smelled of rain. Another storm was brewing.

Avaren dove under the surface and glided home. As she approached the shore, the devastation of the lunar alignment unraveled her emotions. Tears spilled down her cheeks as she swam through floating trash. Dark waters enveloped the piers and the dockside taverns. Fishing boats bobbed like corks in a field of debris that stretched midway up the bulwarks that separated the docks from Reyza's inner districts. Illuminated by fires raging in the slums, orange clouds of roiling smoke shrouded the lower half of the city.

Buildings cowered in darkness, except for the palace. Lit by rows of blazing braziers, the towers of the royal residence shone like beacons. The structure's splendor was rivaled only by the elemental flame burning atop Firehill. The shadowed valley between lighthouse and fortress appeared small and vulnerable against the destructive power of the sea. The flood had toppled foundations and lives—broken hopes made visible.

For a moment, Avaren courted the thought that her grief had summoned the tides to punish her father's betrayers. But the fantasy was one borne of exhaustion. The battle with the anemone had sapped her endurance and addled her mind. Each tail stroke caused her muscles to throb, and the weal on her arm stung with every breath. She needed rest.

The naera veered away from the wrecked harbor and skirted the jagged cliffs until she found the tunnel leading to Ca'd'Cel. The moonstones' unwavering glow revealed a partially flooded passage and an iron door swinging idly in the gentle swells. The creak of rusted hinges echoed in the gloom.

Avaren slipped through the open gate and dragged herself up the stone steps. Her gills flattened, fusing with the skin of her back. Pinpricks needled her lower half as the scales receded, and tails turned to legs. The wintry air raised goosebumps along the length of her body. Out of the buoyant water, she felt as cumbersome as the boulders thrown by competitors during the Feast of Elhinos. The earth pulled on her limbs with merciless vim.

After a few deep breaths, Avaren crawled to her feet and wrung the briny water from her hair. Her chest constricted as her eyes lost their ability to pierce the darkness. The dim bluish glow of the stairwell filled her with dread as she ascended.

At the top of the stairs, Avaren opened the secret door and paused as images of her father's sprawled, blood-splattered corpse drowned her consciousness. Her stomach churned with the memory of Dannia's bruised neck and Paulo's ashen body. The house, which had once been lively and warm, felt as inhospitable as a tomb. Only nightmares and ghosts roamed her halls.

'The scales are weighted against us,' her father used to say. "We must have courage lest we perish," Avaren said, finishing the thought. She clutched the box to her breast and emerged from the passageway. Her heart skipped at the sight of the frame that concealed the mechanism. A few canvas scraps were all that remained of Nephenee Dae'Varis' masterful rendering of Danikos wrangling the Southern Gale.

So much for secrets.

Avaren crept to the base of the grand stair and listened to sounds the way Jarle had taught her. She singled out the cadence of the ocean, the ruffling of nesting doves in the villa's alcoves, the occasional creak of settling floorboards, and the susurration of the wind. She concentrated on tuning out mundane noises and harkened for the telltale signs of habitation—coughs, pacing, the clink of armor, the hush of conversation.

None came. The house was empty.

In the formal hall, many of the furnishings, including her father's cabinet of exotic seashells, stood stockpiled on one side of the room. Canvas tarps hung over the priceless treasures, staving off dust and moisture.

Shivering from the chill, Avaren climbed the curving stair. Her fingertips trembled on the railing as she beheld her father's bed through the bedroom's open doorway. The linens and curtains had been stripped, but the mattress still bore the gruesome stains.

Ven save his soul!

Water pooled at Avaren's feet, and courage threatened to abandon her as Tan'os' voice trembled through her body, *'Take this box and hide it where no one will ever find it. When I die, deliver it to Arcanist Olos at the Collegium. Promise me you will do this.'*

The box in Avaren's hands grew heavy and fell to the floor. The thud banished the memory, but not the supernatural presence. She picked up the coffer and ran across the hall, fearing that if she peered into her father's bedroom once more, she might face his restless specter. Coins did not usher Thrommish souls to the underworld. Only burial in native soil bridged the world of the living with the wasteland of the dead.

Avaren entered Paulo's chamber and slammed the door shut. Bracing the door with her back, she traced the holy blessing of Ven in mid-air. "I vow to deliver the box, Father. I will not fail you." In the desolate room, her promise rang hollow. The

Collegium was a towering fortress surrounded by a walled bailey infested with ferocious creatures. A single, guarded portcullis allowed entrance to expected guests. Admittance required an invitation, and Rigo wanted her dead. She needed protection and a foolproof disguise.

Ambassador Ers could arrange an audience with Olos after she claimed asylum in the Thrommish Embassy. If her father's accolades of Captain Gøran Rarikian held truth, she would be safe under his protection. As for reaching the embassy, she stood a much better chance dressed as a man. Thugs rarely assaulted valets and pages.

Avaren wiped the cold sweat from her forehead and crossed the room. She set the box down on the writing desk and ran her fingers over a dove-shaped inkwell. She had purchased the unmanly bauble for Paulo's nineteenth birthday, never suspecting the role it would play in their affair. The bird's garnet eyes witnessed the penning of countless poems and letters. She imagined Paulo sitting at the table late at night wearing only his nightshirt, his curly brown hair falling over his face as his ink-stained fingers scribbled across the page. It saddened her to think how little she knew about him beyond the steamy confessions immortalized by his quill.

She walked away from the desk and opened the armoire. Folded shirts and cream-colored breeches occupied one shelf. Two dark blue waistcoats, one made of thick wool and the other velvet, hung on hooks above several pairs of riding boots. Avaren brought one of the garments to her nose and inhaled its scent. She recalled the stolen kisses, but the memories held no joy. The man whose letters overflowed with loving sentiments had proved false.

Avaren tossed the velvet coat on the bed and bound her breasts with a pair of stockings. She slipped into one of the linen undershirts and used a spare set of garters to hold up the excess sleeves. Unlike the baggy shirt, the breeches were tight on her hips—a quirk which the waistcoat luckily concealed.

A glance in the mirror confirmed the effectiveness of the disguise. Avaren cast her shoulders back and straightened. If she refrained from speaking, she could pass for a callow page.

Pleased, she twisted her long mane into a bun and stuffed it under the valet's plumed hat. She secured the straps of the dagger sheath around her waist and buttoned the jacket. Only the most scrutinizing observers would ever suspect a woman, but she doubted she could cross the city in Paulo's oversized boots. She needed proper footwear.

Avaren didn't bother to conceal her riflings. She picked up the box and left the room, rounding the balcony to her bedroom. The open door revealed tracks of bloody footprints across the carpet. The vanity drawers lay on the floor, and her privacy screen stood inside the tub. After a month of living like a rustic, her pastel-hued chamber seemed like a child's dollhouse. The florid furnishings belonged to a woman she barely knew, and a life she no longer recognized.

Avaren tossed the box on the mattress and opened the wooden trunk at the foot of her bed. She donned a pair of heeled riding boots and quickly laced them. Stitched with silver thread, the feminine leather boots thwarted her masculine guise, but comfort trumped worry.

After one last look at the bloodstain that marked the assassin's corpse, Avaren grabbed the coffer and fled down the servant stairs. She crossed the kitchen and flung open the back door.

Without the gardener's constant pruning, the orgatha vine had overtaken the garden wall. Defiant of winter, fist-sized flowers, the color of sunset bloomed among the greenery. Avaren kicked over a ceramic pot and snatched a key. She unlocked Ca'd'Cel's rear gate and stepped into a deserted alley.

A drizzle turned the cobbled streets into a warren of slick stones and glinting shadows. Tears threatened as Avaren walked away from her home, hoping never to return. The trappings of title and wealth no longer appealed to her. A noblewoman was a pawn, a tool with which to cajole and bargain. The desire for vengeance still glowed in her heart, but so did something else. In the hidden grotto, cuddled in the arms of her curskin lover, she had fallen in love with the idea of freedom. After she fulfilled her father's last wish, she vowed never again to allow someone else to steer her fate.

MASQUERADE

Shardi, Second of Nommen, 445 A'A'diel

Raindrops streaked down the glass panes of the dome that housed the palace's winter garden. Inside the protected structure, the redolent scent of flowers perfumed the air. Night-blooming jacinth mingled with the crisp fragrance of citrus and pear blossom, creating a heady bouquet.

Irilio peeked under his blindfold in search of his paramour's hiding place while pretending to amble aimlessly along a winding lane. "I'm going to find you, Eloisse," the poet announced, "and when I do, I'm going to devour you."

"Over here, sweet Irilio," came a silky, female voice.

With a smile, the courtier headed in the direction of the sound. Eloisse Gheneveve, five years his senior, was the wife of Councilman Gheneveve—a man so disfigured they called him The Rake. Religious and somewhat shy, the woman had proved an arduous conquest, but the rewards had been plentiful. Once freed from the arms of her boorish husband, Eloisse had become as wanton as Lyssandra's tarts with a body to match. She was petite and curvy with hair the color of night and sultry eyes that could set a man ablaze.

Irilio's hand closed around the contour of a marble urn. He

harkened to the rustle of skirts beneath him, but feigned ignorance to prolong the game. "So close, and yet so far," he said, feeling her gaze upon him. He caressed the basin of the planter, then traced down the edges of the pedestal until his fingers met the luxurious fur of the woman's tippet. Irilio raised his blindfold and smiled, wicked delight dancing in his hazel eyes. The black, glittering half-mask that concealed Eloise's identity stoked his lust. She was a rare beauty, married to one of the most dangerous men in Reyza—an irresistible combination.

Irilio drew the damsel to her feet and pinned her against the marble pedestal. He circled his arm around her waist and brushed his lips against her ear. "By the moons, we dance and play, let this night begin our day."

The woman reached down and stroked his desire. "I see the sun rises presently."

Irilio pulled up her heavy, muslin skirts and luxuriated in the warmth of her body. He wound his hand in her loose, dark curls and ground his hips into her. "May it set between your thighs."

The woman gasped, "Out here?"

Irilio bit her earlobe, breathing heavily into her tresses. "Why not?"

"Come to my villa later," the woman invited, grabbing a fistful of his hair.

Irilio raised her leg and fondled one of her breasts. The thought of bedding Eloisse under her husband's roof quickened his pulse. "I never thought to hear such a bold request. Meeting at The Stallion is safer, don't you think?"

Eloisse closed her eyes and arched her head. Her fingers slid down the poet's back. "Prudent, yes, but cramped. And your friend curses me with her eyes."

"Marcella is harmless." Irilio nuzzled her neck, then paused. Beneath the glittering mask, a scar marked Eloisse's chin. He caressed the pink line with his thumb. "Did the Rake hurt you?"

The woman smiled coquettishly. "No. I accidentally scratched myself with one of my rings."

Reassured, the poet continued his groping. His fingers sank into the pale blue velvet of her bodice. He inhaled the flowery perfume of her hair and lost himself in her arms. "I didn't expect to have a moment with you until after the banquet. Please, say you can stay."

Eloisse shook her head. "I must return before my absence is noted. But later, we shall celebrate. Come to my bed; indulge me. I promise that my husband will sleep soundly."

Irilio nibbled her jaw. "Is that so?"

"I had a rather enlightening conversation with Old Man Warrick at the apothek."

"You have procured something to prevent conception?" the poet asked, unable to quell the excitement in his voice.

"I have managed that and more," purred the woman.

Irilio let go of Eloisse's leg and met her dark eyes. "What do you mean?"

From her cleavage, Eloisse produced a small vial. "It cost me a fortune, but Warrick says that three drops diluted in drink are enough to induce a *profound* sleep. My husband won't even hear the Hounds of Sul should they come for him."

"And four drops?" asked the poet.

Behind the mask, the woman narrowed her eyes. "Four will make me a widow."

Irilio snatched the vial from the woman's hand and took a step back. "Just what do you think you're doing?" he hissed.

"I'm fulfilling your wishes." The woman tried to snatch the bottle. "Give me back the vial."

Irilio ignored her request and tucked the soporific in his pocket. He began walking toward the entrance of the banquet hall, his lustful thoughts quenched by the revelation. He liked his women virtuous, not vile.

The noblewoman hurried after him, breathlessly keeping pace. "I thought you wanted this," she said.

Irilio didn't look at her. "Exactly what gives you that idea?"

"You said just the other night you wished things could be different."

Irilio stopped and turned to face her. He gripped her upper arm and yanked her, pressing her against his chest until their noses nearly touched. Anger fueled his words. "I'm not about to murder one of the most affluent lords of this city for a good lay." His delivery became calculated and direct, "You and I have no future together, Eloisse. I am betrothed, and you are married—this thing we have cannot last, you know that!"

Tears welled up in the woman's eyes. Her bottom lip quivered as she spoke, but her words were full of venom. "Forgive me. Sometimes I forget that I am just your plaything—nothing more than an octet in a long string of vapid sonnets."

Clever—she was clever.

Irilio released her. "An octet?" he asked with amusement. "No. A stanza bestows you too much honor. You are more of a spondee, two very long, *stressed* syllables. Heart-break comes to mind."

"I'll give you two syllables, Irilio. Drop dead!"

Irilio felt as cold as the stone statues that dotted the palace gardens. "Then, we agree. It is over between us."

The woman took a step back. "You can't be serious. I have sacrificed everything for you."

"That's precisely the reason this should end," Irilio said flatly.

The woman grabbed his arm. Her voice trembled as she spoke. "Why are you doing this?"

Fearing that his composure might crumble, Irilio pulled free. He ran a hand through his hair and inhaled sharply. "Because you are fucking insane. Half of Gavalene already suspects that we are having an affair, and what do you do? You run off to purchase a vial of poison right after you ask the apothecary for silphium so you can fornicate to your heart's desire. Just what do you think will happen when your husband dies, Eloisse?"

The woman opened her eyes wide. "I wasn't planning to use it that way."

Irilio's stomach churned at the thought of a noose squeezing his neck. He swallowed hard, his mind drifting to harsher tortures. Eloisse was as beautiful as her husband was grotesque, but her obsession was blinding her to the impossibility of their continued liaison. "Your charms are not worth losing my head over," Irilio asserted.

Turning on his heels, the poet walked away, leaving the woman alone in the shadows of the garden. Behind him came a strangled cry, followed by the sound of sobbing. He had lied when he had compared her to mere syllables. Eloisse was more than a stanza, more even than his most celebrated sonnet. She was an epic poem waiting to be written.

Irilio smoothed the ivory silk of his doublet and tossed away the blindfold. He raised his chin and took a deep breath. Once recovered from the unpleasant exchange, he headed toward the banquet hall's lavish entrance.

As the guards pulled open the glass and steel doors, Irilio feasted on the grandeur before him. It didn't matter how many times he had stood beneath the soaring arches of the great hall. The effect was always awe-inspiring. The grand space rose three stories to culminate in a flat, coffered ceiling that resembled the night sky. Painted in tones of sapphire and lapis, each square panel held at its center a carved star limned in gold. Dual rows of arches perched atop amber columns separated the room into three galleries. On one side, the lancet windows faced the exotic plants of Rigo's winter garden, and on the other, the sea.

The poet's eyes glittered as the servants hoisted the chandeliers upward. Tiny flames danced amid a sea of crystal-cut glass, casting a myriad of reflections on the walls. Reliefs of naeras and tritons frolicking amidst stone-carved surf lined the room, while above them, small porthole-like windows gave the impression of standing inside a magnificent ship.

A long table set with gleaming silverware and crystal goblets ran the length of the room. Pink roses procured from the winter garden jutted from porcelain centerpieces in the shape of conchs. Servants made last-moment adjustments while two musicians tuned their instruments. Irilio hadn't seen such fuss since Jarle Rigo's coronation.

The succulent scent of bacon, garlic, and herbs wafting in from the kitchens caused Irilio's stomach to growl as he crossed the room.

Catching sight of the poet, one of the musicians waved him over. "Hail, Irilio, stealer of hearts. Are you not a bit early?"

Irilio put a hand to his chest and bowed before the duo. "Good evening, Maestro. You know what they say, the early man lives twice."

The musician clapped the poet on the shoulder. "Assuming he stays away from vice—something you wouldn't know anything about."

Out of the corner of his eye, Irilio caught a glimpse of Eloisse. She stumbled into the banquet hall in a flurry of blue skirts, hood drawn over her face. The poet turned his back to her, feigning interest in the Maestro's libretto. *"The Huntsman's Truce for Violin and Lute* is rather dour for a banquet, is it not?"

The players ignored Irilio's question and directed their attention to the fleeing woman. The violinist shook his head and rosined his bow. "Seems you have ruffled some feathers," he said.

Irilio gave the man a terse look as a door slammed at the far end of the hall. "The night is young, sure to be filled with new adventures."

The lutist sighed and shrugged. "Leave it to Irilio to prove there are no faithful wives so long as there are poets."

Once Eloisse departed, Irilio exhaled. He put the libretto back on the easel and crossed his arms. "I was counting on the aid of a harp for my reading, but I suppose a lute will do."

The lutist plucked a couple of chords. He turned the pegs on the head of the instrument and craned his neck to assess the adjustment. "You've written something new for tonight?"

Irilio's face lit up. "Indeed, I have Maestro. I've been working on a few short poems venerating the joys of summer. I almost feel guilty having written them considering the rising tides and the general state of misery in our city."

The violin player took up his instrument and dragged the bow against the strings, producing a melancholy wail. "While our fine city drowns, the poet makes his rounds, whatever has a bosom fair—he pounds."

Irilio laughed. "Not bad, Hemsley. You may yet have a promising future as a jester, or a sheep-shearer."

"Don't mock the boy, Hemsley," said the Maestro, "it's not every day that a prodigy blesses our company. Come, Irilio, favor us with a few lines."

"Here's a thought on love." Irilio cleared his throat. "As grapes are sweet of taste to eager lips, and wine to him who hath well drank, desire traverses golden horizons upon the wings of dreams. And so it seems to the souls that quaff the madness, to the souls who must endure—that the magic of love is pure—while they stoke its tender ache."

The duo looked at each other, then at the poet.

Irilio shifted from one foot to the other. "Well? What do you think?"

Hemsley scratched his head. "I'm no silk-stocking or literary genius by any means, but I say skip that one this evening. You did hear that the Northern Fleet got caught in a nasty storm on their way here, right? Rumor has it the Marchess of Thyra lost her arm to the weather. The last thing she probably wants to hear after her father-in-law's death is sunny love poetry. You'll be safer with something more appropriate—like that one about lasting memories or the one about courage in the face of tragedy."

Irilio pondered the suggestion. "Do you agree, Maestro?"

The lute player sat on an upholstered stool. "Who knows what pleases the court these days? These are troublesome times. Best a man can do is keep his head low and stay out of trouble. Ambassador Neylen instructed us to be demure in our musical offerings. The banquet, we are told, is not a celebration. Taper your poetic offerings accordingly."

Irilio waved his hand, exemplifying the grandeur of the decor. "Well, it certainly isn't a funeral!" His outburst caught the attention of a few servants, who paused briefly before returning to their tasks.

The lutist cocked an eyebrow. "I do not intend rudeness, Majster Irilio, but we need to prepare. The guests will arrive presently."

Hemsley blew his nose on a handkerchief, then sat beside the Maestro. "Surely Reyza's literary love child aspires to better company than lowly musicians."

"All right, all right, I am going," protested Irilio.

The violinist played a quick fiddle, then pointed his bow toward the double doors. "She went that way."

RUFFLED FEATHERS

Shardi, Second of Nommen, 445 A'A'diel

Drawn by four Namurese horses, the whimsical vehicle seemed more like a puff pastry than a carriage. Along the top of the domed gondola ran a carved frieze of waves and open clamshells bearing silver pearls. Two footmen bedecked in the palace's blue and white livery alighted from their perches at the rear of the barouche and opened the gleaming doors of the carriage. Although soaked from the rain, their faces brightened with sunny smiles.

Eva took the footman's hand and stepped into the carriage, followed by the ambassador, Deneven, and Captain Gøran. The interior of the coach was as sumptuous as the exterior. A cut-crystal oil lamp hung from the center of a silk-draped dome, illuminating the champagne-hued upholstery with a warm glow. Upon closing the doors, the footmen took their places on the running boards. Two taps on the roof signaled departure. With a cry and a snap of the reins, the driver guided the transport past the villa's gates.

The carriage lurched to one side when the coachman turned into the street. Years of wagon traffic had ground deep ruts into the city's cobbled roads. Even the most expensive carriages trundled and rocked, resulting in a test of endurance rather than a luxurious journey. The best way to traverse the city was on horseback or by foot, yet no self-respecting noble would resort to such.

They traveled in silence until the horses turned onto Via Elgabarr, a broad avenue that wound up from Old Gate to the palace. Via Elgabarr was one of the few places in Reyza that enjoyed uninterrupted stretches of open space. Amber lanterns and cascading fountains lined the median of the road as it ambled toward the heights of Gavalene. Palatial villas, each more ostentatious than the last, competed for attention on both sides of the thoroughfare. Beyond the gated entrances, onlookers glimpsed grand atriums, fountains, tree-lined driveways, and gardens yet in bloom. The unmitigated display of wealth juxtaposed the crowded chaos of the lower districts.

Gøran assessed the villas through the rain-streaked window. "Trade must be profitable."

"Reyza prospered during the Vise's administration," Deneven admitted. "No one denies that peace is good for commerce.

"Yet the good citizens of Reyza forget who forged the peace they enjoy." Gøran crossed his arms and relaxed into his seat. His gaze flickered to Eva, then to the justiciar. "Not too long ago, Reyzans welcomed our sailors in their taverns; now they cringe in our presence. Are we considered allies only when pirates lurk on the horizon?"

Unsurprised by Gøran's frustration, Deneven chose a guarded response. "Reyza should not be confused with A'diel when it comes to etiquette. Tan'os Ensther may not have been warmly welcomed when he ascended to office, but over time he was accepted— as much as any foreigner could ever hope to be. Reyzans think with their purses, and under the Vise's protection, coin pouches grew fat. But avarice is not all that rules our hearts. A month ago, people were elated over the news of a royal wedding—a welcome distraction from the curse of the Three Sisters. The death of Tan'os and the kidnapping of his daughter, followed by the arrival of what can only be deemed a war fleet, has soured spirits. Fears of bloodshed and rising waters dominate discourse in every corner of the city."

"Perhaps." Gøran eyed Ther'oldo, who pursed his lips.

As the carriage circled a roundabout, Eva looked out the window. "Speaking of war, isn't that a statue of you, Justiciar?"

In the center of the circle, standing upon a pedestal surrounded by jets of water, stood a heroic rendition of the Dragon of Reyza sculpted in white Dessian marble. The youthful rendition of Deneven held a sword in one hand and an upraised torch in the other. The monument was a romanticized recreation of the charge which won the final skirmish of the war and cost him his leg. The statue harkened to a time when Deneven had been a happier man.

"Indeed, it is Marchess. I only wish it were made from limestone rather than marble from that cursed nation," Deneven admitted.

Eva's eyes lingered on the justiciar. "I was too young to remember the war, but I recall the toll the conflict exacted on my family. Every tithe bowl contained coin, and incense constantly burned in the palace's shrines. I believe limestone is too weak a substance to commemorate the efforts of a hero. You fought bravely, Justiciar."

"I would have gladly given my life for Reyza's freedom," said Deneven.

"A rare sentiment these days." Ther'oldo's jaw tightened as he returned to pinched silence.

Eva gave the ambassador a curious look. "Why do you say so?"

"The absence of loyalty is everywhere you care to look," Ther'oldo clipped.

"Truly? Enlighten us," Deneven said.

"Indeed! What is your rationale for such a claim?" Eva asked.

Given leave to speak his mind, Ther'oldo's frustration overflowed. "This city is a den of greedy ingrates who think only of themselves. The mages are deep in their books or chanting useless rituals to prevent their precious tower from sinking into the ocean. Rubbish, if you ask me. The palace is not much better. The Reyzan Court is a maze of traps that even the most skilled diplomats can't navigate. Merchants and commoners alike bicker amongst themselves like starved dogs in pursuit of precious profits. No commerce is too base or immoral when money can be earned. Crime runs rampant; the audacity of the thieves is extraordinary! They run organized guilds! And the city guard charged with enforcing the laws and protecting the citizens? Their corruption and abuses of power are legendary. I believe apes would perform better. Heartfelt fealty from a Reyzan is rarer than mercy from a Sullosian."

Although many of Ther'oldo's observations rang true, Deneven's anger frothed over. "I resent your aspersions, Ambassador! Without the Collegium's long-term efforts, the lower districts would have succumbed to the tides. Raising the very firmament beneath our feet is nothing short of miraculous. As for commerce, we lack land for pasture and crops. Trade is the lifeblood of Reyza; our merchants rival those of A'diel and Terranakis. And your defamation of the Ca'Dezer—"

"Yes, well, what I say is what I see," interrupted Ther'oldo.

The justiciar pursed his lips in an attempt to rein his tongue and failed. "Tell me, Ambassador, if Reyza is such a hopeless midden, why does Thromm continue to offer protection or seek alliance? Why not just let Five Isles annex this miserable maze of traps and be done with it?"

The ambassador's cheeks grew red, and his blue eyes opened wide. He huffed, adjusted his cravat, and prepared to retort when Gøran's hand silenced him. The captain leaned forward and spoke with calm conviction. "One might say Thyra is nothing but a backwash of frozen wooden shacks, skinny sheep, and drunken barbarians, but gods help me should some foreigner badmouth my birthplace in my presence. Apologies, Justiciar."

"Accepted." Deneven relaxed slightly, though his brows remained beetled. More than ever, he felt justified in his decision to conceal much of what he had learned during the investigation.

Ther'oldo was about to speak when Eva cleared her throat. "You have done Thromm a great service, Ambassador, but perhaps the time has come for you to return home."

A pang of empathy tugged Deneven's heartstrings as he watched the ambassador's shoulders droop. He recalled the moment Rigo and Tan'os forced him to retire and frowned. Although he didn't always agree with Ther'oldo, he judged him a competent diplomat and a decent soul.

"I would like nothing more," Ther'oldo blurted. He met Eva's watchful gaze and nodded. The expression on his face revealed that an immense weight had been lifted from his shoulders. "I have not seen my family for a long time. I am a grandfather to four children in name only. And though my wife will likely relegate me to sleeping in the stables, I yearn to return to Carr. I shall seek the Størmman of Blackspur's dispensation. Ten years of service is enough."

Gøran clapped the older man's shoulder. "Better your own outhouse than the most sumptuous foreign palace! May the sea gods grace your voyage with fair weather. As for the stables," Gøran mused, "I am glad I am not married!"

Eva smiled. "Does that explain why you choose to live aboard that creaking pile of bones, Captain?"

Gøran released Ther'oldo and grinned. "You see an old ship whose keel was laid before I was anything more than a twinkle in my father's eyes. That pile of bones has a rich history. She led the attack on Port Serebus, chased Ferencian privateers from the Bay of Guisan, crossed the empty Talantean Ocean to establish the first treaty with Terranakis, and served as our flagship in the War with Five Isles. There is enough Thrommish blood in the *Swoughünd* to make her kinfolk. My beloved ship ushered you to our shores. She is more than a vessel—she is Thyra. She is home." A self-conscious smirk spread upon Gøran's face as he settled back into the cushions. "Us cantankerous old folk are set in our ways, aren't we, Deneven?"

Deneven forced a friendly smile. "A young man is pure conjecture, while we old men are immutable facts."

Eva tucked a strand of hair behind her ear. "I imagine that in your line of work, there are no such things as immutable facts, Justiciar."

The investigator straightened his frock as two taps on the roof, signaled their arrival. "Facts are subject to interpretation, Marchess."

Eva drew the curtains and peered out. "I see the years have not diminished my family's seat of power."

Deneven looked out the window. Perched atop of the foundations of an ancient fortress, the palace with its famed winter garden held commanding views over the harbor. Fortified walls ringed the structure offering a single entry point—a gatehouse with a retractable bridge that spanned a deep gorge. The royal residence was near impregnable from land sieges, but as the marauders from Five Isles had proved, a naval blockade could bring Reyza to its knees. "Rigo has spared no expense in beautifying the royal residence," Deneven said.

"Aye!" chimed Ther'oldo. "He's a vainglorious coxcomb who cares more for fetes and self-aggrandizement than rulership."

Eva let the curtain fall closed. "Tonight we are my brother's guests, and we shall, above all, be gracious," she said. Her eyes fell to Ther'oldo, "Can I count on you, Ambassador?"

The old man sighed. "I shall acquit myself in a manner befitting my station, Marchess. However, my duty is to Blackspur and all of Thromm, not just Thyra."

"Understood," said Eva. "Let us hope my brother lends us proper courtesy."

The staccato clinking of heavy chains filled the air as the barbican portcullis lifted. Every torch along the perimeter of the gatehouse blazed brightly, and candles lined the causeway that led to the inner bailey. The carriage moved through the corridor of foggy light like a ghostly specter. When it entered the courtyard, standard-bearers with long, streaming flags ran alongside them, creating the illusion of undulating golden waves. Trumpets sounded as the carriage rounded a tiered fountain before coming to a stop. A moment later, the door swung open.

Eva fixed her expression to one of regal calmness and stepped out of the vehicle. A crier announced, "Presenting Mejtress Eva Ensther, Marchess of Thyra and the Great Northern Marches, daughter of Jarle Draos Iarris, and sister to his Royal Highness Jarle Rigo Atalios Iarris!"

THE GAMES BEGIN

Shardi, Second of Nommen, 445 A'A'diel

Lael Taelehnn, the Seh'nahiel Emissary to Reyza, lifted his wine glass to the light and swirled. He regarded Mallec, his assistant, and lover, through the syrupy trails clinging to the inner curves of the vessel. "Ferencian Eldenwoen. I am impressed. It appears our host has spared no expense to glorify his sister."

Mallec raised his goblet to Lael's. "I hear Irilio will recite a new work tonight in honor of the Marchess' arrival. Perhaps with enough of this vintage, we can convince the fair poet to favor us with private oratory after the fete."

Lael laughed and clinked the rim of Mallec's glass. "May your wishes reach Sandahria's ears. There isn't another man in Reyza as talented with his tongue; present company excluded."

Mallec tossed a strand of hair back. "Don't be so certain. If rumors are to be believed, the Dessian's tongue reaches so far up Rigo's ass that he uses it to speak."

The companions laughed. They savored the silky fire of the wine while they studied the crowd. The heads of mercantile houses arrived early to stake their claim in the reception hall. Throughout the gallery, courtiers dressed in fanciful clothes and extravagant jewelry gathered in temporary fiefdoms where they held court among their entourages. Diplomatic emissaries from every corner of Laremlis mingled with the wealthiest courtesans. The women glided through the throng like the prismatic peacocks they collected for their dens.

An ayre played by the musicians stationed in the balconet underscored the hum of conversation and laughter. To a casual observer, the assemblage appeared like a gathering of friends, but the camaraderie was deceptive. Beneath the veneer of festivity wars raged.

Lael and Mallec, veterans of those covert battles, displayed the noble aloofness of A'diel with their posture. Bedecked in their most exquisite silks and jewels, they sipped wine on the mezzanine landing. The elevated position provided an unobstructed view of the hall and its occupants while the dramatic arches above their heads conferred importance.

Leaning on the balustrade, Lael observed a lost-looking soul weaving toward the grand stair. The man lumbered through the masses with the subtlety of a thrask dancing a minuet. The diplomat drained the last of the amber wine and straightened. "I fear the flavor of the season from Calantia is about to make his introduction."

Mallec replaced his lover's flute with a full one from the tray of a passing serving girl. "Yes, judging by his appearance and lack of finesse, he'll likely tempt us with the exciting topic of animal husbandry."

Lael smirked. The simple cut and drab colors of the man's dress betrayed his inexperience and bucolic education. Remembering which Dolcarr ruled which city-state in Calantia was more nettlesome than counting flies on a pile of dung. Any Calantian diplomat they dealt with would likely be ousted within the year as civil feuds toppled the ruling houses. "What's his name?" Lael asked.

Mallec chuckled. "I sometimes wonder what you would do without me?"

Lael regarded his companion out of the corner of his eye. "I'd shrivel into a ball and quiver, darling."

"No doubt," agreed Mallec. "The ambassador's name is Cadu. He's the nephew of Minos Morcant, a former envoy from Mencello who was poisoned here at court twenty years ago."

"I don't recall," Lael sighed. "But if his successor's fashion sense is any indication of his intellect, I wager I can broker a ship full of Mencello's finest trade goods in return for a dozen crates of apprentice-crafted swords."

Mallec drained his glass. "Twelve? Too generous. What's the matter, not up for a real challenge tonight?"

"Consider the positive," Lael said to his consort, "this little exchange will entertain us until Marchess Eva arrives."

*
**

The Coral Chamber derived its name from the material on its walls. White plaster traceries of vines and flowers contrasted with the crushed coral veneer. Settees upholstered in aquamarine velvet and urns bursting with exotic blooms lined the vestibule. The pebbled texture and harsh illumination concealed various peepholes scattered throughout the room.

Hidden behind a false wall, Rigo and Neylen spied on Eva and her entourage.

After a quarter-hour of silence, Gøran plopped down on a seat. The wooden frame creaked under his weight. "Depth and substance are both lacking," he groused.

Eva glared at the captain but remained silent.

Across from her, Ther'oldo feigned interest in a rose bloom. "I agree. Everything in this room is fair of surface, but weak of form."

Deneven sat down and massaged his leg. "I don't care for Revivalist decor, but I doubt either of you are referring to the chamber's merits."

"Jarle Rigo's tardiness is an affront to our dignity!" fumed Ther'oldo.

Eva walked to the wall behind which Rigo hid and admired the plaster tracery before moving on. "I have not seen my brother in fifteen years. Another hour won't make a difference."

Rigo backed away from the peephole and stroked Neylen's crotch. "This is worthless," he hissed. "They divulge nothing of value; dullards the lot of them."

Neylen pushed Rigo's hand away and laced his pants. "Judging by their moods, I advise austerity."

Rigo smoothed his doublet and tossed his crimped curls. "I conceded to your counsel and changed into more funerary vesture. However, if I must go through with this charade, I intend to procure some enjoyment. I doubt Eva is capable of loathing me more than she already does."

Neylen bristled at the comment. "You would tempt war for idle amusement?"

"Be at ease. Trust me," soothed Rigo. "I know how to handle that frostbitten cunt. If I do not poke my sister with a needle or two, her suspicions will be inflamed. You do not know her as I do."

"Considering what is at risk, do not prick the lioness too vigorously," cautioned Neylen.

"When it comes to matters of vigorous pricking, I would be a fool to ignore admonitions from a master." A subtle smirk danced at the corner of Rigo's lips. "Look at us! Are we not a pair of proper crows? Let us go and greet our guests. Who knows, I may even shed a tear."

The settee upon which Gøran sat cracked under his weight just as the double doors of the Coral Room flew open.

Ignoring the captain's gaff, Rigo entered the room with arms outstretched. Behind him, Neylen waited; hands clasped behind his back.

Gøran put distance between himself and the broken object and came to stand behind Eva. Both Ther'oldo and Deneven bowed as Rigo embraced his estranged sister.

"Sister!" Rigo beamed, "my heart rejoices in your presence!"

Eva endured her brother's embrace but refused to return the gesture. "Your Highness," she said, her tone cold, "it has been too long."

"Indeed! Your company fills me with gladness, so much so that I momentarily forget my sorrow. I missed you," Rigo said, releasing her.

Eva nodded. "I wish the circumstances for our reunion were merrier."

"I do as well," Rigo affirmed. "The death of Tan'os Ensther affected us deeply. But he is anything but forgotten. Tonight, we shall honor Tan'os' legacy, not merely mourn his passing."

"Tan'os sacrificed much to protect the people of Reyza. Perhaps, in his memory, you should allocate the funds spent on this banquet toward shelter and food for the victims of the tides."

Rigo's eyes narrowed, and his smile faltered. "This is not the first lunar alignment Reyza has weathered. We Reyzans are well versed in surviving calamity and are quite prepared for the worst the Three Sisters have to offer. I have a well-considered plan to safeguard my citizens. Do not let such things concern you."

Eva eyed Rigo, her eyes as intense as those of a snake measuring a mouse. "Forgive me. I am merely perturbed by the scenes of chaos I witnessed in the last few days. It is difficult to discern any strategy amidst widespread panic."

"A few malingerers and vandals failed to evacuate as commanded, but none proved so insidious as the Thrommish sailors who set fire to my harbor." Rigo cocked an eyebrow, "If there is havoc in the streets, your people are to blame."

Ther'oldo cleared his throat before speaking. "Damages have been paid, Your Highness."

Eva quieted Ther'oldo with a hand. "But the destruction remains."

Rigo's smile returned. "Dear sister, I don't wish to bicker. The past is the past. Allow me to introduce my honored guest, Neylen Akkalon, Ambassador of Dessia."

Neylen entered the room and bowed before Eva. "I am humbled," he declared. "It is an honor to meet you, Marchess. You have my deepest condolences. Your father-in-law was a cunning strategist. I had the utmost respect for his skills."

Eva nodded her acknowledgment. "Thank you, Ambassador Akkalon. You are kind to say so."

Rigo sidestepped Neylen. "Enough talk, let us eat. Come, Sister, give me your hand, allow me to escort you to the banquet." When Eva jerked her gloved hand away, Rigo brought his fingers to his lips. "Oh, how insensitive of me. Please, forgive my boorishness. I understand you lost a hand to frostbite during your voyage."

"Your sources are inaccurate," Eva said icily. "Only two of my fingers were amputated."

*
**

"Then it is agreed! One cargo hold of your purest aromatic resins in return for seven crates of A'dielian crafted longswords. May the Dolcarr of Mencello be blessed with many heirs and long-lasting prosperity." Lael raised his goblet in a salute.

Cadu beamed with pride as he lifted his flute. "May Jassindora Althea of House Jezzain reign in sunlight for all her days."

The two diplomats nearly spilled their drinks as the golden double doors opened with a fanfare of trumpets.

Mallec replaced Lael's empty glass with a full one before addressing the Calantian. "Kindly excuse us, Majster Morcant. We must prepare to greet the Marchess of Thyra."

"Of course," Cadu stammered. "Thank you again for your generous deal. I hope you will join me for dinner after the waters settle."

The diplomats ignored him. Lael watched the entrance intently while Mallec adjusted his finery.

At the top of the grand stair, a chamberlain strutted to the balustrade and banged his staff on the floor three times. The crowd fell silent. "Honored guests," he intoned, "give respect to his Royal Highness, Rigo Atalios Iarris, Jarle of Reyza, Beloved of the Gods, Protector of the People, and Master of the Southern Sea."

Amid thunderous applause, Rigo entered and waved.

Mallec leaned over to his lover and whispered in his ear, "Master of the Southern Sea? He has taken Ensther's title! What appellation will he use next?"

"Dessian Lapdog," Lael suggested with a humorless laugh.

The ovation diminished quickly. Rigo moved to one side of the balcony as the chamberlain's rod rang out again. "Please welcome Lady Eva Ensther, Marchess of Thyra and the Great Northern Marches, daughter of Jarle Draos Iarris, and sister to his Royal Highness!"

"Here she comes now!" exclaimed Mallec.

Eva stepped forward and joined Rigo. She appeared genuinely surprised as wild applause filled the room. Moved by her poise, Lael raised his goblet in her honor. His heart skipped as Eva acknowledged the gesture with a smile.

When the acclaim ended, the national anthem of Reyza began to play. The siblings descended the stair, followed by their respective entourages. Courtiers, diplomats, and merchants parted like a shoal of fish to allow the royal procession to cross the reception hall. All persons along their path bowed, some knelt on one knee.

When the doors of the banquet hall opened, Rigo and Eva entered and sat at the head of the table. Distinguished guests selected to join them filed slowly into the room while those less worthy vied for position at the entrance. Lael and Mallec entered last before the doors closed.

"I suspect this evening will be one that we long remember," Lael mused.

Mallec nodded and squeezed his lover's hand. "Look at that table! Even our beloved jassindora would approve."

A large table stretched along the length of the room. White silk runners formed a striped pattern across the surface, offsetting the glittering utensils and plates of burnished gold. Three immense crystal chandeliers illuminated the magnificent tableau with the light of six hundred candles. Ample spacing between chairs ensured all fifty invitees could dine in luxury. Delicate gold-rimmed bowls placed over chargers of crushed ice overflowed with sliced summer fruits—a rare indulgence in winter months.

While guests found their assigned places, servants dressed in ivory livery catered to every need. White-gloved hands held napkins, poured wine, and fussed over the epicurean pleasure of each guest.

Lael and Mallec settled across Eva's retinue. Lael had never met Gøran but knew of his exploits from Mallec's dossiers. The captain was a fine specimen of Thrommish physical prowess, so much so that a massive chair had been provided to accommodate him. On either side of the captain, sat Ther'oldo Ers, and the former Lord Justiciar. There was no mistaking the worry scripted on the men's faces. Something was afoot beyond the palpable tension caused by the Thrommish blockade.

Rigo drummed the rim of his goblet with the butt of his knife to announce a toast. As all eyes turned to their host, Lael leaned and whispered in Mallec's ear, "Let the games begin."

THROUGH THE THICKET

Shardi, Second of Nommen, 445 A'A'diel

The rain masked Avaren's tears as she turned into Lamb Chase, a winding lane famous for its charcuterie market. Shops with shuttered windows and chain-barred doors lined the deserted street. The eerie sound of creaking signs and distant shouts filled her with dread. She rarely traversed the city on foot and had only a vague idea how to reach the Thrommish Embassy. The alleys that branched from the thoroughfare were a cutpurse's paradise where many had lost limb and coin.

Ther'oldo's villa bordered the Thicket, a manicured woodland which offered sanctuary in the summer months when Reyzan tempers flared. Avaren had frequented the park, but always during daylight hours and in the company of Dannia and armed guards. At night, without the aid of recognizable landmarks or main roads, she navigated solely by conjecture.

When Lamb Chase ended, Avaren ambled uphill through the maze of streets in the merchant quarter. Several wrong turns later; she emerged on Beltane Lane, a street renowned for its gem cutters. Unlike Lamb Chase, Beltane thrived with activity. On both sides of the road, refugees huddled beneath makeshift tents while a stream of displaced families lugged what remained of their earthly possessions farther up the hill. The ear-piercing cries of babes joined the cacophony of mounted cavalrymen, the barking of dogs, and the hum of conversation. A few paces ahead of her, an ale keg crashed through a shop window. Frightened screams followed the explosion of sound as shards of glass rained on the cobbles.

Avaren clutched the box to her chest and hid in the shadows as a band of looters emerged. Arms burdened with stolen merchandise; the men ran into a nearby alley. The commotion garnered the attention of the mounted soldiers, who gave chase.

Soaked to the bone, Avaren rushed past the burglarized shop. At the end of Beltane, she entered Bel's Cirque, a roundabout crowned by an oak whose roots protruded from the ground like gnarled fingers. When she was younger, her father had told her stories about Bel's ancient tree and its fairy inhabitants—little people who enjoyed thwarting their larger kin. Looking at the scores of miserable people camped beneath the massive branches, Avaren didn't think the tales far-fetched. The fey had won; the world had gone mad.

Six streets branched from the circle, but Avaren recognized only one—Via Elgabarr. The sight was all thorns and no roses. A contingent of soldiers blocked the road leading to the moneyed parts of Gavalene and turned away all persons seeking higher ground. Not wishing to confront them, Avaren walked through the encampment in search of someone who could provide directions.

Haggard men huddled around campfires. They held their hands out over the flames to keep out the chill while women and children shivered under makeshift tarps. Chiseled by the strokes of suffering and misfortune—terrible sculptors—their bodies hunched against the wind and rain. Melancholy eyes followed her as she trudged through the muck.

Among the evacuees, Avaren spotted a graybeard wrapping a blanket around the shoulders of a child. The man had a fringe of gray-white hair around his mottled scalp and a hand tremor that rendered the task difficult. Avaren lifted the box to conceal the Ensther coat of arms embroidered on the lapel of Paulo's waistcoat and approached the elder. She addressed him in the most masculine voice she could muster. "Pardon, could you point me in the direction of Ghead Hall?"

Although the venerable man swam in the tidewater of his eighth decade, he proved surprisingly agile. He stood to face her and wiped the water from his brow. Thick white eyebrows framed his twinkling eyes as he regarded her. Below him, the child pressed herself against his leg as though seeking refuge beneath a mighty elm. "Why do you seek Ghead Hall?"

Avaren lowered her face and hoped the shadow of the broad-brimmed hat concealed her features. "I have news to deliver to the Ferencian Embassy regarding their warehouses," she lied.

The refugee's forehead furrowed. "Dressed in those fancy clothes, I reckon you would know the way."

Avaren's heart raced. "Simple questions beg for straightforward answers. I don't want any trouble."

The man reached down with a gentle, protective hand and shifted the girl behind him. "There is enough mayhem this night for all. Something tells me you aren't what you seem. Anyone from around these parts knows how to get to the Thicket. Unless, of course, you are from the Tangles." The man glanced at the stationed line of cavalrymen, then lowered his voice, "I take it you wish to avoid the guards?"

Avaren nodded.

The man raised a trembling hand and pointed to the right. "Take Collegium Road until you get to the old watchtower. The street will wind a bit. After it ends, turn left. You will pass a row of clothiers and booksellers before you spot the Pigeon's Roost. At the Roost, make a right and follow the lane to the blue house, it's hard to miss. From there, make another right, and you'll be at the Thicket. Ghead Hall is next to the Thrommish Embassy, across the park." The man rubbed his chin. "You got all that?"

Avaren repeated the directions back to him, grateful when the man corrected a missed turn. "Thank you," she said, tipping her hat.

The man eyed her. "You are shivering. Stay a while; warm yourself by the fire."

Avaren shook her head. "No. I need to be on my way."

The refugee offered a toothless smile. "Ven keep you safe."

"You as well," Avaren said.

Luckily, the landmarks the graybeard singled out were conspicuous. The Pigeon's Roost was a rowdy alehouse, and the blue house was an eyesore of a building with a roof shaped like a corkscrew. By the time she reached the Thicket's gate, every muscle in her body burned, and gnawing hunger rumbled her belly.

The park's gilded entrance stood in contrast to its dilapidated monuments. Past a fountain shaggy with water weeds, stretched rows of mossy statues. Marble nymphs frolicked among the skeletal trees oblivious to the wintry weather. Gusts of rain blew across the bleak landscape, stripping bare whatever foliage remained.

Avaren followed the central avenue to the golden dome peeking above the trees. Every solstice, the Temple of Zezen, with its daevil-faced gargoyles, served as a festival space. Betrothed couples celebrated upcoming unions by tossing glittering offerings into the shrine's thermal waters. For hundreds of years, adventurers in search of castoff treasure plumbed the pool's murky depths only to surface empty-handed—if they surfaced at all. Loremasters believed the pool bottomless, while merchants assumed the tradition a ruse to fatten the city's coffers.

Bracing herself against the wind, Avaren brushed past the hedges and entered the pavilion's columned portico. The walls rose to a magnificent rotunda painted with colorful frescos. The designs depicted joyful Akadian scenes where nymphs and satyrs disported themselves among fields of vines. Addonels circled the wreath of dancing figures, brightening the bucolic faces with gifts of garlands. Inside, the lingering scent of coals and crushed flowers suffused the air.

A pleasant sillage of perfume met Avaren's nose as she approached the center of the shrine. Beams of moonlight filtered through the oculus high above, bathing the black waters in brilliant light. Zezen's statue appeared to welcome the rain with outstretched arms. Droplets of water sparkled in the illuminated shaft before merging with the steaming tarn.

Avaren set her father's box down and began to undress. Her numb fingers throbbed as she undid the bindings of her soaked garment and let it drop. She stared at the water, recalling with dismay the day her most elegant string of Ferencian pearls disappeared in the depths. The day Zezen with her many rows of teats, witnessed her betrothal to Rigo Iarris was one of the worst days of her life.

Naked, Avaren slid into the warm water and welcomed her aquatic form. Scales rippled along her hips and raced down her calves. Her legs elongated into writhing tails and fins unfurled. Beneath the surface, she opened her luminous eyes and breathed, coaxing her gills to suck the life-giving water. The naera hovered, suspended in the velvet blackness, and absorbed the heat into her bones.

The restorative waters alleviated the burns caused by the anemone's tentacles but did little for her cheerless heart. The trickling rain reminded her of the cave and the blissful nights spent in Jarle's embrace. She missed her lover's voice, his strong arms, and his smile. Unlike her father, Jarle had never asked her to sacrifice herself for his love. He had consoled her, and raised her spirits, and she had repaid his kindness with manipulation and lies.

Regret washed over her like the long slow waves of the pool. The thief believed that he loved her, but his feelings were contrived, nothing more than a glamouring born of a naera's most potent weapon—her tears. The seduction which had begun as a means to avenge her father had resulted in a dangerous dance—a gamble that could cost Jarle his life.

Avaren coiled under the water and cried into the emptiness. Suddenly, she envied the temple's sylvan merrymakers trapped in their aestival, plaster prisons. The dancing figures would never experience cold or rain, pain, or sorrow. Reeling with heartache, she implored the ancient deity to safeguard Jarle's journey. She promised Zezen jewels and riches should fate spare him from harm. In the end, no amount of vengeance could ever bring her father back.

THE ELEGY

Shardi, Second of Nommen, 445 A'A'diel

Situated at the rear of the banquet hall and adjacent to the butler's pantry, the Green Room, served as the entertainers' alcove. Irilio stood in the shadow of the doorway and reminisced about Rigo's last fete. The summer Feast of Bel'Tahïm had been a grand celebration during which he wooed a sinuous serpent dancer. The Ghossian girl had proved an able handler of all kinds of snakes.

The memory roused a dreamy smile. It was a pity the regale in Ensther's honor was a bore. He was unaccustomed to standing alone in a room often crowded with performers in outlandish costumes, dancers in mid-stretches, fire breathers, trained animals, musicians, and all manner of diversions.

Irilio shrugged. At least from the alcove, he could enjoy the music and flirt with the endless stream of serving girls. His stomach growled as the servants filed past his vigil carrying trays heaped with aromatic appetizers. Unable to resist, the poet reached out and snatched a meat-filled dumpling from a passing salver. Irilio winked at the girl and popped the morsel into his mouth.

The pastry was blissful—a culinary poem of flaky crust and mouthwatering venison. He marveled at the delicious little treat and wondered what it portended for the rest of the evening's fare.

Irilio lifted a goblet of wine from another tray and sipped while he waited for his cue.

At the head of the table, Rigo droned on about the virtues of Thromm's alliance with Reyza. He bestowed endless praises on the dead Vise—a man everyone knew he loathed. Irilio yawned as he observed the nobles' faces. Some appeared genuinely interested in the acclaim, while others dissembled boredom.

Setting his glass down on a passing tray, the poet cocked his head and sought the one face which could lighten his mood. He spotted Eloisse's husband first and grimaced. Wine trickled from The Rake's deformed lips and stained his bib. Next to him, Eloisse munched on a light tidbit. Her beatific face melted into divine pleasure as she swallowed. Her eyes half-closed, and a tiny smile curled the corners of her mouth.

Irilio fiddled with the vial of poison in his pocket as he watched his lover play the role of obedient wife. Eloisse humored her husband with coquettish smiles and timely blushes. As the charade wore on, he began to lose his appetite. The longer he stared at her, the more certain he became that something wasn't right. Then, it struck him; his mistress had changed her attire and coiffed her hair in a series of interlocking braids. She no longer wore the sky blue gown nor the sapphire jewels from their earlier tryst. Instead, she sported a burgundy bodice with a high lace collar, and a silk cape embroidered with dazzling pearls. Ruby earrings glittered on either side of her flawless complexion, which was, consequently, absent a scar. Perturbed by her drastic alteration, Irilio stole another flute from a roving tray. As he brought the drink to his lips, his name rang out in the banquet hall.

"And now our most gifted poet will commemorate this occasion with his verse. Please, welcome Irilio," announced Rigo.

Irilio set the glass down, swept a hand through his curls, and strode into the light. Applause accompanied him as he ascended a small podium and bowed.

"Capturing the essence of a man is difficult; doubly so when he is an illustrious war hero." Irilio's golden voice rang through the stillness. "I humbly offer tonight's recitation in honor of Tan'os Ensther, the Savior of Reyza.

The audience sat in rapt attention as Irilio's poetry flowed through the room. Swept away by the sobriety of the occasion, the poet's oration grew ever more fierce until his words rang off the walls like thunder at sea. Irilio had crafted an epic paean to the fallen Vise, but it was his performance that elevated the material. He concluded the elegy with a bow and held the position, waiting for applause that failed to arrive. Engrossed in the delivery of the crescendo, he had lost track of his audience.

The poet laureate's stomach tumbled, and his heart pounded. He looked up, expecting to see an enraged regent, but instead, saw only stunned countenances. The performance had stolen the gathering's collective breath. Silence lingered for a long moment until, at last, the hall filled with the crash of applause.

Relieved and delighted, Irilio bowed, humbled by the reception. Even the icy Thrommish Marchess appeared moved. He took a final bow then swaggered back to the shadows of the Green Room. With luck, he might be called upon to recite again, which would result in additional coin and fame.

*
**

"Is the braised boar not to your liking, Your Grace?"

Eva looked across the table to find Neylen smiling at her. "I am not hungry, Ambassador."

"A shame. The flesh is succulent and spiced to perfection." Neylen chewed a forkful of the steaming meat for emphasis. "I confess, Reyzan pork is a guilty pleasure."

Eva drank deeply from her goblet. "Are there no pigs in Dessia?"

"Our hogs are cultivated and lack the flavor of the wilds. Reyza's jungle boars are leaner but far richer in taste. Regardless of spice or cooking method, a free-ranging animal that grazes on a wide variety of forageable food will always be more flavorful than a confined one raised solely on grain."

Eva picked at the herbed tenderloin. "I concede that freedom must certainly taste better than captivity."

Gøran snorted before swallowing a mouthful of pork. "And I thought the only animals that lived in Dessia were jackals and snakes."

Neylen cut into another piece of meat. "That's an understandable perspective considering you spend the majority of your life in a floating barge that cannot reach our shores. Painting foreign lands in unflattering colors is effortless without proper exposure to their cultures. For example, some of my people believe that Thromm is nothing but a frozen wasteland populated by yellow-haired giants with a predilection for drunkenness and violence."

Eva leaned back in her seat, and Gøran tensed, drowning his impolitic retort with a gulp of wine. Nearby guests fell silent as the tension grew.

Ther'oldo cut in, "Diplomacy requires accurate information, especially when dealing with cultures vastly different from one's own. I spent a great deal of time learning about Dessia—including its creatures."

Neylen regarded the ambassador as though considering an upstart child. "Please, enlighten us with your research, Majster Ers."

Ignoring the Dessian's condescending tone, Ther'oldo turned to Eva. "Marchess, people commonly presume that the most deadly animal in Dessia is the jaracca. And while the dust-hued reptile is lethal, it is not the creature that inspires the worst fear in Dessian hearts."

"Let me guess," Gøran growled, "their mothers?"

Before Neylen responded, Ther'oldo's stern tone commanded attention. "From the youngest age, Dessians are taught to respect the plants and animals that share their land. Whether for the king's table or the peasant firepit, each slaughtered animal goes to the afterlife with a prayer. However, there is one exception. The alakret, a scorpion, poetically known as the Widow's Kiss, is so vile that Dessians will destroy the arachnid on sight without hesitation or prayer."

Neylen's black, icy stare challenged Gøran across the table. "You are correct, Ambassador. The sting of a Widow's Kiss is an agonizing ordeal from which no victim ever survives. The venom is so potent that should your captain receive even the slightest prick, he would be dead before he drew three breaths."

Gøran slammed his fist on the table. Guests reached to steady teetering wine glasses amid startled gasps.

Neylen's grin sharpened as he lifted his goblet to the fuming sea captain.

"Eva!" Rigo's voice shattered the tension like a hammer smashing glass. "Dear Sister, I almost forgot to ask you a most important question."

Eva dismissed Neylen with a glance and turned her attention to her brother.

Rigo steepled his fingers. "Speaking of cultures, I know how earnestly the Thrommish grieve, and the importance of burial rites. Please, put my mind at ease and promise me you will ferry Tan'os Ensther's body back to Thyra at your earliest opportunity."

Ther'oldo choked on his wine, then scrambled for a napkin to dab the red droplets from his doublet.

Caught off guard by Ther'oldo's reaction, Eva straightened. "I understand that Collegium mages are properly preserving my father-in-law's remains. Once our investigation ends, and we are satisfied with the findings, we shall return him to native soil."

Ther'oldo's face grew pale as he stammered, "Forgive me, Marchess, I forgot to tell you that—"

Eva cut the ambassador off with a wave of her hand. Anger blazed behind her green eyes. "Tell me what?"

Rigo's eyes bore into Eva's. "Your understanding is only partially correct, Sister. Hours after the tragedy, I pleaded with Majster Ers to ferry Tan'os' body home on one of the two ships of the Southern Fleet still in port, but he refused. Majster Ers disregarded my protestations regarding his decision to keep the body in Reyza until the Northern Fleet arrived. Further, he threatened that if I did not command the mages to magically preserve the bodies of both the Vise and Mejtress Avaren's handmaiden, he would personally see to it that relations between our two nations would come to an abrupt end."

Rigo stood and addressed the ashen-faced gathering. "Ther'oldo Ers has graced the court for many years. While we have not always agreed, I believed him to be a reasonable man until he eschewed his responsibility to Tan'os Ensther, the Savior of Reyza." Rigo ignored Ther'oldo's mortification and focused on Eva. "Sister, you are a Reyzan. You know the incredible cost of both magical talent and coin required to deter putrefaction. I realize this is a grim subject, but one of the utmost importance. I paid the Collegium mages with funds from my coffers because a great man like Tan'os Ensther deserves dignity, and because I care about the future amity of our two cities." Rigo's expression darkened as he continued, "Slowing the initial tidal surge required the skill of every adept in the Collegium. I could not risk the lives of my citizens to save the pride of one diplomat. I had no choice but to direct all efforts toward containing the sea. Even so, the alignment's destruction is vast. Imagine for a moment, a situation far worse."

Eva's stomach lurched. "Tan'os' body must be interred before it decays or his soul will be damned to wander the Endless Waste. What has become of him?"

Rigo shook his head. "The mages preserved his body for many weeks, but during this past week, they halted the conservation rituals. Against my moral inclinations, I ordered his remains packed in sea salt. Despite the efforts of my best embalmers, your father-in-law's corpse is ripening. I am afraid that salt will soon prove inadequate."

"This is an outrage!" Gøran's face glowed red with anger. "I will not sit idly while the body of my friend rots for the sake of political leverage. The soul's passage to the underworld is sacred."

Rigo fixed his gaze on Gøran. "What would you have me do, Captain Rarikian? Your ambassador made the decision—a decision I vehemently contradicted. Ambassador Ers insisted I use the entire Southern Fleet to scour for Mejtress Avaren's whereabouts. Thus, Captain Athanasios searched every cove, fishing village, and smuggler's cay. Forgive my bluntness, but I have done all I can. I will not apologize for choosing to safeguard my people. Do you suppose that raising the ground beneath our feet and halting the power of the tides is a rudimentary feat of magecraft? I assure you, it is not."

Eva's rage fled, leaving the cold calm of resignation in its wake. She felt capsized as Rigo outmaneuvered her. She had no choice but to return Tan'os' corpse to Thyra and end the blockade.

"Captain Rarikian," Eva clipped, "both Jarle Rigo and Ambassador Ers had sensible and compelling reasons for the decisions they made. Your anger cannot aid Tan'os' soul, but your ship can." Eva met Rigo's gaze. "Thank you for your consideration and your efforts, Brother."

"You are welcome," Rigo said, taking a seat. "You implied earlier that your independent investigation had not concluded, but I disagree. I have read Majster D'Neir's report summary and have found no information in its pages to challenge Lord Justiciar Tsardon's conclusions." Rigo paused for dramatic effect. "I think it is time for the Northern Fleet to cease this blockade so that Reyza can rebuild in peace. The Council will interpret a continued military presence as an act of aggression."

The muscles in Eva's jaw twitched. "What of Mejtress Avaren?"

Rigo's smile betrayed the satisfaction of out-witting her. "I give you my solemn word; I will not rest until I find my betrothed. Her uncertain fate grieves us all."

Eva clenched the napkin on her lap. Without hard evidence of a conspiracy or realistic hope of finding Avaren, she could not justify delaying her departure and risking the enmity of allies across the continent. "We will sail after the Sisters' pull wanes, and the fleet reprovisions," Eva stated. "As of this moment, the blockade is over. Ships may enter and depart at will."

"A wise decision," Rigo praised. "I do hope, dear Sister, that camaraderie between our two cities can continue."

"Yes, of course," Eva agreed. "I have the Strommarch's blessings to renew our alliance."

"Excellent!" Rigo's expression brightened. "Let us lighten the mood."

A TALE OF TWO GUARDS

Shardi, Second of Nommen, 445 A'A'diel

Lance Corporal Ionaden Kesner leaned his palm against the warm stones of the hearth while he stirred a boiling cauldron. He lifted the ladle to his lips and savored the stew. The flavor of herbs and braised leeks raised his spirits. He was a far better cook than he was a soldier.

Aside from the occasional argument with Eskander, his assignation to D'Neir had proved worthwhile. The Thrommish embassy's cramped scullery was preferable to the cold rain and the desperate mobs which greeted every cavalryman south of Old Gate.

The irony was not lost on Ionaden as he continued to stir the broth. Deneven had only been half right in his disdainful assessment. Despite his plump cheeks, he was no coddled spawn. His soft hands, adept at preparing food and caring for his armor, had also strangled a man and would do so again given proper cause.

"Lost in the soup again, Kesner?" came a voice from behind him.

Framed by the arched entryway, two armored men stood, adorned in the blue and yellow tabards of Second Company. Calvert and Brent, veterans of countless years of military service, bore a resemblance to one another. Sunken eyes looked out from under heavy brows, and their shoulders slumped from the weight of metal. Age had rendered them incapable of pursuing the sloppiest of cutpurses. Thus, they paced watches unworthy of more vigorous men.

Ionaden grabbed two bowls from a rack above the mantel and filled them to the brim with the chunky stew. "You two make more noise than a pair of Tharsirion jugglers," he said, setting the plates down.

The men ignored the comment and descended the steps into the kitchen. They leaned their polearms against the wall and sat by the fire. Calvert gripped the edge of the bowl with his gauntleted fist and brought it to his lips.

Brent watched with amusement as some of the broth dribbled down his friend's beard. "Did your mother never teach you manners?" he asked.

Calvert winked and gulped down a chunk of parsnip.

Ionaden placed two wooden spoons on the table and fetched a wrapped parcel from the counter "I reckon that's a no," he said to Brent.

Calvert wiped his chin with the back of his hand and smiled a toothy grin. "What you got there, Kesner?"

Ionaden straddled the bench. "This," he said, unwrapping the parcel, "is a loaf of freshly baked rye."

"You are spoiling us. Must be true what the sages say about the moons and madness," said Brent.

Ionaden broke the loaf in half, then handed each man a piece. "Can't a man do a good deed without a nefarious motive?"

Calvert took a bite. "What's ne-far-ee-us?" he asked with his mouth full.

"Another word for wicked," Ionaden explained.

Brent shrugged. "I'm not one to pass up a tasty slice of rye to go with my meal. Thank you."

"Yes, many thanks. This stew has put the heat back into my bones. How did you learn to cook, anyhow?" asked Calvert.

"By the time I came along, my brothers and sisters were already squabbling over inheritances. I grew up in the kitchen, veritably raised by the cook. My toys were garlic bulbs and buckets," Ionaden mused.

"The Kesners are in the textile business, are they not?" asked Brent.

"Not anymore," clipped Ionaden. "A few rotting tapestries and a box of silverware is all the remains of the family fortune."

Calvert pushed his bowl toward Ionaden and changed the subject. "Spare another helping?"

Ionaden took the bowl to the simmering pot and filled it with choice pieces of meat and vegetables. "I'm glad my cooking is to your liking," he said, setting down the stew. "Feel free to help yourselves, but leave some food for the roof retinue. They haven't eaten yet." Ionaden walked to the far side of the room and grabbed his cloak. "I will fetch them."

Brent sopped the broth with a hunk of bread. "I'll stop Calvert from devouring the whole pot, but do us a favor, and don't come back too soon. We're not ready to return to our posts. It's freezing out there."

Ionaden drew the oiled leather hood over his head and stepped outside. The courtyard was quiet save for the sound of water trickling along the gutters. The cold, wet month of Triesse birthed strings of mildew in the cracks of the city's whitewashed masonry that stank like musty rags. Winter in Reyza soured the spirit.

His boots sank into the soggy ground as he skirted the defensive wall of the villa. At the front of the compound, he entered a cramped guardhouse overlooking the Thicket and plopped down on a wooden bench. He unhooked his wineskin from his belt, reclined, and uncorked the vessel. A bouquet of milled herbs and spices replaced the stench of mold as he took a long swallow. After months of watered-down raska, Zherrian Ale tasted like the nipples of Zezen herself.

As the alcohol warmed his belly, Ionaden closed his eyes and imagined himself in the arms of Loli, the tawny-skinned tramp he had bedded in the Tangles before the alignment had unleashed Hel. He gazed out over the woodland and let his gaze settle on the dome of Zezen's temple. Relishing the memory of the harlot's bouncing tits, he raised the wineskin to the goddess. "To Loli!" he toasted before taking another sip.

The cavalryman sat in silence, enjoying memories of the romantic encounter and the honeyed drink. As time passed, the rain ceased, and the moons emerged behind fast rolling clouds. The bladder was half drained when the sound of footsteps interrupted his reverie. Cavalry boots had a distinctive jingle caused by the spurs' rowels clanging against metal shanks. Ionaden wasn't surprised when Eskander appeared in the stone doorway. "Lance Corporal Johar, fancy a drink?"

Eskander stepped forward and snatched the wineskin from Ionaden's hand. He sniffed the contents, then poured the expensive liquor on the earthen floor. "Drinking on duty is punishable by demotion and docked pay. Stealing ale from the house of a foreign dignitary will cost you a hand." Eskander tossed the empty wineskin aside. "Do not let me catch you boozing again, or I'll be forced to report the incident. Surely you value your hand considering all you've done since our assignment is polish your poker."

"What is that awful smell? Wait, I know! It's shit. Maybe if you stopped sucking turds from Deneven's wrinkled asshole, you might discover the joys of a well-polished prick."

"I understand your penchant for self-love. A woman willing to bed a man born of a drunkard and a curskin gutter whore must be difficult to find."

Ionaden launched himself at Eskander with a growl. The two cavalrymen grappled on the muddy ground. Each attempted to gain an advantage over the other.

Ionaden slammed his forehead into his opponent's face. In retaliation, Eskander bashed his fist into Ionaden's ear. The force of the blow sent him reeling into the sodden grass. Ionaden rubbed his ringing ear while his opponent coughed and spat out blood.

"Did I hit a nerve?" Eskander challenged.

Ionaden rolled to his hands and knees and charged. Eskander's foot shot up under Ionaden's hauberk and struck his groin before he could land a blow. Ionaden dropped to the muck like a sack of grain. His balls throbbed with agony. He tried to curse, but only grunts emerged as he fought for breath.

Eskander regained his footing and wiped the blood from his face. "This is going to cost you."

Ionaden clutched his tortured privates. "I think I ruined your pretty face," he gasped.

Eskander took a step forward, fists clenched. "You are an opportunistic caitiff devoid of loyalty and discipline—the product of a disgraced family with no future. I want nothing more than to beat you senseless, but you are not worth the punishment. Enjoy your spurs. You won't be wearing them for long."

Ionaden stood on wobbly legs. He opened his mouth to deliver a barb when, across from him, a shadow darted in the tree line. Startled, Ionaden brushed back his hair and surveyed the woods. "Someone's lurking out there," he said, his voice low.

Eskander cocked an eyebrow. "Do you think I will turn my back on you?"

Ionaden scanned the shadows. "First, you need to stop breaking my balls about the liquor. Second, I'm very serious."

Eskander spat a mouthful of blood and unsheathed his blade. "I will investigate. Stay here and keep watch until relieved."

As the cavalryman entered the Thicket, Ionaden silently implored the gods to punish him. While Eskander had not personally played a role in his family's financial demise, his uncle certainly had. The Johars, a family of ruthless bankers, were admired and despised in equal measure.

Not long after Ionaden returned to the lookout, he spied the source of the movement. Far from where Eskander breached the park, a dark silhouette emerged. Bathed by the light of the moons, the figure ran across the street and tested the iron bars of the embassy's front gate.

Intrigued by the late-night visitor, Ionaden left his post and skirted the wall. He flattened himself against a stone pillar and craned his neck for a better look. The intruder wore the livery of a male valet, but his clothes were ill-fitting. The loose garments reminded him of the outfits thespians sported when mocking the nobility. Strands of pale hair peeked beneath a wide-brimmed, leather hat, and held a parcel in one hand.

The slight man looked the part of a page, but messengers never waited for a distraction to make their presence known. The poorly disguised stranger, he decided, was either a thief, an idiot, or someone possessed by a death wish.

Ionaden drew his sword and stepped into the open. "You there, state your business."

The man shuffled back a few steps, then bolted. He leapt over a row of rose bushes flanking the villa's drive, then ran headlong into the narrow alley leading to the back of the house.

Cursing his heavy maille, Ionaden chased after him. "Intruder!" he shouted. "Alert!"

Brent and Calvert burst out of the rear courtyard and blocked the path with their polearms. The page tumbled in midair to avoid the halberds and landed inside the reach of the weapons with catlike grace. He swung the parcel and connected with Calvert's face with a heavy thud. Dazed, the soldier staggered back.

Brent stepped back to bring his halberd to bear, but the trespasser bypassed his guard. The would-be page delivered a kick to the guard's knee and followed the blow with an elbow to his jaw. When Brent fell to his knees, the figure used his shoulder to propel himself upward. He flew over the disabled soldiers in a clean arc, tumbled, and rolled to his feet.

Beads of sweat soaked the padding beneath Ionaden's armor. He rushed past his stricken cohorts and entered the yard. He trampled a bed of withered irises and plowed through a hedge. "Surrender or die!" he threatened.

Ahead of him, the stranger stopped and whirled to face him. Steel glinted in the moonlight as the intruder brandished a dagger.

Blood rushed to Ionaden's ears as he stared at the gleaming point of the blade. The cries of his compatriots crashed against his senses like a drowning man's lament—distant and garbled. Ionaden felt like a fly trapped in honey. He stood, unmoving as the interloper eased into the shadows.

Ionaden's knuckles whitened as he readied to strike.

"On your left," came a shout from above.

The warning came too late. Ionaden raised his weapon but failed to parry the attack. Sparks flew as the stranger's blade scraped the maille protecting his armpit. The pressure of the blow snapped him from his stupor. The cavalryman pivoted, grabbed his attacker's wrist, and twisted until a shriek pierced the night. The moment the dagger tumbled from his assailant's hand, Ionaden plunged his knee into the man's stomach. The interloper dropped to the ground with a strangled grunt.

Before Ionaden could deliver a killing blow, a cry from the rooftop froze him in place.

"Release!"

A flurry of crossbow bolts whizzed overhead. One of the shafts buried itself into the mud at Ionaden's feet while another flew into the gloom. Two more disappeared into the darkness before the fifth one hit its mark. The page let out a high-pitched yowl as a bolt pierced his thigh.

The injured man dropped the parcel and crawled behind a statue. Hunkered against the stone plinth, he clutched his wounded leg. His breath misted in the cold as he pleaded for his life, "Please, don't kill me. I claim sanctuary."

Surprised by the youthful tenor of the voice, Ionaden strode into the moonlight, where the crossbowmen could see him. "Hold your shots, Gryson. Stand down!"

"Standing down," came the reply. The sound of winches clicking into place followed.

Polearms in hand, Brent and Calvert rallied behind Ionaden. Together, they approached the wounded man.

"What is your business?" Ionaden demanded.

The man's head turned from one guard to the next, then to the men on the roof. Blood oozed from his injury like water from a wellspring, and his chest labored with quick, ragged breaths. "The box... please... Arcanist Olos," he muttered weakly.

No longer faced with the threat of death, Ionaden noticed the seal of the House of Ensther emblazoned on the page's coat. A closer inspection revealed embroidered flowers on his muddy boots and a swathe of pale skin on a slender neck. The blood-soaked fingers which clutched the wound did not belong to a man, and neither did the jewel-like eyes which regarded him.

Avaren Ensther!

Ionaden's mind raced. He imagined his reward—bags full of sequins; hands working the abandoned looms in his family's defunct estate; a culinary school to rival Heridan's!

Fantasies vanished when the figure slumped against the pedestal. Ionaden rushed to her side and lay her down on the wet grass. He unsheathed his boot dagger and cut a long strip of oiled cloth from his cloak. He pushed the woman's legs apart, slipped the makeshift bandage under her thigh and tied a tourniquet above where the quarrel protruded from her leg.

Beside him, Calvert wiped the blood running from the gash on his forehead. "Is that who I think it is?"

Brent clapped his friend's shoulder. "I sense reward in our future."

Ionaden grimaced as the sound of Eskander's spurs met his ears. The man had impeccable timing for doing nothing and reaping praise.

"We will get nothing if she dies," Ionaden said.

Eskander strutted through the garden, his sword drawn like a conquering hero. "What in Hel's unholy fire is going on here?"

Ionaden ignored the query. He wrapped his cloak around the girl's body and tucked the oilcloth beneath her limbs to create a pocket of warmth.

"Who is this lowlife, and why are you bandaging his wounds?" Eskander asked. "Did he not attack you?"

"We've caught ourselves a naera," said Calvert.

"Show him," chimed Brent.

When Ionaden removed the leather hat, Avaren's mane of snow-white hair tumbled free. Beneath the Three Sisters' glow, Avaren's skin shone like mother-of-pearl. All four men stared with awe as her beautiful features quickened their pulse.

Brent was the first to speak. "The little minx almost broke my jaw."

Calvert rubbed his forehead. "She would have done the whole world a favor."

Ionaden mulled over the situation. For months, the city buzzed about the girl's mysterious fate. In the taverns, gamblers wagered about her whereabouts and bards composed songs in her honor. Looking down at her, Ionaden finally understood the obsession. If the gods were real, then Avaren was their masterpiece. He'd be damned if she died on his watch. "She's badly wounded and needs a healer. Let's take her inside."

Eskander shook his head. "Absolutely not! Our orders are to deliver her to the Chancellery of Justice. If we do anything other, we will fail in our duty."

Calvert nodded in agreement. "What do you think will happen to us when the Lord Justiciar finds out we found her and didn't follow orders? I don't know about the rest of you, but I doubt my old bones would benefit from a stretch on the ol' wheel."

"She said something about sanctuary before she passed out. When she sets foot in the embassy, she will claim asylum—a legal provision Majster Ers will enforce. I agree with Eskander," added Brent.

Ionaden stood. "I think she's been hiding—for reasons yet unknown. She needs immediate medical care and may not survive the journey to the Chancellery."

Brent studied Ionaden. "What's gotten into you? The reward for her return is enough to make us all rich. If we take this hellcat inside the embassy, we risk more than the bounty. I'm with Calvert; she's not worth losing our hides."

"What do you think will happen if she dies on our watch?" Ionaden countered.

Behind them, five men in heavy, oiled cloaks bearing crossbows approached. The tallest of them pushed his way between Calvert and Brent while the others remained in the shadows.

Brent and Calvert looked at each other but said nothing as the crossbowman paled. The man lowered his weapon and stared at the bundled girl. "Is that—"

Eskander scowled. "Yes, Gryson, you shot the Vise's daughter. Fortunately, you have poor aim."

Gryson shifted his weight from one foot to the other. "I thought she was a thief! She attacked Ionaden. How was I supposed to know?"

"We need a plan," said Brent. "If she dies, we'll hang."

Gryson's fingers twitched on his crossbow. "Where did I hit her?"

"Thigh," Ionaden answered.

"At this time of night, with the chaos in the streets, we'll never find a healer," lamented Calvert.

"Enough!" commanded Eskander. "I am taking her to the Chancellery. The best place to find a medic is the dispensary."

Out of the corner of his eye, Ionaden studied the box lying in the shadows. He was confident the coffer's contents formed part of the message Avaren sought to deliver. Eskander's inability to question the law and his adherence to duty repulsed him. Like the rest of his damnable family, Eskander Johar lived his life by the numbers. Luckily, he was not hindered by such restrictions.

"You four," Ionaden pointed at the crossbowmen. "Yoke the horses and prepare Ers' carriage. Grab a few pillows and blankets to keep the girl warm. She's soaked to the bone. Brent, Calvert, you'll ride with Eskander and provide protection. Gryson, you drive and ring the bell as you travel. Yell at the top of your lungs; alert everyone that Avaren Ensther is alive. The more people know of our patriotic act, the more likely we are to see Jarle Rigo's gold."

Once they had their orders, the guards hustled down the alleyway.

Eskander waited until the men left before confronting Ionaden. "What are you scheming, Kesner?"

Ionaden bent down and picked Avaren up. "Time is the corrector when judgments err."

"For once, I agree with you," Eskander said.

Ionaden walked along the alley, careful not to aggravate the woman's injury. "Remember to loosen the tourniquet halfway to the dispensary, or she'll lose the leg. Also, leave the quarrel in place. Let the chirurgeon remove the shaft, or she'll bleed out before you get there."

Eskander followed close behind. "Judging by the state of your finances, I would have thought you more interested in the reward."

Ionaden scoffed. "Judging by your closeness with D'Neir, I would have thought you interested in the poor girl's health."

"Feelings shouldn't interfere with duty and loyalty."

"Whoever shoved the pike up your ass did a fine job."

"Goad me no more and explain yourself, Kesner. Why are you staying behind?"

"The Thrommish will be furious with our decision. If Ers returns and finds the embassy unguarded, he may use our dereliction as an excuse to hang us. I don't know if you're aware, but the Ice Queen doesn't much care for us."

"Very well," Eskander sighed in resignation. "Just because I'm taking her to the Chancellery doesn't mean I'm turning my back on her. I will make sure she gets to the palace alive."

"Eskander, the Rescuer has a nice ring," mocked Ionaden.

At the front of the house, the two men found the ambassador's transport hitched to their Namurese mounts. Brent and Calvert stood on either side of the carriage doors, weapons in hand, while Gryson tightened the harnesses.

Eskander took the girl from Ionaden's hands. "With any luck, Captain Gøran will strangle you with his bare hands."

Ionaden sneered. "Don't count on it."

Gryson observed the exchange from the driver's seat, the lines on his face betraying concern. "Enough chatter! Let's go!"

When everyone climbed on board, Ionaden walked up to his mare and ran his hand along the animal's rump. "Ride like the wind, girl."

"We won't let you down, Lance Corporal." With a snap of the reins, Gryson coaxed the horses forward. As the coach rolled into the street, the crossbowman tolled the bell. "Hear, hear, Avaren Ensther lives!" he bellowed.

Once the toll of the bell faded and peace returned to the villa, Ionaden jogged back to the yard where the parcel lay. His night was just beginning.

UNFINISHED STANZAS

Shardi, Second of Nommen, 445 A'A'diel

"Tell me, Salena, has anyone ever written a sonnet about your beautiful eyes?"

Color rose to the maid's cheeks. "Never, Majster Irilio."

The poet slipped his arm around the blushing girl's waist and scooped her closer. "A sin I endeavor to rectify."

An older woman carrying a tray of dirty dishes brushed past them. "Salena, do you plan on attending anyone this evening other than this honey-tongued rooster?"

"I, uh, have to go," Salena protested.

Irilio dipped his head toward his captive's neck, brushing the soft skin under her ear with his lips. "Promise you will meet me at the Fountain of Jynae after the soiree."

Salena twisted free of the poet's grasp. "I will, after I finish the scullery work. Now, please, I must serve these pastries before they get cold."

Irilio plucked a fried croquette from the girl's platter. "Dreams of your eyes will sustain me until then."

Before the hungry poet could enjoy the stolen treat, his patron's voice rang out loud and clear, "Irilio! Come! Recite another poem, something cheerful."

With a rueful sigh, Irilio dropped the honey-drizzled pastry on a passing tray. Ever the performer, he strode out of the shadows with a swagger and a smile. He accepted the scattered applause with a flourish of his hand before ascending the podium. He never tired of acclaim; the thrill was second only to winning the charms of another man's wife. Once the ovation tapered, Irilio bowed with respect. "I would favor Your Highness and his honored guests with something lighter."

Rigo beamed like a cat sated on canary. "Levity is exactly what our feast craves, most gifted of orators. Our ears are yours."

Aside from the occasional ringing of a utensil upon porcelain, silence descended across the room. The odist scanned his rapt audience with satisfaction, each attentive face filling him with pride. On the cusp of his impassioned opening, a distraction soured the moment. A page entered the room, bowed to Rigo, then leaned over Deneven's shoulder. A hushed conversation ensued.

Irilio's anger boiled over when Deneven filed out of the room behind the servant. The abrupt departure stole the crowd's attention. Speculative whispers filled the silence. Stung by the rudeness, the poet cleared his throat. After a dramatic pause, he poured his energy into his recital.

"Wind! Oh, Wind!
Weaving through the tussled moss
Clinging to the lush green
Riddles of the swamp
Wind has seen the tides of time."

Irilio drew his breath for the next stanza but became distracted when Lord Justiciar Tsardon crumpled a napkin in his fist. Tsardon scrutinized Deneven's empty seat before pushing back his chair with thinly veiled anger. The realization that he had paused for too long a beat flustered the poet emeritus. He raised his arm in a full arc to regain the wayward audience's attention and rushed his next lines.

"Wind has seen the tides of time
Caress the earth with wisdom

From glacial ice
To withered stone-wrought
Pounded earth
To calamitous seas
Unleashed."

Tsardon stood and threw the napkin on his plate. He walked over to Neylen, leaned over him, and exchanged words. Shocked by the utter lack of respect, the poet waited for the men to conclude their conversation. He couldn't recall a moment when he had experienced such incivility. When the exchange ended, and Tsardon returned to his seat, Irilio continued.

"Wind has carried love notes
And disease
Arrows and the salty-sweet scent
Of decadence
To the tops of trees
And hallowed valleys
Carved."

Sudden screams and excited shouts cut the poem short. Looking in the direction of the commotion, Irilio stared dumbfounded at the spectacle before him. Rigo's food taster collapsed and began to twitch. The portly man convulsed and flopped about like a landed fish. Foam frothed from the man's open mouth as his bulging eyes rolled wildly.

Irilio swallowed hard. Any ill will over the interruption and stolen glory fled as cries of, "Help! Poison!" echoed through the hall. Several guests ran for the doors to find the way blocked by taciturn guards. Others, including the Thrommish, gathered into a tight group and prepared to defend themselves amid the chaos.

In the center of the room, Lord Justiciar Tsardon barked commands to the guardsmen, intent on restoring order. The main doors opened long enough for Rigo to flee the room before shutting once more. Armed men ushered people against the wall in preparation for the interrogations to follow. The Marchess of Thyra stood to one side; her face unreadable while her sea captain formed a barrier of flesh between her and Tsardon's men. Faces grim, the Seh'nahiel diplomats joined their northern allies.

Irilio's hopes of a midnight rendezvous vanished when the guards corralled Salena along with the kitchen staff into the Green Room. Tsardon didn't measure his words as he harangued and threatened the workers, promising to impale them on spits if they lied.

Chagrin turned to horror as Salena raised her arm and pointed at him. Irilio gripped the podium as the serving girl's shrill cry rang out over the excited mutterings of the crowd. "Irilio! That's who you want. He was picking at the food on our platters all night."

Before Irilio could react to the accusation, other servants chimed in. "Yes! Yes! The poet's fingers were all over our trays!"

Irilio's heart raced. He bolted from the dais only to be stopped by a mailled fist to the face. Rocked by the blow, the poet staggered backward. His head throbbed with pain. "W-wait!" was all he could manage as strong hands seized him and dragged him to the ground.

"Search him," commanded Tsardon.

The guards ignored Irilio's protests as they emptied his pockets. Out of the corner of his eye, Irilio caught sight of Eloisse and called out to her. "Eloisse, tell them this was your idea, please!"

Confusion widened the noblewoman's eyes. Eloisse shook her head, clearly not understanding. She took a step toward Irilio, but The Rake yanked her back.

Time stood still as the guard searching him held up a vial and handed it to the Lord Justiciar. Tsardon uncapped the container and cautiously sniffed the contents. "Poison!" he announced.

The proclamation sent murmurs of shock rolling through the crowd. Desperate, Irilio struggled against his captors. "The serving girl is lying! This is all a terrible mistake!"

"The error is yours, thinking to murder His Royal Highness in his own hall," Tsardon clipped.

Irilio protested as two burly guards gripped his arms. "I would never dream of killing anyone! The vial isn't mine. Someone put it there! How do you know the culprit isn't Deneven D'Neir? I saw him leave before my performance!"

"Give your pathetic excuses to the torturer. I hear he is a

sympathetic fellow," quipped one of the guardsmen as he dragged the terrified poet toward the double doors.

Irilio's bowels turned to ice. He was well versed in the tales of the palace dungeons. "I swear I'm innocent!" On his way out, he caught sight of Salena among the servants. "Why?" he cried out to her, tears streaming down his face.

The girl's response stole his breath along with all hope. Salena responded with a satisfied wink and a cruel little smile. Her features shifted slightly to resemble those of his lover Eloisse. On her chin, he spied a scar. Irilio blinked past his sobs and craned his neck for a second look. As he did so, Salena turned and hugged one of the serving girls.

JUST DESSERTS

Shardi, Second of Nommen, 445 A'A'diel

Deneven followed the young Vendraedi servant past the gilded doors of the banquet hall and into a service corridor. Oil lamps placed at intervals created deep pools of shadow on the downward sloping hallway. As they passed vaulted supply rooms used to store cured meats and cheeses, Deneven studied the youth. The muscular man moved with the swagger of a dancer. His heels never touched the ground, giving his frame the appearance of a bobbing lure.

"What's your name, lad?" Deneven asked.

The servant ran a hand through his dark curls. "Gharth, sir."

Deneven limped beside him. The sound of his cane echoed in the gloom. "Please, slow down for the sake of a crippled man."

The servant waited for Deneven to catch up. "Apologies, Majster D'Neir."

Deneven stared at the row of torches leading to the cellars and frowned. The messenger was agile, robust, and potentially armed. The streets of Reyza were unrepentant teachers, and Gharth appeared well-schooled.

"Lance Corporal Kesner, sir," Gharth answered.

"I see. How long have you worked at the palace?"

"Not long, sir."

Deneven suspected as much. "Your family must be proud of your change in circumstance."

"I'm not sure I understand your meaning."

"You are as lean and as nimble as a cat. If I were to wager—and I am a gambling man—I would think catering to well-fed courtiers is not the highlight of your days, or better yet, your nights?"

Gharth gave the justiciar a sideways glance. "You got me there, sir."

Deneven smiled when they entered a room he hadn't set foot in over a decade. Lit by moonstone orbs, the vaulted wine cellar with its whitewashed walls was as orderly as he remembered it. Oak aging barrels stacked five high formed floor-to-ceiling rows. A copper plate denoting the embarkation point of the vintages marked each cask. Deneven scanned the nameplates with a pang of nostalgia. A cursory audit revealed Ferencian Eldenwoen, Blackvin from Debendelo, a shipment from Hog Cave Cellars in Berinnon, Icevin from Fheydhian Grove, and a dozen rare wines from as far as Xio-Bahnn.

Gharth rapped the barrels with his knuckles as they crossed the room to another set of doors. "Are you a connoisseur, Majster D'Neir?"

Tapping the exotic casks to ascertain their contents was one of the more pleasant duties of his former office. "No, lad. I study wine by drinking it," Deneven replied.

"You are wise," Gharth said. He unlocked the door at the rear of the cellar and waited for Deneven to step through before closing it behind him.

The crude passage linking the Chancellery stables with the stockrooms had fallen into disuse. Patches of brown algae flourished around the dim glow of the moonstone sconces, and the air reeked of rotten cheese. The grooved flagstones glistened with condensation. During the war with Five Isles, the corridor served to ferry reinforcements to and from the palace. Deneven had traversed the stretch many times, but never without a pair of strong legs. The steep, downward grade caused his muscles to cramp with each step.

Halfway to the stables, a patch of slimy mold slowed Deneven down. He took two steps on the morass and slipped. With the speed of a jungle cat, the youth stepped in and grabbed hold of Deneven's upper arm before he touched the ground. "Are you alright?"

Deneven brushed his waistcoat and rubbed his thigh. "The only thing bruised is my pride, young man. Good catch."

Gharth nodded. "Only a few more paces, sir."

The small wooden door leading to the stables glowed with torchlight. Overcome with a desire to escape the tunnel, Deneven loosened his cravat and quickened his pace. "How do you know Corporal Kesner?"

"We have mutual friends," Gharth said. Before Deneven could ask more questions, his escort raced down the hallway and waved to someone beyond the door.

Fresh air, redolent with manure, oiled leather, and sea brine, replaced the stink of mold. Deneven filled his lungs and limped out of the stifling tunnel. "I know my way from here, lad."

The barns occupied two brick-walled buildings with thatched roofs and numerous doorways through which carriages and horses maneuvered. All the entrances were closed to keep out drafts, except one. Silhouetted against the moonlight, Kesner leaned against a beam with the cockiness of a whoremonger on Market Day. Unlike his fellow cavalrymen, the man treated the uniform with contempt. Two saddled Namurese thoroughbreds feasted on a bale of hay near the soldier.

Deneven stopped a few paces from the door. "To what do I owe this rude interruption?"

The cavalryman spat out a reed and brought one of the horses around. "I will explain once we put some distance between us and this place."

"You will elaborate now," insisted Deneven.

"I think not." Kesner slipped his boot into the stirrups of his saddle and straddled his mare. He tugged on the reins and guided the beast next to Deneven's mount. Reaching over the animal's back, he offered Deneven a hand.

The offer affronted his dignity, but Deneven accepted it nonetheless. There had been a time when mounting a horse was as second nature as riding a woman, but those times were long past. With a grunt, he flopped over the beast's back and swung his wooden leg around.

When Deneven settled into the saddle, Kesner poked his horse's ribs and launched himself into the night.

Well-trained Namurese warhorses rarely required spurs. Deneven squeezed his knees and gasped as the tawny beast sprang into a spirited gallop. In the span of a few breaths, the animal overtook the young soldier. Excitement beat at his temples as the wind threatened to dethrone his hat.

As they neared the Chancellery gate, three guards stepped out of the gatehouse and blocked their path. "Who goes?" one of them said, raising a hand. The other two dug the butts of their pikes in the ground and squared off.

Kesner raised his hand in salute. "Lance Corporal Kesner and former Lord Justiciar, D'Neir."

The man-at-arms gave them a cursory glance and nodded. "I meant to commend you earlier, Kesner. You did a good deed."

"I live to serve," Kesner clipped.

"Live to serve, my ass!" The soldier snorted, "Let the rich bastard pass."

The two men rode through the gate and followed the winding hairpins of Commerce Road. Deneven bit his tongue until they cleared the guardhouse, then inquired about the exchange. "What was that all about?"

Ionaden shot him a dark glance. "I assume you haven't heard the news."

"Stop toying with me. What news?"

"Mejtress Avaren is alive."

In the span of a blink, astonishment gave way to worry. Deneven rubbed his brow. He fixed his eagle-like gaze on the young cavalryman. "Start talking, Corporal."

"After your entourage departed, Johar and I relieved the old-timers from their post. We were expressing some differences when I spotted a figure lurking in the shadows. Eskander raced into the Thicket to investigate while I remained at my watch. Opposite where Johar entered the park, a man rushed out. He wore the outfit of a valet, but something about his clothes failed to convince. When he approached the villa, I asked him to identify himself. That's when he ran. Believing him a midnighter, I pursued him into the alley. The chap moved like lightning; hurt Calvert and Brent bad when they got in his way. To make a long-winded story short, the man was no man at all, but Mejtress Avaren disguised. Sadly, none of us discerned the ruse until the rooftop retinue pegged her."

"A bolt?" Deneven's eyes widened; a tic trembled the muscles of his jaw. "Where?"

"Gryson hit her in the thigh."

Deneven pulled on the reins and stopped. "Where is she? I must go to her immediately."

Ionaden guided his mare beside Deneven's stallion. "Impossible. Your bootlicker chose loyalty to his career over Avaren's safety. Eskander insisted on following Tsardon's orders and convinced Ers' retinue to take her to the Chancellery. I protested; tried to persuade them to take her inside the embassy, but they didn't listen."

Deneven's lips went dry. "If she is in Rigo's custody, we will never discover the truth."

"Thanks to, what was it you called me?"—Ionaden pretended to rifle through his memory—"Ah yes, the 'coddled spawn of a lesser merchant,' the noblewoman may yet live to tell her tale."

"Go on." Deneven pursed his lips.

"I realized what might happen if Mejtress Avaren arrived at the palace quietly, especially if your suspicions are true. Thus, I ordered her escort to ring the carriage bell and shout news of her reappearance at the top of their lungs."

"You have been paying attention," Deneven complemented. "Well done."

The guardsman flashed Deneven a sardonic smile. "The stars are about to fall. Did I just receive an accolade from the Dragon of Reyza?"

"What is your problem, Corporal?"

"My problem, D'Neir, is that you are an arrogant prick," Ionaden said. "Had you not been so full of your own shit, you would have recognized Eskander for what he is—Tsardon's tool! That trumped-up promotion-chasing martinet delivered Tan'os' daughter into a den of snakes."

"You have made yourself clear, Kesner." Deneven turned around and began galloping back up the hill.

Ionaden cursed and spurred his mare in pursuit. The cavalryman rushed past Deneven and cut him off. Deneven's mount reared, causing the justiciar to lose his balance. In a remarkable show of horsemanship, the disabled man gripped the horn of the saddle, squeezed his knees and clung to the beast until he regained his bearings.

"Out of my way, Corporal," Deneven growled.

"What do you think you are doing?" spat Ionaden.

"I intend to ensure Mejtress Avaren's safety," Deneven said, urging his horse forward.

The soldier blocked Deneven a second time. "Ven's balls! I'm beginning to think all you have in that skull of yours is a sack of flour. Do you think I summoned you to rescue a damsel in distress? If so, I recommend different bedtime reading. Lord Justiciar Tsardon will not allow you anywhere near Avaren Ensther. Listen for once, you fool!"

Deneven bared his teeth. "Why, then? Why have you sent for me?"

"Tan'os' daughter is with the royal healers, and you've been stripped of authority. Your investigation is officially over, D'Neir; you are nothing more than what you were before all this happened—a retired old man who owns a bakery. What's more, I no longer report to you." Ionaden lowered his voice. "Still, I care about the girl and Reyza. And I possess information which may yet prove useful."

"Who do you work for?" asked Deneven.

"The same mistress as you."

"If your mistress is the city of Reyza, lead on."

Ionaden's lips curled into a smirk. He jerked his knees into his horse and spurred the mighty beast down the cobbled street in the direction of Old Gate.

Keeping pace with him, Deneven followed close behind.

Like most roads in Reyza, Commerce Road wound through the hillside and sloped down through the warren of villas which vied for a seaside view. Through the gaps between buildings, the riders caught glimpses of the disaster below. Only the rooftops of warehouses peaked above the black surface of the floodwaters. A series of unmoored fishing boats littered the blockaded harbor while the underside of others shone like a string of pearls along the base of Minstrel Rock. The torchlight of mercenary guards could be seen circling towers of salvaged goods stacked high on roofs. Bonfires flickered in the distance where camps of refugees huddled in the rain. Formerly abandoned roadside shrines had been cleared of vines and stocked with offerings to the gods. Forlorn pilgrims looked up from beneath sackcloth cowls as they passed, before returning to prayer.

Against the calamitous backdrop, the two men galloped in silence. Before reaching Old Gate, Deneven caught up with the cavalryman. "Do you intend to drown us, Corporal?"

Instead of crossing the old stone portal, Ionaden veered toward higher ground. "I mean to escort you home."

"No need. I know the way well enough," said Deneven.

"Look around, D'Neir. Do these streets appear safe to you?"

Deneven's gaze darted among the shadows. In the gloom, the rain-slicked alleys which hugged the mountainsides converged into a crooked morass. No level ground existed in Reyza save for small plazas interspersed with alleyways and stone tunnels ideal for ambushes. The cavalryman's words took hold of Deneven's imagination, transforming a well-trodden road into a perilous undertaking. "Very well," Deneven conceded. "But I suggest you start talking before I lose my patience with your charade."

"Ride fast," Ionaden warned. "Our mistress has many eyes."

THE CRUSTY LOAF

Shardi, Second of Nommen, 445 A'A'diel

Established by his grandfather, the Crusty Loaf Bakery had achieved a century of profitability, but instead of making Deneven proud, it made him feel old. The cracked marble frontage with its gilded letters may as well have been a tombstone. Deneven continued to run the business at the behest of his deceased parents but held no interest in baking. The cooking was done by a father-and-son duo who churned out some of the best breakfast rolls in Reyza. Some mornings the line at the bakery stretched down Westgalia all the way to Garridan Road.

"We have arrived safely, Corporal," said Deneven from atop his horse. "I think it's time you explained yourself."

Ionaden alighted and unstrapped his saddlebags. "The hour is late, and we are soaked. How about we go inside for a cup of tea and one of your delicious spice rolls."

Deneven threw his crippled leg over the horse's rump too quickly and lost his grip on the reins. For an excruciating moment, he clung sideways to the saddle while his peg leg sought footing. Ionaden's chuckle exhausted what remained of Deneven's patience and sent blood rushing to his face. After regaining his balance, he yanked his cane free from the martingale and tied the beast to a nearby pole. "This way," he urged in as dignified a tone as he could muster.

Ionaden secured his mare and swung the saddlebags over his shoulder. He followed Deneven down the side of the building to a small courtyard littered with kitchen clutter. Old baking pans converted into herb containers circled a mosaic birdbath. Conches of various shapes and sizes, some foreign to Reyzan shores, dotted the small plot.

"You enjoy gardening?" Ionaden asked.

Deneven opened the back door and stepped aside to let the soldier pass. "Retirement affords plenty of free time to an old man," he groused, closing the door.

"I did call you that, didn't I?"

"Yes, you did; it seems everyone is apt to remind me of my age these days." Deneven rummaged through a cupboard drawer until he found a box of emberstems. He struck the stem on exposed masonry and lit a handheld oil lamp.

The back room of the bakery served as a storage space. Orderly cupboards brimming with ingredients lined the walls. In the center of the room, a massive wooden counter held a stack of sheet pans and molds. Dried herbs hung from hooks in the exposed timber ceiling above a trough-style sink.

Piqued by a rack filled with colorful spice jars, Ionaden read the labels out loud, "Anardana, abalor weed, darkpalm, henhazel, blue anise."

Deneven rubbed the back of his neck. "You are literate. Wonderful."

"I have never used any of these," Ionaden mused, perusing the condiments.

"Why would you? Seasonings are the language of cooks, not soldiers."

Ionaden picked up the jar labeled Henhazel. "Might I—may I smell it?"

With a sigh, Deneven surrendered to the whims of his curious guest. He suspected a long night lay ahead of him. "Baking is of interest to you, Corporal?"

Ionaden twisted open the cork and inhaled. The scent caused his face to light up. "I grew up in the kitchens surrounded by food," he said, taking another whiff. "This smells like primrose, but with a grassy undertone. I think this would blend well with a stronger flavor like black walnut." A smile crept across his lips. "I think I've tasted this before—in the Crusty Loaf's Belfast pretzels!"

Deneven leaned his hip against the sink. "I can see now why the blood in Tan'os' villa turned your stomach. Your nose is as keen as a sword."

Ionaden's smile faded as he corked the jar and set it back among the others. "My father insisted I don this uniform, but military service was never my calling. When I receive my share of the reward money for finding the Vise's daughter, I am through with the Ca'Dezer."

"And what will you do?" asked Deneven.

Ionaden shrugged. "I will cook."

"Now, I have heard it all!" Deneven scoffed. "It appears Reyza needs the Thrommish more than ever. If you're interested, I believe we are hiring."

The soldier placed his saddlebags on the wooden slab. "At least I know what I want and don't live in the past."

Deneven's temper bled through his words, "What I would give to be your age, and wear those colors, boy."

"And what would you inherit, old man? The ignoble task of serving pompous pricks? Keep your patriotic preachings to yourself. We both know Reyza is a whore on parade for the highest bidder."

Deneven's hands balled into fists. "There will be no tea or pastries forthcoming," he spat through clenched teeth. "If you have something to say, Corporal, say it and remove yourself from my sight."

Ionaden unbuckled the bag and retrieved a rectangular box. "Avaren Ensther dropped this box in Ers' backyard shortly before we shot her," he said, dropping the case on the counter. "I believe she risked her neck to deliver it—might be important."

"This is why you summoned me?" Deneven stared at the barnacle-crusted object in disbelief. "Is this a jest?"

"I don't like you, D'Neir, but at least you have some integrity. Do what you will with this information; I wipe my hands of this business." Ionaden slung the saddlebag on his back and walked to the door. Before stepping outside, he turned to face Deneven. "Oh, and before I forget, go fuck yourself, D'Neir."

The sound of the door slamming coincided with a clap of thunder. Mirroring Deneven's mood, the sky broke into a ferocious downpour.

"Insolent swine!" Deneven unbuttoned his waistcoat and tugged at his cravat. The sodden silk felt like a noose around his neck. As he gazed at the wooden box, a bitter flush of anger seized him. In a fit of rage, he grabbed one of the baking sheets and swung it into the spice rack. Some of the jars shattered, spilling their contents, while others rolled under the counter.

As anger faded to exhaustion, Deneven tossed the pan into a heap of flour sacks and wiped his face. He picked up the box and the lamp, then limped upstairs to his cold, damp quarters. He deposited the case on a pile of ledgers on his desk and lit the four globes of an ornate oil lamp. The amber firelight lent a semblance of warmth, if not order to the chamber.

Looking around, Deneven grimaced at the disarray. Several dirty plates and unwashed cups peeked from underneath the mess of papers. A half-drained decanter of brandy and an open wine bottle stood by the wood-burning stove. Even in the meager light of the study, he could see the bedroom beyond. His eyes followed a trail of crumbs spread by mice to the foot of the bed, where his sheets wrestled with the fur blankets. A gray film of disuse covered the books on his bookshelves. He couldn't remember the last time he had sat down to read, not from a lack of time, but from the apathy which robbed him of wonder.

Deneven closed the door and hung his coat on a peg. He then stacked several logs into the furnace and stuffed the cracks with a handful of sheets from his father's accounting ledgers. He could care less about the profitability of bread rolls and fruit pies, supply lists, and the endless drudgery of running a bakery. He set fire the pages with the handheld lantern and watched with satisfaction as the papers warped and blackened in the flames.

After the logs began to blaze, Deneven snuffed out the small lamp. He shut the oven's iron grille and extended his hands toward the fire. He flexed his fingers and rubbed his palms together, grateful for the heat. Every winter, the ache in his bones became more of a nuisance.

Leaning on his cane, Deneven rose from his crouching position. He picked up the brandy and shuffled to his writing desk. Most days, the sound his wooden leg made on the floor didn't bother him, but sometimes, when the terror of mortality spread through him like nighttime descending on the world, the hollow echo became unbearable.

With a grunt, he plopped down in his armchair and pushed off his riding boot. Crystal facets shone in the lamplight as he uncorked the decanter and brought the liquor to his lips. The bitter scent of distilled apples enraptured his nostrils before setting fire to his stomach. One sip turned into two, then three, and four, until his insides seethed like a boiling cauldron. Warm at last, Deneven set the bottle down on a dusty pile of books and shifted the clutter aside.

As he studied the mysterious box, thoughts swirled like circling vultures. Whatever the coffer contained was of little consequence. He had failed to rescue Avaren Ensther, solve the Vise's murder, and prove worthy to his employer. As a result, he had squandered his last opportunity at meaningful employment. He was the crippled son of two bakers and as washed out as the docks. History had forgotten him as it had every other lowlife in Reyza.

The cavalryman's brazen summons had saved him from facing the embarrassment of his dismissal and a potentially humiliating confrontation with Eva. By morning, news of Avaren's rescue by Tsardon's men would grace every tongue in the city, and the receding floodwaters would teem with winged predators eager for a meal. "Let the feeding frenzy begin," Deneven said to the darkness.

THE BATHS

Venedi, Third of Nommen, 445 A'A'diel

Referred to as the 'Cave,' the palace's subterranean bathing chamber was a jewel of architecture. Massive slabs of Dessian talderin, a stone prized for its rich asparagus-like facets interspersed with tangerine veins, lined the circular hall. Tall niches sculpted from pock-marked coral contrasted with the smoothness of the marble. Statues of nymphs and tritons, arms brimming with scented toiletries, peered from within the alcoves, their eyes focused on five octagonal pools. The overall effect was one of pampered undersea whimsy.

Only four of the nymphaeum's twenty lamps illuminated the tendrils of steam that curled upward from the largest pool. Rarely, if ever, was the great caldarium cool. Huge boilers kept lit by elemental fires forced a continuous flow of superheated vapor through hidden chambers below the floor and behind the walls.

Throughout the day, the sounds of conversation and laughter echoed from the stonework. From dawn to midday, twenty servants, handpicked for their beauty, tended aristocratic male bathers. In the afternoon, the baths belonged to the female courtiers. After dinner, the palace staff would descend in raucous numbers to enjoy a moment's indulgence. At midnight, a skeleton crew of custodians took possession of the chamber to scrub away the grime and replenish the water.

As they had countless nights before, the cleaning crew finished refilling the last of the smaller pools and headed for the shallow basin in the center of the Cave. Routine removed the need for chatter as they carried their buckets and sponges to their next chore. The foursome was about to unstopper the drains when the front door of the nymphaeum banged open without warning.

The laborers exchanged fearful glances as the Dessian ambassador's elite Durauk Guard fanned in through the doorway. The intruders' kohl-rimmed eyes peeked over the black silk wrappings that concealed their faces.

"Leave!" commanded a leather-clad woman.

The servants offered quick bows to Neylen's bodyguards before scurrying away through the maintenance passage.

One of the Durauks secured the service door while the rest searched the premises. After a moment, one of the masked warriors called out, "The room is clear, Sundaarr Akkalon."

Neylen emerged from the shadow of the outer vestibule, his face grim. Behind him, two Durauks carried a rolled tapestry between them. The ambassador walked to the edge of the saltwater bath and surveyed the lapis and gold mosaic sunburst at the center of the pool. "Seal the doors, Nef'lari, and do not enter regardless of what you may hear."

"As you command, Sundaarr." The woman armored in dark leather rounded up the Durauks with a wave of her hand. All the soldiers except for the pair holding the tapestry filed out.

The flames in the torchieres flickered as the double doors closed. Sweat beaded on the back of Neylen's neck and ran down his spine, soaking through his ivory silk shirt. The humid heat in the Cave offered respite from Reyza's chilly dampness and valuable information. As a result, Neylen bathed frequently. The ministrations of beautiful attendants, robust liquor, and hours of soaking loosened tongues as well as any torturer's rack.

Turning to face the silent Durauks, Neylen eyed the bundle. "Unfurl our prize."

The two guards placed their burden on the floor and unrolled the carpet. As the colorful embroidery gave way, the sounds of rattling chains and faint moans filled the room. A final shove revealed an unconscious, naked girl with pale skin and white hair. Iron rings manacled her wrists, and a length of chain looped over her midriff.

Neylen's gaze lingered on the blood-soaked bandages on the noblewoman's thigh before moving up to the bare mound between her legs, and the rosy peaks of her breasts. The lurid sight of Tan'os Ensther's shackled daughter lying defenseless at his feet inspired delicious tension in his loins.

The Dessian considered his female bodyguards as he approached Avaren. Formidable warriors, Durauks were bred to obey their masters, sworn to chastity, and presumably impervious to the whims of their gender, but Neylen held his doubts. The ambassador peered into one pair of kohl-rimmed eyes, then another, as he pondered the women's capacity to tolerate the lewd acts he wished to perpetrate on his captive.

When cold, reptilian eyes met his gaze, Neylen licked his lips in anticipation. He crouched next to Avaren and coiled a loop of chain around his fist. Restraints in hand, he motioned toward the water. "Toss her in."

The Durauks hoisted the limp girl and carried her to the perimeter of the pool. Neylen followed, allowing the slack of the chain to drag across the tiles. The eerie sound tickled his senses. If Tan'os' daughter was the legendary naera rumors claimed, he was about to experience something extraordinary.

The guards swung the girl twice and released.

Avaren hit the surface with a splash. Water slopped over the lip of the enclosure, draining through the grates at its periphery. The weight of the irons dragged her to the bottom, where she lay face up and listless.

The Durauks drew their swords and assumed a protective stance, ready to strike should the captive threaten their master.

Neylen stood between his bodyguards and peered into the pool. "Our prisoner is not to be harmed."

The sound of whispering steel sang softly as the women sheathed their blades.

When the fabled transformation failed to manifest, Neylen tugged the chain and reeled the submerged girl to the edge.

Avaren's eyes remained closed, and her long hair floated around her like wisps of smoke. She wasn't breathing, but neither was she drowning—she appeared peaceful, as though lost in a dream.

Neylen felt foolish for allowing superstition to override his logic. He had squandered many nights researching the mythical creatures said to inhabit the mist-shrouded coasts of Naiara only to discover that naeras were no different from the skinwalkers of Sullosia, and the goat men from Bel'Ohr.

Complete fiction!

Not one to dwell on failure, Neylen knelt and caressed a strand of Avaren's hair. The Thrommish girl's pale complexion and her strange eyes were rarities any Khadari would desire. Selling her into slavery held merit. He was thousands of sequins in debt with no monetary relief in sight.

Releasing the coiled length of chain, Neylen stood. He wiped his wet hands on his breeches and stepped back. "Pull her out before she drowns."

One of the warriors gripped the girl by the arm, while the other grabbed her leg. They had pulled Avaren halfway out of the water when black, shiny scales raced along her legs like a flood tide. Her lower limbs thickened and elongated into dark, scaly tails. In a heartbeat, the northern waif transformed into a creature of legend—a frightful apparition with sinuous capreolate appendages that thrashed in the gloom like a pair of slaver's whips.

Before the Dessians could react, Avaren let out a blood-curdling shriek. Neylen clutched his ears against the horrifying sound and coughed as an intense itch assaulted his tonsils. He tried to counter the naera's magic, but his concentration fled. In a fog of pain, he stumbled and fell.

Amplified by the marble walls, the unearthly scream increased in pitch and volume. The Durauks released their captive and clapped their hands over their ears in a desperate effort to mute the cacophony. One of the guards collapsed and began to convulse as though struck by the burning palsy. The other staggered aimlessly, howling in agony with hands clamped to the sides of her head.

The half-digested remains of Neylen's supper splattered the tiled floor as he scrabbled in the direction of the closed doors. Through the overwhelming agony, he vowed to rip the abomination's tongue out with his bare hands.

When the ear-splitting scream ended, Neylen turned in time to see a tentacle grab the ambling guard. With a forceful whip of her tail, the naera pulled the flailing warrior into the pool. The woman splashed wildly and fought for breath as a black tail coiled around her waist. Avaren's eyes blazed with savage fury as she slammed the guard's skull against the floor. Amid a spreading cloud of scarlet water, the Durauk grew still.

Neylen had barely recovered from the horror when Avaren lobbed the broken corpse in his direction. The dead guard flew over his head and landed behind him with a sodden thump. In the pool, he saw no sign of the fragile beauty who had been bandaged by the royal healer. In her place stood a monster with flaring nostrils, and baleful, hate-filled eyes. The creature rose up out of the water balanced on its powerful tails and unsheathed the convulsing guard's blade with her bound hands. Beads of water dripped down her shoulders and sparkled in the torchlight as she stabbed the woman, ending her life.

At last, Neylen understood the dread inherent in the retelling of the ancient myths. The Collegium's collection of etchings detailing splintered ships and drowning men clawing their ears took on new meaning. The depictions were not the result of fanciful imaginations but accurate accounts.

Neylen rolled to his feet and circled the creature at a safe distance. His eyes shifted to the crumpled form of his guard and the armed naera whose dark tails rose behind her like black serpents. As the pain in his head ebbed, he tried to imagine how Tan'os Ensther had survived such a fiend long enough to breed.

The Dessian considered summoning his contingent then changed his mind. The guards would chop the monster down to safeguard his life and in so doing, destroy all hopes of profit. Avaren, a fabled freak of nature, was no use to him dead.

Raising his arms, Neylen began to chant in the sonorous language of the Rehi—the crag-dwelling adepts who had taught him magic. As the torches dimmed, shadows swallowed the statues in the niches. A breeze swirled around the room and strengthened as the Dessian called forth his power.

The powerful vortex gathered the heat of the elemental

furnaces and swirled toward Avaren. The surface of the water sloshed and steamed, forcing the naera to seek refuge underwater.

The distraction proved useful. Beneath Neylen's shirt, his muscles bulged and popped. Perspiration poured from his face and ran down his back as his body enlarged. Gritting his teeth, he unfastened his jeweled belt and tossed it aside. His legs trembled and shook as his thighs tore through his velvet breeches. When the spell ended, he stood as tall and broad as the Yerr'draki of legend.

With newfound strength flowing through his frame, Neylen banished the whirlwind. "Epicures claim the seafood in Reyza is the finest in the world. I'm inclined to agree."

In a single leap, Neylen landed in the pool and grabbed hold of the chain. He reeled the sea monster in with forceful yanks until the writhing girl swam within reach. When Avaren opened her mouth to shriek, Neylen plunged his fist into her side.

A stream of bubbles raced to the surface as the injured naera lost her grip on the blade. She flayed the Dessian's back with her tail, but the blow failed to dissuade her attacker.

Heedless of the bloody tracks across his back, Neylen coiled his arm around one of the fiend's tails and wrestled her to the floor. Beneath him, the facedown girl struggled like a wriggling worm on a hook.

In the churn, Neylen examined the reddish lines across the naera's back. The membranes, similar to those of a fish, flapped open and close as the struggle wore on. If the Collegium's illustrations proved accurate, Avaren would be forced to change into her weaker form once out of the water.

The Yerr'draki sorcerer pinned her down with his knee and struck her gills with the heel of his palm. Avaren coughed and raked the mosaics with her bound hands. Her face turned red.

Neylen exploited the weakness, hitting his adversary's lungs over and over again until she grew still. Satisfied with his catch, the Dessian gathered the unconscious half-breed and tossed her out of the water. After clambering out, he ripped apart his silk shirt and stuffed a wad of cloth into the naera's mouth. With the gag secured, he waited for the noblewoman's unearthly transformation to begin.

STOKING AMBITION

Venedi, Third of Nommen, 445 A'A'diel

Deneven examined the barnacle-encrusted box with a magnifying glass. Pieces of reddish coral filled the gaps between the odiferous shells. The coral was moist to the touch, but the wood showed no evidence of rot or bloating. The exotic purple and brown striated hardwood hailed from the heart of Bel'Ohr. Draengale trees grew as hard as iron and could only be felled and forged with elemental magic. In antiquity, territorial wars had waged in the coveted woodlands. In all his years, he had seen only one weapon made of the precious resource—the longbow carried by Redmane.

Intrigued, Deneven traced the bluish seam where the wooden halves met. The mysterious box lacked latches and hinges and appeared to be sealed by tension. He grabbed a letter opener and pried away some of the coral embedded in the barnacles. After a few scrapes, the brittle particles disintegrated into strawberry-hued dust.

Blood coral carpeted the shallows of the northern coast. Only the most daring oyster trawlers braved the chop of the treacherous reef. Judging by the profusion of coral, Deneven estimated the box had lain submerged for several years. How Avaren managed to wrest the coffer from the sea defied logic as surely as her mysterious escape.

Perplexed, Deneven indulged another sip of brandy. He picked up the box and shook it, but the action revealed only a slight shift in weight. Next, he applied pressure to different corners, but the result was the same—the lids didn't budge. Finally, he wedged the small knife into the groove but didn't get far. The coffer was magically sealed. "Barnacled bastard!" he cursed.

"I am surprised you didn't try a hammer," mocked a feminine voice.

Startled, Deneven swiveled his chair and scanned the shadows. "Who goes there? Show yourself!"

Laughter came from the darkness, followed by the sound of the shutters banging in the wind. "And if I refuse?"

Deneven stood, clutching the letter opener. His eyes darted to his cane near the fireplace. "What sorcery is this?"

The answer came from multiple places at once. "The kind that is beyond your comprehension. Now sit down. I can kill you three times over by the time you reach your walking stick."

"What does an adept want with a retired old man?"

"First, you are short-sighted to think me a wet-behind-the-ears elementalist. Second, I find it amusing that you wish the world to perceive you as something more than a retiree, yet you eagerly become one when the situation suits you. Tell me, D'Neir, which are you—a dragon or an old codger worthy of my pity?"

"Legends say the Three Sisters exert their influence on men's minds, not just the tides. If I continue to speak with the darkness, some might claim I am demented," retorted Deneven.

"I admire your wit. Perhaps I should remain a shadow and garner further amusement."

"I have always believed darkness and shadow to be of feminine disposition." Deneven set the letter-opener down. "Night is softer, less vulgar than the garish day—a time when a man can become more than the sum of his fragments and dream."

"Hero, gambler, and romantic. I am beginning to see why Fhaen fell in love with you."

Deneven narrowed his eyes. "What do you know about Fhaen?"

"Too much."

"You work with her?"

"Sometimes, I work with her, and sometimes I work against her—just like you."

The lines in Deneven's forehead grew tense. He unearthed an unwashed glass from the pile of papers on his desk and filled it with a splash of brandy. "My strained relationship with the Mistress of Rats is no secret." In the glow of the lamp, the liquor shone like a fading sunset. "Apologies for my lack of decorum," he said, raising the cup. "Please, Shadow, join me for a drink."

The air in the room became suffused with a dulcet odor reminiscent of the perfumeries along Tennabac Road. The shadows in the room shifted eerily in the opposite direction of the light. A sudden rush of heat like that of an open furnace warmed Deneven's back. The presence turned physical, pressed against his buttocks, and drove his pelvis into the edge of the desk. Slender fingers curved over his ribs and caressed upwards.

Every hair on Deneven's body stood in rapt attention as strong hands prevented him from turning around. The liquid in the cup trembled. "What do you desire, Shadow? Speak."

The woman took the offered glass and whispered in his ear with a familiar voice. "To get to know you better, of course."

Deneven swallowed hard. "You sound like Fhaen, but you are not."

The sorceress drank the brandy and set the glass down. "How long has it been since you inhaled her scent and savored her nails on your back?

"Too long," Deneven confessed.

Fhaen's impostor stroked the front of Deneven's breeches until he stiffened. "Long enough to lose yourself in the illusion?"

Aside from sounding like his beloved Fhaen—the silken daevil was bold and dangerous—a combination he found irresistible. Deneven reached back and grabbed a handful of her leather-clad ass. "I am not so old as to have outlived enthusiasm."

The uninvited guest entwined her fingers in his graying hair and yanked his head back. Her breath warmed his neck. "Or ambition."

"Are we to play games all night?"

"Are you in a rush?"

The sorceress behind him invoked the same thrilling, out-of-control excitement he once shared with his former lover. Whoever or whatever the entity was, she knew how to stoke his lust. Deneven shifted his hand to her front and massaged her crotch. "Abuse patience and see it turn to savagery."

The intruder encouraged Deneven's handling by grinding her hips against his buttocks. "Does a dragon yet stir beneath the facade of self-control?"

After his falling out with Fhaen, Deneven had indulged a handful of lovers, but none captured his imagination or his heart. He thrust two fingers into the pliant leather groove between the woman's thighs and stroked her with slow, deliberate circles. The women he craved couldn't be bought at a cathouse. "You seem to have me all figured out, you tell me."

The stranger stepped sideways and kicked the chair into place behind Deneven's legs. The momentum caused him to fall back. Once he was seated, the mysterious woman circled and sat on the edge of the desk.

Deneven gripped the armrests as the claws of remembrance dug into his heart. The slender beauty wore a tailored leather outfit that hugged her curves like black oil. Her long, reddish mane fell in loose rivulets around her elfin features. Delicate brows arched in amusement over almond-shaped eyes the color of woodland moss. Her lips were soft and pink, her skin smooth as caramel. An unfamiliar scar on her chin was the only flaw in an otherwise perfect illusion. She was a vision of youthful beauty—Fhaen—when he first laid eyes on her years ago. "Am I dreaming?"

The sorceress let out an amused laugh and pressed the tip of her boot into his groin. "Fate has been unkind to you, D'Neir. You found love in the bosom of a criminal, while your passion exults in lawfulness. You fought for a dream, defended this city with your blood, only to find yourself rejected."

She lifted her foot, then straddled Deneven's lap, pinning his forearms with her thighs. "I watched you rise, and I watched you fall." She straightened until her breasts pushed up against Deneven's scruff, then began unlacing the bindings of her leather suit. "I appreciate the depravities that lurk in your shuttered, sharp-witted mind."

Deneven inched his head forward, took the peak of a leather-clad breast into his mouth, and bit down until he felt her nipple stiffen. He pulled away and gave her a long, shrewd look. "Shadow, take warning, you are inching ever closer to the end of my patience."

The seductress shrugged off her top. "I time my arrival to coincide with your exhaustion. Unlike you, I do not gamble."

Deneven freed his arms and cupped the sorceress' hips. He feasted on her nakedness. Her bosom was like Fhaen's—ample and caressible with high, pointed nipples that quivered with every movement. "Why does my past come to haunt me?"

The woman gasped as Deneven squeezed her buttocks. "I come to elevate you."

Deneven released her ass and focused on her breasts. He kneaded the flesh, rubbing the rosy peaks with his thumbs. "Aye, you have done so."

The sorceress reached down and stroked Deneven's stiffness through his pants. "You tried to straighten the skew of Reyza's streets and wash out the grime of her soul, but you failed. You continue to sulk over the loss of your precious Chancellery, endlessly plodding down the trodden path like an old horse with blinders. You sacrificed your love, for the useless title of Lord Justiciar. Why you desire your former office is beyond my comprehension."

"I want no such thing," Deneven lied.

Fhaen's doppelganger stood. She peeled her breeches to her knees and revealed her stark, hairless nakedness. She tossed her mane of reddish curls and turned around, bending over Deneven's cluttered desk. The lamplight shone golden over the globes of her buttocks, accentuating the shadowy groove between her legs. "You lie. I know men's desires, D'Neir."

Deneven wanted to discover how far his uninvited guest would go to impersonate Fhaen. Leaning forward, he grasped her loins and buried his face in the offered prize. He devoured her slick cunny like a ripe fruit. She tasted different from Fhaen but just as delightful. To his surprise, she did not shrink from the attention. With a heady moan, she reached back and held herself open, granting him with that obscene, inviting gesture, the permission he sought to sate his lust. With the exuberance of a youth, Deneven rose from his chair and unlaced his breeches. His prick bobbed out, large and heavy, its size disproportionate to his body. His girth had distressed all his lovers except Fhaen—beautiful Fhaen, whom he had spurned. "Give me a name, Shadow, or I will call you a moniker you don't deserve," Deneven said hoarsely.

"Let's dance," the woman said, arching into him.

Deneven opened a desk drawer and produced a flask of oil he had not tapped in many months. He unstoppered the bottle and poured the substance liberally over the woman's rump before discarding it. The fragrant liquid dripped over her hips, between the groove of buttocks, and down the back of her thighs. He pushed her hands away and worked both her openings with his fingers until she cried out in a quivering, desirous mess. As her climax peaked, he spanked her ass so hard his hand left a reddened imprint. "You want my cock? Take it."

The young woman moved so fast she became a blur. Deneven's head hit the back of the seat as she pushed him back and squatted before him. "You are in my graces because of your usefulness, D'Neir. The day you are not,"—she prodded his manhood—"you may find yourself poisoned with forkleaf."

Deneven's heart skipped as his shaft bobbed in the cold emptiness. "You killed Tan'os? Who are you?"

"Maél Aodhan assassinated the Vise."

Deneven grabbed a handful of her hair. "Who do you work for?"

The half-naked woman looked down at Deneven's erection and smiled. "I am fascinated by how virile the memory of Fhaen remains, yet I suspect you would prefer the company of shadows."

"I'm listening."

"Do you know how Tan'os Ensther achieved power?"

Deneven lowered his gaze to his exposed privates before meeting the woman's eyes. "Even the most obstinate flag-waver can answer that question," he scoffed. "Ensther won favor by liberating Reyza from Five Isles."

"Waging war on the pirates made him wealthy and earned him the admiration of the people, but the victory didn't grant him his title. He became Vise by ensuring Rigo, Draos' illegitimate son, inherited the throne."

"Lies and rumors."

"No, D'Neir, think back. Draos scorned Leila for her inability to bear him a male heir. He bedded her maidens in waiting. One, in particular, obsessed him if you recall."

"Reanne Badradeis. Sad ending."

The woman stood and pulled up her pants but did not lace them. "Yes, she jumped to her death from the highest tower. You investigated her suicide."

The topic quenched Deneven's passion. He covered his privates with his shirt. "The beating deformed Reanne's face and ruined her future. She was disturbed and opted to end her life. I found no evidence of foul play."

"Of course not."

"What are you getting at, Shadow? Stop talking in circles."

"Do you recall what happened after Leila attacked Reanne?"

"Draos announced his wife was with child and ordered her taken to the Retreat of Silos citing concern for her health."

"Who escorted her?"

"Tan'os"—Deneven narrowed his eyes—"Draos' trusted ally. The sorceress smiled. "Did you ever lay eyes on Leila Osueldo again?"

Deneven shook his head. "The Jarleina died during childbirth. Several healers attended her in her final hours."

"Trust me; she was never pregnant. The doctors were part of the conspiracy to lead the public on. When Leila refused to accept Reanne's son as the rightful heir to the throne, Draos entreated Tan'os to silence her.

"Preposterous. What proof do you offer?"

The woman tapped her fingers on the edge of the desk. "I aided Ensther during this trying time. I became his advisor on matters of Reyzan life and culture."

Deneven cocked an eyebrow. "Life and culture?"

"You are a smart man, D'Neir. What do you think I do for a living?"

"I will venture to guess you are good at pulling strings. Answer my question. Where is the evidence?"

Reaching into thin air, the mysterious woman produced a wooden scroll case. "This," she said, placing the cylinder on a heap of papers, "contains the writ signed and sealed by Jarle Draos Iarris promising Tan'os Ensther the position of Vise upon the assassination of his wife. I inveigled Tan'os to demand such a document for his protection. Shortly afterward, I stole the incriminating writ—a circumstance the newly minted Vise found rather disagreeable."

"You blackmailed him."

"Of course. How else is anything accomplished in this city? In exchange for a reasonable income, I helped Tan'os rise to power. I aligned the guilds and coerced the Council. To use your phrasing, I pulled strings."

"Why didn't Tan'os simply kill you?"

"He tried, but alas shadows are faceless and nameless."

Deneven blinked as his guest vanished, and her disembodied voice echoed from multiple places at once. "Reyza is my dominion. Tan'os believed he could beat me at my own game. He began to make backroom deals with my contacts and cut into my profits. I would have let his offenses slide had he not threatened to expose me. The Vise's arrogance proved deadly."

Deneven squinted into the shadows. "Why are you telling me all this?"

"Come now, D'Neir, who in this city stands to gain most from the death of the Vise? Impress me with your vaunted powers of deduction."

Deneven rolled his eyes, recalling his conversation with The Mistress of Rats. "Ambassador Akkalon, but I have no evidence linking him to the murder."

"You're in luck," the intruder whispered in his ear. "The scroll case on your desk contains the proof of Rigo's illegitimacy as well as a letter written in code, promising a substantial sum to Mast for the assassination of Tan'os and his household. Neylen signed the document and sealed it with the official seal of Cartuj. The key to deciphering the contract is *Heart of the Blade* by Taif Que'kin, a warfare classic currently on your bookshelf."

The more the mysterious woman divulged, the more Deneven needed to know. "How did you obtain this document?"

"I arranged for its delivery."

"So, you conspired with Neylen to kill Tan'os."

"Neylen arrived in Reyza with an agenda and a fortune in jewels. I saw an opportunity to capitalize and eliminate an enemy at the same time. Can you blame me?"

Deneven felt like a rabbit in an eagle's sight. "Why massacre the Vise's entire household? Why butcher his servants and his daughter? What kind of monster are you?"

"Me? I delivered the letter, not the killing blow. Rigo was incensed with the arranged marriage to Avaren—an emotion Neylen fanned into a bonfire. I doubt Rigo would have agreed to the plot without the assurance that Avaren would die. As for leaving witnesses, well, you know the risks of sloppy work."

Deneven shook his head. "Yet, Avaren lives."

The woman ran her hands down Deneven's chest. "Yes. Jarle Jadien complicated matters. Regardless, Tan'os' daughter poses no threat to us."

"Us?"

"Yes," she said, circling to face him. "Which brings me to my proposition."

Deneven laughed. "I'll be thrice-damned before I collaborate with the daevil."

The young woman's eyes sparkled. "Daevil? No, but close. I am the Hand of Fate."

A tremor ran the length of Deneven's spine. The entity who inhabited the body of Fhaen was already a legend by the time he was a boy. As Lord Justiciar, he never bothered to investigate a mystery he believed to be nothing more than Reyzan superstition. "Can it be?"

"In the flesh," she said, pushing off her thigh-high leather boots.

Deneven sat transfixed as she disrobed. In his mind, her voice changed pitch, becoming rich and vibrant, like the middle notes of a cello. She no longer sounded like Fhaen. "You want Eva to depose her brother?"

The woman's gratified smile confirmed his conclusion. His heart beat wildly as she knelt before him and wrapped her fingers around his cock.

Deneven's voice hitched when the supple hand began to stroke his member. "If Neylen gets his way, Dessia will cease paying tariffs to A'diel. Their coffers will swell, and their armies will march across the desert. Reyza will be annexed."

"They are rich, missing only a port from which to ship their goods. Maintaining balance requires a delicate touch." The Hand of Fate looked up with a knowing smile. "Stability leads to profit, but extended peace provokes stagnation. Strong economies require occasional chaos, the timely pruning of an uncooperative official, et cetera. Conversely, conflict is far more destructive than it is profitable. In this, we agree. You lied to the Marchess to prevent a war. Not the best tactic, but I respect the effort."

"Gamblers play the hand they're dealt."

"Rogues do not. I am offering you the tools you need to put a definitive end to the conflict with Thyra. With these documents, you can restore the rightful heir to the Reyzan throne. Foreigners have meddled too long. Join me and seize your true aspirations. Become Vise."

"Vise?" Deneven shook his head. "How?"

The naked woman stood and straddled Deneven's lap, draping her legs over the chair's armrests. She guided his stiff rod inside her and took him to the root.

A strangled moan burst from Deneven's lips as his mysterious guest began to ride him with ferocious abandon. He circled his arms around her waist and jerked his thighs upwards to please her. The woman's beautiful green eyes locked on his, and her warm palms caressed his neck. At that moment, the Fate became Fhaen, and every woman he had ever desired. Her passion raged like the violent storm outside his window. Questions fell away, forgotten in the seductress' moans, and the pressure building in his loins. "Fuck me," he begged, "by the gods, fuck me."

"Patience." The woman slowed her tempo. She ground against Deneven's hips, arched forward to offer a pert nipple to his lips. "The Thrommish fleet sails soon. Go to Eva with the documents. She is canny enough to recognize the opportunity you are presenting. Impress upon her that you are uniquely qualified to affirm her claim. She knows the people admire you; support among the commoners is invaluable. If she hesitates, remind her how Reyza is truly ruled."

Deneven lifted his mouth from her breast. "What of the

Collegium?"

"The mages do not care who reigns. So long as you do not threaten their domain, they will not intervene."

"Eva will never agree to this."

"I know her ambitions, Dragon. Eva does not wish to destroy her home. War is the last recourse, one which Rigo neutralized when he publicly shamed her into ferrying Tan'os' corpse back to Thyra. She lusts for the throne."

Deneven grabbed her buttocks and quickened the pace. "If the office of Vise is my price, then what is yours?"

"Oooh," the sorceress gasped. "Deliver twenty thousand sequins to the *Jiulia* docked on the northernmost slip and grant the vessel passage, Do so, and I will wrangle the political clout you and Eva need to seize power."

Deneven groaned as the woman gyrated. Her body trembled, and her teeth clamped down on his neck as she neared a breathless climax. The sensation pushed him over the edge. Deneven buried himself into the farthest reaches of her tightness and shared the ecstasy of a mutual orgasm. He held her tight as he ejaculated with a guttural cry.

The sound of the crackling flames filled the room as the duo relaxed. Soft, tender kisses replaced scheming. Deneven stroked the Fate's long, flaming hair. The young woman looked so much like his Fhaen that he surrendered to the fantasy. He didn't care if the wanton straddled atop him was an assassin, a soulbinder, or the daevil herself. He wanted her. "If I do this, will I see you again?"

The woman disengaged from the embrace. Her red hair shone like wildfire in the light as she began to get dressed. "Timing is vital. Take the evidence to Eva before the fleet sets sail. Convince her."

"Is that a yes?" Deneven drank in the sight of her body as she shimmied into the leather outfit.

The woman remained silent as she pulled on her boots. When she finished, she grabbed the box from Deneven's desk. Her eyes gleamed as she stroked his chin. "When the bells begin to toll, all you desire will come true."

Deneven's gaze fell on the draengale case. "What's in the box?"

The Fate stepped into the shadows and vanished. "My only

weakness."

"You came for the box all along?" Deneven asked, incredulously.

"Think of it as an advance for services rendered. Do not fail me."

Deneven stood. "Wait," he cried into the darkness. "Don't go, not yet."

"Be satisfied." The mellifluous, disembodied voice echoed. "It's not every day you get fucked by Fate."

In Neylen's Hands

Venedi, Third of Nommen, 445 A'A'diel

Avaren awoke to the sound of voices. She screamed, but only a muffled groan escaped her lips. A crumpled, bitter-tasting wad of fabric clogged her mouth, and a dark swathe covered her eyes. Every inhalation caused a burst of pain along her back, where Neylen had pummeled her gills. Movement proved impossible. She was tied spread-eagled on a bed with only a thin nightdress to protect her modesty. Her protests did little to dissuade the conversation taking place around her. She recognized two of the three voices.

"My sister is demanding proof that she is alive," said Rigo.

"We shall put Marchess Eva's mind at ease, won't we, Master Healer?" A hint of amusement tinged the Dessian's voice.

A chair scraped along the wooden floor. A stranger with a raspy drawl spoke, his cadence slow. "The lady suffered much. She was nearly killed and possibly raped; such tragedies weigh heavily on a woman's mind. Only the gods know if she will ever be herself again."

Avaren flexed her arms and pulled against her restraints, bucking and twisting. The effort left her winded.

Footsteps neared the bed. "We must ensure that she poses no

threat to the Marchess when she arrives to see her," said Neylen.

When a gentle hand smoothed back her hair, Avaren struggled once more, but the bonds held firm.

The healer spoke again. "There are ways of taming the wayward will. One need only look to the plant kingdom, Your Highness. True and tried remedies can work wonders on the temperaments of reticent brides and madmen alike."

A pitcher scraped, and liquid poured. "Enlighten us," Rigo said.

"There is a man named Warrick, old in years like myself. He owns an apothek in the Tangles, which stocks the palace's medicinal stores. No one in Reyza surpasses his pharmacological skills. Rich and poor alike seek his expertise. He is, however, how should I say"—the creaking voice paused then lowered in tone—"unscrupulous. He has been accused of poisoning by the families of some persons now deceased."

Rigo scoffed, "Can he keep his tongue still?"

The healer coughed. "Warrick's skill in alchemy and wildcrafting is as great as his desire to remain a free man. He is devoted to his son, a feebleminded boy unable to fend for himself. I believe I can persuade him to your cause."

Rigo walked away from the bed, then paused. "This man sounds rather unsavory."

"Perhaps, Sire, but I know of no one else capable of fulfilling your wishes."

Avaren tugged the ropes and groaned in protest. Neylen stroked one of her outstretched arms. "Excellent. What of the other matter we discussed?"

The old man's footfalls grew louder as he neared. "Violent intercourse can, on occasion, render the womb infertile. I summoned a respectable member of the Venestrae to ascertain the condition of the lady's virtue. Prioress Chan'tahl can confirm or deny her ability to bear a royal heir."

Rigo huffed, "Well, let us get on with it."

The old healer limped across the room. A door opened, followed by the sound of padded footsteps and rustling skirts.

"Rise, Prioress. Thank you for your discretion in this sensitive matter," said Rigo.

The woman's voice held a nervous tremor, "Honored to serve, Your Highness."

The door shut with a soft click. Avaren peeked out the bottom of her blindfold and discerned several dark shapes silhouetted against the sunlight.

"Prioress, I must warn you," the old man said, "the lady endured a horrific ordeal and is not in control of her faculties. We took precautions against her outbursts, but even restrained, she may prove difficult. The ambassador and I are prepared to assist in your examination. Direct our humble hands as you require."

The conversation fell into silence as the holy woman circled the bed and placed a parcel next to Avaren's hips. The mattress dipped as the priestess sat opposite Neylen.

"Mejtress Ensther, I am Chan'tahl, Second Prioress of the Temple of Ven on Minstrel Rock. I vow to be as quick and as gentle as possible." The priestess' voice took on a serene tone as she offered an ancient supplication to the death god, "Ven, redeemer of souls, guide my hand and absolve me with your divine favor. Bestow this young woman forbearance during this difficult time."

When the orison ended, the woman rummaged through the contents of her parcel. Avaren's heart thundered as the sound of metal instruments filled the silence. The hollow pop of an uncorked jar aroused a fresh wave of panic. She gagged on the sodden cloth as Chan'tahl positioned herself between her legs and pushed her gown up to her waist. Avaren squeezed her thighs in protest as soft hands coaxed her open. Never had she felt so exposed—so humiliated!

The harder the prioress insisted, the more Avaren resisted. Her thigh muscles ached with the effort of keeping her legs closed, but she did not relent. At long last, Chan'tahl released her hold and sat back. "Lady, you must allow me to perform my task, or else these men will force you. I don't believe that is something either of us desires. I won't ask kindly again."

Avaren weighed her options. She could continue to thwart the holy woman and suffer further abuses in Neylen's hands or cooperate and hope the degradation ended quickly. Trapped as she was, she had little choice. Defiantly she spread her knees as far as the rope permitted and ceased to struggle.

The priestess placed her palm on Avaren's groin and pressed down. Using her other hand, she inserted two slippery fingers into her vagina and probed deep.

Avaren's breaths hitched as the cleric prodded and tapped along her abdomen, running the tips of her digits over her pelvic mound. Although she could not see them, she sensed the men clamoring closer for a better view. Their lascivious stares burned like hot ingots on her flesh. Disgusted, she cursed them a thousand times while simultaneously praying for relief.

After what felt like an eternity, the prioress withdrew her fingers, but the respite was short-lived. The woman reached under Avaren's thighs and positioned the tip of something hard and cold against her opening. "This instrument will aid me in gauging the health of the womb," she announced.

"Do not rush," offered Neylen. "His Highness must be sure."

Rage-fueled teardrops soaked Avaren's blindfold as a bulbous steel tool pushed deep inside her. She gripped the bedposts and bit down on her gag as the pressure increased. Every time the woman moved her hand, the sensation in her vulva intensified. A fearful shiver rippled down her spine as the infernal device stretched her wider and wider, exposing her most intimate place to the leering audience. Just when she thought she might be torn apart from the inside out, the cruel expansion stopped. A pillow was propped beneath her trembling hips.

The priestess shifted on the bed, her face so close that her breath washed over Avaren's exposed sex. "Away with you, I need light."

Time slowed to a glacial crawl. Avaren thrust her shoulders into the bedding as another tool intruded. Discomfort turned into pain.

"Well!?" For once, Rigo's outburst was a welcomed distraction. "Can you tell me if my future wife can bear me children, or are you content to idly stare at her cunny?"

"Her maidenhead is torn. Her organ bears signs of recent sexual intercourse. I cannot substantiate whether she was raped or not."

Avaren chewed on the rag as her tormenter tinkered with the implement. With each jostle, the pressure eased. A sense of relief washed through her when the invasive tool withdrew.

Rigo moved closer. "You haven't answered my question."

The Venestrae rose from the bed. She pulled the pillow from beneath Avaren and smoothed the gown over her body. "She is strong and healthy and—"

Prioress Chan'tahl's pause agitated Rigo and Avaren alike.

"And?" demanded Rigo.

"Capable of bearing children, Sire."

Dread replaced humiliation. Avaren wailed and thrashed until the ropes that bound her dug deep into her wrists. The bedframe shook, and the headboard slammed against the wall.

Chan'tahl gathered her instruments. "Hush, child," she hissed, "Ven does not abandon his flock in time of need. Keep the faith."

"As you can see, her lucidity comes and goes," said the old man. "Thank you for coming on such short notice, Prioress."

Avaren's heart sank at the sound of jingling coins. The priestess would not aid her. No one would.

"Ven bless you for your generous donation, Master Healer."

Skirts brushed over the floor. The door opened and closed.

"What now?" Rigo asked.

"We follow our plan," said Neylen.

"You and your plans!"

"The throne needs an heir, Sire," the old man added. "The discovery and return of Mejtress Avaren is a sign of providence."

"Fool!" snapped Rigo. "She is like a rabid animal. She would sooner bite off my cock than agree to marry me."

"The ceremony does not need to be a public one," mumbled the healer.

"This alchemist of yours, this Warrick, what can he do to fix this?" Neylen's interjection was thick with frustration.

"F-fix? Well, that depends. The mind is a delicate realm. Warrick is an expert in exotic unguents and herbs. Some substances can erase a person's memories or paralyze the body. If his concoctions do not suffice, there is also a surgical procedure I developed for dealing with dangerous madmen. A sharp instrument inserted into the nasal cavity can—"

Rigo cut him off. "Yank out her tongue if you have to, just make sure she is unable to say a word to my sister when she arrives this evening. Fail me in this, and I will feed you your own hide."

"Fetch the alchemist," commanded Neylen.

Rigo shouted when the old man tarried. "Go. Now!"

"Yes, my liege." A slammed door accentuated the healer's hasty departure.

For a few moments, the only sound was that of angry pacing. Avaren tensed when a sudden crash broke the silence. Wood splintered, and glass shattered.

Rigo flung his words like daggers. "You whore. I should hang you for this mess!"

For an instant, Avaren believed Rigo was addressing her, but Neylen's response proved he wasn't.

"Calm down," soothed the Dessian. "Once you convince Eva to leave her behind, you will wed and gain the approval of your people. Reyza will hail you as a hero for following through on your promise to marry Ensther's daughter despite her tragic ordeal. Shortly after the marriage, she will become pregnant. You will relinquish her care to the Master Healer, who will keep her secluded and silent. Once she delivers a male heir, she will die during childbirth. A grand funeral will follow. You will feign heartbreak and devote your life to your child. A year from now, this will be nothing but a memory."

"I am tired of listening to you, you black-eyed, Ven-damned, landlocked snake-licker." Rigo's voice grew shrill. "I swear I could claw your eyes out. You assured me she would be dead, and yet, here she is!"

Words gave way to an intense scuffle followed by the meaty thud of men grappling on the wooden floor. "This conspiracy will never work. I have no intention of marrying the bitch or bedding her. I suggest you give me one good reason why I shouldn't expose you for the murdering daevil you are."

A table fell over.

"Because you love me," Neylen hissed.

"Arrogant prick. I will never give you what you want."

Clothing ripped as the commotion escalated.

Avaren peeked under her blindfold and caught a blur of movement. She couldn't discern if Neylen and Rigo were trading to blows or engaged in something else entirely.

"You will give this arrogant snake-licker all he desires and more—much more," growled Neylen.

Rigo choked back a sob, and Neylen let out a lustful sigh. Slurping and sucking filled the gaps between heavy breaths.

Avaren clenched her eyes tight. Pins and needles assaulted the tips of her toes and fingers. Suddenly, revenge tasted every bit as bitter as the rag stuffed in her mouth.

The noises of thrusting and licking, coupled with the sound of Rigo gagging and moaning went on for a long time. Neylen reached his climax with a guttural groan that left the younger man gasping for air.

There was another quiet altercation before Neylen spoke again, this time in a hushed, harsh whisper. "Go and wait for me. I am not finished with you."

Rigo said nothing more. The regent's footsteps faded as he stomped off.

A thrill of fear ran the length of Avaren's body as the door clicked, and the Dessian approached the bed. Her revolting nightmare seemed to have no end.

"Are you thirsty?" Neylen inquired.

Avaren nodded. Her throat was too parched to allow prideful abstinence.

Neylen sat beside her. "I apologize for my rudeness. As you may have surmised, I have a short temper when it comes to our beloved ruler. He grinds my nerves at the most inopportune moments."

Avaren froze when the Dessian's palm grasped the bare curve of her calf. He caressed upwards, squeezing her thigh before continuing to her midriff. "When I asked the healer to examine you, I sought to humiliate you—something I accomplished rather well."

Avaren's heart thundered as Neylen rubbed her abdomen and leaned down to whisper in her ear. "Don't be shy, we're alone now. Tell me, where can I find the mongrel who calls himself Jarle Jadien."

Neylen's hand moved upward and took hold of Avaren's breast. He kneaded the flesh between his fingers. "Oh, wait," Neylen mused, tweaking her nipple, "you can't speak, can you?

Look at you all tied up, swimming in your own sweat, panting with anticipation. You're at my mercy. I wager you are wondering what it's like to take a Yerr'draki cock between those lovely thighs. Let me give you a hint—you will soon be yearning for the metal toy the priestess teased you with."

Neylen relinquished one nipple to focus on the other. "I don't blame you for being excited," he purred, pinching the delicate flesh. "Since I'm feeling generous, I will remove this rag and provide you with some water, but only if you promise not to scream. Shriek, and I promise you will never sing again."

When Avaren gave no hint of understanding, Neylen pinched the nipple harder. "Understand?"

Avaren groaned, then nodded.

When Neylen extracted the gag, Avaren licked her lips. "The man you speak of helped me escape in exchange for my jewelry. He took me out of the city along the South Road. We journeyed together for two days, then parted ways. I have not seen him since."

Neylen lifted Avaren's head and brought the rim of the glass to her mouth. Avaren gulped the water, causing it to spill over her chin.

"Traveled the South Road, did you?" Neylen set the vessel down. "While that may be true, I think you also spread your legs for that curskin son of a whore."

Avaren gasped when the Dessian grabbed a fistful of her hair. "Listen carefully, you slithering, fish-tailed bitch. If you want to live, you better start telling me where I can find this Jars."

"I don't know where he is!" Avaren cried.

"That's unfortunate." Neylen stuffed the fabric back into Avaren's mouth. He groped Avaren's body under the nightdress before smoothing it back into place. "I know a few soulbinders and anatomists who would be interested in studying a naera."

The Dessian rose to his feet. "I must depart, but I implore you not to exhaust yourself. Rigo has no interest in bedding you, so I shall have to devise an alternate means of seeding a child in your belly. I will make certain that your wedding night is unforgettable."

No consolation came from Neylen's departure. Icy despair clutched Avaren's heart. She tugged violently against her bindings and howled into the emptiness. No one heard her.

THE SPIDER WEB

Venedi, Third of Nommen, 445 A'A'diel

Warrick looked at his son with chagrin. In the afternoon sunlight streaming through the window, the youth's complexion glowed beneath the hood of his apothecary's robe. Aldorf stood tall and broad and possessed enviable good looks, but despite his nineteen seasons, he was still a child.

A tremor shook the old man's hands as he unlatched the chest that held his alchemical supplies. "Aldorf, boy, I need your help."

Fascinated by a spider rappelling down a silken thread, the youth did not heed his father's call. His eyes widened, and a wonder-filled smile spread across his face as the insect landed on the windowsill and began to weave a web.

Warrick huffed and let the lid drop with a thud. "Aldorf!"

Aldorf twitched and bowed his head. He stepped down from the window's alcove and trudged over to where his father hunched. Without a word, he unpacked the portable alchemy chest. His nimble hands arranged the beakers, measuring cylinders, condensers, funnels, tinctures, powder-filled jars, and pouches of dried components on a wooden table. He finished emptying the contents and commenced the careful assembly of the metal and glass parts of an extractor.

Warrick observed his apprentice with a hawk's eye. "The flask with two necks goes in the other way. Remember the story of the two geese needing to swim up the narrow stream?"

The young man's face lit up. He turned the tube in his hand and nodded. Absorbed by the many fittings of the apparatus, he recited his learnings. "Paa says thimble-holder hangs inside the solvent flask. Still pot clamped while solvent is added with a slow, steady drip. Once chamber is full, flush it with a siphon to send the solvent running down the distillation flask. Thimble, like Nana's sewing thimble, ensures that the motion of the solvent does not transport any solid into the still pot." Aldorf adjusted the tubes that connected the interlocking glass cylinders. "Paa says that during each cycle, a portion of the non-volatile compound dissolves in the solvent. Need water and fire now, Paa, water, and fire. What we making, Paa?"

Warrick grunted with approval. "We have a few hours, boy, best to take our time and brew something fresh."

Aldorf poked his finger in his nose and chortled. "Fresh, Aldorf likes fresh. What we making, Paa?"

The alchemist glanced up from the cluttered table and licked his lips. The gagged, struggling girl tied to the bed was soaked in sweat. Beneath her gossamer gown, her naked flesh shone pink. "We're making something to calm the lady down."

"Water, Paa, measure water. How much water?"

Warrick ignited the oil burner under the still, then tapped the top of the measuring cylinder. "Three counts."

Aldorf dug under his robe until his fingers closed around his water skin. He unhooked the bladder, freed the cap, and filled the vessel. "Lady shakes and sweats. Shaking and sweating require rutaceae, allium, snakeskin powder, blue morret root, tincture of vertis, and, and, wild boar meat? No, not boar meat, peat. Peat!"

"No, boy, she is afflicted by a different sort of illness. Listen carefully and be very precise with your measurements."

"Not shakes, different shakes. Yes, Paa, which measurements? What to add to Nana's thimble?" A smile grew on the apprentice's face. "Nana, Nana, Nana has a thimble. Which measurements, Paa? Which?"

"A pinch of white acacia blossoms, six leaves of birdsfoot lotus, a small dash of yellow jessamine, eight ligula oil of castor, two seeds of cramp bark, and a pinch of powdered scorpion stings."

Midway through counting the dry, slim leaves Aldorf's face twisted into a snarl. "Bad Paa, bad Paa, yellow jessamine and cramp bark, bad. Lady will not wake up, Paa. Cramp bark killed alley cat, Paa. Remember? Cat ate cramp bark and died."

Warrick reached up and patted the boy's shoulder. "Easy, son. What have I always explained about ratios and proportions? You are correct, cramp bark and jessamine are poisonous when combined, but the lady is much larger than the cat. We will brew a tonic that will merely relax her muscles. She will not lose consciousness. Measure out what I dictated and learn something new."

Aldorf calmed down. "Learn something new, Aldorf likes fresh. Measure correct to relax muscles. Lady feels better."

Warrick checked Aldorf's proportions and made adjustments. He removed minute amounts of specific ingredients and added more of others. Once satisfied, the alchemist poured the substances into the extractor. He opened a wood case and withdrew an hourglass made of carved bone. "Excellent work, boy. The tincture requires an hour and a half, plus a few minutes to cool. While we wait for the distillation, I want to teach you something about female anatomy."

Aldorf tapped his fingers on the work table and blinked several times. He gazed at the spider web spanning the open window. In the center of the skein, a small brown moth fluttered in the threads. The insect flapped its wings, becoming more entangled with every movement. In the fading sunlight, the network of trembling filaments shone a brilliant gold. Aldorf flinched when Avaren tugged on her restraints. "Paa, girl would feel better if she were not caught?"

Warrick hobbled to the edge of the bed where his charge lay. He swept Avaren's hair back. "Son, this woman is Starborn and dangerous."

The tempo of Aldorf's finger-tapping increased. "What she done, Paa? Am I Starborn?"

"Come, Aldorf, come see her eyes. They burn like fire opals."

Aldorf looked back at the spider. The moth had stopped moving and was being encased in silk. "I should watch the brew,

Paa. Watch the brew."

Warrick bent forward and whispered in the girl's ear. "Avaren Ensther, I knew your father. He always paid well." Warrick rested his hand on her belly. "Under different circumstances, who knows, you might have even sought my services. I am here to perform a duty that will violate your dignity." He kneaded the slight curve between her hip bones with trembling fingers. "Forgive me."

Aldorf jumped when the strapped girl lunged at his father. The bedframe shook as the woman strained against the bonds that held her.

"Have it your way, be as difficult as you like. The outcome shall be the same, regardless of resistance." Warrick tucked a strand of white hair behind his ear and straightened. "Boy, bring me that washbasin by the door and fill it."

Aldorf surveyed the room. Aside from the oak table upon which their brewing supplies lay strewn, the room's furnishings consisted of two sumptuous chairs, an oversized, reinforced trunk, and a copper washbasin on an iron pedestal. Nearby stood two ceramic ewers and a basket with washcloths and toiletries.

Aldorf's robe dragged on the planks as he moved about the room. He tucked the basin under one arm and pulled the pedestal across the wooden floor, gouging a groove. Warrick's menacing stare stopped him in his tracks. "Sorry, Paa."

"One thing at a time, Aldorf. We are in the palace!" Warrick admonished. "How many times did I tell you? We need to be careful!"

"Twenty-one times, Paa."

Warrick opened his mouth to retort but instead snapped it shut. He hobbled over to his son and snagged the washbasin from his grasp. "Fetch the water."

Aldorf placed the stand beside the bed. He set the bowl on the iron framework, then fetched the two ewers. He smiled at his father as he filled the container with water. "You mean to bathe her, Father?"

The word, father, softened Warrick's demeanor. It was in these rare moments that he saw a dashing young man on the cusp of adulthood, instead of the forgetful, clumsy creature who had damaged the royal floor. "Yes, we must make her presentable."

Aldorf's bright gray eyes traveled the length of the girl's displayed body and settled on the dark, raised peaks of her nipples. Heat rose to his cheeks. "She is beautiful, Father. Who is she?"

Warrick crossed the room, grabbed the hamper of toiletries, and returned. "She is an honored guest here at the palace and is very sick. We are to care for her."

Aldorf gazed down at the struggling girl. "She is like a rabid dog," he said, adjusting his breeches. "May I touch her?"

Warrick eyed his son and wondered how long Aldorf's normalcy would linger. Hope never lasted long; nonetheless, his son's curiosity about the girl roused a sense of pride. The old man set the basket down on the foot of the bed and dropped a washcloth into the basin. "We should undress her if we are to bathe her, yes?"

Aldorf gathered his cassock and knelt on the mattress. He hovered over the trapped girl and brought his face as near to hers as he dared. The woman's eyes were pools of fire and ice. With one hand, Aldorf yanked the nightgown upward over her haunches, then again, until her privates were exposed.

Warrick narrowed his eyes. The delight he had taken in the transparency of the sweat-soaked garment clinging to her curves paled to the feast her nakedness provided. Warrick placed his hand on Aldorf's shoulder and eased the boy backward. "Get the scalpel."

Aldorf stared at the rolling swells of the full, pale breasts with slack-jawed amazement.

Warrick snapped at the dumbfounded boy. "Aldorf! Scalpel!"

Aldorf slid away with a frustrated sigh. He rummaged through the trunk in search of the blade—the contents of every drawer alien to his awakened mind. "Where is it?"

Warrick ignored him. He shoved his nose into the girl's sweltering cleft and inhaled deep. The grossness of the act, coupled with Avaren's jerking thighs, inspired a subtle stirring in the alchemist's loins. In that heavenly moment, surrounded by the scent of sex, the geezer wished himself young again, but no concoction brewed by mortal hand could grant such a wish. "It is a shame we have to clean her up; she's quite fine as is."

After throwing open the drawers of the small cabinets inside the chest, Aldorf found the surgical knife in a cinched leather bag.

He handed it to his father and crawled on the bed.

Warrick cut the gown down the center then slit both sleeves until the garment fell away. The girl clenched her thighs shut, but her modesty only served to amuse him.

The mystique surrounding Avaren Ensther had been on the tongues of Reyzans for several years. Without the heavy veils, the covered carriage, and armed guards, she was no more and no less mysterious than any other noblewoman. She was beautiful, but Warrick saw no basis for the stranger rumors. He saw no fish scales, gills, nor any other deformity.

The alchemist tossed the tattered rag aside, stepped back, and gave his son an approving nod. "She's all yours, boy. Make sure you scrub behind her ears and be gentle with the wound on her leg."

Aldorf undid the belt that held his soutane closed and let it drop. He then stripped down to his breechcloth and undershirt and set to work.

Warrick pretended to make adjustments to the extractor while he watched the boy. Despite his excitement, Aldorf paced himself. He added herbal salts to the water, then began to wipe Avaren's body with a damp washcloth. Aldorf's every touch caused a jerk or muffled growl to escape the bound woman.

Warrick leaned forward on the work table. "Cooperate, dear, or you will leave me no recourse but to sedate you."

Aldorf grinned when his father's threat appeared to have some effect. Beneath him, the girl ceased her tossing, but the anger in her eyes continued to smolder.

Aldorf massaged her ribs and belly with the soft cloth. He brought it upwards along the valley of her bosom, avoiding her breasts. Every time Aldorf drew closer to the pale globes, his hands trembled, and he lost his nerve. When he could no longer avoid them, the youth swallowed hard and ran the towel over the voluptuous peaks. The contact caused his face to contort with sudden, frightful anguish. Trembling like a child doused with frigid water, he shrieked, "Nana! I love Nana! Nana!"

Warrick sighed as Aldorf threw the washcloth down and began scratching his thighs. Aldorf's moments of clarity were sporadic and tenuous. He waited for the tantrum to pass before approaching his son. "I know you love Nana, boy, as you should.

She raised you. It's all right, boy, you're all right."

Aldorf's tear-stained eyes darted to the window. The moth was gone, transformed into a cocoon of spider silk. "I'm all right, Paa," he sobbed, "I'm all right."

Warrick embraced the youth and rubbed his back. "Shhh, this girl is not Nana, and you have not harmed her. You have not done anything wrong."

"I thought she was sick, Paa, needed cramp bark brew." Aldorf sniffled and let go of his father. "Is she sick or just caught, Paa?"

"My clever boy. Go check on our distillation."

Aldorf took up his robe and slipped it on. He neared the bed to pick up his belt but changed his mind when the girl glowered in his direction. He scurried behind the table, squatted down, and shut his eyes to the world.

Warrick studied his shaking progeny with dismay. Without supervision, guidance, or wealth, Aldorf faced a grim future—either as a beggar in Reyza's rat-infested alleys or, worse, one of the lost souls who wailed day and night behind bars in the Collegium's insanity wards. Only the gods knew what secret experiments the arcanists inflicted on their deranged captives.

Warrick peered down at the naked girl. Avaren was a few years younger than Aldorf, orphaned by a tragedy and likely to suffer much more before she met her end. In exchange for cruelty and secrecy, the Dessian paid him a small fortune and promised to pardon his legal troubles. Going against Rigo's wishes would not bode well for him or his son.

Warrick tottered to his alchemy trunk. He took out a corked jar containing a gelatinous substance, opened it, and sat on the side of Avaren's bed. He inserted two bony fingers into the pot and scooped out the unguent. In response to the girl's muffled protests, Warrick shook his head. "Listen, girl, I've been hired to torment you, but old age has tempered my vices. My boy"—Warrick pointed to the youth huddled under the table—"is my treasure and my chain in this life. I do what I must for him."

Warrick climbed between Avaren's legs and spread her flailing thighs with his knees. He glopped the glistening gel into her vagina and began to work his fingers in and out, coating her channel generously. Once finished with her front, the alchemist scooped more of the goo. Warrick ignored her whimpers as he worked his fingers into her anus. Satisfied that the girl was well lubricated, the geezer took up the washcloth and dabbed the excess lubricant.

"I know this feels unpleasant, but trust me when I tell you that it will make what will come later less painful." Warrick lowered his voice. "That Dessian snake is intent on sowing a child in your belly, and his methods won't be gentle. He's lined up a score of men whose bloodlines match Rigo's. Knowing him, he'll indulge his lust and put his cock where he likes it most, and by that, I don't mean your cunny." Warrick patted her thigh. "Unlike him, I am not an animal."

When Avaren started to sob and heave, Warrick frowned. "Mejtress, I promise to comfort you as best I can short of sedating you completely. Don't despair; my brew will help you forget this ugliness. You won't feel a thing."

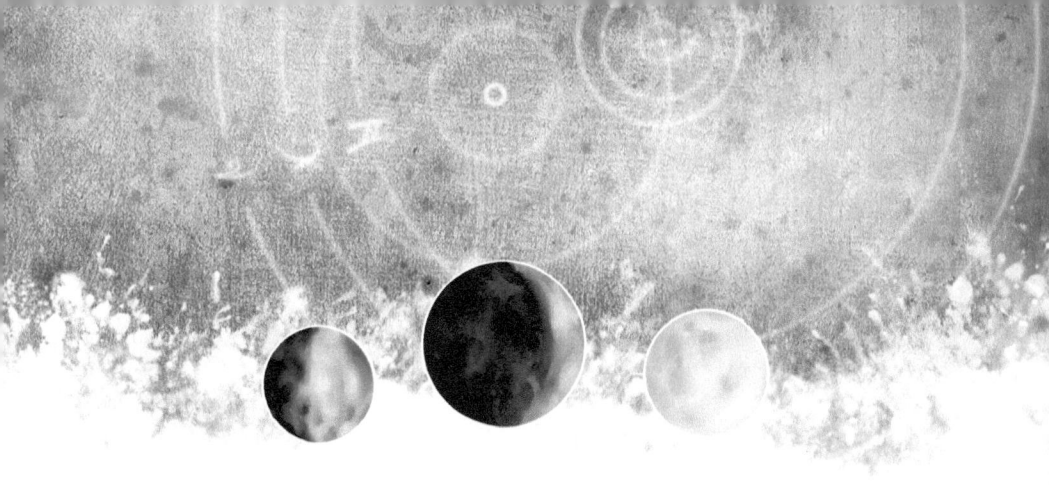

HOMECOMING

Venedi, Third of Nommen, 445 A'A'diel

The rain clouds had scattered, and the cold wind that blew inland from the sea drove plumes of smoke past the northern wall. Jarle drew the grimmalkin pelt over his head as he moved among the shadows of the crowded encampment outside Reyza's defensive perimeter. He caressed the lush fur with a twinge of regret. The time had come to discard the hide—a rarity bound to draw the wrong sort of attention.

The thief wound past the tents and wagons, pausing behind a barouche to survey the fortification. Built by Reyza's founders, the battlements that marked the border between civilization and the wilds, stretched a dozen manlengths into the sky. The rains of many winters had gouged away the mortar, exposing a web of cracks and handholds in the gray stone blocks. Braziers spanned the length of the ramparts, lighting the way for heavily armored patrols.

As Jarle surveyed the refugees in search of a potential disguise, a snore caught his attention. Peering under the wagon, he spied a cloaked greybeard sprawled in the mud. The man's bony fingers clutched a jar of raska, and he stank of piss and alcohol.

The thief crawled under the wagon and peeled the filthy

vestment from the drunkard's shoulders. "Old timer," he said, draping the grimmalkin hide on the man's back, "tonight's your lucky night." Jarle smeared the stolen cloak with horse dung, then donned the tattered rag. With a grimace, he pulled the cowl over his head and slipped out from under the cart.

Jarle walked across the camp and joined a group of men, warming their hands around a campfire. The vantage point afforded a better view of the Jungle Gate and its forlorn traffic. Muddy evacuees intermingled with boisterous inebriates looking for a place to sleep and hawkers seeking quick profits from the discomforts of the homeless. On one side of the portal, a trio of pikemen watched the refugees with bored half interest. The youngest of the three, a broad-shouldered man with a long ponytail, took pleasure in accosting random citizens as they crossed—a pretty girl was as likely a target as a geezer for a moment's sport.

"If I were younger, I'd give that armored turd a piece of my mind," said one of the huddled men.

"You'd think they'd find something better to do than harass us at a time like this," chimed Jarle.

"Aye," agreed another. "Makes you wonder if any of these whore sons ever had mothers or sisters."

Jarle maintained his vigil, waiting for an opportunity to slip past the sentries. As he indulged in idle chatter, he noticed a woman struggling to carry a limp girl toward the portal. The distressed mother sobbed as her feet sank into the muck.

Jarle abandoned the fire and jogged over to her. "A thousand pardons, I couldn't ignore your plight. What ails your child?" he asked.

"A fight broke out between two men," she said, her voice fraught with worry. "One knocked the other into our tent and landed on my daughter. Now I can't wake her. She needs a healer."

The girl's breathing was labored, and a red lump discolored her temple. "The public infirmary is far from here," Jarle said. "You are tired; let me help you."

Fresh tears tracked down the woman's cheeks. "You are the first person to offer aid. Ven bless you."

Jarle took the unconscious girl into his arms. She was about ten seasons old but as light as a feather.

The guardsmen studied them as they neared the gate. Behind them, tacked on a wooden post, a stained parchment read:

BY ORDER OF THE COUNCIL
WANTED
– JARLE 'JARS' JADIEN –
FOR MURDER AND ABDUCTION
FIVE THOUSAND SEQUINS
DEAD OR ALIVE

Beneath the block letters, a crude sketch of his face held a remarkable likeness. Jarle's heart skipped a beat. He dipped his cowled face toward the child in his arms and appeared like a worried father. He hadn't fought his way through the wilderness only to be captured by slipshod gate monkeys.

Pike in hand, the young bully stepped forward. An officious smirk curled under his thin mustache. "Here now, what's your hurry?"

The woman bowed and uttered a desperate rush of words, "Please, sir, my daughter is hurt and needs a healer."

"Lots of people need help tonight. What makes you think the healers will see you?"

"My baby is barely breathing." Tears tracked down the woman's face. "Please, let us pass."

Another guard with a long beard and a hooked nose examined the battered girl. Without raising his head, Jarle spoke with a strangled voice. "My little one was trampled by ruffians." He cradled the girl as his tone grew thicker with pathos. "Please, don't let her die, kind sirs. She's all we have in the world."

The bearded guard scowled at his companion. "Tarlock, you've had your fun." He stood back and waved them toward the city. "Let them pass."

"Gratitude, sir." Jarle rushed through the entrance before Tarlock could respond. Past the gate, they walked briskly through the deserted streets. At the intersection of Berengor Lane and the South Road, Jarle stopped and eased the child into her mother's arms.

"Why are you stopping?" the woman asked, looking around the empty crossroads.

"This is as far as I go," Jarle said. "Your daughter received a nasty blow, but I think she'll recover. The infirmary is around the bend."

The woman's confusion gave way to curiosity as she cradled her child. "What is your name so that I may thank you properly once this madness ends?"

The thief lowered his head. "I am merely a concerned citizen. May Addonel aid you." With those words, Jarle turned and jogged down the Southern Road.

Nestled between the shuttered shops on Clothier's Row and the sprawling warehouses of the Sailmakers' Union, a four-story tavern shone like a beacon. The light of a score of braziers danced on the ivory façade of The Stallion. A multitude of people occupied the tables beneath the hoofs of a carved, rearing horse. Serving girls and table boys hustled platters and flagons in an endless flow through the arched entrance of the inn.

The interior bustled with activity. Patrons clamored among the rows of trestle tables in the vaulted hall. On the stage, a sextet of musicians performed before a black velvet backdrop woven with crystals to resemble stars. The harmony of hammerans, ertalangs, and sunderdrums provided a counterpoint to the buzz of excited conversations. The music built to a majestic crescendo then faded into a crash of applause and satisfied hollers.

When the clapping waned, the percussionists sounded a lively tattoo. People cheered as the strummers played the introduction of a well-known ditty.

A barefoot woman with dark hair and skin the color of weathered bronze wove a sensuous path among the musicians. She wore a gown of thin golden chains and shimmering scales that teased the eyes. Her full breasts jiggled as she slapped a tambourine festooned with colorful ribbons. A roll of her hips offered a glimpse of thigh beneath the swirling fetters.

White teeth and sapphire eyes flashed as she urged the enthusiastic crowd to join her in the ribald tune. "Nine wise men with knowledge so fine, created a cunny to their design. First was a butcher, with a quick wit, and using a knife, he gave it a slit."

Patrons cheered and howled, joining her for the next stanza. "Second was a carpenter, strong and bold, with a mallet and chisel, he gave it a hole."

Jarle sat in a corner not far from the bar and ordered a bowl of stew and a mug of ale. He laughed as the seductress climbed on a table and slapped her rump with the tambourine.

"Third, I'm told was a tailor, tall and thin, using red velvet, he lined it within." The performer's eyes glittered with delight as she gazed at the rowdy audience. "Fourth was a hunter, short and stout, took some fox fur and lined it without."

Tankards crashed on wooden tables as laughter rang out. Once again, the crowd chimed in, "Fifth was a fisherman, nasty as Hel, threw in a fish to give it a smell!"

The woman shimmied her hips as she waggled an admonishing finger at her audience. "Now you and I know a good cunny smells wonderful. So don't you listen to what they say about that idiot fisherman." People roared with approval as she continued. "Sixth was a priest, whose name was Ran' dee, touched it and blessed it, and said it could pee!"

Cheers echoed as the mob responded, "Seventh was a banker who pondered some more, if the hole could store a cock, then profits would soar."

"Where can I get one?" cried an old man.

"I love you, Myrsi!" someone else shouted.

The dark-haired minx twirled and shook her tambourine at the geezer. "Be like the sailor, you dirty, old runt, who sucked it and fucked it, and called it a cunt!"

When his food arrived, Jarle hunched over the bowl and shoveled spoonful after spoonful of the spicy meal into his mouth. He chewed the succulent chunks of lamb with the appreciation of a starved wolf before washing it down with a mouthful of dark beer. After a month of unseasoned fish, he had almost forgotten the fiery pleasures of The Stallion's fare.

Behind the bar, the proprietor, Doshmaan Suvi, grinned and clapped his barkeep on the shoulder. "Start pouring now, Croy. There will be many a parched throat when Myrsi finishes her act."

"They're drinking us dry." The barkeep returned the smile as he twisted the spigot into a keg. "This is the fifth pipe of Ghossian lager I've tapped since sundown. Also, we are down to the last two cases of Zherrian Summerwine."

"Double the price on the Summerwine." Doshmaan stroked his black goatee. "Push the Debendelo Red. We have two tuns of that taking up valuable cellar space. How is the Terranakan rum moving?"

"Too expensive for this crowd." Croy stole a mug from a passing tray and handed it to his boss. "I mixed it with some of our faster-moving stock, and it's selling well."

The tavern-keeper sniffed the drink. "Tanjerfruit and—is that Kynet?" When Croy nodded, Doshmaan took a swig. "By Ghaddo's prodigious balls! What do you call this potion?"

Croy gave him a wink and a smirk. "Milk of Zezen!"

The sight of the innkeeper's happy smile plucked Jarle's heartstrings. He regretted not saying goodbye to Doshmaan and his wives, Irilio, his closest friend, or Marcella. The less they knew about him, the better.

The sextet finished the lewd ditty with a flourish and commenced playing a mellower tune. The dark-skinned woman flirted with the crowd as she sang a romantic ballad. The rhythmic inflections of her Ellaian accent imbued the song with sensuality. The beauty of her voice roused memories of Avaren.

Jarle grabbed a crusty piece of bread, tore off a chunk, and sopped the last bit of thick gravy from the side of his bowl. Near him, three young nobles engaged in a lively discussion.

"I swear it!" said one of the young dandies. "My father was at the banquet and heard everything. Rigo was in top form." Clad in royal blue sateen with crimson piping, the nobleman leaned back and considered his goblet. "His skillful maneuvering left Marchess Eva positively fuming."

His companion, a youth with long blond curls, asked, "Will the embargo end? My father's business will suffer if the Thrommish armada lingers."

Jarle paused mid drink, his mind racing. He hadn't anticipated Thyra would send an entire fleet, let alone blockade the city. Silently, he cursed his luck and sipped the ale without savoring it.

"I don't know. My father thinks the Marchess will ferry the Vise's body back to Thyra with a ship or two and leave the rest here to assert her influence." The blue-clad fop drained his glass with a flippant swig, then wiped his mouth with a napkin. "I wager twenty sequins on the Thrommish clogging the harbor until New Year's Day."

The news soured Jarle's disposition. He slammed his tankard down and rubbed his forehead under the hood.

A blockade, of course! Why would the gods make his life simple?

No longer able to enjoy the respite, Jarle rose from his chair and shouldered his way through the crowd. He avoided eye contact and kept his head bowed as he walked to the rear of the tavern.

With Myrsi's performance in full sway, the people he passed were too drunk or too enthralled by her undulations to notice another seemingly inebriated guest heading up to his rooms. In the stairwell, a pair of women recommended he bathe before rushing past him.

On the fourth floor, Jarle paused at the landing and listened until he was sure the hallway was vacant. When he heard nothing beyond the dull roar of applause from the hall below, he strode along the dim corridor to his door. Thoughts of the blockade vanished with the anticipation of resting in his own bed—if only for a nap.

The thief pressed his ear to the door. Reassured by the silence, he withdrew the leather wallet from his jerkin and removed two slender lengths of steel. He slipped the picks into the keyhole and worked with the ease borne of habit. When the click of the mechanism rewarded his ears, he stowed away his tools and cracked open the door.

Peeking inside, Jarle scowled. His furniture was rearranged, and frilly garments littered the floor. Two dressmaker's forms, half-clothed in swathes of silk and lace, faced the armoire. An open trunk filled with rumpled dresses and women's shoes occupied the space where his ironbound, triple-lock chest had once stood. Perfume bottles, makeup sponges, used wine glasses, and a myriad of spools, scissors, and tailoring tools crowded his bureau.

Jarle entered the room and paled. Vartan Lieris' masterwork, Nemserati Worshiping Bel's Effigy, was gone. All that remained of his beloved painting was a clean rectangle of white surrounded by smoke-dimmed plaster.

Closing the door, Jarle moved to the bed and shoved it an armlength away from the wall. He knelt and worked the tip of his dagger between the grooves of the floorboards and pried loose the planks. Upon finding the hidden compartment untouched, he sighed with relief.

The thief retrieved a dusty wooden case and opened it. Nestled in a bed of blue velvet, lay a pair of Calantian combat daggers and a leather pouch bulging with coins.

Jarle sheathed the blades and pocketed the money, then stuffed the coffer back under the floor. After tapping the planks into place, he pushed the bed against the wall. As he had suspected, The Stallion was no longer safe.

OLD FRIENDS

Venedi, Third of Nommen, 445 A'A'diel

Marcella lined up three crystal goblets on the Stallion's bar while the owner opened a dusty green bottle. "Don't skimp! This lot is as generous as they are thirsty, and I intend to test their limits."

"Generous, are they?" Doshmaan's dark eyes twinkled as the deep purple wine trickled into the delicate glasses. "I think you will sleep well tonight."

The late-night hostess yawned and rested her arms on the rail. "My feet cannot wait for this night to end."

A dusky-skinned Ellaian woman with a wild mane of jet black curls crept behind the innkeeper. She exchanged conspiratorial winks with the serving girl as the unsuspecting man placed the wine glasses on a tray. The waitress' bemusement bloomed into laughter when the stealthy woman slid her hand down the back of Doshmaan's loose silk pants.

Doshmaan did not turn around. He handed the platter to Marcella and sent her on her way with a nudge of his goatee. Once the girl departed, Doshmaan half-turned his head to his bartender and whispered with theatrical loudness. "Croy, have I warned you about my wives? They cannot resist grabbing a perfect bum."

The woman squeezed a handful of his rump. "Truer words were never spoken!"

Croy shook his head and laughed. "Leave me out of this, you two. I am busy enough with this ravenous horde."

Doshmaan cocked his hips, driving his backside deeper into the woman's grasp. "Myrri, *m'ne sheh'durry*, how I adore you."

Myrena pulled her hand free then playfully smacked Doshmaan's ass. Her eyes gleamed with mischievous intent. "I need to speak with you about the ledgers."

"Ah, yes, I had forgotten you wished to review our finances." The innkeeper brushed back his hair and turned to face his wife. He gazed at her as though for the first time. Her bronze skin, full lips, and alluring blue eyes proudly proclaimed her Ellaian ancestry. Myrena was the mirror image of Myrsi, her twin sister.

Lost in his beloved's sapphire eyes, Doshmaan recalled his grandfather's tales of the bewitchments of Ellaian women. "Baba'ga warned me—"

"Yes, yes. Don't look those daevil girls in the eyes, my boy, or you will sell your soul for a single kiss," she mocked. "Despite his warnings, you went and seduced two Ellaian women—sisters no less!"

Doshmaan loosed a winsome sigh. "My wives are the two most wonderful and beautiful women in all Laremlis."

"That golden tongue of yours is matched only by your wicked mind."

"You mentioned something about our books?"

"Yes. In the office—now." Myrena grabbed her husband by the hand and pulled him away from the bar and into the bustling kitchen.

The scullery harkened back to ancient Chaia. Rings of mortared stone hemmed in mounds of embers upon which rested iron grilling grates heaped with sizzling, smoking meats. In the back corner, a cauldron bubbled and steamed. The aroma of pungent spices filled the air amid the din of shouted orders while a half dozen cooks scurried about in the chaos of the dinner rush.

Doshmaan and his wife ignored the knowing glances and lurid comments among the staff as they disappeared between a row of supply cabinets. Obscured from view by shelves stuffed with crates of vegetables, smoked chops, and netted cheeses, Myrena drew the Chaian into an embrace. "I need you, *m'ne shehdur*. I need you now." The seductress devoured him with insatiate kisses and pressed her hips against his groin.

Doshmaan returned his wife's passion with equal enthusiasm. He stroked and grasped her soft curves while stumbling toward the door of the back room.

Myrena moaned as Doshmaan fumbled with the doorknob. When the door popped open, they tumbled into the cramped storage room that doubled as the inn's office. Myrena tugged her husband's shirt free to reveal his muscular burnished flesh.

Consumed with desire, Doshmaan kicked the door shut. He slipped his hands under his wife's blouse but froze when a man's voice interrupted the tryst.

"I hate to be hair in your pudding, but why have you let my room to a pair of seamstresses?"

Myrena smoothed down her shirt. She rolled free of her husband and ran a quick hand through her hair.

A brilliant smile split Doshmaan's face as he faced the intruder. "Jars, welcome back!"

Jarle tapped his fingers against the edge of the desk. "Why don't you speak louder? I don't think the guards can quite hear you up on Firehill."

Doshmaan's voice dropped to an excited whisper as he adjusted his pants. "Forgive my exuberance, old friend. It is good to see you."

"You gave away my room, old friend."

Doshmaan flipped his palms upward and spread his arms. "What was I to do? We experienced an infestation of inquisitive rats after you disappeared."

"Rats, eh?" Jarle narrowed his eyes. "How did Fhaen discover my apartment?"

"Come now, Jarle, if she didn't know you lived here, she suspected as much." The Chaian lowered his hands. "The Vise wasn't dead a day before your friends Golias and Ianto showed up and tore the place up looking for you."

Jarle slipped back his hood, revealing a dour expression. "Those drunk-rolling, back-alley thugs are no friends of mine."

"Of course not. I meant no disrespect." Doshmaan's smile wavered. His lips flattened to a thin line of concern. "You do remember who your real friends are, yes?"

"I thought I did until I found the lock on my door changed and all my things missing." Jarle rose from the chair and walked around to lean on the desk with folded arms. "Where are my belongings?"

Myrena pushed past her husband. "Jars Jadien! How dare you doubt our friendship!"

"*M'ne sheh'durry*, let me—" A glare from his wife silenced Doshmaan.

The raven-haired woman eyed Jarle with a venomous stare. "After you killed the Vise and stole his daughter away to Daugga knows where we were left to face the storm that followed. Are you aware of how much trouble you caused us?" Myrena shot her finger at the silent thief as she continued her tirade. "The entire city knows that you and that cock-brained Irilio spend your evenings drinking here. Everyone questioned us—the justiciars, the Ca'Dezer, and the Mistress' rats. For weeks, no one would dare come to the Stallion for fear of being accosted. What balls you have to come into our home and infer that we are not your friends—especially since we covered for you and safeguarded your things. To the River of Dust with you, Jarle Jadien. You are the one who is no friend."

"Myrena, enough." Doshmaan wrapped his arms around his angry wife. He whispered into her ear, mellow and soothing, "Enough."

"I didn't assassinate Tan'os," Jarle said.

"I know, Jars"—Doshmaan smiled over his wife's shoulder—"and so does Myrena. We are aware you are no assassin, but you must understand, the whole ordeal was rough on us. The Stallion was closed by royal order and under investigation for two weeks. The day we reopened, we did so with guards posted at our doors. You can imagine how our business was affected, but if fortunes continue to improve, we shall recoup our losses. As for your belongings, they are safe."

Doshmaan released his wife with a quick kiss on her cheek. He stepped past Jarle to the wall at the back of the office and slid open a section of paneling to reveal a hidden closet. Doshmaan yanked a massive ironbound chest out of the storage space and pushed it with his foot in front of Jarle. He patted the lid with a smile. "Here is your lockbox. As soon as we heard you had been accused of killing the Vise, I went to your rooms and removed everything."

Myrena's expression softened. "Your obscene painting is safe too. Nemserati graces our bedroom wall—for inspiration."

Jarle smiled. "You three don't need inspiration in that particular room—or any room for that matter."

Myrena relaxed and nodded. "Truth, indeed."

Doshmaan pulled another crate from the compartment. "This is the rest—clothing, toiletries, and everything else. I changed the lock before the justiciars arrived and rented the room to the Parron sisters."

Jarle placed his foot on top of the chest. "I should have known you would not betray me. Thank you, Dosh, you too, Myrena."

"It is nothing, old friend." Doshmaan gave Jarle a fierce hug. "I am overjoyed you are alive."

"As am I. Please forgive my accusations." Jarle returned the embrace with equal intensity. He broke off from the innkeeper to accept a warm, welcoming hug from Myrena. "Life has not been easy for me, either. Most days, I wonder if the gods favor or despise me."

"You are forgiven. By us, at least." Myrena released Jarle to look at him, her cobalt eyes intense with concern. "Placards bearing your likeness are posted all over Reyza, offering a fortune in sequins for your handsome ass—dead or alive. However, the Mistress promises to pay double the official reward if you are brought to her instead. She intends to make an example out of you for acting without her blessing."

Jarle pursed his lips and nodded. "Why am I not surprised? I am sorry that you suffered on my behalf."

"We Chaians are resilient—unconquerable even," boasted Doshmaan.

"Full of the desert wind, he means." Myrena's features softened. "I am glad to see you, Jars. We all missed you."

Jarle arched an eyebrow. "You scared me a moment ago."

"No, I didn't. No woman ever frightened you, or Irilio." At the mention of the bard's name, Myrena's mirth evaporated.

"Irilio, how is he?" Jarle asked.

Doshmaan laid a hand upon Jarle's shoulder. "He was apprehended yesterday."

Jarle paled. "Why?"

"Jars, this is not about you or the Vise. They questioned him regarding your acquaintance weeks ago, of course, but he played with his inquisitors until they tired of having their wits insulted. I am sure they suspected he knew something but didn't press him too hard because of his father's influence.

"So why was he arrested, Dosh?"

The Chaian tightened his grip on Jarle's shoulder. "Irilio is accused of attempted assassination. The rumor is he tried to poison Jarle Rigo at the banquet last night."

Jarle slammed his palms on the desk. "Thrask shit! Irilio has broken a few hearts, but he's incapable of murder."

"We know it is a mistake," Doshmaan paused, "or worse."

Jarle's features sharpened with anger. "A setup?"

"Irilio and Eloisse Gheneveve were lovers. They rented rooms here often enough. Considering the throng of cuckolded husbands Irilio left in his wake; I'm surprised he survived thirty seasons. The scorpions at court are as vicious as the rats in the Tangles."

"When is his trial?"

"There will be no trial. Rigo has condemned the poet to the dungeons, Ghaddo have mercy on his soul."

Jarle's head snapped up, and his body tensed. "They can't kill him if they don't have him."

Doshmaan shook his head. "Consider your actions carefully. I understand your impulse to help him, but Caz'd'Reyza is nigh impregnable—the prison even more so. Irilio will be in the deepest, most secure cell. The palace is swarming with Ambassador Akkalon's thrice-damned Durauk Guard. That fiend's tongue is so far up His Royal Highness' ass, Rigo sings like a Dessian songbird. A rescue with even the slimmest chance of success will take more days to prepare than Irilio has left. While I cannot say it is hopeless, there is no gambler desperate or degenerate enough to wager on those odds. I fear Irilio may have bedded his last conquest."

"Bel's hairy balls! The gods are bastards." Jarle gritted his teeth, closed his eyes, and ran a hand through his hair. "Fuck!"

Doshmaan cocked his head, "Jars, leave Irilio's defense to his father. I am sure he will muster all resources to save his heir. The longer you stay in Reyza, the shorter your lifespan. In a day or so, the fleet will depart for Thromm. Everything will settle down now that the girl has reappeared."

Jarle met his friend's eyes. "What girl?"

"Avaren Ensther!"

"What!?"

Doshmaan nodded. "She was discovered two days ago and taken to the palace."

"Discovered? Where? Tell me everything."

"A Ca'Dezer officer found her wounded and wandering in the rain near the Thrommish Embassy."

Jarle's face contorted with confusion and shock. "What you are telling me cannot be true—makes no sense at all."

The intensity of Jarle's reaction shocked Doshmaan. "Yes, the wag-tongues say she was bleeding and near death when she reached the infirmary. They say she was hurt escaping from you. Is that true?"

Myrena glanced at her husband then back to Jarle. "You did not abduct her?"

"No. Yes. It's complicated." Jarle closed his eyes.

Doshmaan knitted his brow and remained silent.

"Fuck!" Jarle slammed the heel of his fist on the desk. "Of course, she didn't wait!"

Myrena crossed her arms. "You were together all this time?"

Jarle dropped down and tinkered with the padlock on his chest. He pulled out his spare armor and bandolier and heaped pieces of black leather armor on the floor. He kicked off his boots and cast off the filthy marauder's jerkin.

The couple watched in stunned silence as their friend withdrew a bag of coins from his pocket and dropped it beside the open chest. When Jarle turned away and peeled off his torn breeches, Doshmaan nudged his wife and darted his eyes toward the office door.

Myrena wrinkled her nose as she gathered the discarded gear.

"I will fetch some water and a towel."

The thief stripped his undergarments. "No time."

Myrena dumped the soiled armor in the hidden compartment and stormed past the two men. "Make time. You smell like a dead animal."

"She is right, my friend. You stink like a sun-fermented corpse." The moment the door shut behind his wife, the Chaian crossed his arms and squared up to Jarle. "Spill it."

"You are in enough peril already."

Doshmaan's warm brown eyes flashed. "I am waiting."

Jarle sighed and leaned back on the desk, "I didn't kidnap Avaren, Dosh, but in my desperation to save her from the assassins sent to kill her father, I may have twisted her arm a bit."

"Finally—a story that makes sense. We never believed the rapist yarn the palace spun." Doshmaan grinned. When Jarle did not return the smile, his visage darkened. "What happened?"

Jarle shook his head. "You wouldn't believe me if I told you."

"Try me."

"I fell in love."

Doshmaan's mouth fell open. "Only Irilio matches your ability to break hearts like a cook breaks eggs for omelets. In a thousand years, I never expected to hear those words from your mouth."

"Nonetheless—it's true. I love Avaren."

"And she?"

Jarle opened his arms. "Could you resist this body?"

The dusky-skinned man didn't answer. He tugged at his whiskers and paced. "If I had to guess, you hid somewhere while you waited for the firestorm to settle. Thrust together by unfortunate events, you and the noble girl found common ground, but—"

"What, Dosh?"

"The gossips say she was raving like a lunatic when they found her roaming the embassy grounds."

"She may be a lot of things, but she is not insane!" Jarle's brow creased. "The palace is likely spreading this rumor to discredit her. The last thing Rigo wants is for Avaren to divulge the details of her father's murder as such information would incriminate him."

"These are dark times." Doshmaan leaned on the desk next

to Jarle. "With the Vise no longer an obstacle, the Dessian openly exerts influence. The Council does nothing to oppose Rigo's new advisor, which bodes ill for our homelands. Chaia and Ellaia will fall under Dessian occupation if Akkalon negotiates a new trade route. But enough politics. How can I help you, my friend?"

Jarle rubbed his forehead. "I need to book passage on a ship and do so quietly."

"There is only one man who can arrange such a miracle during a blockade—the Golden Snake."

"Is there no one else?" Jarle's shoulders drooped enough to warrant a sympathetic clap on the back from his friend.

"The Lord Justiciar is on a crusade to destroy the guilds. Since the Vise's death, dozens have succumbed to the wheel. Many rats languish in the dungeons, and the black-market dealers fear raids. The only broker still in business aside from the Mistress of Rats is the cunning Snake."

The door handle jiggled, capturing the men's attention. Jarle covered his privates while Doshmaan moved away from the desk.

The door opened to reveal Myrena carrying a pail of steaming water and some towels. She rolled her eyes at them. "Get the door, you fool."

Doshmaan closed the door behind her while Myrena placed the bucket and towel on the floor. "I brought some soap too."

"Thank you, Myrena," Jarle faced the wall, so only his backside was exposed.

Myrena kissed her husband, then stood back as the thief bathed. Her eyes followed the slow trickle of water as it curved over the man's muscular shoulders and down the valley of his spine. A little frown graced her lips when Doshmaan pulled her away to relate what he had learned in the tongue of the nomads.

Jarle scrubbed away the grime with rapid strokes of the thick cloth. When he finished, he dried himself and began to don his armor.

Myrena giggled as her husband concluded his briefing. "So, Jars Jadien, thief of hearts, went and fell in love? The prophets were right; the world is indeed coming to an end."

"This isn't a jest, Myrena." Jarle squatted down and wrung out the towel. He swished it on the floor to sop up the filthy water.

Myrena snatched the towel from Jarle's grasp. "You don't have time for that. How can we help?"

Jarle strapped on his weapon belt. "You have both done enough. I appreciate it, but I fear this may be goodbye."

Doshmaan smiled without mirth. "You are going after her, aren't you?"

Jarle gripped the handles of his daggers and nodded. "I have a promise to fulfill."

The Chaian strode past his friend and reached up to the top of one of the shelves. He pulled down a crock and set it on the desk. When he lifted the cover, the office filled with the sour aroma of *lugha*, a Chaian liquor of fermented mare's milk, and other unsavory ingredients.

"If you think I am going to share that with you, think again. I love you, Dosh, but there are limits."

Doshmaan ignored the jibe, rolled up his sleeves, and inserted his hand into the opaque fluid. He fished out a smaller jar, sealed with wax. After quickly wiping the foul-smelling residue from his arm and the container, the innkeeper slid a thin-bladed dagger from his boot and cut the wax from the lid. Only then did he look into Myrena's eyes. Cheered by her nod of approval, Doshmaan handed the opened pot to Jarle. "If this is goodbye, please accept a parting gift."

Jarle shook his head, "No, I can't! You said it yourself; you are barely staying in business."

"To refuse a gift from a friend is to deny friendship." Doshmaan pressed the jar into Jarle's hands.

"I am not one to take gifts without reciprocating."

"Oh, but you already gave us a magnificent gift, or have you forgotten?" Myrena said, a saucy smirk dancing on her lips.

Jarle's eyes widened. "Aye, the masterwork by Vartan! The day you wish for a life of leisure, take the painting to the Grinding Wheel, and speak to Lyssandra. She can find a buyer."

"That filthy canvas will be the death of me," huffed Doshmaan.

Jarle added the sequins in the ceramic jar to his money pouch. "You are the best friends a man could ever want."

The couple took turns embracing him. "Until we meet again," Doshmaan said.

Jarle nodded. "Please say goodbye to Myrsi and Marcella for me."

"We will. When you rescue that girl of yours, ask her to marry you. I have just the wedding gift."

Myrena jabbed her husband in the ribs. "That painting isn't going anywhere."

Jarle shoved the money bag into his pocket and wrapped his fingers around a handheld crossbow. "I will, but first I must speak to a man about a boat."

GHOSTS

Venedi, Third of Nommen, 445 A'A'diel

Eva's black dress snaked behind her as she climbed the marble staircase to the upper floors of the palace. Beside her, clad in scale armor worthy of Thromm's fiercest champions, walked Gøran. The captain's leaden steps drowned the silken rustle of the woman's skirts. Two royal footmen, whose mannered graces rivaled their comeliness, led the Thrommish entourage.

Behind Eva and Gøran, six Thyran warriors followed. Their wary eyes scanned the wrapped faces and kohl-lined eyes of the Durauks stationed along the winding stair.

Eva's gaze deviated from the backsides of the young escorts and darted to Gøran. "Why do you suppose Deneven D'Neir insisted on an appointment at such a late hour? I thought I made myself quite plain when I ended his employment. Truly, I am in no mood to listen to tiresome apologies."

Gøran placed a respectful hand on Eva's lower back and leaned in close. "The Dragon is like a bloodthirsty wolf when pursuing a case. News of Lady Avaren's reappearance must have reached his ears by now. Perhaps he wishes to provide information on this development."

"Fine. When we return to the ambassador's house, dispatch a

runner, and inform him a meeting is agreeable."

"As you wish, Marchess."

Eva shot a glance to one of the Durauks, lingering for a moment on the curve of the leather breastplate. "Tell me, Captain, do you believe the rumors about the Dessian elite guard? Can they truly all be female?"

Gøran eyed the closest sentry. "This one certainly is."

"I am told they are formidable warriors. I imagine a man must feel a great deal of humiliation when bested by a woman."

Gøran winked at the Durauk as he passed her, but the action went unacknowledged. The soldier continued to stare straight ahead. "I'm not sure. I think some men might find defeat in the hands of a woman delightful."

Eva cocked her head. "Yes, I suppose you are right. There are only two types of people in this world, the conquerors and the conquered. Sadly, my gender often falls prey to the latter."

Gøran sighed. "Why do you enjoy philosophical absolutes so much? You are stronger than most men and wield the naval power of Northern Fleet. I dare say there isn't a single meek bone in your body."

"You are too bold." Eva sniffed in mock indignation. "To insinuate that you are familiar with my bones or my body is quite unbecoming, Captain Rarikian. I shall forgive you only because I am aware of how you spend your days and nights—eating foul meals and partaking in the vulgar roughness of the sea."

Gøran bowed his head. "Apologies for my crassness, my liege."

"Proper loyalty never requires forgiveness." Eva grasped her skirts and quickened her pace, moving up the stair past the captain.

The escorts hurried to stay ahead of their charge. The party climbed to the third floor, where the royal apartments stretched along an open colonnade that faced the harbor, then veered down a corridor with resplendent floors tiled with aquamarine mosaics. In the candlelight, the arcade glowed a rich amber. The warm tones of the columns complimented the dark cliffs and the indigo expanse of the ocean. The salty scent of the sea and the aroma of larqbark incense reminded Eva of her childhood. Growing up, she had played hide-and-seek in the southern wing.

The valets led the entourage through a series of corridors

before ushering them into a sparse antechamber furnished with low settees arranged around a table.

Eva's brows knitted at the sight of the azure double doors on the far side of the room. Her mother once occupied the cluster of chambers past the blue portal during the last year of her life. "I abhor my brother's sense of drama," Eva said loud enough for all to hear.

Unabated, the footmen bowed and opened the grand doors that led to the apartments. The taller of the two spoke, "His Royal Highness, Jarle Rigo Iarris, awaits."

Gøran peered into the darkness beyond the entrance with a concerned expression. "Allow me to accompany you, Marchess."

Eva raised her hand. "I must go alone. If I am not back in a quarter bell, follow my orders."

"As you command."

Eva didn't need an escort to navigate the audience chamber past the vestibule. She moved through the hall like a ghost, only vaguely aware of the changes the rooms had undergone since her mother's death. Her footsteps resounded in the candlelit gloom as she drew ever closer to the shadowy door at the end of the windowless chamber. Her skin crawled with the discomfort of memory, and her chest ached with injustice. The shadows deepened and swelled with echoes of her childhood grief.

Convinced that if she paused, she would turn and run, Eva kept walking. Her trembling legs carried her through to the former Jarleina's dressing room, where the air smelled stale and musty. Two oil sconces illuminated the ivory-colored dust cloths covering the tables, mirrors, and vanities. Only her mother's favorite chair, unmoved from its place near the hearth, remained uncovered. A thick film of dust dulled every exposed surface except for a tract of polished marble that ended at the doorway of the last place she ever intended revisiting—her mother's bedroom.

On the other side of the open door, a figure paced back and forth before her mother's curtained bed. Eva gritted her teeth and clenched her fists as the urge to flee intensified. Fear choked her throat as she entered the room and faced her worst nightmare.

A pillar candelabrum with five arms provided illumination. The room appeared as Eva remembered it save for the bedcurtains.

Her mother had always preferred purple and gold and had insisted on sheer embroidered bolts from A'diel. Solid black curtains without ornamentation presently concealed the interior of the bed. The bedchamber resembled a crypt.

Rigo approached his sister and bowed. "Dear Sister, how kind of you to answer my summons. Please forgive the secrecy and the dust. I did not wish to involve servants until we had an opportunity to talk. Wagging tongues can be rather insensitive."

"Where is Avaren Ensther?" Eva said, her tone reserved.

"So direct," Rigo scolded. He escorted her to a pair of armchairs. "Please, sit. We have some matters to discuss."

Eva sat and folded her hands on her lap. "I am listening."

Oblivious to the chill and the dingy darkness, Rigo crossed his legs and relaxed into the chair. "As you know, Mejtress Ensther and I are betrothed. Our marriage was scheduled to take place a few days after the unfortunate sacking of Ca'd'Cel. The abduction of my bride has occupied every waking moment with indescribable worry." Rigo bent forward and clasped his hands. "Sister, you must believe me when I tell you that, contrary to what you may have heard, I am very much in love with Tan'os' daughter. Now that we are reunited, I cannot bear to part with her once more. If you decide to take her back to Thromm, I will respect your decision, but I implore you to consider the diplomatic relations of our nations."

Eva fixed her gaze on her brother. Rigo wore an elegant doublet of crushed blue velvet with black piping and cream-colored hose. "Brother, I will ask again, where is my sister-in-law?"

"There is more to this matter than my feelings, of course," Rigo continued. "When my cavalrymen found her, she was not well. We must consider her safety."

"I am not interested in your games," clipped Eva.

Rigo sighed with exasperation. "To be blunt, the court physician believes Avaren was violated—repeatedly. The suffering she undoubtedly endured has fractured her mind. In short, she is raving mad."

Eva straightened on the chair. "Go on."

"Reyza is in crisis—ravaged by the Three Sisters, shaken to the core by brutal murders, and blockaded by your fleet. I do not exaggerate when I say that the last few months have been the most trying of my life. The people need something good to raise their spirits. What can be better than a happy ending?" Rigo's voice grew calm and steady. "I intend to fulfill my promise to marry Avaren in spite of her condition. I believe there is a way to salvage some hope from all this by way of an heir."

Eva's jaw twitched. "What are you proposing?"

Rigo looked into his sister's eyes with a steady, even gaze. "Let us talk candidly—not as jousting siblings but as two rulers concerned for the future of our lands. Avaren Ensther is the sister of the Strommarch of Thyra, ruler of the largest and most profitable province of Thromm. She is a princess and heiress and shares the status of your husband's station. If you bring her to Thromm, you risk undermining the authority of your sons."

In a swirl of black skirts, Eva rose from her chair and walked away to hide her disgust. "What do you care about hope and love, Rigo? You fete while your people drown. Why should I trust you? How do I know Avaren hasn't been mistreated by that despicable Dessian you so flagrantly indulge or by your men?"

"You don't, Eva. In all such things, the truth is unknowable; it is as fickle and as ungraspable as the wind. I doubt any of my assurances will win your favor, so let us focus on practicality instead."

Eva turned and faced the bed, dreading whatever sight lay beyond the black curtains. Phantasms of her screaming mother plagued her mind. A chill ran down her spine. "Let me see her."

Rigo stood and approached the bed. He gripped the curtains and slid them open without overture.

For a moment, Eva wasn't sure if she was looking at a ghost or a flesh-and-blood woman. Avaren Ensther reclined on a tower of upholstered pillows. She wore a sleeveless, white lace gown that matched the pallor of her skin and hair. Her bare arms rested on her belly, and her head listed sideways. The girl's opalescent eyes flashed and shifted from one side of the room to the other as though following the flight of an invisible bird. When her lips parted, a trickle of moisture trailed down her chin.

Rigo withdrew a lacy handkerchief and dabbed the dribbled saliva from the girl's gaping mouth. "Even in this pitiable state, she is beautiful."

Eva neared the bed and took Avaren's hand in hers. The contact allowed the young woman's life energy to seep into her consciousness. Avaren's mind felt distant and muted—trapped in a fog that threatened to consume her. "Is she drugged?" she asked, knowing the answer.

Rigo caressed Avaren's hair. "She has been medicated to prevent self-harm. We found her clad in men's clothing, acting like a rabid beast. She assaulted several soldiers and wounded two before they shot her with a crossbow bolt. It was dark; my guards had no way of knowing they were being attacked by a woman, least of all, Lady Ensther. Upon capture, she experienced convulsions that put her in a delirious state. My physicians theorize that severe trauma and stress can cause the falling sickness. In truth, we do not know what is wrong with her. She has not uttered a sensible word since she opened her eyes."

Eva released Avaren's hand and let it fall limp. She possessed the power to rescue Avaren from Rigo's clutches and restore her health, but what then? The girl was a Thyran Marchette with the same authority as her husband and endowed with a legendary countenance. Even without her virtue, she would attract an ambitious Blackspur Skül. She paced away from the bed and stood before a wall mirror. She didn't recognize the icy eyes staring back at her. "With beauty such as hers, it would be a simple task to find her a suitor."

"Yes, but I doubt her brother would accept an offer from some backwater chieftain looking to improve his position. I don't presume to know your husband, Eva, but Strommarch Rhiess strikes me as the sort of man who values family above all else. He will not allow his sister to languish in obscurity after all she has endured. I suspect he will dote on her and insist she stay in Thyra. Regardless, as Rhiess' successor, I doubt she will be mending your dresses or drawing your baths."

The barb ignited Eva's cheeks. She pressed her palms against her midriff and silently cursed the tight laces of her bodice. She took a few steps toward the door and paused, her mind roiling in a vortex of thoughts. Rigo was lying about his intentions, but she could not refute his logic. The idea of her authority undermined by the offspring of a man she loathed offended her. Her sudden rage brought an awful realization; she was not beyond giving Avaren Ensther a taste of the wrongs Tan'os Ensther had visited upon her mother. Dooming her felt like justice.

"Sister?"

Eva braced her shoulders and lifted her chin. She wrung her clammy hands and stood unmoving, refusing to face her half-brother. Her words were cold and measured. "Strommarch Rhiess is a wonderful husband and father. My stay in Reyza has delayed our reunion long enough. You have demonstrated that Mejtress Ensther is receiving proper care from your physicians. I see no reason to tear her from your loving arms and force her to endure a perilous voyage that may aggravate her affliction. I grant you your wish, Rigo. In honor of Tan'os Ensther, I hope your union will solidify the goodwill that exists between our people."

Rigo closed the bedcurtains. "I admire your wisdom, dear Sister."

Eva nodded. "Lastly, you can expect a replacement for Ambassador Ers from Blackspur in a few months. Ers wishes to return home and will sail with us."

"I look forward to engaging with his successor," said Rigo.

Without further words, Eva walked away from her brother, her memories, and the oppressive darkness of Reyza. Her footsteps sounded as bleak as a funeral drum.

THE SNAKE'S DEN

Venedi, Third of Nommen, 445 A'A'diel

On the southern fringe of Reyza where the tenements of the Tangles butted up against dockside warehouses, five streets converged at a circular intersection. In the center of the junction stood a villa of awkward dimensions, the result of merging three shops into a unified structure. In a heroic attempt to forge cohesion, the proprietor spared no expense during a lengthy renovation, which added columns, verandas, and trim. The sides of the building were painted the deep yellow hue of summer roses, while the carved floral frieze was plated in copper. The monstrosity stood out in garish contrast to the gray, rain-stained tenements. The owner, Leoros Hroka, dubbed the complex Cos'd'Nala, the Snake's Den, but the locals referred to it by a more colorful appellation: Caz'd'Huisca, the Palace of Piss.

Muck, debris, dead fish, and noisome remnants of the receding tide choked the narrow streets surrounding the estate, but Cos'd'Nala survived the tidal surge intact. Protected by a thick ring of mortared bricks around its base, the villa proved impervious to the tides. Perched on the villa's parapets and balconies, guards armored in maille and matching yellow tunics stood vigil.

In the master bedroom on the topmost floor, Leoros lay

sprawled on a round bed ample enough for six people. Discarded goblets and empty wine bottles littered the crimson carpet around the bed along with platters of fruit and half-eaten pastries. Leoros snored softly with one arm draped across the thigh of his sleeping lover. The slumbering broker scratched the swell of his belly and turned to his side, pulling the blue, crinkled-crepe sheets around his body.

The plump man dreamt of a lush forest. He smiled in his sleep as he splashed with his companion in a clear stream in the noonday sun. Sunlight warmed his skin, and his ears filled with the melody of laughter and the lively burble of water. Slowly, the sound of rushing water morphed into the familiar, soft clinking of metal. The incongruity chased the smile from his face. With a yawn, Leoros stirred. He rubbed his bald head and leaned over the edge of the bed to poke among the bottles of wine.

When the metallic sound from his dream persisted, Leoros sat up and opened his eyes wide. A masked man dressed in black leathers stood at the foot of his bed. The stranger held a pouch in one hand and a crossbow in the other.

Tingles of fear chilled Leoros' blood as he stared at the glinting tip of the bolt aimed at his heart. "Please," he said, raising his hands in a placating gesture. "Don't hurt us."

The black-clad man gestured with the sack toward the doorway of the adjoining parlor, beckoning Leoros to move.

Assured by his lover's peaceful breaths, Leoros obeyed. He swung his legs from under the sheets and stood without making a sound. The muffled chink of coins piqued his curiosity enough to override his worst fears. If the masked housebreaker sought his death, he would have met his end in his sleep. The Golden Snake had not survived Reyza's turbulent underworld by letting his emotions trump his greed. He smelled business.

Middle-aged and hairless, Leoros Hroka was unremarkable in physique save for an intricate yellow and black tattoo of a serpent. The tail started on his left calf, snaked up his back, circled his shoulder and angled down over his belly to end at his penis, which formed the animal's head. The merchant snatched his red silk robe from the floor, knotted the belt loosely around his waist, and wound his way through the scattered remains of the feast.

Leoros followed the midnighter into the parlor and closed the door. In the pale moonlight streaming through the single arched window, the parlor's garish red hues transformed into deep purples. Two stuffed armchairs, upholstered in crimson velvet, flanked a golden-footed table topped with a slab of black marble. Opposite the window, crystal decanters, glasses, and barware crowded a long console. Two dead tree trunks formed an arch above the improvised bar. Wrapped around one of the leafless branches slept a muscular yellow python.

Seemingly oblivious to the armed stranger, Leoros paused by the tree and picked up the constrictor snake, "Hello, Sunshine. Sorry to wake you, my sweet." He coiled the docile reptile on his neck before retrieving an emberstem from the embersafe. He struck a light on the rough bark of the stump and lit an oil lamp. In the warm glow, the serpent's glossy black eyes contrasted with the daffodil-yellow of its scales.

After snuffing the emberstem in a tumbler half-filled with brandy, he eyed the intruder through narrowed eyes. "Drink?" When the man shook his head, Leoros grabbed a clean glass and shrugged. "Suit yourself."

The Golden Snake's fingers danced upon the polished hardwood of the console before he selected a thin bottle filled with amber liquid. He poured a generous portion into his glass and sipped. The bloom of warmth in his belly calmed his nerves. In a swallow, the unsettled Leoros Hroka transformed into the confident Golden Snake. "Sunshine, since I am still breathing, I assume our uninvited guest is here to discuss business and not to murder us."

The masked man's crossbow tracked Leoros as he walked over to the chair and sank into the soft cushions.

The broker took another sip and gestured to the empty seat across the table. "Please, let's be comfortable. Put away that awful weapon. Everyone knows I abhor violence. Threats unnerve me; anxiety only serves to complicate negotiations. You have my attention and my word that I will not summon the buffoons who steal my money by calling themselves guards."

The intruder removed the bolt and uncocked the crossbow before taking a seat.

Pleased with the stranger's change in mood, the Golden Snake lifted his pet to his face and spoke with a childish lilt. "Well, Sunshine, I am beginning to think our guest is mute. Unless he happens to be an exceptionally gifted mime, I suppose we shall divine his wishes."

"Passage out of Reyza," the man in leather said flatly.

Leoros set his glass down. "He speaks! Our mystery man breaks into our home in the night, threatens our lives, and offers us nothing but a small bag of coins in exchange for passage out of Reyza during a naval blockade! Sunshine, does this man not realize we are neck-deep in the alignment and teetering on the precipice of war? Has he not seen the Thrommish juggernauts choking the harbor?" Leoros nuzzled his snake. "Judging by our leather-clad friend's scary mask, his egregious lack of a proper appointment, and his aversion to parley, it appears our prospective employer requires both anonymity and secrecy."

A nod from the masked man prompted the Snake to continue. "A challenging and expensive proposition. Isn't that right, Sunshine? How fortunate for him, that is exactly the type of scheme in which I specialize." Leoros turned his gaze to the man seated across from him. "You will need a bigger sack if you want to command my attention—not to mention my aid."

The leather-clad man dropped the heavy pouch in his lap and pulled it open. He reached in with a gloved hand and withdrew a fistful of coins and jewels. The jangle of spilled currency on the marble surface echoed in the small room. In a fluid motion, Leoros lunged forward and caught a gold coin the moment it rolled off the edge of the table.

The fence reclined back in his chair and held the coin up to the light. "A Ferencian Rilkh in uncirculated condition." He tossed the gold piece over his shoulder and retrieved a thick lozenge of silver with embossed glyphs. "A Seh'nahiel trade bar, also pristine." He sorted through the rest of the treasure and stacked the coins with their peers as he named them. He examined the jewels and rings with the scrutiny of a lapidary appraising a fresh-cut diamond.

For the first time in memory, Leoros struggled to remain calm and detached in the presence of money. The scattered wealth doubled the amount he intended to demand at the opening of negotiations. Leoros weighed the silver ingot in his hand while he considered his mysterious guest.

"Fate smiles upon you, my silent friend. It just so happens I am well acquainted with the captain of the *Jiulia*, a Terranakan ship currently anchored in our harbor." The Golden Snake's eyes glinted as he twirled the bar between his fingers. "I am confident I can persuade Captain Haukon to accommodate one passenger."

"Three."

"Three?" Leoros set the trade barback on the pile and reclined into his seat. "Even if I owned the ship, this"—he nudged his chin toward the coins—"is not enough by half."

The stranger lobbed the entire sack on the table, scattering the carefully arranged piles. "Three."

The Snake snatched up the pouch with the directness of a viper striking a mouse and began to extract the contents. Foreign coins joined the heap, followed by sparkling gems and glittering pieces of jewelry. The thrill of avarice sent his heart racing. Wealth equivalent to half a year's profits crowded the tabletop, and the bag was still a quarter full. *Fuck her*, Leoros thought as he examined a ring with a diamond the size of a pea. What the Fate didn't know— hopefully—wouldn't hurt him.

"Listen carefully," Leoros said. "The ship sets sail when the first light of dawn touches the banners on Firehill at six bells. You must be prompt; the *Jiulia* waits for no one. Boarding will not be a problem if you and your fellows follow my instructions. On Savarass Road, between Masaga's Ropehouse and the rigging lofts, stands a green, unmarked warehouse. Go around to the blue door and knock in this sequence: two knocks, pause for two breaths, then four knocks. After two more breaths, two final hard knocks. Repeat it."

"Green warehouse, blue door. Two knocks, two breaths, four knocks, two breaths, two loud knocks."

"Good. Do not forget the order. My warehouse employees are far more disciplined than the idiots on my rooftop and will not grant entry to Sherzadeen herself unless you follow the pattern. I suggest you arrive by five bells, at the latest." Leoros continued to pull jewels from the bag. Each trinket proved a joyous revelation. "I caution you, many other travelers will be present; some of

Reyza's finest citizens seeking respite from the threat of war and the cold. You and your party will wait in a separate room, away from curious eyes." The dealer looked up, "When the time comes, your group will be smuggled aboard a covered cart and taken to the docks in cargo crates. From there, a dory will ferry you to the *Jiulia*. Once aboard, you will be escorted directly to a private cabin. Since you are a generous man, I will include supplies for you during the voyage. Deal?"

When the masked man did not respond, Leoros spoke to his pet. "Ah, Sunshine, our mysterious employer is a wary one. At this very moment, he is wondering whether I will betray him. Understandable concerns were he dealing with a flea-bitten scoundrel in some dingy hogwash." The broker met his guest's eyes. "You came to me because I am Leoros Hroka—the Golden Snake—the only person in this city who can help you. My word is my bond. Once we agree, I will fulfill our deal, as stated. My clients, legal and otherwise, recognize and rely on my integrity. I also happen to enjoy the respect my reputation provides, the freedom to travel any street without looking over my shoulder. One betrayal, no matter how profitable, would destroy everything I have worked so long to build." Leoros scooted to the edge of his chair. "Quiet passage for three out of Reyza aboard the *Jiulia*, tomorrow at dawn. I ask again, do we have an accord?"

The intruder rose to his feet, adjusted his armor, and nodded. "We do."

"Excellent! Once underway, Captain Haukon will provide you with your options for discreet disembarkation along his route. Officially he is sailing to Dar'bas by way of Stellae and the Crossroads, but his true destination is the port of Goizonne." Leoros returned his attention to emptying the bag. "I'm sure you can find your way out. Do not worry about disturbing my companion, with the amount of wine he drank; I doubt Jubbal's bulls could rouse him."

The masked man crossed the room to the door. He was about to leave when Leoros' polite cough interrupted his departure. "Before you go, there is one more matter to discuss."

When the intruder turned and faced him, Leoros held up a necklace between his fingers. A fire opal framed by two lavender jewels flared in the lamplight. "This is a magnificent piece, a true masterwork from a gifted jeweler." The Golden Snake's eyes did not leave the choker as he spoke. "Most people would be captivated by the opal pendant. Indeed, the gem is an exquisite specimen—look how it blazes. But the wonder of this piece is the pair of spectacular leadochrite trilliants that frame the focal point. Although pretty and difficult to procure, leadochrites are prosaic and lifeless when mounted alone. When cut by an exceptional lapidary and mounted with other jewels, their magnificence is unbound. There is but a single jeweler in Reyza with hands steady enough to release the brilliant magic of leadochrite to this degree. This artisan demands perfect specimens, strong in color, and completely devoid of inclusions. Dessian stones won't do. Leadochrite gems of this purity come from a single mine in Castan. As it happens, I am the sole importer of Castanian leadochrite."

Leoros locked gazes with the stranger. A thin smile spread on his lips. "I recognize these gemstones. They were specially ordered by Ba'Las Gordhiello to create his dowry gift to win the hand of Mejtress Avaren Ensther—a treasure that was stolen. I know this necklace, and I know you, Jarle 'Jars' Jadien. You of all people should grasp the value of these jewels—thief."

When the stranger didn't respond to the accusation, the Golden Snake held up the priceless necklace and studied it in the light. "Do not distress yourself, Majster Jadien. A deal is a deal, and I am a man of honor. I completely understand your desire for anonymity; however, I have business partners whose interests conflict with my own. Keeping such volatile information from one's peers can be damaging to trust—damage I am willing to sustain for proper compensation."

Jarle stood motionless. "How much?" he asked between clenched teeth.

"Well, you are a much sought-after man, desired by people with the ability to make my life short and painful should they discover I helped you. You are aware of the bounties on your head, are you not?"

Without a word, Jarle reached into one of his many pockets and withdrew the velvet sack he retrieved from his chest at the Stallion. He tossed the parcel on the table, where it burst open, spilling coins everywhere.

The Golden Snake bent down to scoop the riches from the carpet but stopped suddenly when the sharp edge of a dagger pressed against his jugular.

"My silence is golden!" Leoros squealed.

Jarle whispered into the broker's ear, "Break your word, and you will die—slowly. Fugitive or not, I have friends in this city— unforgiving friends. Understand?"

"Y-yes, of course!" Leoros swallowed. "We can only benefit from mutual silence."

The dagger did not move. "I gave you enough wealth to buy three ships, and you still try to wrangle more out of me?"

"You are risky business," Leoros said, instantly regretting his words.

"Are we done haggling?" Jarle growled.

"Your payment is acceptable. I will negotiate passage and grant you my eternal silence." When the pressure of the blade eased, Leoros exhaled and rubbed his throat. He watched Jarle cross the room. "Wait," he croaked.

Jarle spun around with such celerity that Leoros nearly screamed. The wide-eyed broker held up his hands. "I wish to offer compensation for my insult."

"No need."

"My network of contacts is useful for more than trading goods. If it were my mother, I would want the truth."

"What about my mother?" Jarle clipped.

"The justiciars arrested her. They took her to the dungeons for questioning. Officially she is being detained for aiding you." Leoros grimaced. "I am sorry to be the one to tell you this."

"Speak."

"They tortured her for information regarding your whereabouts. When they wrenched every last detail from her, Ambassador Akkalon ordered her execution."

Jarle clenched his fists. "How?"

"The sea caves. They fed your mother to the crabs."

Jarle let out a strangled sound and punched the door so hard he cracked a panel. The outburst frightened Leoros Hroka to the core. He wrapped his hands around his snake and closed his eyes, grateful when he heard the door to his parlor slam shut.

Dawn rose before Leoros mustered the nerve to finish his drink and indulge in his newfound wealth. Six bells and Jarle's departure from Reyza could not come soon enough.

WARRICK & SON

Venedi, Third of Nommen, 445 A'A'diel

The Warrick & Son Apothek formed the terminus of a dead-end street. Ivy covered the villa's crumbling façade and framed a cavernous entryway which housed a reinforced door. Above the portal, a rust-streaked oval sign of a mortar and pestle provided the only clue of the building's purpose.

Across from the shop, Jarle stood in the shadows. He held no illusions about the nature of his relationship with the alchemist. A quick and cordial transaction was hopeless. The man would betray him faster than a harlot spitting cum.

Warrick was a private man, averse to small talk and pleasantry. Jarle's curiosity on the matter of poisons and their antidotes had prompted occasional discourse, but never friendly banter.

Years ago, after an enthusiastic exchange regarding the effects of tree frog venom, the old man invited Jarle to his laboratory. The tour had been brief, but Jarle's memory of the premises remained vivid. The back of the first floor of Warrick's home housed work tables cluttered with glass tubes, bottles, alembics, and burners. Dozens of different-sized mortars and pestles occupied shelves stuffed with every curious appurtenance of the alchemical trade.

Questions had tumbled from his lips as he tried to comprehend the alchemist's methods for creating antidotes. Amused, or perhaps flattered, Warrick answered all the queries posed until the conversation turned to the subject of the laboratory's greenhouse. In an instant, Warrick transformed into a surly host. During his hasty departure, Jarle caught sight of Aldorf emerging from a nearby closet. One glance revealed racks of potions, salves, elixirs, and powders organized and labeled beyond the storeroom door.

The thief hoisted himself to the top of the decrepit wall and circled to the rear of the property. In the waning moonlight, the riotous tumble of foliage within the wall's perimeter appeared sinister. Leafy plants and twisting vines touched by the wilting hand of frost covered the grounds in mounding heaps, separated by meandering paths of crushed stone.

Overgrown planters and maroon-glazed urns planted with herbs bordered the walkways. The red, stippled leaves of dardensa warned of stubborn rashes while a row of aromatic rillweed scented the night breeze. A triple-tiered marble fountain dominated the center of the frost-bitten garden; its mossy, waterless basins brimmed with an assortment of jugs containing herbs in oil. At the far end of the yard, a rectangular iron and glass conservatory adjoined the house.

A few strides from the entrance, Jarle paused. He plucked a leaf from a shrub, rolled it into a tight bundle, and popped it into his mouth. As he chewed, he snapped off more leaves and tucked them into his belt pouch. Tingling warmth spread through his limbs and washed away his fatigue, but not his trepidation.

He wanted to believe his prickling nerves were the result of the energy-bestowing herb, but he knew otherwise. The poisons and creatures said to inhabit the conservatory terrified him.

Jarle gritted his teeth as he picked the lock and opened the door. Wet, warm air billowed out, redolent with the scent of decay. Pots and planters containing innumerable botanical specimens from around the world crammed the shelves of Warrick's greenhouse. Creeping vines hung down in tangles from suspended trellises in amorphous mounds. No space went unused, including the floor, where moldy-paned glass bins teeming with aquatic plants lay stowed beneath the countertops.

Jarle entered and closed the door behind him. Inside the

terrariums, shadowy shapes slithered and climbed, seeking escape from their dank prisons. Some enclosures contained pit vipers illegally imported from Xio-Bahnn. Others were choked with thick webs crawling with spiders and lesser-known venomous creatures. Scorpions and centipedes roamed over rotten logs while vibrantly colored tree frogs and bilious toads stared at him with enormous, golden eyes.

Beads of sweat broke on Jarle's brow as he crept through the humid hothouse. With each step, he fought nightmares of broken latches and escaped prisoners slithering among the vegetation. Less than a half dozen paces from the door to the laboratory, a heavy thump of meat on glass caused his heart to leap to his throat. Trapped in one of the boxes, a red and black-scaled snake lunged, mashing its square nose against the transparent barrier. Hissing and twisting, the hateful creature followed his movements with its slitted eyes as it banged the enclosure with malevolent zeal.

The thief's skin crawled, and his scalp tingled. His instincts screamed for him to flee. Shaken, he gripped the handles of his blades and hurried past the snake to the doorway leading to the villa. His hand shook as he reached for the lever, anxious to escape the nightmarish greenhouse.

Jarle froze when muffled voices came from the lab.

"Aldorf, stop fiddling with yourself and do what I told you," Warrick said. "Clean the instruments and restock the cart. Use only the freshest supplies. I want nothing to go wrong when we return."

"Yes, Paa, fresh herbs, new unguents, clean instruments. Wash, rinse, dry. Everything goes in its proper place. Just so, just so."

"Do not dally. We have but two bells before we are due back at the palace. I need to refresh her dose before eleven. It would not do for the girl to regain her wits at an inopportune moment. Our employers are not forgiving men."

Jarle's mind raced. He cracked the door and listened.

Aldorf shuffled some vials as he spoke. "Pretty lady, smooth skin, like milk. Not like Nana, not like Nana."

"Yes, my boy, she is a pretty one. If we hurry, we will have some time alone with her."

"Alone with Starborn lady?" Aldorf's tone held an edge of

worry. "I don't want to be alone, Paa, not alone."

"Boy, this is an opportunity. You cannot remain chaste forever."

Jarle's knuckles whitened on the door handle. He nearly burst into the room when Aldorf's cries froze him in place.

"No, Paa! Nooo! I belong to Nana—to Nana. I am her good, good boy!"

"Aldorf, calm down, of course, you are Nana's good boy. I am not talking about leaving you there." Warrick let out a frustrated huff. "Replenish the cart while I go upstairs to fetch some dinner."

"Yes, Paa, wash, rinse, dry, return. Everything must go in its rightful place. Just so, just so."

Jarle pushed the door a little wider and peered inside.

The old man trundled out of the laboratory and disappeared from view, leaving the boy to empty a cumbersome apothecary cart.

Jarle slid his daggers from their sheaths, slipped through the doorway, and soft-stepped between the crowded tables. As the apprentice bent down to rinse a beaker, Jarle snuck behind him and slammed the pommel of his dagger into his skull. The alchemist's son gasped and crumpled backward into the thief's waiting arms.

Jarle eased Aldorf to the ground and listened with the blade at his throat. Assured that the attack had gone undetected, he stepped over the unconscious youth and snuck into the storeroom.

The small room was an alchemical bonanza. Potions of every conceivable substance occupied floor-to-ceiling shelves. Jarle shook his head; the jars and bottles were consigned in nonsensical fashion despite the orderliness of their placement. Aldorf alone understood the logic of the assortment.

Jarle located his customary antidotes and restocked his bandolier. After a moment's deliberation, he grabbed a vial labeled bitter ogium. The substance acted as a muscle paralyzer and was not lethal in its own right, but could prove deadly if a wounded victim could not stop the flow of blood. He had long ago vowed never to use poison on his weapons, but desperate times called for extreme measures.

Jarle slipped the vial into a pocket and rummaged through the shelves for anything else of value. A solid green bottle on a high shelf drew his eye. He took it from its resting place and examined the inscription. Extract of Lirica was the only known cure for canensis poisoning. In all his years, he had never laid eyes on the legendary antidote. He thought it all but a myth.

For years the alchemist rebuffed his questions, claiming the formula was beyond his skills. Jarle rolled the container in his palm, watching the lamplight play on the metal. "Warrick, you lying pile of thrask shit!"

Where there was lirica, there was canensis oil, a painless, unstoppable poison that induced a slumber that deepened with time until the heart stilled forever. Jarle tucked the potion inside his jerkin and began rifling through the substances in search of the poisonous soporific. Upon finding the vial, he stashed it in his pocket opposite the lirica.

The thief continued to search the shelves until he found sweetsleep, an ordinary medicinal syrup used to calm nerves and induce sleep. He removed a flask from the back where a casual glance would fail to note its absence and closed the door. He returned to where Aldorf lay unconscious and dripped the sweetsleep elixir into the boy's slack mouth.

Aldorf instinctively swallowed. Soon his breaths grew deep, and his body relaxed. Jarle pocketed the empty vessel and wiped the creamy remnants of the sleeping potion from Aldorf's lips. Next, he withdrew the canensis oil, opened it, and poured most of it into a potted cactus. He smeared the few drops that remained on Aldorf's chin and placed the empty vial in Aldorf's hand. The substance smelled as bitter as he felt.

Satisfied with the tableau, Jarle hid behind one of the laboratory tables and waited.

Moments later, the hobbling alchemist appeared carrying a platter with bread, cheese, and fruit. "I hope you finished your chores, boy. I brought us something to eat." When the old man saw his son sprawled on the ground, he dropped the tray and scurried toward his son. The tinkle of the canensis vial tumbling from senseless fingers drew Warrick's gaze. He bent and sniffed the boy's mouth before a high, thin wail of despair filled the room. "Aldorf, what happened?" he wailed. "What have you done, my handsome, foolish boy?"

The frantic alchemist laid his son down and scrambled to his feet, knocking over several flasks in his urgency. He rushed to the storage room and flung the door open with a bang. "I will fix this!" he cried as his bony fingers scrabbled at the rows of vials. Bottles crashed to the floor as the geezer searched for the antidote. After a moment, Warrick stumbled out of the closet and tore at his wisps of graying hair. Tears streamed from his rheumy eyes.

Jarle emerged from the shadows and held up the green potion. "Looking for this?"

"You!?" The alchemist lunged at Jarle with a cry, hands grasping for the vial.

Jarle sidestepped the desperate attack and rewarded the old man with a cuff to the back of the head.

Warrick collapsed in a heap. He scuttled toward Jarle like a supplicant before a priest, "Please, Jars, please give me the antidote, don't kill my baby boy!"

Jarle kicked away the man's appealing hands. "In due time. Canensis oil takes a full day to end a life."

The cold anger in the thief's eyes sobered the old man into submission. "What do you want?"

"You are going to help me rescue Avaren Ensther."

Warrick paled. "Impossible!"

"Then, your son dies." Jarle walked toward the door.

"Wait!" Tears streamed from Warrick's eyes. "She is in Jarle Rigo's chambers, under heavy guard. How can I possibly help?"

Jarle stopped and turned around. "You and your son are due at Caz'd'Reyza in a few hours, to drug her, are you not?"

"Yes, but—"

"I will wear your son's cloak and hood. If you want your boy to live, you will convince the guards there is nothing amiss." When the old man began to protest, Jarle cut him off. "If you so much as think of betraying me, Aldorf will die. Aid me, and see him cured."

Warrick wiped the snots from his nose. "We will be crab food if they catch us!"

Jarle's voice was as hard as granite. "After you take me to her, your fate is your own. You can confess to Rigo's inquisitors and tell them I coerced you. If you doubt your ability to inspire compassion in Rigo, you might consider relocating to the jungle. The wilds are lovely this time of year."

The old man's shoulders drooped as he looked at his comatose son. "You are a cruel, heartless bastard."

Jarle gave the alchemist a shark's smile. "Looked in the mirror lately?"

Warrick crawled to his son's side. He stroked the sleeping boy's peaceful face before meeting Jarle's gaze. "Even if your ruse works, how will you sneak the girl past the guards?"

Jarle pointed to the large apothecary cart. "Those shelves come out, do they not?"

Warrick frowned in confusion, then nodded.

"Avaren can fit inside if carefully positioned."

Warrick's mouth flapped with incredulity. "You—you cannot be serious!"

"As serious as canensis poisoning. Unless you have a better idea, in which case I am listening."

When the alchemist failed to answer, Jarle grabbed Warrick by the collar and pulled him to his feet. He leaned in until he could smell the stink of the old man's breath and said in a reasonable mimicry of Aldorf's drawl, "My life is in your hands, Paa!"

Tears reappeared in the alchemist's eyes but did not spill down his cheeks. "You are mad!"

"Undoubtedly," Jarle said, shoving him against the worktable. "I suggest you concoct an antidote for whatever foulness you gave Avaren while I coat my blades in some of your finer wares. Hurry, time is wasting."

INTO THE CRUCIBLE

Venedi, Third of Nommen, 445 A'A'diel

As Jarle leaned his head on the paneled interior of the barouche that sped him and the alchemist to the palace, a crack of thunder rumbled from sea to mountainside. The thief shook from the sudden sound, twitchy with exhaustion. He wore Aldorf's clothes—a heavy woolen robe over a linen undershirt, and soft calfskin breeches—yet the damp cold of Reyza seeped in from all sides.

Jarle thought of his unfortunate mother, trapped in the bowels of the dungeon, crying and pleading to the gods as the waters rose, then of Avaren and Irilio. He rubbed his face with both hands, powerless against the anguish and hopelessness that threatened to bring him to tears. Warrick's confession left little doubt of Avaren's future should he fail to rescue her. Dark thoughts caused him to glare at the old man with murderous intent. The bastard was alive only by the grace of his skill to cure whatever malady he had inflicted on his lover.

Jarle leaned across the trunk and gripped the alchemist by the neck. "Betray my identity to the royal guard, and I swear by all that is holy that your son will not see another sunrise."

Warrick shook his head and spoke so low, the horses' clatter nearly drowned his voice. "The guards will surely search us. I doubt either of us will live till dawn. We are doomed."

"If you continue to stare at the box like it's caught fire, you will arouse suspicion!" Jarle squeezed the man's neck. "For your son's sake, get a hold of yourself."

"Aldorf walks with a sideways gait and stays behind me with our things," Warrick offered.

Jarle released him with a shove, then settled back into his seat. "I will do my part."

Outside, swift-moving clouds drenched the streets and the coach in a sudden violent downpour. Tree branches tossed in a wind that boded a tempest. Jarle grimaced when the cold breeze laden with the stench of seaweed, salt, and rotting things assaulted his nostrils. Curtains of pelting rain overflowed gutters. The weather was as miserable as his mood.

The carriage wound upwards through the many hairpin turns of Via Gabrillé, past shuttered shops, and deserted side streets. They passed shrines and niches where fleeing refugees prayed and made twelfth-hour offerings to the gods. Rats picked at what remained of soaked bread loaves and bowls of rice. Some covered candles still burned in the downpour.

Jarle crossed himself as they sped past the shrouded figure of Ven, the god of death and patron of Reyza. At the Circ of Muses where sister statues danced, forever bound in gaiety, the barouche emerged from claustrophobic street and merged with the broader avenue of Oldisseta. The hour was late, but souls yet wandered upwards away from the flooded port in search of mercy and warmth. People trudged along the cobbles with sacks on their backs, eyes downcast.

Oldisseta's rowhouses quartered the city's ragattieri—linen sellers, drapery vendors, flax workers, and tailors. The Ragattiers were a populous but lowly guild that had gained a footing in the Council in recent years. The shops' colorful signs swayed in the wind, each more embellished than the next.

With a crack of the whip, the coachman directed the horses seaward to merge on Via Elgabarr. Modest dwellings gave way to spacious villas surrounded by needle pines and wrought-iron gates that offered glimpses of the moonlit bay. The glittering waters had swelled beyond the docks, swallowing taverns, warehouses, and tenements. Flotsam jammed the streets of the Tangles, pushed inland by the tides. High above the floodwaters stood Caz'd'Reyza, its ramparts blazing with torchlit banners fit for a festival day.

Sickened by the contrast, Jarle turned away and closed his eyes, grateful for a moment's rest.

*
**

"You two, help the boy with that trunk—and be gentle, the ambassador is in one of his moods."

At the sound of the sergeant's voice, two dark-skinned guards dressed in palace livery emerged from the gatehouse and advanced to the parked carriage. Their breastplates shone in the torchlit courtyard as they clambered into the coach and began to fumble with the alchemical cart.

The middle-aged sergeant watched his men with a hint of amusement. "You arrive earlier than expected, Majster Warrick."

The alchemist rubbed his palms together. "Yes, well, you see, my boy realized that my calculations for the time needed to distill gru'danrice leaves with tincture of junari root were inaccurate, and when he brought it to my attention, I rushed back."

"I do not need to know your business. However, allow me to give you a word of advice; don't proclaim your errors. Failure doesn't bode well with our betters."

The color blanched from Warrick's face, and his eyes bulged. "I did not mean to imply that we did anything wrong. Not at all. My son and I, we are experts in our trade. Alchemy is a p-precise science, but not a perfect one." Warrick took a deep breath. "What I meant to say was, what I'm trying to explain, Majster Sergeant Gandas—sir—is that we have only the best intentions."

Jarle shifted his weight from one foot to the other and twitched his right arm. "Cold, Paa, cold," he complained in Aldorf's monotone drawl.

"We will be warm soon."

Behind them, one of the guards hoisting the pushcart lost his grip, causing the wheel to slam down on his toes. "Ven's balls," he yelped. "I thought you worked with herbs. What is in this thing, a bunch of boulders?"

The alchemist turned his head at the sound of rattling glass and frowned.

Jarle's movements grew agitated. "Yes, yes, fresh herbs, clean instruments. Wash, rinse, dry, return. Everything goes in its rightful place. Just so, just so."

Warrick slapped Jarle in the back of the head. "Quiet, boy."

The thief gritted his teeth and returned to swaying.

"Check the contents," ordered Gandas.

The injured guard threw the chest lid open.

"Please be careful," Warrick pleaded. "I have fragile instruments in there without which I cannot perform my duties."

"We are just doing our job. Are you carrying any weapons?"

The alchemist shook his head. "Ven, no, of course not!"

One of the guards held up two strange beakers and shrugged before putting the items back into the cart.

Sergeant Gandas drew up his cloak to counter a gust that blew up from the bluffs. He moved behind the alchemist and began to pat his voluminous robes in search of weapons. Warrick raised his arms to give the guard access to his sides.

"You are clear. Please advise your boy to be still so that I may frisk him."

The demand triggered a surge of adrenalin through Jarle's core. He continued the charade, his gaze locked on the cobbles.

"He is just an innocent. I assure you he is unarmed."

Gandas approached Jarle and grabbed hold of his arm. "I will judge for myself."

Jarle clenched and unclenched his fists. "Don't touch! Don't touch!" he raved until Warrick patted his back.

"You want to be warm, don't you?" Warrick asked.

"Yes, Paa," Jarle relaxed his hands. "Good to be warm."

"Then you must hold still so the kind sergeant can search you like he did earlier today."

"Yes, Paa. Still."

Sergeant Gandas gave a silent signal to his men. One of them wheeled the heavy cart toward the guardhouse; the other approached the barouche.

The sergeant patted down Jarle with cursory interest. Satisfied, he motioned for father and son to follow him. "Boij and Vandro will escort you to the first floor. At the head of the stairs, the Durauk will meet you. When she asks about the birds you will answer with the phrase, '*Taékkog al eéndrre shah nestee far.*'"

While the alchemist repeated the words, Jarle exhaled. They had conquered the first checkpoint.

Beyond the square gatehouse, the rear of the palace was as penumbral as a Cer'belian tomb. The squat windows that lined the vaulted passage were shuttered against the wind and secured with latches. Every fourth torch was lit, creating long stretches of darkness. Within the pools of flickering torchlight, soot-stained murals, conjured images of war and bloodshed. In panel after panel, footmen and cavalry clashed with savage fury.

Jarle shuffled next to Warrick; head bowed to conceal his features. In front of them, the guard named Boij dragged the wheeled trunk, whistling a bawdy tune as he went. He walked through the damp passage with the casual demeanor of someone strolling along the shore on a summer's eve. Vandro lagged several manlengths behind and locked doors as they passed.

Jarle winced at a painted panel of skewered, screaming men. The creak of a door and the jingle of keys grated his ears. The hallway felt like a trap. "It's dark, Paa. Dark! Why do we go to a dark place?" Jarle tugged on Warrick's sleeve.

Neither Boij nor Vandro reacted to the outburst.

The alchemist pinched Jarle's forearm. "We are almost there."

Boij paused before a grated door and stepped aside to let Vandro pass. The seasoned guard knocked; three, quick, flat-palmed taps, a long pause, then five knuckle taps.

The door grate opened to reveal a pair of solid black, kohl-rimmed eyes. "At evening, do the flocks fly downward, on extended wings?" The woman sounded stern; her words heavily accented.

Vandro looked at Boij, who looked at Warrick.

The old man approached and repeated the phrase given to him by Sergeant Gandas, "*Takkeeg al endroo she nest fa.*"

The exotic eyes lost their sharpness. Her tone sang with amusement. "Dessian does not agree upon your tongue."

"Humble apologies." Warrick fumbled with his hands.

The grate closed, and the latch lifted. As the door swung open,

Jarle was surprised to see a lone woman standing in the hall. She was short of stature and dressed in a series of dark leather wrappings that concealed the entirety of her body save for her outlined eyes. Short swords with curved blades, sharp and unsheathed, hung from each of her hips.

The Dessian rested her foot on the lip of an upside-down wooden bucket that doubled as a stepstool. She gripped the handles of her blades and sauntered past the guards. "Sergeant Gandas wishes to shame you," she said to Warrick. "The polite answer is, '*Takshah'al áendre shah'nest'i faeh,*' which means, intelligence without will is, a bird that never flaps."

The alchemist's cheeks reddened. Jarle didn't want to know what blunder the dotard had committed with his mangled response.

"Intelligence without willpower is a flightless bird," Vandro corrected.

"*Kai! Kai!* Flaaightless," the woman repeated.

Boij looked around. "You alone tonight, Mij?"

"Zuhaa took lantern to privy, will return in a short time."

Vandro motioned in the direction of the stairwell beyond the door. "Go. I will wait here until Zuhaa returns."

Mij's kohl-lined eyes rested on the trunk, then rose to meet Vandro's. "That is acceptable. Follow."

Jarle and Warrick fell into step behind the Dessian while Boij pulled the cart. The hallway turned right and opened to a staircase that led to the second floor.

At the base of the stairs, Mij paused. "You," she said, pointing at Jarle, "help Boij with box."

Jarle stepped to the other side of the guard, grabbed the handle, and lifted. Between the two of them, they hoisted the chest upstairs. Behind them, Warrick held the handrail and hobbled as fast as his knees allowed. "I'm too old for this," he groused.

On the second-floor, Boij and Jarle set the pushcart down. The young guard looked at the struggling old man and scoffed. "Thought you apothecaries concocted remedies for everything."

"Rejoice, boy," Warrick said, raising a bushy white eyebrow. "Today is the youngest you will ever be."

Boij threw him a sour look. "I can't believe people pay for

such thrask-shit."

The Dessian guard walked beside the alchemist, matching his pace. She took his elbow in her hand and helped him. "In Cartuj, my home, we respect wise old ones," she said.

Boij sneered. "In my country, we do not enslave orphan women and force them into military servitude."

"No, you do not," Mij clipped, "Instead, you make them slaves to your kitchens."

Boij opened his mouth to retort when Warrick interjected. "Thank you for your help, dear."

"My pleasure, honored guest of my master." Mij gave Warrick a respectful bow. "Please, this way."

As the group made their way, Jarle took mental note of their route. They passed wood stoves with ornate grills and grand mantles that provided warmth while oil sconces illuminated the soaring, ice-blue paneled walls. Antique tapestries interspersed with paintings hung on either side of the passageway. An open door offered a glimpse into an endless corridor of darkened apartments.

The hall ended at a white marble staircase that ascended by dignified degrees to the third floor. Once more, Jarle and Boij carried the cumbersome trunk while Mij assisted the old man.

"I return to my post now," Boij declared at the top.

The Durauk paused midway up the stairs with Warrick in tow and gave the young palace soldier a cursory glance. Her eyes shone like black pearls. "Advise Sergeant Gandas to polish his Dessian. I suspect you will hear more of my language spoken in your streets very soon."

Boij bounded down and faced the female guard. He leaned forward and whispered in her ear loud enough for all to hear. "The captain would love for you to tutor him. He's eager to learn the secrets of your tongue."

The woman's eyes smiled. "Men are the same in all places."

Boij laughed. "Not so! In some places, some of us are longer."

Mij suppressed a chuckle. "Become lost!"

Boij continued down. "You must mean, 'get lost.'"

"*Kai! Pa'chien éh'le kéq,*" Mij cursed without anger.

At the top of the staircase, the woman unlocked a door that led to a spacious foyer. An eight-armed torchiere on a marble-topped table illuminated a rectangular anteroom. Brocaded curtains of a similar hue partially obscured two doorways opposite where they stood.

The Durauk walked to the furthest door, knocked twice, paused, and repeated the pattern three more times.

The brass knobs glinted in the firelight as the door opened from the other side.

Turning to face them, Mij crossed her arms over her chest and kowtowed in traditional Dessian fashion. "My sisters will accompany you from here."

Jarle shifted and rocked. "Paa, is girl this way, Paa?"

"Yes," Warrick hissed. "Go!"

Two black-clad guards escorted them through a lavish corridor. The floor shone with the distinctive aquamarine color made famous by Reyzan ceramicists. The hexagonal mosaic tiles formed a subtle pattern that lent the ground a sense of watery motion. Panes of clear glass held together by delicate veins of metal offered a view of the moonlit sea. Opposite the arched colonnade stood three double doors, all white, with ostentatious lintels upon which carved tritons frolicked in the waves. One of the Durauks stepped forward and opened one of the doors while her comrade took a position beside the entry.

Warrick licked his lips nervously and stepped into the room. Jarle loosened his grip on the cart's handle lest the guards notice his white-knuckled tension, and entered.

Two doors led from the vestibule. In the four corners of the room, carved, white arms protruded from the walls. Each limb held a moonstone globe in its hand that radiated a dim, bluish glow. Friezes carved with mollusks, starfish, and seashells adorned the top of the lofty chamber. A polished table and a settee with crab legs for feet occupied the space.

Warrick accidentally smacked his hip against the table and caused the slender vase at its center to teeter. Instinctively, Jarle caught the object before it shattered.

"Gods have mercy!" Disaster averted, Warrick turned and waved his hands at the Durauk. "Th-thank you for escorting me and my son, kind lady—person—you, but now there is work to be done, and I c-certainly cannot do it with you staring at me with those beady eyes. Oh, no."

When the Durauk didn't budge, Warrick swept his cane in a clean arc in the direction of the door. "Out! Out you go."

The guard crossed her arms over her chest and bowed. "My master wishes to speak with you," she said. Her voice was soft—a stark contrast to the tension in her frame.

"He knows where to find us."

When the woman left the room, Warrick closed the door with trembling hands.

Jarle pointed to one door then the other. "Which?" he mouthed.

Warrick indicated the door opposite the entry with a weak jab of his cane. "Go, boy," he croaked, "I will be right behind you."

Something about the alchemist's feeble tone alarmed him. Jarle turned in time to see Warrick slump against the wall with his eyes upturned. His face blanched as he grasped his chest with a liver-spotted hand. A thin, wheezing sound underscored his breaths.

"Ven's scaly cock! I swear I am cursed," Jarle spat under his breath. Moving quickly, he lifted the trunk's lid and began to stack the decoy items on the floor. Sweat broke on his brow as he poked around the bottom of the box for his bandolier. Remedies flashed through Jarle's mind as the raspy breathing worsened. Jarle shook his head at the irony of saving the life of a man he wanted to strangle.

Upon finding the leather sash containing his antidotes, Jarle pulled out one of the vials and scrambled to Warrick's side. "Do not dare die on me," Jarle threatened, grasping the old man by his collar. "Drink!"

Warrick attempted to speak, but only a hollow sound escaped his lips. His eyes opened wide as he examined the offered vial. He snatched the medicine with a quivering hand and chugged it down.

Jarle grabbed Warrick by his arm and helped him to the crab-legged settee. He propped him up with an overstuffed pillow and loosened a few buttons of his overcoat. "Focus on breathing. I gave you Essence of Goralis to ease your nerves."

"They are coming for us!" Warrick's worried gaze darted to the door beyond which the Durauks stood watch.

The thief froze and listened. When only the muffled sounds of the sea reached his ears, he tugged the woolen robe over his head and tossed it aside. He returned to the chest and removed the upper tray to reveal his gear. Jarle retrieved the bundled armor and unwrapped it, careful not to make a sound. He placed his daggers and throwing dirks aside, and disrobed down to his braies. He pulled on the thick leather breeches and boots, then tied the laces. After donning his black silk shirt, he proceeded to lace the leather cuirass with its many pockets and crisscrossed reinforced bands. Once his vambraces and cuisses were secured, Jarle slipped on his bandolier and buckled his scabbards. His armor was well oiled and his blades, all nine of them, keen and ready to kill. The thought of his envenomed daggers filled him with dread. The slightest nick could send him to the afterlife.

When he finished, he no longer looked the part of fumbling apprentice, but that of the famed moonlighter from the Reyzan underworld. Jarle caught his reflection in one of the mirrors. In the dim light, he appeared more shadow than a man.

Somewhat recovered, Warrick leaned forward on the settee and picked up his son's robe. "Put this back on," he hissed. "Hurry."

Jarle donned the robe and drew the cowl over his head. Quickly, he began to pile the alchemical equipment back in the chest. "Can you walk?" he asked Warrick.

"My medicines are effective." Warrick wiped his face then used his cane to rise to his feet. He hobbled to the door that led to the girl's chamber. "I am sure you saved my life only to see it taken more gruesomely."

Jarle closed the lid. "My reason for saving your miserable hide does not concern your welfare."

"Of course not. The pretty ones inspire reckless devotion." Warrick opened the door and started down the corridor. "Without fools like you ensnared by beauty, love, and lust, I would be out of business."

"Mind your tongue, lest you find yourself without one."

Warrick paused before an imposing door with a golden knocker in the shape of a seahorse. "She's in here."

The thief tightened his grip on the dirk hidden in his sleeve as a heavy sensation settled over his heart. He had no inkling what to expect; no idea what horrible abuses Avaren had endured, or if she would even recognize him.

"Open it."

"You should know that she will not be herself. I gave her—" Warrick's words died when a cold blade threatened his neck.

Jarle's features twisted into a mask of quiet rage. "You will make her well, or I swear to make you suffer before you die."

"Worry not. What I did can be undone." Warrick's wheezing returned as he eased Jarle's hand away from his throat. "For my son's sake, Jars, promise me that if I don't survive, you will cure my boy."

"Your son's life depends entirely on you." Jarle withdrew the unpoisoned blade, but his eyes did not lose their fire.

Warrick gripped the handle and pushed the door open, to reveal a sparsely furnished salon. The room was chilly and smelled of sea salt and rain. White curtains flapped against an open window, casting long shadows on the floor.

The two men dragged the cart into the room and closed the door. Jarle scanned the empty room, "Where is she?"

"She was here, right here!" Warrick's voice betrayed his panic.

Jarle's face flushed with rage. He grabbed Warrick by the collar and pulled him into a chokehold, the tip of his blade pressed into the old man's ribs. "Be very careful with the next words you utter."

"The bed was there!" he said, pointing to the wall.

"You need to do better than that, much better."

Tears welled up in Warrick's eyes. "I swear on the life of my son; I did not trick you. Please, have mercy."

The blade bit ever so slightly into soft flesh. "Give me the antidote Avaren needs."

"In the cart!" Warrick wheezed.

The sound of the doorknob turning startled them. Jarle tucked the dagger into his sleeve while Warrick burst into a nervous fit of coughing.

The door swung open to reveal Ambassador Akkalon. The Dessian wore a loose embroidered robe over tight black breeches and calfskin boots. Large golden hoops dangled from his ears as he entered. The two Durauks who had escorted them earlier stood behind their master.

"What is in the cart?" Neylen asked.

Jarle lowered his head and pretended to comfort the alchemist. "Paa's medicine. And herbs and instruments and flasks. Everything in its place. Just so, just so."

Warrick shooed Jarle's hands away and bowed. "M-majster Neylen."

Neylen spared Jarle a disdainful glance before settling his black gaze on Warrick. "Fetch your medicine, Majster Apothek."

Warrick flung open the lid of the cart and rummaged through the contents until he found a vial filled with milky-white liquid. He unstoppered the bottle, took a small sip, and thrust the container into Jarle's hand. "Hold on to this, boy, in case this detestable cough returns."

Jarle corked the vial and rocked back and forth. "Aldorf holds on to Paa's medicine. Aldorf keeps Paa's medicine safe for Paa."

With a swish of his robes, Neylen turned and strutted out the door. "Come."

The guards returned to their posts, while their master crossed the chamber to the door yet unopened. Warrick hobbled behind the imposing Dessian while Jarle followed with the cart.

The thief assessed the ambassador with the intensity of a lion studying its prey. Neylen carried himself with regal bearing, but his movements denoted confidence and strength. The man's shifting robes concealed thick, muscled arms and an athletic build. The Dessian was no soft courtier.

Past the blue door they strode through a series of rooms outfitted with immense wealth: a marble-paneled escritoire with views of the sea, a library with gilded shelves and priceless tomes, a portrait gallery, a sitting room with a fireplace carved to resemble smoky sylphs, and a grand music room complete with the spiraling pipes of an A'dielian organ. They entered through a set of double doors and into a smaller hallway adorned with portraits of the royal family. The low ceiling of the hall guided the eye to the delicately painted faces.

Neylen paused before a door with such suddenness that the alchemist bumped into him.

"Apologies, Majster Akkalon," Warrick groveled.

Undisturbed by the blunder, Neylen opened the door and

extended his arm. "Your patient is here. Be warned; you are now in Jarle Iarris' private wing. Touch nothing, and do not leave this room until I return. Do you understand?"

Warrick bowed twice in succession. "Yes, yes, as you wish, of course, we shall be careful."

Neylen's eyes sparkled, and his lips curved into a half-smile. "I expect the field will be fertile and ready for sowing. Succeed, and you will discover the abundance of my generosity."

Blood roared in Jarle's ears. The implication of the Dessian's words tested his willpower. The desire to feel his blades sink into bronzed flesh was near overwhelming.

Sensing the thief's rage, Warrick stepped between them and bowed again. "Thank you, Majster Akkalon, thank you. Be assured; my son and I will not fail."

Neylen brought a palm to his chest and offered the alchemist a courteous nod, after which he turned and walked away.

Jarle's gut tightened. Warrick was right; breaking into the palace was madness.

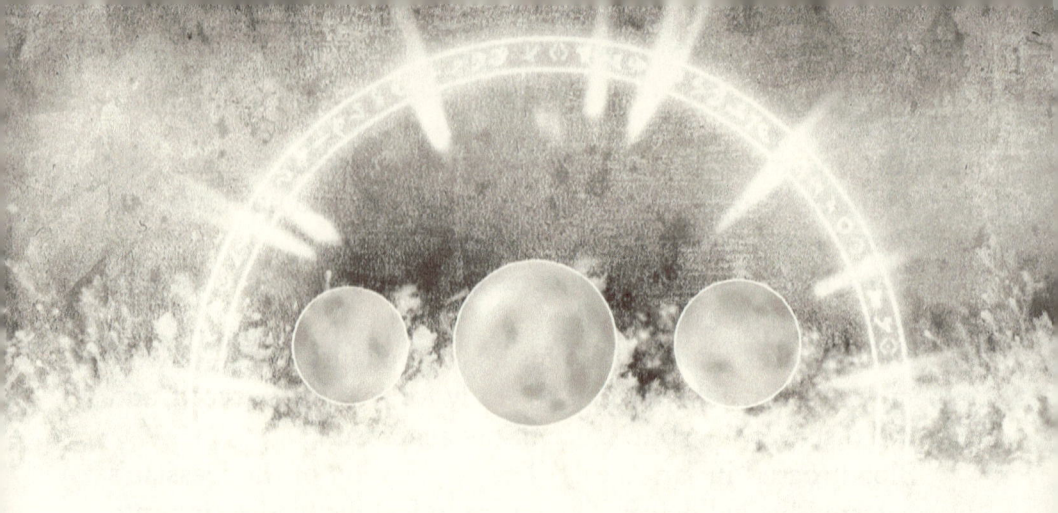

A COLD, DARK PRAYER

Venedi, Third of Nommen, 445 A'A'diel

The sight of Avaren struck Jarle with the force of a gut punch. He stood frozen, breathless—his mind a storm of emotion. He clutched the doorframe to steady himself.

Avaren lay undressed on a grandiose bed whose towering, draped baldaquin dwarfed her. She reclined on a heap of embroidered pillows the color of midnight. In the dim glow of the moonstone sconces, her skin shone pale, lending her a ghastly visage. Save for the gentle rise and fall of her belly; she was utterly still, lips parted as though about to speak. Her once-bright eyes were as dull as the moonstones that illuminated the horrific scene.

When the alchemist laid his hand upon the thief's shoulder, the spell broke. Jarle rushed into the room and climbed on the bed. He cradled Avaren in his arms while pulling the bedding to cover her nakedness. He kissed her lips and cheeks; stroked her hair. "Warrick, what did you do? Please, help her."

Warrick raised his hand in a placating motion and dragged the cart to the bed. "She is catatonic but still conscious—quite alive, I assure you. I must coax her gradually from the paralysis to minimize the risk of dementia."

The implications of the alchemist's words were as vile as the sorrowful ache in Jarle's stomach. He breathed in the scent of Avaren's hair and closed his eyes. Avaren would sooner die than be violated by the monsters who conspired against her father. "How much time do we have?"

The geezer looked down at his gaunt, liver-spotted hands and shook his head. "The Dessian will return within the hour."

Jarle blinked away tears. He was trembling with exhaustion, and his eyes burned from sleeplessness. Clutching the limp girl, he began to recite a prayer to the patron deity of Reyza—Death—whose eternal embrace seemed near. "Ven, Lord of Souls, at this, my coldest and darkest hour, I honor you. I implore you to guard our mortal shadows. Protect us and grant us forbearance until the day of our final journey."

Warrick approached the bed. "Ven forgive me, but prayer is an indulgence our time cannot accommodate."

Jarle slipped his hand inside the robe's sleeve and withdrew the vial the alchemist had bade him keep, and handed it to Warrick. "Do what you can."

The alchemist's hand trembled as he took the bottle. "Did you resupply your doses of bushtooth?"

Jarle lay Avaren down among the pillows. "What?"

"The tonic of Bland Bushtooth smells like licorice. Did you take some from my cabinet?"

Realizing what he was babbling about, the thief reached under the robe and plucked the antidote from his bandolier. "Will it help?"

"Mixed with the milk of conabina speciosa, the substance creates a powerful stimulant."

Jarle handed the potion over with some trepidation. "Conabina by itself, jolts the heart. Are you certain?"

The alchemist held the milky-white extract to the light of the moonstone and offered Jarle a smile. "I have performed the procedure before. Now help me or remove yourself."

"What should I do?"

Warrick's gaze fell on a nightgown folded neatly atop a bedside bench. The old man opened the alchemical chest and withdrew a thin glass cylinder. "Dress her while I prepare the dosage. I doubt we will have another opportunity to clothe her in something warm."

Jarle shook out the linen gown and draped it over Avaren's head. He threaded her limp arms through the sleeves while Warrick worked.

The old man attached a long, hollow needle to the end of the glass tube etched with fine measurement lines. He fitted a metal cylinder into the device to act as a plunger.

Jarle knitted his brows and shook his head. The contraption looked painful. "You must be jesting."

Warrick set the instrument down. "Trust me; the syringe appears more severe than the pain it inflicts."

"This here mechanism ensures a consistent dosage over time. Too much or too little can mean the difference between life and death." Warrick pointed to the bed's curtains with a nudge of his chin. "Bind her wrists and ankles with those tiebacks."

Disbelief turned to anger. Jarle rose from the bed and grabbed the alchemist by the arm. "Do not play games with me, old man. Why does she need to be bound?"

Warrick fixed the thief with a scowl. "If you wish to argue over every one of my instructions, then all is lost. Allow me to do what you brought me here to do."

Jarle ran both hands through his hair and exhaled in frustration. He pulled the cords holding the drapery back and untied them. He knotted the curtain tiebacks together into one long rope, eased Avaren onto her side, and secured her limbs. "Answer my question, Warrick."

"Hush," said Warrick, licking his lips. "I have to measure this precisely. One finger of conabina, two drops of bushtooth."

The alchemist muttered as he poured the substances one after the other into a glass measuring tube. "Just so—just so." He put the vials aside and extracted his waterskin from the cart. "Two fingers of water, which we incorporate." He shook the container until the liquid inside shone a translucent white. Warrick examined the fluid in the light, then assessed the bound girl. He bit his bottom lip and nodded to himself before adding another few drips of the bushtooth.

"This method is not ideal, but it works fast. When sensation returns, your sweetheart will experience an acute euphoria bordering on madness. The bindings will prevent self-harm. Stuff her mouth so she won't alert the guards when her lethargy fades."

The thief cast a venomous glare at the greybeard. He slashed a square of cloth from the bedsheet and knelt on the bed. "I am sorry, my love," he said, stuffing the fabric between her lips.

"This doesn't seem safe," Jarle said, staring at the sharp point of the needle.

Warrick filled the device's barrel and fitted the metal plunger. "She is young and healthy, and my dosage is precise, but Ven only knows. Cures are never without risk. Do you wish her lively or not?"

Jarle smoothed Avaren's hair with his palm. Seeing his lover gagged and bound made his heartache with despair, and his throat tighten. "Do what you must."

Warrick approached with the syringe upright to prevent the medicine from escaping. "Pull her head back and, for the love of Ven, keep her still no matter how she reacts."

Jarle tilted Avaren's head and revealed the pale skin of her throat. Warrick depressed the plunger and let some fluid drip before driving the needle into the jugular vein.

Almost immediately, Avaren opened her eyes and began to convulse. She bucked against her restraints and gnashed on the gag. She screamed, but only muffled growls emerged.

Using his body weight, Jarle held her down. "What is happening to her!?"

The struggle prevented the alchemist from administering the full dose. "Hold her still! It is almost over."

Something in the tone of the old man's voice froze his heart. "You bastard; you're killing her!" Jarle tore the needle from the girl's neck and slammed his fist into the alchemist's face.

Warrick stumbled backward. The instrument dropped from his hand as he held his bloodied nose. "You doomed my son," he hissed. "One life for another!"

Jarle tackled the geezer to the floor. He grabbed Warrick by his collar and shook him violently. "What did you give her?"

Warrick reached frantically into one of his pockets and flung a pouch of brown dust in Jarle's face. "Death, boy. Death! None of us will leave here!"

Pain followed disorientation.

Jarle recoiled and twisted away but failed to avoid the dust cloud. He expelled his breath forcefully as he rolled away from the alchemist. His chest constricted; every inhalation seared his lungs. The room's contours melted into splotches of dizzying swirls.

Blinded, Jarle shut his eyes and focused on the sounds around him. Avaren was still writhing and screaming. The tap of a cane and hoarse breathing revealed the alchemist's position.

Warrick was close.

Jarle moved in the directions of Avaren's groans until he found the bed. He knelt at the edge of the mattress and traced down the girl's arm to her wrists, then to her bonds. When his fingers closed on the loop that secured the knot, he pulled it loose.

The effort left him breathless. Jarle sucked air in agonized gulps as he slumped down. When he opened his eyes, the disorienting, pulsating blotches transformed into a dark whirlwind of movement.

Stars exploded in Jarle's head as Warrick's walking stick struck his brow. Blood trickled over his left eye as bright ribbons of distorted light flooded his vision with each frenzied whack.

Jarle drew his dagger and swung in an arc but missed his mark. The stick cracked down on his ribs, knuckles, and whipped his back over and over as he gasped for air. He tumbled away from the blows and attempted to stand, but his legs failed him. Helpless, he rolled into a ball, hands clutching his head, while the assault continued.

When the beating stopped, Jarle sensed Warrick stoop over him. Bony hands yanked up his robe and rifled through his bandolier.

"Where is it? Where is it? I must save my boy." The alchemist's words sounded faint and distant. Jarle tried one last time to push him away as the brilliant tapestry of whirling colors faded to a sea of black.

THE GLIMMERING SYLPH

Venedi, Third of Nommen, 445 A'A'diel

Every nerve in Avaren's body tingled. Behind her eyes, a pounding headache magnified every sound into a maddening din. The concoction the alchemist had given her churned her stomach and scrambled her senses. Her heart thumped as the mortal struggle near her bed continued. She bit back a scream as the alchemist's cane smashed down on Jarle's defenseless body.

Avaren pushed past the pain and focused on piercing the drug-induced fog. Her hands shook as she untied her ankles and slid off the bed.

The sight of Warrick hunched over her motionless lover filled her with dark fury. Avaren wound the curtain tiebacks around her palms and crept behind the frenzied alchemist. Bending over the geezer, she looped the improvised garrote over his head and yanked with all of her might.

The garrotte bit into the old man's flesh with surprising ease. Warrick's cane clattered on the floor as he clawed at the rope around his windpipe. He gurgled and spat. His hands flailed wildly to try to dislodge his attacker.

Avaren drove her knee between her victim's shoulder blades and pushed her victim to the ground. Once he was on his belly, she straddled his back and tightened her grip. When the man attempted to roll out from under her, she stopped him with a sustained tug that caused every muscle in her arms to burn. "Don't despair," she hissed, enjoying the geezer's suffering, "you won't feel a thing."

Warrick twisted against the chokehold; his mouth opened and closed yet drew no air. The cord dug into Avaren's knuckles as she arched backward. The memory of Warrick's disgusting, probing fingers lent strength to her efforts. "Die," she spat. "Die! Die!"

With each affirmation, Warrick's struggles weakened, until at last, his body surrendered its spark. With a violent shudder and a final wheeze, the old man ceased to struggle.

The alchemist was dead, yet Avaren continued to pull and wish for his death until her rage cooled to bone-chilling terror. Abruptly aware that she had killed a man in the same manner as the assassin who tried to murder her, she released the rope and scrambled backward.

The alchemist's purpled face and bulging, bloodshot eyes seemed fixed in her direction. Warrick's mouth was agape, and his tongue extended—frozen in the final moment of death. His curled, bony fingers resembled talons that might still reach for her if she came too close. Avaren averted her gaze, but she could not extinguish the nightmarish vision of her father's lifeless eyes.

Tears came in a sudden gush as she crawled to her lover's side. "Jarle, please don't die; don't leave me alone in this ugly world!"

Jarle lay unconscious. A nasty bruise bulged on his forehead, and his respiration was shallow. Avaren tilted his chin back, placed her mouth over his, and forced air into his lungs. After several long breaths, his legs twitched.

"That's it, just breathe," she coaxed, stroking his hair.

"Avi?" Jarle groaned.

Avaren grasped his hand as fresh tears welled behind her eyes. She missed him. "I'm here."

Jarle opened his eyes and gazed up at her. "Thank gods you're alive," he whispered, winding his fingers in her hair. He pulled her down and showered her with kisses. He nuzzled into her neck and caressed her arms. "I love you."

Avaren embraced her lover and kissed him. Jarle tasted dark and deliciously male, reminding her of the summer storms that had thundered through their cave. She had never intended to love him, but she could no longer deny her heart. "Sweet Jarle," she murmured against his mouth, "If this madness in my soul is what this world calls love, then I love you with all that I am. I am sorry that I lied to you; that I judged you. I realize now that you were right—about everything. I should have never come back here. Can you forgive me?"

"Hush, there is nothing to forgive." Jarle stroked her cheek. "You could draw me to fire, to ruin, and disgrace and I would gladly follow. My heart beats only for you."

"My lies have trapped us both," Avaren said with regret.

Jarle sat up to face his lover. He grasped her cheeks and tenderly ran his thumbs over her silky skin. "Avi, my sight is blurred, and I can't seem to catch my breath. Warrick threw something in my face. I don't know how long the effects will last. Neylen will return at any moment. We need to act now, or our journey in the waking world will end."

Avaren glanced toward the door. "Neylen is powerful. I have seen firsthand the power of his incantations. He can manipulate the elements and augment his strength."

"Then we shall have to take him by surprise."

Avaren squeezed her lover's hand and helped him wobble to his feet. "Tell me what I must do."

After a long pause, Jarle smiled. "Take your clothes off."

*
**

The chamber door swung open without a sound. Four men dressed in robes of black silk and soft slippers stepped inside, followed by Neylen. After locking the door, Neylen strode forward past his silent companions. The Dessian's unbound robe swirled open to reveal the sharp furrows of his naked physique. His thick cock jutted before him like the prow of a warship, erect and bejeweled with a row of piercings.

He gave a final passing inspection to the men he had selected to impregnate Avaren. Two were young palace guards with expressions that barely concealed their terror. Both were more attractive and kind-hearted than he preferred, but they could be counted on to follow orders without hesitation. The third man, a Council member and a long-time supporter of Dessia, stood alert and dignified. His long, graying hair and aquiline features harkened to distant Seh'nahiel ancestry. The fourth was middle-aged and wiry—one of the dungeon's notorious torturers with talented hands. Neylen exchanged a knowing glance with the gaunt man and nodded when sadist acknowledged his scrutiny with a shark-like smile

The Dessian moved toward his prize: the nubile, naked girl splayed on the bed. The thought of his enemy's daughter's suffering aroused him far more than the sexual liberty he would take with her. Fixated on the daydream of her desecration, he nearly failed to notice the absence of the alchemist. The cart was by the footboard, along with his idiot apprentice, but there was no sign of Warrick.

Neylen halted his entourage with a raised hand as he approached his prey. He ran a finger along Avaren's jaw as he addressed the youth. "Boy, where is your father?"

The hooded youth refused to lift his face to address him. He clenched his hands and shifted from foot to foot as though he were standing on a hot grill. "Paa, where is Paa? Privy, privy! Told me to say girl is ready. She is sleeping, sleeping."

The naera possessed a sublime radiance. Neylen marveled at the stark contrast of his bronzed skin against her ivory pallor as he traced her full lips with his finger. The corner of his mouth curled into a grin. Neylen addressed the apprentice without sparing him a glance. "Take your equipment and find your father, boy. Tell him to wait for me in the blue room."

"Yes, yes, tell Paa to go to the room with the sea things." The boy kept his head bowed and began to roll the cart in the direction of the robed men.

Neylen sat at the edge of the bed. He inserted two fingers into Avaren's mouth and observed as her belly rippled with frantic breaths. The alchemist's concoction was indeed a daevilish delight. A different, more merciful man, would have allowed the girl the dignity of unconsciousness, but alas, he was not that man. His pleasure demanded awareness, if not cooperation. He wished the firebrand to experience every moment of her degradation.

Surprised gasps and agonized yelps tore Neylen from his erotic reveries. He turned toward the commotion in time to see Aldorf scuffling with his studs. The two young guards hunched over and clutched their bellies while the other two men wrestled with the youth. Neylen scowled. The last thing he wanted to do was administer a beating, but violence would have to serve as foreplay.

Neylen turned away from Avaren and rose to his feet. He took but a single step before a hard, penetrating impact in the small of his back induced blinding pain. Neylen inhaled sharply and found himself unable to scream. He clutched the wound on his back and felt hot blood flow over his fingers.

Agonizing waves of pain and dizziness threatened to steal his consciousness as he staggered forward. When his legs buckled, Neylen fell and hit his head on the floor. Fighting for control over his body, he flopped to his side and faced his ambusher.

Through the haze of pain, he saw Avaren staring down at him. Her opalescent eyes whorled with baleful fire. Again, he attempted to cry for help, but no sound emerged. Icy oblivion traveled through his veins, dulling all sensation. Time slowed until every detail became lucid and profound. Neylen gawked at the dagger in the girl's hand, aghast with the realization that the dripping blood on its edge was his. Helplessly, he watched the naked waif kneel and draw the weapon back only to thrust once more. His eyes followed the awful trajectory of the blade as it stabbed below his sternum. All conscious thought vanished in a thunderclap of white-hot pain.

Neylen lay rigid while the poison ravaged his nerves. A thrill of horror swept through him as his eyes met those of the dead alchemist under the bed. He exerted his will to shout and summon the fortifying magic of the Rehi but was powerless to do so. Saliva drooled from his slack, open mouth as warm wet urine soaked his thighs.

Suddenly, Neylen rued the ill-considered decision to dismiss his Durauks for the evening. He regretted dealing with the daevil named Vess and ever setting foot in Reyza. He cursed Tan'os Ensther, Rigo, and the entirety of mankind before beseeching the gods to grant him a quick death.

*
**

The fight was over before it began.

Four would-be rapists lay paralyzed on the floor; their half-naked bodies contorted in a gruesome asymmetry. In Jarle's damaged eyes, their bloody corpses were nothing more than dark, hazy shapes in a field of azure. Satisfied they would never rise again, he turned toward Avaren.

Through the opaline haze of his vision, Jarle beheld an apparition gliding toward him—a glimmering sylph from childhood tales. Relief thrilled through his core and set his heart racing. He reached out and pulled the trembling girl into an embrace. "You are all right, my love. We've done it."

Avaren wrapped her arms around Jarle's waist, "How long before Neylen dies?"

Jarle stroked his lover's pale hair. "Quarter bell for us, but a cursèd eternity for him." He raised his voice for the Dessian to hear him. "That piece of shit will perish slowly with no one to mourn his passing. He will never hurt you or anyone else again."

Avaren gently pulled free. She stepped over the corpse of a dead man and walked back toward Neylen.

Jarle followed but kept silent. All he could discern was a glowing silhouette hovering over a dark, motionless shape.

The silvery apparition withdrew the blade stuck in Neylen's belly and wiped it to a gleam on the silk of the man's robe. Blood seeped from the wound with each of Neylen's labored breaths. "My father waits for you in the afterlife."

As Neylen bled to death, Jarle's vision improved. He placed his ear to the door and listened. Satisfied by the silence in the hallway outside, he returned to Avaren's side and slipped out of Aldorf's robe.

"Put this on," he said, handing the cassock to Avaren. "And grab some slippers from one of those bastards. I'll wear Warrick's robe."

Avaren set the dagger down and pulled the hooded garment over her head. "I know a way out of the palace," she said, curling her hair into a bun at the base of her skull.

"Now would be an ideal time to divulge that information." Jarle crouched under the bed, took one of the dead alchemist's arms and tugged. He rolled the cadaver face down and set about disrobing him.

Avaren selected the smallest pair of slippers and put them on. "I know where my *betrothed* sleeps."

"You bastard!" Jarle yanked harder when the damnable woolen robe refused to part with its host. As though listening from beyond, Warrick's corpse voided its bowels in a grotesque, bubbling rush. Jarle covered his nose and grimaced. He backed away and fanned the odiferous stench. "On second thought, never mind."

Avaren used the hem of her robe to retrieve the poisoned blades from the fallen thugs. "Rigo's bedchamber is past the recital room," she said, handing Jarle the daggers. "It would be a shame to depart without saying goodbye, don't you think?"

Jarle sheathed his weapons, feeling both exhilarated and saddened by Avaren's bloodlust. He pulled her into an embrace and kissed her head, allowing the mad intensity of her emotions to flood through him. "Rigo's a poor host, the least we can do is express our displeasure." Jarle released her and extended his arm toward the door. "After you."

Avaren clutched the handle of her dagger so fiercely her knuckles grew white. She pressed down on the latch and pulled the door open.

The hall was empty.

Assured by the absence of footsteps or voices, they traversed the portrait gallery and cracked the door at the end of the passage. Brilliant flashes of lightning flickered through the tall windows of the deserted music room.

Framed by coral branches and sea nymphs sounding conchs, the lovers' reflection danced on the polished mirrors that lined the walls. Their wavering doppelgangers paced with them as they crossed the room and stepped inside a shadowed window niche.

Avaren loosened one of the curtains to conceal their presence then drew Jarle close. "Past the recital room doors stretches a promenade with windows facing the sea. Rigo's chamber faces the terrace that circles the palace. The way is probably clear. Rigo forbid most of his staff from entering this wing to keep my condition a secret. Only those dreaded Durauks are on vigil." Avaren gazed into Jarle's dark eyes. "How are you feeling?"

"Better. My sight is as good as a drunkard's on a festival day." The girl's proximity and the scent of her skin intoxicated him. Surrendering to a rush of longing, he curled his arms around her waist and kissed her. Arousal flooded his loins as her silky tongue twined with his, and her fingers wound through his hair. "You are my every desire," Jarle said, moving sinuously against her.

Avaren reciprocated by clasping his buttocks and grinding against him with lusty need. "And you are mine."

Jarle kissed along her jaw to her neck, suckling the moist flesh beneath which her pulse skittered. His hands roamed, kneading, caressing, and possessing. The taste of her, the way her body conformed to his, the delight of her mere presence was beyond the articulation of the most eloquent of poets—a song no chanteuse could vocalize. The naera was elemental. She captivated him as surely as a burning flame enthralled a lowly insect. So long as they were together, he could face whatever dangers lurked ahead.

Avaren massaged the bulge in the thief's breeches and smiled against his lips. "We should go."

The aroused edge in her voice thrilled him. "Aye, romance can wait until we're far away from this nightmarish place."

"You know, you shouldn't always agree with me," she teased.

"Bloody Hel," Jarle gasped. "How am I supposed to rescue you with this cockstand?"

Avaren suppressed a laugh. "Who's rescuing who?"

Jarle adjusted his pants and led her out of the alcove. "Come on, Trouble, time to leave."

THE THIRTEENTH HOUR

Brindi, Fourth of Nommen, 445 A'A'diel

The knock on the door to the royal quarters in the Thrommish Embassy coincided with the first of thirteen bells. Eva ignored the summons and raised a gold-limned teacup to her lips. She watched the play of firelight and shadow in the streets of the stricken city as she sipped. The lateness of the appointment irked her. Worse, Deneven was an hour overdue.

After the second knock, she set the porcelain cup and saucer down. "Enter," she said, turning to face the door.

Brueck, the broad-shouldered sailor, entrusted to ensure her safety while the fleet prepared for departure, stood in the doorway. "Majster Deneven D'Neir is here, Marchess. He is not alone; a woman is with him."

"Who is she?"

"Majster Deneven told me to tell you that her identity is for your ears only."

"Ask Ambassador Ers to entertain our uninvited guest and bring D'Neir to me."

"As you command, Marchess."

Eva returned to the window. Since Avaren's attempted break-in, Ers had doubled the guard. Undeterred by the rain, soldiers paced beyond the embassy gates with timely precision, yet the sight offered no comfort. Avaren's drug-induced desperation sang in her blood and would color her dreams for days to come. The girl's cloying aura of vulnerability and fear was unsettling.

A rap on the door caused Eva to regain her composure. She smoothed her dress and straightened her shoulders. "Come."

Deneven D'Neir entered and bowed. His greatcoat was soaked, and gray strands of hair clung to his face. He held a leather satchel under one arm and appeared every bit as disturbed as she felt. "Good evening, Marchess."

"Please, wait outside, Brueck." Eva waited until they were alone before addressing the former justiciar. "The hour is late, and I depart at dawn. Therefore, please divulge your purpose quickly and without formality."

"I shall get right to it then." Deneven crossed the room and set his valise on the drawing-room table. "I know the truth about Rigo."

Eva narrowed her eyes. "Truly? Do tell."

"Your mother was murdered to enable a bastard to ascend to the throne. Rigo is that bastard."

Eva's jaw slacked, and her belly tightened. She gripped the back of a chair to steady herself. "How did you learn this?"

"You are the rightful heir," Deneven pressed.

"Indeed." Eva's fingers dimpled the plush velvet padding of the chair. She inhaled deeply then exhaled with restraint until her heart stopped thumping. "Of course, such a revelation matters little now. You, yourself, conducted the official inquiry into my mother's demise and deemed her death a suicide!"

"I was wrong."

"How grand, the relentless seeker of justice admits he erred. Is that why you came here tonight, to assuage your guilt over your gross incompetence? Or perhaps you saw an opportunity to needle me before we part? I never took you for a petty man, D'Neir."

"Neither accusation is correct, Marchess." Whether her insinuations stung Deneven's pride or not, his tone remained calm. "I am here to apologize and redress the suffering that my failure wrought upon you."

Eva turned away and rubbed her forehead. "Knowing what

happened won't change anything without proof—then or now. And said evidence does not exist."

"That is where you are wrong. I possess incontrovertible proof."

Eva shot upright. "I am listening."

Deneven tapped his valise. "This case contains a writ penned by Draos Iarris, with his royal seal, empowering Tan'os Ensther to arrange for the murder of your mother in return for the title of Vise."

The floor tilted beneath Eva's feet. Her eyes darted to the valise as a myriad of questions fought for dominance. "Do not jest with me."

"I do not. Now is the time to litigate your rightful claim and invoke justice. This opportunity will not reappear."

Eva met the investigator's eyes. "What do you want, Dragon? No one in this treacherous city divulges incendiary information without recompense."

Deneven met her stare with cold conviction. "I want what is best for Reyza."

"And that is?"

"Reyza governed by you, the legitimate heir, with me beside you—as Vise."

Eva laughed without mirth.

"You find my suggestion humorous?"

"No. I am merely caught off guard by your directness."

"The hour is late, and you asked me to eschew formality."

Eva's body thrummed with excitement. The possibility of seizing the throne and securing the future of her children was nigh, yet something gave her pause, some variable yet undiscovered. "Even if the document you speak of is not a forgery, Rigo will claim it is. Evidence or not, politicians will stall and grant favor to anyone wealthy enough to sway their feckless loyalties. I fear that Cartuj's pockets are deeper than Thyra's. What you propose is as contentious as staging a coup."

Deneven shook his head. "You control both the Northern and Southern Fleets. Do not underestimate the might of naval supremacy to mitigate resistance. My support gains you the Chancellery, the loyalty of the Ca'Dezer, and the approval of the people. Reyzans see Rigo is a vainglorious fop and will gladly see him replaced. As for the Council, I know someone who can guarantee their unanimous support. Agree, and Reyza will be yours within the week."

"You are an optimist, indeed! The Council can't even agree on the color of festival pennants. Am I to understand that the woman waiting in the parlor is a miracle maker?"

Deneven nodded. "Marchess, you need to speak with her. I give you my oath; she will detail everything to your satisfaction."

Eva eyed Deneven. Something in his manner aroused suspicion. "Does this mysterious benefactor have a name?"

"She goes by the name of Vess. And like me, she holds Reyza in utmost esteem. She procured the writ proving your mother's homicide. She also possesses a coded letter from Ambassador Neylen Akkalon in which he guarantees a fortune in trade bars to the assassin Maél Aodhan in exchange for the deaths of Tan'os Ensther and his daughter."

"Akkalon!?" The revelation caused Eva's blood to roar in her ears. "When did you discover that the Dessian arranged the assassination? I recall asking you what you discovered, D'Neir! You made me look like a fool."

"Regretfully, I did not possess this evidence until mere hours ago, Marchess."

Eva poured two brandies and handed Deneven a glass. "Drink, put some heat back in your bones."

"Thank you." Deneven chugged the alcohol and set the tumbler down. "This night is fit for a whole bottle."

"Aye. Ghosts and spirits are afoot." Eva walked to the door and opened it. "Brueck, please fetch Majster D'Neir's companion."

Deneven leaned on his cane. "If I may change the subject for a moment, I hoped to find Mejtress Avaren in the company of her people. Have you seen her?"

Eva drank as a shudder ran down her spine. "I went to the palace earlier to see her. She was mentally unstable and badly wounded. I thought it best that she remain in the care of the royal physicians. An arduous sea crossing bodes ill for her health."

"Marchess, I fear her life is in danger so long as she is in Rigo's grasp," warned Deneven.

Before Eva could answer, Brueck returned with a Vendraedi woman of approximately thirty seasons with long black hair tied in a ponytail. Her dark eyes possessed casual confidence, and she moved with the grace of cats and nighttime predators.

"Marchess," Deneven said with a flair of his hand, "allow me to introduce you to Vess, our ally."

When the woman nodded, Eva noted the scar on her chin. "Thank you, Majster D'Neir. Please wait in the parlor while Vess and I become better acquainted."

"This way," said Brueck.

Deneven hesitated. "But, Marchess, I—"

Eva raised her hand. "We both understand who holds the cards in this game. You will wait downstairs until summoned."

Chastened, Deneven bowed and hobbled out of the room. The leather valise remained on the table.

Eva and her cloaked guest waited in silence until the door shut, and the soft clunk of Deneven's peg leg faded.

"Vess, is it?"

"Yes, Marchess, or should I call you, Eva the Jarleina?"

"Let's not be coy; I have neither the patience nor the inclination to parse rhymes."

Vess' eyes sparkled with amusement. "I like you already."

Eva set the tumbler down. "A sentiment which I assure you is one-sided. I imagine you obtained evidence of my mother's murder and Tan'os' assassination via some unsavory means. Therefore, you are either a thief or complicit in these dealings. Why would I ally myself with someone as despicable as you?"

Vess settled into Eva's cushioned chair. "You offered Deneven a drink. Will you not extend the hospitality to me?"

"Certainly not as that would prove your insolence welcome."

Vess met the remark with a smile. She picked up the tea kettle and filled Eva's teacup. After taking a sip, she put the cup down and crossed her legs. "Welcome or not, you will work with me because the throne is your heart's desire. The documents in Deneven's valise are legitimate and will withstand the utmost scrutiny. Regardless, as I am sure you are aware, papers alone can't secure the desired outcome."

Eva nodded. "Yes, Deneven made his price clear. I believe this is the part where you attempt to extort me. Surely, you think you possess some leverage over me, or you wouldn't be sitting there gloating like the cat who's eaten the songbird."

"Extortion implies a threat and a one-sided deal, and you are no songbird. I have the connections required to restore your legacy. Should my services not be compensated? Come now, this is Reyza."

"Connections? Services? You mean blackmail."

"The Council is made up of mortal men and women. Like everyone else, they possess weaknesses and failings, misdeeds they wish to remain hidden." Vess clasped her knee with both hands. "I am gifted in the art of discovering and disseminating secrets, call my skills what you will."

"I do not need you to take what is rightfully mine."

"If you had the power to seize the crown, you would not be sailing at dawn with your tail tucked between your legs like a whipped bitch."

"How dare you speak to me like that!?"

"I dare because I know you, Eva Iarris Ensther."

Eva felt a chill tighten her belly at the dismissive inflection of her husband's last name. "You know nothing."

"You are vindictive enough to leave your husband's sister drugged and helpless in the care of those who would murder and rape her," Vess said with a cold, controlled tone. "The irony cannot be lost on you. You inflict misery on the girl just as Tan'os inflicted harm on your mother. Your thirst for vengeance is limitless."

The condemnation struck like a physical blow. Eva clutched her stomach. "Your talent is no idle boast. How have you gleaned this information? Rigo and I were alone."

Vess stood and offered Eva the chair. "Please sit, you look pale."

"No, I shall stand." Eva sucked in a lungful of air and released it in a long exhalation. "I admit; I am at a disadvantage."

"Only if you make it so." Vess returned to her seat. She dropped three cubes of sugar in the cup and stirred.

The tinkle of the spoon on the delicate ceramic grated Eva's ears. "Whom do you work for?"

Vess sipped. "The highest bidder; soon to be you."

"How much?"

"Eighty thousand sequins in trade bars delivered to the Jiulia before dawn. The sum will seal our agreement, certify the Council's vote, and appease Reyza's trading partners. After you seize power, I will remain in your employ and guarantee the obedience of your subjects for a mere eight thousand a month."

Eva reeled. The amount was no coincidence. Eighty thousand sequins represented the entire fleet treasury, secured in four ironbound chests concealed in Gøran's quarters. "If I agree, how will you reassure me that I am not handing over a fortune for a handful of empty promises?"

Vess nodded toward Deneven's satchel. "Keep the writ and the letter as tokens of my goodwill and evidence of my sincerity."

Eva sat on the bed. Her head spun with the consequences of realizing her lifelong dream. Rhiess would never surrender his title, but neither would he prevent her from seizing hers. They would be married in name only, ruling their dominions at opposite ends of the world. "What of Rigo? He won't step down without a fight."

"Deliver the money and assemble your forces before dawn. Leave the rest to me."

"You speak as though I have accepted your proposal."

Vess stood and met her gaze. "I assume nothing. I will consider the deal sealed when the payment is in my hands."

"Deneven said you would detail everything to my satisfaction. I see now that was a hopeful boast." Eva rose and escorted her guest to the door. "Good night."

"May our paths cross again," said Vess stepping into the hallway.

Brueck appeared in the doorway. "Is there anything you need, Marchess?"

"Escort our guests out and send word to Captain Gøran. Tell him I need to meet with him—immediately."

A HUMBLED JARLE

Brindi, Fourth of Nommen, 445 A'A'diel

The maze of rooms beyond the recital chamber bore painted depictions of the legends of antiquity. Colorful, mythological scenes adorned ceilings, walls, friezes, and mantels. The eye roamed, unable to rest within that frivolous space as it wandered from countenance to naked breast, to sword-wielding hand, to winged shoulders. Between the gilt-framed paintings flowed a sea of marble of every hue and pattern. Pale green veins met burgundy swirls and bluish slabs in garish geometric wainscoting.

Unlit crystal chandeliers hovered high above the salons while branched candlesticks offered illumination. Tapestried seats complemented tables of inlaid wood and ebony curios limned in gold. Pedestals of porphyry supported urns that overflowed with exotic blooms. A breeze stirred the fragrant air, rustling the brocaded curtains that obscured all traces of the outside world.

Although his vision was blurry, Jarle's other senses remained keen. The smell of wilting flowers, incense, and expensive perfume assaulted his nostrils. The masculine sillage contained vetiveria and citrus blended in some unknowable ratio with helichrysum. The earthy, soothing mixture was the sort of fragrance nature might produce in an idealized corner of Laremlis where the sun always shone. An even more exotic blend lingered in the mix—rockrose and sage—the scent of the Durauks. The thief grasped Avaren's wrist and drew her into the shadow of a column. "We are not alone," he mouthed.

Jarle looked in every direction, searching for anything that might confirm his suspicions. He tightened his grip on his dagger and pulled Avaren against him. The tension became almost nauseating as they waited and listened with their backs to the pillar. The tick of the pendulum in the parlor clock became deafening.

With glacial slowness, Jarle palmed one of his throwing dirks and focused his hearing, filtering out the hiss of their breaths and the soughing of the waves below the cliffs. Soon, the familiar chorus of sounds faded and revealed a faint fluttering akin to the ruffling of a sparrow's wings. Accompanied by a breeze, which was scarcely more than a whisper, the susurrus caused Jarle's throat to tingle.

"Behind you!" Avaren's warning arrived a heartbeat too late.

The attack came fast. The edge of a blade glinted before slicing through the black leather bracer on Jarle's forearm as he parried. A spatter of bright red blood stained the marble.

Jarle shoved Avaren away to protect her from the unseen assailant. "Find cover!"

Sparks flew as the second blow scraped along the column, narrowly missing Jarle's neck. The thief stumbled backward, unable to comprehend the vision before him. Twisting, whirling darkness swallowed the scant pools of candlelight. The shadowy mass that engulfed him resembled a sandstorm—a vortex of glinting blades that slashed and stabbed in multiple directions. Jarle ducked and dodged as he deflected the attacker's blows with sparking parries. The strident ringing of clashing metal filled the room as the flurry of slashes grew more determined. A line of searing pain scorched Jarle's ribcage. Another burned his shoulder beneath his pauldron.

Despite his best efforts, the whirlwind of sharp edges scored more hits. Sand clogged his nostrils and stung his eyes.

Half-blind and wounded in a dozen places, Jarle fought by instinct alone. A gash on his thigh caused him to tumble. Desperate to avoid the churning morass, he kicked a brazier in the thing's path before rolling to his feet. The silhouette in the center of the vortex rushed toward him. When his back hit the wall, and he could retreat no farther, he warned Avaren. "Go! Run!"

Following his admonition, a high-pitched scream swept through the room. Delicate vases shook then shattered; chandelier prisms rattled; windowpanes cracked.

Sheer agony assaulted Jarle's skull. He dropped his weapons and clapped his hands over his ears, but the horrific wail continued unabated. Clutching his head, he fell to his knees and spilled the food in his belly with heaving retches. He was near madness when two curved swords clanged to the marble tiles. The sandy wind ebbed to reveal a black-clad Durauk covering her ears. Heedless of anything but the harrowing sound, the guard vomited.

Jarle looked away from his crippled foe to where he had last seen his lover. Avaren's eyes glowed like twin embers beneath the shadowed recesses of a table. He watched in stunned awe as she emerged from hiding, mouth open as though delivering an aria.

Above his head, window panes exploded into tiny fragments. Jarle shielded his face from the rain of glass, before losing the battle against the insufferable sound.

*
**

Avaren channeled the unearthly shriek as she crawled out of hiding. Her knuckles grew white on the handle of the knife as she stepped over Jarle. The scream ended at the precise moment she plunged the blade into the Durauk's back.

The wounded adept lunged upward with shocking alacrity and clutched Avaren by the throat. The two women wrangled on the floor, locked in a mortal struggle.

Avaren twisted the dagger with all her strength before letting it slip from her blood-drenched hand. She turned her head to the side to alleviate the pressure on her neck, then gouged the Dessian's eyes with her thumbs. When her opponent's hold relented, she reached for the nearest weapon. Her scrabbling fingers found the woman's scimitar and held tight. With a savage growl, she slammed the pommel into the guard's skull. Blood coated the sword's snake-shaped hilt and splattered on her face, but Avaren did not relent. She clobbered her adversary's head until her cheek caved, in a mess of crushed flesh and bone.

With a half-gasped curse, the woman slumped forward and convulsed. When her trembling limbs grew still, Avaren pushed her aside. She dropped the sword and scrambled to Jarle's side. "Wake up," she said, shaking him. "Come back to me."

Before Jarle roused, the brass repoussé doors of Rigo's bedchamber flew open. Rigo stormed into the salon, bare-chested and barefoot, his long, ash-blond hair wafting down his back. His luxurious, peacock-patterned robe swirled around his athletic frame, exposing lithe, muscular thighs as he stomped in her direction. His puffy face and unhappy scowl gave testimony of a rude awakening.

"Neylen! Guards!" Rigo bellowed. "Who in Ven's name is screaming at this hour!?"

The sight of her father's killer boiled Avaren's blood. She gathered her scattered impulses into a passionate act of courage and picked up her dagger. Eyes gleaming, teeth bared, she charged.

Rigo twisted sideways and evaded the attack. The knife sliced through his silk robe.

"You?" Rigo growled, incredulously. "I will flay you alive!"

Misdirection is your ally. Jarle's words echoed in Avaren's mind as she dropped to the floor and kicked Rigo's knee with her heel. The unexpected blow buckled the regent's leg and toppled him. The man hit the ground with a howl. When he attempted to stand, Avaren swung for his gut.

Eyes wild with bloodlust, Rigo intercepted Avaren's wrist and twisted until the weapon slid from her grasp. The blade landed with a leaden clang. "You should have died with your father!"

As unimaginable pain traveled the length of her arm, Avaren collapsed and cried out. Inspired by her anguish, Rigo forced her face down and yanked so violently that her shoulder joint nearly popped the socket. "Stupid cunt! Did you think killing me would be that easy?"

Across the salon, the doors burst open. Several Durauks brandishing swords fanned out into the room, followed by a score of palace guards. An urgent voice rose above the soldiers' clanking footsteps. "Protect His Royal Highness!"

Tears streamed down Avaren's cheeks. She opened her mouth

to scream when a familiar sight stayed her.

Dagger in hand, her lover crept silently among the flickering shadows. He came up behind Rigo, grasped a handful of his blond curls, and pressed the knife to his neck.

"Let go of her," Jarle said with icy menace.

Led by a goatish-looking man, the soldiers rushed forward. Their advance suddenly ceased when Jarle's blade bit into the regent's throat. Thin crimson lines wormed down Rigo's chest and stained his robe. "Take one more step, and I will send this miserable bastard to the River of Dust. Please," he said, daring the guards, "test me."

Avaren grabbed her dagger and scurried behind Jarle. Shoulder pain and the sight of more soldiers weakened her knees and churned her stomach.

Jarle gave Rigo's hair a forceful tug. "Listen to me carefully, you piece of shit. I am fucking weary of this place. Tell your lackeys to withdraw, or you will taste more of my blade." For emphasis, the edge bit deep enough to elicit a strangled sob.

"Leave!" Rigo shooed his men with trembling hands, but the nervous quaver in his voice failed to rally them.

"What he means is," Jarle corrected, "clear the fucking room and bar the door!" Jarle's knuckles whitened around the handle of the blade. "Isn't that right? Your Highness?"

"Y-yes!" Rigo's voice rose in pitch. "Go! NOW!"

Recognition flickered in the guard captain's eyes. He lowered his sword a notch but did not budge. "Jarle Jars Jadien, you are accused of murder, theft, kidnapping, and rape. Release His Royal Highness unharmed, and I promise you the mercy of a quick death."

The Durauks exchanged glances as though communicating some silent plan. Their bodies grew tense, ready to strike.

Avaren's temper flared. "Rigo Iarris ordered the assassination of my father. Jarle Jadien is the only reason I live."

Jarle sank his knife into the soft tissue of Rigo's clavicle. The point pierced his shoulder joint, eliciting a yelp that intensified into a scream.

Tears burst from Rigo's eyes, and the color flushed from his cheeks. His blood-curdling howls echoed in the hall. Blood seeped down the sleeve of his robe and soaked into the silk. Rigo waved his hand in an angry sweep toward his guards. "Captain Arinda, disobey me again, and I will personally feed your family to the crabs! Do as he says! Now!"

Avaren pulled on Jarle's bandolier, urging him backward. "This way."

Jarle returned his blade to Rigo's throat. He fixed his gaze on the commanding officer. "Are you willing to risk your family's life for this asslicker?"

Captain Arinda's eyes danced from Rigo to Jarle. He sheathed his sword with a disgusted snort and turned to his men. "You heard His Royal Highness! Fall back. Retreat and secure the entry." He gestured to the Durauks. "You also or I swear on my honor that whatever misfortune happens on account of your insubordination will fall on your liege!"

The Dessian's padded boots made no sound as they retreated along with the palace retinue. When the last guard exited, the Captain backed away with slow, deliberate steps. "This is not over, street rat."

After the doors slammed shut, and the thud of a heavy latch filled the silence, Jarle threw an arm around Rigo's neck and locked him in a chokehold. When Rigo struggled, he pressed the knife to his testicles. "Do as I say, or you will meet Tan'os in the afterlife without your balls."

Rigo's face twisted into a mask of terror as Jarle dragged him backward toward the royal bedroom. Snot and tears dribbled over his lips in gooey strings as he pleaded, "P-please, let me go. I promise you amnesty, passage out of Reyza! I can grant you gold, jewels, titles. Be reasonable."

Avaren waited until the men crossed the bedroom's threshold before closing the doors. She pushed the bolt into place, confident the metal slab could halt an invading army.

Rigo's bedchamber was sumptuously appointed. Pale marble walls soared upward to a gilded ceiling. Portraits of former rulers hung in overbearing frames, illuminated by flickering orbs of elemental flame. An ostentatious bed heaped with cushions perched on a raised platform. The painted dome above the stately berth depicted an allegory of Ahitsura. Flanked by monstrous waves, the goddess rose from the sea to threaten the most profitable nations of Ibea: A'diel, Thromm, Dessia, Belvaaste, and Bel'Ohr. Not coincidentally, Five Isles appeared capsized in the pictorial deluge, while Reyza remained untouched.

Avaren grabbed hold of a flame-bearing elemental orb and circled the room. "According to my father, there is a secret passage here—somewhere."

Rigo shook his head. "The only way out is the cliffs."

Jarle's blade dug into his groin. "Are you certain?"

Rigo stood on his toes to avoid losing his scrotum. "No!" he screeched.

Avaren felt along the wall, searching for a draft, a groove, anything that might reveal a tunnel. "Where is it?"

When no answer came, Jarle dragged the tip of the blade up the inside of Rigo's inner thigh. Bright blood flowed in its wake.

Rigo shuddered and sobbed. "Please, stop! Mercy."

"Mercy!?" Jarle's voice dripped with darkness. "Which mercy do you wish? Shall I grant you the same mercy you showed my mother? How about the mercy you scripted for the Vise and his daughter? Or perhaps that which you inflicted on Irilio?"

Avaren's head whipped in Jarle's direction. The look that passed between them required no words. Jarle had lost everyone he cared about and loved to aid her. Guilt and sadness joined her rage. She wanted to leave Reyza and never return, but the fire of revenge still burned bright.

A light crept into Rigo's tearful, blue eyes. "Irilio is not dead. Spare my life, and I will release him."

"Liar!" countered Avaren.

"No, I swear! The poet lives. I can take you to him."

The possibility that Jarle's best friend could still be alive gave Avaren hope. "Start talking. Where is the passage?"

Rigo raised a trembling finger toward the platform. "Under the bed."

Avaren climbed the steps and lay on her belly. She pushed up the linens and peered beneath the imposing piece of furniture. The frame was carved from solid ash and adorned with cast-bronze fleurons. Perched on clawed feet, the monstrosity stood an armlength above the floor.

She held out the elemental orb and spied two brass rings inset into the wooden platform. "Found it! Looks like a door."

"Can you open it?" Jarle asked.

Avaren grabbed hold of the rings and tried to lift the slab, but the stone did not budge. "No."

Jarle shoved Rigo closer to the dais. "Tell us how it works willingly, or I will slice the answer out of you."

"It slides for gods' sake." Rigo's voice quaked with fear. "Pull both rings toward the headboard. You will see a tunnel and a stairway down."

Avaren crawled under the bed. She set the orb down and pulled the loops. The panel slid easily to reveal a gentle ramp of polished marble. "Damnation!" Avaren cried as the effort caused her shoulder to throb.

"You alright?"

"I'll live," Avaren said, illuminating the narrow chute.

"Talk to me. What's under there?" asked Jarle.

The smooth corridor opened to a small landing from which a crudely carved, steep stairway descended through the stone foundation. "A passage leads down; very tight. I will go first."

"Be careful," Jarle cautioned.

Avaren slid on her stomach and placed her feet into the chute. She lowered herself slowly until her toes grazed the ground. With the dagger in one hand and the glowing orb in the other, she dropped down.

In the passage, the air reeked of dust and cobwebs. Pebbles dug into the soles of her slippers as she ventured a few paces into the darkness. "Send Rigo down," she called out. "I will stab him to death if he tries anything."

Rigo slid down ungracefully, followed by Jarle, who closed the panel after him. Without a word, the trio set off.

For a long while, they walked in silence, each of them locked in their dark thoughts. The tunnel wound through interminable turns interspersed with sudden, severe descents. Moisture, mold, and age had transformed the once neatly chiseled steps into crumbling, rounded mounds. The corridor bore no resemblance to the polish of the palace, harking back to a time when Reyza required fortresses, not villas.

Avaren led the procession and illuminated the path. The captive followed with Jarle close behind, ready to prod him with the tip of his blade should he lag. The way Rigo pranced on the stones biting into his bare feet lent him the appearance of a spirited filly. Wealth and power offered little protection against the ailments of the body. Suffering and discomfort were classless.

"How much farther?" Jarle asked.

Rigo dabbed the wound on his shoulder. "No idea," he snapped. "I have never traversed this filthy hole."

Avaren stopped and turned to face Rigo. Her dagger glinted in the glow of the orb as she threatened his belly. "We should kill him—now."

Rigo's mouth opened and closed like a frog's while catching flies before words emerged. "I—I think I know where we are going. This tunnel is part of the old fortress. My father told me about it before he died."

Jarle raised his hand to steady Avaren. "Where does it lead?"

"The old granary below the kitchens, not far from the prison."

"Move," motioned Jarle.

"Neylen. Is he—"

"Dead," Avaren cut in. Her eyes glimmered, and her lips curved into a cruel grin.

"I am sorry you have suffered," Rigo said apologetically. "Your father's death was not my idea, you know. Neylen, he made me—"

Avaren wanted to sink her knife into Rigo's gut and twist, but she controlled the urge for Irilio's sake. "Mention my father or that Dessian mongrel again, and I will rip your tongue out."

Rigo backed away and bumped into the thief. "Apologies."

When Avaren trudged down the tunnel, Jarle pushed Rigo forward. "The next time you speak, your words better be relevant to our escape."

Rigo whimpered but offered nothing further. Thoroughly shaken, he moved through the darkness in silence.

A myriad of turns and descents later, the passage ended in a cobwebbed impasse. Avaren approached the webs and raised the elemental orb. The magically contained flame sizzled and hissed, sending up sparks as it touched the gossamer tangle. As the dusty skeins thinned, an outline became visible.

"I think we found the way out," Avaren said.

Jarle cut loose a swathe of cloth from Rigo's robe and used it to tie the regent's hands behind his back. He dug his fingers into the man's wounded shoulder and brought him to his knees. "Avi, watch him while I investigate."

Avaren set the orb in a rough niche and slipped behind the captive. Her heart thundered in her chest as Jarle squeezed past her. For all she knew, the entire palace garrison waited beyond the secret door.

The iron portal hung askew on hinges that time and moisture had whittled to rusted slats. Jarle sat on his haunches and kicked the bottom corner of the rotted casement with both legs, dislodging the lower hinge. Jarle jumped up and steadied the listing door with his hands. He worked the portal back and forth until the top hinge fell. The reinforced door came loose and crashed against something on the other side. A large wooden cabinet concealed the exit.

Jarle braced against the wall and pushed the door with all the strength left in his limbs. The shove jarred the cabinet, causing it to topple with a crash. The din of breaking wood and shattered glass echoed in the passage. A moment later, the massive portal collapsed on the splintered cupboard.

"So much for stealth," Avaren muttered, prodding Rigo forward.

They emerged into a storeroom that stank of honey and fermented yeast. Hollowed out long ago by pickaxe and chisel, the moldy walls housed shelves of mead-filled crocks that would not see daylight until Midsummer Feast. A single moonstone sconce illuminated the cavernous space.

Jarle grabbed Rigo by the hair and brought him to his feet. "Which way to Irilio?"

"He is in the dungeon, stretched out on the torturer's rack." Hatred flashed across Rigo's eyes. "I suspect he's grown as a person since last you spoke."

With a backhand, Jarle sent the insolent man reeling into the wall.

Rigo licked his split lip; managed a smile. "Kill me, and you will never free him."

"I used to play down here when I was a child," Avaren said, gaining her bearings. "I know where the prisons are."

"Hear that?"—Jarle punched Rigo in the stomach—"We don't need you anymore."

Rigo doubled over; caught his breath. "You do!" he said, raising a placating hand. "The palace is on full alert. Without me, you won't get past the sentries."

Avaren sighed. "I hate to agree with the bastard, but he's right."

Jarle clapped Rigo on his injured shoulder and extended his hand in invitation. "After you, Your Highness."

DESCENT INTO DARKNESS

Brindi, Fourth of Nommen, 445 A'A'diel

The fine-boned palace Ingues D'Commenzeur, the fifth Jarle of Reyza, built with its lofty heights and architectural excess concealed the grotesque foundations of an ancient fortress. Elegant Caz'd'Reyza rested on rough-hewn stones laid long ago by fearful hands more concerned with security than aesthetics. The thick, artless walls of the dank corridors that wound down to the dungeons had stifled the pitiful cries of countless prisoners. In places where the rainwater seeped through the masonry, moldy pools marked depressions on the floors.

Avaren led Jarle and Rigo through the maze of abandoned storerooms, whose iron doors slumped on rusted hinges like lopsided tombstones. Every glimpse into the darkness beyond summoned phantasms of demise.

Jarle slipped an arm around Avaren's shoulders and kissed the top of her head. "How do you know your way through these passages?"

Avaren leaned into her lover's embrace. "Toward the end of his life, Jarle Draos insisted we relocate to the palace. My father reluctantly agreed, and for a while, this place became home. I was nine years old and pure mischief. When I got bored, I snuck away and explored all the places my father told me to avoid."

"That must have riled him."

Avaren shrugged. "His anger was preferable to his indifference. Most of the time, I felt invisible."

Jarle gave Rigo a shove to keep him moving. "Hard to respect a man who can be everything to everybody except a parent to his child."

Avaren glanced down at her torn slippers. "My father believed every man built the world in his image. In Tan'os Ensther's world, everyone was either a tool or a pawn. I suppose I was both. His desire for the throne blinded him. He resented my mother, and I think that feeling colored his feelings toward me."

"I was a responsibility my mother never wanted." Jarle squeezed her shoulder. "We do not choose our families."

"No, but we choose our friends. What happened to Irilio? What did you find out?"

Jarle glowered at Rigo. "Word on the street is that he tried to poison Majster Maggot here. Irilio may possess questionable morals, but he's not a murderer. I suspect he was arrested because of me."

Rigo responded with a disgusted sigh.

Avaren tensed in Jarle's arms as the sound of muffled shouts, and armored footsteps echoed in the passageway. "Did you hear that?"

"Damnation!" Jarle cursed. "Run!"

Rigo chanced a glance over his shoulder, then threw himself on the ground. He curled into a fetal position with hands over his head and shrieked at the top of his lungs. "Guards! Help!"

Jarle kicked him. "Get up, or by the gods, I will gut you."

"Kill me, and you will never get past the gates."

Jarle grabbed a fistful of the regent's hair and yanked him upright. He slammed his fist into the side of his head. "Try that again, and I will flay the flesh from your bones."

Dazed by the blow, Rigo stumbled. "Curskin, son of a dead whore! I hope you roast in Hel!"

Avaren raked the tip of her dagger along Rigo's back. The stroke slit the silk garment and opened a bloody gash. "This blade killed your lover and is hungry for blood. Make another sound, and I will speed you to the afterlife."

Jarle cut another strip of cloth from Rigo's robe and stuffed it into the man's mouth. Satisfied with the gag, he pushed the man forward. "Move."

The noise of approaching footsteps and excited shouts spurred the trio into a run down a decrepit stairwell.

After a dozen steps, Rigo slipped on a patch of mold, and fell backward, knocking the flaming orb from Avaren's hands. The glass ball bounced twice and shattered in a fiery flash, leaving them in near darkness.

Avaren landed a kick on Rigo's rump. "Jackass!"

"Avi, forget it. How far to the dungeon?" Jarle asked, pulling the fumbling regent to his feet.

"Three floors down, on the opposite side of the palace."

"Ven have mercy."

Avaren winced as pebbles dug into her soles. "Our best chance of remaining undetected is an old, sealed stairway one floor above the prison."

"What do you mean by sealed off?"

"The stairs used to go all the way up the cliff, but part of the shaft crumbled. All but the last two stories were mortared closed."

Using the spine of his dagger, Jarle pried open the rusted metal claws of one of the moonstone sconces. He lifted the dimly glowing stone from its prison and handed it to Avaren. "Let's go. Mind the broken glass."

The sound of pursuing footsteps faded as they rushed through forgotten halls and oppressive stairwells. Strands of greenish mold threatened their footing while damp coldness prickled their skin. Upon reaching the abandoned shaft, Jarle cuffed Rigo and forced him into the crawlspace. One story down, a partially collapsed landing offered access to the hallway beyond.

Avaren tucked the glowing crystal under her arm and crouched next to Jarle. "I think we are on the same level as the dungeon."

Jarle crawled to the opening. "If the pigfucker moves prick him where it hurts. I'm going to scout ahead."

Avaren stopped Jarle before he exited the stairwell. Her eyes darted to his blood-stained pauldron before meeting his. "Please, be careful."

Despite his anxiety and discomfort, Jarle smiled. He cupped his lover's cheek and kissed her tenderly. "I will, I promise."

Beyond the landing, a curving, soot-stained thoroughfare led to the prison entrance. The hall reeked of tallow, mildew, and sweat. Oil lamps placed at regular intervals shed a meager glow on the blackened stonework.

Hidden in the flickering shadows, Jarle spied a fortified gatehouse with two doors. The first barrier was an iron portcullis behind which stood two sentinels, and the second, a wooden door reinforced with steel plates.

As he retreated, each footstep tormented him with the fear of discovery. Every urchin in the streets of Reyza had heard the tales of the Salon of Inquest. The barbaric amphitheater was said to be furnished with nail-studded benches upon which the accused sat, forced to witness the preparations for their interrogation. Some rooms contained immense iron rings, which compressed the limbs, while others were outfitted with contrivances to elongate them. A shudder raised the scruff on his neck as he imagined his mother trapped in the grisly place.

Once in the safety of the collapsed stairwell, Jarle caught his breath. "We are close to the entrance," he said, wiping his forehead. "The gatehouse is a barbican with a portcullis and a reinforced door. The lack of a grille on the solid door tells me they probably use a knock or passphrase to gain access." Jarle brushed his fingers through his hair. "Even if we get past the guards, more pitfalls may await us."

Avaren shone the moonstone in Rigo's face. "How many doors are there? What can we expect?"

Jarle withdrew the rag from Rigo's mouth. "Speak."

"Two." Rigo sucked in air and leaned his head against the cold stone. "The sentries are armed with crossbows. I suggest you untie me and let me do the talking."

The lovers exchanged worried glances over the proposal.

Jarle pecked Avaren's cheek. "We must act, Avi. The longer we wait, the slimmer our chances become."

With a swipe of her knife, Avaren freed Rigo's hands. "You do anything and I'll—"

"Yes, yes, if I so much as breathe wrong, you will skin me alive and chop me into tiny bits." Rigo rubbed the circulation back into his wrists. "Your threats lack creativity, but I'm not about to test their sincerity."

Jarle booted Rigo out of the stairwell. He hid the dagger under the collar of the regent's robe and pretended to drape a friendly arm around him. "Stay close," he instructed Avaren.

Avaren positioned herself behind the men and followed them as they walked down the hallway.

The soldiers guarding portcullis lifted their crossbows and aimed. "Halt. Identify yourselves!"

"Bark at me again, and I will have you disemboweled." Rigo's imperious tone rang off the stone walls.

The pair squinted for a better look, but neither lowered his weapon.

Rigo brushed back a dirty strand of hair and clucked his cheek. "Put down your arbalests before I shove them up your asses."

The younger of the two guards shifted his weight from one foot to the other. The steel of his helmet glinted as he looked to his counterpart. "But—"

The young man's protest was cut short by Rigo's outburst. "What, you turtle-brained oaf? How dare you defy me?"

The turnkeys lowered their crossbows and snapped upright.

"Apologies, Sire," said the youth.

Rigo huffed with exasperation. "If you are done playing with your cunts, open the fucking gate!"

A stout man with a scruffy beard and face resembling a plate of boiled dumplings faced his companion and nudged his chin toward the door. "Yes, Sire. Immediately, Sire!"

The gawky youth unhooked an iron key from the wall. His hand shook as he inserted the key in the lock. "Simmon, the man with him, is—"

"Quiet!" The man named Simmon pushed his comrade aside and took over his task. A moment later, the gate swung open. "Your Highness," he said, taking a bow, "I beg your pardon. Young Radolf here started only two weeks ago and has much to learn."

"If the ape does not know how to obey an order from his sovereign, then perhaps his trainer should be reprimanded."

The color fled from Simmon's cheeks. "Forgive us, Sire. Please, accept our most humble apologies."

Rigo tightened what remained of his tattered robe. "You are fortunate that my friends and I are in a rush, or else I would enjoy tossing your carcasses into the pit."

The heavy-set man genuflected. "Thank you, Your Highness. You are merciful and wise."

Jarle locked eyes with the seasoned soldier. "Do as your ruler commands, and avoid a tragedy. No need to be a hero."

The sentries tensed when they beheld the blade threatening Rigo's throat.

"Open the damned door," Rigo said, his voice cracking.

Though their eyes burned with anger, the guards obeyed. The pair grunted with effort as they lifted the crossbar that sealed the dungeon from the palace. They let the heavy brace fall with a thud.

Simmon eyed the myriad of cuts and bruises on his liege's body before settling once more on the dagger. "Should I give the passcode, Sire?'

"Go on," Rigo motioned.

"Lenora!" Two kicks against the iron-plated door punctuated the name.

The rusty creak of hinges followed the sound of a bolt lifting on the other side. The imposing door opened to reveal two men-at-arms blocking a wooden drawbridge spanning a natural chasm.

The stench of feces, sweat, and piss flowed from the dungeons in an eye-stinging miasma that soured the tongue. Beyond the bridge, the glow of braziers cast a lurid dance of shadow and light. From somewhere in the stony confines, a man wailed, while numerous others moaned in agony.

At the sight of the intruders, the guards readied their swords.

"Stand down!" Rigo commanded.

"Come out and lie face down in the hall where I can see you," Jarle said to the soldiers.

The turnkeys' eyes widened, but they quietly obeyed. After the last of them lay prone, the trio entered the gatehouse.

Avaren locked the portcullis and tucked the key into Jarle's belt. "That should hold them a while."

Jarle used Rigo as a shield as he backed away from the bars. When they were through the oaken door, Avaren kicked it shut.

"Listen carefully, you piece of shit"—Jarle untied Rigo's binds—"I can't lift the crossbar alone, so you're going to help me. Understand?"

Rigo opened his mouth to protest, but the tip of Avaren's blade cowed him. He shuffled to one end of the brace and hoisted alongside the thief until the massive bar slid into place.

The weary regent didn't complain when Avaren bound his wrists or when Jarle shoved him toward the drawbridge. His bare feet left bloody prints as he plodded across the planks. Dozens of gashes had turned his robe into a threadbare rag, and loss of blood imbued his skin a ghastly pastiness. A chilly breeze wafted up from the moat's watery depths and tossed Rigo's hair, bestowing him the wraith-like semblance.

On the other side of the shadowy cleft, the vaulted passage opened to a grand chamber surrounded by cells. The room served as a terrifying auditorium for the captive audience imprisoned around its periphery. The executioner, a broad-shouldered brute clad in bloodied leathers, was busy mutilating a prisoner's toes with a pair of smoking pincers. The victim's groans swelled to an ear-piercing shriek before fading to quiet sobs.

Exasperated, Jarle prodded Rigo forward and entered the room. "Cease!"

The shout caused the instrument to drop from the torturer's hand. The man ran gloved fingers through his greasy hair to appear presentable and bowed. "Sire! I was not informed you would be honoring us with your presence. A thousand pardons!"

Anger flared behind Rigo's eyes. "You presume I should advise you before visiting my own dungeon?"

"Certainly not, Esteemed Highness." The torturer eyed Avaren lustily and crossed his hands behind his back. "How may I be of service?"

"What have you done with the poet?"

"I did as you commanded, Sire. I stretched Majster Errion on a bed of nails and gave him a cold-water bath. He is in the Guest Room now, enjoying darkness and solitude while he reflects on his crimes. Shall I fetch him?"

"No. Place the key to his cell on your workbench and leave."

The leather-clad man unbuckled the keyring from his belt,

singled out a key, and laid it flat on his unconscious victim's chest. He smiled at Avaren, took off his gloves, and sauntered past them.

"Begone!" Jarle clenched his dagger, fighting the urge to slay the brute.

"Look! It's Jars! He's got Rigo, hostage," a weak prisoner cried out.

"Kill him, Jars! Kill him and set us free," another man echoed.

Around the hall, haggard captives stumbled to the edge of their cages. Their malnourished arms protruded between the bars, their fingers spread as though to receive a blessing from the gods. Desperate eyes gleamed from broken countenances.

"Lady Addonel, save us," a toothless geezer pleaded.

The sudden crash of splintering wood drowned the chorus of voices.

Jarle turned in time to see Captain Arinda's retinue of elite guards enter along with a cloaked figure. The taste of magic tickled his throat.

Seizing the distraction, Rigo smashed his forehead into Jarle's jaw. As Jarle recoiled from the pain, Rigo rolled from his grasp and bolted for the gatehouse.

"Free us!" shouted the prisoners. "For Cel's sake, let us out!"

Disoriented, Jarle spun around. Several passages led from the theater of torture. All appeared to be wobbling. "Irilio!?" he called, hoping against reason that his friend would answer.

Avaren dove for the bench and grabbed the keyring, careful to keep the key to Irilio's cell separate. "Time to leave!"

Guards fanned out when Rigo reached the drawbridge and blocked the entrance. From within their midst, Rigo shouted orders. "Bring me their fucking heads!"

Jarle and Avaren were about to flee when an ear-splitting scream froze them in place. Turning to face the commotion, they witnessed a perplexing sight.

Several soldiers held the shrieking torturer aloft, then flung the man into the abyss. Heedless of the executioner's demise, Rigo continued to bark orders. "After them, imbeciles! What are you doing?"

"Free us!" Panic intensified the prisoners' pleas. "Free us before it's too late."

The mob of guards surged forward and surrounded Rigo, penning him in with their shields. In the chaos, a woman's voice rang out. "Now!"

Jarle's blood chilled when the soldiers' swords flashed in the torchlight. The blades rose and fell in unison, time and again. Rigo's blood-curdling screams merged with the cacophony of the captives. For a moment, Jarle thought the guards were responding to the chant of the prisoners, but Avaren's strangled gasp brought the stark, horrifying truth into focus.

Rigo was being assassinated.

A prisoner banged a metal plate against the bars of his cell, snapping Jarle from shock. When the thief glanced in his direction, the old man waved him over. "Give me the keys, boy, and I'll tell you where your friend is."

Beads of sweat rolled down Jarle's forehead. He took the keyring from his lover's trembling fingers and unhooked Irilio's cell key. His attention shifted between the murderous coup and Avaren, who stood beside him, shivering. "Where are they keeping him?" Jarle asked, shoving the keys into the geezer's hands.

The convict began to work on the lock. His knobby fingers fumbled with each key in search of the right one. "Left corridor, all the way down. When it opens up, you'll find him. Third hole on the right."

Jarle grabbed Avaren's wrist and ran headlong into the indicated passage. When she lost a slipper, he tossed her over his shoulder and rushed down the stairs, skipping two steps at a time. As the echoes of butchered men reached his ears, he felt sick. Even if they managed to escape the palace alive, he would be a fugitive for the rest of his life. No place in Ibea would be safe for a king killer.

OUT TO SEA

Brindi, Fourth of Nommen, 445 A'A'diel

The black walls studded with ring bolts, and dangling chains echoed the screams of dying prisoners. The sound of steel scraping stone punctuated unintelligible curses and pleas for mercy that would never come. All witnesses of Rigo's butchery would pay with spilled blood.

"Irilio!" Jarle's desperate cries joined the terrifying echoes as he trudged down the tunnel in search of his friend.

Rusted gates barred rough cells, which were little more than damp burrows. Opposite the openings, small windows offered scant glimpses of moonlight and cold drafts from the ocean below.

Avaren covered her mouth with her robe to block the choking stench of the tunnels. Each step on the slippery muck filled her with terror. She shone the moonstone into the dark recesses of the cells, recoiling at the sight of mice and forgotten bones. Her eyes stung, and her lungs struggled for air in the oppressive dankness. Twice, she nearly retched.

Far from just, the prison was an instrument of vengeance and a hotbed of disease—an affront to civilization. The dungeons reeked of barbarity.

Avaren spat in hopes of dislodging the disgusting taste of rot from her tongue. "Did we make a wrong turn?"

Jarle steadied her. "The old man said left corridor, third cell, but we've passed at least twenty. If we double back, we will perish. Our only option is to keep going."

They rushed down a slick ramp that opened into a broad passage with larger cells. At the rear of one of the stone-carved hollows, a figure huddled on the moldy straw.

Avaren's heart leapt. "This one," she said, shining the light.

Jarle stepped up to the bars, his face a strange mask of fear and hope. "Irilio, is that you?"

The startled man hugged his knees into his chest and shrank from the illumination.

Jarle jammed the iron key in the lock. When it failed to turn, he kicked the gate. "Fuck Sherzi with a pole! That bastard singled out the wrong key!"

"No, it can't be! Try it again," urged Avaren. The sounds of men fighting and dying echoed through the passage. "Hurry."

The captive sat up unsteadily. "Jarle, is that you? Does my fevered mind conjure phantasms?"

With a disgusted grunt, Jarle flung the key into the cell. "I'm no ghost. To say you owe me one is a dramatic understatement."

Avaren suppressed a gasp as Irilio crawled across the filthy floor. The poet's garb was a mess of soiled rags that hung from his abused body like moss from an ancient oak. Patches of his scalp shone in places where hair once grew. Bug bites and angry rashes littered his limbs, and a bloody rag covered his eyes.

"What did they do to you?" Jarle asked, unable to keep the shock from his voice.

The poet grabbed hold of the bars and pulled himself up. "They stole the light from my world."

Tears welled up in Avaren's eyes. She clasped Irilio's bruised forearm through the gate and steadied him. "We're going to free you."

The broken poet turned his head toward the sound of carnage. He placed a hand on Avaren's and shook his head. "Fair lady, whoever you are, do not risk life and limb for a doomed poet. Go now, do not die here."

"Now's not the time for poetry." Jarle crouched in front of

the lock. He withdrew a crooked feeler hook and a crosspick from his leather tool wallet and began to work. The lock's size was intimidating, but the mechanism was rudimentary. He steadied his breathing, wiped his brow, and tinkered with the cylinder. With a deft twist, the tumblers clicked, and the bolt slid open.

Jarle kissed his lockpicks before slipping them back in his pocket. He rose to his feet, pushed open the creaky door, and grabbed Irilio's arm. "Can you walk?"

Irilio nodded. "I will crawl if I must. You have a plan, I hope."

"When have you known me to have a plan—for anything?" Jarle circled his arm around his friend's waist and guided him into the passage.

"I suppose 'tis better to die in good company." Irilio offered a weak smile. "You, Jarle Jadien, are one crazy bastard. For that, I thank you."

Avaren added her support to Irilio's other side. "We are close to the sea, but I don't know where this corridor leads."

Jarle gritted his teeth. "Only one way to find out."

Together, they helped Irilio down a set of rickety wooden stairs and past a series of dark, empty cells created to house prisoners for months or years. Glimpses into the prisons unveiled leg irons, inverted spiked collars, and the insufferable sound of scurrying rats. Genius and industry could not invent a worse place to erode a person's passion for freedom.

Avaren fought the urge to scream as a wet mass slithered against her foot. Her body ached, and her eyes burned with sleeplessness, but the desire to escape drove her forward.

Beside her, Irilio struggled with each step. His shaky footfalls slapped the flagstones, and his breath exploded from his nostrils. Just when she thought he could go no farther, the poet broke the silence. "The night we parted on Parthinia's terrace, I was certain I would never see you again."

"Not your best pun." Jarle hefted the poet's weight to take the brunt off of Avaren's shoulders. "I'm sorry for what you've suffered. I never intended to cause misery for my friends and family."

"Do not blame yourself. I am responsible for my choices and losses." Irilio sighed. "I can't wait to see the look on your face when

I tell you the strange tale of my downfall."

"You won't believe your ears when you learn what we've endured. This night is cursed."

"I concur," said Irilio. "The gods are pricks."

Avaren sneezed. "We will make it out of here, you'll see."

"Jarle, will you not introduce me to the addonel at my side?"

"Her name is, Unavailable," Jarle quipped.

The poet mustered a weak smile. "Is that a challenge?"

Jarle scoffed. "Have you not had your fill of chasing dangerous women?"

"Unavailable and dangerous, the mystery deepens."

The thief smiled. "You have no idea."

"When the torturer asked me if I knew something about your acquaintance with Avaren Ensther, I laughed." Irilio's tone took on a playful note. "I told him a beauty like her would never look twice at the likes of you."

"And this is why poets are the bane of men."

Despite her misery, Avaren laughed. The poet's spirit had fared better than his body. "And lowly thieves the bane of women."

"I knew it!" Irilio shook his head. "Leave it to fate to take my sight on the eve of meeting a goddess." Irilio squeezed Avaren's shoulder. "A pleasure to meet you, my lady."

"I like him," teased Avaren.

Jarle helped Irilio when his knees buckled. "I have a feeling this is going to be a long journey."

"Sounds like you two have a scheme beyond this scenic stroll. I admit I'm intrigued."

Jarle grunted when Irilio accidentally aggravated the wound on his shoulder. "I've booked us passage on the *Jiulia*. She sails for Goizonne at dawn."

"Fancy! How did you manifest this miracle?"

"Compliments of the Golden Snake."

The mention of the sinister name coupled with a chilling wind wafting in from the sea ended the repartee.

The trio descended to a split in the corridor and followed the least traveled path. Rough walls caked with salt and rotting seaweed closed in on them as they ventured toward the sound of crashing surf.

Avaren screamed when a rat dropped from the ceiling and landed on her head. The moonstone crystal tumbled from her hands as she flailed wildly to dislodge the furry beast.

The thief grabbed the clawing abomination by the tail and crushed it under his heel, but not before Avaren squealed with nervous tremors. "I hate this place!" she cried, rubbing her scalp.

Jarle wrapped his arms around her and soothed her with loving kisses. "I'm sorry you are tired and cold. This nightmare will hopefully end soon."

Avaren returned the embrace with a fatigued sigh. "I will feel better once we reach the sea."

Jarle picked up the glowing moonstone and handed it to her. "I can handle Irilio. All you need to do is illuminate our path."

Avaren shuffled ahead of them. The tunnel sloped down at a gradual angle and became progressively wet. Several times Irilio slipped on the moss-covered stones but found the will to keep going. The sound of waves buffeting the outer wall of the palace filled the corridor with a hollow roar.

They wandered in the damp twilight—tired and hungry, sleepless and bleeding—until the passageway ended.

"You are not going to like this," Avaren said, turning to face Jarle.

Several armlengths past her feet, a flooded stairwell descended into blackness. The waters rose and fell with the swells, engulfing six to seven rungs at a time.

"What's happening?" asked Irilio.

Jarle managed a cavalier tone for his friend's sake, "We're going for a moonlight swim."

"I take it our mosey through the field of rats wasn't thrilling enough?" A visible shudder shook Irilio's limbs.

Avaren handed Jarle the crystal. She removed her filthy clothes and took a few uneasy steps down the mossy stairs. "Wait here. I'll find a way out."

Jarle helped Irilio to the ground and sat beside him. "Please, be careful."

Avaren stepped into the swirling, black water, and sighed with relief as the sea soothed her tortured feet. Tingles of delight raced along her spine as her body shifted. Bruised, aching legs, transformed into powerful, writhing tails as her gills quaffed the ocean's air. When her mysterious eyes turned darkness into light, she broke the surface.

In the stark brightness, both men appeared worn thin. Worry creased Jarle's forehead, and shivers wracked Irilio's frame. The sight of them huddled at the water's edge brought tears to her eyes.

Avaren caressed Jarle's leg with one of her tails. When their eyes met, her heart somersaulted. Never again would she forsake him. "I love you," she mouthed before disappearing beneath the restless tide.

THE JIULIA

Brindi, Fourth of Nommen, 445 A'A'diel

The trio of refugees sat huddled in a dinghy that slowly drew closer to a low-slung ship anchored away from the intimidating hulks of the Thrommish fleet. In the silver light, the *Jiulia* appeared alien. She lacked the armored heft of the warships and the liquid lines of Seh'nahiel frigates. The Terranakan vessel's sharp angles presented the impression of predatory speed. Despite the assurances of their guide, and international treaties which afforded ships from Terranakis unhindered passage, Jarle did not trust the Golden Snake. The man was a leech capable of selling his own mother.

Jarle draped his arm on the poet's trembling shoulders. Across from him, Avaren sat between two rowing sailors, her jewel-like eyes glittering in the darkness. He offered her a smile but felt no mirth.

As they neared the vessel, a sheet of fog rolled in and obscured the northern juggernauts until only their lanterns shone through. The blurry orbs bobbed in an arc around the harbor—a pageant that caused Jarle's palms to sweat and his stomach to tighten. Assuming the ship sailed past the blockade, he had no clue how he was going to go to ground with a blind man and a woman with such unforgettable eyes.

The rippling black water was hypnotic, yet all Jarle saw was his parents' grave. The sudden bitterness swept the cobwebs from his mind, and he clenched the handle of his dagger beneath the tarp. "Row faster," he said, thinking out loud.

The sailors ignored the outburst and continued to tread water at a steady pace. The old salt sitting beside him spoke, "We are almost there, Majster Curro. Focus on the horizon to ease your stomach."

The alias grated Jarle's ears. The fact that the surname was one syllable away from curskin was no coincidence. He would be Julius Curro for the remainder of the voyage as punishment for his unwelcome visit. Irilio and Avaren, known to the crew, as Devodro and Rosalin, fared better.

"Is my discomfort so obvious?" Jarle asked.

The sailor nodded. "I have seen gaffed galefin with more composure. Rest easy land-walker; the *Jiulia* runs as smooth as mother's milk."

A sly smile crept over Avaren's face. "My husband abhors seafaring."

"Aye. My brother clings to land like a drunkard to a bottle," said Irilio.

Jarle released the blade and gave Irilio a playful shake. "Is it any wonder why I always need a drink?"

"I'll happily switch places with you," said a young sailor behind him.

The poet hunched forward as though to shield himself from some internal pain. "In hindsight marrying Lynyah would have been a blessing. I am a fool."

Jarle's eyes darted to Avaren. Revealing their real identities would not bode well. "Now is not the time to dwell on the past, Devodro."

The bow of the Jiulia emerged, trailing fog-wreaths on either side like steam from the maw of a leviathan. The men raised their oars and allowed the dinghy to glide the rest of the way. When they bumped the side of the hull, the crew lowered ropes from davits to bring the small boat and her passengers on board.

On deck, a lean, middle-aged man with sun-leathered skin

and blond hair tied in a queue leaned on the ship's railing. He wore a trim, black uniform and ran a speculative eye over them. "Welcome aboard. I am Jhondolo Merritt, the quartermaster. You are about to set foot on Terranakis and sail under our protection.

As the boat neared the deck, Jhondolo ordered the sailors with a robust and commanding voice. Jarle didn't understand the crew's musical language but sensed their intentions were benign when a stair was brought to bridge deck and dinghy.

After the rowers alighted, Jarle helped his lover alight. "Stay close."

Avaren fluffed her wet skirts. "I won't get far in these."

"I will free you from your stays soon, dear *wife*."

Irilio grabbed Jarle's hand and wobbled to his feet on the rocking boat. "You two are enjoying this charade too much."

Jarle guided the poet down the stairs. Once on deck, he clasped the quartermaster's hand. "Thank you for honoring such a late arrangement."

"I am pleased to help a friend of Leoros. Please, go with my men. You will be warm and comfortable in the kitchen while we prepare your berth."

Pierced by the shaft of the foremast, the galley of the Jiulia was cheerful and warm. Carved beams framed polished mahogany cabinets and shelves brimming with supplies. Rows of glass jars containing preserved jellies and vegetables shared space with a multitude of condiments and specialty bottles of liquor. Dry-cured hams smoked sausages, and brined cheeses swayed from hooks with the Jiulia's bobbing motion.

Shiny copper pots stacked four high teetered on a worktable near a hulking, iron oven. Reclined against the metal bar that safeguarded the hot surface, the ship's cook waited for a tea kettle to boil.

Jarle shot the man a suspicious glance as they sat around an oaken table. The cook's face was scored like a dry fig, and his eyes were narrow and wideset. Catching Jarle mid-stare, the man smiled, flashing a set of sharp canine teeth. The unnerving sight confirmed the man's Iah'gren bloodline.

Turning away from the cook, Jarle assessed his companions. Dressed in gentleman's garb, Irilio appeared much more himself, but his constant scratching told of his misery. Though he could not see his eyes, he suspected that his friend hovered at the edge of slumber. Sitting beside the poet, Avaren hunched forward with her head propped on one arm. She looked every bit like a wilted daffodil in a piss-yellow dress and matching cloak. The Golden Snake's humor was not amusing.

Jarle unlaced the sodden leather cuirass that nearly cost him his life during their underwater escape. The movement caused the gash on his forearm to bleed anew. "Ven be damned," he said, applying pressure to his arm.

"Let me see," Avaren said, unlacing his vambrace.

"Wait," said the cook.

"What for?" asked Avaren.

The Iah'gren wrinkled his nose. "The medic. I don't enjoy scrubbing curskin blood from my kitchen."

Jarle went to stand, but Avaren halted him. "If you do not want a mess, then I suggest you hand me something to bind his wound," she said flatly. "And fetch the healer at once."

The beady-eyed man tossed them a clean dish rag before busying himself with several jars of herbs. Oblivious to the command, he hummed a tune as he crushed dried leaves into a strainer. "Medicine cures the man who is fated not to die. I will prepare a calmative to heal you and ease your pain."

Avaren wrapped Jarle's forearm in the cloth and applied pressure. "Thank you."

Jarle ignored the strange man and cocked his ear toward the ceiling. The faint sound of footsteps and the cries of sailors joined the creak of the ship's wooden walls. Instinctively, he drew his blade. "What's happening?"

The cook poured steaming water into three mugs. As he did so, a grassy, soothing scent suffused the room. "I can tell that Angry Curskin, Bright Star, and Blind Man had a long, trying day. Worry no more for you are safe in my kitchen, and the *Jiulia* is as swift as a starling."

Jarle bristled. "I have a name."

The cook responded with a toothy grin. "I have a name too."

Avaren wrapped the cloak around her shoulders a little tighter. "Mind telling us what is going on upstairs?"

The man placed the mugs on a tray and brought them to the table. He set a cup in front of each of them. "*Jiulia* sails early."

Jarle slammed his fist down. The cups rattled. "That double-crossing snake!"

Irilio, who had dozed off, awoke with a start. "W-what? Where?"

Avaren guided the poet's hand to a mug. "The ship's cook brewed us some tea. Careful, it's hot."

"Thank you." Irilio circled his fingers around the warm drink. "What did I miss?"

Jarle rubbed his face with his hands. "The Golden Snake lied to me about the time of departure. We are setting sail hours ahead of time. Had we but delayed a half-hour, we might not have boarded."

Avaren met Jarle's eyes. "The sooner we leave, the better, don't you think?"

Irilio frowned. "I never imagined I would ever leave Reyza. Gods know my parents must be worried stiff. They were excited about my marriage and expecting grandchildren, and now—" The poet sighed— "who knows."

Avaren stroked Irilio's back. "You will s—." She pursed her lips. "Meet them again."

The cook considered the blind man. "In Xio-Bahnn, we have an old saying, 'Love looks with the mind, not the eyes.'"

Jarle cringed at the comment, then exhaled. Anger would solve nothing. "Thank you for the tea."

The fanged man gave a curt bow. "Are you hungry?"

"Yes!" Irilio burst out.

"Very," added Avaren.

The cook beamed. "Bright Star, your beauty reminds me of my eldest granddaughter. I shall prepare for you her favorite meal, a traditional Jinquo-yun breakfast."

Avaren smiled. "Please, don't trouble yourself, Majster—"

"Kian-ido."

"My name is Rosalin, and this is my husband, Julius, and his brother Devodro. Some bread or fruit is fine. We don't wish to be a burden."

"Please, call me Kian." The cook walked back to the counter, where he opened and closed cabinets in his search of ingredients. "I am pleased to make a meal for honored guests. Drink and loosen up while your quarters are made ready."

"Honored guests?" Jarle arched an eyebrow.

Kian gathered some yams and commenced peeling. "Yes. The captain said we should show you all due"—the cook paused, searching for the right word—"gentility." A low chuckle followed the word.

Rife with suspicion, Jarle sniffed the tea. "What did you say was in this?"

"I did not say."

Irilio took the first sip and shrugged. "Not bad."

The thief scowled. His friend was far too trusting. "Will this put us to sleep?"

"Yes," said Kian-ido. "My tea is a magnificent curative for many aches and ills."

Avaren clinked Jarle's cup. "To freedom."

Irilio yawned. "And rest."

After a cautious sniff, Jarle brought the steaming beverage to his lips. Kian-ido's concoction was a nauseous mess of flavors, but each sip diminished the ache in his muscles. Slightly less tense, he reached out and caressed Avaren's cheek. "How are you?"

Avaren was about to reply when the door swung open. A barefoot, olive-skinned boy in sailor's garb ran into the galley and stopped a few paces from where they sat. He removed his cap and bowed. "Greetings. My name is Nicola, but you can call me Nico. I will be your steward." The boy's eyes widened as he took in the sight of Irilio's bandaged eyes and Jarle's bloody bandage. "Apologies, I didn't realize you were hurt."

Jarle eyed the youth. Nico sported a tousled mop of dark hair and bright, intelligent eyes. His accent marked him as Zherrian. "You were saying?"

When the boy laid eyes on Avaren, he began to fidget. "I'm your cabin boy during the voyage. Anything you need, you just tell me, and I'll do my best to make you feel welcome."

Jarle drained his mug. "Thank you, Nico, but we have no coin with which to retain your services."

The steward gave Jarle an odd look. "The cost of your fare

includes my services." His face lit up. "I hope you are pleased. Aside from the captain's quarters, your cabin is the finest in the entire ship."

Avaren shot Jarle a glance. "Is that so?"

"Oh yes, Mejtress Curro. Your cuddy is large enough for four passengers with two sets of windows from which you can gaze out over the sea. There is a sitting area furnished with finery and berths stuffed with feathers. I arranged your belongings and stowed away your trunks."

Irilio straightened. "Trunks?"

"Splendid!" Jarle declared, discouraging further comments from the poet.

"Please, call me Rosalin, and my husband, Julius. No need for formality," said Avaren.

"As you wish, beautiful lady."

What do your duties entail?" asked Jarle.

The youth threw his shoulders back and lifted his chin. "As your steward, I arrange your meals, tidy your cabin, draw water for your baths, borrow books for your leisure from the captain's library, and answer questions about our voyage. If you like," he said excitedly, "I can show you how to tie knots like a sailor!"

"You will discover that the lady is already quite adept at tying knots," said Jarle.

The boy's eyes sparkled as he regarded Avaren. "Excellent! We can hold a wager."

Avaren finished her tea, then rose. "Perhaps, after we've had some time to rest. Please, show us to our quarters."

Kian stopped chopping and turned to address the youngster. "Come back in a quarter bell for their breakfast and make sure they are stitched up."

The boy acknowledged the cook with a tip of his hat. "Follow me," he said, walking toward the exit.

Jarle stood and moved around the table to help Irilio.

The poet slung his arm around Jarle's waist, and together they hobbled after the youth. "I have heard tales of men going blind from the spices in Xio-Bahnnese dishes. I suppose there's no danger of that."

Jarle helped Irilio up the galley stairs. "Can't be worse than eating kelp and áels for months."

"Kelp? Áels? Do I want to know?" asked Irilio.

Jarle and Avaren replied in unison, "No!"

*
**

Overhead the dawn sky was clear with a promise of swift sailing. The bowsprit of the *Jiulia* turned, and the ship dipped in the southwesterly swell. The captain laid a course to skirt the Reyzan peninsula before heading north into the Xarxet Main. Barefooted sailors scrambled along the ship's shrouds, chanting while they unfurled the mainsails in preparation for a full run toward the open sea.

The air freshened after the storm, and all square sails were set, with the foresail reefed to allow the lookouts a clear view ahead.

Across the harbor, the bell atop the Collegium began to toll.

The somber sound had not been heard in Reyza for nearly a decade. The mournful knell announced the death of a regent. Rigo Iarris, the Jarle of Reyza, lay dead.

After a long, respectful pause, the bells of every shrine joined the dolorous tolling. For some, the clarion call signaled a tragedy, for others, a celebration. The devastated city had more to rebuild than flooded streets and damaged buildings.

Running fast before a gay wind, the *Jiulia* listed to her port side. With each luff of her sails, Reyza faded in the distance.

Jarle and Avaren cuddled in the upper bunk of their posh cabin, while Irilio snored softly below them.

Avaren laid her head on Jarle's chest and traced the linen bandages wrapped around his forearm. "Kian-ido is odd, but his cooking is faultless. Those yam fritters were divine."

Jarle smiled. "I didn't know what to expect when he said he was preparing a Xio-Bahnnese breakfast. Food from the Crescent Isle is rumored to be so spicy that Chaian cuisine tastes bland in comparison. Guess I was wrong."

Avaren grew serious. "Who do you think was that woman who ordered Rigo's death? Do you think she will come for us?"

Jarle stroked Avaren's hair, reassured by the steady beat of his lover's heart. "By now, the Thrommish fleet is behind us. Even the

Whisperers cannot catch a Terranakan barque on the open sea."

"People say that the cities in Terranakis float like corks on the water and that the Xio-Bahnnese can light up the sky with explosive powder."

Jarle looked at Avaren. He doubted he would ever grow tired of gazing into her breathtaking eyes. "Before meeting you, I would have dubbed those rumors legends, but now"—Jarle smiled—"I refrain from passing judgment on unbelievable things."

Avaren sighed. "I fear for Irilio. I can't imagine what it must be like to lose one's sight."

Jarle shut his eyes and cradled Avaren close. "He's lost his sight, but not his vision. I hope you are prepared to become his muse."

Avaren's breathing grew steady and deep. Her eyes slowly closed. "Tell me about Goizonne," she whispered.

Jarle caressed the girl's arm. "The island is on the other side of the world, far away from Reyza and Thromm. It is a land of beauty and peace where the wine flows in rivers and bread grows on trees, or so the tales go. We can disappear and be whoever we wish to be—together."

"We can live like áels in a cozy cave," Avaren said, groggy with slumber.

Jarle's chest swelled with hope. He kissed her forehead. "Áels in a cave sounds wonderful."

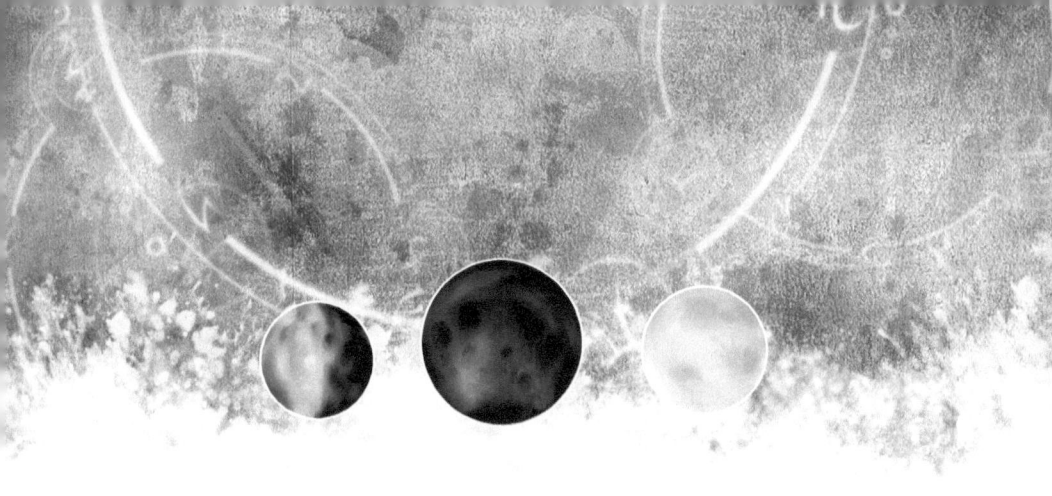

EPILOGUE

— Three Months Later —

Mir'kadi, Twelfth of Lusc, 446 A'A'diel

Deneven propped himself up on his pillow, careful not to wake his lover. Every morning, as the mantle of sleep lifted, the weight of a thousand responsibilities returned.

Toil and turmoil followed Rigo's death. In the aftermath of the flood, the once vibrant city succumbed into a quiet uncertainty—a mood that was palpable in every alley and tavern, drawing room and bedroom.

The Council legitimized Eva's ascension, but she inspired little confidence. Neylen's murder, and Thromm's maritime chokehold, eroded trade relations with Dessia beyond reconciliation. Within weeks, marble and precious stones disappeared from the markets engendering the wrath of the Mistress of Rats.

The Jewelers' Guild consolidated their diamond reserves, which in turn affected lenders and inflated prices throughout the city. As the cost of building materials, labor, and goods soared, reconstruction in the most afflicted parts of Reyza slowed to a crawl. With the dockside warehouses in shambles, trade tapered to one or two ships a month.

Deneven grabbed a decanter of brandy from the bedside table and poured himself a drink. The liquor burned his nostrils before blossoming with soothing warmth in his belly. His meteoric rise to Vise and the woes that followed made him wary of the woman who shared his bed.

The daevil who called herself the Hand of Fate was as mercurial as she was lubricious. She came and went, often disappearing for days. All attempts to pry into her nature resulted in periods of prolonged absence that triggered bouts of limerence he hadn't felt in years.

Deneven set the glass down and studied his sleeping lover. The shapeshifter lay curled in the woolen blankets, appearing every bit the ingénue who tended him at the baths the previous evening. She had long dark hair and a boyish build with small breasts, and a heart-shaped face worthy of a sculptor's chisel.

Deneven brushed a lock of hair from her face to reveal the reddish scar that never healed. In his mind, the permanent mark had become her only true identity.

The sorceress was a phantom—an enigma who thrilled him with sexual games beyond his imaginings. He surmised she watched him, as her invitations almost always came on stressful days when he needed a reprieve.

Each time they met, they did so in a different place. And when they made love, she never wore the same skin twice. Sometimes the Fate impersonated familiar people, other times, strangers. More than once, she came to him as a man.

The abandoned house where they had spent the night was silent except for the moaning wind and the crashing waves. When his lover insisted they meet at the scene of the crime, the one place where no one would dare to search for them, Deneven had not been surprised. Despite loathing himself for associating with so vile a personage, he did not wish to end the affair. The depraved rendezvous rekindled a fraction of his youth—a thrill he was unwilling to forsake.

Deneven pushed off the blanket and sat at the edge of Tan'os Ensther's bed. As he reached for his peg leg, his eyes lingered on the spot where the Northman's great sword had lain. Though the bloodstains were gone, the message was clear. If he ever crossed her, he would join the former Vise in the afterlife. As the woman stirred, Deneven frowned. "Ah, the Shadow awakens."

Girlish fingers tickled his midriff. "Leaving so soon?"

Deneven buckled the straps that held his wooden leg in place. "I'm due at Criers' Corner at noon. The Jarleina believes that going shopping on the first Market Day of the year will raise sour spirits."

"And what do you think?"

Deneven rubbed his face with both hands. "I don't think people give a damn about seeing us purchase this morning's catch. If we don't settle trade with Dessia soon, A'diel's coffers will overflow while Reyzans starve."

The Fate rolled out of bed and walked to the fireplace. She uttered some unintelligible susurration that brought the spent embers back to life. In a flash, the ashes transformed into tongues of flame that licked the blackened stones. "I suspect Kha Shanin is already regretting his decision to sever ties with Reyza. Many Dessians are of Yerr'draki lineage, and Seh'nahiel grudges are eternal."

Deneven shuddered as the petite, naked girl fed the last two logs into the unnatural fire. She seemed so at ease in Tan'os' bedchamber—so smug—that he couldn't help but wonder if they had once been lovers. "Why have you brought me to this grisly place?"

The sorceress grabbed hold of the sheets that covered the fireside chairs and pulled, sending a cloud of dust into the air. "I think it's time you learned how to play Thrarttas. Besides, this place holds pleasant memories for me. Tan'os and I weren't always adversaries."

"You were lovers."

The Fate shrugged. "Are you jealous?"

Deneven rubbed his thigh muscles before standing, then limped to the fire. The warmth was not sufficient to thaw the chilling, murderous emotions that surged through him at the thought of being another one of her pawns. He seized the Fate's throat and squeezed, never fearing he could harm her. "Every day, I struggle with my feelings for you. I live in perpetual expectancy. When we are together, time slips away as though in a dream. When we part, I realize what a fool I've been."

The girl's dark eyes shone. The guise of innocence, coupled with the wanton look in her eyes, proved irresistible. Deneven released her and circled his arms around her waist. He lifted her off the ground and carried her to one of the chairs where they fell back awkwardly. Kneeling before her, he suckled her nipple hard enough for her to cry out. "Have you nothing to say?"

The sorceress reached down and fondled his erection. She gave him a saucy smile, then grew serious. "Hush, someone comes."

Deneven listened. Somewhere in the empty house, a board creaked, then another.

In a blur of motion, the woman escaped his grasp and grabbed her daggers.

Deneven scarcely had time to hobble to the bed and grab his cane before a rude knock disturbed the stillness.

"Announce yourself," said the Fate.

"Apologies for disturbing you, Mistress," came a feminine voice.

The Hand of Fate chuckled at Deneven's defensive stance. Using the tip of her dagger, she motioned to his clothes. "One moment, Ily."

Deneven slung a blanket over his shoulders, then tossed a sheet in her direction. The woman caught it with flair, transforming before his eyes into someone altogether different. The girlish façade melted to reveal a woman of more seasons with a mane of dark curls and pale blue eyes. When she opened the door, a disheveled young girl wearing leather armor stepped into the room.

The woman glanced nervously between the two of them, then brushed her palms against her pants. "I bring news of the *Jiulia*."

Deneven grabbed the decanter and poured the informant a drink. He rounded the bed and walked to the door. "Apologies for my attire. Here," he said, handing her the goblet, "allow me to improve your morning."

Ily took the cup and chugged back the brandy. She curled her lips over her teeth, then exhaled with a hiss. "I doubt it, but thank you."

The Hand of Fate crossed her arms. "Speak."

"The ship arrived in Goizonne, as scheduled, but"—the young

woman winced, as though the words caused her pain—"Merritt claims Captain Haukon went mad and tossed your chests into the harbor. He sent word with the Whisperers."

A sudden, scalding wind banished the morning chill. "Surely, Merritt retrieved the cargo!"

The messenger handed Deneven back the glass and took a step back. "He used diving bells, and his men found the strongboxes, but they were empty. Your money is gone."

Song
– OF –
ISONEI

By Narcisse Navarre

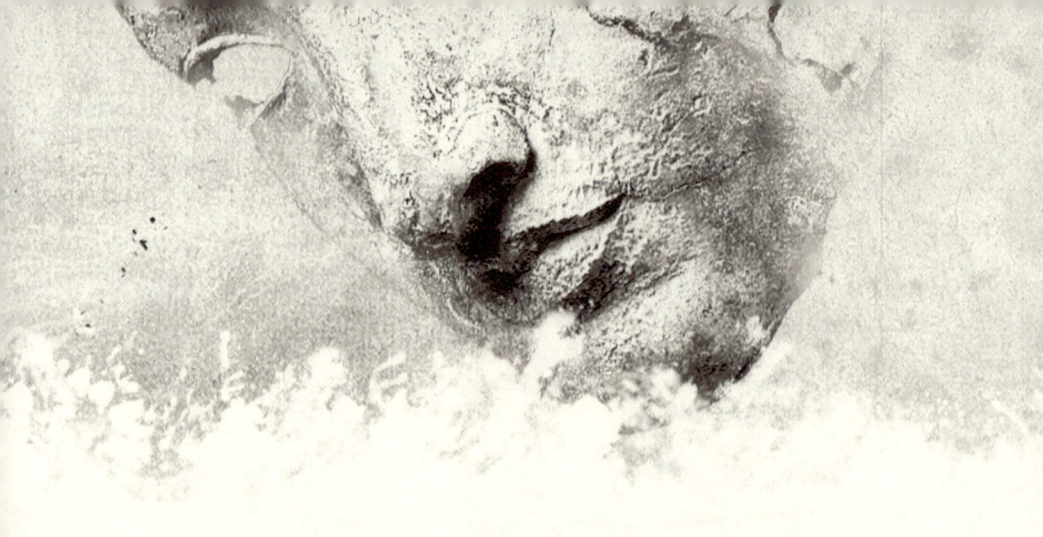

THE SONG OF ISONEI

— One Year Earlier —

Brindi, Fourth of Sund'im, 444 A'A'diel

At dusk, the young poet Irilio descended from his family's forlorn villa perched high in the hills of Gavalene and entered the city's only park. Cleared of courtiers and merchants by the late hour, the expanse of woods with its enchanting nooks was an oasis of tranquility, but Irilio felt no peace. His father's tirade of the merits of marriage and news of his betrothal to the dullest woman in Laremlis ruined his day, and possibly his life.

Feeling powerless, the courtier walked through the verdant lanes and lashed out at the clusters of dark shrubbery. He smacked the bushes with his walking stick; poked the marble pedestals of nymphs and shouted his displeasure to the moons. Above the trees, loomed the Temple of Zezen where couples seeking happiness tossed jewels into the goddess' well. The pavilion's golden dome shone brightly against the serrated silhouettes of needle pines—a stark reminder of his future.

Irilio bent down and picked up a rock. He weighed the object in his hand, and upon finding it too light, threw it aside. He jogged along the gravel path to a crumbled statue and rummaged through the rubble. The merry nymph's head, cleaved in two by time and moisture, provided a heavy chunk of marble.

"Perfect!" he mused, holding her broken face to the moonlight. "You, dear girl, are prettier than my future bride, and likely more intelligent. Thus, I impose the cow's name on you with great chagrin. You are hereby known as Lynyah."

The poet tucked the decrepit head under his arm and made for the temple. His footsteps crunched on the path as he whistled a bawdy tune. He had a year and a half to enjoy the pleasures of bachelorhood before the yoke of marriage slammed down on dalliance. He would start by showing his disgust with the marital institution by dumping his bride's proxy into the sacred well. No jewels, nor wishes for happiness with Lynyah would be forthcoming.

Irilio entered the building through the columned portico. The walls rose to a frescoed rotunda depicting joyful Akadian scenes. The light of elemental orbs illuminated carvings of nymphs and satyrs. Winged addonels blessed the bucolic figures with garlands and summer fruit. Inside, a soothing sillage of burnt resin and crushed petals suffused the air. Beams of moonlight filtered through the oculus high above, bathing the steaming font in brilliant light.

Irilio spread his arms in mockery of the welcoming effigy and smiled at the multi-breasted goddess. He set down his cane on the lip of the well and held the stone head over the water. "I come with an offering; my future wife's head!"

"Most unwise," came a masculine voice.

Startled, Irilio lost his grip. The statue's head tumbled from his hands and splashed into the black waters of the pool. Whipping around, the poet scrabbled for his dagger. "Who goes?"

Mailled footsteps echoed in the pavilion as a guard wearing the palace livery stepped forward. The man, whose face betrayed forty seasons, held his helmet under his arm. His graying hair was slicked back and his eyes filled with pathos. His pauldrons and vambraces glinted in the flamelight as he approached. "At ease, I am no foe."

Irilio sheathed his blade and smoothed his tunic. He gave the rippling water a cursory glance before addressing the man. "I did not see you when I came in."

"I was sitting in the shadows."

"Praying for a sweetheart?"

The semblance of a smile crossed the soldier's face. "Something like that."

The young courtier extended his hand. "Irilio."

"I know who you are." The man shook his hand. "Name's Matello."

"What you witnessed; let's keep it between us, yes?"

Matello gazed longingly at the pool. "I will hold my tongue, but I doubt the underdweller will forgive you."

"You believe that nonsense?" Irilio scoffed.

"Aye. The spirit of the water calls herself Isonei." The guard sighed. "This was once a place that delighted me as a boy."

Intrigued, the courtier sat on the ledge. "There is no fitter place for a poet to dream of love and commune with the beings of his imagination, but you do not strike me as one, sir."

The soldier chuckled. "Indeed, I am no rimer, but I tell you, I have been very happy here, in the company of this pool and its watery dweller."

"Tell me your story then."

Matello set his helmet down and joined Irilio. He sat at the edge of the basin and stretched his legs. "I shall but only if you promise to pen a ballad."

"Since I cannot vouch for my own happiness, I will rejoice in yours. You have my vow."

"I grew up in a family of means and as a boy, I often played here. One autumn evening I heard a beautiful song. I followed the melody through the wood and wandered past the arcade. I was five or six at the time; not allowed near the temple. My parents were afraid I would drown."

"A female voice, I presume?" asked Irilio.

"Aye, an addonel's voice, sweet and sublime." Matello stared into the flickering darkness for a moment before unhooking his wineskin. He uncorked it and took a sip, then handed the bladder to Irilio.

The poet took a swig and grimaced at the watered-down ale. "Gratitude," he said handing it back. "Please, continue."

"The sound led me to this very place where I beheld a sparkle. I climbed up over there for a better look," he said pointing to the base of the statue.

"What did you see?"

"Hundreds of tiny glints, like a school of silverfish moving beneath the water. At the time, I was too young to realize I had seen her tails. As I grew older, and our meetings became more intimate, I began to make sense of her mysteries."

"What man can make sense of any woman, sir? Even a character as fictitious as your friend is unknowable."

The passionate outburst inspired a hearty laugh from the soldier. "You misunderstand my meaning."

"Wild legends have the most powerful charm when least artfully told."

"I will try not to insult you with my paean, laureate Irilio."

"I am far from grievance. Elucidate me."

Matello corked the wineskin. "From the moment I saw her, I loved her. She was a fresh, cool, dewy thing, sunny and shadowy, full of pleasant little mischiefs, fitful and changeable with the whim of the occasion, yet as constant as her native pool." Matello took another sip. "She ruled my thoughts day and night. At first, we were playmates. I would sneak away to meet her, and we would race around this room. Some evenings she would tell me stories of her kin and worlds beyond ours. Other nights we frolicked in the trees. She taught me how to call her from her balmy source, and we spent many a happy hour together in the enthusiasm of summer days. Often as I sat waiting for her, she would summon a shower of sunny raindrops and a rainbow, and soak me to the bone. She was as frolicsome as the breeze and would dazzle me for the sake of my laughter, which she loved to hear."

"So she had legs?"

"Oh yes, beautiful, long, slender legs when on land. Her skin was as pale as spun sugar and her hair the color of the shallows. Lovely," he said, his voice trailing off.

"Did anyone else see her?"

"Our meetings were secretive. As I grew older, I came later and later and avoided the cutpurses that lurked in the wood. The Thicket is dangerous after dusk."

Irilio's hackles rose as he considered his companion. The man wore the colors of the palace, but his livery could be a ruse. What better way to ambush a courtier then in the guise of a royal soldier? The man could steal his purse and backhand him into Zezen's well before he could defend himself. "Then I am glad to be in your company. Who did you say was your commanding officer?"

"I did not say, but if you must know, I serve under Captain Arinda."

"Ah, Jarle Rigo's personal guard. Prestigious."

The soldier crossed his arms and nodded.

Relieved, Irilio audibly exhaled. "Please, sir, continue. I suspect we have yet to reach the crux of your tale."

"Kind maiden that she was, she transformed stifling summer nights into cool and deliciously fragrant occasions. Even the water of this sweltering reservoir became cold when I bent down to drink. Often, a pair of rosy lips came up out of the depths and touched mine. I still smile when I think of the dewy bliss."

"Sounds delightful," observed Irilio, "but the deportment of your watery lady must have had a chilling influence in midwinter. Very literally, a cold reception!"

"In winter the air bent to her will and caressed us with the joys of summer. The coldest days were the most carefree. I would join her in her balmy waters, and we would make love under the stars. Sometimes we would swim to the bottom and languish in her lair until dawn. She slept among the glittering treasures lovers cast into the well. Hers is the domain of purity and innocence; each jewel holds a special memory. She told me once she could sense intention in every object. I believe she, not the goddess, curses dishonest unions."

"Here I thought the well was a cleverly derived custom to fatten the city's coffers." Irilio shook his head. "Come now; surely the palace collects the baubles."

"Not so. My beloved spirit guards over them."

Irilio listened as Matello went on to relate, that for a long while, he found infinite pleasure and comfort in the arms of the naera. In his merriest hours, she gladdened him with her wit and quenched his lust with her body. If ever he was annoyed with earthly trouble, she laid her moist hand upon his brow and charmed the fret and fever entirely away. But one fatal night the young soldier came rushing with quick and irregular steps to the pool. He called the spirit; but—no doubt because there was something unusual and frightful in his tone—she did not answer him.

Sensing his companion's melancholy, Irilio placed a hand on his shoulder. "What happened?"

"I flung myself down, and washed my hands and bathed my feverish brow in the cool, pure water, but the water shrank away leaving me as feverish as before. Then a mournful sound resounded in the wood. Perhaps it was my lover's voice or maybe the sighing of the wind. But I heard it still."

Matello came to a dead pause.

"Why did the water shrink?" inquired the poet.

"Because blood stained my hands!" the soldier said, in a horror-stricken whisper.

"Whose blood?"

"An innocent."

"How?"

Matello looked down at his hands. "My family procured a position for me in the illustrious Ca'Dezer, and I became a cavalryman. That summer I squashed a revolt in The Tangles and trampled a child. Even if my beautiful naera could comfort my sorrow, she could not cleanse my conscience."

Irilio slid to the edge of the basin. "Did you ever see her again?"

"Once, years ago," replied his companion. "Isonei appeared as a reflection in the pool turned red from my guilt. I mourn her absence still and come here to make peace. Since that day, my hands have claimed more lives. Such is the burden of a soldier."

Irilio found a certain charm to the legend. Whether intended or not, he understood the guard's confession as an apologue. The soothing effects of intercourse with nature in all ordinary cares and griefs were vast, but such mild influences fell short on ruder passions and became altogether powerless against the deadly chill of guilt.

A long time passed in silence as they sat listening to the quiet bubbling of the pool. When at last Irilio spoke, he did so quietly. "I suppose she will curse me for my ill-begotten offering."

The soldier picked up his helm and stood. He clapped the poet in the back and nodded. "We curse ourselves with bad choices. Please, allow me to escort you. I wouldn't want you to meet ill before you have had the chance to pen my story."

The two men walked away from the pool. Outside the temple, Irilio looked back. The Song of Isonei had a nice ring to it.

— *The End* —

ABOUT THE AUTHORS

Narcisse and Marzio met at a rambunctious game of Dungeons & Dragons® in 2007 and have been friends ever since. They are both cat people. Marzio has a black cat who goes for the throat and Narcisse, a sugary white puffball who loves to cuddle. Each of them enjoys travel, gaming, geekery, and getting their hands dirty in the garden. Both of them believe in magic and impossible things before breakfast, though good luck getting either of them up early. Cowriting brings out the pyromaniac in each of them, so threats of burning manuscripts are not uncommon.

To follow their writing journey, subscribe to InkSorcery.com.

This book is typeset
in "Italian Old Style"
a British Monotype
font based on William
Morris's Golden Type.

SECOND

EDITION

PAPERBACK

www.ingramcontent.com/pod-product-compliance
Lightning Source LLC
Chambersburg PA
CBHW021833010726
47493CB00005B/1378